PHINEAS POE

kiss me, judas

penny dreadful

hell's half acre

3 NOVELS BY **WILL CHRISTOPHER BAER**

PHINEAS POE

kiss me, judas

penny dreadful

hell's half acre

3 NOVELS BY **WILL CHRISTOPHER BAER**

MacAdam/Cage

MacAdam/Cage
155 Sansome Street, Suite 550
San Francisco, CA 94104
www.macadamcage.com
Copyright © Will Christopher Baer 2004
ALL RIGHTS RESERVED.

Library of Congress Cataloging-in-Publication Data

Baer, Will Christopher.
  Kiss me, Judas / by Will Christopher Baer.
    p. cm.
  ISBN 1-931561-80-X (hardcover : alk. paper)
    1. Kidneys—Transplantation—Fiction. 2. Ex-mental patients—Fiction. 3. Ex-police
officers—Fiction. 4. Loss (psychology)—Fiction. 5. Denver (Colo.)—Fiction. 6. Drug traffic—
Fiction. 7. Prostitutes—Fiction. 8. Widowers—Fiction. I. Title.
  PS3552.A3323K57 2004
  813'.54—dc22

                                                                                    2004014846

Baer, Will Christopher.
  Penny dreadful / by Will Christopher Baer.
    p. cm.
  ISBN 1-931561-81-8 (hardcover : alk. paper)
    1. Ex-mental patients—Fiction. 2. Ex-police officers—Fiction. 3. Missing persons—
Fiction. 4. Denver (Colo.)—Fiction. 5. Punk culture—Fiction. I. Title

  PS3552.A3323P46 2004
  813'.54—dc22

                                                                                    2004015758

Baer, Will Christopher.
  Hell's half acre / by Will Christopher Baer.
    p. cm.
  ISBN 1-931561-82-6 (hardcover : alk. paper)
    1. Ex-mental patients—Fiction. 2. Ex-police officers—Fiction.
  3. San Francisco (Calif.)—Fiction. 4. Revenge—Fiction. I. Title

  PS3552.A3323H45 2004
  813'.54—dc22

                                                                                    2004015292

Paperback Compilation: October 2005
ISBN: 1-59692-151-X

Manufactured in the United States of America.
10 9 8 7 6 5 4 3 2 1

Book and cover design by Dorothy Carico Smith.

For Elias McCulloch Baer

kiss me, judas

obscurely through my brain
like shadows dim
sweep awful thoughts, rapid and
thick. I feel
faint, like one mingled in entwining love;
yet 'tis not pleasure.

—Prometheus Unbound, *Percy Bysshe Shelley*

one.

I MUST BE DEAD for there is nothing but blue snow and the furious silence of a gunshot. Two birds crash blindly against the glass surface of a lake. I'm cold, religiously cold. The birds burst from the water, their wings like silver. One has a fish twisting in its grip. The other dives again and now I hold my breath. Now the snow has stopped and the sky is endless and white and I'm so cold I must have left my body.

I drift down an elevator shaft to the hotel lobby. I see myself walking across a gold carpet. Time is slowed to a crawl and I'm looking through a filter but it's me. The familiar skull shaved to stubble and the eyes like shadows. The gray skin pulled tight on my face and my hands flashing white as if cut from paper. I wear a black suit and tie and a dirty white shirt. The clothes hang loose, as if borrowed. The truth is I am losing weight. I look like I'm dying of cancer. I stop and turn a slow circle. I think I'm looking for the bar. The prick of nausea. Someone else is watching me. A woman in a red dress. She sits in a leather armchair, long legs crossed and yellow. She has long black hair streaked with blond. Her lips part slightly and I can see her teeth. I pass behind a marble column and disappear. I slip inside myself again and I can hear the sound of a piano.

I sit at the bar and order vodka.
     Vodka how? the man says.

I don't know. With a lemon and some ice.

He brings me a glass. I sip it and feel better. The woman in red sits down beside me. She is younger than I thought. It's been too long since I sat so close to a woman and my first impulse is to move away. I loosen my tie and look at her. She has a scar at the edge of her mouth and disturbing eyes. She doesn't seem to blink. Her body is like a knife. A dull black stone, shaped like a teardrop, dangles from a string of silver in the cold hollow of flesh above her collarbone.

Are you a tourist? she says.

I'm not even sure what city this is.

Denver.

I'm a salesman.

That's funny. You look like a cop.

I've just been released from a mental hospital.

Perfect, she says.

I finish my drink and push it aside. She dips two fingers into the glass and I see her nails are painted blue. She fishes out the twist of lemon and eats the pulp. I turn my head slightly and her face is two inches from mine. She takes a deep breath and exhales slowly. I breathe her dead air.

You must be a terrible salesman, she says.

I am.

Do you want to buy me a drink?

I'm not dead. Terribly cold but my eyes are open. I'm staring directly into a white overhead light and when I close my eyes I still see it, as if the white is burned into my brain. I try to take shallow breaths. I'm in a bathtub. I'm naked and the tub seems to be filled with glass. I don't think I'm bleeding. I'm fine, really. The glass is smooth and somehow comforting. There's a strange tickle down my left side, below the ribs. I want to scratch it but I can't move my arms.

She says her name is Jude.

What are you drinking?

Silly question. Tequila sunrise, she says.

Why is it silly?

Look around. It's island night.

I swivel on my stool. The waitresses are barefoot and wear plastic flowers in their hair. They serve multicolored drinks that sport happy little umbrellas like hats. On the dance floor are belly dancers cut from card-board. Surf music drones in the distance.

The dancers, I say.

What about them?

They're not real.

She laughs. You are clever.

The bartender brings us a glowing pitcher of tequila sunrises and two tall glasses. I drink cautiously from mine. It tastes like children's vitamins. Jude drinks hers with a straw.

I used to be a dancer, she says. I was thirteen and I wanted to be famous.

How sad.

Don't you want to be famous?

No.

She gazes at me, her mouth crooked.

There's something wrong with you, she says.

I stare down at my limp body. Wet black hairs against the white skin of my torso. The genitals shrunken as those of a corpse. The scar of a bullet on my left thigh like the mouth of an unborn twin. My knees blue with cold. What I thought was glass is in fact ice, and it has a familiar smell. The trapped air of a hospital, a morgue. Disinfectant or formaldehyde. The ice is red but I don't see a wound.

The tequila is gone and by now I have one hand well up Jude's dress. She has swimmer's muscles and goose bumps along her thigh and she is so sweet and lovely I might weep.

Do you want to go upstairs?

Oh, yes. I pat my pockets but can't find my key.

Room 411, she says. A key dangles between her blue nails.

That's my key.

Of course it is.

I try to fondle her in the elevator but she isn't having it.

This is going to cost you two hundred, she says.

The elevator stops at the second floor but no one gets on.

Do you have two hundred?

I'm sure I do.

The elevator rises, groaning. She stares at the floor.

What's wrong with you? she says.

My reflection in the mirrored doors is shadowy, grotesque. I must look like a corpse to her.

Why don't you want to be famous?

I'm terrified of crowds.

In the room she drops her purse on the bed. It's square and black, oddly like a doctor's bag. It looks heavy. Jude pulls her dress over her head. There is a strange tattoo between her shoulder blades: a third eye, staring at me. I fumble through my wallet and come up with a wad of bills I can't bear to count and a decayed-looking condom. She takes the cash and puts it in her shoe. I try to tear open the condom and she takes it away.

Don't you worry about disease?

I never worry, she says.

A stranger's blood can kill you.

It's okay, she says. I'm sure your blood is clean.

She puts her arms around me and finds the gun clipped to my belt. She holds it up with a smile and I shrug. She already has my money. She tosses the gun aside and says, you don't need it. I push her to the floor and she surprises me with a tender kiss on the mouth.

I'm awake. Shivering so badly I have to lock my teeth to keep from biting off my tongue. The ice has melted and the water feels oily, like mucus. There's a complimentary bathrobe hanging from a hook behind the door, less than three feet away. It looks warm and soft and I can't move. I can't move. I don't think I can sleep anymore. I have been asleep in the ice for a day, for two days. In my left hand is a piece of paper. Black ink in round girlish script.

kiss me, judas

If you want to live call 911.

There's a telephone between the tub and the toilet. I keep reading the note over and over and finally reach for the phone. It takes at least five minutes for me to dial.

Emergency operator.

I need some help.

Please describe your situation.

I'm in a bathtub.

Are you injured, sir?

I was with a woman, a prostitute. Now I'm in a bathtub full of ice and I might be dreaming.

Are you injured?

I'm cold. And there's blood coming from somewhere.

I'm sending an ambulance right away. You are at the Hotel Peacock, is that correct?

Room 411.

Can you determine the source of the blood? It will help the paramedics.

It's coming from my left side.

Try to reach it. You may have been shot.

I can feel thin pieces of metal, a half inch apart. Like staples.

Did you say staples, sir?

I'm pretty sure.

Remain calm, sir. Help is coming.

What did she do? What the fuck did she do?

Silence.

Remain calm, sir.

Please tell me. I've got staples in me.

The paramedics wear black rubber coats. They touch me so delicately, as if I'm a bomb. They strap an oxygen mask over my face and give me a shot. I wake up as they load me into a helicopter, the blades beating furiously. I hear someone whisper in a low sexless voice. *Don't worry, you really only*

9

need one. I'm sure it is Jude's voice. We lift off and for a moment the city lights glow like an overturned Christmas tree and I feel fine.

two.

I SLEEP FOREVER. I drag up bits and pieces of memory and slowly reconstruct a bad dream. She must have put some kind of horse tranquilizer in my tequila because I was never really unconscious. I was brain dead and paralyzed but my eyes and ears were functioning. The flash of a scalpel. Gloved fingers against my skin. She said she was sorry and rolled me over. Funny that she wore latex gloves to cut me open and ten minutes earlier I was inside her without a condom. It's a wonder I could even point my dick in the right direction but I have a feeling the sex was not bad.

I remember two things: Jude talks to herself when she's nervous and she kissed my eyelids before she left. I think she fell for me.

A part of me still sleeps beside her, twitching and bloody in a cooler meant for soft drinks. I see her driving a stolen car with the windows down and country music on the radio. She sings softly to herself and I'm sure she has a lovely voice. She's taking my kidney to Las Vegas. She's going to trade it to the devil for a record contract. I will find her. I will come to her dressing room with champagne and chocolates and I will kill her.

This isn't a dream. I'm alive and this is a hospital room like any other. I'm hooked up to an IV rig and a pale liquid drips into me. There's a tube up my nose. It's a rude feeling and I want to remove it. I flex my hands. They aren't restrained and I tell myself it's not that kind of hospital. I wonder if the tube is keeping me alive and then I pull it out. There's a little blood but no immediate change in my condition. I try to sit up and the pain is so bad I think I pass out for a while. My belly is made of fire and I could use a morphine button. I have to pee badly and I'm aware that my dick is very sore. It feels like she fucked me to pieces. I tell myself it's not funny. She ruined me. I must have heard the nurses talking while I was out because I know that my left kidney is gone and that it was crude but professional work. Or else I would be dead. I realize there's another tube extending from my dick and I gratefully empty my bladder. I'm wearing a sexy little gown and I hope my clothes are here somewhere. It's really time to go.

I sleep some more. There's a police guard outside my door. He's a big boy, a chunk of meat in blue. He stands with his legs wide apart, like a tree. I can't see his face and the back of his neck is less than comforting. I'm not sure if he's meant to keep people out or keep me in.

The next time I wake up I disconnect the catheter. It's not so easy and it makes a terrible mess. Then I manage to stand up without screaming out loud. I want to wait a few minutes before I jerk the needle from my arm. The IV must be doing me some good. I drag it to the little bathroom and pee weakly into the toilet. I don't want to but I take a peek in the mirror. I suppose I could look worse. I seem to be growing a beard. I tell myself it's a disguise. The front of my gown is smeared with blood and snot and other uncertain fluids. There's a small closet and I'm surprised to find my clothes inside. Everything is there. My shoes and my pitifully small suitcase. A plastic bag containing my personal items: keys and wallet with no money, pocketknife and wristwatch, silver cigarette lighter that my dead wife gave me but no cigarettes, hotel room key number 411, a broken silver chain with a black stone shaped like a tear. Jude might have left it for me; something of hers in exchange for something of mine. But the chain is broken and it must have happened while we were fucking. She just didn't notice. The cops must have found it and thought it was mine. I look at it closely and it appears to be a locket, but I'm too stupid to open it. I slip it into my pocket and suddenly feel sick. I've lost my gun.

The date on my watch is December 21, the first day of winter. It certainly feels like winter. I'm naked and cold and nearly dead and it hurts to laugh. I was out for a day and a half and I wonder if they call that a coma. I wasn't planning anything special for Christmas. Maybe a nicer hotel room. A bottle of spiced rum and an expensive whore. That's out of the question, of course. But the last place I want to be is the hospital. I pull the IV, trembling slightly. I don't care for needles. I get dressed slowly, hoping no one comes in. I turn in the mirror to look at my wound. I have frantic black stitches halfway around my belly and back, like ants marching. I assume they yanked the staples and poked around in there, then sewed me up. The surrounding flesh is raw and puckered and I feel as if my head will float away.

Slow hiss as the door swings open and I have plainclothes cops in my room. One of them is Detective Moon from the 9th. I'm glad to see that he hasn't changed; he wears the same gray corduroy jacket and the same wide blue tie with a single yellow fish. He wears white pants that are too short for him and I can see his socks. He is short and heavy and wears glasses that make his eyes forever vague. I investigated Moon once, in connection with a case of prostitutes being executed by cops. His partner was a suspect, but Moon never was. He was curiously agreeable about the inquiry, as if he were bored and lonely and a little scandal might brighten his day. The other guy is a stranger. He has a massive fever blister on his upper lip and a white bandage over his right eye. His face is bruised and puffy as a toad. His face is wrecked. He has oily brown hair, hanging over his eyes and ears like a helmet. I had a haircut like that when I was six.

Detective Moon sits down on my bed. He looks miserable.
 Hello.
 Moon doesn't quite look at me. The Blister stands with his back to the door and his arms crossed and I can tell he's going to be difficult. He wears white gloves and he wants to do all the talking.
 It hurts to smile, doesn't it?
 He doesn't seem to breathe. How do you mean?

Your face is a disaster, I say.

The Blister examines his tie and flicks a gloved finger at nothing, at an invisible soup stain, at the lost wing of a fly.

I glance at Moon. Do you still bite your fingernails?

He blinks and coughs. Sometimes, yeah.

I toss my shoe at him. See what you can do with that knot.

The Blister clears his throat.

Can I help you? I say.

Your name is Phineas Poe, is that correct?

Yes, it is.

What are you doing in Denver?

Passing through.

What did I tell you? says Moon. He doesn't like strangers.

The Blister licks his lip. You were a cop in this town for six years.

Oh, well.

There's a fat file on you.

I'm sure.

A special agent in the Internal Affairs Division.

Moon is whistling softly as he works on the knot.

I stare at the Blister. And you hate IAD. What's new?

You were assigned to investigate Internal Affairs from within.

The rat among rats. I was never even sure where my orders came from.

You must have had some problems with trust.

I must have.

The Blister puts a cigarette in his mouth and smiles.

Have you got another one of those?

No. I don't.

I'm sorry about your face, I say.

How did you lose your shield? says the Blister.

Moon growls. Is this shit really necessary?

I shrug. It's okay, Moon. Tell him.

Moon shrugs. Nervous breakdown, he says.

The Blister laughs, looking at me. I read the incident reports. You lost it on the firing range and started shooting at imaginary people. You took an ounce of crystal meth from an informant and later spooned it into your coffee. You locked yourself in the cage with a female prisoner and allowed her to urinate on you.

It's an uncommon sensation. Try it sometime.

I don't suppose your kidney was removed by imaginary people?

Fuck you. Take your wrecked face and go home.

The Blister steps close to me. His eyes are slitted and he looks dangerous.

Moon, I say. I don't like your friend.

Then who did this to you? says the Blister.

I don't know.

Wasn't there an accident involving your wife? says the Blister.

I open my eyes wide. My face feels blank, a piece of ice.

A hunting accident, I think it was.

Okay, says Moon. Shut the fuck up.

The Blister forces a smile. Well. Let's save that for later.

I sit on the floor for a long time after they leave. I hear myself whistling and it occurs to me that I never did see the Blister's badge. He might not have been a cop. He had poor Moon squirming under his thumb like a bug, though. He could have been a fed, an assassin, a bill collector. It doesn't matter, really. I'm sure I will see him again. Jude is my problem. I put my shoe on and look out the window. It's snowing, small hard flakes swirling in the dark. I don't want the cops involved. I have nothing to hide. I just don't like cops.

I wonder how long a kidney will keep on ice. Human tissue surely goes bad in a hurry. If I were receiving a foreign kidney I would want it to be fresh.

I poke my head out of the room cautiously. I have a vague idea that I might ask the police guard for the correct time. Engage him in some friendly banter. Invite him into my room to watch Letterman do stupid pet tricks. Smoke cigarettes and argue about hockey and which nurse has the best pair of legs. Lull him to sleep with a song. Then disarm him and leave him hogtied in my tiny bathroom. Something like that. But he's gone and I'm not sure he was ever there.

I'm gathering myself to leave and a single word chimes in my head: *antibiotics.* My poor torso is surely alive with infection. I decide to improvise. I leave my things in the room and wander down the hall. Two doors down I get lucky. A woman lies unconscious and alone. She's a burn victim, on heavy life support. There's a med cart beside her bed. Ordinarily I would grab condoms and sterile gloves and other novelty items, but I ignore this shit and look for the drugs. I find a tray of ampoules marked penicillin. Pills would be better but what can you do. I take a handful and start looking for needles. The thought makes me ill. I'm going to fucking faint every time I have to shoot up.

I turn to go and the woman stirs. Is that you, Joey?

I hesitate. Her face is heavily bandaged and she can't see.

It's me, I whisper.

Did you feed my Groucho? He likes his milk warm.

Of course, I say.

On rainy days I give him the canned salmon.

Don't worry about a thing.

I'm so afraid, Joey. Will you pray for me?

She extends a veined hand the color of stone. I have nothing to lose.

I crouch beside her bed and stumble through the only prayer I know: *now I lay me down to sleep and pray the Lord my soul to keep.* It's appropriate, I think. And still I feel worthless. I want to comfort her, to chase her fears into the snow. But sympathy is buried in me, like a stone in the belly of a goat. And the goat is the rare animal that will eat garbage. I hold her hand until she falls asleep, then steal fifty dollars from her purse.

three.

THE WEIGHT OF MY SUITCASE PULLS ME SLIGHTLY OFF-BALANCE and stretches my damaged skin. If I put it down I will have to bend over again. I ride down the elevator grinning like a jackal. The emergency room is so silent it makes me nervous. Two morose students in green scrubs sip coffee and stare at the clock. I get the feeling they're waiting for a truckload of bodies. One of them is looking at me, staring at me. She has dark, crooked eyes and red hair. Her skin is like milk.

Can I help you, sir?

I hope so. Would you call a cab for me? I was just discharged.

Gladly, sir.

Please don't call me sir. It depresses me.

She smiles, a shadow. She picks up the phone as I sit gingerly on a bench.

A few minutes later she taps me on the shoulder. I'm sorry, she says. The cabs are swamped because of the snow. It's going to be at least an hour.

Oh, I say. I'm in no hurry.

Are you all right?

My forehead is sweating ropes and I feel shattered. I'm fine, I say.

You don't look well.

I just want to go home.

She presses her lips together for a moment and when she pulls them apart they look frozen and pale as a scar and then the blood rushes back into them. She fingers her stethoscope like a rosary. She stands on one foot as if it helps her think.

My shift is almost over, she says. I could give you a ride.

Do you know karate?

No, she says. Why do you ask?

I might be a strangler.

Oh, yeah. You look pretty feeble. What happened to you?

My kidney was stolen by a prostitute.

She laughs, nervous. No, really.

I have an irregular heartbeat and sometimes it just stops.

Well. Then you had better come with me.

What's your name?

She holds out her hand, the fingernails unpainted.

I'm Rose White, she says.

She carries my suitcase for me. The parking lot is slippery and I take small birdlike steps. The snow stings my face and it feels good. Rose jingles her keys and points at a little black Mustang.

This is me, she says.

She unlocks the passenger door and her car alarm begins to whoop.

Did you steal this car?

Rose doesn't laugh. She whispers to herself, oh you motherfucker. She fumbles with the keys for a long angry moment and the alarm finally stops. She smiles and puts my suitcase in the backseat. My head throbs.

The car hums quietly over the fresh snow. She hasn't asked me where I'm going. I can't breathe and I crack my window. She lights a cigarette and mutters an apology. I want one but don't ask. I don't like this at all. She's either a cop or a freak. The Blister knew I would run. He pulled the fat uniform from my door because he was too easy. He threw me a knuckleball: a nurse with eyes like a virgin. Or else she's a freak. She looks like a schoolteacher but she's really a pervert. She has a fetish for nearly dead strangers. She takes them home and euthanizes them on red satin sheets. I remember a piece of soft porn I saw years ago. A sweet young girl with thick glasses and a nervous stutter and a body like a centerfold. Her father rapes her when she's sixteen. He visits her bed every morning and one day dies of a heart attack upon entering her. The girl goes slowly insane. She leaves the corpse in her bed and begins to bring home men she finds sleeping in alleyways. She kills them in her father's bed. She waits until they roll away from her and begin to snore, then stabs an ice pick deep into their ears. She believes she is retrieving her virginity.

I'm curious. Why did you bother with me?
    I don't know what you mean?
    Do you know me?
    Rose glances at me then away. Her cigarette glows bright.
    No, she says. You haven't even told me your name.
    And no one assigned you to watch me?
    She blows smoke. I don't like this conversation.
    Are you really a doctor?
    I'm a medical student.
    I thought cigarettes would kill you.
    They do, she says. But it takes a long time. What's your problem?
    I want to know if I can trust you. Why did you offer me a ride?
    She stops the car suddenly and we slide onto the sidewalk.
    Because you have a sweet face. You look like someone broke your heart.
    Then this isn't a sex thing.
    She laughs at that. I'm not sure I like you.
    The engine dies and we sit in cold silence.
    My name is Phineas.
    It's nice to meet you, Phineas. Do you want to walk home in the snow?
    No, I don't. I would be dead by morning.
    She restarts the Mustang and revs the engine. Then stop talking crazy. Are you hungry?
    Rose smiles. Yes. In fact, I'm starving.
    Let me buy you breakfast.

The diner is busy with people caught in the snow. The floors are slick and waitresses move in slow motion. Rose eats an omelet with bright yellow cheese. I look at her closely now. Her hair isn't naturally red. She takes small bites. I have a Belgian waffle under a mound of whipped cream. My blood races with sugar and I remember that I haven't eaten solid food in days. I ask Rose if she's ever been involved in an organ transplant.

She flinches. Why?

I'm just curious.

Not really, she says. I was on duty once when a donor died on the table. I held the sponge and bucket while the doctors harvested his liver.

Interesting. What happens next?

What do you mean? Rose reaches across the table and dips her fingers in my whipped cream. There is a birthmark in the shape of an hourglass on the back of her hand.

She licks the finger quickly and smiles and briefly I adore her.

I mean do you toss it in the freezer until someone needs it?

Someone always needs it, she says. The organ is transported immediately.

It's packed in ice, though.

Of course. But it has to be sterile ice.

I guess regular ice from the foodmart is no good.

She laughs. Ice from the foodmart is crawling with bacteria. The organ would be contaminated.

And where do you find sterile ice?

Why do you want to know? Her eyes are slanted and dark.

Oh, you never know when someone is going to die in your kitchen with a perfectly good heart.

No, she says softly. You never know.

Rose drops me off at the Hotel Peacock. The snow has stopped.

I'm sorry.

What for?

For not trusting you. I was rude.

It's okay, she says. You have to be careful.

You remind me of someone, I say.

Who?

Never mind.

She laughs. Who?

My wife, I say.

Is that a good thing?

I lean over and give her a gentle kiss on the side of the mouth. Her skin is warm and I'm tempted to ask her up to my room. But I doubt she would be interested. I've seen myself in the mirror. I'm a fucking wreck. And I'm far too weak and distracted. I can see her in a small apartment with a cat; she watches television with the sound off and eats ice cream. She takes a bath before bed and masturbates.

But she surprises me. Why don't you come home with me, she says.

No. I don't think so.

Are you sure it's safe here?

I'm not sure of anything.

Rose gives me a phone number and says, please call me.

Thank you, I say.

She drives away, headlights swinging across the snow.

Her hair is slightly askew. Like an ill-fitting wig. Maybe that's why she reminded me of my wife, my dead wife. The hair sends echoes through my body.

I still have my room key and I try to cruise through the lobby as if I live there. I don't have a care in the world and no one pays any attention to me. I share the elevator with a little old man who loudly chews his lips. The door to my room is bright with yellow tape. *Police Line Do Not Cross.* I reach for my knife to cut the tape and I see that it has already been cut. A nearly invisible slit, fine as an eyelash. Maybe one of the cops forgot something. Maybe Jude came back for me.

four.

THE ROOM IS UNFAMILIAR. I might have been born in this room and I might never have been here before. It doesn't even look like a hotel room and I realize this is because it hasn't been cleaned. The sheets are ripped and dangling from the mattress. There's a pillow on the floor and I pick it up. It smells and I turn it over. It's been burned. The smell is scorched foam. Nothing else looks touched. I never slept in this room. I didn't unpack and I didn't use the toilet. I had twisting, violent sex with a woman and I had unexpected surgery. I get down on my hands and knees and crawl the floor like a dog. I find a spot on the rug that could be semen. I think of Rose, her arms white with whipped cream. I have a partial erection and I move my hips, trying to remember Jude.

Skin raw and painful. She had a perfect ass, curved like an egg. No rubber between us and I didn't want to bleed. She could be a carrier, or I could be. Her third eye staring at me, watching me.

I can't find a drop of blood in the room. It doesn't seem possible and I feel a peculiar ache like loneliness. My blood is missing. I have lost some blood and I want to see the stains. I want to touch, to be sure that it's mine. I crawl into the bathroom and soon my head clears. I sit on the toilet staring at the claw feet of the tub. Jude was in this room. I glance at the mirror, half expecting to see her there.

Blue and white tiles and the mirror gray with steam. Lightbulb hanging. Shadows of arms and legs stretching, melting into torsos. Naked on a sheet of plastic. Gloved fingers elegant and fierce. Mechanical birds. Smell of disinfectant and blood. The sound of television and someone vomiting. Dark reflection in a window. A fat man with sideburns, a cast on his arm. The glow of a cigarette and the toilet flushing. Jude's lips touching my eyes soft as butterfly shadows. Her breath was tequila and smoke.

A bathroom is the perfect place to torture someone. Hard shiny surfaces and mirrors and running water. Forced intimacy and screams falling hollow, trapped in a claustrophobic box. It will be months or years before I relax in a bathroom. I limp to the bed and realize I'm holding my belly. The pain is visual, an endless white space. I can go inside it and disappear and I wonder if it was a good idea to leave the hospital. I lie back on the bed and try not to think. I'm afraid to dream and I'm afraid not to. Sleep is effortless, merciful.

Pale morning half awake. Tangled sheets between my legs. Noise of garbage trucks and a woman screaming far away fuck you fuck you. My face is wet. I'm crying and I can't stop. My nose is bleeding. Jude is in the room. I can smell her perfume. She's in the next bed pretending to be asleep. The next bed is a lifeboat drifting on a dead calm sea. Blank blue eyes and a naked yellow sun. Two people in the boat, a man and a woman. The man is drunk or catatonic and something is wrong with the woman. The top of her head is blown off and she has a gun in her hand.

I search the room again and my missing gun is nowhere. Some idiot cop put it in his pocket. It wasn't evidence. He picked it up and muttered, say hello to my new unregistered weapon. He filed the serial numbers down that very night. I tell myself bad dreams are good for you. My clothes stink. I need to bathe but I can't face the bathroom. I open my little suitcase and stare at the contents briefly before closing it. Socks and underwear and a slightly less stinking shirt. I must have other clothes somewhere. Then I remember the car. My car is parked in a garage two blocks from here.

Let's just get our shit together, I say.

I straighten my tie and tuck in my shirt and generally pull myself together. Outside the room I start feeling better. The hallway is painted a soothing mint green and the carpet is geometric green and white. A room service tray has been left outside the next room. I pour myself a cup of coffee and stroll to the elevator.

The lobby is a wasp's nest. Too many people and voices and I feel a panic attack coming. The sun is very bright through high windows and the floor is wet with mud and melted snow. I keep hearing a distant tinkling noise like glass touching glass. The noise is coming from me.

May I help you, sir?

What?

I slap at my pockets to find the noise. I pull out a fistful of glass vials. The penicillin.

Of course.

Sir?

For the infection, I say.

The man staring at me wears a bow tie and a name tag. He must work here. His face is cocked sideways, waiting. I pull back and realize that I have instinctively drifted to the front desk. My heart is like a hammer. He presses his lips together and rolls his blue eyes at me.

I have a sudden and arousing urge to claw those eyes out and I can't help smiling.

Do I have any messages? The name is Poe.

One moment.

I turn to face the lobby and take deep breaths. A cluster of tourists waiting for taxis and staring grimly at their luggage. A man and a woman groping each other on a sofa. Two salesmen with visible hangovers. One blond woman in black jeans and a leather coat reading a newspaper. Detective Moon sitting in a sunken blue armchair with a glum face. He sips orange juice through a straw and his cheeks are bright red. I force a mad grin but I don't see the Blister anywhere.

Here you are, sir.

The desk clerk is brandishing a bright yellow envelope with my name on it. The handwriting is familiar and I recoil slightly. If you want to live call 911.

Excuse me, sir?

Nothing, thank you.

I take the envelope without looking at it and turn to face Detective Moon. He doesn't smile and I remember something. He was one of the few cops who sent flowers after Lucy died. I hold out my hand and his grip is like a vise.

It's good to see you, Moon.

Wish I could say the same. He touches his upper lip, which is freshly shaved and dotted with sweat.

I glance around. Where is your shadow?

That motherfucker, he says. He's not my partner.

I'm glad. He was a nasty one.

You look terrible, says Moon. If you don't mind. Like a junkie with no friends.

Thanks.

You want to talk outside, maybe?

Yes, I say. Outside is better.

Let's grab a bite, then. He is clearly tempted to take me by the sleeve but stops himself. I walk with him into bright and awful sunlight. There is a café next door and I follow him, a few steps behind.

Moon orders coffee and a Texas omelet. I force another smile and say I will have the same. Moon stirs his coffee for a long time and doesn't say anything. I wonder if I'm still dreaming and I stare at the fish on his tie as if it will transport me to another place.

How long have you been out of Fort Logan? he says.

Only a few days.

And you checked into the Peacock right away. What was your state of mind?

How do you mean?

Were you cured or rehabilitated or anything? Did they noodle with your brain or was it all jigsaws and watercolors and quiet time?

They diagnosed me with borderline personality. I'm paranoid and antisocial and I have an unusual indifference to violence. They said I don't believe the rest of the world is real and consequently I don't trust anyone and I don't mind hurting people and what else is new? I used to be a cop. That shit is normal. It's perfectly normal.

Moon licks his lips and looks around for the waitress.

They put me on drugs, I say. Lithium and synthetic dopamine inhibitors and god knows what. Some kind of sensory deprivator. But my hands shook all the time and I had insomnia. The drugs made my skin itch and fucked up my vision. I had to stop taking them.

He nods and loosens his tie.

Listen, he says. I came by the hospital this morning and was told that you released yourself. The doctors didn't think that was such a good idea.

No, it wasn't. I think I'm dying here.

Moon smiles. I wanted to apologize about last night.

And who was the fucker, exactly?

Lee Harvey Oswald, says Moon. He might as well be. He claims to be with Internal Affairs, right. He comes in the station yesterday and flashes a badge and a pocketful of attitude and nobody says boo. They don't want any static with IAD and plus, they don't like you anyway.

Imagine that. Do you have any aspirin?

Our food arrives and Moon shovels in a mouthful of steaming eggs with green peppers and bits of meat. He swallows and wipes oil from his chin.

Yeah, he says. Imagine.

Moon is a violent eater. I watch him destroy his food for a while.

Anyway, says Moon. The guy doesn't smell right. He's a fucking spook. But he's somebody, and he's slick enough to fool a roomful of cops.

Did he fool you?

He made me nervous, says Moon.

The waitress appears from nowhere, her pink dress stained and cut low in the front. The edge of white lace peeks out, brownish from grease and smoke. It does nothing for my appetite. She bends to fill my coffee cup and I look away.

I talked to the bartender who was working that night, says Moon. He said you were with a girl that looked like a whore but wasn't. There was something military about her. Like she could kill you as easy as blowing her nose.

I shrug and poke at my eggs.

He put her at five foot seven and one hundred twenty-five pounds. White girl with maybe a touch of Asian blood. Black hair with blond streaks and wearing a red dress that didn't hide much.

I barely looked at her, I say.

Did you get a name or anything?

I shake my head. She put something in my drink. I don't remember anything.

You took her upstairs and woke up in the bathtub missing a vital organ.

It was painful. It was like being born.

She didn't say anything that might help us trace her.

No, she didn't. She didn't tell me anything. I gave her two hundred dollars for a half hour and she took my kidney for fun.

Moon pushes his plate away. Well. She's probably in London or Tokyo by now and she won't be back. Organ smuggling is good money, I'm sure.

I have to go. I have to get out of here.

Wait, he says. Let's go for a ride.

I don't trust you. I'm sorry.

Come on, he says. Five minutes.

I'm not going anywhere with you, Moon.

Phineas.

I need some air and I back away from the table. The idea that Jude has left the country is like a thousand pounds of freshly turned earth on my chest.

I'm sorry, Moon. I will call you if I need anything but I doubt it. And thanks. Thanks for breakfast.

Salt and gravel and black snow. The sidewalk is flooded by a puddle deep enough to drown a horse. Moon didn't say a word about my gun. A crosswalk and the sign says walk, don't walk. It beeps for blind people. I stand against a brick wall and shiver. He could be saving the gun for later. Or maybe my new friend the Blister has it. The light changes again and again, still beeping. My feet are wet and numb. I watch the flow of people until I feel serene.

five.

I FIND THE PARKING GARAGE WITHOUT DIFFICULTY. The kid in the booth is reading a comic book. He asks for my claim ticket. I don't panic. I'm sure it's in my wallet and it is. The kid rings me up and says I'm looking at fifty dollars even. Fabulous. I slap a credit card on the counter and I have no idea if it's still good. I whistle as he runs it through. The card is good. The kid slides me the keys and tells me to have a nice day.

The car still surprises me. It's a silver Volkswagen Bug, a convertible. I don't remember buying it. It seems I picked it up at some point during the lost time. The hours and days I spent underwater. I lost my job and my apartment in early July. The last thing I remember is beating a cab driver half to death during a hailstorm. Then six weeks of consciousness disappeared. And in September I checked myself into the hospital at Fort Logan. I had this car and some clothes and maybe four hundred dollars.

The Bug is not bad. The body and interior are nicely restored and the engine purrs like a fat cat. The only flaw is the passenger seat; it's cut or torn and messily patched with duct tape. I climb into the backseat to change clothes. It's high time I stopped dressing like a cop. I strip down and stop to examine my shirt. I'm leaking a lot of blood and I try not to freak out. I tell myself to get dressed and go see Crumb. If anyone can fix this for me, he can. I dump out a duffel bag looking for clean socks. I find my lucky knife, the tanto. It's a Japanese fighting knife; the blade is four inches of Damascus steel with a slanted, almost blunt tip. The handle is hammered white chrome. The tanto slides into a wrist sheath that I can wear under my shirt or coat. It's almost undetectable; I once wore it with a tuxedo. I find one unregistered handgun, a Smith & Wesson I took off a dead pimp. It's a sexy little gun, a killer's gun. It's a lightweight alloy .38 with an enclosed hammer and a hollow grip. I wear it in an ankle holster and I feel better as soon as I put it on.

My registered weapon was a Browning 9mm; it was surrendered with my badge soon after the accident. They were going to use it against me but I stole it from a rookie cop who was half asleep, working the evidence room on a graveyard shift. And it's almost funny. I always dreaded the day I might lose my gun, or have it taken from me. The very idea made me feel green. I always thought I would rather chew off my foot than lose my gun. And now I've lost it twice. It doesn't feel quite as bad as the new yawning hole in my belly, but I do want that fucking gun.

I don't want to but I get out the penicillin. I break the protective seal on one vial, then unwrap a hypo. The needle thin and bright. I draw out ten cc's and look at my arm. Muscle or vein. I can't decide. I roll the back window down. The muscle seems safer. I do it quickly and promptly throw up.

A man walks past my car twirling an umbrella. He gives me a funny look and I don't blame him. I'm still sitting in the backseat. I'm bleeding and naked except for the ankle holster and my shorts. I'm clutching a needle and there's puke down the side of my car. I dig through my clothes for something inconspicuous that won't show blood. I find jeans and a black T-shirt. I try to wiggle into the jeans without ripping open my side. I put on steel-toed shoes and leave them unlaced. And my leather coat is so stained I don't think a little blood will make any difference.

I open the envelope. It's scented and my head whirls. The dark smell of musk, of earth. I think of animals in cages, pressed close against each other.

The note is from Jude: *when I'm depressed I go bowling.*

I roll out of the garage and a long white Lincoln sits across the street, dark windows rolled halfway down. The Blister drinks coffee from a Thermos, steam swirling merrily. I can hear music coming from his radio. He stares right at me, then looks away. After a moment, I see the white car in my rearview mirror, bobbing along like a cheerful little cloud.

A red light and I find myself staring at the passenger seat. The duct tape doesn't make sense and I peel it back. The leather is slit open as if by a razor. I reach inside and pull out a brown envelope full of cash. It's at least three thousand dollars. I'm dumb with nausea and glee. I must have stashed the money in a paranoid funk. I'm pleased by my own cleverness but I shudder to think what else I'm going to find. I take out a thousand and stuff the rest back into the seat.

I'm sure Crumb will tell me I'm a dead man.

The Witch's Teat is a little sex shop downtown. Next door is a coffeehouse that features questionable poetry readings. It's always dark in the Teat and the music is so loud I feel sick. Drums and horns and venomous distortion. The air itself throbs. A girl sits behind a glass display case of S&M gear. She is perhaps eighteen and bored to death, flipping the pages of a magazine. She wears a black rubber bra and her eyebrows are shaved off. Her shoulders and cheekbones are marked with ornamental scars and burns. I tell her I need to see Crumb and she shrugs; she wiggles her tongue at me and goes back to the magazine. Her tongue is dyed black and my stomach twitches.

I lean close to her. The magazine is opened to a spread featuring genital piercing.

Do that again, I say.

The tongue darts out, black as ink. I try to grab it, to snatch it from the air like a housefly. The tip of her tongue slips from my fingers, warm and velvety.

She grins at me. I'm Eve.

Lovely, I say. Where is Crumb?

She points at a sheer blue curtain, like a veil.

Through the blue and the terrible horns grow louder. Crumb sits on a stool before a wall of mirrors. He holds a scissors in one hand and a small mirror in the other. He wears a bath towel around his waist. He's cutting his hair, badly. It looks like a dog got hold of his head and it makes me a little nervous. Crumb ignores me for a moment, then puts down the scissors. He flicks off the music and examines his hair.

What the fuck was that?

Sun Ra, he says. Intergalactic death blues.

A poor choice, I think.

He laughs. Whatever do you mean?

Look in the mirror.

I am looking in the mirror. I'm a handsome bastard.

I'm sure you are. But your hair is mangled.

Crumb smiles and puts aside the mirror. He motions for me to sit down. I sink onto a very soft purple sofa and think I might like to close my eyes and die there. Crumb removes the towel and reaches for a pair of pants. It's so nice to see you, Phineas. I'm afraid you don't look well.

Is there anything to drink?

Tea or gin? he says.

Both, I think.

Crumb disappears to boil water. He comes back with a pint of gin. He sits down next to me on the sofa. I take small, careful sips from the bottle and tell him what happened. The kettle begins to whine.

I think I had better have a look at you, he says.

Crumb isn't really a doctor. He does cheap abortions and gunshot wounds and even dental work for the mad and desperate. Crumb reads a lot. He has a closet full of old surgical textbooks and a lot of stolen equipment. And he doesn't try to fake it. If you come to him with a ruptured bowel or a crushed spine he gives you a cup of tea and sends you to the hospital.

A half hour passes. I lay naked and ashamed on Crumb's table, my clothes crumpled and damp beside me. The shame is curious. I didn't do this to myself. And it could have happened to anyone. Jude was an efficient predator, a cat. I was a mouse with a bad leg.

What's the story?

You are nearly dead. In fact, I'm surprised you are walking.

Crumb holds a hypo to the light, tapping it for bubbles. I stare at the bubbles until I think I can hear them. But that's impossible. The noise is my heartbeat.

I can hear my heart, I say. If I can hear it I must be fine.

Crumb sighs. Are you listening? he says. The external wound itself is not so bad and there's no sign of infection thus far. How much of the penicillin did you take?

Ten cc's, I say. Straight into the muscle.

It should be enough, I think. If you're still alive in ten days you might take another dose. For good measure. As for immediate concerns, your white cell count is very low. You are dehydrated and you have a fever of 102 degrees. You have some bleeding inside. I can't say what else without opening you up.

But I feel strong. Almost high.

Adrenaline and loss of blood, he says. Invigorating but alas, temporary.

He comes toward me, the hypo pointed like a hideous eleventh finger. I look away.

Roll over, please.

The needle stings and I feel warm. A detailed map of Denver dissolves in my head. I'm looking for bowling alleys.

What should I do?

Be very careful, says Crumb. Do not fight or fuck anyone. Those stitches could easily tear.

My face feels strange. I think I must be smiling. Every muscle in my body is like a piece of nylon rope. What kind of shot was that? I speak slowly. The words pass my lips dense and textured as meat.

A mild speedball. Morphine for the pain. A touch of methamphetamine to give you energy. Do you have any money?

Money, I say. Oh, yeah. What do I owe you?

No, he says. This visit was free. But I suggest you pick up whatever drugs you can find on the street. When that shot wears off you will realize how much pain you are in.

I start to get dressed but Crumb's face bothers me. He has the expression of someone who wishes the rain would stop.

My wife had leukemia. Her own blood cells were attacking her. When she was twenty-six a doctor told her she would be lucky to live another year. She had one failed bone marrow transplant, she had a seemingly endless course of chemical therapy. Her fine black hair dropped out, it fell away like dust. She began to collect wigs. She had a grim drawer of phony hair. Glittering blond and impossible red and gunmetal blue. She didn't want anything that looked like her own short black hair. She rarely let me see her bare skull. She had a few stubborn and lingering strands, gray wisps. She hated them, she said. When she was very weak, she would ask me to bathe her. Heavy silence would fall between us as I washed her failing flesh. She wouldn't let me touch her head. I would turn away as she raised her skinny arms to pour water over herself. Whenever I stared into her wide black eyes I saw a terrified girl who would never grow old, and for a moment I could feel how it was to be dying. It was heartbreaking and I rarely felt closer to her.

Lucy's dead now and the doctors were wrong. She lived to be twenty-nine.

Eve glides through the blue curtain. She gives me a cool stare. Her lipstick is silver and I wonder if her pubic hair is shaved to match her eyebrows.

Crumb, she says. You have a phone call.

Thank you, dear.

Crumb reaches for a portable phone and begins to murmur. Eve stands with her pelvis thrust forward. She wears a leather miniskirt slung low across her hips. I'm sure she doesn't wear underpants. And I doubt she would blink if I asked about her pubic hair.

Eve, I say. If you were to go bowling, where would you go?

That's easy, she says. The Inferno.

Her belly is smooth and the skin transparent and I'm aware that I'm high as a kite.

Well. Are you in the mood?

Am I in the mood?

To go bowling?

She grins. Always.

I can't help smiling.

Give me five minutes, she says. And she disappears through the curtain.

Crumb puts down the phone. I believe she fancies you.

Does she have a driver's license?

Crumb frowns and pours more gin. I'm sure I said that sex in your condition would likely kill you. And definitely so with one such as Eve.

Oh no, I say. I think I need her to drive.

Five minutes or five hours later and I haven't moved. Eve leans close and blows on my face. The scars beneath her eyes are like fallen petals. The effect is lovely. As if she's been crying and she's too proud to dry the tears. I notice that she has painted on slim blue eyebrows. There's no sign of Crumb.

Hello, I say. I can't feel my legs.

Let me help you, she says.

She pulls me up and now I'm light as a feather. I take a few steps. My muscles are fluid and distant. Eve has changed into boots and jeans and a long leather coat. She still wears the black bra and I crouch down to examine her belly. It appears normal.

Come on, she says.

She leads me outside. I'm surprised by the dark and I take deep breaths. The air is cold and thick in my lungs. I spread my arms like wings and close my eyes and I hear a thousand televisions.

Where is your car? says Eve.

I don't know. It's silver. A silver Bug.

six.

EVE DRIVES. I sit in the passenger seat and whisper.

Every time I close my eyes I'm dreaming. I am in the woods. My reflection is a knife blade. Throat and chest scratched and bloody, burned by the sun. The face blackened, hollow. Lips cracked and white with salt. I move in widening circles, away from the lake. I can still hear the water. She floats. Her face is gone. When the sun rises again I press the knife into my arm to make the ninth cut.

An endless red light. Eve smiles at me. I turn my face to the window. There is a long white car stopped alongside us. The driver stares at me. His face is familiar and I realize it's the cop from the hospital. The man with the blister on his mouth. I get out of the car and stand there clutching my stomach.

Open the fucking window.

I fall against the white car and slap at the roof. The window glides down with a soft electric hum.

What's the trouble, young fellow?

I thrust my face into the car spitting like a cat.

Piece of shit, I say. Follow me and find yourself dead in the morning.

I beg your pardon, the man says. An elderly man in a camel hair coat. He wears glasses and has a fine white mustache. A black silk scarf is tucked around his neck. In the passenger seat is a woman wrapped in fur and heavy perfume. The old man is pointing a small antique gun at me; I think it's a Derringer, of all things.

I'm very sorry.

The light is green and I get back in the Bug. Eve is smoking a cigarette. I look over my shoulder and the white car is nowhere to be seen. Eve doesn't say a word. It has to be the drugs. I chew on my finger to convince myself I'm awake.

What are we looking for? she says.

I'm distracted, trying to find something on the radio that doesn't make my skin throb. Eve hits the left turn signal. I look up and see the word *Inferno* blinking in red neon. What?

She slides the car in between a cruiser on jacked-up wheels and a hump of gray snow. The engine dies abruptly. I notice that my fingers are stiff and brittle from the cold.

Listen, she says. I like you. You have a nice face and in another lifetime I might find you mildly attractive. But Crumb says you're dying and you're obviously too pitiful to swing a bowling ball and you don't think this is a date, do you?

Oh, boy.

And you're old, she says. You're ancient. It would be like having my stepfather grope me.

I'm thirty-three.

She smiles and lights another cigarette. Are you cold?

Why do you ask?

Because your lips are blue.

I'm fine, I say. Let me have a drag.

She leans over and holds the cigarette to my mouth. Her lipstick tastes like licorice. I blow smoke and try to smile. The facial muscles are still a bit vague from the morphine. Eve is patient.

I want to know what we're looking for, she says.

A woman. Her name is Jude. White or possibly Asian and approximately twenty-five years old. A little taller than you and a nice body. Black hair with blond streaks. Tattoo of an eye between her shoulder blades. Last seen wearing a red dress. She has something of mine.

Eve laughs. And you want my help?

Of course. And by the way. In another lifetime I would gladly drink your bathwater. But Crumb advised me not to touch you, which reminds me. How old are you?

Today is my birthday. I'm nineteen and I pee in my bathwater.

My god.

Let's go. This is gonna be fun.

Did you say it was your birthday?

Yeah, she says. Why?

I have a superstition. If someone tells me it's his birthday, I give him something on the spot. A present from my pocket, whatever is there. I have given away some nice things: knives and watches and expensive cigars. On a few occasions I have had nothing in my pocket but loose change and chewing gum and I offered it as humbly as I could. I reach into my pocket and pull out Jude's necklace, the black teardrop. I give it to Eve and she is so surprised and pleased that she kisses me.

Inside the Inferno. A schizophrenic coupling of honky-tonk and gothic. Sawdust on the floor. Mirrors cracked and gleaming on every wall. Antique farm equipment and weapons hang from the ceiling. Hammers and sickles, a massive yoke and harness, crossbows and axes and bayonets. Christmas lights swing from the rafters. The bar is a long slab of unfinished oak and the bartender wears a monk's robe. The waitresses are dressed as prostitutes and schoolgirls and French maids. Eve leads me to a dark table. I'm surprised to see actual bowling lanes; on several of them people are even bowling. A schoolgirl comes to take our order. She wears knee socks and an obscenely short skirt.

Eve asks for beer and a whiskey shot.

Two, I say. And bring me a glass of milk.

The girl blinks and scratches her thigh. We don't have milk.

You must have water.

She rolls her eyes. It's a dollar if you want ice.

I tell her I don't care but she's already walking away. I like this place, I say.

Eve isn't listening. She puts her arm around my neck and leans close. Her tongue flicks the edge of my ear. Someone's watching you, she says.

Where?

It's too easy if I tell you, she says.

I let my eyes relax and wander. I've been a civilian too long. My senses are dull. But this is obvious. At the end of the bar is a knot of bikers. One of them has a big belly and white muscle shirt that's too small. It clings to him like it's pasted to his skin. Leather riding chaps and army boots. His left arm is in a cast smeared with oil and Magic Markers. He has matted blond hair and sideburns like the ears of a lazy hound. He is staring at me like I'm a sandwich and I've seen him before.

Fat man with the broken arm.

Gotcha, says Eve.

The schoolgirl returns with our drinks. She brings two beers and two shots and a glass of tepid water.

Enjoy, she says. Eve gives her ten dollars and tells her to keep it. I drink some of the water and wash it down with beer.

I'll be back in a minute, I say.

I get up and walk straight for the fat man. He blinks rapidly and his face turns faintly red. He is surprisingly handsome, in a brutish way. I come close enough to shake his hand, to feel his pulse.

Don't I know you? I say.

Then I veer off and head for the bathroom. I can see him in three different mirrors, splintered and turning to follow me. I step inside the bathroom and turn off the lights. Someone grunts and curses in a stall.

Very sorry, I say.

I lift my leg and palm the Smith & Wesson. I take a long shallow breath. The air is sour, like artificial fruit. It smells like violence. I take another breath and ignore my rattling heart. The bathroom door swings open and the fat man pauses, confused. The doorway a halo around him. I grab him by the throat and pull him inside, then switch on the light. I jam the gun into his left eye.

Oh fuck me, he says. You're the guy.

That's right. Who are you?

I'm nobody.

Did you hold me down, I say. Did you actually touch my kidney? Did you put your fucking fingers inside me?

I don't know you.

But you do. You were in that bathroom the other night, at the Peacock.

I don't know you, he says. I don't want to know you.

And you watched her cut me open.

His face falls. It was terrible, he says. I puked my guts.

I don't say anything. I hold the gun like it's a feather.

He eyes me carefully. Are you even supposed to be walking around?

I'm fine, thank you. I'm a new man.

He laughs and I jab him with the gun.

Who are you?

He squirms. My name is Winston but my friends call me Pooh. Like Winnie-the-Pooh.

I poke him with the gun once more and he whimpers. This pleases me, but I shrug as if I'm bored and I might put a bullet in him for laughs. It was very nice meeting you, I say.

Hold your horses. This isn't the way it goes.

Did she send you to scare me, Winston? Because you aren't very scary.

I'm stoned, he says. When I'm stoned I get soft.

The skin is turning white around his eye. I pull the gun back but leave it in his face. Then I notice the sheen of tears on his cheeks.

What the fuck. Are you crying?

This isn't the way it goes. You weren't supposed to fuck her, he says. She slips you the little orange pill and you go to sleep and she cuts you open. You don't fuck her. You don't fuck my girlfriend.

She's your girlfriend, huh. Your sweetheart.

Yeah, that's right.

Come on. Are you gonna marry her and move out to the suburbs? Fill her belly with little Winstons and hope she doesn't burn the pot roast?

His face turns red.

Be realistic, Winston. How long have you known her?

A week, he says. Five days. But I'm the only one who fucks her. And I should be the one holding a gun, okay. I got a gun.

I frisk him quickly and find a snub-nose .32 in his waistband, the barrel clammy with his sweat. In his pocket I find a film canister. I pop it open with my thumb and there are a dozen small blue capsules inside.

Muscle relaxers, he says. Blue moons. For my busted arm and some good shit, too. Ease the pain and make you happy as a cat sucking himself. I could get you some at low cost.

That's nice, I say. Where is Jude?

One hundred dollars. For a hundred I can get you twenty of 'em.

I give him my warmest smile. Winston, I say. Don't be so fucking greedy.

He grins, sheepish. Okay. For you I could do thirty for a hundred.

It's getting hot in here, I say.

I might need the hundred up front, of course.

Of course.

I smile and he swings his cast at me like a chunk of firewood. I duck under it, stupid and shocked. I didn't think he had it in him. But he narrowly misses smashing the cast to bits, his exposed fingers thumping into the side of the white sink behind me. He grunts in pain and shoves the fingers in his mouth.

Oh, fuck me.

I pull him close and hug him like a brother. He smells faintly of Jude. I fill my lungs with that smell. I stroke the back of his neck and take a fistful of his hair. I don't pull it, not yet. His face is crumpled.

I'm sorry, he says. I'm so fucking sorry.

Take it easy, I say.

What about a load of smack, he says. I can get you a ton of the pure white shit. It's straight out of Turkey or someplace. It's the best shit. It's going to the top, with a fucking bullet.

That sounds too good to be true.

Believe it, he says. This shit is the truth.

Winston, I say. I'm not a buyer. I'm the guy you're looking for. Jude sent you to find me. To tell me something or do something to me. Remember.

Pooh sniffs. She didn't send me to do anything. I come here all the damn time. The beer is cheap and I like to throw darts. I meet lots of chicks here.

I'm sure. But where is she?

Well, he says. I don't exactly know. But I do have a rendezvous with her tomorrow.

A rendezvous.

He shrugs. Business and pleasure. Has to do with the smack.

Listen, Pooh. I'm tired of this and I have to pee and I'm going to shoot you in the eye if you don't tell me the time and place.

Tomorrow morning at the train station. Eleven o'clock. Jude likes to sleep late.

I drop his pills in my pocket. Why don't you stay home tomorrow? Watch cartoons and forget about Jude. I want to talk to her alone.

He frowns and I can almost see his brain scrambling.

Or else I could just shoot you.

Pooh smiles. I think I will stay home tomorrow, after all.

Do you like surprises?

Oh, I love a good surprise.

Then don't tell her I'm coming.

Okay.

My legs are feeling watery and I suddenly want Pooh to go away. I give him twenty dollars and tell him to go have a beer.

Hey, he says. Don't tell her I cried.

Don't worry. I'll tell her you scared me half to death.

Pooh scratches himself. Can I have my gun back? It's not even loaded.

Are you ticklish? I say.

He hesitates as if it's a trick question. No, he says.

Close your eyes, then. Think good thoughts.

I press the .32 to his soft belly and pull the trigger. He flinches.

When I come out of the bathroom Eve is arguing with another woman. I sit down and sip my whiskey. It tastes like burnt wood. The woman is long and skinny and bald. She turns to glare at me.

Is there a problem? I say.

She flicks her finger at me. Eve is with me, she says.

I look at Eve and she shrugs. This is Georgia.

My heart is still banging too fast after the encounter with Pooh. The stitches have begun to itch, far away and maddening. My hands are cold and damp and I hold one out to Georgia.

I don't think so, she says.

Delighted, I say.

Eve sits between us, her eyes closed. She looks so young. I retract my hand like a piece of machinery. Eve stands up and I see the blood rush into her face.

Let's go, she says. Do you want to go?

I'm finished here.

Georgia leans forward and gives me a curved shard of glass from a mirror, thin as my finger. I glance at it and see only my eyes. I'll see you later, she says.

In the parking lot Eve rubs snow on her face.

It stops me from crying, she says.

I take a breath and the frozen air stings my throat like nettles. I'm a bit dizzy.

Are there any motels nearby?

No, she says. You're coming home with me.

Home, I say.

She takes my hand.

It's not far. Georgia lives with me.

I lift her small, cold hand and hold it to my lips. I want to tell her how tired I am.

It's okay, she says. You can sleep on the couch. It's velvet.

seven.

THE WATER IS WARM, the temperature of blood. I swim through it, laboring. My limbs so heavy and strange. Lift my head to breathe and I can see the boat. Adrift, barely moving. A woman's arm dangling over one side. Her fingertips gliding at the surface of the water like the legs of a spider, leaving no trace. The sun is high in a cloudless sky. Her skin is fair and will burn easily. I close my eyes and swim. I hear terrible echoes. When I open my eyes I am alongside the boat, near enough to kiss the woman's hand. I pull myself up to look at her. She wears a short blond wig that seems to crouch on her head like a yellow, flightless bird. She is naked, as if she fell asleep sunbathing. She has small, delicate feet. Her face is a giant black hole that moves and shifts in the light. Tiny particles detach themselves from the hole and drift away to land on her thigh and I comprehend that this is a mass of flies. My handgun is in the floor of the boat. I pull it overboard and let its weight drag me under. I'm sinking fast and the water is much colder below. There is almost no light and I'm swallowing water, breathing it as I push the gun into soft black mud. I want to leave it but I can't. There will be no fingerprints but mine and I don't care. I push myself to the surface and choke in the open air. I swim away from the boat and regain consciousness on a cold floor beside a velvet couch.

There is a dark face leaning over mine. The breath is hot and sickly sweet.

Get on your fucking feet, she says.

Georgia, I say.

She flicks on a lamp and thrusts her arm at me. A dog bit me, she says.

I blink in the yellow light. Her lips are raw; she's chewing them.

My arm, she says. Look at my arm.

She has smooth skin, the color of chocolate. There is a small, crescent scar on her biceps and the mark of a recent needle. The flesh is otherwise undamaged.

Don't you see it? she says. She's breathing rapidly. Her eyes are like sunspots.

There's nothing there, I say. Close your eyes and it will go away.

It's still bleeding, she says. There's blood everywhere.

What kind of dog was it?

Her face goes blank. There is a sharp pain in my foot. She's squeezing it like a lump of dough.

A black dog. Or yellow, I think.

I pull my foot away from her and begin putting on my shoes.

Do you want something to drink? I say. A glass of water?

She hisses at me. Water is poison.

I shake my head. Water is good.

It's rabies. I could have rabies, she says.

Oh, yeah. You might be right.

The basement, she says. You should lock me in the basement. If it's rabies you will have to shoot me in the morning, shoot me dead.

I fish out the blue muscle relaxers I took from Pooh. There are only ten of them.

Open your mouth, Georgia.

And her mouth pops open. As if she's ten and I'm her uncle who always has gum. I place one pill on her tongue and push her mouth closed. I slip another one into her hand and she makes a fist.

This should make you feel better, I say. If not, take the other one.

And I lead her down the hall to the closet. There's no basement, I say.

She kneels obediently on some dirty sheets and blankets.

I'm going to go out for a while, I tell her.

Her face contorts and I'm afraid she will start screaming.

Don't worry, I say. If it's rabies, I promise I will shoot you in the morning.

Georgia smiles, rocking back and forth. I leave the door cracked. In one of the bedrooms I find Eve. She is curled into a ball in the middle of her bed, shivering. Her blankets are on the floor and I pull them over her. I sit on the edge of her bed and watch her sleep. I bend close enough to smell her breath. It is sweet, like toothpaste. It would be nice to have a daughter.

My wife and I tried to make a baby. When things were good between us, when she wasn't dying. She wanted one so badly, and we tried. Every night for months. I thought this was fine at first. All the sex I wanted and we did it in every room of the house. The idea was that the bathroom might be luckier than the kitchen and so on. We tried different positions that might improve the sperm's ascent. I fucked her underwater and upside down. We used leather and dogs and vegetables and ice and cellophane and hand-cuffs to make it interesting. I fucked her fully clothed in the rain. Her face was ever a grim mask. She couldn't enjoy it, she said. Because she had to concentrate. I fucked her until I had nothing left, until my penis shrank at the thought of her. None of it mattered because one of us was sterile. I took the weight because Lucy stank of death already, but when the doctors fingered me for it she pulled away from me with thousand-yard eyes.

Then outside. The snow has stopped. My watch says it is four. The sun will be up soon and I start to walk. I limp slightly, to the left. This eases the pain in my side but I have to be careful not to fall off the sidewalk. I buy cigarettes at the glowing foodmart. Six hours until I meet Jude and I have no idea what I will do to her. I'm wide awake and almost happy but on the edge of weeping. As if I'm thinking of a lover and I can't wait to see her. It's pitiful and I bite my lip to clear my head. The wind is picking up and I duck into a phone booth to smoke a cigarette. I need someone to talk to and I decide to call Crumb. But I don't know his number. I don't know anyone's number.

I call my old number and get a recording that says disconnected, try again. I dig through my wallet and find two scraps of paper. One is the original note from Jude. If you want to live call 911. It's wrinkled and the ink is a little smeared. The handwriting is curved and sharp, girlish but bright with intent. She has strong fingers. I can almost see her. I can smell her cold yellow skin. The other bit of paper is from Rose White. Her name and phone number. Her handwriting is softer, dreamier than Jude's. I pick up the phone and drop a quarter.

Hello, she says. She is suspicious but awake.

Rose, I say. It's Phineas.

Oh. Good morning.

I'm sorry. Did I wake you?

No, I'm glad you called. Are you okay?

I don't know. I need to tell you something.

What is it?

My wife is dead.

Oh, I'm so sorry.

It happened six months ago. I just wanted you to know.

Where are you?

I'm nowhere. A phone booth.

I think you should be in bed. You're not well.

It wasn't my fault.

What?

My wife. It was an accident.

Do you want me to come get you?

The thing is, I taught her how to handle a gun. She knew.

Phineas, listen to me. Where are you?

I don't know what to do.

What do you want to do?

I have to meet Jude at the train station.

Who is she?

She stole something from me and I have to get it back.

Okay. What time are you meeting her?

At eleven o'clock. She took my kidney.

Of course. Your kidney.

Do you know the story of the goose and the golden eggs?

She sighs. I hope you're not the goose.

I'm the fucking egg.

Phineas, she says. Let me come get you.

My wife was a good shot. She could take the head off a bottle.

Tell me about her.

Jude? She's a hell of a woman. Mean as a snake but nice to look at, god love her.

Your wife, tell me about your wife.

My wife. Her name was Lucy and she was a teacher. Ninth-grade math.

What did she look like?

She had short black hair, cut like an elf from a fairy tale. When I first met her I was sure she had pointed ears. Her eyes were dark and a little slanted.

What about her body? Was she smaller than me?

Lucy was soft. She had a nice round ass and strong legs. A little bit of a tummy.

And did she dress like an elf?

She wore sharp little designer suits. Like a short gray flannel skirt with matching jacket. High-heel shoes and she loved white stockings. She was a sweetheart but she had a dirty mind. Because she was dying and she wanted a little excitement. She didn't wear underpants sometimes and she said the boys in her class could sense it and they got pretty hot and couldn't tell you five plus six.

She sounds like fun. Did she like to dance?

I don't want to talk about her anymore. She's dead and sometimes I'm glad.

You don't mean that. You don't.

She was always dying. And then she was dead.

Phineas, you're scaring me. Tell me where you are.

Why do you want to know?

Because I can take care of you. I'm a nurse.

I'm weak. I need to be strong when I see Jude.

Let me help you.

No. I need to do this alone.

What are you going to do?

I'm going to take her to a hotel room.

I don't want to know. I really don't.

I'm going to drug her and fuck her senseless.

Phineas. That's enough.

Then I'm going to kill her.

The phone is chirping in my hand and the sky is turning pink. It's morning and I'm stiff with cold. My left hand is a claw, frozen to the phone. On the back of my hand is a note to myself. Blue ink and my uneven handwriting. *Rose 1013 Alpine 2 P.M.* There's a burnt stub of cigarette in my other hand. Rose must have hung up on me and I fell asleep or blacked out. Either way I'm still standing. And it looks like Rose and I have a date. Maybe she wants to go to a matinee. Two o'clock. I can take care of Jude by then, I'm sure. I'm hungry and I drop the phone. There's a diner down the street.

I must look bad. The waitress asks if I have any money before she will give me a menu. I show her twenty dollars and still she is slow with the coffee. I'm the only customer. I stare at the eggs on my plate. I asked for them sunny side up because it sounded cheerful and now they won't stop jiggling. I chew a piece of bacon for a long time, grinding it into tasteless paste.

This was a bad idea.

Excuse me? The waitress sucks the end of her pencil and stares at me.

The food, I say. Sometimes I hate to eat.

What's wrong with it?

I would rather be a machine. Or else just take a pill and be done.

Listen, mister. If you don't like it you can take your funny ideas someplace else.

You don't understand. This place is the same as any other. It's the need to consume food every day in order to sustain the flesh. It depresses me.

I'm sorry you got problems. But mostly I don't care.

I gouge the eggs with my fork and the yolk is bright and putrid.

Is there more coffee?

But she doesn't look up. I drop a few crumpled dollars on my plate and go.

eight.

A LONG WHITE LINCOLN IDLES IN AN ALLEYWAY. The windows are tinted but I know who it is. I walk to the driver's side and stand there until the black glass slides down.

Are you feeling better? says the Blister. He still wears the white leather gloves.

Oh, I'm a peach.

The engine growls. The Blister is nervously tapping the accelerator. My breath swirls away from me thick as smoke. The Blister wears a black fur coat and a red silk tie. The coat hangs open and I see he's got a small cannon in his shoulder holster.

I had a funny idea, I say.

What's that? says the Blister. The gloves squeal and pop as he grips the wheel.

The idea is that you aren't a cop. I never saw your badge.

That's a scream, says the Blister.

But I really don't mind you following me. It's comforting.

The Blister shrugs and his big gun is pressed gently into my testicles. I never saw him move. He leans out the window, as if he wants directions. I'm not a cop, he says. I'm a bunny rabbit. Now get in the car.

He kicks open the passenger door and I stroll around to get in. I suppose I could run. But I'm so feeble it would be embarrassing. He could smoke two cigarettes and daydream awhile, then go have a bite and still drop me from fifty yards with that gun.

I fasten my seat belt and the Blister rests the barrel of his gun on my shoulder.

Get used to that feeling, he says.

Where are we going?

The Blister smiles through me. A vein in his neck throbs visibly. The silence is crushing. The car gleams as if new. The seats are a soft, pale leather that must have come from baby calves. The dash is oiled mahogany. The car feels computerized, climate-controlled.

I love the car, I say. Very glamorous.

Isn't it fantastic. I just drove it off the lot the other day.

Oh, yeah. It's a fucking beauty.

I hope so, he says. It cost a small fortune.

Too bad, though. It smells like a dead boy's asshole.

He glares at me. Be careful with your tongue.

Do you have a name? Or a serial number?

Silence.

The gun at my ear twitches and I realize he's trembling. His face is dreamy, unfocused. I'm crazy, of course. But I think he's got a little erection and there is a brief unwanted rush of blood in my own genitals, because there is nothing so arousing as fear and submission and the threat of violence. And he could easily blow my head off when we hit a patch of ice.

My mouth is very dry. Do you mind if I smoke a cigarette?

If you like, says the Blister. You are not a prisoner, Mr. Poe.

This isn't the way to make friends.

If I meant to kill you I would have done so. If you were a prisoner, you would be riding in the trunk with a broken collarbone.

The collarbone?

Very painful. It leaves you extremely docile.

What about the gun in my ear?

Oh, well. A gun is only a tool.

Why don't you stop driving in circles and tell me what you want?

The Blister sighs and pulls over. He kills the engine. Now, he says. I will get to the point. In less than an hour you are meeting a woman named Jude at the train station. I will be watching you.

I smoke and try to appear undaunted.

The Blister taps the wheel with a gloved finger. I don't want to kill you. I want to help you. And perhaps you can help me.

Thanks. But I don't like you.

Don't be clever. That's the last thing you want to be.

This isn't happening.

I'm afraid it is. The minute you took Jude up to your room you entered into a world of shit.

Unlucky in love, I say.

The Blister smiles. Jude works for me, he says. Rather, she once did.

Okay. Who is she and why does she want my kidney?

It doesn't matter who she is, he says. She can be whoever you want her to be. And she doesn't want your kidney.

Oh, well. Someone must want it.

Indeed.

I stare at him, growing irritated. Who?

The Blister smiles like a generous king. I might want it, he says.

You hired her to steal my kidney.

He shrugs. My dear brother is dying.

And she gave you those bruises. She fucked you up. What did you do to her?

I'm a gentleman, he says.

Let me guess. You didn't want to pay her and she decided to keep my poor kidney.

It is no longer your kidney, says the Blister. It is mine. Or my brother's to be exact. Unfortunately, Jude has failed to deliver it.

My knife is out of the wrist sheath, fast and silent as a cat's heart. I slash upward and think, if I cut his lips off he might stop talking like such a wanker. The Blister brings the barrel of his gun down on my wrist and I drop the knife; my fingers are numb and I hope the wrist isn't broken. I hope I don't cry like a baby when the feeling returns to my hand. The Blister picks up the fallen knife, holding it by the blade with two fingers.

He gives it back to me without a word.

Listen very carefully, he says. If you try that again, I will cut off your thumb.

I apologize. I tell him I'm a little sensitive about my body parts.

A natural reaction, he says.

Okay, I say. Tell me what you want.

I want you to kill her and return the kidney to me. I will pay you one hundred thousand dollars.

Your little scenario is flawed.

Why do you say that?

Because I already have a plan. I'm going to kill Jude this afternoon for fun. And then eat my own putrid kidney for dinner. This will bring me strength and good fortune.

The Blister laughs. You won't kill her. Not yet.

Oh, really. Why not?

Because I can see it in your eyes. You can't wait to touch her, to fuck her again.

She fucked me, I say.

Whatever you say. But when you get tired of her, you will kill her for me.

I blow smoke and try to connect the dots between Pooh and Jude and the Blister. I try to open my window but the button doesn't work. The Blister has a master switch on his side and I'm sure it pleases him to control everyone's window. He seems like a control freak, a little Hitler with equally bad hair. I turn my head and the gun is at my Adam's apple. The Blister's face is blank as the gray sun. He's suddenly a thousand miles away and his left hand is busily squeezing and poking at a pimple on his chin. He's eager to pop it but he needs both hands. He needs to take off those stupid gloves.

Aren't you neglecting something? I say.

He blinks at me.

What about the heroin?

The Blister turns a delicious shade of pink. Heroin?

Heroin, I say.

The Blister waves a hand and stutters. It's nothing. Jude is simply killing two birds with one stone.

I laugh. Am I a bird or a stone?

If you must know, she is using you as a mule. When she removed your kidney she also made a deposit. There is a large amount of raw heroin in your lower intestine. Today she will pretend to be surprised and angry to see you; she may even threaten to kill you. Then she will allow you to gain the upper hand; she will reluctantly invite you to become her partner. You will travel to El Paso with her and cross the border. Then she will sell you to her buyer, as if you were a package, or a dog. The buyer will remove the heroin by whatever method he chooses.

You just made that up, I say.

I did not, he says.

Come on. Are you trying to tell me she is letting me walk around town with a balloon full of smack in my belly, unaware? What if I accidentally shit it out in some public toilet?

When was your last bowel movement?

I don't really know. Maybe three days ago. Before I met her.

Precisely, he says. She has no doubt made alterations to your digestive system. Staples in your stomach perhaps, for the very purpose of protecting her merchandise. And I'm sure she drugged you. I assume you have no appetite? Food repulses you, am I right?

I just had breakfast, I say. Bacon and eggs. Fucking delicious, too.

Whatever you say; the heroin is irrelevant to me. My only interest is eliminating Jude and recovering the kidney.

I look at the Blister, amused. A large quantity of heroin is never irrelevant.

His gloved fingers clench and relax as if they are stiff with cold. He starts the car.

I could use something to drink, the Blister says. Where shall we go?

There's a drive-through burger place down the street.

The Blister drives pitifully slow, as if he's not used to driving on snow. He's staring at the road like he's afraid it might disappear. I rub my belly, reluctant to believe that there is anything inside but empty space and disconnected wiring. Blood and white noise.

Let's make it two hundred thousand, I say.

One hundred. Not a penny more.

Easy money. Like falling out of bed.

A piece of advice, says the Blister. Don't take her too lightly. Jude is a very dangerous girl. She has tasted your blood and she enjoys it. Likewise, you wouldn't want to disappoint me.

I'm sorry. But you just aren't as dreadful as you mean to be. I think you might want to shave your head and grow a little goatee. And you could use a foreign accent, maybe French.

Imagine, says the Blister. Imagine waking up with no vocal cords and your eyes like jelly, your hands and feet cut off and soaked in acid, your teeth removed and crushed to powder.

I try to smile, to savor this moment.

At the drive-up window the Blister orders for both of us. A diet soda for himself and coffee for me. I reach for my wallet but the Blister waves it away. He parks the car and leaves it running. I light a cigarette and offer him one. He takes it and smiles. Thank you.

For a few silent minutes we blow smoke at each other, like best friends.

The Blister glances at his watch and when I finish my coffee, he presses a button that unlocks my door.

Good-bye, he says. I will find you when Jude is dead.

Excuse me. I haven't agreed to anything. And I think a little money up front would be a nice gesture.

The Blister smiles through white and yellow teeth. He pulls a slim leather wallet from his breast pocket and counts out five thousand dollars.

The rest upon completion, he says.

What is this. A little cigarette money?

Don't be rude, he says. Take the money and go.

Who the fuck are you?

This time he doesn't smile. I wait for him to whip out that big foolish gun.

I'm afraid it's time for you to go, he says.

It's snowing, I say. The least you could do is give me a ride.

Don't be foolish. Jude will be watching.

Tell me again: why should I do this?

The money. Do it for the money. Then you can buy your wife a new dress.

My wife is dead.

Of course she is.

What do you know about it? I say. I'm disgusted by the sound of my voice.

He shrugs. I might know who killed her. Or who didn't.

I look at my hands; there is no blood on them. I tell the Blister I will think about it.

nine.

It's a long walk to the train station.

Five minutes until eleven. The station is old and cavernous. It echoes like a cathedral. I stand in the center and let people stream past me. The panic of faces and thoughts colliding. Slow breaths and a half smile. I am a fool. I told Jude I was afraid of crowds and she will use it against me. I turn a slow circle but I don't see her anywhere. I close my eyes and sniff the air. I try to feel her. I was sure that she would arrive early and take the high ground. But she's expecting Pooh and she isn't worried. She might still be sleeping, white sheets wrinkled around her yellow skin. Her fists clenched, her eyelids fluttering. She might be dreaming of me.

Twenty minutes later I'm sitting on a wooden bench. I'm watching two kids argue over a video game. Jude sits down beside me. She's chewing her lip, angry. But her eyes glow.

You should never have come here, she says.

It's twenty-nine degrees outside and snowing. Jude is wearing a short white ski jacket. A black dress that stops halfway down her thighs and cowboy boots the color of wine. Her knees are pale and cold. She has her hands buried in her pockets. She looks everywhere but at me.

Are you insane? I say.

She crosses her legs. I have very warm blood.

I might want to kill you.

And I might say the same thing.

But you're glad to see me.

Hardly.

My senses are jangled and the pain is becoming unbearable. I remove Pooh's film canister from my pocket. I rattle the pills around, trying to think. Jude watches me, amused. One pill could leave me too goofy to function and I would rather she didn't know I was high.

She grins. Did you like Pooh?

Her hair is slightly frozen, as if she just washed it. Her eyes are impossibly green and I wonder if she's wearing colored lenses. She unzips the jacket a few inches to show her tender throat. She's wearing lipstick and suddenly I want to crush my mouth against hers. I want to suck her blood.

Pooh is a sad tomato, I say. He's in love with you.

Of course he is.

He must have a massive dick.

I'm sure he does. Like a horse. But I wouldn't know.

Oh, really. Pooh tells me a different story.

And who do you believe?

I don't believe anyone.

She laughs. Pooh is terrified of me. His penis would run and hide if I uncrossed my legs.

Then what use is he?

He carried eleven bags of ice up four flights of stairs to keep you alive. He never even complained.

That shuts me up. I pop one blue muscle relaxer into my mouth and roll it between my teeth. I bite it in two before it dissolves. I swallow half and spit the other into the palm of my hand.

Let's pretend to be friends, I say.

Close friends, she says.

I hold the bitten pill out to Jude and she bends to take it with her lips.

Where is my kidney? I say.

It's hot in here, don't you think?

Did you know I used to be a cop? I could make you disappear.

Disappear, she says. I love that word.

She crosses and uncrosses her legs. A muscle like rope along her inner thigh.

Let's go somewhere less public, she says.

Why not, I say. But I sit like a statue, a stone frog crouching in someone's garden.

Don't be afraid, she says.

The urge to kill her returns and I feel warm, as if the sun has slipped from behind a cloud.

Why would I be afraid?

I've already wounded you, she says.

Terribly.

But I can't hurt you anymore, she says.

No, I say.

She stands and I can hear every whisper and rustle of her clothes. I can almost see her body through the nylon and leather. I can nearly see the organs beneath her skin, clustered and purple. Busily pumping and thrusting, keeping her alive. For a moment I wonder if my kidney is in there, knitting itself to her flesh. I tell myself I want to kill her, to punish her. I want my kidney back. But such thoughts only float away, foreign and weightless. I feel myself dissolve. She dangles a gloved hand and I take it.

Jude and I stand on the street corner waiting for the light to change. I still hold her hand. I'm afraid she will run away. The wind is bitter and I want to shield her from it. I have this ridiculous idea that I can protect her, that she needs me to. Three nights ago she took me apart like a dog eating stolen meat. She tore into me.

Across from the train station is a nameless motel.

It's ugly, she says. But it does have room service.

I step out into the street, her hand still in mine. She flinches and I look around me. Pooh is standing behind a streetlamp; his face is hidden but his arms and shoulders and half his belly are clearly visible. His dirty white cast is bright against the dark mist in the air. I'm weirdly embarrassed by his incompetence. Jude growls and reaches into her purse. She comes out with a square black hairbrush, gripping it with the bristles turned down. She pulls away from me and takes several steps toward the streetlamp, holding the brush out like a gun. Pooh's arms begin to flail and I am reminded of a children's puppet show. Then he turns and runs down the sidewalk. Jude turns back to me, smiling and I shrug, as if she has just chased away a cowardly mugger.

The parking lot is black with snow.

Jude leads me up a flight of stairs to room 212. The door is heavy and swings shut slowly. Jude sits down on the bed and takes off her cowboy boots, dropping them to the floor. She reaches for the remote control and flicks on the television. She finds a soap opera and turns down the volume. I still stand by the door. The gun is in my ankle holster. I could have it in my hand. I could shoot her between the eyes and go. I could kill her with my knife. I could sit down beside her and offer to rub her feet and when she smiles I could grab her by the hair and pull her head back and cut her throat. I could keep the Blister's insulting money and take Eve to Disney World.

Jude glances at me. Why don't you sit down?

I bend to one knee and remove the Smith & Wesson. Jude watches me, unconcerned. I place the gun on top of the television, then put my knife down beside it.

Jude smiles. In my left boot, she says. I have a stinger, like a wasp.

I pick up the boot. The leather is slick and smells new. There is a sheath sewn into the inner wall of the boot and I pull out what appears to be a sharpened dentist's surgical tool, much like a stiletto with a hooked tip. It's a nasty little thing. The silver grip is slightly curved and wrapped in leather cord. I fold my hand around the grip and slash at the air and I like the feel of it.

Did you use this to rip me open?

She laughs. Of course not. It's not meant for such delicate work.

I put the stinger down. What else do you have? I say.

Jude unzips the ski jacket. Her dress is cut low across the neck and her collarbones are sharply defined. The flash of a black satin strap. I roll my eyes away and try to concentrate. She pulls a small silver automatic from the inside pocket of her coat. She tosses the gun at me, a Beretta .25 with a skeleton grip.

It suits you, I say.

Jude shrugs. I always wanted to fuck James Bond.

Dreams are all we have. But I'm looking for another gun, a 9mm.

I don't have a nine, she says. I don't care for big loud guns.

But I did have one. The night I met you. And now I can't seem to find it.

She lounges back against the pillows, her legs like scissors. The black dress is like tissue and I'm dying to touch her. I'm sorry, she says. But I didn't take it. Maybe the cops have it, or the bellboy. Even Pooh could have it. He was in the room and he has very sticky fingers.

Detective Moon has it in his desk drawer and he hasn't decided what to do with it. I should close my eyes and walk out of here. I should go down to the station and walk in like I'm coming home. I hope you boys are thirsty because I got money to burn and by the way, Moon: where's my fucking gun? But he might just laugh at me and say whatever do you mean? I take off my coat and drop it to the floor.

Tell me about yourself, I say.

I'm an only child.

Only children tend to be spoiled.

They are selfish, she says. They never had to share their mother's breast.

The shadows in her room are short and malformed, squatting in the corners like sullen trolls.

Are your legs cold?

Very, she says.

I touch her knee with the tip of a finger. Slowly trace a line down to her ankle. There's a fine black stubble, barely visible but rough as stone.

Let me rub your feet, I say.

She uncocks the left leg and drops her foot in my lap. I look at it without touching. A small pale foot, with a high arch. A crooked purple vein. The heel is callused. The toes are well shaped, evenly spaced. The nails painted blue as a clear sky. I begin to stroke and fondle her foot as if I'm petting a kitten.

I'm curious, she says. What's so special about that gun?

Silence.

I used to be a cop.

She stares up at the ceiling, bored. That cloud looks like a lizard, she says.

I could easily break her ankle. I could twist her fucking foot off.

So you used to be a cop. So what?

A cop doesn't like to lose his gun. It makes him nervous, I say.

Is that the only reason?

I whisper for her to shut up and bend to kiss her, to bite her.

Jude reaches for the phone. She says she's starving.

She orders blueberry pancakes and coffee for two. I look down at my hands, clasped around her foot. They are strange to me, unfamiliar. I look at the television instead. Two actors are kissing vigorously on a phony riverfront as white smoke swirls around them.

Jude lights two cigarettes and gives me one.

For ten minutes we smoke and watch the silent soap opera. Jude tries to explain the intricacies of each character's sexual history but I'm not really listening.

They have money and posh cars but they're still a lot of inbreds, she says.

A gentle knock at the door. I go to answer it and a boy in a red suit stands there with a tray of food. I sign the slip and give him five dollars. Jude tells me to hang the DO NOT DISTURB card. I ignore her and set the tray down on the bed. Jude moves to crouch like a wolf over the food. She uncovers the steaming pancakes. They are stained by the burst blueberries and the smell is heavy and sweet. Jude smears them with butter and eats them without syrup. She pours coffee and hands me a cup.

Look in the bathroom, she says. There's a bottle of brandy in the sink.

For the first time I look closely at the room. It is clean and neat; house-keeping must have come recently. Still, there are no random possessions laying about. There are no clothes hanging in the closet. A compact black garment bag dangles from a hook. I would dearly love to poke through it but it is zippered shut and tight as a drum. I have a feeling Jude is ever ready to walk out the door. Even in the bathroom there is little sign of her presence. No clumps of tissue, no toothbrush and feminine gear. A half bottle of brandy in the sink. A green rubber icebox on the floor. I unscrew the brandy and take a short swallow. The hairs in my nose shrink as if on fire. The icebox is padlocked.

Jude has disposed of her pancakes and is freshening her lipstick. I give her the brandy and sit down to smoke a cigarette. You should eat, she says. The pancakes are getting cold.

I'm not hungry.

It's a shame. They're delicious.

I blow smoke and watch it swirl toward her.

Why didn't you meet me last night?

What do you mean, dear?

You left me a note. When I'm depressed I go bowling…

Oh, she says. I suppose I changed my mind. And you found me anyway.

Strains of early afternoon light. Pooh's blue moon gives everything a fine glassy sheen. The room is thick with electric heat and it's difficult to breathe. The soap opera has given way to thumb-sucking midget versions of Bugs Bunny and friends. The sound is muted but I keep thinking I can hear their helium voices. Above the television is a large round mirror and a watercolor of a duck. I sit in a chair beside the bed. On the nightstand there is a phone book and a *TV Guide* and the Gideons' Bible. The chair has no arms and I don't know what to do with my hands. My pants are unbuttoned and Jude kneels before me with my dick in her mouth. Her teeth are small and sharp and it's like her mouth is full of powdered glass. She may have drawn blood and I can't separate the pleasure from pain. I don't want her to stop. Jude lifts her head before I come. She breathes and smiles. The lipstick is gone and her lips are pale. She climbs into the chair and I'm inside her and I remember Crumb telling me to be careful, that sex could kill me.

The brandy is gone. Jude lies with her head in my lap. We share a cigarette back and forth. She is naked and has thrown the sheets off the bed. I am memorizing her body and I really don't need to. She is already as familiar to me as a recurring dream. Her eyes are wide apart and shaped like lemons; the lids are hooded and I remember my mother telling me those were mongoloid eyes, the devil's eyes. She has fine white teeth, slightly crooked and sharp. Her skin is a pale creamy yellow. She has small breasts with nipples the color of wet leather. Her belly and thighs are long, muscular. Her pubic hair is shaved like the narrow wing of a baby crow.

Phineas, she says.

What?

You saw the icebox.

Yes. Didn't you want me to?

I suppose.

It has my kidney in it.

She doesn't say anything. I stroke her throat and she passes me the cigarette.

It's strange, I say. At first it was like my wallet was gone and I wanted it back. And now I don't feel anything. It's just used flesh. It's garbage.

It's not garbage. It's worth a lot of money.

Who is the buyer?

A land developer in El Paso named Gore. One of his children has a bone disease or something.

What if the kidney isn't compatible?

Don't worry. I took tissue samples and had DNA tests done. Mr. Gore wasn't the only prospect. It could have easily gone to a baseball player or a politician in Canada.

Jude is never completely still. She twists a piece of string between her fin-

gers and her foot bounces up and down. Her whole body seems to vibrate.
I watch her face closely and her eyes never fade. She doesn't scratch her nose
or twist her lip or change colors. I'm sure she's lying and then I'm not sure.

I have two tickets to El Paso, she says. A cozy little sleeper car.
  I don't want to but I smile. What are you saying?
  I'm willing to give you half.
  Only half.
  I've done all the legwork, she says.
  Why give me any of it?
  I need a partner. Someone to watch my back. And I kept thinking of you.
  That's nice. How much are we talking about?
  A lot, she says.
  When I was ten years old, I thought fifty dollars was a lot of money.
  I think it's impolite to discuss money.
  There's nothing polite about any of this.
  She sighs. It's quite cheap, really. Two hundred and fifty thousand.

I slide out from under her and begin to get dressed. Two hundred and fifty
thousand. It seems ridiculous. The kidney is a small lump of fatty tissue
that processes waste and sends it along to the bladder in liquid form. The
kidney makes urine all day. Then again, someone might have a daughter
whose life depends on a used kidney and how much is that worth? I am
very sore and my brain is like a dead balloon. I am hoping that sex with
Jude will eventually make me stronger. For now, she will have to help me
put my boots on. I stop and smile at our weapons lined up in a neat row.
I take my gun and stroll into the bathroom. I pick up the icebox and I'm
almost disappointed. It should be heavier, somehow. I come out of the
bathroom, my gun pointed lazily at Jude. She is still naked. She doesn't
blink and she doesn't pull a gun from her ear like a coin.
  I'm taking this with me, I say.
  What will you do with it?
  I feel like screaming.
  I don't know. I might put it back where it belongs. I might fry it up

with some purple onions and have it for lunch. I might just sell it myself.

You could never find a buyer. Not in a thousand days.

When does the train leave?

Tomorrow at nine thirty-five A.M.

Give me my fucking ticket.

Are you going to kill me?

I thought so, earlier. Or I wanted to think so.

Jude rolls onto her stomach. The eye tattoo black beneath her strewn hair. I adore her strong sleek ass. She reaches for the white ski jacket and pulls out a blue and white ticket, flashing it like a trump card.

ten.

THE AVERAGE DRUG MULE SWALLOWS A DOZEN OR MORE fat, skin-tight latex packets shaped like bullets and filled with heroin or coke. He or she has perhaps thirty-six hours to make delivery; otherwise the digestive system breaks down the latex, dissolving it. The drug is released into the bloodstream, and the host is dead within minutes. I have long passed thirty-six hours and I'm still breathing.

I could care less about heroin that may not exist. But Jude has her teeth deep in my heart.

Everyone is throwing money at me today and I'm feeling like a car wreck. I decide to live a little and take a taxi. It's ten after two. I'm late for Rose but I think she'll understand. I haven't been myself.

The driver is a young guy, slouched down in his seat. I tell him the address. He grunts, chews his gum. I'm lucky and he doesn't want to talk. The radio is tuned to an oldies station. A little Johnny Mathis and then the Temptations. I stare out the window at faces in passing cars.

A green Volvo station wagon pulls alongside the cab. There is a woman at the wheel, perhaps forty with severe hair. Her lipstick is a ferocious red that is smeared along her jaw and in the back window I see naked faces pressed against the glass, dirty and emaciated. Lost children, tortured and pleading for help. The faces dissolve and waver and become ordinary children, five and seven. The woman is their mother and there is something wrong with me.

I bounce around in my seat, manic and juiced. My skin doesn't feel right. It feels rubbery and stretched, as if two people are sharing it. Soon it will come apart. I'm stupidly high, of course. Jude could have slipped me something. Or Pooh might have lied. Perhaps those little blue pills were not muscle relaxers at all, and I remember poor Georgia. I hope she has come down from Pluto and is no longer rabid as I would hate to shoot her. I hope she suffered no ill effects from the pills I gave her. She was already on a bad cocktail of some kind; heroin and ecstasy perhaps, with a dash of crystal for kicks. Sudden death is always an eyelash away and I hope she didn't perish in that closet. Eve might find her while innocently looking for toilet paper.

What will I tell Eve, I wonder. What will I tell Rose. That I decided not to kill Jude. In fact, I massaged her feet and had breakfast with her. I take out my pocketknife and begin to trim my nails. I let her suck me like she was stealing gasoline and then I fucked her as if there was no tomorrow. The knife slips back and forth across my fingertips and white slivers fall to my chest. She has me wrapped around her little toe and I like it. I cut my thumbnail too short and soon it starts to bleed.

Is this it?

The cab has stopped at a haunted little bungalow with dark red shutters and a black tile roof with a weather vane. A curved hardwood front door, like a Hobbit hole. There's a gargoyle birdbath in the front yard, and a FOR SALE sign.

Is this it?

How do I know, man? It's the address you said—1013 Alpine.

It's way the hell across town.

Yeah. And you owe me thirteen dollars.

I stare at the house. I was half asleep when I spoke to Rose. I could have written down the wrong address. There's a scrap of paper tacked to the door, white and twisting in the wind. It might be a note.

I think I've been here before.

That's great, man. Do you want out or what?

I pass the kid some money and tell him to keep it. I get out and watch him drive away. I'm immediately very cold and I can tell by looking at the house that no one's home.

The note is unsigned, addressed to no one. *If I'm not here at three please wait.* I press my face to the cold windows. Dark rooms with minimalist décor. Wooden furniture and thick red carpets. No sign of life. I sit on the stoop to smoke. The wind is picking up and I waste a dozen matches before I get a light. It's quarter to three. How long do I want to wait? It's cold enough to die out here and I need to see Eve before I leave town. I want to have a shower and pack a few things and ask her to keep the Bug for me. And I should really see Crumb. Perhaps he can reinstall my kidney for a small fee. At the very least, he can give me a cup of tea and a little sympathy.

A car pulls up at the curb, a red Subaru wagon. A woman gets out and it's not Rose. She wears a long gray overcoat and rubber boots. A bright blue scarf and gold earrings. She holds a leather briefcase in one gloved hand. She's obviously a real estate agent.

Hello. Her voice is practiced, friendly. Are you my three o'clock?

I nod and smile and apologize for being early. She eyes the green icebox and I shrug. Some people carry briefcases, some don't.

That's fine. What about your wife?

She's not going to make it. I'm all alone.

Super, she says. Are you ready to see the house?

Please. I'm nearly frozen.

I offer my hand as she approaches the steps. She smiles and produces a massive ring of keys. The door swings open and heat rushes out. There's a damp smell of cats.

After you, I say.

Do you have children?

No…I don't.

There's a lovely little bedroom upstairs. Perfect for a baby's room.

I drift through the front room and look for details, photographs. There is almost nothing. Not a book or candlestick or ceramic ashtray. Behind me the woman is reciting square feet and water pressure and morning light and nearby schools. I tell her I was hoping to meet the owner.

I'm afraid Miss Hunt is not well. She's quite old, you know.

I try to mirror her expression of polite but uninterested pity.

It's hard to be old, I say. What is she like, Miss Hunt?

Actually, I have never met her. A lawyer arranged for the sale.

But she has a daughter, then?

A daughter, no. I don't think she was ever married.

I stare at her, nodding. Is there a telephone I can use?

She shows me the phone and hovers nearby as I dial the number Rose gave me. She watches me with nervous brown eyes. Three times I get a busy signal. I give up and call for another cab.

eleven.

THE SECOND CAB DRIVER IS FAT AND CHEERFUL. He wants to talk about football but I'm not in the mood. I tell him I don't like football and he turns around to glare at me, as if I'm a pervert. Eventually we arrive at the address I gave him and he gets a good look at the Witch's Teat. He nods and mutters to himself, eager to get me out of his cab. I give him a big tip anyway.

Crumb is watching the store and he doesn't look too happy about it. He grunts when I walk in. He holds a sleek leather riding crop in one hand.

I'm killing flies, he says.

Where is little Eve?

She never came in. He swats at a fat winter fly and misses.

Maybe she's not feeling well.

I don't care, he says. She knows I don't like to work the counter. The customers are a lot of freaks.

Do you ever get any customers in here?

Well. It's a little slow today. But sometimes it gets crazy around Valentine's Day.

I'm sure. I stare at a grotesque display of vibrators shaped like rodents.

What can I do for you? he says.

I lift the green icebox like a trophy, like the head of a deer.

Crumb shudders. Is that what I think it is?

Have you had your lunch?

I'm not hungry.

Excellent. This will be easier on an empty stomach.

Phineas, he says. I helped a woman give birth once. It was a difficult procedure and she very nearly died. But she didn't. I kept her alive and she delivered a healthy baby girl. Six and a half pounds. The woman was so grateful that she asked me to help her eat the placenta. I was ill for days and I could never eat meat again.

I laugh helplessly. I'm sorry.

What is so fucking funny.

I'm not going to eat it. And if I were, I wouldn't share it with you.

Oh, I see. Phineas was making a little joke.

Not a very good one, it seems. I didn't even know you were a vegetarian.

Crumb sniffs. What do you want, then?

I want you to cut me open and put this little jewel back where it belongs.

Crumb locks the front door without a word. He hangs a sign in the window that says he has gone fishing. He grins faintly and tells me the sign was stolen from a barbershop. I follow him into the back and he motions for me to sit down. He bustles about as before, boiling water for tea and tinkering with the radio until he finds a moody Bach fugue. I sit on the purple sofa and flip through a magazine that is five years old.

Crumb finally sits down.

This is not a good idea, he says.

Why not?

When was the kidney removed?

Three days ago. Maybe four.

Then it is surely worthless.

I stare at him, insulted.

He sighs. I never went to medical school, remember. I don't know everything about transplant technology. But I don't think human tissue can survive outside the body much longer than a day.

But there's a chance, I say.

It's very doubtful.

Then let's open it and have a look.

Do you have the key?

No. But we could probably pry it open.

If the kidney is still viable, then forcibly opening the icebox would probably fuck it up. I would need all sorts of fancy equipment and two or three extra hands to do the operation. And I would have to do a little reading on the subject first.

Well. That's just fucking great.

Listen, he says. You have had something terrible done to you. It's like being mugged, or raped. You have been violently invaded and you aren't thinking straight.

Fuck you. Don't you think I know that?

Crumb closes his eyes. Where the hell is Eve? he says.

I light a cigarette and immediately put it out. I wish she were here.

What do you expect from me, Phineas?

The kettle has been whistling tunelessly for several minutes now.

I just want some tea, okay.

Crumb serves the tea with a tray of stale English cookies. I chew on a cookie and Crumb smokes his pipe. Steam twists from our cups and the Bach fugue gives way to an unknown cello piece that is frantic as razors against glass. I do have another problem, I say.

What's this?

I may be carrying around a bag of heroin in my belly.

Are you serious?

I don't know. The information is unreliable.

My, my. That would be diabolical. To steal your kidney and leave such a package in its place. I'm not sure it makes a lot of sense, though. What if you had died, for instance? The heroin would be largely unretrievable.

No shit. The plan is so full of holes you could swim through it. But then who would hassle a wounded ex-cop at the border?

Interesting. What do you want to do about it?

I don't want to choke down a handful of laxatives and spend the day on your toilet. Especially if someone is only fucking with me.

I have an idea, he says. But don't laugh.

Crumb is making a lot of noise. It sounds like he's kicking a cardboard box to death. I can hear him wheezing and cursing and for once I wonder how old he is. Finally he drags a grocery cart with jammed wheels from his closet. The cart contains a machine that looks like the vile offspring of an old black-and-white television and a microwave. A variety of wires and dusty cords extend from its guts. It reminds me of a broken stereo I used to have. It was such a piece of shit that no one would steal it if I left it on my front porch.

What the hell is that?

Your ignorance betrays you, boy. This is a slightly used but perfectly functional ultrasound machine. I stole it many years ago from a hospital supply company.

Oh, boy.

Take off your shirt, he says.

Again I stretch out on Crumb's table and wonder how many strangers have lain bleeding here. Crumb plugs in the machine and adjusts the small humming screen so that I can see it. He smears cold, odorless jelly over my skin that looks innocently like spermicide, like a friendly lubricant.

That goo is the same shit the paramedics use before they shock your dead heart, isn't it?

Your heart is fine, he says.

And when they electrocute you. They smear that same jelly on your skull.

Crumb whispers for me to hush. He shows me a round black paddle that is wired to the machine and looks a lot like a Ping-Pong paddle.

This sends sound waves into your abdominal cavity, he says. The waves bounce around in there and the machine uses the information to construct an image. Submarines and bats navigate by the same basic principle.

Fantastic.

Crumb rubs the paddle over my belly like a magic wand. I watch the screen but it remains black. My belly is a bottomless pit. A small child could crawl in there and take a nap.

You're a quack, I say. A hopeless fucking quack.

He grunts and fiddles with the machinery, and finally a grainy image appears on the screen. Random black and white shapes, endlessly shifting. I could be staring through the dark leaves of a tree against the gray sky before a storm. I remember watching television in the middle of the night when I was a kid; the broadcast would abruptly end at four in the morning and I was left staring at a window of blinding snow, at a thousand insects killing each other.

Have you ever seen anyone make sausage? I say. They take all the nasty leftover bits of a cow or pig and grind them up until they look exactly like this.

Shut up.

Weather patterns, I say.

That large chaotic mass is your large intestine, he says. Nothing unusual.

Thanks. What about that gray area?

What gray area?

Lurking off the coast of California, I say.

Oh, that could be anything. Scar tissue or undigested cabbage.

I don't like cabbage.

And he mutters dryly, it could be a bomb.

Jesus, I say. Why can't you just lie to me like a normal doctor? Tell me it's my appendix. Tell me it's an undescended testicle or something.

Crumb has a wicked laugh. The bomb could be wired to your heart. If your heart stops, the bomb loses an electrical charge and good-bye, Phineas.

Oh, you motherfucker. Doesn't my heart stop whenever I sneeze?

Sorry, he says. I was up late last night, watching a bad spy movie.

Last night was a hundred years ago. I dreamt of Lucy last night.

I've only actually used this machine once, says Crumb. And I mistakenly told a woman she was carrying twin girls. For all I know, you have a bag of shit in there the size of my head. Or you might well be pregnant with a litter of puppies.

I feel so much better.

Latex would have surely dissolved by now, he says.

Of course. But drug smugglers are pretty imaginative these days. They may have come up with indestructible baggies made of bulletproof Kevlar.

Well, he says. Then I suppose you can't be fucked.

twelve.

IT'S A SHORT WALK TO EVE'S PLACE. The snow has stopped but the wind is still vicious. My shirt sticks against my skin where Crumb rubbed that foul jelly. I wiped most of it off but a fine sheen remains. I decide not to worry about the heroin. I will pretend it's another imaginary tumor. I often dream that I have a brain tumor, and in the dream, I take strange comfort in the idea that I know how I will die but not when.

But I may as well go with Jude to El Paso. I'm pitifully drawn to her, like a moth. I remember when I was seventeen; I always went running back to the girls who tore my heart out. The kidney is apparently worthless, but I can still kill Jude if I want to. But I will kill her for my own reasons. The Blister can rot.

My car still sits where Eve left it, a friendly pink parking ticket fluttering on the windshield. I climb in and start shoving things into the duffel bag. A box of ammunition, razor and toothbrush, most of my clothes. I count my money and decide to leave some of it with Eve. I might die before I spend it all.

Her apartment is dark and quiet, as if no one's home. I'm wondering if I can break in through a window but I try the door anyway. It's unlocked. The air smells faintly of lemons and smoke. I step inside and flick on a light. The apartment has been torn apart; clothes and papers are strewn everywhere, like garbage ripped apart by dogs. Silverware and books and toiletries lay scattered. Someone came looking for me, for something I have. Perhaps the kidney in my icebox is not so worthless. It might have been the Blister, but this isn't quite his style. He wouldn't have left a trace. The person who did this was furious, manic.

I take off my shoes and slip through the kitchen. I hold my weapon like a bird's egg. I hear my grandfather's voice: *Hold it tight, now. But don't try to crush it. Pretend she's a bird's egg.* And I told Lucy the same thing when I taught her to use my gun. First I circle through the living room to be sure. Nothing has changed and I move down the hall in silence. Stop and poke the door of the linen closet with my foot; it creaks open. Empty and I keep moving. The bathroom. Toilet and sink and clothes hamper. A window too small for an adult to pass. Push back the shower curtain and Georgia is there, naked and shivering. She is unharmed, but she looks at me with terrible eyes. Her pupils have swallowed her eyes. She looks like a tortured dog. She spits at me and I want to throttle her, to hold her head underwater until she comes out of it. But I know she's already tipped over the edge.

Eve's room, she says finally.

Walk down the hall, don't run. Remain calm and be sure no one is behind me. Push open the door to Eve's room and enter at a crouch. The gun is an extension of my arm. Eve is facedown on her bed, naked. Her wrists are bound with tape and tethered to the bed frame. Her ankles are thrown wide apart and tied to either bedpost. She isn't moving and I smell blood. I cut the cords from her hands and feet, roll her over and there is so much tape around her face and skull I'm not sure she's breathing. Even her eyes are masked. I ease the tape away from her mouth and she gasps for air. I tell myself she's alive, she's alive. She doesn't make a sound and I hug her to me with my left arm, my back to the wall. The gun in my right hand trembles ever so slightly.

Where is he? I say.

She points at the window, the fire escape. I want to hold her but I need to examine her. I tell her I'm sorry and lay her gently down. There are bruises on her thighs and breasts and I've seen their kind before. The sheets are bloody. I know she hasn't been shot or cut but I have to check her anyway. Georgia is in the doorway, weeping.

Eve is alive, I say. She needs you.

Georgia creeps into the room as if she's moving through water. She stops crying and holds Eve to her chest like a mother with a child. There's a phone beside the bed and I call 911 for an ambulance. I bend to kiss Eve and she pulls away from me. I touch Georgia's cheek.

Listen to me, I say. You will have to talk to the police. Your attacker was unknown to you. He left the scene and you freed yourselves. I wasn't here. I was never here.

When I hear the sirens I too climb out the window. I close my eyes and listen for voices. I try to become someone else. I think of Pooh, his heavy, clumsy body. His stinking flesh and his giant hands. Pooh saw me with Eve; he followed us home. I pick up a chunk of broken cement and whirl around in a circle and finally let it go at my own car. The windshield becomes a spider's web but doesn't break and I have something to remind me of this.

The stitches in my side are screaming.

I drive with one hand. The other hand is torn between smoking a cigarette and clutching my wound to keep my guts from spilling out. The pain begins to ease and I let myself have a cigarette. I glance at my watch. I have nowhere to be until the train leaves tomorrow morning. I can take care of Pooh at my leisure. I'm not worried about finding him. He's a creature of habit. He will be thirsty. I don't believe he really has the stomach for this kind of thing and his knees will be rubber before long. And he will go somewhere familiar, somewhere comfortable. He will go to the Inferno and I will get there before he finishes his first beer. And then we will see. I have revenge to spare today; suffering that was meant for Jude will not be wasted. I will give it to him.

Late afternoon and the Inferno is empty and cold. It smells of dead fish and beer. Sick yellow sunshine filters through unwashed skylights. Two waitresses sit at the bar, bored and smoking cigarettes. They wear ill-fitting dominatrix gear: gleaming leather and vinyl and too much exposed flesh. Their faces are blank and humorless. A bartender dressed as a hunchback stands half in shadows. He is drinking a glass of milk. I circle through the bathroom and back to the bar. I don't see any sign of Pooh. I realize I'm walking like a cop. I become a junkie and force myself to walk as if I have stomach cramps. It isn't hard at all. I chew my thumb and stare at the floor. The bartender gazes at me like I'm a bug he can't be bothered to kill.

You seen Pooh, I say.

Don't think so, partner.

I need to find him. I need to find him in the worst way.

The bartender adjusts his hump and is silent. One of the women takes out black lipstick and a small mirror. She examines her face. The other one gives me a thin smile. Her eyes are blue and gentle.

You must be Christopher Robin.

I laugh like a chicken.

What's the matter with you?

I'm sick. Can't you see I'm sick.

The bartender sighs. I already mopped. I don't need any junkie regurgitating his lunch in here so why don't you get the fuck out?

There is a long silence. I scratch myself and cough. I stare mournfully at those soft blue eyes. Then turn and limp outside. I crouch down like a beggar and begin picking up wet cigarette butts.

After a minute she comes outside. I know what it's like, she says.

I'm dying here, I say.

I know, she says. And you need to get a fix. Everybody looks right through you.

It's like I'm a leper and my nose is fallin' off. How could you not notice that?

My knees buckle and I'm sinking but she catches me. Her touch is tender. She digs through her handbag and comes up with a slightly mashed chocolate bar.

Eat this. The sugar will make you feel better.

I'm afraid I'm going to laugh. I cover my face and moan as if I'm sobbing.

You're a nice person, I say.

I can tell you where Pooh lives.

The sun drifts behind a cloud and I look at her with my eyes open. She is dressed like a vampire, a cyberpunk whore. Her face is painted white. Her hair is an impossible black, almost blue. It must be synthetic. Her breasts are fake, round and plump as grapefruits. Her lips are bloated with fat taken from her ass. But her eyes are like pools of new rain. I eat the chocolate bar gratefully. I let her hold my hand and soon I am almost sorry for deceiving her.

thirteen.

MY WIFE USED TO SAY I WAS A TERRIBLE LIAR, that it was the only time I smiled. But she was wrong; I smiled when I was telling the truth.

On a winter morning one year ago I told her, without smiling, that she wasn't dead. She was sitting on the kitchen floor, crying. And she kept saying that she was dead. She wasn't supposed to live this long and I could hear the boy still breathing in our bedroom. I caught them together and it was embarrassing. They were fully dressed watching television and their thighs were barely touching. I wanted to be furious but I wasn't.

I don't remember when she started bringing home the high school boys, but I had been aware of it for months and pretended not to be. The house was wired for sound and video. Hidden cameras in every room. I didn't intend to watch her. I had been having blackouts and long episodes of sleeplessness and I didn't trust my memory. I wanted to watch myself. I wanted to know what I was doing when I disappeared, and I found myself watching Lucy instead. She brought home boys who barely had pubic hair. She let them see her naked, the odd glimpse as she came out of the shower, the flash of a breast where her robe fell open. They hung around for the possibility of more. Lucy helped them with their homework, she combed their hair and let them watch TV in bed with her. She asked them about girls and cars and baseball. She asked them what were they afraid of, what they dreamed of, and she pretended they were the children I couldn't give her.

The days became chasms, waiting for her to die. Sometimes I watched myself fuck her in the middle of the night, when I was unconscious and dreaming of my former self. Her shrunken body crushed under mine, her bald head glowing like an egg.

I told her I didn't care about the boys. Lucy borrowed youth and time and strength from them, things she couldn't get from me. I told her I had problems of my own and I wanted her to be happy. I told her she wasn't dead; the doctors were wrong and she had years to live. I told her I loved her and I didn't smile, because I wanted her to believe me.

The boy in the bedroom had asthma and later I would sit in the dark and listen to his terrible wheezing on my headphones.

Pooh lives in a basement apartment. The windows are covered from within by greased wax paper. I can already imagine the smell. The door is easily forced open. There is one room plus a closet with toilet and sink. Television and mattress and refrigerator and strewn clothes. The carpet foul and stained. I squat in the center of the room and breathe his air. I gather saliva in my mouth and spit. In the refrigerator is a box of aged jelly doughnuts. I poke through his clothes and find only pennies and bits of tobacco and strands of hair. In a metal crate beside his bed are comic books. A small collection, perhaps a hundred. They are well cared for. Each is in a plastic sheath to protect it from dust and moisture and bugs. I pull out a *Spider-Man* from twenty years ago and light a cigarette.

Spider-Man is tangling with Doctor Octopus and getting the shit pounded out of him. He keeps the wisecracks coming and manages to slap a glowing spider tracer on Doc Oc's leg before he gets away. Then the cops give him a hard time and he goes to see MaryJane and she's pissed because he is two hours late and I'm thinking: She never sleeps with you anyway so why bother? Then he drags himself home and has soup and sandwiches with his feeble Aunt May before he has to go hunt down the Octopus.

Pooh followed me and Eve home from the Inferno the other night. He was stupid with drink and he wanted to do something to me. He fell asleep and when he woke up he was sober and there was bile in his mouth. He went inside. He told himself he was going to kill me but I doubt that. He just wanted to scare me, to squeeze me for some money but I was gone. Instead he found two girls naked and cuddling on the couch and he just went crazy. Pooh would certainly hate lesbians. They would offend his moral sensibilities. He screamed at them and waved the gun around and said he would cut out their tongues. Then he tied them up and preached hellfire and motherhood and how they hadn't been fucked by the right fellow. He was going to leave but one of them said something to him. He took the little one and her smart mouth back to the bedroom and stripped her down and gave her a piece of Pooh.

I gave her a piece of Pooh.

The washed gray light before dawn. My head rests on Pooh's pillow and I am clutching his ratty blue blanket in one hand. My clothes smell like Pooh. For a moment I think I am Pooh. I have a grim and throbbing erection and I'm sick to realize I dreamed of raping Eve. My watch says it is six A.M. and I must have slept over fifteen hours. I was underwater, unconscious. I wasn't myself. I'm confused at first because I feel good. I feel rested. I go to Pooh's little bathroom and piss in his toilet. I drink from his faucet and eat some of his toothpaste.

The *Spider-Man* comic still lays open on the bed. I glance at it once more before I leave. The pages are slightly faded and the corners are worn soft and I imagine Pooh has read this a thousand times. He washes his hands every time and is careful not to crease the pages.

I have to get out of here before I lose the taste for killing him.

I step out Pooh's front door and there is Detective Moon. He is sitting on the top step with two cups of coffee. He looks tired and cold and slightly ill. His breath is white.

I was waiting for you to come out, he says. I thought it would be less complicated than trying to explain why you're asleep in a drug dealer's bed.

Is one of those coffees for me?

No, he says. I like to have two on a day like this. But I'm willing to share.

I sit down beside him and light a cigarette, glancing at my watch. The train leaves in a little over three hours and I'm going to be on it.

I don't normally work rape cases, he says. They make my stomach hurt. But your description came up when the uniforms questioned the neighbors. A little old lady, somebody's granny. She said you climbed out the window and looked exactly like a rapist. He laughs. What does a rapist look like?

He looks like a beggar, I say. A lawyer, a thief. He looks like somebody's brother. He has a sister, a mother. He has a granny that loves him.

This particular granny watches a lot of TV. And she was hot to come in and work with a sketch artist. In about eighteen hours your happy face will land on a lot of desks.

I never wanted to be famous.

Your name is already dogshit at the station.

Listen to me, Moon. This isn't connected to that other thing. Eve is a friend of mine. I'm just trying to find the guy who did this. Once a cop, you know.

But you aren't a cop, are you? And you're looking like a bad guy.

I'm not a bad guy. I'm not.

Let's take a ride, Phineas.

I take the coffee from him and gulp half of it. It's cold and too sweet and I dump it into ashen snow, splattering Moon's feet. If he has my gun, why doesn't he just say so? I can't let him arrest me. I'm in no condition to fight, but I'm not going downtown. I will rip open my wrists with my teeth before he puts me in a cage. I don't think Moon will shoot me but you never know. I shake my head. Moon openly stares at the green icebox I hold on my lap, and I realize it's like a deformity, a third leg. Some people stare at it and others pretend it's not there.

Have you found what you were looking for? he says.

Maybe.

There's an unverified story going around, he says. Five days ago a beautiful woman with dark hair walked into an emergency room in Colorado Springs. She wore a long white coat and she was carrying a Styrofoam ice chest. She handed the ice chest to a nurse and walked away. She disappeared. The ice chest contained a viable human kidney. It was used to save the life of a little girl in Phoenix. Some people are calling the woman an angel.

That is a terrible story. It's fucking nonsense. And it has nothing to do with me.

Moon looks to the east, at the colorless sky.

Every day, he says. The sun has to eat its way through clouds and smoke and poison.

Spare me, I say.

I danced with your wife once, he says. At the Christmas party last year. She told me you were in the bathroom and I danced with her. She said you were sick.

I close my eyes. She wore a little white dress. As smooth and tight as new skin.

Moon licks his lips and looks embarrassed. She told me her underpants were green velvet. This made me nervous and I offered to go see if you were okay. I thought you must have passed out in the toilet. She said you weren't sick from drinking. She said you were sitting in the last stall with your gun in your mouth. She said you were losing your mind and every day you put the gun in your mouth and thought about it.

She was drunk, I say. The doctors said she wasn't supposed to drink but she did.

She was dancing real close to me, says Moon. She was smiling and all

I could think about were those little green panties and how it would be to slide them down around her ankles and I started to panic. I wasn't like that. I went out in the parking lot and smoked a joint with some guys from the arson squad and they said they were going to the Black Heart to shoot pool and did I want to come. I was glad to go and an hour later I was lining up the two ball in the side pocket and it hit me. That maybe you were in that bathroom about to eat your own gun and I didn't do anything about it. I didn't try to save you from yourself or even go see if you needed saving because I was too busy trying to visualize your wife's panties.

Moon looks at me. His face is miserable. A lot of guys wanted to fuck my wife. She was a terribly sexy woman. She could have fucked them, all of them. I wouldn't have blamed her. But she never did. She waited for me to touch her again. I was too busy disappearing; I woke up next to her one morning and asked her who she was. I am tempted to put my arms around Moon and tell him not to worry, but I don't. I want to know if he has my gun. I scoop up a handful of snow and pack it into a hard gray ball of ice.

I remember those panties. They smelled like eucalyptus.

She didn't want me, he says. She was dying and she wanted you to love her.

I did love her. I loved her.

The next day I waited for my phone to ring, he says. For the voice that would tell me some poor bastard from Internal Affairs had blown his brains out and isn't it a damn shame, ho ho ho.

Do you have my gun?

What fucking gun?

My registered weapon, a Browning 9mm. The gun that may or may not have killed Lucy. It disappeared from evidence, remember?

Is this some kind of confession?

This is a conversation. Let me put it this way. The gun disappeared from evidence and came into my possession. I had it, and now I don't have it.

I don't have your gun, Phineas.

I still have the ball of ice in my left hand. I give it to Moon and tell him to let it melt, to forget he saw me here. He doesn't say anything and I know that he will let me disappear for now. But he will search Pooh's apartment after I'm gone and he will question Eve. If he finds anything that points to me then he will forget about Lucy's green panties. He will come after me without pity.

fourteen.

I EASE THE LITTLE BUG INTO THE PARKING LOT of Jude's motel. There's a red pickup truck parked crazily, sideways. It's jacked up on fat tires with mud-flaps that read: *Jesus was a U.S. Marine.* I don't like the look of this but maybe it's nothing. I'm breathing hard and the pain in my side has resumed its high-pitched whine. Moon made me nervous and my body is not well. I sit on the hood of my car to rest for a while and I find myself staring at the red truck. It's a beauty. The phallic but nervously whiplike antenna for a police scanner and the requisite gun rack above the back windshield. A small animal skull hangs from the rearview mirror. The hood is painted to resemble the American flag, with Playboy bunnies in place of stars. I can't wait to meet the owner. Then I notice the custom hood ornament: it's Winnie-the-Pooh flashing a killer smile.

He's with Jude. I don't know why I didn't think of it sooner. Of course he would run to her. I climb the stairs to room 212. Air escapes my chest as if I've been punched. I sit down on the frozen steps. I don't want to do this. I'm too tired. The taste of metal is gone from my mouth. When I saw Eve I wanted to kill him carefully. I wanted to use the tanto, to take him apart very slowly. Now I want to be done with him. I want him to walk out of room 212 with his hat in his hands and a big satisfied grin on his face. Then he will turn and see me, the gun in my hand. He will never hear the shot. And he will drop softly, like a scarecrow. The stuffing will come out of him and dogs will rise out of the snow to tear at his shoes. I feel unclean and I realize how badly I need a shave and a bath. I want to soak in painfully hot water and wrap myself in one of those thin white motel towels and lie down next to a woman. I want her to stroke my hair and whisper nonsense into my ear.

None of this happens. I sit there until I'm stiff with cold. I wonder what he's doing in there. I can't imagine Jude bothering to sleep with him. He's so clumsy and foul. Of course, she slept with me and I'm hardly a prize. I smoke two cigarettes and watch the end of the sunrise. The sky turns the color of mucus streaked with dirt. Finally I knock on the door of room 212 and Jude throws it open. She is dressed for travel; her hair is sleek and pulled back. A white silk shirt buttoned to the throat with a big French collar. Dark red lipstick but no jewelry. Black pants that cling to her hips and thighs and flare at the ankles. She's barefoot.

Are you ready? she says.

I'm looking for Pooh.

He's in the bathroom.

Her voice is flat and cold. As if she's annoyed that I look like shit and I still haven't kissed her. I hand her the icebox and smile. A gift, I say. She steps aside and I slip past her. I pull my gun and try the bathroom door. It's locked and I glance at Jude. He likes his privacy, she says.

I poke the door. Pooh. Let's go, boy. The bell tolls.

There's no answer.

When did he get here?

I don't know. Midnight, I suppose.

He's not really in there, is he?

Kick it down if you don't believe me.

She lights a cigarette, smiling. I lean against the door and look at her. This isn't a movie, I say. Doors are not so easy to kick down.

Jude rolls her eyes and sucks at her cigarette.

I talked to the cops, I say.

Oh, really.

They don't seem to have my gun.

She smiles. That's strange.

Someone has that fucking gun.

Who are you going to believe?

The door is compressed sawdust. I stab my knife in and wiggle it until the doorknob pops. Pooh is wedged naked between the wall and the toilet. His hair is wet. His skin is pale and turning blue. He sits in a small puddle of blood. There's a wide gash on his left thigh; the femoral artery has been cut.

There's not much blood, I say.

I did it in the shower.

Why did you move him?

She drops her cigarette in the toilet. I had to wash my hair.

I sit on the edge of the tub. Pooh has a simple, placid face. The backs of his thighs and buttocks are purple with the puddle wealth of his blood. Tomorrow he will be an unclaimed corpse at the coroner's office, soon to be cut apart by bored and restless medical students.

And why did you do it?

Oh. We had a fight about money, about you.

Well, I say. I was going to kill him myself.

Why did you want to? she says.

I think he hurt someone, a friend of mine. He raped her.

She nods and her eyes slide away from mine.

I know, she says. He told me about it. He said it wasn't really rape because he didn't come.

She sits down next to me and kisses my ear, my throat.

What is her name?

Eve, I say. She's nineteen.

I'm very sorry. I know what it's like.

Merry Christmas, I say.

She isn't wearing a bra and I can't help running my hand up her shirt. I love the feel of silk. She pulls away from me and goes to the mirror. She wets her fingers and smoothes her hair. Her lipstick is smeared. She takes a tissue and wipes the rest of it away. The color has disappeared from her face. She looks sick.

My toothbrush is in my purse, she says. Will you get it?

I don't like to dig through a woman's purse. It doesn't feel right. I think of
the old woman in the hospital. She was dying and thought I was her son
and I stole from her. And I think of my wife. She kept secrets in her purse.
Jude's is soft black leather and no bigger than my head. Still there seem to
be a hundred things inside. I dump it out and find a plastic tube that holds
a travel toothbrush and paste. I find a small black device, shaped like a
stereo remote control. It's a stun gun, very powerful and certainly illegal. I
have no choice but to confiscate it. There is also a small silver key on a ring,
the kind of key that fits a padlock. I glance at the lock on the icebox and I'm
surprised. The icebox contains valuable merchandise and the key would be
so much safer around her neck. I believe she trusts me. How touching. I put
the key in my pocket and replace everything else from her purse.

I give her the toothbrush and watch as she smears it with blue gel. She
leans against the sink with her face bent forward. She brushes her teeth
slowly, methodically. I look at Pooh.
What should we do with him?
She spits. Did you want to take a shower?
A bath, really.
She looks at her watch. It will have to be fast. Then we move him back
into the tub and lock the door. The room is registered in his name. It might
pass for suicide.
The cast is on his left arm. The cut on his left thigh is at such an angle
that it could have been self-inflicted. I uncurl the fingers of his right hand.
There are no defensive wounds, no signs of a struggle at all. She said she
killed him in the shower, and the curtain isn't even pulled down. She
would have had to spread his thighs apart and push the knife in at a difficult angle, then pull the blade up and away.
Was he asleep when you did this?
No, she says. But his eyes were closed.
Jude rinses her toothbrush. I am still kneeling behind her. She turns
and stands over me and I stare up at her. The black pants fit her like a

glove. My mouth is two inches from the curve of her crotch.

It was like this, I say. Wasn't it? He was in the shower and you asked if you could join him. Oh, you dirty girl. The knife behind your back. You knelt in his bathwater and took his dick in your mouth and brought the knife up when he closed his eyes.

His dick was in my hand, she says. If you must know. I wanted to cut the fucking thing off. But that would hardly pass as suicide.

And the blood came down like rain. That's why you had to wash your hair.

It was terrible. And it was glorious, too.

You're much braver than me.

She smiles, embarrassed. I take her hands and pull her down on me. We kneel before Pooh's body and grin at each other like two kids with a secret.

I fill the tub with hot water and begin to undress. Jude tells me to turn around so she can inspect my wound. The dressing Crumb gave it is filthy but holding fast. Her touch is cool and efficient.

It looks okay, she says. I want to clean it, though.

Are you a doctor?

Not exactly. I had paramedical training in the army.

Please tell me you have some painkillers.

She goes to get her medical bag and I sit naked on the toilet beside Pooh. There's a mirror on the opposite wall and I decide I look nearly as bad as he does. Jude comes back wearing surgical gloves. She gives me a shot of liquid Valium and I don't look at the needle. I think of the last time she drugged me, and I think of Prometheus. He pissed the gods off and they chained him to a rock; a bird came and ate his liver and the liver grew back while he slept. The bird returned every day, to eat his liver again and again.

I trust you, I say. I don't know why.

There is a sudden fist of warmth at the base of my spine.

Jude smiles and wipes down the wound with a damp, sterile cloth. She smears on a clear jelly that stinks of iodine and then gives me a fresh dressing.

I hate to tell you this, she says.

Am I dying?

She laughs. No, you aren't dying. But I can't let you take a bath. The wound shouldn't get wet. These stitches are made of a soluble plastic. In ten days you can take a bath and let them dissolve.

Jude, please. I haven't had a bath in days. You must have noticed I'm getting ripe.

I like the way you smell. She grins at me. You can take a shower if you're very careful.

Oh, no. A shower is no good. Anyway I would slip on the soap and crack my skull. I just want to smell like I'm not dying.

She pulls me to my feet. If you were still in the hospital, you would be getting a sponge bath every day. From a pretty little nurse, if you were lucky.

I'm anything but lucky.

Jude spreads a few towels on the floor. She fills an ice bucket with liquid soap and warm water from the bath. I stand on the towels, naked and feeling a little foolish. I'm not crippled, I say.

She ignores me. The only sound is humming lights, the drip of water. Jude takes a washcloth and soaks it in the ice bucket. She washes my feet first, and slowly works her way up my body. Every few minutes she stops to wring out the washcloth. In the mirror she is thin and beautiful and serious. She is a priestess, preparing a corpse for burial. I think I love her and I tell myself it's the Valium. She washes my face, the blunt stubble on top of my head. When she's finished I feel a thousand times better.

Together we move Pooh to the bathtub. We both wear gloves. He's heavy, and he's not stiff yet. It's like moving a drunk. The hot water makes the blood run from his leg and the bath turns a dull shade of brown. It still doesn't look right. There's not enough blood. After a minute I pull the plug. The bloody water drains away and Pooh lies there, bloated and pale as a fish. I turn the shower on and the water hammers down. It seems insulting but more realistic. Jude puts the knife in his hand.

It's his knife, she says.

She wipes down every surface in the room. I carry her bags outside. The moon is orange and still visible. It shares the sky with a glaring sun. The sound of the shower is disturbing my Valium haze. I'm not sure why, but I leave the green icebox on the bed. It might be a show of good faith to let Jude carry it for a while.

I smoke a cigarette and after a minute Jude comes out with the icebox. She is wearing the wine-colored boots and for a second I think she's stepped in blood. The door swings shut and is locked. I want to look at the room again, to be sure we didn't forget anything. But the keys are inside. Jude left them on the bed, with Pooh's wallet. She has a dark look in her eyes.

What are you staring at? she says.

Nothing. I think it might be a nice day.

She glances at the sky. The moon is orange, she says. It's a bad sign.

I smile. Why?

The blood of a stranger will be spilled.

It's pollution, I say. It's atmospheric weirdness. The sky is toxic and it doesn't mean anything.

I'm sorry, she says. I think I'm getting my period.

I stare at her dumbly.

This isn't going to work, she says. The suicide angle.

No, I say. It doesn't matter now.

Let's go, she says. We have a train to catch.

I follow her across the street. She walks with one arm protecting her belly. The green icebox swings at her side and for a moment I see a small child walking on the beach with a pail full of sand.

fifteen.

THE BLISTER WAS LYING. Or I have decided he was. He wants me to kill Jude, and he fed me the heroin story to give me the trembles. I don't believe him. I don't believe him. Heroin is cheap and plentiful in South America. No one smuggles smack from the north. It would make as much sense to sneak a box of snow into Canada. It's funny though. The balloon or glove or whatever it is could dissolve at any time and fill my bloodstream with heroin, killing me like an internal supernova. And the idea electrifies me. It calms me at the same time. I felt this way once before, stepping out onto a dark highway and staring into the lights of oncoming traffic.

Jude sits on a bench, one arm dangling protectively over the green icebox. She crosses her legs and asks me twice if I have any gum. Her voice has taken on a menstrual edge. I'm distracted and I tell her I'm going to the men's room. She says she needs gum and magazines and tampons. She's examining her nails. I think I'm going to scream, she says. Her face is blank. Maybe she didn't say anything. The voice came from inside me. I can hear the blood in my ears and my fingers tingle and for a second I think I'm going to hit her.

Don't scream, I say.

She doesn't even look up. Is something wrong?

I'm going to the men's room.

Fine, she says. Don't be long.

I pass a wall of telephones and I think of Eve. I should call her but I'm not in the mood. I would have to call the hospital and listen to static and soft jazz and a weather report as I was placed on hold. I would be transferred to her room and I would have to speak to her mother or sister or someone else before they let me speak to her. I would have to be a normal person, a friend. I would have to pretend I didn't find her naked and bloody in her own bed.

The men's room is silent. One guy stands at a urinal, his eyes cast up at the ceiling. Another bends over a sink, one side of his face white with foam. The other side is shiny and pink and he is holding his thumb against a bleeding cut. There is hair on the floor around him, a straight razor in his hand. He's disposing of a beard. Our eyes meet and I know he is on the run from someone. I shrug and close my eyes. He lifts the razor to his face. I push open the door to each stall but there's no one else. I'm sure the Blister is here somewhere, watching me. I don't care. But I would love to say hello and see that cocksure smile fade from his mouth. I would ask him why he's so afraid of little Jude. I go into the last stall and force myself to vomit. It's not hard, really. I close my eyes and think of Pooh. Dead bodies never fail. My nostrils burn but I feel better. There's a streak of blood in the toilet but I hardly notice it. I flush it away and go to wash my hands.

I stand beside the shaving man. He is bleeding in several places now and doesn't seem to mind. The blade scrapes his face in long, urgent strokes. I hold my hands under a stream of cold water until they are numb. I stare into my own face. The eyes pale and gray, like dirty ice. The sockets are sunken and black. The shaving man has one brown eye, the other a fierce blue. His lips are thick and meaty and his nose is crooked. My own beard is getting thick, blond with traces of red. The shaving man is wearing a white shirt and a blue down vest. I am wearing the black T-shirt and jeans I put on two days ago, the filthy leather jacket. The man has finished shaving, his face bright and sore. His eyes find mine in the mirror.

Are you looking at me, brother?

I'm sorry. I'm looking at myself.

He wipes his mouth. Don't take me wrong. But you look like shit, brother.

He is wearing a faded green baseball cap with the word *Crash* across the front. It looks like a lucky hat. He takes it off and a mass of dark hair falls to his shoulders. He reaches into a brown paper bag for scissors and a bottle of peroxide. My hands are starting to hurt from the cold and I turn off the water. I wipe my fingers dry against my chest. The man is cutting his hair in fistfuls.

I like that ring, he says. That gold ring.

He means my wedding ring. I never took it off after Lucy died and I don't know why. I don't think it will come off; it feels grafted there, melded to my flesh. But I'm wrong. It slides over my knuckle as if my hands are oiled. I have lost so much weight. I lift it to the light and turn it before my eyes. It is so smooth, almost unmarked. Gold is a soft metal; it should be cut and scarred by five years of marriage.

I could use it, he says. For my new identity.

Who are you?

I don't know, brother. How do you like the name Henry?

You could do worse.

That's what I'm thinking. And Henry sounds like a guy that's married.

I give him the ring without pause. He slips it on his ring finger and smiles.

It looks good, he says. I'll give you fifty bucks.

I don't need any money.

Come on. You must want something.

Jude is stalking around our luggage like a panther that hasn't had dinner. I duck out of the rest room with Henry's lucky hat pulled low over my eyes. I go to the newsstand and grab a stack of magazines: *Vogue* and *Rolling Stone*, *Penthouse*, *Sports Illustrated* and *Mother Jones*. I get sugarless bubble gum and a carton of cigarettes and a box of nontoxic superabsorbent tampons.

I return to Jude bearing these gifts. She eyes my new hat but doesn't say a word. I tear open the gum and she takes two sticks, crushing them in her mouth. In a parallel universe, I might kiss her.

What's the problem?

The train is delayed. They won't say how long.

It's Christmas Eve. Be patient.

Where did you get that ridiculous hat?

Listen, fuck you. Take a pill or something. Go wash your face.

She turns and walks away, her bootheels flashing like hammers. I like the way she walks. She takes long arrogant strides, her ass and hips swinging. She holds her head high, her shoulders back like a dancer. Everyone gets out of her way, I notice. I sit down beside the green icebox, smiling. It's been a long time since I argued pointlessly with a woman and I forgot how much fun it could be.

I look around. There's still no sign of the Blister and I decide not to worry about him. I flip through a magazine and smoke half a cigarette before a little girl gives me a long dirty look and points at the NO SMOKING sign. I look up and see Jude near the ticket window. She's talking to a woman with short black hair. Their faces are just inches apart and they could be fighting. They could be leaning to kiss. Jude glances my way and she knows I'm watching her. She looks furious. Her face is cold and white, her hands clenched. She whispers something to the woman and they separate. The woman with black hair looks familiar. She wears high heels, white stockings. But she walks away and I never see her face. Jude comes toward me with an expression that says *don't say a fucking word.* She sits down beside me.

Jude, I say.

Don't say a fucking word.

Who was that woman?

She was no one. She was someone I used to work with.

Not a friend, then.

No, she says. Definitely not.

Funny, I say. She looked very familiar.

Henry steps out of the bathroom, his hair bleached and wet and cut like a fright wig. His eyes linger on Jude before he turns away.

Minutes crawl past us on all fours. The Valium is wearing off and I feel a rush of clarity. I want to be sweet to Jude, to make her laugh. I show her a funny picture of a man taking a bath with a pig. She barely smiles. She takes a single tampon from the box and goes to the bathroom. She comes back silent, skulking. She tells me she hates to bleed. I take her hand and kiss it.

Sorry, she says. I'll feel better when we're on the train.

Have you ever done this before?

What? she says.

Have you ever cozied up with one of your victims?

I've never wanted to.

She puts her head in my lap and I flinch, then reach to stroke her hair. I think I'm embarrassed by her sudden affection, her trust. I'm fifteen and I don't want anyone to know she's my girlfriend.

Jude falls asleep. I hold my breath for a minute, afraid to move and wake her. I take off my jacket and fold it square. I slip it under her head and go to a pay phone. I watch Jude sleep and then look away as I dial the hospital. I turn Henry's baseball cap around backward and force a sheepish grin onto my face. I am immediately put on hold. I snap my fingers and continue to grin. Thank you, I say. I listen to elevator music for three minutes. I watch the second hand on my watch. A nurse comes on and asks if I'm a family member. I'm Frank, I say. I'm Eve's older brother. I am put on hold again.

Eve's voice is thin and tough. I don't have a brother, she says.

It's me.

Phineas. Where are you?

Are you okay?

I'm fine. They kept me overnight but I'm okay.

I'm sorry.

Will you come see me?

I can't. I wish I could.

Crumb is here, she says. He's taking care of me.

I smile and wonder what manner of equipment Crumb is stealing from Eve's room.

What about Georgia?

I don't know, she says. She's missing. She never came to the hospital with me and I don't know where she is. I'm going to kill her.

She's okay, I say. She was on a lot of drugs and she probably freaked out when the cops came. She's crashing on somebody's floor.

The necklace you gave me, she says. The black locket. It's gone.

I'm sorry. I tell myself not to be sorry, not to care. But I can't help it.

There's a woman sitting on a bench across from me. It could be the woman I saw talking to Jude. Her face is buried in a magazine. She has short, muscular legs in white stockings. A short gray dress. She crosses her legs and smoothes the nylon along one thigh with her palm. The dress slips and I see the lace of a garter. My knees weaken. My wife used to wear a garter when she was feeling like a dirty girl.

Phineas, did you hear what I said?

I close my eyes and hold them shut.

What? What did you say?

It wasn't rape.

Eve, please. Listen to me. The man who did this is dead. He's dead.

No, she says. It wasn't rape.

Okay, I say. It's okay.

This might sound crazy, she says. But sometimes I think it was a woman. A very strong woman.

I open my eyes and the woman is gone. The crossed white legs and flash of garter were an illusion. I turn to look at Jude. She still sleeps, her face innocent and dreaming and I tell myself nothing sounds crazy.

What did she look like? What color was her hair?

I'm sorry, Eve says. I don't know.

What about the police? What do they think?

They think I'm in shock and I'm nineteen. They think I'm a lesbian.

I love the cops.

They asked me a thousand questions about you, she says.

And Georgia is missing, I say.

It was Georgia, she says.

I don't say a word. I watch Jude sleep. I can hear Eve breathing. I tell her to lock her doors, to be careful of strangers. I tell her I can't talk anymore.

The phone buzzes in my hand. I hang up and call the hospital again. I ask for the emergency room and I am put on hold. The same void. The same churning in my belly. I watch Jude sleep and finally a sexless voice comes on the line. Emergency room. Can I help you?

I need to speak with Rose.

I'm sorry. The voice coughs, or chokes. Rose?

Rose White. She's an intern. A student.

Perhaps you would like to leave a message.

Perhaps perhaps perhaps.

Excuse me, sir?

I want to speak with her.

Hold on. And papers rattle. A metallic whine and other voices distorted, underwater. A male voice comes on the line, suspicious and cold. He asks me to identify myself.

I know who I am. Who are you?

The voice hesitates, then tells me that there is no one in the emergency room named Rose White.

I'm hearing things. The ticket clerk chews a breath mint and I hear the delicate crunch of teeth against bone. A boy with gold hair is tossing pennies at a wax paper cup and the coins ring against the floor like high heels. An old woman with pale, stretched cheeks has sewage in her lungs and every time she takes a breath, I can hear the liquid rattle in her chest. I didn't have the wrong address when I went to the little Hobbit house to meet Rose. The Blister got there before me with a crew of federal agents dressed up like exterminators and plumbers. She opened the door with a trusting smile and they swarmed inside and devoured her. They drugged her and rolled her up in a faded Turkish rug that she found at a flea market for a real bargain and stuffed her into an unmarked white van. Then they emptied her house and surgically erased all evidence of her existence. They left the FOR SALE sign in her yard and sent the real estate agent along to deal with me.

The phone is buzzing, disconnected. I say thank you and feel myself slinking. I sit down with my back against the wall and watch Jude sleep. I close my eyes and see a brightly colored beach ball, kicked and punched and abused by sunburned drunks until it is nearly ragged, deflated. Soon the ball is pulled high by the wind and allowed to drift for a while.

I feed my last quarter into the machine and dial Moon.

He grunts, hello. And I try to sound casual, uninterested. I ask him to look into the disappearance of a young woman named Rose White.

Are you kidding.

I am silent for a long time and Moon asks if I'm okay.

It's important, I say.

Moon wants to know where I'm calling from and I hang up on him.

sixteen.

THE SOUND OF METAL AGAINST METAL. The train doesn't move. Jude sits with her eyes closed and her gloved fingers pressed to her temples. It's been thirty minutes since they allowed us to board and nothing is happening. I sit across from her and I see a woman in a ski mask with her fist between Eve's thighs. I wonder when the bar will open. A tall glass of vodka with ice might empty my head. I was drinking the very same thing the night I met Jude.

Why did you choose me? I say.

Her eyes become green slits. What?

At the hotel. Why me and not the bald guy with the gold watch? The midget with bad teeth or the transvestite behind door number three?

Jude smiles and I realize that my feelings will be hurt if it was pure chance. She removes one glove and bites the edge of her fingers. The tip of her tongue, fleshy and pink.

Don't be offended, she says. But you were an easy target. You were weak and disoriented and I knew you were the one as soon as I saw you.

It was fate, then.

Did you think it was your smile? Your sexy blue eyes, maybe.

Maybe.

I slide down in my seat and stare at her until a bright red dot appears between her eyes. I close my eyes and I still see the dot. I tell myself I will put the bullet there, when the time comes. I will kill her. I will kill her. But

I'm such a liar.

I was wondering about Pooh, I say.
 What about him?
 Before you killed him. What did he say, exactly?
 Jude removes the other glove and looks at her watch.
 We should be leaving soon.

I cross the compartment to sit beside her. I slip my left hand between her narrow thighs and stroke her with my middle finger. The black pants are so tight. The heat from her body is intense and I remember she's menstruating.

What did Pooh say? I'm just curious.
 Jude moves her hips against my hand. It wasn't rape, she says.
 Her breath is quick and I wonder if she's even wearing panties.
 Pooh was never there. It was a woman, I whisper.
 Oh, that's nonsense.
 She is surging against my hand. I feel sick. I think I might come in my own pants.
 I heard a rumor, I say. A sexy bit of gossip. An angel walked into a hospital in Colorado Springs and turned in a lost kidney. It was used to save a little boy.
 Don't believe it, she says. Don't.
 I pull my hand away and wipe it across my jeans. Jude lets her head sink back against the foam cushion. Her face and throat are flushed, her hands limp as sleeping birds.
 Why did you choose me. Why?
 There's a knock at the door and the train begins to move.
 A young black guy in a stiff blue suit. Tickets, please.
 I give him the tickets and ask for directions to the lounge car.

Jude doesn't want a drink. She takes her boots off and unbuttons her blouse. Her bra is red lace and again I see blood when I look at her. And something else catches my eye; around her neck is a small, tear-shaped black locket that I've seen before. Pooh took it from Eve as a souvenir, a trophy. And Jude took it away from him. I wonder just how stupid she thinks I am. I place my hands on the sides of my head to keep it from spinning off. I'm ten years old and I'm soaking wet. I'm standing in the rain and I refuse to believe that the sun isn't shining. Look around, I say. It's coming down in fucking ropes.

What are you talking about? she says.

Nothing.

I have a headache, she says.

Lucy used to have awful headaches. She would go blind. There was nothing I could do for her and I hated her for it. I go to the sink and soak a washcloth in cold water.

Jude drapes it over her eyes and says thank you.

I want to kiss you, I say.

You stink of guilt, she says.

The lounge car has curved windows, like bubbles in the roof. The sky is blank. I take a seat at the bar and ask for vodka with orange juice. I figure the vitamins will be good for me. The bartender is at least a hundred years old and he pours my drink with trembling hands.

Henry takes a seat on the stool next to me. I barely recognize him. His ragged white hair is slicked back with gel that looks hard to the touch. He is dressed in a charcoal gray suit, with a crisp white shirt and black tie. My wedding ring winks at me from his creased and sun-hardened left hand.

He smiles. Greetings, brother.

Henry, I say. Care for a drink?

It's too early for me. Coffee, he says.

I didn't know you were taking the train.

Didn't I mention it?

I gaze at the pale orange drink before me and I remember Jude's strange lament. *The blood of a stranger must be spilled.* The bartender places a cup and saucer on the bar and pours the coffee without spilling a drop. I watch Henry dump several packets of sugar into his cup but no cream.

No, I say. I don't think you did.

Oh, well. It is the only way to travel. Unless you're in a hurry, that is.

The stranger could be anyone. It could be me.

In the mirror behind the bar I see Jude. She lies on a narrow bed in our compartment, black silk legs bent like a grasshopper. She is hot and has taken off her shirt. One red bra strap falls from her shoulder. She lazily flips through a magazine. She unbends her legs and rests her bare feet on the green icebox that contains my kidney. Shouldn't we hurry, I say. Before the ice melts.

She smiles at me. Oh, please. Don't worry so much.

Henry is looking at me, amused. Do you always talk to yourself?

My teeth are chattering and I sip my drink. There's no kidney in that icebox. It's money or a bomb or a sock full of dirt. I should wait until she falls asleep and have a look. I do have the key. But if it is my kidney I might fuck it up by exposing it to the world. And if it's a bomb, then Jude is a liar and I will have to kill her. I don't want to kill her. I have loved two women and one of them is already dead.

Not always, I say.

Henry finishes his coffee and runs one hand through his stiff, plastic hair.

How is your new identity working out? I say.

He smiles. It's not bad, brother. There's a truckload of details to consider, though. What's my favorite color, my birthday. What do I eat for breakfast and how do I take my coffee. Where am I from and all that shit. My wife's name and what does she look like. Speaking of which. I saw that little tiger lily you're with and riddle me this, is she as mean as she looks?

I smile. She's mean, I say. I turned my back on her once and she cut me open.

Henry laughs. The best woman is like a gun.

Henry is a good actor. He could talk trash and tell lies about women and baseball and money with anybody. I want to tell him it's unnecessary but something stops me. I don't trust him yet. After a while he stands up and pulls out a silver clip fat with new money. He drops a few bills on the bar and says he will see me later. I watch him walk away and I wonder who he's running from.

Jude is exactly as I imagined. Mostly naked and reading a magazine. The green icebox beneath one bare foot. I bend and kiss her toes and listen but the icebox isn't ticking.

Your face is sweating, she says. Is it the pain?

I sit down across from her and look out the window. The train is going west, chasing the sun.

Jude, I say. The bartender told me this train is going to Los Angeles.

That's right. Then we take another train down to El Paso.

She goes back to her magazine. She licks her finger and turns the pages slowly. They crackle with alarming volume. Everywhere I look there's a sign that says NO SMOKING. I stare at the green icebox that may or may not contain a piece of me. The key is in my pants pocket. But I am no closer to opening the icebox than I was yesterday. Nothing good would come of such a betrayal. Something would only perish. My flesh, my strange feelings for Jude.

It seems like a roundabout way to get there. We could have rented a car and gotten there tonight.

What's the rush? she says. Relax. This is like a honeymoon.

You're a scream. Isn't our merchandise perishable?

Oh, that. Listen to me. That is no ordinary icebox. The kidney is vacuum-sealed and encased in a brick of dry ice. You could thaw it next summer and it would be as good as new.

Beautiful.

Your teeth are chattering, she says.

My head is floating on warm black water like a dirty life vest.

That note you left me at the hotel, I say. Why did you want to see me?

I don't know, she says. I was feeling daffy and I thought I might give you your kidney back. But then I changed my mind. The money was more tempting.

You. You are such a good liar.

I did give it back to you. Eventually.

No. I took it from you.

Irrelevant, isn't it?

I wrap my arms around my belly, suddenly cold. The pain is very bad, I say.

Jude smiles and reaches for her medical gear. I watch her prepare a hypo with the liquid Valium. She holds it to the light and I see it's a lovely gold color. Jude crosses the compartment and straddles my clenched knees. A length of rubber tube between her teeth like a rose. Give me your arm, she says.

I bare my left arm and I think of dogs. When a dog meets another dog in the park, the weaker dog rolls over and exposes his genitals, his naked belly. The stronger dog can rip open his belly and eat his genitals if he chooses. The weaker dog trusts him not to do so. Jude ties off my arm with the rubber tube and quickly finds a fat blue vein. The shot spreads through me, cold and then warm and I'm at the edge of dream and sleep. I feel myself slipping but I want to stay awake and still dream. Every sound and smell is hazy and somehow clarified and Jude's dark yellow skin is hot and porous and unstable as dry sand. I kiss and lick greedily at her breasts and fumble with the straps of her bra and my mouth is wet and I realize I'm weeping. Jude ties my wrists together with the rubber tube and pushes me back against the seat and I think oh I'm going to like this but she whispers hush, hush. She strokes my hair until I fall asleep.

seventeen.

AND IT'S POSSIBLE THAT I FOLLOWED ROSE HOME THAT NIGHT. She dropped me off at the Hotel Peacock and I watched her drive away. I hailed a cab and said with a crooked smile, follow that car. It was a long silent drive, snowflakes hypnotically rushing at the headlights. Her little red truck pulled into a curved driveway and disappeared behind snow-covered bushes. The address was 1013 Alpine, a red and white house with a round front door. I told the driver to stop. I gave him fifty dollars and asked him to forget he ever saw me. I walked up to her door, weak from blood loss but alive with the rush and promise of her. Rose opened the door and she wasn't surprised to see me. Her red hair was pulled back into a ponytail, and her lips were wet, as if she had been washing her face when the door-bell rang. She wore faded green and black pajamas; the shirt was missing two buttons and her belly showed white. She pulled the door open and I limped past her and I smiled when I saw the cat. He was a fat bastard, gray and black with Persian blood. He lounged in a windowsill and regarded me with disdain. Rose said his name was Castro. I took a seat on the couch and it felt very good to sink into the soft cushions; I became weightless for a moment. Rose asked if I was hungry and I said I would love some ice cream. She smiled and disappeared. I opened my suitcase and took out the 9mm; I touched my lips to the silent metal and asked the gods for luck and forgiveness. I slipped the gun between two pillows as Rose returned. She had a gallon of cookie dough ice cream and two spoons. We passed the ice cream back and forth and shared our spoons and watched the evening news without sound. I wanted to kiss her, to taste her mouth and it was hopeless. I wondered if she would feel my pain at all and slowly pulled the gun from the pillows.

I hear voices but I'm blind. Something soft and translucent covers my eyes and I try to remove it but my wrists are still bound. Jude is talking to someone, another woman. Jude is so cold. She measures her words like spoonfuls of salt. The other woman is asking for something. She is almost begging but not quite. There's too much hate in her voice, liquid and untouchable as mercury. The voice is familiar.

I never went to the little Hobbit house and chatted with any real estate agent about copper plumbing and afternoon light and a lovely baby's room. That was a false memory. That was something Lucy did. When she was trying to get pregnant she often went looking at houses and station wagons and patio furniture. Lucy must have told me about that little house with the gargoyle birdbath. I was never there. I was at Eve's apartment that day; I wore a black ski mask and I climbed the fire escape like a monkey. I pushed open her window and found her in bed with Georgia. They were so graceful together, so sweet. And I knew I wouldn't need my gun. I pulled Georgia from Eve's arms and pressed my knife to her throat. I gave her the duct tape and watched, impatient and hot, as Georgia fumbled with the tape. She was furious, breathing through her teeth as she taped Eve's hands and feet together. I was sick with desire. Georgia came at me spitting and slashing; she was very strong and finally I punched her in the throat. She dropped to the floor, gasping. I dragged her to the bathroom and shoved a rag in her mouth. I hoped she would suffocate because I couldn't bear to kill her. I went back to Eve's room and took off my pants. She lay silent, waiting. I cut the tape from her feet and rolled her onto her belly.

I wake again and my hands are free. The cloth covering my face is a red gauze scarf of Jude's. It smells of honey and dirt. I sit up and flex my hands. The compartment is empty. The green icebox and Jude's black bag are gone. I am terribly thirsty, as if my tongue were cut out and replaced by a chunk of rotten wood. I go to the sink and fill my belly with tepid, sterile water. I splash my face and take a look in the mirror and I see that my reflection is misproportioned, its movements unrelated to my own. If I concentrate I might appear normal. I examine my teeth, blunt and white and all present. I stroke my beard and consider shaving it but I decide it makes me look less gaunt and malnourished. My hair is growing back, blond and fine. I wet my hands and slick it back. I change into a clean shirt and go to look for Jude.

Pooh was easy to kill. I found him asleep in his truck, parked in a hump of snow outside Jude's motel room. It was five in the morning and the sky was turning a dreamy pink. Pooh lay across the front seat like a dead cow. The windows bright with long cracked fingers of ice. I climbed into the truck and checked his pulse; it was steady as a clock. I unfastened his belt and pulled his filthy jeans down around his ankles. He woke up then, snarling and grunting at me. I pulled him into the parking lot and he tried to fight but his own tangled jeans pulled him down. I kicked him in the head, the belly, until my legs were sore and my feet heavy as stones. He was unconscious. I stripped the rest of his clothes off and buried my knife in his thigh.

There is some difficulty walking. My legs are strangely distant, removed from my nervous system. The floor appears to move but doesn't. I fall to my knees and laugh at myself. Perhaps I'm thinking about it too much. I stare straight ahead and walk. I pass a smoke lounge and duck inside and the air is literally blue. I try to make out faces but there are only eyes and disembodied mouths, fingers and wristwatches and burning stubs. I smoke two cigarettes and slip away gasping.

I killed Lucy, of course. And that made everything else possible. I killed her in the boat. I waited until she was drunk and her words fell apart in her mouth. The sun was behind a cloud when I shot her, and the first bullet took her face apart. She was still alive, breathing through shredded nostrils. One eyes was dark with blood and extraordinarily calm. I put the gun just above her ear and shot her again. I was half naked and a little drunk myself. The water pulled me over the edge of the boat and I let myself sink. The gun so heavy but I couldn't let it go. I swam back to the boat and climbed in, nearly tipping it over. She already stank, and the flies were terrible. I put the gun in her hand and swam ashore; I had a knife and nothing else. I don't know when her body was found. For ten days I was incoherent. I drank rainwater that pooled among rocks. I ate dandelions and chewed on the bark of a young ash. I chased my shadow like a dog. I made another cut in my arm at each sunset; I was slowly bleeding myself to death. When the state troopers found me, my tongue was swollen to the size of my fist. I couldn't speak for days.

Children stare at me. Their mothers and fathers are discreet and look away, smiling. I bite my lip until it bleeds and I'm surely awake this time. I seem to walk for miles and then I pass through a doorway into the dining car. White tablecloths and cheap silverware and plastic flowers in blue vases. The smell of chicken and rosemary. A woman drinks iced tea with a bright twist of lemon and I have an urge to take it from her hands and pour it over my face. A man in a white jacket moves to intercept me. He holds a menu in one hand and his fingers are long and so white I think he's wearing gloves, but his fingernails are sharp and yellow as bone.

Pardon me, sir. This dining car is for first-class passengers only.

Yes, I say. Of course. What does that mean?

He sighs. Are you traveling by coach or in a private compartment?

In a compartment. A box.

I see. And the number?

I'm not hungry. I just want some of that iced tea.

He smiles and shows me a mouthful of teeth. I'm glad he finds this amusing and I'm about to say so when Jude steps forward, a white napkin in her left hand.

Hello, I say.

This is my husband, she says. He's easily confused, that's all.

The man mutters his apologies and offers me a menu. I smile with lips that feel drained of blood.

I want some of that iced tea.

Of course, sir. He bites each word.

Jude takes my hand. Come on, dear. I have already ordered for you.

She leads me like a donkey. I follow and practice my smile. It doesn't feel right and I want to ask her what she thinks. What's wrong with you? she says.

Nothing's wrong. A bit high.

You must be joking. If there had been a security guard on this car I think he would have shot you.

Why? I'm wearing a clean shirt. I have a nice smile.

You were leaning over that woman like you might rip out her throat.

The woman with the tea. I look back over my shoulder and she is pale as a ghost. Her husband is consoling her and the waiter is bringing a tray of complimentary pies.

Jude stops at our booth and I turn to see that we are not dining alone.

Now be nice, she whispers.

eighteen.

SOMETIMES THERE IS NOTHING SO HORRIBLE AS A FAMILIAR FACE. The woman at Jude's table, however, is a mutant. She's two or three women at once. I see the woman from the train station. The same black high heels and white lace garter belt. A short wool dress the color of a cloudy day. Her hair is short as a young boy's and black. She touches a napkin to her mouth and it comes away marked with red lipstick. She looks like an elf, a woodland fairy. I see the sweet young medical student from the emergency room. Rose White. She had bright red hair and pale white skin, I'm sure. I try to summon her face but I see only ashes. The hair and clothes are exactly like my dead wife's. But she isn't Lucy. She smiles across the table.

Phineas, says Jude. This is Isabel, someone I used to know. I haven't seen her in years and then today I run into her on a train. Isn't it a small world?

I sit down across from Isabel and take a sip of water. Jude's medical bag dangles from a hook on the wall; the green icebox is nowhere to be seen. Jude is busily composing her face. I look under the table and between her legs. I look over my shoulder and under the butter dish.

Jude. Where is the icebox?

She bites my ear and whispers for me to shut up.

Isabel is preening herself. She touches up her lipstick, her bloody mouth. She frowns at her nose and snaps shut a compact mirror. I stare at her hair and wonder if it's a wig. If I try to pull it off and it's real there might be a lot of excitement and confusion. The waiter brings my iced tea on a silver dish.

Isabel grins at me. It's very nice to meet you, Phineas.

I lift my glass and I can feel Jude watching me. Her fingers dance along my thigh.

It's a pleasure, I say.

Isabel takes a roll from the bread basket and daintily smears it with butter. She tears off a small piece and it disappears between her teeth. She chews silently and swallows.

Oh, she says. I almost forgot. Congratulations.

I chew a piece of ice. For what?

Jude tells me you just got married.

That's right. We just ran off like a couple of kids.

It must be nice, she says. To be in love.

Love is a reptile, I say. Don't you think? If you cut off its tail it grows another one.

I stare at Isabel without blinking. I stare until I can see the pale roots of her natural hair and the expensive skin cream that changed her skin from milk to olive and the colored lenses that gave her yellow eyes and I wonder how she changed her breasts and ass and shortened her legs. I stare at her until her eyes are pointed and her teeth glitter like fangs and I have to close my eyes. If she said her name was Lucy and she faked her death I would believe her.

Jude pokes me and asks if I want chicken or beef.

Isabel shifts in her seat.

Chicken, I say.

Why are you staring at me? says Isabel.

Because you have an unusual face. Did anyone ever say that you look exactly like someone else?

She frowns. Of course.

Phineas, says Jude.

But you look like two or three people at once. Isn't that funny?

Phineas, says Jude.

What?

Let go of the glass, she says. Let go.

I look down and the iced tea glass in my hand is cracked. A brown stain is forming on the tablecloth as tea and melted ice drip from my wrist. I let go and the glass falls apart. Two busboys appear and whisk away the tablecloth and everything on it.

Are you bleeding? Jude says. Her voice sounds funny, as if it's about to come apart like the glass. I look at her closely and I see how red her eyes are, how colorless her lips. She looks like she wants to throw up. I lift my dripping hand so she can see there's no blood.

I'm sorry.

I notice you aren't wearing a wedding ring, says Isabel.

Jude shrugs. She opens her mouth and someone starts to laugh.

Well, brother. I thought I might find you here.

Henry is standing over us and the sun is coming through the window behind him. His face is completely obscured by shadow. His laugh is thick and lecherous. He sits down next to Isabel and offers her his hand. I'm Henry, he says. Phineas and I are associates. Which one of you is his beautiful wife?

With the slightest shudder of her thin shoulders, Jude asks Isabel and Henry to join us in our compartment for a drink. Henry grins so wide I can see the metal in his teeth. As we leave the dining car, Isabel asks us to excuse her; there's a phone call she must make. Jude narrows her eyes and says that will be fine.

My stomach hurts and I realize that I'm starving. I never touched my chicken.

The drugs have faded and I am aware of my body again. Henry bows and offers to escort Isabel to her compartment. The train enters a tunnel and I automatically close my eyes. Everything is pink and I see shadow images. I open my eyes and see Henry leaning to whisper at Jude's ear. His hand on her shoulder as if he's pressing her down. She nods and says something, her lips barely moving. Henry winks at me and hurries to catch up with Isabel.

I grab Jude by the wrist and I feel the electricity in her. She's full of juice.

What did he say?

She pushes me into a vacant bathroom the size of a coffin. I pull her close to me and it's the first time I've held her without thinking of sex or violence.

His name isn't Henry, she says.

I know. It's his new identity.

How do you know him?

From the station. He gave me the lucky hat.

Jude rolls her eyes. Who the fuck is he?

He's no one. He's a drifter. An escaped convict.

No, she says. He's more than that.

What about Isabel? Don't tell me she was your college roommate.

She kisses me quickly. Let's go. I want to be ready for them.

A cocktail party, I say. What were you thinking?

She shakes her head. It's a game. Isabel wants to play and I'm going to let her.

I've met her before, you know.

Jude turns pale. What?

She was at the hospital. She was a medical student, a nurse. But she was different. She had red hair and pale skin and she was thinner, with kind of a flat chest. She gave me a ride. She gave me her phone number.

Jude doesn't say anything. There is a trace of embarrassment in her eyes, as if I have just described an imaginary friend and she doesn't have the heart to tell me that my friend isn't real.

Her name was Rose White, I say.

Rose White. What a delicious name.

I close my eyes and try to remember. I was in shock and I was drugged and she was fucking real. I'm sure of it. But I hesitate to tell Jude that this person has transformed into the body of my dead wife.

Don't worry about it, Jude says. It doesn't matter what you saw or thought you saw. She's here and we have to deal with her.

Why don't you tell me who she is?

Isabel is my partner, she says. We do the organ routine together, like a dance. We choose a target, someone that's on the edge. Someone that just stepped out of prison or rehab, someone still blinded by the sun and confused as a newborn. She seduces the target and I do the surgery. But we had a little fight about money, and I split. I decided to try a solo run, and I chose you. Is that what you want to hear?

You bitch, I whisper.

Jude smiles and touches my cheek. Oh, dear. Are you hearing voices again?

The fuck.

I will tell you the truth, she says. Soon.

I follow Jude back down the narrow passageway. It is completely unfamiliar and I shake my head. I did just come this way. Jude stops in the lounge and I think yes, a drink is a good idea. I wait behind her like a shadow, obedient and uninformed. She briskly tells the bartender that she wants to buy a bottle of mescal. He says, oh I'm sorry miss. No alcohol leaves the lounge. Jude hits him with a charge of animal heat; she gives him bottomless eyes and hard nipples, a voice like bone marrow and a palmed fifty. The old man rolls over panting. He provides a sack of limes and a shaker of salt. Jude thanks him, twirling a shot glass on her finger.

I crack the seal on the bottle before we reach our compartment. I ask her again where the icebox is. She tells me not to worry and takes the bottle from me.

Take it easy, she says. I don't want you to get stupid.

I am stupid. I am the foolishness of flesh. Drinking gives me charm and texture.

She laughs and begins to straighten the tiny living area. She unfolds one bed.

The icebox, I say.

Jude points to a locked closet. It's safe, okay?

I take another drink from the bottle and decide she might be right; I don't need to get drunk. I am already blindfolded. I have no control, no focus. The icebox is all I can think of, but I can't bear to open it, to look inside. The kidney is a chunk of repressed memory, buried deep and crushed by heavy earth. I'm unraveling and I'm soft inside. I need to be sharp. I need to be cruel. Jude is undressing. Her body is terribly distracting and I am tempted to take her from behind in a sudden, staggering rush. I loosen my belt.

She gives me her cool stare. I don't think so, she says.

I watch her change into pale silver pajamas; the material is sheer and clings to her and the effect is maddening. I assume that's what she intended. She reclines on the bed.

Why did you tell them we were married? I say.

Instinct, she says. Off the top of my head.

I like the sound of it.

Please. Don't get misty on me.

This train stops in Vegas. We could be married in an hour.

She sighs and reaches for a magazine. The drugs are talking, she says.

I'm going to get some air, I say.

nineteen.

I STAND IN THE PASSAGEWAY and try to meditate, to clear my head. I concentrate on the train beneath my feet. The constant motion, the plunge. The barely perceptible clicking of the tracks, rapid as a terrified pulse.

Henry and Isabel come toward me, their arms entwined. They have become fast friends, I see. Isabel has changed clothes. She wears a slinky black thing that might be called a dress. It might be a nightgown. She is certainly naked beneath it. I can feel blood swelling in my face and I open my mouth to tell Henry to get his hands off my wife. I laugh abruptly, grinning. I hold out my hand and Isabel looks at it with shiny contempt.

Henry laughs. Hello, brother. Why are you lurking here in the hall? You look as nervous as a thief. Or did the wife send you out for a gallon of milk?

Jude is inside, I say. I would like to speak with Isabel alone.

Certainly, he says. He kisses Isabel on the wrist and says, she is yours.

He disappears inside and I hear Jude tell him to sit down, to make himself at home. I take Isabel by the wrist, the same wrist kissed by Henry, and I imagine I can feel the warmth of his lips. I press her small bones between my thumb and fingers. She doesn't resist. She barely seems to notice me. I pull her along to a section of coach. There are two empty seats and I tell her to sit down.

What is your name?

How feeble your memory is. My name is Isabel.

Are you sure? I can call you Rose if you like.

I don't know what you mean. She carefully removes my hand from her arm and rubs the skin, but there is already a bluish mark in the shape of my thumb. I'm enjoying this. I can feel it in my teeth, like I have just bitten aluminum. This is silly, I say. I take long whistling breaths.

Yes, it is. And really unnecessary. If you are interested in me, just say so.

What?

You want to sleep with me.

Is that what you think?

It's obvious. And charming, of course. But at the moment I'm rather more attracted to your friend.

Henry? He's not really my friend.

Oh, really? That's your loss, I'm sure.

I look at her full, pouting lips. She doesn't talk quite like Rose; her voice is too bitter and jagged. And she doesn't really look like Lucy. I stare at the line of her jaw, searching for evidence of makeup. An artificial tan, a bronze cream. There is nothing to see. Her small ears, her silky black hair. The heavy, round breasts. A slight tummy and hard, muscular legs.

You look nothing like the girl I remember.

And which girl do you remember, she says.

The one at the hospital. She gave me a ride to my hotel. Then on the telephone. I told her my life story and she gave me the wrong address. We had a date.

I'm sorry, she says. I'm sure I don't know who you're talking about. And you seem to be a very confused person. Delusional, I suppose. I have never seen you before today.

I do love your hair.

She smiles and cocks her head like a curious bird. I stroke a soft black wisp behind her ear, then tug it gently between my thumb and finger. It feels real.

I'm glad you like it, she says.

Oh, yes. You look exactly like Lucy, my dead wife.

Isabel presses her lips together and her face becomes pale and gaunt.

I hope so, she whispers. Jude designed me to look like her, to become her.

I could kill you.

She sighs. I didn't really care for the idea, at first.

I could kill you a thousand times.

But I played along and I really think it's a smash, don't you?

She leans forward, smiling richly. Her teeth are long and curved and there is a bright trickle of sweat down her left cheek. I'm sure it would taste like ashes.

It's perfect, I say. My head suddenly feels like it has been disconnected.

I touch the thin slip of her dress. The material feels like it might melt between my fingers. Her white thigh is smooth as porcelain and I pull my hand away.

What is most precious to you? she says.

Nothing, I say. My arms and legs.

Do you have any brothers and sisters? she says.

I have a little brother. But I haven't heard from him in five or six years.

He could be dead, she says.

He's not dead.

Isabel makes a soft clucking sound, like a hen. Did you adore him? she says.

Not really. I tolerated him most of the time.

Did you protect him?

He was my brother, I say. I periodically beat the crap out of him. But if I had a candy bar or a few dollars, I gave him half.

Then you understand, she says.

No, I don't.

What was his name? she says.

Fuck you.

I have a brother, she says. He's seventeen. He's made of glass. If I could hold him in the palm of my hand or keep him safe in my pocket, I would.

Who are you?

She sighs. It doesn't matter.

But you have seen me before, haven't you?

I chose you, she says.

No, I say. Jude chose me.

Jude preys on thieves, she says. On prostitutes and drug addicts.

I'm a drug addict.

She shakes her head. You are only confused.

Did you come to steal me away from Jude?

I came to watch over you, she says.

Like an angel.

Jude is very dangerous, says Isabel. She is not what she seems.

No one is.

Even so. You would be much safer traveling with me.

Isabel takes my hand and pushes it into the soft fold of her crotch. I suck in my breath and beg Jude to forgive me. I want to kiss this stranger, to see if her mouth is like Lucy's.

My brother's name is Everson, I say. Everson Poe.

I feel sorry for you, she says.

Why?

Your brother could be dead and you feel nothing.

My brother is in Africa. He wanders.

Isabel leans close, her lips dark and bursting with blood. I kiss her hard enough to bruise and I don't feel anything but dead skin and elusive shame.

You're not real, are you? I'm dreaming again.

She shrugs and pushes past me.

Come on, she says. They are waiting for us.

Henry juggles limes with little success. His chest is brown and smooth as stone. Isabel kicks off her shoes and crouches on the floor. The thin black dress is impossibly short; she is naked to the hip. She drops one hand between her thighs to hide her crotch, to touch herself. Limes roll in every direction and I crouch and begin to gather them. I try not to look at Isabel but I can't help it. I can't take my eyes off her.

Throw me one of those limes, brother. Don't be shy.

I flip a lime at Henry.

Now where the Christ is that bottle?

Jude takes a long drink and comes to kiss me, her mouth hot with mescal. I bite her softly and suck the breath from her and I am still hungry.

I don't like your friend.

He's harmless.

Look at him. He's a shark.

It's too late, I'm afraid.

Henry lies back on the floor and dumps salt on his slick belly. He tucks a chunk of lime between his teeth, the pale flesh outward. Isabel bends to lick the salt from his belly and drinks long from the bottle, then chews the lime in his mouth. Yellow liquor and juice run down their throats.

Henry gives me a brutal smile.

I kneel beside Isabel and crush half a lime in my fist; the juice gathers in the hollow of her throat. I lick the salt between her breasts and drink, then lick and bite at her soft throat. She laughs as if it tickles, as if we are dear friends.

Does it feel good?

It's like a fish, nibbling at me.

I look at you and I see a dead woman.

What a thing to say.

Isabel wraps her strong bare thighs around me and shrugs and suddenly I am on my back. I'm a specimen, a corpse beneath her. She bends to kiss my throat and my penis swells terribly.

Jude is silent, she's invisible.

Isabel pulls up my shirt and exposes my belly, my wound. I feel a hot, wet trickle like blood or tears and I think she's cut herself, she's menstruating and I remember Lucy saying that she and her sister were forever bleeding on the same cycle. But this isn't blood, it's urine. Jude drags her away from me, a fistful of Isabel's hair in her left hand. Their faces are almost touching.

Oh, you fucking coward.

Are you a woman or a dog?

You should be careful where you sleep.

And you should never have fucked me.

Isabel pulls off her torn dress and sits naked on the other bed. She licks salt from her hand and I see her sitting across from me at the waffle house, slowly licking whipped cream from her finger.

You have beautiful hands, I say.

She holds out her hands, grinning. Her left hand bears the hourglass birthmark. I take a drink and the worm slips between my teeth. I chew it, tasting dirt.

twenty.

Sleep is black and lifeless for me. I edge to the surface and try to dream of Lucy but nothing comes. I take myself back to a bright, hot morning. The lake is shaped like a horse's head. I rent a flat-bottom boat from a toothless, shirtless man who wears striped suspenders to hold up his pants. Lucy wears a red bikini top and short cutoff army pants that barely cover her skeletal ass. She wears a baseball cap to keep her hair from blowing away. The boat has an ancient motor; it wheezes and dies again and again as we cross the lake. There is no wind. My gun is sealed in a plastic bag to keep it dry. It sits in the bottom of a Styrofoam cooler with sandwiches and fruit and cheese. I'm going to teach her to shoot. The motor dies again and I can't get it to roll over. There are no paddles and the boat begins to drift. I curse the toothless man. Lucy takes off her bikini top to get some sun on her breasts. I open a bottle of wine and drink. The boat drifts under the staring sun. I tell Lucy to be careful she doesn't burn. She doesn't answer and I think she's asleep. The boat drifts and time is elastic. The bottle is empty. I take off my shirt and use it to cover Lucy. She's turning red now and I check the pockets of my shorts. I have a knife and nothing else. No identification. I slip over the side of the boat.

Jude is curled and silent beside me, her face pressed against my ribs.

Whoa, girl. Take it easy, now.

Jude sits naked on Henry's chest, she throws his face back with her left
hand and her little stinger barely touches his exposed throat. I never heard
her move. She's a cat.

What are you looking for? she whispers.

My cigarette lighter. It's nickel-plated and I'd hate to lose it.

Don't lie, she says. It's insulting.

Do you mind putting that thing away? You seem a little too eager to
cut me a new smile.

Isabel is snoring in the other bed and I am struck by the thought that
I don't remember if Lucy snored. I always slept like a dead man, with her.
That was a lifetime ago and now I sleep like a lizard; I breathe through my
eyelids.

I don't like you, Henry. I don't know you and you make me very
fucking nervous.

Henry breathes evenly. I do have that effect on some people.

It's a liability, she says. Who are you?

My name is John Henry King. I was born July fourth, 1961. I sell
speedboats and orange is my favorite color. I like my coffee with sugar, no
cream. I don't eat breakfast unless I'm on vacation. I have a wife named
Josephine back in St. Louis. She's a law student.

And what about Isabel? You seem pretty friendly with her for a married man.

My wife and I are estranged. Isabel is but a daydream, an illusion.

Jude is silent and I know she doesn't believe him. But she doesn't have
much choice and she really doesn't want to kill him. Dead bodies aren't so
easy to hide on a train.

I'm sorry, says Henry. I'm still working on that story. I have another
one where I'm running from the federal witness protection program, but
it's too bloody for polite company.

Jude laughs reluctantly, then pulls her stinger away and stands up.
Henry rubs his throat and watches her. She covers her breasts and says, did
you get a good look?

Oh yes, ma'am.

I'm glad, she says. I hope it keeps you awake at night. Now get out, please.

As you wish.

Jude glares at Isabel, passive and drunk in the next bed. She sneers.

Take that bitch with you.

Henry gathers himself and lifts Isabel as if she's made of air. Her arms and legs dangle. She growls and grunts, still sleeping.

Jude leans over me, perhaps to kiss me.

Did you believe him?

Jude smiles. Oh, you're awake.

She sits on the edge of the little bed, turning the stinger in her hands. It seems to comfort her.

I roll over onto my side, the blankets pulled tight around me.

Of course I didn't believe him. He's too smooth, too frightening. He's like a stockbroker with a meat cleaver in his briefcase.

I like him, I say.

She bites her lip. I may be paranoid. But I'm thinking he works for Gore and maybe Gore has decided he doesn't want to pay. Maybe he wants to kill the messenger.

I smile in the dark. But you said Gore was a nice land developer, a tax-payer.

Jude hugs her knees.

Okay, she says. I might have lied to you. Luscious Gore is hardly a land developer.

That's a shame.

Jude smiles.

Tell me the truth, I say. My teeth clash together and I marvel at my own foolishness.

The stories are better than the truth, she says. He's a bored, sick millionaire. He's a rich pervert who wants to be the big bad wolf. He likes boys, he likes farm animals…ho-hum. He wants to be a terrorist, but he has no political agenda. He loves a good bombing and random assassinations. He killed two of his own children.

She is grinning like a fool.

Okay. If Luscious Gore is so high on the food chain, why does he run the double-cross?

He might double-cross me because it's raining, because he can't find his socks. It's not about the money with him, it's about sport. Henry makes things interesting.

And what about Isabel. Isn't she interesting?

She only wants to fuck with me and send you screaming back to the nuthouse.

Hold the phone. I'm not crazy.

Oh, Phineas.

I sit up with the sheets around my waist. Bits and pieces of the sun break through cracks in the heavy curtains, and Jude's face flickers in and out of the dark. She is still naked. She plays with the stinger now, running her thumb across the cruel point.

I know about your wife, she says. And I know what she looked like. Don't you think I would check you out before I asked you to come on this joyride?

And what did you find?

I found a pack of lies and misinformation. Your wife was killed last spring and you resigned from the police department in a cloud of smoke. One newspaper said it was suicide and another said it was a boating accident. She was buried in a closed casket and there was no autopsy. One newspaper hinted that the body was never even found. You surrendered your gun and then it disappeared from evidence. The district attorney wanted to crucify you but the case was dropped suddenly.

Five years with the cops, I say. And you learn how to kill an investigation. To make a fine mess of things.

So what really happened?

My wife was killed by a gun, by my gun. Her face was blown off. There was no autopsy simply because I arranged for the medical examiner to lose the body among the Jane Does. She was cremated with a dozen nameless women.

And the gun?

I helped it disappear from evidence. I carried it around for months like a dead albatross. Then I lost it the night I met you.

Purely a coincidence.

Or fate.

Her face was blown off, says Jude. Are you sure it was her body?

This isn't television. Of course I'm sure.

And who pulled the trigger?

There is silence between us.

The bright steel against her yellow skin is too much for me. The sheets have formed a ridiculous tent between my legs. I take the stinger from Jude and she leans to take me in her mouth but I stop her. I pull my knife from its sheath and softly kiss her fingers, the back of her hand. The pale underside of her wrist. I touch the dark veins with the blade, with my tongue. The bend of her elbow is soft, vulnerable. The biceps are sleek and curved and her skin smells like almonds. Is this supposed to be fun? she says.

Trust me, I say.

I press the knife's edge into her shoulder and pull it away quickly. The cut is as long as my pinkie and maybe a quarter inch deep. Her body shudders once, then relaxes. She trusts me. She wants me to hurt her, perhaps. I push her onto her stomach; she is numb and doesn't resist. The cut is bleeding profusely now. I use the knife to cut a long white strip from the sheet and tie it around her shoulder. The blood slows, but the cut will likely require stitches. I press the blade against the back of her thigh, barely below the soft flesh of her ass. She jerks and makes a small sound. The blade leaves a mark but there is no blood. I place the knife at her tailbone and trace a hair-thin cut along the pale bikini line. The skin hesitates then opens slightly and blood appears, as if she has cut herself shaving. I move the knife to the area of her right kidney and scratch a mark that is like my own cut but will not scar. I am nearly bursting now, and my left elbow is trembling under my weight. I push her legs apart and let my body fall over hers, heavy as a blanket of snow. I drop my knife on the bed where she can reach it and I am inside her.

Minutes later I am kissing her ear, her neck. I tell her I'm sorry.

I haven't earned your tenderness, she says.

Jude is asleep on her belly and the sheets are dark with blood. Her mouth is open slightly and her lips glisten with spit. I allow myself to hate her, briefly. Then I wake her with a hurried kiss, whispering her name and she answers me in a purring, drunken voice.

Tell me about Isabel, I say.

I feel good, she says. Don't spoil it.

This is important.

Jude rolls over and uses her folded arms as a pillow. The shoulder is painful, I can tell.

Isabel is Luscious Gore's daughter, she says.

I close my eyes and I see Lucy's face.

And she doesn't have any bone disease, does she?

Jude sighs and I don't think I'm in the mood for this, not really.

I'm sorry. But I don't think I've told the truth in over a year.

A year is nothing, I say. And the truth drifts, like smoke.

I'm not in the army, she says. I'm attached to a deep-cover unit called the Platypus Project. It's a bastard child of the CIA and totally unprotected.

You're a secret agent, I say.

It sounds silly, doesn't it? But yes. For the past two years I have been undercover, living as Luscious Gore's bodyguard.

And the organ snatching? That's a hobby.

The kidney is actually intended for Isabel's brother, Horatio. He's a coke addict and he slipped into a coma four weeks ago. Almost total renal failure. He needs a transplant right away, and even if he was a legitimate citizen he would go on a waiting list. But Horatio is wanted for a dozen capital crimes; he can't just walk into the emergency room and flash his Blue Shield card.

Oh, yeah. It must be inconvenient.

Jude smiles through shadows.

Anyway, she says. Isabel disappeared one night and came back at two in the morning with a bloody, mutilated kidney in a shoebox. She had gutted a male prostitute in downtown Dallas.

I love it. Then what.

Everyone was hysterical. They had to sedate her. The funny thing is that Luscious can't stand Horatio. He would gladly pull the plug and call it a day. But Isabel adores him, so he promised her a kidney. He knew I had the surgical background to do it right, and he offered me a lot of money. It would have blown my cover to refuse. I told him I would take care of it, and I went to Denver alone. Isabel followed me.

Denver, I say. Why not Albuquerque?

It was just far enough away and removed from Gore's sphere. And no one knew me. To be honest, I wish I had gone to New Orleans. It's my favorite city in the world. It's crawling with vampires and voodoo queens. No one would have noticed a missing kidney.

Now, I say. Why did you fucking choose me?

Isabel chose you, she says. She said you were a perfect tissue match, a rare find.

I'm special.

Very.

Why not just give the damn thing to Isabel?

She doesn't have the money, says Jude. And I like to watch her twist.

It's an excellent story but I don't believe her for a minute. Jude is an organ smuggler, a flesh thief. She made the crucial error of falling in love with her victim and now she's trying to dazzle me with a lot of intrigue. Isabel is her estranged partner, perhaps her lover. Her resemblance to Lucy is all in my fucking head.

Do you know anything about Greek mythology? she says.

I stare at her. You aren't going to change me into a pig, are you?

Jude laughs. I was thinking of Orpheus, the poet. His wife was killed and he was so shattered by grief that he followed her to the underworld.

Poor bastard.

Orpheus begged the gods to release his wife, but they refused.

I light a cigarette. I really don't like this story.

For years he charmed them with his pitiful music and finally the gods couldn't stand it anymore. They agreed to let Orpheus take his wife back to the living, on one condition.

The gods always have to fuck with you. It's not enough to just kill you.

But Orpheus was given such a simple task, she says. Like a walk in the park. All he had to do was lead his wife out of the underworld without looking back. And he almost made it. At the very end, he turned to look at his wife. He loved her and he didn't quite trust her. He wasn't sure she would follow him. When he looked at her, she vanished and was gone.

That's just great.

There's no smoking in here, says Jude.

It's cool. I disabled the smoke detectors.

I might love you, she says.

Yeah. And what happened to Orpheus?

Don't laugh, but he was killed at an orgy. He was torn apart by a pack of young girls.

My face is suddenly cold. I feel something like a rush of stupidity and I don't know the difference between love and sorrow.

Something bothers me, she says.

What?

You never kiss me on the mouth.

I know you will betray me in the end, I say.

She smiles. I wouldn't do that.

I stroke her foot. What is your real name?

My only name is Jude.

Jude gives me a brief lesson in undercover field medicine. I'm doubtful but she convinces me to sterilize her wound, then seal it with Krazy Glue. She shows me how to make a butterfly bandage and it feels good to take care of her. I help her get dressed and she lets me pick out her clothes. I'm tired of her cold European goddess clothes and I choose torn blue jeans that are a little too big for her and hang loose at the hips, the burgundy boots and a tiny white T-shirt that clings to her like it's wet. Her nipples are round and dark and clearly visible.

Do you want me to look like a tart? she says.

I smile. You look like you're nineteen and you're sore from too much fucking.

You look pale, she says. Is it the pain?

I realize my hands are slick with sweat. My teeth hurt from clenching them and I've been shivering for the last hour. My eyes ache and my belly is a pool of acid. I don't really want another shot but I can't say no.

twenty-one.

JUDE IS HUNGRY. She tries to talk me into having breakfast but the shot has settled into my muscles and blood, my bone structure. I am happy to watch shadows race across the floor. And I'm in no mood to see Isabel and Henry. The speedboat salesman, I say. Whoever the fuck he is. I'm bored with his game.

Jude sighs. You are so innocent, aren't you.

Bring me a piece of bread, maybe some fruit.

Okay, she says. But don't wander off without me. I don't want you to get lost again.

Don't worry. I'm safe as a bug in a glass.

This makes me giggle foolishly and Jude shrugs. She takes the blood-soiled sheets to leave elsewhere and I hear a massive click as she locks the door behind her. This isn't like any Valium I ever had. My sensory perception is ridiculously heightened and I feel shifting waves of ecstasy and paranoia. I can't say I don't like it. I watch as silent rushing trees and slabs of rock and yawning open space blur behind the window. If I listen carefully I can hear unseen animals breathing and chirping, scratching and chewing. I can even hear the sun. It sounds like a jet taking off in the middle of the night. I stare at my hands for five minutes and I see endless scars and wrinkled, discolored flesh and there is a taste like chrome in my throat. An inhuman voice invades my head and I tell myself it is only the conductor, he's telling me the train will be stopping shortly in Las Vegas. I laugh out loud and clap my hands like a monkey because I want to get off the train.

But I'm not going anywhere without the little green icebox. It's still locked in the complimentary storage compartment, a little white cupboard made of brightly painted plywood. The lock is flimsy, the kind that takes a miniature key. I'm sure Jude could pick it with a paper clip, with her eyebrow tweezers. But I was never any good at that. I use my knife to pry one hinge, but the other won't give. I manage to slide my fingers into a tiny gap and with strength that surprises me simply rip the door apart.

The icebox is maddeningly weightless, as always. She told me it was packed in dry ice and I believed her. But I can't help thinking the ice has melted and my kidney is wrapped in aluminum foil like a ham sandwich; it's floating around in there with a few cans of beer and a piece of pie.

I'm suddenly nervous about metal detectors and I drop my knife and gun on the bed. I still have Jude's little stun gun. It's graphite and plastic and it looks so harmless, like a toy.

I drift along the passageway, mumbling and schizophrenic. The train is so still, so silent. The constant motion was sickening but now it's gone and I feel lost. Isabel comes toward me, her yellow eyes bright. She's wearing a short blond wig and a black and white dress that could have come from Lucy's closet. I try to remember what I did with her clothes after the funeral but all I see are haze and yellow clouds.

What's in the box, dear?

Nothing, I say. My pet rabbit.

Oh, let me see.

Don't touch it, I say. My teeth are chattering. I really want to get off the train.

She laughs. You don't really think there's a kidney in there, do you? Let me tell you a small medical truth. An organ intended for transplant cannot survive longer than twenty-four hours without oxygen.

It's packed in dry ice. Dry ice.

It could be packed in amber and it would still be worthless, she says. It would be a dead piece of meat.

Why should I believe you? My voice is so faint I could be underwater.

Don't then, she says. Let's open it.

I don't have the key.

That hardly matters. Do you have a gun, a knife?

I push past her, hugging the icebox to my belly.

The kidney is fine, I say. Jude knows what she's doing.

Isabel blows me a kiss and against a bleeding red filter I see myself drop the icebox and grab her shoulders and snap her fine neck with the raw, damp noise of bone and tissue separating. I pull the clothes from her shattered body and watch her eyes become coins. I set fire to her hair and now she smiles and says, you will see me again.

Outside and I bend to touch the untrembling earth, the dead wood of the platform. I feel the liquid, visible heat coming from the train. A man in a shiny blue uniform tells me I have thirty minutes before the train leaves. I walk into the station, my lucky hat pulled low over my eyes. I see everything with uncomfortable clarity and I try not to whisper and giggle but the incessant bells and lights of slot machines send me into a shivering panic. The crush of people waiting in lines and talking on cell phones and waving tickets drops me to my knees. I crouch before a short, burly vending machine; it's blue and white and I think of R2D2, the droll little robot that endlessly beeped and whistled in a faraway galaxy where everyone was so polite and sometimes I wished Luke had the testicles to just vaporize him. The machine before me dispenses newspapers and I glare at one through the glass. The headlines are meaningless but the date in the left corner reads December 25. The sky outside has the impossible color and texture of morning. It's been only twenty-four hours since we left Denver.

I fucking hate Christmas. It always drags on, as if it's dying. I tried to be happy when I was with Lucy. She thought every Christmas might be her last. Everything was thick with symbolism. Every little thing took on the weight of a body, of a dead person. I spent too much money on presents and helped her decorate the tree. I tolerated the music, the smell of orange peels and cinnamon. But it all struck me as a waste of time. I wasn't any happier than I ever was. In the end, I could only get drunk and make Lucy cry. She would sit on the couch, two miles away and silent. Her face dirty with tears and her legs bent beneath her.

I crawl and stagger into a frozen yogurt shop and throw myself into a plastic booth. I want to get back on the train. I need Jude to soothe me, to make everyone stop staring at me. There is a salt shaker on the table and I unscrew the lid with twitching fingers. I pour salt into my hand and eat it, choking. It calms me down a bit. I rest my cheek on the cool yellow surface of the table. I breathe in and out until my pulse is normal. I want to get back on the train but I'm not ready to go outside, not yet. A pair of white pants enters my field of vision. The thick fur coat made from some scrawny animal whose meat is probably too bitter to eat. A black leather belt with a bright silver buckle. I look down at polished black boots and then up, at the smiling face of the Blister. He still wears the bright white gloves and I wonder if they hide prosthetic hands. He holds two sugar cones of soft chocolate yogurt, and he licks one of them boyishly. He slides into the booth and hands me the other cone and I stare at it in wonder. I touch it hesitantly with my raw tongue and it tastes impossibly good.

Are you having fun yet? he says.
    Did you ever notice that frozen yogurt doesn't really melt? It uncongeals, I say. As if the molecular bond is only temporary.
    I see that Jude is keeping you well anesthetized, he says. For the pain, I'm sure.
    He wipes chocolate from his lips. There is a bubble of silence around our table and the churning faces of the station seem far away. But there isn't enough oxygen for the two of us and the bubble will soon burst.
    I don't mind the pain so much, I say. But the drugs are a nice distraction.

His tongue flicks across his teeth. I wanted to give you a little pep talk.

I glance at my wrist and I'm surprised to see my watch is actually there. The porter said thirty minutes but that could have been hours ago.

Let's make it fast, I say.

The Blister smiles and I notice how red his lips are.

Don't worry.

I'm not worried.

A knot of chocolate surfaces at the back of my throat, apparently rejected by my stomach. I place the unfinished cone in the center of the yellow tabletop. The Blister glares at it.

I'm afraid that you are losing focus, he says. That your infatuation with Jude might distract you from your purpose. There's a lot of money involved and I have to be careful.

I don't really need your money, I say.

The Blister bites forcefully into his sugar cone. I was hoping you would say that. I enjoy conflict, now and then. It allows me to apply a little leverage.

I could use a little leverage.

Did you know that you have become quite popular with the police? Your name is on everyone's lips and they are dying to meet you in Los Angeles.

What are you talking about?

Murder, of course. And a rape for good measure.

I stare at him. You raped Eve, of course.

Don't be silly, he says. That would be far too pedestrian for me, too messy.

I'm sure you hate a mess.

He chews for a moment. The point is that the police think you raped her.

Oh, well. Then I must have raped her. And killed a person, too.

You must have, he says. He grins at me. A local drug dealer named Winston Jones. He was a piece of garbage, but still. The evidence against you may as well be on a silver platter.

Oh you motherfucker.

I am told that Mr. Jones had a daughter, the Blister says. A sweet little girl who suddenly has no daddy.

My fingers are tingling and I laugh out loud.

How are your bowels? he says. Has there been any activity?

Nothing yet. But I have my fingers crossed.

You are casual, he says. For a man with a bag of poison in his abdominal cavity.

The only bag of poison is my heart.

Oh, the drama. The Blister sighs. Jude bothers me and I want you to kill her, very soon. If not, I may be forced to do it myself. And I can just as easily lay the blame on you.

The drugs are waning. I look down at the table, at the decomposing yogurt.

Then go ahead and kill her, I say. But I don't think Jude will die easily.

The table is perhaps three feet across, half a body length. I place the icebox in the center like a bouquet of flowers. The Blister stares at it, his shoulders twitching.

Give it to me, he says.

Silence.

I insist, he says.

Everyone tells me the kidney is worthless. A sad piece of meat you couldn't feed to a dog.

It is hardly worthless.

I'm curious. Are you Luscious Gore?

He laughs. One day, perhaps. I will be.

I don't like this answer. I push the icebox to one side and lean forward as if I have a secret. The Blister bends toward me, his head slightly cocked to one side. I grab him by the ears and smash his forehead with mine. I've seen this little maneuver in a dozen movies but never actually tried it. It's absurdly painful. My eyes are hot with tears and for a second I think I may have done him a favor: I've knocked myself silly. But then his mouth turns to jelly and his cheeks are the color of cigarette ash. He slumps sideways and I come out of my seat in mock horror. My friend is drunk, I say.

No one pays any attention. This is Las Vegas and the tourists drop like flies. I slide in next to the Blister and he is trying to sit up. I find his carotid artery with my thumb and crush it. I count to five, six, seven, and let go. Unconsciousness is a delicate thing and it too easily becomes death.

twenty-two.

A YEAR AGO I MIGHT HAVE CARRIED THE BLISTER up a flight of stairs. But I'm so much weaker than I used to be. I'm a fucking flower, lately. I listen to him breathe beside me. I wonder if he's dreaming. I'm bored and worried that the train will leave soon. I lean over the Blister and remove one of his white gloves. His hand is ropy and gray with scar tissue, with old, poorly healed burns. His hand is like a prehistoric claw, the gross extremity of some cave-dwelling troll. It could probably use some sunlight. I pull the slick glove over my own hand. There is still a puddle of melted yogurt on the table. With one alien finger, I trace out a wobbly heart in the sweet brown goo. I stare at the top of my finger, at the dripping white leather. The Blister breathes, in and out. His face is stupid with trust. I shrug and wipe the glove clean, then slip it back onto his hand. He comes to life suddenly, eyes rolling and incoherent. He doesn't seem to know where he is. I guide him to the bathroom, smiling and apologizing to anyone that will listen. My friend is drunk, I whisper.

The Blister says he wants to lie down. He wants to go back to sleep. I say nothing. I don't want to weaken. I drag him unprotesting to the handicap stall and prop him up on the toilet, his head dangling like meat on a string. I slap his pockets, smiling when I find a set of handcuffs and still smiling as I shackle him to the guardrail. I take his gun from the shoulder holster and unload it. I open his wallet. He has a stack of hundred-dollar bills and a startling array of false identification; he's a cop and a U.S. marshal and a secret service agent and a military investigator. He has a dozen names. I pocket the money and drop his wallet into the toilet. The Blister is made of rubber. I feel the rush, the trill of reckoning and I know that I am making a mistake. I have changed the game and now everything is personal. There will be no frozen yogurt next time and I don't mind. I have been patient for so long. The Blister has a cell phone in his jacket pocket, slim as a cigarette lighter, and I slip it into my pocket. I clumsily pull his shoes and pants off. He has very hairy legs and he wears black bikini underpants. He has also wet himself. I take the panties off with care and I'm vaguely pleased to see that his penis is uncircumcised, ugly, and quite small. Now he wears only the gloves. His eyes flutter and he begins to make unhappy noises. I kiss him on the lips and whisper, wake up sweet Romeo.

The Blister's eyes are boiling. He yanks at the handcuffs and groans like a horse. I shrug as he presses his knees together to hide his crotch. He waits for me to speak and I realize I don't know what I want from him. I crouch and stare at him for a moment, wondering if I should gag him. The men's room is suddenly alive with noise. The drone of pipes and crashing footsteps, the hum of urine against tile. Someone blows his nose bloodily. Two stalls over, a giant takes a long and terrifying shit. It sounds like he's drowning someone. The Blister becomes calm. I imagine he doesn't want anyone to notice us, but I don't really care.

Let's open the icebox, I say. Shall we?

The Blister is blank now. He looks at me as if I am speaking a foreign language.

You must be a tiny bit curious.

He doesn't answer and I decide to ignore him. I dig through my pockets and come up with the key that I took from Jude's purse. That was a hundred years ago. I take a deep breath and stare at the icebox until I feel disconnected. If my kidney is inside, I will chew it up like hamburger and go home. I sniff the air and wonder what stinks, but it's only me. I smell of sulfur, of fear. I'm slick with sweat and my hands are pale as fish. I'm afraid to open the box, to gaze on the lost, bloodied piece of myself. I put the key in my mouth and it's bitter beneath my tongue.

For a long shimmering moment I point the Blister's gun at the icebox and I'm tempted to just fill it with holes. The Blister is soon laughing at me, his voice forced and artificial.

What?

There is a bomb in that box, he says. And I would dearly hate to perish with my pants down.

Do I have a stupid face? Why does everyone think they can sell me a pack of lies?

The Blister laughs like a demented wind-up toy. He's trying to give me the trembles again and it's working. I reach into the toilet and splash chemical blue water onto his thigh. And still he laughs, his voice nearly cracking and I pull out the little stun gun. I press it against his wet skin and give him a nice jolt and it doesn't seem to make a real impression so I stun him again and again and soon he begins to shriek. His face is twisting and purple and I wonder if I might have really hurt him.

I'm very sorry, I say.

His skin is the wrong color and his eyes are wandering, but he never loses consciousness.

How did you burn your hands? I say.

The Blister glances at his left hand, still gloved and shackled to the silver rail.

You will be dead before nightfall, he says. His voice is slushy.

Not likely. How did you burn your hands?

A household accident, he says. It was a stupid, childish thing.

What happened?

Did you ever hurt anyone? he says.

I blink at him. A thousand times.

No, he says. Didn't you ever hurt an animal or a child, someone that was weak?

Just for fun?

Curiosity, he says.

Oh, I say. You're ten years old and you find a frog in the woods. He's too far from the water and the sun is about to cook him. He's dragging himself through the dust and you know he's not gonna make it. You could carry him to water and save his life, or you could just sit there and poke him with a stick and watch him bleed for a while. Because it's more interesting. Is that what you mean?

Yes, he says. Because you don't feel anything.

The Blister is a strange bird. He crackles and pops with some kind of nervous rage, but he can't sustain it. He wants to be supercool and dangerous but he's too self-conscious. His face betrays him readily and his ordinary fears spill around his feet, glittering like gasoline in a puddle.

I stare at him for a long time and he barks, What?

Everyone is afraid of sympathy, I say. Everyone is cruel.

Why would I listen to you? He sneers. You were in an institution.

And children are the worst, aren't they?

He crashes around, cursing me. I slip the key into the lock easily, sexually. Then crack the lid of the icebox so carefully I might be stealing a peek at a solar eclipse. I expect a rush of liquid smoke, a spill of maggots. But I bend to sniff at the crack in the lid and smell only vinyl.

Five plastic bags of heroin. I guess ten, maybe twelve ounces each. Five tight little pouches, barely two sorry kilos. I stroke one of them as if it were flesh and the plastic is smooth and cool and soft as a young girl's breast. I bite it open with my teeth and poke my tongue in through the tear. It's unpleasantly pure and I may have swallowed too much. The spine uncoils lazily and I suffer false impressions of underwater breathing and the bitter taste of melancholy. But the spiral is only temporary and I can soon form words.

Is this a fucking joke?

The Blister glares at me with such pure loathing it's almost sexy.

The street value of your kidney, he says. An unloved organ, an accessory you never really needed until you found it missing.

This is what you want?

Oh, yes.

I slit the bag open like the belly of a kitten and the Blister howls. I twirl the bag at him, then another. And soon his face and torso and wretched genitals are white. He's naked and handcuffed and in another lifetime he might be someone's lover, squealing like a baby and dipped in sugar. I drop the remaining bags into the toilet.

I'm sure they will float, I say.

The Blister is speechless. I stuff his clothing into the icebox and lock it shut.

Don't you have anything to say?

He shrugs like a sullen child and I release him from the handcuffs. I offer him the fur coat.

Comfort from the rain, I say.

It's been too long. I'm shivering and my legs are asleep but I feel like I might grow wings. The train will surely pull away any moment and I run through the station grinning and sweating like a maniac. I have to find Jude before the train leaves. I stop and break the glass on a fire alarm and laugh like a kid as the Klaxons start to whoop. The crowd disintegrates and I become terribly calm.

I reboard the train and hurry to the dining car. I see Jude from behind. Her thick black and blond hair like sun and shadow joined. The knots of her spine faintly reptilian through the tiny white T-shirt. Henry and Isabel sit across from her. I walk toward them, slowly. Isabel yawns lazily. Her lips are swollen and she glows with sex. Henry winks at me, twirling a chunk of sausage on his fork. Jude sucks at a piece of ice and looks at me like a stranger. I take her hand and mutter something about borrowing my wife. Isabel chews the edge of her thumb and the color stubbornly clings to her face.

What's going on? Jude says. You look insane.

I'm fine. I'm fucking great actually. I hold her hand so tightly I might crush it. I smile and say excuse me to a pair of frail old men who are maddeningly slow to get out of our way. I drag Jude behind me until she stops and pulls her hand free and I remember how strong she is.

Did you know that you have two black eyes?

What? I touch my face and I'm surprised to feel the swollen and tender bones around my eyes. The Blister's face must be a regular sunset.

Oh, well. I had a little trouble in the bathroom.

She touches my cheek and her hand hangs briefly in the air and I stare at the tip of her finger until I notice a fine white dust on her sharp blue nails. I wait for her to taste it but she doesn't even blink. She doesn't glance at the icebox. Where are we going? she says.

I don't answer and she follows me anyway. I push open the door to our compartment and tell her to get her things. We're getting off the train, I say.

Oh, no. That's what she wants. She wants me to run.

I shove my face close to hers. The adrenaline is rushing between us like visible heat.

I'm serious, Jude. Let's go.

She doesn't move. Her face is two inches away and all I see are flared nostrils, sharp teeth and cheekbones cut from stone. I wouldn't want to fight her. But she breathes with me and her face softens, she backs away. She picks up her garment bag and looks around the tiny room. The train begins to rumble.

What's happened. Who are you running from?

My own personal boogeyman. And yours.

She doesn't blink. I hope you know what you're doing, she says.

twenty-three.

I STEP OFF THE TRAIN INTO RAZOR SUNSHINE as the conductor howls all aboard. The sirens have died away and two or three firemen wander irritably through the station. Jude is behind me. I walk through the thinning crowd, my eyes and ears trying to take in everything. A fat lady hunched over a nickel slot machine, her heavy right hand dipping with strange grace into a cup full of coins and in the same motion feeding a coin into the machine and pulling the handle and dipping into the cup again. A little boy eating a hot dog. His young mother has a body like a tree branch and when she bends over him the front of her dress falls open and I see her small bare breasts and narrow ribs, a flash of silver in her navel and tiny white panties. A man and woman sitting exhausted on a wooden bench. He wears no socks and there is a line of pale skin at his wrist where his watch used to be. His wife has eyes like sand; she is incapable of crying anymore and I wonder how much money they lost. The Blister is nowhere to be seen. I can't even feel his presence and I suppose he's already slithered away. Or possibly the cops have grabbed him up. A naked man with three dripping bags of heroin is not something you see every day. Jude takes my hand and squeezes it.

There is a line of taxicabs out front. I open the door to the first one and Jude climbs in. The cabbie is a skinny kid with a mustache and he hops out to put our bags into the trunk.

Where can I take you? he says.

I put my arm around him and pull him close. He is soft and smells of peanut butter. I slap one of the Blister's hundred-dollar bills into his palm.

Don't blink, I say. But that is Lisa Marie Presley in the backseat and I need to hire a private plane. Maybe you know a small, inconspicuous airport?

The kid grins. We're there in a half hour, he says.

The cab growls through slow-moving traffic. The city is naked and grim under the morning sun, clogged with too many people. Bits of paper swirl and twist in the air. Jude sits against the cracked vinyl in the backseat, her face to the window. She hasn't spoken. I rest my hand on her thigh and feel her warmth. I take the Blister's cell phone from my jacket pocket and flip it open, then take a deep breath and dial. I touch her shoulder and she looks at me. I give her the phone and tell her to ask for Detective Moon. She is put on hold and I take the phone from her. What are you doing to us? she says.

Hush. I need you to trust me.

Moon comes on the line, his voice heavy with smoke. I hesitate, nervous and shameful. As if I am fifteen and I have wrecked the car. I ran away from home and two days have passed and I'm calling my father to see how bad the damage is. Moon, I say. It's Phineas Poe.

Do you have a screw loose? he says. I'm going to hang up now.

No, I say. Talk to me, please. Tell me what you have.

I have you, he says. I have you fucking gift-wrapped. All I need to do is find you.

Don't bother tracing this.

I'm not. I don't want to look like a bigger fool than I am.

What do you have?

I have smoke and mirrors. I have a fistful of physical evidence that says you raped Eve McBride. Your fingerprints were everywhere. Your hair was in her bed, your blood between her legs. But she swears it wasn't you and I believe her.

My blood. How do you know it's mine?

Remember. The lab did everything but stool samples on you after Lucy died. And they save it all for a rainy day.

Wonderful. But it wasn't me.

Maybe. Why don't you come home and we'll talk.

No, thanks. I talked to Eve yesterday. She said it wasn't rape and maybe it was a woman.

He grunts. I'm not her husband and she doesn't have to sell me any mind games. But she's asking for some expensive therapy, if you ask me. And if it was a woman, she had a big dick. The rape kit showed massive vaginal damage.

I'm a sucker, a deaf-and-dumb asshole. I wanted to believe her, to spare her.

Do me a favor, I say. Put a car outside her apartment for a few days.

My pleasure, he says.

Thanks. And what else do you have on me.

I have a possible suicide by the name of Winston "Pooh" Jones: white male, age thirty. The funny thing is that he was also a suspect in the McBride rape. And you slept in his bed and ate his last Twinkies that same night. Pooh is then found dead in a motel room, apparently by his own hand. But it looks a lot like murder dressed up as suicide. He used a knife to cut his fucking leg open and bleed himself to death. Meanwhile, he had a perfectly good shotgun in his truck outside, and a lot of blood on the front seat. I'm supposed to think he cut his leg open in the truck, then went up to his room and took a shower? Hair and fibers came up empty; everything was clean as a whistle. Nothing but his own blood and prints.

I'm sorry to hear that.

Of course you are. And one might think that you killed him to shut him up. But it doesn't matter because those charges are fucking gravy, they're parsley. My idiot brother could get those thrown out.

I take a breath and look at Jude. I stare at her ear until it becomes the bent and fragile leaf of a dried flower. Her reflection in the window is cut in half and I see her lips. They are moving, just barely. I wonder if she's singing, if she's counting cars. I wonder what she did with my kidney. Did she trade it for a box of heroin or did she give it up for a dying boy in Phoenix?

I also found your missing gun, he says. It was in the front seat of a black Ford Mustang.

My brain takes a spin and I see wild horses, their lips white with foam. Whose car is it? I say.

The missing Rose White, he says. A pediatric surgeon at the same hospital where you recently did time. Dr. White was found in the trunk of her car, shot twice by your gun.

I stare at Jude's slender throat. I wonder if it will be easier to kill her than to save her.

When, I say. When was she killed?

She was pretty stiff, maybe four days old and we checked her work schedule. She never showed for her shift on the twenty-first.

The first day of winter. The day I woke up in the hospital.

Oh, yeah. Moon is eerily cheerful. The cool weather kept her fresh.

What did she look like?

She was bald, says Moon. Which was a little creepy. Her friends say she usually wore a red wig. And she was naked, but that's normal. Otherwise she was your typical dead white female.

How did she lose her hair?

What kind of question is that? She had cancer.

Did you get any prints from my gun?

Of course not. But I'm afraid your blood was found in the car.

My blood is everywhere.

Where did you find the car? I say.

1013 Alpine, he says. It was parked in the driveway of a nice little two-bedroom house for sale. The real estate agent called it in.

I stare at the back of my hand. The ink is faded to a spidery blue like the veins beneath my skin but I can still read it. *Rose 1013 Alpine 2 P.M.* I never made a date with Rose White and she never really existed. She was already dead. Isabel answered the phone that night and she gave me the bogus address. She strapped on a detachable penis and raped Eve while I was looking at the Hobbit house with a lovely room for the baby. Or maybe it was Pooh. He was looking for me, for the heroin. And he found Eve. She was a prize; she was the ring that glows in the dark, buried in a box of Cracker Jack.

It doesn't matter. Because the wound in my belly was leaking like a sieve.

I was leaving my blood behind me, in the dead woman's car and Eve's bed.

Do you have a recent photo of me? I say. You might want to show it to the real estate agent.

Phineas, says Moon. Come home and we'll work this out.

I laugh like a chump and Jude glances at me, then away. Lucy faked her death and she's having a lot of fun with me. She killed this Rose White with my gun and now she's setting me up as a killer, a rapist. She couldn't do this alone; her heart isn't hard enough and she wouldn't know how. She would need help and she would get it with melting black eyes and the voice of a dove, with the promise of velvet panties. Moon could have helped her. It would be easy for him. Moon's voice has become static and I think, satellites are crashing and my blood is everywhere. *I'm the stranger.* I drop the Blister's phone out the window and turn to watch it shatter. I feel sick and I want to hit someone, to crush a familiar face.

Lucy is alive, I say. She's killing people and Henry has my wedding ring. He stole my identity and she's going to kill him next.

It's not possible, Jude says. Your wife is dead, okay?

My stomach churns with dread and nausea. Nothing is what it seems.

twenty-four.

I LEAN AND WHISPER SICKLY TO JUDE. Do you know how to fly?

She shrugs. Of course.

The cab turns down a narrow gravel road. Ahead I can see a half dozen hangars in a scattered semicircle. Two small planes sit on the runway. A car is parked beside one of them, and a man and woman move back and forth in the skeletal shadow of the plane. I tell the cabbie to park alongside their car. He leaves the engine running and jumps out to open the door for Jude. He bobs his head, clutching her hand.

It's a real pleasure, Miss Presley.

Jude frowns and I step between them. He lets go of her hand.

What's your name, kid? I say.

Bobby. My name is Robert but no one calls me that.

That's fine. Bobby, I want to thank you.

He looks nervous. What for?

For a smooth ride. For a cab that didn't smell like fried eggs. And for your professional attitude, of course. I give him another hundred. And I hope you can keep a secret. Miss Presley is a private person.

He shakes his head. Don't you worry. I'm like a priest. Nothing leaves the backseat.

Interesting analogy, says Jude.

Bobby backs away from her. No problem, he says.

He drives away and Jude turns to me, squinting. That little secret will last five minutes.

I know. But it made his day and sometimes confusion is better than nothing.

Well, she says. I assume you have a plan.

Not really. I lift the green icebox. But I'm feeling lucky.

The plane is an old twin-engine, blue and white. It has shining black propellers and I think it will be a miracle if it ever gets off the ground. The man and woman watch as we walk toward them. They appear to be in their sixties and they look friendly enough. The woman wears a yellow pantsuit and a white hat. The man wears madras shorts and a golf shirt. He holds a wrench in one hand. They might be Elvis fans but they aren't as stupid as Bobby. And I don't think they need our money.

Morning to you, the man says.

I bend over to tie my shoes and remove my gun from the ankle holster.

That's a beautiful little plane, says Jude. She drops her bag to the tarmac.

Thank you. What can I do for you?

Let us borrow it, I say.

His eyes flicker. Don't be ridiculous, young man.

I feel terrible but I bring the gun up and point it at his wife. She puts one hand to her throat. I know I'm not going to shoot her and I'm afraid the man knows it too. Jude is ten or fifteen feet away from him but she is so quick. It isn't natural. She is like a water bug, a skipping stone. I blink and she is swinging the stinger at him, a tight backhand slash like a blurred raindrop, a magician's veil. The man cries out and drops the wrench and his arm is pouring blood.

I help the lady to the car. She says her name is Marian. She hangs on to my arm and she doesn't weigh more than eighty pounds. I open the driver's side door and place her on the seat as if she might shatter. Her legs aren't nearly long enough to reach the pedals. I adjust the seat for her and she clutches at the wheel. I'm afraid she's going to faint. There's a bottle of warm water in the backseat and I make her take small swallows.

I'm very sorry, I say. I wasn't going to shoot you.

She looks at me with glazed, milky eyes.

You don't look like a nice boy, she says.

Jude brings the man over to the car. He walks unsteadily, leaning on her. She has bandaged his arm but it's already showing blood. She hands me the car keys and I lean in to start the engine. It's not a stick shift, at least. I think they might make it to the hospital.

My purse is on the plane, says Marian. It has my driver's license.

Jude offers to get it and the old woman starts to tremble at the sound of her voice.

Don't worry, I say. I'll get it.

Jude turns away from the wind and lights a cigarette. I run to the plane and bring back the purse and a leather suitcase that bears faded stickers from more countries than I can count. I give the purse to Marian and slide the suitcase into the backseat. The old man sits crumpled in the passenger seat, his face pale.

Take him straight to the hospital, I say. And be careful.

The car pulls away feebly, and I know she won't go faster than twenty miles per hour. Maybe a cop will stop her. Jude stands facing me and I ask for a drag of her cigarette. She flicks it away and walks to the plane. I look out at the desert and I remember what it's like to be alone. After a minute I follow her.

Jude is in the cockpit, her eyes dark behind sunglasses. She is looking over some charts and muttering to herself. I scan the instrument panel and feel a rush of vertigo.

This isn't like stealing a car, she says. You don't just cover the plates with mud and disappear on some back road. You go up without a registered flight plan and you get sucked into the tailwind of a passenger jet. You do a Patsy Cline and run into a fucking mountain.

I sit down in the copilot's chair. What's the problem?

There's no problem. Ma and Pa back there were headed for Taos and we will have barely enough fuel to make El Paso. We need to deviate from their flight plan a little, a lot. If we stay below the commercial flight paths and don't draw attention to ourselves we might be okay. As long as we don't stumble into a snowstorm.

She speaks without looking at me, spitting her words in a controlled monotone.

I'm glad, I say. I'm glad there's no problem.

What were you thinking? she says. If you could just be patient I would have had that old man begging us to take the plane. But you pulled your gun and you weren't going to shoot her. It was written all over your face. And you were a cop. What is the first rule in a hostage situation?

I close my eyes. Don't point your weapon at anyone unless you are willing to shoot him.

That's right. And why is that?

Because you have no power. If your bluff is called you lose.

I open my eyes and look at her. The thin white T-shirt is damp with sweat and she might as well be naked. She folds her arms across her chest and a pretty blue vein stands out in her throat.

I cut her husband because I had to do something, she says. It would have been easier and safer to kill them both and bring their bodies along. Then it looks like they went to Taos as planned and no one's the wiser. But I didn't kill him. I saved you from making a decision and you looked at me like I was the Wicked Witch.

Jude, I say.

She hits me once in the face and I know she's holding back. She could probably kill me with two fingers. Her fist is sharp as a stone. After a minute, she lets me hold her.

I don't want you to look at me that way, she says. Ever again.

The engines cough and roar to life and the propellers become ragged, blurred eyes. Jude runs the twin throttles as far as they will go and the plane trembles as if it will fall apart. I sit beside her, uneasy but strangely happy. I wish I had a mouthful of bubble gum. The plane lunges forward as she releases the brakes, and we roll down the runway in a hammering rush. I can't take my eyes off Jude. She is as calm as a cat lying half asleep, watching birds bathe themselves out of reach. Her dark lips are slightly parted and the muscles stand out along her arms. Her body is all piano wires and sinew. I hold my breath as the plane leaves the earth and Jude turns to me, her face shining.

twenty-five.

THE CELL IS A SOOTHING, SICKENING BLUE.

I meet Lucy when I'm still new with the cops. I'm a fool. I'm living in a rathole apartment with rented furniture. A wide-screen television and a water bed. The kind of shit that you pay nineteen bucks a week for, and as soon as you miss a payment you're looking at stained gray carpet and balls of hair and chewed fingernails and you're sleeping on the floor wrapped in a beach towel. I'm a drug dealer.

There are no windows. No sharp edges anywhere. The bed is ordinary but for the locking clamps that hold my hands and feet in place. There is a toilet in the corner. A camera is mounted above me, the lens glowing orange. I can feel the caress of foreign eyes on my flesh, like the tickle of imagined insects.

The silly thing is that I'm supposed to be an incompetent drug dealer. Someone who is dumb enough to sell to cops. I have dyed my hair black, to make me look even more pale and sick. But the dye is cheap and my hair just looks green in the light. I have been drinking too much beer and I have a new belly that peeks out from the waistband of my pants. I watch cartoons all day and wait for my telephone to ring. I am a lot like my recently dead friend Pooh.

Two men come to my room; they wear white, silent shoes. Their faces are hidden behind surgical masks, as if I am a carrier, a plague victim. I beg them to show me their faces, to speak. They give me a shot and a handful of pills to swallow. I stare at the thin red wall of my inner eyelid and listen to my skin and I can't be sure how the medication is affecting me. I can't remember how I'm supposed to feel. I can't remember my name. I have never seen my face.

Lucy lives upstairs. Her clothes are torn and don't really fit her but she's strangely beautiful. She doesn't teach ninth-grade math yet. She isn't dying yet. Her blue jeans are splattered with paint all the time and her hair is shaved to stubble. I think she wants to be an artist. I see her outside sometimes, talking to the squirrels and feeding them brightly colored cereal from her pale, stained hand. On a chilly morning I ask her what the hell she is feeding them and she doesn't flinch. Her voice is lovely, a whisper that reminds me of blown glass. I notice her ears then, sharp and pointed. She smiles quickly and says it's Cap'n Crunch. The animals love it.

I am a white male with one identifying mark, a bullet hole scar on my left leg. I stare at the cracked blue ceiling with such intensity that it drips and ripples like a ruined map of the universe. I have no shoes and my feet are pale and shrunken. I am disappearing. They feed me only liquids, and I'm rapidly losing weight. I must have done something terrible but I can remember only these blue walls. There is nothing else and my head is as empty and silent as a church.

Lucy tries to avoid me. I am a rather dirty and pathetic drug seller, after all. There is a narrow black path to my door, trodden by agitated speed freaks and slouching homeless guys and nimble hippie kids and poorly disguised cops. I watch her come and go, and I try to think of reasons I might knock on her door. I need a cup of sugar, an egg. I doubt she even has sugar. I can hear her moving above me when I mute my droning television. Her feet are small and she scurries around like a mouse.

The two men come back with a wheelchair. I am confident that I can walk but they are robotic and unsmiling. They don't seem to breathe. They lift me from the bed like I'm made of sticks, and I let them strap me into the chair. I'm a child, a ragged doll. They wheel me down a long white hall that glistens so brightly the floor and ceiling melt into one. The hall grows narrow in the distance and I try to become smaller, to pull my head into my body. I close my eyes and wait. I listen but the wheelchair makes no sound.

Lucy stops at my door one morning. She asks if I have any milk. I'm surprised and I mutter something incoherent. The truth is I do have milk. But for some reason I don't want to admit it. I stare at the floor, at Lucy's feet. She isn't wearing shoes and I briefly fall in love with her. But her legs are odd, malformed somehow, and I realize that one of them is writhing like a spider's egg sac before it bursts and I wonder if I'm taking too many of my own drugs.

Everything is oiled and waxed and padded and there is only silence.

Lucy's pants are not full of spiders. She has a kitten hiding in there. I tell her there are no cats allowed in the building and we both laugh. I'm a known drug dealer, but there are no cats allowed. She tells me she found the little guy in a cardboard box with his three dead brothers. Someone didn't want kittens and didn't have the energy to kill them. Again she asks if I have milk and stupidly I try to touch her face, to brush away an eyelash. She ducks away like my own shadow and I apologize.

The faint swish of an electronic door: brief and lovely, like the breath of a sparrow. I open my eyes and find myself sealed in a glass box; there's a row of holes in the glass and I can feel cool air against my face. Behind the glass are pale green walls, the color of leaves with the sun shining through them.

Two cops show up at my door and I can tell they aren't interested in buying drugs. They close the door behind them and I feel a sudden fever. On my loud, rented television Andy Griffith is telling Opie that it's really not okay to judge people by the color of their skin. The two cops tell me they know I'm working for Internal Affairs and they want to talk. I'm lucky and they merely beat the shit out of me. They don't kill me. Four hours later Lucy finds me in the stairwell. Apparently I went to get my mail and I was so tired that I sat down and fell asleep. She's horrified by my face. It's okay, I say. I can still walk. She takes me back to my apartment and cleans me up. She disconnects the telephone and tells me I'm out of business for a while. It's painful to laugh. Lucy turns off the television and tells me a story about a little boy named Edward who choked on a peach. The kitten chases himself in endless circles on my filthy carpet and I smile, watching him.

I become aware of a voice, androgynous and without emotion. The voice is like silk and shadow and I might have heard the voice for hours without realizing it. The voice has the texture of unconscious thought and I wonder if I'm dreaming, if the voice is my own. But my own thoughts, faint and muffled as a heartbeat, are distinct from the voice. I am aware of my body; it is separate from me, dead and useless.

Lucy tells me that my hair looks terrible. I don't want to dye it blond again; it would only look worse. I allow her to shave my head and now we could be brother and sister. She kisses me when I'm distracted and uneasy. I'm washing dishes and worrying about the fucking mess I've made of my job when I feel her lips on my cheek. I am easily consumed by her.

The voice tells me that my name is Phineas Poe. I am a policeman living in Denver. I recently suffered a nervous breakdown. I had been in Internal Affairs for six years. My wife is dead, apparently by suicide. Her name was Lucy and we had no children.

The kitten slips out of Lucy's window one morning and gets himself stuck in the rain gutter. I can hear him yowling up there but I ignore it. I assume he's hungry and Lucy isn't fast enough with his food. I'm trying to write out a report. My assignment is over, a failure. I haven't told Lucy that I'm a cop and I'm not sure what she will say. Then I hear a noise like someone has thrown a suitcase off the roof and Lucy never screams at all. She sits in the grass and tries not to look at her broken leg. The kitten is walking around and around her as if he can reverse time. I take Lucy to the hospital and part of me is glad her leg is broken. She won't be able to run away from me. In the waiting area I kiss her and tell her I'm a cop. Lucy is relieved. Because you really weren't a very good drug dealer, she says. The doctor soon puts her back together again and calmly says he wants to talk to her alone. It's about her blood, he says. There's something wrong with her blood.

I open my eyes and I am in the blue room again. I study my new identity, wondering if the voice was telling the truth. My name is Phineas Poe. It might as well be.

I am shaking to pieces. But I'm only sleeping and Jude is trying to wake me. It's black outside the bubble of the cockpit and when I open my eyes, the night sky rushes at me and I'm sure that we are crashing.

Are we crashing? I say.

Jude slaps me. Wake up, please.

I'm awake. Are we crashing?

No, she says. We're somewhere over Texas.

In the glow of the controls her face is blue and stretched as a skull.

Then why did you wake me?

Because you talk in your sleep. I couldn't listen to another word.

I touch my cheek to the window. I try to remember what I was dreaming of but there's only black sky and cold skin. What did I say?

Nothing that made any sense. But it made me very uncomfortable.

I grope for the chain of thoughts that would bring the dream back to me but I can summon only the color blue. I feel a surge of nausea and I slap at the belt buckle. Jude leans over and releases me. I stagger to the back of the plane and vomit into a storage bin. My stomach holds nothing solid and what comes up is like oily water that smells of blood.

Jude calls out to me. When did you last eat anything?

I don't know.

You need to eat, okay. You look like a corpse. If you get a little protein into your system, you might stop hallucinating all the time.

I can barely stand up and I know she's right. But starvation isn't my only problem.

What's in those shots you keep giving me?

I told you, it's pharmaceutical Valium. The kind the dentist uses. It's for the pain.

Then why do I feel like a fucking junkie. I suddenly can't stop shaking and all I can think about is getting another shot. Jude gets out of her seat and comes toward me.

Are you insane? I say. We're going to crash.

Relax, she says. It's on autopilot.

She puts her arms around me and hugs me. I feel like I might break.

I never had Valium like that, I say. Never.

Do you want another shot? she says.

Fuck you. Fuck you.

Listen. You have to trust me, okay. I want to take care of you.

You should have cut out my heart.

If you don't want another shot, I won't make you. But if you don't eat, you will die.

What have you done to me? I say. What have you done?

I removed your kidney, she says. It's a simple procedure.

No, I say. You altered me somehow. You stapled my stomach into a fucking knot. And you left something inside, didn't you? Something to remember you by.

Do you hear yourself?

I'm dying, Jude.

What? she says. I can't hear you.

Never mind.

You're still alive, she says. You have one good kidney.

And if the kidney in the icebox is no good?

Then the buyer is fucked.

No. You could still offer my remaining kidney to Gore.

She doesn't smile. I never thought of that. But yes.

I hear Lucy laughing and crying in the dark and I wonder why it's so easy to pretend that my kidney is in the icebox, that I still believe.

Oh, you never thought of it.

Are you stupid? she says. If I wanted to kill you, I would have.

I'm sorry.

It's okay, she says. I saw a picnic basket in the back. I'm sure that little old lady packed a nice, wholesome dinner. I want you to sit down while I take a look. Okay?

I return to my seat, vaguely uneasy that the pilot's chair is empty. Jude comes out of the dark with turkey sandwiches, two bananas and a chocolate chip brownie. There's even a Thermos of sweet coffee. Jude sits down at the controls and examines the instruments. I take small, cautious bites of turkey. I don't feel immediately better but I don't throw up either.

We will be there soon, says Jude.

twenty-six.

JUDE SETS THE PLANE DOWN in a dead wheat field as gently as she might kiss a baby. A mile away, lights crawl along a two-lane road.

How far to El Paso? I say.

Ten miles, twenty. It doesn't matter.

I look around in the dark. The country is flat as my hand and the city lights are a tiny glow over the horizon. I have had the dry heaves for a half hour now; the turkey sandwich did not sit well and my mouth is full of acid and blood and I am inclined to think it does matter. But Jude is cool and unconcerned. I despise myself but I would love to push up my sleeve and offer her my naked arm. To close my eyes and wait for the needle. But I don't want her to know how badly I want it, and I shrug when she asks how I feel.

I watch as she unloads the gear and I realize there's more than we can carry. Jude opens her massive garment bag and produces a sleek little backpack, purple and gold with an internal frame. She transfers her purse, a few pieces of clothing and toiletries, tools and a number of small, compact items that I can't identify. She knows what she's doing, certainly. One thing catches my eye: a fat file folder with leather straps.

Jude turns to me. What can you unload? It's hot where we're going and we may do some walking.

I shake my head, hefting my duffel bag.

Give it to me, she says.

She unzips it and pokes around.

There's really nothing in there, I say. A change of clothes. Some disposable razors and a toothbrush.

She holds up a pale blond wig and I nearly swallow my tongue.

That sneaky bitch, I say.

You should be more careful, she says.

Jude.

Well, she says. This is a lot of wasted space.

Before I can say anything she transfers my meager possessions to her
backpack, then tosses my empty bag onto the pile. She stands up and looks
around. I pick up the green icebox and she grins at me. I'm a fool, I know.
But she has a good smile.

Jude moves the discarded things several yards from the plane and makes a
neat pile. She holds up Isabel's wig like a stolen scalp, then takes a book of
matches from her pocket. She strikes one and there's a teardrop of blue and
red at her fingertips. I blink and the hair catches fire, the flames coiling
greedily around her arm. Jude drops it and patiently blows on the little fire,
as if she's camping.

Let's go, she says.

I bend to touch the ground and the earth is damp. Not damp enough,
perhaps.

The plane may go up, I say. The whole fucking field.

I don't care. No one is connecting that plane to me.

She wears the bulging pack and I carry the icebox in one hand, her
medical bag in the other. I feel a bit like a bellboy, my arms loose in their
sockets. There is no sound but the crunch of sand, the faraway cry of geese
overhead. I am a few steps behind Jude, and every few minutes I turn to
look back. The small fire still burns, but it appears to be contained.

What now? The road stretches black in either direction.

Nothing, she says. She begins to walk along the shoulder.

The sweep of headlights from the north and Jude tells me to get out of sight. There are no trees and little brush. A single rock the size of my head. I drop my bag and the icebox and lie facedown in the dirt. I can hear Jude cracking her knuckles, one by one. The car slows and an electric window glides down. Jude leans in to ask the driver for a ride. He says he will be happy to help and there is a sudden, fleshy noise. Then silence.

Are you coming? says Jude.

I stand up and see a long black car, the right turn signal still blinking. Jude sits on the driver's side. The car has a slick leather interior and smells new. I look over my shoulder and there is a long-legged man with no hair sleeping soundly in the backseat.

Very nice, I say. Did you give him a Vulcan nerve pinch?

Something like that, says Jude. He will wake up in El Paso, his car undamaged and his wallet intact. He will even feel refreshed, and he will have a fantastic story to tell his friends.

God as my witness but I was abducted by a hot little number, boys. She did experiments on me and tossed me back like a bad fish.

Jude doesn't laugh. Her face is blank. I think she is too tired.

She drives with one hand on the wheel. She asks me to find a radio station and I spin the dial. I find a jazz station and she says for me to leave it there. A green sign looms in the dark: EL PASO 19 MILES.

What's going to happen in El Paso? I say.

We are going to a motel called the Seventh Son, she says. Then we wait.

For what?

The explosion is like a thousand pounds of air sucked into a soda bottle, the bottle bursts and the air expands to its normal dimensions with shocking force. I look over my shoulder and see the ball of fire that was the plane. It seems to hover, as if it wants to rise and return to the clouds. Minutes later, emergency vehicles rush past. One laughable fire truck and two cop cars, their sirens screaming through us.

Jude maintains her speed at exactly the limit.

She never tells me who or what we will be waiting for.

The Seventh Son has beds that vibrate. Jude laughs and digs in her pockets for change. She feeds two quarters into the slot and the bed comes to life. She lies down with her eyes closed, her body humming.

Come on, Phineas. It feels so nice.

I drop my bag on the floor and shake my head.

If I go near that thing I will fall to pieces.

Oh, she says. I won't let it hurt you.

But I'm not in the mood. I go into the bathroom, looking for a place to hide the icebox. I shove it in a small closet and cover it with a bath towel. I pull off my clothes and stand before the mirror. Every bone in my body pushes at the surface of my white skin. I can see veins and tendons and unprotected muscle. My face is a grinning mask. I turn to examine my wound. I remove the dressing and see that the flesh is a little red, possibly infected. But the skin does seem to have closed, rejoined itself where Jude made her cut. I shudder to think of letting her open me up again, even to replace my lost kidney. I sit down on the toilet and remind myself that the precious green icebox is now stuffed with the Blister's dirty clothes. I empty my bladder like an old man, too feeble to stand.

The bed has stopped vibrating. Jude gives me another sponge bath and smears antibiotic cream over the infected skin. She leaves the wound exposed and says it needs air. She kisses me, softly at first. I am slow to respond. I put my hands on her hips, her muscular waist. She tells me to undress her. My teeth feel like they are falling out and finally I can't stand it anymore. I want to feel reborn, even if it's artificial and temporary. I want to make love to her and I need the drugs to give me strength.

I want another shot, Jude.

Are you sure? she says.

She sits cross-legged at the end of the bed while I lay collapsed on the pillows. She appears to be at least a hundred feet away. I can't move to touch her. If I could, I would kiss her bare feet and bite her toes. I would stroke her thighs through blue jeans faded white. I would lick the exposed tummy, the long muscles in her arms, I would close my eyes and touch the dark and gold hair that falls and falls. She chews a thumbnail briefly, her eyes on me.

Haven't I warned you about getting sappy on me? she says.
     The shot, I say. Then talk and sex, okay.

Jude prepares the hypo in the bathroom. I don't want to watch, anymore. I don't need to. The thought of a needle once made me ill, now my skin tingles. I lie naked on the bed, my arms outstretched as if I am nailed there. I close my eyes and wait. Jude ties back my arm, stopping the blood. She finds the vein; I breathe through my teeth and try to think of the needle as a lover's bite.

The body is composed of water and little else. I can feel the waves inside me.

I open my eyes. I want to ask Jude the color of electricity. She is naked, crouched over me and glowing with sweat and fever. She isn't listening. Her hair is everywhere and I can't see her face. She rises and falls, impaling herself on my surprisingly erect penis. I can't feel it at all. My body, it seems, is too enamored of the drug to be bothered by ordinary sex. Jude doesn't seem to mind, she rides me like she would her own hand, and I watch her, removed and soon dreaming.

The dark swallows me. There is rough carpet beneath my naked shoulders and I'm crushed, folded into an impossible position. My knees are pain-lessly tucked beneath my chin. The road hums beneath me. I'm in a car, the trunk of a car. My face hurts like a raw, open wound and I snake one hand free to touch it, to feel the mass of chewed flesh and shattered bone. My face is gone and I seem to be bald as a stone. I touch my throat and I have no pulse. I hug myself and my fingers find my belly, my breasts. I'm a dead woman and I have no hair.

twenty-seven.

Sorrow is like the ocean and sometimes I wish my heart would stop.

Jude is gone. I am staring at nothing, at an unremarkable white wall. I dimly remember her whispering to me that she was going, that I wasn't to worry. I have no idea how long ago that was.

I swing my legs over the edge of the bed and my feet find the floor. I stand up and I feel fine. In a far corner of my mind, I am aware that my physical condition is misleading. I am weak from the surgery, from hunger. But when I'm drugged, I feel like a king and I can't be killed. Jude is drugging me for the pain but the true pain arrives when I am not drugged. Two minus two equals two and there is a shrinking window between the fading of the drug and the arrival of pain, when I can see and think clearly. But I will take this up with Jude later. I'm thirsty and I want a cigarette. I'm naked and shivering and I can't find my pants.

I dig through Jude's heavy backpack and vaguely remember the bound file folder. It would be worth a few minutes of my time, I think. But it isn't there, she has taken it with her. I stand half naked in the corner of the room, Jude's hairbrush in one hand and a crushed pack of cigarettes in the other.

The hairs in her brush appear dry and brittle, stripped of color like a winter sky.

I look down at the strewn contents of Jude's pack and realize that I will never put everything back so neatly, so efficiently. She will know I searched her pack, that I was looking for the folder. I tear the cellophane from the cigarettes and try to imagine the contents of the folder. There could be an extensive file on Gore, on Isabel. There could be any number of files and reports on me, the police are relentless chroniclers of their own misfortunes. And the doctors at Fort Logan must have written a telephone book on my delusions and theories, my borderline fantasies.

I remember the green room, the voice. I see two possible realities. I was a nameless mental patient, drooling and eating my fingers and killing time on the ward. I was chosen for physical reasons, nothing more. They took great pains to implant a new identity for some dark purpose.

Or I was truly Phineas Poe, fractured and suicidal ex-cop. They were merely reconstructing my identity.

I couldn't have killed Lucy. I might have thought about it, dreamed of recreating myself in the wake of her death. But then I would find myself staring at her as she watered the plants or read a magazine, and I would tell myself she was a piece of me. I could as easily cut off a hand or foot. She would feel my eyes, then. And without looking up, she would ask me if something was the matter.

She was precious, a rare bird. Even when I was coming undone. Even when I regained consciousness on a street corner, unsure of the time or day. Unsure of where I had been. I could see myself in unrelated flashes of memory, in poor camera angles. I could see only my feet, the back of my head. I saw obscene close-ups of my face, a gray fleshy landscape with massive pink lips and scar tissue, small black hairs protruding from dead skin. I saw myself through glass, through a sheet of cracked enamel. I saw unnatural detail. I saw body parts that couldn't be mine. I heard my own voice from within, from underwater. Distorted, crashing against bone fragments.

And whenever I returned to her, I saw myself through her eyes and I was barely human. I was never the husband she remembered.

I remember waking up to find I was a dead woman with no hair. I could scream and scream until my voice is gone and I will never get that out of my head.

I find my pants in the bathroom, they are so dirty they seem to shine. I put them on anyway and sit down to drink a glass of tap water. The water is warm and slightly brown with rust. It smells of chemical treatment and it would taste much better with ice. I am wondering if it would be worth the effort to leave the room and look for an ice machine, and I find myself staring at the small closet where the green icebox was hidden. Jude took it with her and I remind myself that it's worthless now. It's worthless. And I guess she doesn't really trust me.

Jude feeds me one lie after another and I gobble them up like a baby eating mush. I suppose I know it to be mush, but I want to like it. I want her to hurt me, to betray me. And as long as I pretend to believe her, I can make excuses for not killing her. But I have no excuses now. I have nothing but a sad little drug habit and the twisting notion that I might love her.

There's a telephone beside the bed, and I'm tempted to call Moon and tell him where I am. I'm in Texas on a vibrating bed. My new girlfriend is a secret agent and she traded my kidney for a box of smack. She loves me. She loves me not and I want you to come down here with a big fucking net and take me back to Fort Logan. I need forty-eight hours of observation. I pick up the phone and dial Eve's number.

What are you doing? I say.

Phineas, she says. Her voice is fragile, terrible.

Are you alone?

Why?

I just want to talk. I want to know if anyone's listening.

No one is here, she says. I'm lying on the couch under about ten blankets. I'm watching the news and I'm waiting for them to flash your face on the screen: have you seen this man?

I'm invisible, I say. I'm safe.

Are you? That cop was here yesterday, Detective Moon. He seems to be worried about you.

Oh, yeah. He wants to arrest me.

No, she says. I don't think so.

What did he say?

He said there's a lot of evidence against you. But he said it was too easy, too perfect. He doesn't think you did anything.

And what do you think?

Silence.

I was raped, Phineas. I was raped.

Eve, I say. You don't have to talk about it.

I'm okay, she says. I'm really okay. I have a gun under the blankets. Two days ago I was like a puppy that someone had tortured. I screamed when I heard a car door slam. And now I want to kill someone and it makes me feel good. It feels really good.

I know the feeling. It comes and goes.

Where are you? she says.

What kind of gun do you have under those blankets?

I don't know, she says. A little bitty gun, like a toy. But it's loaded.

That's fine. Is this gun an automatic?

No, she says. The chambers spin around in case you want to play Russian roulette.

Okay, Eve. It's okay.

A six-shooter, she says. In another lifetime I was Calamity Jane.

She laughs and her voice is like thin ice.

Eve, please. No one else is going to hurt you, I say. The cops are watching your apartment and the man who did this is dead.

It wasn't a man, she says. I told you it was a woman.

Eve, I say. Forgive me. But when did you last have sex with a man?

I was sixteen, she says. Three years ago. I did it with a boy who stuttered. It lasted two minutes, maybe. What are you trying to say? That I wouldn't recognize a penis?

I'm not saying anything. Tell me what happened.

Eve takes a long painful breath.

It was dark in my room, she says. I have these heavy velvet curtains that block out the sun and I was trying to sleep. Georgia was home but she couldn't talk. She was hiding in the closet and whenever I tried to touch her she growled at me, so I left her alone. I wanted to sleep. I never heard a noise, not a whisper. I always sleep on my stomach. Ever since I was a kid. And when I felt a hand on my neck I thought it might be Georgia but the hand was so strong. I tried to roll over and I saw a shadow leaning over me, slender like a woman and a black ski mask over her face. I think I still believed it was Georgia and this was one of her sex games. She liked to dress up in different clothes and pretend we were strangers. But then she started wrapping the tape around my face and I was a little scared. And the fear was exciting at first. She tied my hands and feet and cut off my T-shirt and underpants and I felt the knife against my skin. Then she started beating me and she pushed my legs apart and she shoved things inside me.

What things, I say.

Eve is crying now and I start to babble that I'm sorry, that I don't want to know.

I think there was a wooden spoon, she says. A shampoo bottle and a portable phone. And something very cold, like a gun. But maybe that was only my imagination.

My fucking god.

Now, she says. Do you think it was Georgia?

I may never know and I can't say I'm sorry anymore. I don't think I can stand the sound of my voice. I listen as she walks down the hall with the portable phone, her footsteps soft and faraway. She goes into the bathroom and I hear her pull back the shower curtain. She locks the door and I listen as she puts her finger down her throat and throws up. She does this twice, her throat racked and hoarse. She sits on the toilet and I listen to her pee. She brings the phone to her mouth and I listen to her breathe.

I'm going to go to sleep now, she says. Will you stay on the phone awhile?

twenty-eight.

EVE IS ASLEEP A THOUSAND MILES AWAY and I lie on a rented bed, the telephone heavy on my chest.

There's a knock at the door and I tell myself it's Jude, she's forgotten her key. But she is too careful for that and I check the peephole. Distorted and grotesque through the fisheye is Isabel, and she's alone. She is smiling and confident. She wears her own hair, short and dark. She wears a new dress, silver with a metallic texture. Lucy would have looked fabulous in it. She might have a gun behind her back but I really don't care. I want to smash something. I open the door and there's nothing there. I'm only hallucinating again.

Now I wonder where Jude has gone. She does covet the air of mystery, and perhaps she has only disappeared to make me nervous. Maybe she's gone to sell the heroin and won't she be surprised when she finds the Blister's soiled clothes? Maybe she is meeting one of Gore's wraithlike henchmen, negotiating the final terms of the exchange for my remaining organ, for me. And so she had to leave me behind. I would only be cumbersome and dull. I might ask silly questions. Or else she is chatting on a cell phone with another agent back at headquarters. But she may well be down the street at the bar of a much nicer hotel, killing time and nursing a drink. Lazily eyeing a fat, torpid lawyer. He is drinking bourbon on the rocks as if tomorrow will never come and she decides his kidney may be worthless, but perhaps she could move his corneas.

I want to tell her I don't care anymore, that I can forgive her. I only want to kiss her sweet lips and go to sleep. And I'm such a liar. In two days or a week, I would wake beside her sore and stinking of sex and my mouth dry as dust. I would look for flaws in her face and body, imperfections that would prove her heart was never pure. I would not love her. I would not.

I try to remember the way I felt when I first felt her eyes on me. I felt cold, as if I had touched a piece of metal or just walked into a dark movie theater.

I feel extraordinarily calm. It's time for me to run. And it's possible that Jude wants me to run. She wants me to save myself, to disappear. Perhaps she merely wants to hunt me. I roll off the bed and reach for my shoes. I fumble with the laces like a toddler and I try not to worry about the unraveling that will take place inside me when my body begins to crave the phantom drug and I find myself weeping for Jude to save me. I need to get out of here before I change my mind. Before Jude appears, warm and bending to kill me. I take almost nothing with me: knife and gun and a box of .38 ammunition. The torn and filthy clothes I am wearing and a fat wad of cash. I hesitate, then leave half of my money for Jude. I resolve to buy myself some new clothes and a hot meal.

Crushing white sunlight and I feel numb, shocked. I was so sure that it was night. I slouch away from the motel, feeling strangely naked without the icebox and I'm sure that everyone on the street is turning to look at me. Every passing car fills me with dread. I cross the street and hurry into an alley. The smell of rotting food drifts from the back of a restaurant and I doubt if I will be able to eat. I need to sit down, to rest. There is a discarded mattress tucked behind a garbage pail and I'm tempted to flop down on it but I'm afraid I would fall asleep and wake up in jail. But my knees are numb and soon I am sitting on a cinder block in the inelegant, squatting position of a man on a child's toilet.

My body is so cold. The sun comes and goes and the light that lingers is lifeless. Nothing has a shadow. I lift my hand to my face and there is no definition. The skin is smooth, transparent. As if I'm wearing latex gloves and the real skin glows through them.

I'm a scarecrow gloomily watching over a cornfield in winter. The goose bumps along my arm are painful to the touch. There are insects beneath my scalp, in my veins and teeth. I think I'm going to faint. I sit on the cinder block, muttering. I twist sideways and wrench the fragile, newly healed skin of my wound. The pain is an electric shock, and soon the insects subside.

Laughter. And a pack of kids swerves down the alley, their movements spidery and sudden and I think they are looking to torment the cripple. Bludgeon the drunk, the homeless man. One of them picks up my fallen baseball cap and hands it to me. I grunt and smile. They spew something in Spanish and float away.

Hundreds of eyes and the chirp and giggle of voices, the drone of engines. The urge to flee is a high-pitched whistle and I stare into a black cavity of space that stinks of urine and dead flowers. Of rotting oranges and leather and spray paint. I crawl into the space and find a corner. I stare into the shadows and I see several corpselike figures, coiled in burlap sacks around me. Sleeping drunks with the faces of dogs, of horses. I blink and they're not there.

I sit very still, until I am sure I won't vomit. Then I walk slowly around the building, to the front of the restaurant. There is a faded mural sprawled across the wall near the entrance, depicting a surreal bullfight. A cartoon-like bull paws at the earth, fire spewing from his massive nostrils. The body of a dead boy lies before him. A police car with a flat tire circles the scene, a rodeo clown at the wheel. In the foreground is a matador bearing a guitar. The audience is made up of young girls, howling and tearing at

their clothes. I peer through the windows of the café, shameful as a beggar.
A busboy with bright red acne scars wearily mops the floor. I'm reluctant
to go inside. I've been in the shadows too long, speaking to no one. I'm
afraid of the faces.

I take a seat at a booth in the corner. I'm glad to see the cushions are plush
red vinyl, in case I feel faint. Through a mirrored window I can see the Seventh Son. A young man comes to take my order. He is very young, perhaps
sixteen. He has the beginnings of a mustache, soft as a baby dog's fur. He
looks at me nervously.

What's the matter? I croak.

I'm sorry, sir. The owner says you should go.

Why?

He turns to look at a fat man with a belly like wet cement, leaning on
the bar. The owner, presumably. He could break me in two with his little
finger.

You don't look so good, the boy says.

I have money, I say. I want a steak and a bottle of wine.

The owner wants you to leave. Please, sir.

I throw some money on the table and stand up. The fat man comes
around the bar, his movements surprisingly fluid. His eyes are impassive as
pools of ink.

I'm sure you don't pay this boy enough, I say.

Get the fuck out of here, he says. You piece of trash.

On the street again, staring at my reflection in a shop window. I need new
clothes, clearly. I need something. When I was with Jude, I might have
passed for an eccentric junkie. A suicidal cancer patient with a beautiful
wife. An extraterrestrial with a credit card. Without her I'm a leper.

I walk into a men's clothing store and drop five thousand dollars on the
counter. The nearest salesperson is a thin man with wispy blond hair and
bright pink skin. I'm sure he's an albino and I just can't deal with it right
now. It's hard enough to try on pants under normal conditions. But in my

state of mind, under the silky cold gaze of rat pink eyes, I think I might come to pieces. I might tell him about the inevitable death of the sun and how those of us that are used to living in shadows will be the new gods. But I look closely at his eyes and they are an ordinary brown. I realize he only has a sunburn.

His lip curls slightly but he shrugs when he sees the money.

I need some new clothes, I say.

The salesman hesitates, then smiles. I should say so, he says.

He isn't a bad guy, the sunburned salesman. His name is Alexander. He's reluctant at first, but he agrees to hold on to my money. There's no one else in the store, thank god. I can't stand the artificial silence and shared humiliation that seep from the mirrors in a room full of expensive, empty clothing. Alexander takes me gently by the elbow, as if I am his blind girlfriend, his arthritic mother. He helps me pick out some gray wool pants; they are cut like military pants, with multiple pockets and fat belt loops and those small, riveted holes in the crotch that will prevent them from filling with water if I have to slog through a river. I come out of the dressing room and stand before him.

These are some nice pants, I say.

They are fantastic, he says. He turns his head sideways.

I glance at the price tag, I could get six pairs of pants at the army surplus store for that kind of cash. I sigh and realize I don't care. Money has been irrelevant to me, lately. Alexander crouches before me to tug at the hem of my pants. I wait for him to notice the gun at my ankle, and I can't decide if I will shrug and smile or kick him in the mouth like a dog. He doesn't notice it.

I need some new T-shirts, I say.

Alexander raises his left eyebrow, but says nothing. He shows me where the T-shirts are. They seem to be plain cotton T-shirts. But they are apparently designed by a French clothing guru and woven of silver thread. They cost a hundred dollars each. I choose two of them, one black and one green. Alexander coaxes me into taking a white dress shirt as well, in case I need to wear a tie. I laugh weakly at that, and he laughs with me.

What else. Does it get cold here?

At night it gets quite chilly, he says.

A jacket then. And shoes, I think.

Alexander smiles. He disappears for a moment and returns with a long, sleek jacket of heavy brown calfskin. I slip it on and the weight of it feels good. It feels like armor. I realize that my old jacket has been clinging to me like the skin of a dead rat. This jacket will give me the heart of a lion, the penis of a horse. It will cost me the price of a small Japanese car.

Alexander reaches to adjust my lapel, then trails his fingers softly, slowly down my arms.

I'll take it.

Excellent, he says.

I try on several pairs of boots, and finally settle for the simple black ones that zip up the side. I'm glad I won't need to bother with laces for a while.

Alexander looks at me awkwardly. Don't be offended, he says. But you smell like death. I really think you should have a shower before you wear these new things.

I shake my head. Nothing offends me. But I'm a little bit homeless at the moment.

There's a shower in the employee bathroom, he says. I insist.

It can't hurt, I say.

He shows me to the little bathroom and I feel like a holiday house-guest. It feels good to trust someone, if only for a few minutes. The shower is a small box with a sliding glass door. I stand under hot, pounding water and stare down at the stitches in my skin. They coil around me like the rotting skin of a snake, and I wonder if they will dissolve before my eyes. The door to the bathroom opens and I can see Alexander through the steamed glass. He has come to shoot me. Or else he wants to get in the shower with me. I don't really like either idea.

I brought you a towel, he says.

There is another customer in the shop when I come out of the bathroom. A woman, her back turned to me. She has gray hairs and a thick web of blue veins on the backs of her legs. She's no one, a stranger and still I flinch. Alexander cocks his head and puckers his mouth as if to whistle when he sees me. It's foolish, but the new clothes have changed the way I walk. They have given me a temporary sheen of confidence that will be rubbed away in a few hours. Alexander hands me a stack of bills and a leather shoulder bag. The extra shirts are inside, he says. And the money is what's left of my wad. It feels too thick and I thumb through it. A little more than three thousand in matted hundreds and twenties.

I gave you a discount, says Alexander. And I threw in a pair of silk boxers.

Thanks.

A smile creeps across my face and I reach to touch his hand. Kindness from strangers is rare and strange, it makes me weak. I want to tell him that I don't wear boxers, that I don't wear any underwear at all.

twenty-nine.

I NEARLY ASK ALEXANDER TO HAVE A DRINK WITH ME. My tastes don't really run to thin, fair-haired men. It would just be nice to drink with someone who is normal, who isn't lying to me with every breath. I have had the odd moments, though. Some men are disturbingly pretty. The dark, heavy lips and knifelike bones and the feline muscles in their shoulders. Lucy used to drag me to one particularly damp museum in Denver. She loved a lot of postmodern shit, and I would follow her around, generally stoned and indifferent. After an hour or two I would drift away from her until I found the torso. It was a headless fragment, the broken remains of an early Roman statue. The chest and belly of a dying man, dying or twisting in pain. It was carved in marble so smooth it looked wet, and I always wanted to touch it.

I'm coming to pieces and I want to go home.

I wonder if I can pull myself together and hitchhike back to Denver. Then I can get myself a nice job at a gas station, maybe a video store. I can change my name to Freddie and I can mutter to myself and chew on my hair and tell outrageous stories to anyone who will listen. I can meet Eve for coffee and maybe a movie. I can write bad poems for her. I know she has a girlfriend but there's always hope, there's always boredom and the goofy bliss of unrequited love. But I'm far too weak. I'm feeling the first tug of chemical loss in my belly, in the palms of my hands. A stomach full of bland, heavy food will dull the need. I drag myself back to the café that banished me before, hoping the new clothes will do their thing.

The fat man still leans against the bar. His eyebrows twitch when he sees me, but that's all. I sit in the same booth, and this time a girl appears. I tell her to bring me a plate of beans and rice, a shot of tequila and a pot of coffee. The girl is perhaps fourteen and she seems to walk on her toes. She brings me a glass of fresh orange juice, on the house. She says I look very pale. Her only words to me. I drink the juice, and it sloshes around with the coffee and tequila. The beans and rice sit before me, untouched. They are barely warm when I begin to eat. I chew each bite monotonously, tirelessly. And the food stays down.

I am drinking my fourth shot of tequila, feeling slightly damp and bloated and staring out the big glass window as if it's a television and I can't be bothered to change the channel. There is nothing to see. A thousand cars pass, blurry and colorless.

Jude appears from the west, the orange sun falling behind her like a ring of fire. Her face is a shadow. She is light on her feet, as if she couldn't be happier. She carries the icebox and a dozen roses, and a tickle of guilt rises in my throat. Jude disappears around the corner to our room and I hold my breath. I count to five and she comes out of the motel at a half run, her hands empty. She looks up and down the street, and for a moment she glares right at me. I'm sure she sees me. But I shrink back into my booth and she looks away. Finally she turns and returns to the room. I finish my drink and sit there, smoking.

Time shivers and Jude is on the street again. She has changed into fresh clothes: black jeans and a tight silver shirt that barely covers her stomach, a black trench coat that appears to be made of velvet. Heavy boots and a little black hat that clings to her head. Her backpack is slung over one shoulder. She stands on the street corner for a moment, her face gray as stone. She still holds the icebox. Either she is about to burst into tears, or she is patiently waiting for a bomb to go off. I can never be sure. A car whips past her, then a man on a motorcycle. In their wake, Jude holds out her closed fist for a heartbeat before the torn rose petals tumble away from her open hand. She walks down the street, away from me.

I drop some money on the table and walk out of the café into bruised light. Jude has vanished. I turn in widening circles. She was never there and I don't even feel myself collapse.

Lucy and I were married one year after she fell from the roof. I knew she had leukemia, that I was borrowing her. I should have taken her to France, to the moon. But we tried to shove our lives into a box. Lucy packed away her paints and brushes and let her hair grow. She became a teacher. She begged me for children. I went deeper and deeper with Internal Affairs, until I disappeared. I was underwater. I couldn't be trusted. Lucy was a meteor, burning up as she entered the atmosphere.

I spent nine weeks as a mole with Vice. I was posing as an involuntary transfer from Narcotics. I was posing as another fuck-up and it wasn't hard. My name was Stephen Crow. I had a green convertible and a little apartment two blocks from home and Lucy knew little about it. She called it my artificial life. She was teaching math to snotty kids with penetrating eyes and rapidly mutating bodies. The kids were itching to fuck each other, to kill each other. Lucy was trying to keep a straight face about death. I was supposed to get close to some rogue from Internal Affairs who was selling expensive protection to dirty cops in Vice. Of course, I never found him.

But I did get tangled up with a male prostitute. His name was T. and he had the soft, liquid brown eyes of a German shepherd. The kid was dangling on a hook between good cops and bad cops. Everybody was squeezing him and the pale brown shit was running out of his ass and mouth. The bad guys were feeding him bogus information and he was selling it to the good guys, and some of the good guys were getting killed. I casually decided to look into it, as if I were trying on a new hat. I had nothing to lose. My own assignment was dead, it was a stuffed animal. This prostitute could have been big for me. He could have been huge. I thought I could tie a string around his toe and follow him to a nest of filthy cops.

I got close to little T. without any trouble. I had some heroin I was willing to share, and all it would cost him was a little love. I shared a needle with him and we nodded for hours together in his shadowy room. He tried to feed me some of his bad information but I wasn't listening. I was staring at his long dark eyelashes, his perfect nose. He had the skin of a baby and I knew he would be dead soon. T. was arrogant and rude but not entirely stupid. He smelled the badge on me and still he gave me the most stunning blow job I ever had. He left me nearly in tears. T. sat back against the wall in a yellow splash of sunlight that fell over his bare futon and rolled a lumpy cigarette. He was pleased with himself. There was a gold fleck of tobacco on his lower lip.

He eyed my wedding ring and said, Does your wife know?

I stared at him without smiling. It was fascinating, really, that I could be so stupid, so careless. Stephen Crow was surely not married.

Does she know what? I said.

He grinned. That you like boys.

I drank flat beer from a green bottle and resisted the urge to pluck the tobacco from his lip, to twist the lip until it turned white between my fingers.

It isn't about that, I said. You could be a little girl or a dog.

T. blew smoke rings, his mouth dark and pouting.

It's about alien flesh and misplaced sympathy.

Why don't you speak English?

My wife is dying, I said. And she's so close to me that I can't touch her. I don't know you but I can see her in you. I see death in you and it's so much easier to give myself to you.

T. flicked his cigarette at a withered aloe plant.

It's a terrible feeling, I said.

But I'm not dying, he said.

I can see your dead body when I close my eyes, I said. And it makes you glow a little more brightly.

T. pulled a blue plaid shirt across his lap. I'm not dying, he said.

But you are, I said. You have fucking killed yourself. If I don't kill you, someone else will.

He threw my shoes at me and told me to get the fuck out. I marveled at how easily tenderness became cruelty and took the stairs two at a time, manic and cheerful. The kid was dead two days later. One of the good cops decided it was no fun being good all the time, and little T. was found in bed with both brown eyes gouged out and a bullet in the back of his head.

I went home to Lucy and made frantic love to her on the floor beside our bed. The sun fell in shreds. She wrapped her legs around me and told me outrageous stories about her students. Lucy told me how the kids looked at her, how she felt naked before them. She told me that she was never going to die. I couldn't tell her anything. I still had an apartment two streets away. I want to say: I saw you. Two weeks ago, when my name was Stephen Crow and I was barely awake, smoking a cigarette at my window. You walked right past me and I was a ghost behind glass. Your car must have died and you had to catch the bus. I stared at you so hard that I could see through your clothes. I could see the cancer in your blood and I was made of tin.

Lucy never asked if I had other lovers when I was undercover, when I was artificial. There's a bumpy road beneath me and I wake up choking. I blink my eyes and I'm in a fucking ambulance. I'm strapped down like a bug, my poor skull rattling. The funny thing is that no one is busy trying to save my life. I'm hooked up to no machinery. In fact, the paramedics are studiously ignoring me. The siren is off. I twist my neck around and peer at a female medic sitting in the jump seat, a clipboard in hand. She has dark skin and cropped black hair, a weirdly muscular face. She wears navy blue pants and a white shirt and polished black desert boots.

What happened? I say.

Her eyes fix on me, narrow and blue. You were asleep in the middle of the road.

I'm not dying.

She sighs. No.

Then remove these straps, please.

Relax, she says.

Take off the fucking straps and let me out.

Relax, she says. Those are for your safety.

Where are you taking me?

She squints at me. The hospital.

Oh, yeah. And who is paying for this?

The woman shrugs, then writes a few words on the clipboard. The rapid click of a mechanical pencil as she ejects a piece of broken lead. Her hand moves lazily. She could be deciding my future, or merely doodling. She could be sketching a three-dimensional box, as if she's on the phone with a dull salesman.

You are, she says. Or your next of kin.

At the hospital, I refuse to change into one of those foolish gowns. I don't want any sticky questions about weapons. I'm poked and prodded by one unsmiling male intern who assumes I came in to beg for painkillers. I have no insurance and I'm wasting his time. He asks about my scar and I tell him I recently had some work done on my bladder. He doesn't laugh. Alexander pushes through the powder blue curtain that hides one exam area from its neighbors. His cheeks are rosy as ever, his hair thin as silk. He smiles when he sees me. The intern wipes sweat from his upper lip and scowls at me. I'm not only a malnourished junkie found crumpled before oncoming traffic, but I must be queer as well. The horror. I'm tempted to roll off the table and cut his throat or at least force him to watch me give Alexander a long, sloppy kiss but really I'm too tired to do anything but flap my hand.

How is he? says Alexander.

He's dehydrated, says the intern. Among other things.

Alexander looks mildly disappointed. The intern shrugs and tells me to roll over.

Why?

I'm going to give you a shot.

No, thanks.

He stares at me, his eyes hooded. He looks like he hasn't slept in a while.

What's your name? he says.

I smile. I don't want a shot.

This is a nutritional supplement, he says.

You don't care if I take it or not, do you?

No, he says. I don't care.

Okay, then.

I slide my pants down and I'm sure my skinny ass is a sorry sight. The intern is rude and unsympathetic but he's good with a needle. I barely feel a thing. Then he tells me to relax, to wait. He disappears and I'm alone with Alexander, who sits on a stool, spinning around like a kid.

I found you, he says. I went out for coffee and I just happened to glance down the road. I saw a shadowy lump and I thought someone had run over a dog. But then I recognized your pants.

My ass is getting sore and I rub it briefly, staring at him.

I like these pants, I say.

Anyhow, he says. I checked your pulse and everything and called the ambulance.

Did you drag me out of the road?

No, he says. I didn't want to move you. In case you had a spinal injury.

I laugh at that and my mind drifts. Something else is wrong with me. The bag of smack that Jude supposedly planted in my guts, for instance.

Alexander smiles. I waved the traffic around you, like a cop. I always wanted to do that.

I hear Crumb's dry voice: *maybe there's a bomb inside you, a tumor.*

Or a litter of puppies, I say.

Excuse me? says Alexander.

Nothing.

The paramedics didn't want to take you at first, he says. They said you were drunk.

I was drunk. But that offends me.

Anyhow, I talked them into it. I told them I was a friend of yours.

A friend, I say. The word floats between us like a speck of dust.

I thought so, he says.

Silence.

Alexander plays with a discarded stethoscope. I close my eyes and listen to my gurgling belly. There's nothing in there. The intern pokes his head through the curtain.

You're finished, he says.

Alexander frowns. Are you sure?

There's nothing wrong with him.

I was wondering, I say. How much for a couple of X rays?

What? he says. You don't need X rays.

Humor me.

Well, he says. It depends on your deductible. And the radiologist's fee.

I don't have insurance. And radiologists are overpaid geeks.

He glares at me. Don't waste my time.

How much?

Two thousand dollars, maybe.

I whistle and sigh, then pull out my wallet and start counting.

This isn't a barbershop. You don't just get X rays because you feel like it.

Would you deny me medical treatment?

Alexander clears his throat. Why do you want X rays?

I lift my shirt to expose the scar. There's something inside me.

The intern laughs. Like what?

I whisper and twitch as if stricken by palsy. Rosemary's fucking baby. I don't know, okay. I don't know. That's why I want X rays.

Calm down, says Alexander.

Please, says the intern. Take your friend home and tuck him into bed.

He's not my friend, I say. He's just a salesman who was nice to me.

I see. Have you had episodes like this before?

Every day, I say.

The intern shakes his head. I will be happy to call for a psych exam.

I have a gun, I say. And I want those X rays.

This is sad, he says.

Oh, you motherfucker. I want to talk to someone else.

The intern backs away smiling and he calls for someone else. He calls security. Alexander has become green and I think he's sick to his stomach, as if he just realized he is terribly lost in the woods. I walk out with a fat rented cop who breathes through his mouth. He tells me he has sinus trouble and I want to tell him that he should keep his weaknesses private, that sometimes I'm guilty of the same random intimacy. I pay nine hundred dollars for the ambulance and the B12 shot. I call for a cab. Alexander and the cop with sinus trouble wait outside with me. Alexander scratches compulsively at his sunburn, the dead skin falling from his arm in gray flakes. I'm an asshole and I try to apologize. I nearly offer him money. He chews at the side of his mouth and doesn't look at me.

thirty.

THE CAB UNLOADS ME BEFORE THE SEVENTH SON and I slink across the parking lot to my room, to our room. I imagine the roses lie half crushed on the floor, on the bed. One of the maids will find them tomorrow. She will be a single mother, overweight and uneducated. She will hate to see such pretty things wasted. She will put the roses in water and watch them die and I laugh at myself. The roses were not real.

I push open the door to our room and Isabel turns to grin at me like a car, her mouth bright with feathers. She wears the red wig, the dead stolen hair of Rose White.

Are you lonely? she says.

Terribly.

She stands on one foot, her arms uncoiled at her sides. She is pale and fleshy.

I could strangle you with that hair.

Isabel laughs. Jude told me you were easily excited, she says.

She lazily adjusts the wig, her bare arms raised above her head. She tucks a stray red wisp behind her ears. She licks her lips and sits down on the bed. I might be a madman but I think she's wearing the same silver dress as before. Perhaps I'm dreaming again. I'm only looking through a peephole. I watch her cross her legs and I have to tell myself she's not Lucy. My mouth is hot.

It didn't take you long to find us, I say.

Jude is so predictable, she says. She's like a bird, returning to nest.

How did you get in?

The manager, she says. I told him I was your wife and I wanted to surprise you.

Oh, I love a surprise.

I sink into a chair, wishing I had a glass of gin to swirl casually in my
left hand.

Where is the dear girl? says Isabel.

She walks around the room, touching things. She reclines on the bed,
her legs slightly apart. She's wearing the white garter belt again and this
time it's cartoonish. I could bash her skull with a hammer and it would
only bounce off. She would give me a wacky smile as her rubber skull
popped back into place.

Jude isn't coming back, I say.

What a pity.

But I'm glad you're here. I was just thinking of you.

Nice thoughts, I hope.

Did you have any fun in Denver?

I was such a slug, she says. A fat, lazy slug.

But you did find time to kill a woman named Rose White.

And the weather was positively beastly, she says.

Did you kill her for her stethoscope? I say. And her little green scrubs?

I painted my nails and ate room service all day.

Because you can buy that shit at any drugstore.

She smiles. I love those little shrimp cocktails.

You stole her fucking hair.

She hisses at me. I invented Rose White. She never existed.

Her body was found yesterday, in the trunk of a black Mustang.

That's so strange.

Tell me one thing. Where did you get my gun?

Oh, she says. It fell into my lap. Your little wife gave it to me.

Jude, you mean.

Who else?

The tiny room spins and I smile. What do you want from me?

I want you, she says.

Fuck you.

Where is the icebox? she says.

I gave it away. I sold it to an ugly little man in Las Vegas.

She blinks rapidly and I study her. She doesn't look like Lucy at all, not really. The hair and clothes and the body are the same. But her face is a fucking mask. Her eyes look right through me. I swivel my head around woodenly. There must be something to drink in this room. The toilet flushes with a sudden boom and I turn to look at Isabel. Are we not alone, I say. The Blister walks out of the bathroom, drying his hands on a white towel. He wears the fur coat and a white silk tie and a smile like dry ice.

Oh, this gets better and better.

I believe you know my ugly little brother, says Isabel.

The Blister sits down gingerly, as if the furniture is simply too cheap and dirty.

Hello, I say. My name is Phineas Poe.

He sneers. Such wit.

What is your fucking name?

Isabel sighs. His name is Jerome Gore.

I sink into the bed. I have had such a long day.

Isabel takes off the red wig and tosses it aside. It crouches on the floor like a headless animal and my mind is coming apart, like a frayed and tangled piece of rope. The Blister laughs, or chokes. I tell myself to think of him as Jerry. My hands float before my face, disconnected and useless. Isabel runs fingers through her own sleek black hair. It is cut exactly like Lucy's was, before she lost it. She smiles and wets her lips with a flashing tongue.

Which do you prefer, she says. Sex or violence?

I try to smile. What's the difference, really.

And I slap at my pockets, desperate for a cigarette. I'm about to ask Jerry if he has any when Isabel takes two steps and she's so close to me I can smell her. She stinks of eucalyptus. She flips open an engraved silver case and slides a cigarette between my lips. Thick black smoke drifts between us and I feel better.

Just knock him on the head and be done with it, says the Blister.

Shut up, she says.

He sighs. Have your fun, then.

Isabel reaches between her breasts and unzips the silver dress to her waist. She wears a white lace bustier. Her skin is bright with warm, thick blood moving beneath the surface. She's alive, she's Lucy and I just want to touch her. I want to pull her close and tell her how sorry I am. I want to push her gently to the floor and kiss the pulse in her throat. I want to breathe her new life. I want to tell her a thousand things and close my eyes and disappear into her. But she's an illusion, a specter.

The Blister groans loudly and flicks on the television. He finds a tennis match on cable and settles back in his chair. Isabel picks up the telephone and the Blister glances at her.

Are you calling room service? he says. Because I would love a cup of tea.

Isabel yanks the plug from the wall and throws the telephone at him. It barely misses his head and he gives her a filthy look.

Turn it off, she says. Or else I'm going to make you wait outside.

Don't be such a slut, he says.

Maybe I should wait outside, I say.

No, says Isabel.

The Blister mutes the television and shrugs.

Isabel is naked now and my eyes betray me. I steal a long, hungry look at her. Her breasts are larger than Jude's, her belly softer. She has a wild black bush of pubic hair, and her thighs are creamy white and not so long and muscular. I can imagine them wrapped around my head. They are Lucy's legs.

She smiles and says, do you like me?

No. I don't like you.

Look at me, she says. Touch me. I could be your wife.

I throw a towel at her. Have some shame.

Yes, the Blister says loudly. Do us a fucking favor.

Why, she says. Why did you give the icebox to such a pig?

I shrug. He seemed to want it.

But it was empty, she says.

Oh, no. It was packed full of heroin.

Heroin, she says. Her face grows slowly, frighteningly dark.

It was excellent stuff, I say. The best.

Whose was it?

I believe it was Jerry's.

Isabel walks across the room, slowly. Her bare ass swaying as if it's Saturday night and she can't decide whether to go out or just wash her hair.

Jerome, she says. Where did the heroin come from?

The Blister stares at the silent tennis match. He takes out a giant gun exactly like the one I took from him in Vegas. He gives me a faint smile and places the gun on his thigh. Isabel laughs at him.

You spent the money on heroin, didn't you. What else did you buy?

That was a slick Lincoln town car you were driving around Denver, I say.

He looks at me. You're a mouse, he says. A bug.

And that's a nice fur coat, I say.

Isabel takes the Blister's gun from him and unloads it. She drops the bullets to the floor like shiny pebbles. She slips the gun back into his lap, snug against his crotch. The Blister's face is changing colors, humming with blood and I imagine his little penis swollen and pulsing under her thumb. He wants to fuck her, to kill her. He's terrified of her. I can almost sympathize.

My. That is a lovely fur, she says. Is it otter?

Take your hand off me, sister.

Isabel looks at me over one shoulder.

This is so embarrassing, she says. My youngest brother, Horatio, is dying. He has an immune deficiency disorder and he badly needs a kidney.

The Blister shows his teeth. Horatio has AIDS, you stupid cow. He's queer as a blue moon.

Be careful, she says.

Your brother needs a kidney, I say. He needs my kidney.

Yes, she says. I hired Jude to find a suitable donor. And she found five.

Five, I say.

Isabel shrugs and explains that Jude accessed the medical files of nine hundred inmates and medical patients. Eleven of them matched Horatio's blood and tissue type, five of them were scheduled for release. And then it was a matter of elimination. One suffered chronic hepatitis, another tuberculosis. Two of them were very unattractive, she says. They were genetically inferior.

What?

She smiles. You were the best-looking, by far.

What difference does that make?

None, she says.

I stare at her. Would you borrow a pair of shoes from an ugly girl?

What kind of shoes?

Oh, god.

She bites her lip. Ironic, isn't it?

Oh, yes. It's bad poetry.

It was really a simple transaction, she says. It was like ordering lingerie from a catalog. But my father foolishly gave Jerome a suitcase full of money and sent him to make the exchange.

I was unstoppable, says the Blister.

A disaster, she says.

I was the spy that came in from the cold and the cops were licking my bootheels.

Isabel laughs as if her head will fly off.

Jerome came home in a fury, she says. He said that Jude cheated him, that she took the kidney to another buyer. He needed his little sister's help.

Isabel touches her fingers to the Blister's lips.

Oh you wet bitch, he whispers.

Actually, I say. I think she gave the kidney to some orphan.

The Blister bites into Isabel's hand as if it were a piece of fruit. Her face turns white.

I still have my knife in the wrist sheath and I shrug and it's in my hand, cool and untrembling. My knees are like water, though. I take two endless steps through mud and black sand and push the point of the tanto into the Blister's ear. If I sneeze or flinch or tremble, the Blister has brain damage. He opens his mouth, blood on his lips. Isabel jerks her hand free and whirls away from him, screeching like a mad bird. I'm not sure if she's dancing, if she's about to attack. I glace at the Blister and he too is uneasy. Isabel whirls prettily and kicks him in the mouth with her bare heel. The Blister rolls to his knees, the big gun in his left hand. He picks up two of his loose bullets and reloads, spitting blood. I stare at him lazily. I don't even reach for my gun. The Blister backs away from us, the gun pointed at Isabel, then at me. He pulls the trigger and the hammer falls on an empty chamber with a vaguely disappointing little click. The Blister throws open the door and is gone.

Isabel is breathing hard, drunk with her own blood.

That was beautiful, she says.

It was interesting.

She licks her lips and leans close to me.

What's the matter? she says.

Are you kidding?

I would have spared you this, she says.

Yeah.

The room is shrinking. I'm stupid with hunger.

My brother is such a pill, she says.

What happened to his hands? I say.

Oh, god. I'm so tired of that story.

What happened?

Isabel is so close to me that I can feel her body vibrating. She reminds me of an electric carving knife, the blade that hums effortlessly through meat. She seems to occupy more space than I do. Isabel claps her hands together and I jump at the sound. She laughs merrily and abruptly reaches for her metallic dress, then pulls it like a sack over her head. She zips it to the throat. She asks me to find her panties. I glance around and spot a clump of white lace on the floor, barely touching Jude's hairbrush. I flick them at her and watch as she pulls them slowly up her thighs to disappear beneath her dress.

She ignores the wig and bustier. I kick them under the bed, feeling suddenly sweaty.

Are you leaving? I say.

I'm sorry, she says. I hope you didn't want to fuck me.

I see myself, bent and jerking at her unresponding body in fierce rabbit strokes. Isabel is staring at her fingernails, perhaps thinking that what she needs is an expensive manicure. She shrugs and begins to tidy the room. She picks up the fallen telephone.

Not really, I say. I wanted to reject you.

Could you?

Fuck you. What was that, then?

That was pure theater. I call it amusing Jerome.

Why?

He deserves it.

Because of the heroin?

I take a step forward and her eyes flicker. Among other things.

Does he want your brother to die?

She takes a shallow breath and spits. He wants to be famous.

What does that mean? He wants to be on television?

He wants to be my father.

I step closer. Would your father have tried to double-cross Jude?

Isabel forces herself to shrug and she looks briefly weak. I step closer and she smiles, muscles flexing in her neck.

It's not safe here, she says.

I tell her to lock the door and she shudders. I step close enough to touch her, to hurt her. She wants me, she's pulling me in. Her eyes are downcast and she lets her body go limp. I should cut her throat or run away but my hands slip around her waist and my brain drones like television and I don't even ask myself what I'm doing and then I hear the odd jingle of the telephone as she swings it in a narrow, intimate arc that crashes into the side of my skull.

I swim through a prolonged black void to find that my arms and legs are gone. I'm sure they will come back to me when it's too late. My spine is like soup. I seem to be stretched like a corpse on my own vibrating bed. Though it's mercilessly not vibrating, currently. Isabel circles around me, her body weirdly contorted and legless. My vision must be fucked. A nice blow to the head will do that. I am so stupid, so easily foiled. It's really almost funny. If I could lift a finger I would gladly kill myself. Isabel rummages through Jude's things and cheerfully produces a set of handcuffs. She gives them a shake and they ring like new money.

What the fuck is this?

You are supposed to be asleep.

You hit me with a telephone.

I'm sorry, she says. I still need your kidney.

Oh, well. I'm afraid it's gone.

Funny, she says.

Do you know what you're doing? I say.

Hush, she says.

Jude told me that you butchered a male prostitute.

Oh, she says. That's true, actually.

She uses my own knife to cut away my fine new shirt. The room yawns around me and I wish I had gone to have a quiet drink with Alexander. Isabel shackles my hands together, gently. My face is at such an angle that I can only see the television. The silent tennis match defies gravity. Isabel washes my chest with rubbing alcohol and uses my own disposable razor to shave the hair from the right side of my torso. I wonder if the two scars will meet, if they will make a circle. I never hear the door open and I don't hear footsteps. I hear a soft, sleepy noise like air escaping. I'm aware that Isabel is twisting, falling. Then she becomes still and Jude is leaning over me and her lips are soft as shadows.

You should have run, she says. You should have run when I gave you the chance.

thirty-one.

THE TOE OF A BOOT AGAINST MY RIBS. I wake from the gray landscape of empty dreams.

Jude, I say.

Apologies, brother. But I'm not gonna kiss you. Henry's voice.

He crouches beside me and strikes a match. His face is dirty, unshaven in the flickering glow. He smells like rain and he doesn't smile. He offers me his hand and I let him pull me to my feet. I stare blankly at my watch. One in the morning, says Henry.

I thought I had seen the last of you.

Never fear.

How did you find me?

I have a keen sense of smell, he says. I can sniff out a fuck-up from miles away.

I reach for a cigarette and say nothing. I'm still half asleep. The room is dark and I wonder if Jude knocked out the electricity. I can't see a thing but I'm sure Jude has disappeared. She is reluctant to linger, to leave a trace. Henry lights another match and I see that the bed is neatly made. There are no signs of love or struggle and Jude's things are gone.

You must be the stupidest motherfucker I ever saw, he says. Or the luckiest.

I was born under a dying star, a red dwarf.

Let's go, says Henry. I want to show you something.

He lights another match. Isabel is in the bathtub and the air is ripe with the copper smell of blood. She's curled in a ball, feline and beautiful in the unstable light.

The power comes on with a tremble. There is a long smear of black feces on the white floor, marked by a single smallish footprint that can only be Jude's. Blood seeps from Isabel's mouth and from her swollen left eye. Her lips are sewn shut. There is a sleek, unhurried cut across her breasts. Her feet bear tiny, bloodless puncture wounds. I lean over the toilet but it's full of blood. I turn and throw up calmly in the sink.

Your girlfriend, says Henry. She's a real daydream.
    Oh, yeah. She'll make a nice little wife, one day.
    I wipe my mouth on a towel.
    This is a terrible fucking thing, says Henry.
    Did you call the cops?
    He grunts. Do you want to talk to the cops?
    Not really.
    Then shut the fuck up.
    How long was I asleep?
    I don't have a clue, brother. I missed the little tea party.
    Jude is gone, then. I've lost her.
    Henry leans against the door. He produces a cigar and pokes it between his lips.
    Take it easy, little Joe. We just might catch up with her.
    I sit on the edge of the bloody toilet. I notice that he has abandoned the slick, homicidal stockbroker look. He has become the drifter again, the ex-convict. He chews the cigar and grins at me.
    Where is she, I say.
    I have a few ideas, he says.
    Let's get out of here, I say. Before the earth swallows her.
    One more thing, says Henry. He pokes Isabel, who twitches like a rubber doll.

My god.

Interesting, isn't it? The body can survive a lot.

Tell me about it.

Blank blue eyes and a naked yellow sun. Two people in a boat, a man and a woman. The man is drunk or catatonic. Something is wrong with the woman and Isabel doesn't move or try to speak. There is so much blood in the bathtub that I can't believe she's alive.

She's dead. She's dead, Henry.

The dead don't move, he says.

They fucking do, I say. It's some kind of postmortem electric weirdness. I've seen it in the morgue. The dead bodies sit up and roll over and have erections and say hello all the time. It's like a party in there.

Henry smiles. I'm telling you she's alive.

You're sick.

Touch her, says Henry.

I hesitate, then jab at the body with one finger. I feel like a kid who's been dared to touch an unidentified object in the park. A decomposing squirrel, a lump of moldy clothes and garbage. Nothing happens. Isabel doesn't move. I pull out my little pocketknife and carefully cut the stitches from her lips. Fluid spills from her mouth and it's a wonder she didn't vomit and drown herself. She tries to speak but her words are like slush, malformed. The gibberish of a monkey.

What the hell is wrong with her?

Look at her left eye, says Henry.

Yeah. It's fucked.

No, he says. The eye isn't the point.

What is the point, Henry?

Jude didn't mean to blind this girl, he says. The wound is just above the eyeball.

The frontal lobe, I say.

Nice piece of work, isn't it? He chews the cigar and spits violently.

That fucking dental tool. I close my eyes and I can see Jude carefully, calmly stabbing it in beneath the ridge of bone and guiding the sleek, curved tip up and into her brain.

Henry shrugs. I thought you might want to kill her. Or shall I do it?

The boat drifts under the staring sun. I tell Lucy to be careful she doesn't burn. She doesn't answer and I think she's asleep. Time becomes elastic and the bottle is empty. I take off my shirt and use it to cover her. She's turning red now and I check the pockets of my shorts. I have a knife and nothing else. No identification. I slip over the side of the boat.

I don't want to kill her. I can't.

Someone needs to kill her.

Shut up.

Isabel sighs wetly. She's like a kid born with brain damage. She will need someone to feed her, to bathe her. I look into her mutilated eye. Do you want a doctor, I say. An ambulance?

That's enough, says Henry.

I'm going to call 911, I say.

No, says Henry.

I turn around as he pulls a gun from inside his jean jacket. Unpolished chrome 9 mm, with a black rubber grip. The barrel has been fitted with a silencer. He offers it to me like a gift and my lips are cracked, white with salt. I move in widening circles, away from the lake. I can still hear the water. She floats. Her face is gone. When the sun rises again I press the knife into my arm to make the ninth cut.

I don't want the gun.

Henry pushes me gently to one side. He bends to kiss Isabel on the cheek, then steps back. He rips the shower curtain down and wraps it around himself. Isabel screams, nodding her head madly and drumming the tub with her heels until Henry puts two quick bullets in her brain.

Henry and I sit next to each other on the bed. Henry holds his cigar and shivers, staring at the television. His face is glossy with tears. A black and white cowboy movie flickers on the screen. Isabel is a bundle of bloody rags, a dummy. She will soon be placed in a drawer in a huge, windowless room. She's not Lucy and she never was and I'm anxious to get away from her. If I turn my head slightly to the left, I can see a string of her blood stretching across the floor.

Henry sits against the wall, silent and furious. I smash the television to pieces and the room fills with smoke. I crush a cheap wooden chair with my fists and I love the rage. I wish it were mine. But it will soon disappear, like everything else. Henry rips the sheets from the bed and staggers into the bathroom to cover the body.

A half hour passes and I feel a little better. I catch a glimpse of myself in the mirror and I'm naked to the waist. Isabel cut off my shirt, I remember. I glance at my new pants and their thousand pockets. I find the leather bag that Alexander gave me and try on one of the priceless T-shirts. I slip into my new leather coat and I'm born again. Henry tells me a bad cowboy joke, about two cowboys and a hatful of water. They are taking turns guarding the hat while the other one sleeps. Soon the water seeps through the hat, and the cowboys are at each other's throat. Henry forgets the punch line, and the joke falls apart.

thirty-two.

I FOLLOW HIM OUT TO HIS CAR, a long red monster with whitewall tires.

Very inconspicuous, I say.

I swear by American cars, he says. The first car I ever loved a woman in was a Cutlass Supreme. You can't maneuver properly in a little Nissan.

That's the trouble with this country, I say. Too much room for fucking.

Henry laughs and climbs in. The engine roars like a wounded elephant. I shrug and get in, happy to sit down. I want to sleep for two days. I toss my bag on the backseat and we glide out of the parking lot and onto the dark highway. The sky is still black, nearly purple. There's no moon yet, or it's in hiding.

I close my eyes and try to float.

Something is wrong with you, he says.

I can't even count the ways.

Did you ever see a crippled animal on the highway? Its back legs shattered so it has to drag itself off the road and it makes you sick to look at it.

Maybe, I say. So what?

Didn't you have the decency to stop and kill the fucking thing or did you keep driving.

Fuck you. I know what's decent.

Mercy, he says. What about mercy?

It's easy to kill someone and call it mercy.

I stare at the black, rippling road. If one is confronted with a creature that is dying, that is weak, it's easier to look away than to kill. And what did I tell the Blister in Las Vegas? That it's more interesting to torture a frog than to save it. But there is another choice that is harder than any of these.

There is silence for a mile or two. Henry offers me a cigar.

No, thanks. I think I would throw up.

You're just kicking, he says. I've seen it a thousand times.

I'm kicking. And what do you know about it?

I know Jude was shooting you up regular. Some kind of magic shit, too. You were hallucinating and paranoid and pitiful and generally falling out of your skin.

Falling out of my skin, I say. I like the sound of that.

Let me tell you right now, he says. I don't care for junkies. They got the mentality of a cockroach and they're twice as pathetic. A cockroach at least has pride. I know you didn't get hooked on purpose or anything like that. However. When I see an addict, I personally want to kick his sorry ass. Especially if he's crying like a baby, laying around in his own piss and puke. I'd be happy to put a bullet in his belly.

That's beautiful, I say. It's heartwarming, really.

The reason I mention it, he says. If you're gonna get like that, you need to warn me. Otherwise, I will stop this car and push your ass out. I will leave you in the desert to die.

Don't worry, I say. I'm right as rain. I haven't puked in an hour, at least.

I'm serious, he says. You get sick in my car and we're gonna have some words. Just kick the shit quietly, like a cowboy. Then I'll be your best friend.

My only fucking friend, more like it.

You could do worse.

Who the fuck are you?

Henry Love, he says. He turns slightly, and offers me his hand. I grasp it, weirdly grateful.

And what is your real name?

That's it. On my mother's soul and god rest her.

Henry, I say. I think it's high time we had a little chat.

Indeed.

Who do you work for?

I'm an independent contractor.

Whatever you say. But how are you involved in this game?

You and I have a mutual friend. Funny-looking bastard called Detective Moon. I spoke to him yesterday, matter of fact. And he said to say hello for him.

Moon sent you? I don't believe it.

Eucalyptus, says Henry.

What?

It's a code, goddammit.

Eucalyptus, I say.

Something about velvet panties. Moon said you would know what it means.

The cigar glows orange in his mouth.

I suppose it means I should trust you.

Moon was worried about you, brother. He said you were on the stinky end of something bad, and you were all fucked up. He said a five-year-old could hand your ass to you.

That's nice of him.

He wasn't half wrong, says Henry.

And so you came down out of the sky to save me. Are you Batman or is Moon throwing you some money?

Henry laughs. Moon doesn't have any money. He bets on everything but the weather.

Then you do know him, I say.

Maybe he made an outstanding warrant or two go away, says Henry. As a favor. And I looked into your situation, as a favor.

Warrants for what?

Just shut up and I'll tell you my life story, he says. If you're so interested.

Please, I say. I love a good story.

He drives with one hand. The other dangles out his window. I used to be a fed, he says. A long time ago, five years ago at least. I can't really believe it myself. And it wasn't much fun. A lot of pencil pushing, mostly. Like I was an insurance agent. It wasn't what I signed up for, believe me. I wanted to hunt down a serial killer or two and have a few epic gunfights with the mob, you know what I mean.

I sigh. The man from U.N.C.L.E.

Exactly, he says. That's the shit.

Television, I say. The stuff of dreams.

Henry shrugs. Whatever. It was a fucking bore. Then one fine day, I got a little too creative and maybe a little violent. I broke another agent's neck during a simulation and I was bounced out of there like a bad salesman. I drifted around for a while and figured I'd use my skills to make a little cash. I ran drugs for a while, but like I said, I developed a serious dislike for junkies. I took up bounty hunting, over in Arizona mostly. It's not half bad, it's like hunting rabbits.

I don't know. Rabbits are pretty clever.

No shit. And fast little fuckers. Humans are easier to catch. Anyway, that's how I came to encounter your pal Moon. I retrieved a boy that had jumped bail on a carjacking charge in Colorado, and Moon came to collect him. The kid was still unconscious in the back of my truck when Moon got there. And Moon didn't want to move him, see. I was a good host and broke out a bottle. Moon and me, we got drunk and stayed up half the night.

I'm curious. Why was the kid unconscious, exactly?

Henry laughs. Oh, well. I used tranquilizer darts on him. The kind the animal control uses when a mad dog gets loose in somebody's tomato garden.

That is creative. And very funny.

Then a year ago I fucked up. One of my rabbits had himself a seizure and almost perished. I had to take him to the emergency room and he was all bruised and cut up. The cops came to sort it out and I got charged with excessive force, illegal weapons, assault on a cop and contempt of court and a pile of other shit. The judge didn't much care for me and managed to hit me with the maximum for everything. I got out two months ago and found out I had bench warrants in California and Tennessee for a handful of failure charges.

I stare into the dark and wonder what color the moon will be tonight.

What kind of charges?

Failure charges, he says. Failure to pay, failure to appear, failure to comply. Moon took care of them for me and here I am. It's like a little vacation, really.

You used to be a fed, huh? That's funny. It seems like everybody wants to be a secret agent.

Who do you mean?

Jude, I say. She gave me some smoke about being in the CIA.

That's horseshit, he says. As a former agent, that offends me. Besides. I checked her out. She was in the army for a while, special forces. But she didn't last. She received a dishonorable discharge five years ago, for non-specific fucked-up reasons. Then she became a ghost.

Or a shape-shifter, I say.

Henry grins. In those five years, there have been twelve other cases of some poor fucker just like you. They wake up in a bathtub full of ice, with staples in their guts. They all describe a different woman, but it's her. Each guy had just been released from jail or the nuthouse.

Thirteen human kidneys, I say. And you've got enough blood pudding for the queen.

Relax, brother.

I'm fucking relaxed. I'm like butter. Where did you get this information?

I still have a friend or two up at Quantico. They have some really big computers, you know.

Henry slows the car as we approach a decayed roadhouse on the left. A blinking neon sign: THE BROKEN HEART. A wide gravel lot, with a dozen cars and trucks.

Beautiful, says Henry. I would kill my granny for a beer right now.

What do you want? I say. Everybody wants something.

I told you. Moon asked me to look out for you, that's all. And it wasn't hard. I took a liking to you right away, in that bathroom. You were like a dying saint or something. The way you handed over your wedding ring for a hat.

Oh, yeah. Then why didn't you state your true purpose?

Because I wasn't sure how deep you were in with her.

You were sniffing around like a pure grifter. Looking for a crack to wiggle through.

That was an unfortunate tactic, he says. I apologize. But I wanted to see how you reacted to various stimuli. Then you got a mighty bug up your ass and hopped off the train. Which was irritating, by the way.

Stimuli, I say. Like you fucking my wife.

Your wife?

Yeah. My dead wife, Lucy. You couldn't help yourself, I guess.

Listen to yourself, brother.

Get the fuck out of the car, I say. Just get out.

Phineas.

No weapons, I say.

Henry laughs. You don't want to fight me, Phineas.

thirty-three.

THE HUM AND BUZZ OF MUSIC AND DOGS AND PEOPLE.

Our boots crunch in the gravel. The sky is black. Henry wobbles before me and I feel like I'm on a boat. I swing at him, my arm suddenly ten feet long. He ducks under it easily and punches me in the stomach and I am on my knees, trying to breathe. I see Lucy, naked and coiled around him. His hands gripped her soft ass like a piece of dough. I stand up, slowly. Henry watches me, his hands loose and relaxed at his sides. He has a small, sad smile on his face.

You know those fat houseflies that drift around in the winter? he says.
Like cows with wings, I say.
Exactly. You have the reflexes of a cow.
I push off the car and spin, sending a wild high kick at his head. He steps out of the way and hits me in the side of the neck, then brings his forearm up to crush my nose.

Are you finished? he says. Because this is embarrassing.
I'm finished.
Henry pulls me up. What's wrong with you? he says.
I'm so tired. And I want to hurt somebody.
Sure, he says. But I haven't done anything to you. That girl on the train was Isabel. And Moon told me your wife is dead and buried, anyhow.

I know it was Isabel on the train. But she was Lucy's shadow.

Okay, he says. It's okay. I understand.

Henry does something amazing, baffling. He hugs me. I lock my jaw to stop from weeping. He pulls away and sticks his ring finger in his mouth, tugging my wedding ring off with his teeth. He drops it in my hand and it feels warm to my skin.

Thank you, I say.

How do you feel?

I'm not bad. A little dizzy and my nose hurts.

Let's get a drink, he says. And maybe say hello to Jude.

How do you know she's here?

He winks at me. I'm psychic.

Two of the buildings are skeletal and empty, ruined by fire. The third is alive and thumping. The music growls, thick and menacing and distorted, as if it's coming from under ground. Henry and I approach the front steps. A man sits on a stool beside the door, he looks sleepy and fat with muscle. A baseball bat rests between his legs. Beside him is a shiny new shotgun. He regards me with the eyes of a polar bear at the zoo. His arms are crossed, and his hands are moving slightly, fluttering and mothlike. As if he's stroking his armpits.

Don't believe I know you boys, he says.

Not to worry, says Henry.

His elbow brushes mine and I can feel a tingle like static electricity. He's itching to hit someone, after tasting a little blood with me. I pull out a wad of cash.

What's your name, I say.

Junior, he says.

I pass him a fifty.

You a cop, he says. He examines the bill, suspiciously.

I laugh softly, and a splash of blood bubbles from my nose. He stares at it.

Henry smiles fiercely. Open the door, Junior.

Smoke. The sound of a piano and a woman singing. The only light comes from behind the bar, a long low slab of unfinished wood. There is a ragged crowd of white men and a few very young girls. The girls have black hair and skin that ranges from yellow to chocolate. They are beautiful and bright with despair. Henry drifts away and comes back with two glass jars of uncertain liquid.

This smells of death, I say.
  Drink it slow.
  She isn't here, I say.
  Downstairs, he says. I believe the real action is in the basement.

A long, narrow room with a dirt floor and a very low ceiling. Every table is crowded with men and women hunched on plastic chairs. The women are older than the sad whores upstairs, and most of them are white. There is no music now, only the crackle and static of voices. The thick noise of impatience. At one end of the room is a shallow pit surrounded by thick chicken wire. The wire is a dull reddish color like rust. Now a murmur snakes through the crowd. A man with thick red hair and dark glasses approaches the pit. He wears a three-piece suit the color of lead. He surveys the crowd, a crooked smile on his face. Two men enter from a rear door, dressed in blue jeans and sleeveless shirts, leather gloves. One of them leads a brindle pit bull on a short chain. The dog is muzzled, silent and lunging. Another man appears leading a mottled blue dog with powerful legs and a square, wolflike head. The dog appears wild, nervous and high-strung. He wears no muzzle and doesn't make a sound.

Their vocal cords are removed, Henry says. It's creepy, isn't it?

The man with red hair begins to speak. He introduces the first dog as Spider, three years old and weighing fifty-five pounds; sired by the infamous Diablo and the winner of thirteen blood matches. The crowd howls with love and pride. The challenger is the Blue Ghost, two years old and sixty pounds. Fathered by a nameless, chicken-killing coyote. This will be his first match. The crowd whistles and jeers. The Blue Ghost is trembling now, with fear or rage. The announcer waves his arms for silence. The Ghost's mother, he says, was Bloody Mary. She was the Australian cattle dog that killed a mountain lion in the summer of '92. The crowd is pleased and soon begins to whisper and sign, placing bets.

Henry squints at me through cigarette smoke. Are you a fucking monk or something?

What do you mean?

You want to tell me what happened back there, at the Seventh Son?

Well, I say. Isabel was getting ready to gut me.

That's just pitiful, says Henry.

She was eager to take my last kidney.

How long can a young man live with no kidney at all?

Not fucking long, brother.

Henry laughs.

Jude came out of nowhere, I say. She saved my ass.

Maybe the sky is falling, he says.

Maybe she loves me, I say.

Henry turns to a burly man at the next table. A hundred on the Ghost, he says.

The man laughs. Easy money. You never seen the Spider, have you?

The men are allowed to massage and prep their dogs for a few minutes. The Blue Ghost's owner is a young kid, perhaps twenty. He whispers to his dog, stroking him and rubbing his ears. The kid is pale, biting his lip. The kid loves his dog and I feel bad for him. He should be taking his dog out to chase rabbits in the high yellow grass. The Blue Ghost is calm again. He holds his head up and stares at the Spider. The Spider's handlers poke and jab at him with a sharpened stick. They curse and snarl at him and splash chicken's blood on his face. He is soon in a frenzy, foaming through the muzzle. He gnaws at the leather, his teeth drawing blood from his own gums. His handlers smile and hold him back.

That kid owes somebody money, I say. His momma is in the hospital. They need a new roof, something. He doesn't want to fight that dog.

Henry nods. Maybe. So what?

I could help him, I say.

How are you gonna help that kid?

I could give him a couple thousand. Then he could take his dog and go home.

No, he says. The kid is proud.

I look at the kid, his face hard and glazed with tears. Henry is right, I'm sure. The kid would cut his wrists before he took money from a stranger.

The dogs are placed in the pit and the crowd surges to the edge. The kid rubs his mouth and sighs. Henry finishes his whiskey and asks if I want mine. I shake my head. The one swallow I took still churns in my belly like liquid nitrogen. I was sure it would kill me.

The dogs circle each other, slow and hypnotic, then striking in a blur of teeth and fur. The Blue Ghost is strong and unafraid. He fights well enough, using his strong legs to knock the Spider down. He opens shallow wounds on the Spider's chest and shoulders. But the Ghost lacks the proper fury. The Spider is relentless and terribly fast, moving with strange chaos and grace.

Henry is mesmerized, his mouth wet.

The Ghost is in trouble, moving clumsily and bleeding from the mouth. He has a broken rib, a puncture lung. The Spider toys with him, slashing at his legs.

The crowd is wailing like Christians in a big tent.

I look away, at the kid. He holds his face in both hands. The Spider finally takes down the Ghost, his massive jaws closed on the throat. The Ghost is a filthy, bloody lump. His neck is broken and the Spider doesn't let go until his handlers enter the pit and beat at him with rubber hoses. The kid is silent.

Henry shakes his head and drops a clump of money on the burly man's slick, wet table. He turns to me, smiling. I lean close to whisper in his ear, where the fuck is Jude.

thirty-four.

THE MOON IS A FRAGMENT, disappearing behind clouds. Henry and I smoke cigarettes and throw stones into the dark. We make such a lovely pair. He is dangerously drunk and I'm trembling, a morphine addict. The stitches in my belly feel like they might be alive.

Is your arm made of glass? he says.
    Fuck you.
    Brother, he says. You throw like a pretty boy.
    Enough of this shit, I say. Tell me where she is.
    Keep your pants on.
    What are you waiting for?
    I don't know. I thought we might go find some action.
    Sex or violence, I say.
    He grins at me. Isabel was a hell of a girl, he says.
    She was a mad hatter, I say.
    Anyway, he says. There must be a decent whorehouse around here.
This is Texas.
    Please. I'm on my last legs.
    Or we could go home.
    Home?
    Denver, he says.
    No. There's nothing there.

Moon asked me to bring you back.

I shuffle away from him with the grace and ferocity of a diseased kid begging for spare change. I only need space to breathe. He watches me, amused. I mutter an apology and remove the gun from my ankle holster. Henry shakes his head.

Are you serious?

I probably wouldn't shoot you.

Thanks, he says.

But I'm not going back to Denver. Let's get that fucking straight.

Think of your loved ones.

What loved ones?

Don't you have a dog or a cat?

You're insane.

I'm sentimental, he says.

Do you want me to shoot you?

Listen, he says. I'm just fucking with you.

Do you know where Jude is?

Of course, he says. She's in the trunk of my car.

The dark swallows me. I'm a dead woman with no hair.

What did you say?

It's cool, he says. I grabbed her when she was coming out of the Seventh Son.

You didn't kill her.

No, he says. Oh, hell no. She fights like a goddamn tiger, though. I finally poked her with one of those tranquilizer darts I mentioned earlier.

Oh, you dumb motherfucker. Let her out and pray she doesn't kill you.

Henry fumbles with his keys and I hold my breath. He mutters that the icebox is also in the trunk, in case I still want it. I'm afraid I might start laughing and I won't be able to stop. He bends over the trunk of his car and he's too casual. He doesn't exactly have groceries in there. The key turns with the sound of a hammer against metal and I pull him away from the car.

You want to stand clear, I say.

The trunk swings open and Jude bursts free. She breathes slowly, through her teeth.

Jude, I say.

She regards Henry with a long, piteous stare.

Jude.

I'm gonna take a walk, says Henry.

My heart uncoils in my chest. Jude relaxes, and I see that her legs are trembling. I grip her thin, hard body as if I might hurt her. She whispers to me and I bite her hair, her neck.

Henry drifts back to us and he appears sober, dangerous. I wonder if he's been faking it.

I thought you two would be snuggling like rabbits. He doesn't smile.

It's time to go, I say.

Is she coming with us?

Yes, I say.

He frowns. Let's put her back in the trunk.

Forget it.

The bitch could stab me in the neck.

I trust her, I say.

You are a fucking fool.

Didn't you take her weapons when you tranquilized her?

Yeah, he says. But I could have missed something.

Do you want me to frisk her?

Please.

Of course, she could kill you with her fingernails.

Fuck you. Just do it.

I tell her I'm sorry and she shrugs. Jude turns lazily and spreads her hands on the hood. I kick her feet apart and gently slap her down. She trembles when I touch her thigh, as if it tickles. I slide my hands over her ass and crotch, suddenly shy.

This is hopeless, I say.

Jude looks at me, her green eyes unblinking.

Do you have any weapons? I say.

No, she says.

I can barely look at Henry.

Oh, he says. I feel much better.

Jude kisses my left eye. Don't worry.

Where are we going? says Henry. And what do you want?

I stare out the dark window and wonder about that. Henry drives, muttering. He has found nothing but gospel on the radio. It reminds him of his childhood, he says. Jude sits beside him, silent. Her head is bent, waiting for the sun. The green icebox sits beside me on the backseat. I still have the little key in my pocket and soon I slip it into the lock. I open the icebox, oddly nervous. Part of me still expects to find my kidney inside. It only holds the Blister's clothes, now torn and cut to shreds. His clothes were whole when I last touched them. I smile at the back of Jude's head. I don't know what I want.

Time disappears. I recite the laws of inertia. A body placed in motion will not rest until acted up by another body. It's bullshit, I know. But I want to keep moving. I want Jude to stop me.

I lean over the seat and breathe against Jude's throat. Where is Luscious Gore?

She shrugs. I think he has a summer house around here somewhere.

I'm serious.

Phineas, she says. What are you thinking?

Do you know where he is?

Of course.

The miles pass and the sun rises behind us, as if we are running from it.

I tell Henry to stop the car. He ignores me.

Humor me, I say.

He pulls to the shoulder and grunts about needing to piss anyway. There is a fine mist in the air, cool against our skin. Henry and I stand side by side, peeing noisily against rocks as the sky changes colors around us. Jude refuses to get out of the car. I tell her it could be hours before she has another chance, but she doesn't answer. I feel better now, having seen the sunrise. The landscape is barren and deathly quiet, stretching into the distance without pause. The silent, jagged beauty like a map of the moon.

This isn't quite over, I say.

What do you mean? says Henry.

Luscious Gore is waiting for us, I say.

No, he says. I don't really like this idea.

You don't have to come with us.

Shit, brother. I have nowhere else to be.

Then indulge me.

I get in the car and tell Jude to give him directions. She asks if I have a pen and Henry turns to give her a heavy dose of his face. Henry's face is not ugly, exactly. It's fearsome though, and deeply textured. The eyes are hard, and disturbing in their contrast. The blue one is bright as a knife blade, the brown one a hole in the earth. His beard is thick and speckled with gray. And his blunt, ragged hair is still mostly white.

Don't even think about stabbing me with a fucking pen, he says.

Jude laughs softly. You have nothing to fear.

He glances at me. You're the one who should be afraid.

I am curiously calm, and I want to tell him that Jude will take care of me, that everything will be fine. But I'm not sure I believe it. Jude pulls a crisp five-dollar bill from her pocket and quickly draws out a map across Lincoln's long, sad face. She gives the bill to Henry, like a tip.

thirty-five.

HALF AN HOUR PASSES AND I'M BORED SILLY. Jude says we have maybe twenty miles to go and the road bleeds away from us, an endless black rope. I play with the window, rolling it up and down. I let my hand float and drift in the rush of air. Henry chews his cigar and looks at me with one eye. The other is closed, as if seeing something else. I look away, into the distance, hoping to see a jackrabbit.

Do they test nuclear weapons out here? I say.

Go to sleep, says Henry.

I'm not tired.

Talk to your girlfriend, then.

I light two cigarettes and pass one to Jude.

This is what you wanted, I say. All along.

No, she says. It was your idea to come to Texas.

Oh, yeah. And when I'm depressed I go bowling.

But I stood you up, she says.

Why?

It was a stupid idea, she says.

I whisper, but you had two tickets to El Paso. A cozy sleeper car.

Jude shows her teeth.

The other ticket was for that idiot Pooh. He was my entertainment and muscle. And then you drifted back into my life and I was forced to improvise.

How romantic, says Henry.

It's a pile of shit, I say.

When did you stop believing me? says Jude. When did you start, for that matter?

Maybe the other ticket was for Isabel, I say.

Jude laughs. I couldn't stand Isabel.

You gave her my gun, I say. Didn't you?

Isabel is dead, she says. And she's still tying you in knots.

What did you do with my kidney?

She looks straight through me. It's in the icebox, isn't it?

What did you do with it?

I gave it to a little black bird, she says. The bird carried it for miles and miles and finally dropped it into the ocean, where a fish ate it. The fish was caught by a young boy, who took it home and gave it to his sister. The sister cleaned the fish and cooked it, and fed it to her family.

I study the shape of her face, the angle of her neck. She has effortlessly burned herself into my brain. Jerome tried to fuck her somehow. He had mysteriously blown the money on a ridiculous new car and a fur coat while his own brother lay dying. He had poor impulse control and he wanted Isabel's pet to die. Jimmy crack corn and I don't care. Black hair streaked with blond and eyes wide apart, hooded and shaped like lemons. *They are mongoloid eyes, the devil's eyes.* Jerome tried to pay her with heroin, maybe he refused to pay her at all. Jude was not amused either way. She beat him half to death and disappeared, a box of heroin in one hand and a nearly rotten kidney in the other. A scar at the edge of her mouth and fine white teeth, slightly crooked and sharp. She could have dropped the kidney down a laundry chute or found another buyer but I like to think she walked into that emergency room in Colorado Springs like an angel with snow in her hair. The stone around her neck, the horrible teardrop. It still dangles from a string of silver in a cold hollow of flesh and you had a thousand chances, I say. To cut me open a second time.

She never answers me. She doesn't need to.

The sickness comes on abruptly. It resumes, as if to remind me that I'm still alive. I have a coughing fit that nearly tears me apart. I think my intestines are unraveling. I touch my throat, my face. The skin is damp and cold as the bottom of my shoe. Jude is watching me with alien tenderness.

I'm okay, I say. I'm like a house on fire.

She sighs. You don't look well.

It's only loneliness.

Did you really miss me?

Yes. I was lost without you.

You should have run, she says.

I could use one of those shots, I say.

I'm sorry, she says. But I've misplaced my medical bag.

Henry mutters. I tossed it into a Dumpster.

She looks at him. You're dying to be my friend, aren't you?

What happened to you? he says. In the army?

Jude rolls down her window and leans out. The wind whips at her hair and I watch the dark and light streaks merge and flail apart. An almost invisible blur, like insect wings. Even when pale and shattered by withdrawals, I am still fascinated by the most meager stimuli.

Why do you ask? she says.

I like to know who I'm traveling with.

Or who you carelessly shove in the trunk of your car.

Maybe, he says.

I was in Israel, she says dreamily. During some recent foolishness that never even made the newspapers.

Oh I love this fucking country, says Henry.

I close my eyes and Jude's voice drifts. She was lost in the desert for five weeks, she says. The sand was in her bowels, her blood. But she wasn't alone. There were two boys with her. Felix was nineteen. He stuttered under pressure but he was fearless in a fight. He was a good Christian and a virgin. Cody was twenty. He was from California and he thought the world was his. He never took his eyes off her. It was so cold at night that the three of them slept together like newborn rats, huddled so close that their breath and skin mingled and became one. Felix soon went mad. He stared at the sun until his eyes were white. Jude had to tie a nylon rope to his wrist and drag him along behind her. Cody was so afraid of dying that he never shut up and he begged her to sleep with him, to have his baby. Then one day he stepped on a land mine and blew himself to bits and Jude was glad. Because she wouldn't have to listen to him anymore. She wished she had killed him herself. On the twenty-ninth day she killed Felix with a knife, because there wasn't enough water for both of them. It was like killing a dog, and her heart shrank. Jude came out of the desert, alone and slightly insane. She received a section eight discharge one month later.

That's a very good story, says Henry.

Jude stares at him, a vein turning faintly blue in her left temple.

Henry examines the map and slows the car, stopping at a dirt road. He stares at it bleakly, and I follow his gaze. The road is gutted with holes, ugly with rocks. The road is a mud slide, a disaster area. The road is uphill. Henry's car would be ruined and wheezing, bottomed out after twenty yards.

How long is this road? he says.

Jude grins at him. Ten miles, perhaps.

Beautiful, he says. Why didn't you say we would need a fucking all-terrain vehicle?

It slipped my mind.

It's okay, I say. We can turn around and go back to El Paso, steal a truck and come back. Or we can walk. Personally, I don't care.

Nice day, says Jude. Let's walk.

Oh, no. This is bullshit, says Henry.

What? I say.

This is the end, okay. This is as far as we go. I'm not a lovesick junkie and I'm not a fucking serial killer. I'm the only one thinking straight.

Jude squints at him, as if he is blurry around the edges.

Henry, I say.

Listen, he says. I'm not letting you go up that road with this bitch. Don't you know she will slaughter you like a goddamn chicken? I can see it in her eyes.

Poor thing, says Jude. You don't know me at all.

I hold my face in my hands, suddenly very tired.

Phineas, he says. I would rather kill you myself than let you go with her.

That's nice of you, I say.

Or I could drag your sorry ass back to Denver.

Please, says Jude. This is so dull.

Shut the fuck up, says Henry.

Jude leans close to him. Are you going to do something? Or just talk.

Henry slaps her with the back of his hand and she rocks back against the passenger door. I could kill him. He yanks the gun out of his jean jacket in an easy, fluid motion. The same gun he killed Isabel with, the gun I refused to hold. He points it at Jude's face, so close that she could put her lips around it and he may or may not be ready to shoot her. It doesn't really matter, does it? Because she takes it away from him in a flickering reflex, sudden and reptilian, and before I can make a sound she is on top of him, the gun in his eye and the shot is silenced, as if fired underwater. My hair and clothes are washed in his blood.

I fall out of the car, numb and nearly paralyzed by the rush of claustrophobia. I walk in circles, fumbling in my pockets for a cigarette. Henry's blood is in my mouth and I have to sit down.

He provoked her. He was begging for it. He shot her with an animal tranquilizer and he dumped her in the trunk of his car like a sack of fertilizer. He left her there to choke on dust for a few hours. He was rude to her. He hit her with an open hand and he all but offered her his gun.

Jude comes toward me, the sky crashing behind her and the gun in her left hand. She spreads her arms out wide and she looks pale and ghastly as a vampire.

I won't apologize, she says.

And I haven't asked you to.

I go back to the car and, like a robot, open the driver's door and shove at Henry with both hands to keep him from spilling onto the dirt road and he is so heavy, so warm, and for a moment I think I might collapse under his weight, that he will crush me like a drunken lover and now I hammer at his chest and shoulders with my fists until he falls sideways over the seat and I can slide in next to him and start the car, my foot sharing the gas pedal with his, and I drive as far up the road as I can and finally steer the giant car off the dirt and into a rocky, rainswept gully bounded by cherry trees that may just hide the car from the road and I kill the engine with a sigh, slipping from behind the wheel and without looking at Henry, I grab him by the armpits and struggle to pull him from the car but his foot is lodged somehow and my hands are soaked with sweat and blood and I am screaming, my head pounding when Jude wraps her arms around me from behind and holds me, holds me.

Minutes or hours later and I relax. She helps me pull Henry from the car and drag him through the dust to a piece of high ground. I am exhausted, destroyed. I sit beneath a deformed little tree and smoke cigarettes while she patiently, silently buries Henry under a mound of rocks that will keep the beasts from his remains, for a day or two.

thirty-six.

I WALK A DOZEN OR SO YARDS BEHIND HER. The only sound is my own rattling breath. Jude is shrinking, disappearing ahead.

In the woods, as before. My hands are unfamiliar. Carrion birds circle overhead and I wait for them to find Lucy. She floats still, on the lake, but I can't see her for the trees. I don't think I could bear to look at her ruined face. I am bleeding to death, starving and never happier. I pull strange plants from the earth and devour the roots. Lick and suck the dew from green leaves.

When I was a child, I believed there was a sun-god. My father told me never to look directly at it, that the sun would punish you.

Two kids spot me on the ninth day. I wave to them and shout hello, my voice dusty and strange. They run from me. Soon the state police arrive, with dogs. They find me easily, and surround me. They don't expect me to fight, to strangle one of their beautiful dogs. I cry over the dog and raise my hands. One of the cops is furious, however. He screams at me and puts a single bullet in my leg. They bind my hands and feet and place me in the back of a car. One of them takes pity on me, he pours water over my cracked and blistered face. I talk to them through the iron mesh, telling them that I killed my wife. But they don't believe me. They deny that a body has been found on the lake.

My feet drag like stones over dry yellow earth. I stumble and fall and dumbly notice that I'm clutching the green icebox. I can't let go of it. Jude stops to wait for me.

    I assume you have read *The Hobbit*?

    Are you kidding, I say. What about it?

    Gollum, she says. The wretched, stinking cave dweller.

    I smile at her. My precious, I say.

They take me to the station and drop me on the floor of a tiny cell, removing the chains from my feet. No one comes to question me. A silent doctor comes to examine my leg. He smells like stale smoke. There are murmurs through the walls. They have uncovered my identity. I'm a cop from the city, from Internal Affairs. I'm a vulture, a plague dog. They come into the cell and beat me with electrical cords, they laugh and smoke cigarettes. I lose count of days and nights and on a sunny morning I am placed on a special transport bus. I am taken back to the city without ceremony or comment. Lucy's body is found several days later, and my life comes apart like a love letter in the rain.

Jude is still up ahead, farther now. She's running from me.

They first thought it was murder. Lucy was shot twice and her body mutilated. After further examination, it was decided that the first bullet was self-inflicted. She was then shot once more, and mutilated sometime later. Apparently by her husband.

The end is near. I can't go much further. Jude waits for me in a patch of shade, her hands folded like scissors in her lap.

    You have been miles away, says Jude.

    I'm thinking of my wife, I say.

    What do you see?

    I hesitate.

In your mind, says Jude. Is she alive or dead?

She's asleep.

I don't believe you, says Jude.

Why should you? I say.

A butterfly flicks past my face. I try to follow its flight but my eyes are numb. My reflexes are gone. I take a breath and listen to my body. There is pain, abstract and gray. Infinite, barely noticed. There is euphoria, like the buzzing of a disconnected telephone. Drugs would have little effect on me now.

I wish I had known her, says Jude.

The butterfly returns and I smile with unfamiliar muscles.

Why, I say.

She shrugs. We might have been friends.

I don't think so.

Jude lights a cigarette.

Other women aren't safe from you, I say.

Jude doesn't blink. She disappears. She becomes the color of stone, of dust. Her tongue flicks at the air and I tell myself not to be sorry. I extend two fingers and she gives me the cigarette.

How did Lucy die? says Jude.

I take a long rotten breath and I see everything so clearly.

She shot herself with my gun and it was one of those freakish, terrible things. The bullet should have punched through her skull and into her brain but it didn't, it skated around her head like she was made of ice and tore off her left ear and she was shocked to be alive. The pain must have been incredible and she couldn't hold the gun. She asked me to finish her and I took the gun from her too slowly and I was afraid. I hesitated and by the time I could bring myself to shoot her she was already dead. I couldn't help her.

Jude is sorry, she's so sorry. But of course she is. Her heart would have to be made of sun-bleached bone to listen to that story and shrug.

I sat in the boat with Lucy for hours. Finally I shot her once in the face and swam away.

Do you smell something dreadful? says Jude.

I shrug. Cherry blossoms and cow manure.

Jude looks around. It smells of death, she says.

I walk a few feet from the road and find the body of a dead dog. He's a big puppy, a black mongrel. He was shot recently and dragged himself there. Maybe he was stealing somebody's chickens, maybe not. This is cattle country. A strange dog might be shot merely for stepping on somebody's land.

Let's keep moving, says Jude.

Wait a minute, I say.

I pull out my knife and bend over the dead dog, holding my breath. His body is soft and pliable, rigor mortis a mere memory. I roll him over onto his back; his paws are limp and I scratch as his chest briefly. Blackflies crawl listlessly through his fur, but he might be sleeping. I stroke his ears and tell myself he was a good dog. He was no thief. I slip the tanto into his belly, just above his genitals.

The smell is awful.

My eyes burn and I can barely see. I wipe at them furiously, then relax.

I look down at the poor dog's spilling bowels and tell myself I'm dissecting a frog in the ninth grade. I have gym class next period, and the new girl from Virginia has an ass like a peach. Her gym shorts are too little and when she sweats they tend to get caught up in her sweet little crack. She plucks them out so daintily, so carelessly that I fall in love with her every day.

Sink my hands into the dog's open belly, startled by the heat.

Push through the organs until I find a slippery, purplish lump of tissue the size of my fist. It could be liver or kidney or bladder, I can't be sure. But it doesn't matter and I cut it loose without difficulty. It seems so small, maybe three or four ounces. I hold it in the palm of my hand like a raw chicken breast, an aborted fetus.

I wrap it carefully in a shred of my shirt and tell Jude to hand me the icebox.

She gives me a long, shivering dark look. But she brings it to me.

I unlock it and throw the Blister's clothes onto the skeletal rosebush. They hang there like a vagrant's laundry. I place the small, bloody package in the icebox and close the lid.

How long have you known? she says.

Irrelevant, I say.

But you stayed with me.

The air swirls with dust. It's strange, because there is no wind at all.

Why? she says.

I've had three or four good chances to kill you.

And you had at least one chance to run.

Oh, I tried to run. I did. I was a wreck without you.

Jude gives a false laugh and drops Henry's gun in the dust. She removes the little stinger, the dentist's tool, from the slim waistband of her panties. I stare at it and she shrugs.

I lied, she says. When you asked if I had any weapons.

Of course you did.

She drops the stinger carelessly and stares at me.

Do you think you could kill me with your bare hands?

Yes, she says.

I do have one valuable kidney, safe in my belly.

So you keep telling me.

Isn't that why you brought me here?

For once she doesn't stare at my eyes. Her gaze drifts between my teeth and throat and I think she's preparing to kill me. The tanto is in my left hand, slick with the dog's blood. I shift it to my right hand and remember the last time I cut her. She was naked and she trusted me. I couldn't bear to cut her again. I pull the .38 from my ankle holster and lift it slowly, as if it weighs ten pounds. I aim at her chest, at the cool hollow between her breasts.

Maybe, she says. Maybe I thought I could still deliver you to Gore. But it was a bad risk. Then you threw yourself in my lap and you practically begged me to come here.

And you had two fucking tickets to El Paso.

You idiot, she says. I gave you my ticket and bought another one later.

I tell myself she's full of shit. She stinks of it. The other ticket was for Isabel. They were working some kind of switch on brother Jerome and it went bad somehow. I stare at her, trying to summon the laser red dot that will make her a faceless target. Her hair is damp and hangs to her shoulders in black twists. The skin beneath her sharp green eyes is swollen. Her mouth is a pale red slash. I wonder when she last slept.

She is unflinching.

When did you change your mind? I say. Or why.

Jude smiles. Irrelevant.

Oh, you're adorable.

Do you ever wonder what I did with it? she says. Your kidney.

I would rather daydream, I say.

I like that about you. She takes a step toward me.

And the heroin, I say. Do you wonder what I did with it?

Heroin, she says. I wouldn't be caught dead moving that shit.

I shrug and gaze up at the sun. Jude takes another step.

Listen, she says. When I found that wig in your bag I was jealous.

I see a thousand red dots. Jude takes the gun away from me. I don't resist and it slips from my fingers like a shared piece of fruit.

Listen to me, she says. I don't get jealous, ever.

I don't believe you.

She glances at my gun and smiles.

The safety is on, she says.

That's funny.

You might kiss me, she says.

I give her a quick, dry kiss on the side of her mouth. The kiss of a brother. My knees buckle and I crouch down beneath the sun, waiting for it to finish me. I don't look up. Jude gathers our weapons and helps me to my feet.

What now? she says.

I would love to kill somebody. But I'm so tired.

She grins. Luscious Gore lives just around the bend.

Maybe he could buy us dinner.

Okay, she says. It's okay.

The heat is unreal. I take off my expensive leather jacket, murmur an apology to Alexander and leave it in the sun.

The road twists and doubles back, intestinal. The little green icebox holds the vital organ of an anonymous dog. Again we rest. I take off my pants and sit on the ground, my thighs white and skeletal. Jude gives me a look and I tell her I might as well get a tan.

We walk side by side, now. Jude carries the icebox.

This will be putrid before dark, she says.

There's nowhere to buy ice in the desert, I say. Diamonds are easier to come by.

She looks at me oddly. What happened to that silly hat? she says. The one Henry gave you.

It's in my pocket.

Please put it on. Before you have a stroke.

A fork in the road and we are forced to choose. Jude says she doesn't remember a fork. I sit down and hold my head in my hands. Jude walks to the top of a rise and stares into the distance.

Haven't you been here before?

Never, she says.

I thought you were a secret agent.

She laughs.

The platypus, I say. Is that a duck or a fish?

Shut up.

Flip a fucking coin.

No, she says. I believe it's to the left.

Why? We haven't seen any tracks for miles.

Only because it's so dry and stony.

Why the left, though?

I just feel it, she says.

Water. A dirty, crippled little stream but it's beautiful. I drink cautiously, and I remember Henry's warning that he would kill me if I should throw up in his car. I laugh and cry and roll in the dust as if I'm simple. Jude squats on her haunches, wolflike and brown from the sun. Water glows like silver on her lips.

I'm worried about you, she says.

And I'm not sure what I expect to find. An armed compound, with impenetrable walls and watchtowers manned by lazy snipers. Electric fences and spotlights and Dobermans. A teardrop-shaped swimming pool, with a dozen unemployed actresses sunning themselves.

An hour before sunset and the apparent prize lies before us. A dozen stone buildings, sprawling in a broken circle. A small chapel and a crumbling bell tower. An ancient rock well. It looks like a monastery, deserted years ago. The monks long dead. One building is larger than the others. Several cars and trucks are parked in front. There is a short runway to the south, an airplane hangar and a landing pad for a helicopter. A few dogs sleep in the shade of a flatbed truck, but there are no humans about.

There are no guards, Jude says.

It doesn't matter, I say. We aren't going to sack the place.

Do you have a plan?

No. I'm going to walk up to the front door and knock.

Look at us, she says. Bloody as two thieves.

You look beautiful.

Together we sit down in a rare circle of grass to inventory our weapons. She has Henry's gun and the little stinger. She has a book of matches and a melted chocolate bar that she gives to me. I eat it and feel dizzy. She has nothing else. No identification, no money.

We don't need any money, she says.

It's true. I have three or four thousand dollars in my wallet, as useless as yesterday's newspaper. I have the .38 and six extra cartridges. The small silver pocketknife and the slim tanto. A dented pack of cigarettes and a lighter with no fluid. I have a ballpoint pen and a dog's kidney.

Jude says we should sleep for a few hours, and I agree.

I sink into the grass and close my eyes, wishing I were in a bathtub full of ice.

Her tongue drifts across my lips and her hand slips into my pants and squeezes my soft, sleeping penis. I open my eyes and Jude is bent over me. She takes off her shirt and I raise my mouth to her breasts but the black stone locket swings like a bitter, shrunken plum before my eyes and I reach for her throat.

I unbutton her pants and she lifts her pelvis slightly, to help me pull them down to her knees.

Her underpants are black and damp and I rip them off her.

Her teeth find my neck.

I have two fingers inside her and I whisper, is this how it was with Eve?

Her body shudders and I tell her I'm sorry I don't have a wooden spoon. Or a portable phone. But Jude is much stronger than me. She easily kicks herself free and I now sit in the dust, wearily wondering if I want to shoot her. I'm sure she would kill me first.

Phineas, she says.

Tell me the fucking truth, for once.

I was there, she says. I was looking for you. But I never touched that girl.

You destroyed her.

No, she says. The girl was sleeping when I got there, and she was sleeping when I left.

Her name is Eve, I say. And that locket was around her neck.

Then she must have taken it off before she got in the shower. Because I found it on the bathroom sink, curled up like a little spider.

thirty-seven.

IT'S DARK WHEN I AWAKE. Jude is sleeping silently on the stony ground. I look at her and I know she's a scorpion, a killer. But I want to believe her and if this is my undoing then I will smile and swallow the poison of my choice. My throat is sore and I'm tempted to walk back to the dirty little creek, but it's too far. I smoke one of my few remaining cigarettes and this numbs the pain. I poke Jude with my foot and she wakes with a shrug.

We walk down to the monastery, casually, as if we have come home. Perhaps we have.

I stop at the well and haul the bucket up for a drink. The water is sweet and cool. Jude doesn't want any, and I let the bucket fall. I approach the main building, Jude behind me. When we are twenty yards away, motion-sensitive lights wash over us. A dog begins to bark. The front door swings open, and the shadow of a woman waits to greet us.

Hello, I say. My name is Phineas Poe.

The woman has the ancient, silent air of an untouchable, an indentured servant. Her face is like eroded rock. She stares at me for a long moment, then pulls the door wide.

I want to see Mr. Gore.

She coughs. Mr. Gore is having his dinner, sir.

That's okay, says Jude.

She turns without another word and leads us through a dark, stony room where two black dogs sleep among weapons and umbrellas and expensive coats. Antique swords and longbows are mounted on one wall. There are several humped coatracks and countless pairs of shoes and dusty boots. A glass case holds hunting rifles and a few handguns. The woman walks slowly, her long brown skirt rustling with the sound of fallen leaves.

Jude nudges me. What are we doing here, Phineas?

I don't know. I really don't know.

Aren't you the least bit afraid? she says.

Of what?

Aren't you afraid that I might come at you with a knife, that I might cut you open again?

Not really. I don't think Gore has any more money.

Is that the only reason?

You warned me about getting misty with you.

The old woman takes us through another doorway, into a room that is lit with perhaps a hundred candles. The walls are lined with bookshelves and the furniture is leather, cracked and dusty. In the center of the room is an empty hospital bed, the sheets turned back. The bed faces a wide-screen television.

The boy is dead, Jude says. He didn't make it.

No, I say. The sheets would be stripped.

The woman leads us to the kitchen. It is brightly lit and warm. The table is set for dinner, with fine silver and china. On one side of the table is an upholstered wingback chair that must have been dragged in from the living room. A young man is curled in the chair, apparently asleep. He is wrapped in blue and yellow blankets, faded and worn thin. His skin is extraordinarily white, his hair long and fine and seemingly colorless. The boy is dreaming and his eyes flicker rapidly behind lids so thin they can hardly block out the light. He is impossibly skinny, and I wonder if he weighs more than ninety pounds. I wonder if my kidney would have done him any good, if he might have lived even six undeserved months. At the head of the table is a heavy, bald man in an electric wheelchair. His skin is dark and cracked as leather, his eyes naked and gray as oysters. One arm is shriveled and useless, a distended flipper, an evolutionary error. The other arm is grotesquely muscled.

Who is it? he says. Who's there?

Phineas Poe, I say. And this is Jude.

Do I know you?

No. I don't think so.

Jude says softly, we know your son.

I have two sons, he says.

Jerome, I say. We know Jerome.

He wheels around and stops before me and he is obviously not feeble. I hold out my hand and smile as he crushes it. He is clearly blind, but he seems to smell me or operate by sonar. I wonder if he sleeps upside down. Gore smiles, and his teeth are shaped unlike any human teeth I have ever seen. They glitter like bits of glass and small sharp stones on the beach. If I waved my hand before his face, like a child fascinated by the blind man, I think I would lose a finger.

He is gentle with Jude's hand, which amuses me.

I'm sorry, he says. Jerome is not here. He's gone on a long business trip and I don't know when he will return. To be true, I had hoped he would be home by now.

His eyes are like sundials. They don't waver. I am uncomfortable, standing over him. He relaxes his gaze and points at the table.

Please, he says. Sit down. You must be tired.

I clear my throat. I have a small gift for you, Mr. Gore.

Jude glances at the icebox, then at me. Her eyes are bright with disgust.

How kind, says Gore. And please, call me Luscious.

He sniffs the air as I remove the dog's kidney, still wrapped in my shirt. I lay it gently on his plate, and watch as he slowly unwraps it with one hand. The kidney is surely putrid, alive with maggots, but it might as well be a box of chocolates. His expression doesn't change. I wildly remind myself that he's blind, he's blind. And he doesn't know who the hell I am.

I'm afraid I don't understand, says Gore.

And I have made a terrible mistake, I say. This was meant for Jerome.

I put the plate down on the floor, whistling softly. The two black dogs appear and quickly eat the organ of their cousin, growling at each other. The shame surges through me like a forgotten bodily fluid.

Will you please join us for supper? says Luscious.

I stand over the dogs like a mummy, fascinated by the simplicity of this transaction. I imagine the flesh of rabbits and mice that passed through the dead dog, the worms that burrowed through his corpse and into the earth. I see the blackflies that picked through his fur and wonder if the eggs they left behind have hatched. Soon the two black dogs lick the plate clean and wander away. Jude grabs at my sleeve and whispers for me to sit down. Luscious rings a silver bell, and now the old woman appears to serve us a simple meal. She places a loaf of fresh bread in the center of the table, with a brick of yellow cheese and a knife. She brings us each a steaming bowl of stew and a plate of rice and fruit.

Jude leans close to me. You're a freak.

I wonder, says Luscious. Would you mind not whispering? It makes me anxious.

Jude flushes and I don't think I've ever seen her embarrassed.

I'm so sorry, she says.

Oh, he says. It's all right.

Jude looks away, her eyes drifting over the stone walls.

I love the house, she says.

Thank you. It's fallen into disrepair, I'm afraid.

Was it ever a monastery? she says.

Yes, he says. Two hundred years ago, when this was Mexican territory. A rather eccentric order of Franciscan monks.

How were they eccentric? she says.

They took the Eucharist quite literally.

What does that mean, she says. They were cannibals?

I like to think so, he says. But the order died off abruptly, in 1809. A yellow fever epidemic, mass suicide. There were numerous stories. Most of their records were destroyed by looters.

Perfect, says Jude.

The hunger in me is stunning. I eat for several minutes without pause, and I feel the blood respond in my starved limbs. Jude picks moodily at her food.

I'm not sure how long the boy has been awake, but I feel his eyes on me like arthritic hands. I turn to look at him. His eyes are such a dark brown they seem bottomless in his white face. He has the thin, curved lips of a young girl, and his fine cheekbones are sharp, too sharp. I glance at Jude and she frowns, as if to say yes, he's painfully beautiful.

Strangers, he says. What a treat.

His voice is a scratched whisper, cold and curiously threatening.

Horatio, says Luscious. How do you feel, boy?

Better, he says.

Would you like a drop of wine? says Luscious.

Please introduce me to our guests.

I extend my hand. Phineas, I say. And my wife, Jude.

Jude sinks her fingernails lightly into my thigh.

Hello, she says.

They are your brother's friends, says Luscious.

Horatio smiles. Somehow, I don't think so.

What do you mean, boy?

I just have a feeling, he says.

Our clothes are bloody, of course. And our faces.

Horatio shakes his head as if he can hear my thoughts. Jerome likes to be surrounded by people who are afraid of him, he says.

Hush, boy.

Oh, but it's true.

Jerome has countless flaws, says Luscious. But they are not for you to number.

Fingers crawl my legs like a gang of insects and I know that Jude is restless.

Does anyone have a cigarette? says Horatio.

I hesitate, then extract my nearly crushed box of cigarettes. There are seven left. I place one between his lips and light a match for him. His skin is smooth and pink in the glow and I have a sudden uncomfortable desire to see his chest, his torso. To see if it is the color of marble, if it looks wet.

My son is ill, says Luscious.

Isn't it obvious? the boy says.

I light a cigarette to share with Jude.

What's wrong with you? she says.

Horatio smiles, a brief flicker.

I suppose my most immediate problem is that my kidneys are failing and I will soon be unable to process my own waste. He laughs. I have a problem with sewage.

Luscious sighs. You were always nasty, even as a child.

I'm sorry, he says. I just think it's funny.

How old are you? I say.

Seventeen, he says.

One of the best years.

I thought so, he says.

Of course, high school is unpleasant.

Luscious waves his good hand and Jude watches it like a diving moth.

He isn't in high school, says Luscious. He finished last year.

Good for you, says Jude.

Horatio sneers. I'm going to Stanford, in the fall.

The serving woman drifts through unseen, clearing away the dishes.

Hetty, says Luscious. We will have coffee, please. And perhaps cake.

Horatio lounges in his chair, withered and delicate in his blankets. The cigarette I gave him has shrunk to a nub, and there are ashes scattered on his chest like dirty snowflakes. He closes his eyes and Hetty leans over him to pluck the butt gently from his mouth and for a moment I think she will breathe into his mouth the way animals pass predigested foods from their mouths to the mouths of their feeble young.

thirty-eight.

WHEN I WAS A SMALL CHILD, says Horatio. My father took the three of us to Rome. It was one of the few times we did anything as a family, a normal family.

It was soon after your mother passed, says Gore.

It was September and gray and one day we had breakfast in a little plaza near the Colosseum. There were a thousand pigeons flapping about, pecking for crumbs you know. They were fearless, and they would take bread from your hand if you sat very still.

They were vicious beasts, says Gore.

Horatio ignores him. There was a photographer there, and he offered to take our family portrait with the birds. Don't you remember, Father? The photo used to hang in the guest bathroom.

I remember, says Luscious. I remember well.

Anyway, says Horatio. My brother and sister were older than me and they had no trouble coaxing the wild pigeons to eat from their hands. And in the photo they each have birds on their outstretched fingers, the wings a mad blur. My father, too. But I was so young, so impatient that the photographer had to place a tame pigeon, a pet bird, on my left arm. And it sat there as if it were nailed there, as if it were stuffed. In the photo, my bird appears to be dead, and every time I look at it I think I am cursed.

That's ridiculous, says Luscious. It's morbid and adolescent.

Hetty returns, pushing a little table on wheels. Her arms tremble as she silently serves around coffee in small white cups. I am tempted to ask if she needs any help, but I'm sure that Luscious would frown on it. She places cream and sugar in the center of the table, then gives us each a slice of black bundt cake.

I'm curious, says Jude. If your kidneys are failing, shouldn't you be hooked up to a machine?

I like you, says Horatio.

She smiles, eerily flirting.

But yes, he says. The dreaded machine. I'm shackled to it for hours at a time. Maybe you would like to watch television with me later, if you can stand it.

I would be happy to, she says.

The machine has seen its last days, says Luscious. He takes a bite of cake and his sharp teeth flash. Jerome is arranging for the purchase of a replacement kidney, as we speak.

That's fantastic, I say.

Jude claws at my leg.

It's a waste of money, says Horatio. And I doubt he will ever come back.

Why do you say such a thing? says Luscious. Why can you not be silent? He bites his words and the veins rise in his blackened face.

Father, he says. Jerome is a plunger. He's a hyena. He will take the money you gave him and run like the wind.

Perhaps, says Luscious. If I had sent him to buy a car, yes. But this is different.

Horatio mutters. And why do you suppose Isabel has disappeared?

Damn your eyes, says Luscious. You wretched boy.

Jude had finished her cake and now begins to eat mine, which I have barely touched.

I am feeling suddenly weak, says Horatio.

Let me ring for Hetty, says Luscious. His voice becomes so gentle.

Jude grips my right hand and whispers for me to relax. She's crushing my fingers and I love her strength. But there is something sharp poking through my shirt, like a needle or tooth. I look down and she is pressing her sharp little dentist's tool into the narrow space between my second and third rib. I glance into her pretty green eyes and I recognize her, I do.

Excuse me, she says.

Luscious Gore turns his dead eyes toward her.

If I offered to give you a kidney, what would you say?

Are you joking, girl?

I cough. She has almost no sense of humor.

Hypothetical, she says.

There would be a question of compatibility, he says. My son has a rare blood type.

Jude shrugs. This is make-believe.

Then I would say thank you, if it were a gift.

And if it wasn't. If it was expensive? she says.

Then I would be the man dying of thirst in a lifeboat, he says. He blows imaginary dust from his fingers and smiles crookedly. Because I have no money left.

Horatio spits. Excellent metaphor, Dad. But wouldn't I be the one in the lifeboat?

The old man turns slightly green.

My apologies, says Jude. I was only curious.

Silence.

Jude blows into my ear and I remember to breathe. She slips the stinger into my pocket and places her slender, empty hands alongside her plate. The palms turned upward in a sweet, meaningless gesture. She is sure she can kill me with her bare hands.

I'm actually aroused, I mutter.

Don't go to sleep on me, she says softly.

Whispers, says Gore. I hear whispers.

I wonder, says Horatio. Would one of you mind helping me to my bed.

You are so trusting, says Jude.

Should we not trust you? says Gore.

I want to help you, I say. I want to be trusted. But my muscles fail me.

The table is two miles wide and the sun is shrinking in a blue sky. The boat drifts and everyone is staring at me.

Jude pushes back her chair. Let me do it, she says.

Thank you. I am so tired of Hetty's cold hands. Horatio smiles, his lips thin as paper.

Jude wipes her mouth and I watch silently as she lifts Horatio from his chair as if he's made of straw. His arm swings free and it's so thin it doesn't look human. Lucy was never that skinny. Even on her worse days.

I try not to stare at Luscious Gore. I'm sure that he can sense it, that he can reverse my thoughts and send them back at me, twisted and viral. He has loomed so long at the edge of my consciousness, hideous and bloated and vaguely imagined as my own private Jabba the Hutt. I expected to hate and fear him at once. He set the machine in motion that summoned me here and he doesn't even recognize me. He doesn't know me. He released Isabel and Jerome into the world like chaotic birds of prey and they fell on me purely by accident.

I have heard stories about you, I say.

He makes a wet sound in his throat, an approximate laugh.

The truth pales, doesn't it?

He sighs and pushes aside his plate.

I must be off to bed, he says. Hetty will show you the guest quarters.

What century is this? I say.

He peers at me.

Do you offer a bed to every unwashed stranger that turns up on your doorstep?

He laughs softly. It is irregular. We don't often have visitors, here. But you are hardly a stranger.

Do you know me?

No, he says. But you are Jerome's friend. You told me so.

This staggers me.

Besides, he says. I have nothing left to steal, and death already lives in my home.

I feel slightly unhinged and I can't decide if I would rather punish this man for his faith, or prove myself worthy of it. I wish Jude would come back. Luscious rings the silver bell. He waits a moment, then rings it again.

Oh, bother.

What's the matter?

Hetty has gotten so deaf, he says. And the battery is rather low in my chair.

May I help somehow?

If you could give me push, he says. That would be tremendous.

No problem.

The main hall is silent and shadowy, a few gas lamps flickering. I push the heavy chair along a thick burgundy carpet. Luscious is nodding, half asleep. He points to a door on the right. I stop and wait as he pushes a button and the door swings open. His room is dark and cold. Soft electric lights come on automatically as we enter. The room is minimally furnished. There is a huge bed with numerous pillows, a chest of drawers, a dressing table and mirror, a sink and toilet with handicap rails. Everything is very low to the floor. There is a lot of scattered artwork: dozens, possibly a hundred charcoal drawings of the crucifixion on yellowed paper and three abstract iron sculptures of Christ on the cross, dying alongside two anonymous thieves.

Well, then. Good night, I say.

Just a moment, he says. If you could just help me from my chair, and onto the bed. I am feeling terribly weak. It will only take a moment.

Yes. Of course, I say.

It's awkward, but I lift him from the chair in a fireman's embrace. His legs are weightless, barely there. His pants are soaking wet. I lay him down on the bed and stand up.

Your pants are wet, I say.

So they are. I suppose I lost control of my bladder, over coffee. It gets more difficult every day. We shall have to change them, won't we?

I can only nod and smile, a thin bloodless smile.

Thank you, he says.

It's nothing, I say. Really.

Luscious manages to unbutton the pants himself, but getting them off is
another thing. I kneel on the bed and peel them off him like the loose skin
of a banana. His legs are rather shocking. They are not legs at all, but the
boneless, unformed tentacles of some sea creature. They are blue and gray
and hairless. I glance away and take a small breath. His penis appears
normal and is quite large.

There is a long silence.

I understand, says Luscious. That masturbation can be a man's single
greatest pleasure.

My mind spins weightlessly. Oh, I say. It is a reliable source.

He lifts his head to gaze forlornly in the direction of his own awesome
appendage. I can manipulate it and ejaculate with some success, he says.
But I can't feel anything. I cannot even see it.

I stand over him and try to think of something, anything to say. I'm
not unsympathetic.

It's lonely in this house, isn't it?

Terribly so.

The room is shrinking and I stand there nodding like a puppet.

I will just run along now, I say. If there's nothing else.

But I do need a diaper, he says. Isn't that a thing of poetry? A man like
myself, of wealth and power. To sleep in a diaper.

I thought your money was gone.

He gives a dry chuckle. Quite right.

Where are the diapers? The sweat slides down my back.

They are beneath the bed, he says.

I crouch and pull out one adult diaper. With a little difficulty and
coaching from Luscious, I wrestle him into the thing and fasten the sticky
tape. I only pray that he doesn't ask me to powder his bottom. As I lean
across him to adjust the tape he whispers in my ear.

My son is dying, he says. He's dying very badly.

I shake my head. What is a good death?

It isn't comedy, says Gore.

Haven't you read Shakespeare?

Gore smiles. *Othello* is rather funny, I suppose.

I sit reluctantly at the edge of his bed.

What happened to your family? I say.

He frowns. How do you mean?

This house, I say. It's like a crushed skull.

It's gloomy when my daughter is away.

She isn't coming back, I say.

Gore sucks at his teeth. What?

Trust me.

How do you know?

It's just a feeling.

Isabel will be back, says Gore. She adores Horatio.

There is a long, widening silence. Lucy and Isabel slither around in my head, sleeping restlessly and twined together as if their arms and legs were one. I stare at the dull black crucifix over Gore's bed and I wonder if he has any funny ideas about the nature of his own firstborn son.

What about Jerome?

My pride, he says.

But he's flawed.

He has fears, says Gore. The same as you.

I laugh softly. Jerome is not like me.

But you are friends, are you not?

Again, silence. I feel vaguely unclean.

How did Jerome burn his hands? I say.

Gore licks his lips with a long gray tongue. He breathes.

When you were a child, he says. Did you ever play with fire?

Of course.

I used to collect cars, he says. The most beautiful cars. I had five vintage Corvettes and several old Thunderbirds. A red Cadillac convertible from 1965. They were like a ring of jewels around my house, glowing the sun. My wife was still alive, then. There were rosebushes everywhere, red and white. Three lovely children and I had more money than God. I bought cars that I never intended to drive. The boys often played in them.

Jerome called the Cadillac his castle.

American cars, I say. Henry would approve.

Thirteen years ago, says Gore. Thanksgiving Day and the sun was shining. I was asleep in my chair. A football game on the television with the sound off and I woke to hear screaming. Horatio was playing in the Cadillac when it caught fire. He was three, perhaps four. Jerome saved him.

Was the boy hurt?

His hair was barely singed.

But Jerome's hands were ruined, I say.

Terrible third-degree burns, says Gore. From the tips of his fingers to his wrists.

He set the fire, I say. He had gasoline on his hands.

Perhaps, says Gore. I choose not to think so.

He wants the boy to die.

It doesn't matter what he wants. The boy is dying nonetheless.

I turn and walk away as he wriggles under the sheets like a snake. The lights dim as I leave the room, and the door closes with a whisper behind me.

thirty-nine.

I HURRY DOWN THE NARROW HALLWAY and the carpet is so soft I can't hear my own footsteps and I'm sure that I will soon turn a corner and wander into a labyrinth. That I will be lost for days and when I find my way to the surface and into the sun, I will have clawed out my hair and Jude will have vanished. She will have left me.

Back through the kitchen.

Hetty has not yet cleared away the coffee and cake. I stop and pour myself a cup of the cold coffee and drink it quickly. My hands are not shaking, and I don't think I'm seeing things.

Maybe I'm through the worst of it. Maybe not.

If Jude offers to shoot me up again, I might rip my skin open looking for a vein.

The library still flickers with candlelight. The wide-screen television is on, low and murmuring. A commercial gives way to an old episode of *Star Trek,* and the color is very bad. Mr. Spock's face is green, his shirt gray. Horatio is a fetal lump on the hospital bed, white as an egg but for the black cord that extends from him and hangs limply between the bed and a humming machine.

Jude sits in a stuffed chair, a book open on her lap. It's too dark to read, however. She stares blankly at Horatio, at me. I sit on the arm of her chair and we simply hold hands. As if we are home for the holidays and after a day of spooky relatives we are finally alone.

I liked your little puppet show, I say.

Jude exhales. You weren't afraid I would gut you at the dinner table?

Not really.

Trust, she says.

A wasp crawls along your arm, I say. And you sit perfectly still, telling yourself that he won't sting you unless you flinch, unless you try to kill him. You hold your breath and hope he won't sting you and probably he doesn't want to. But that's not trust, is it. It's fear and fascination.

I want to get out of here, she says.

I'm not stopping you.

She frowns. I want you to come with me.

Not yet. My voice is cracking.

What's wrong with you? she says.

I feel sick.

You owe these people nothing, she says. Nothing.

This kid wanted to borrow life from me.

Jude laughs. You're a stranger, she says. You are no one to him.

I'm the stranger.

The fragile new scar around my torso feels so cold, as if it's blue with electricity. I clutch at the skin of my stomach and stare at the television without really seeing it. The candles stink of eucalyptus but surely that's my imagination. Jude puts her arms around me. She touches my face and I shiver from the cold. I take her ring finger between my lips and suck at it like an anxious child. She smiles and strokes the edge of my teeth.

The kid is beautiful, isn't he?

You shouldn't confuse sympathy with desire, she says.

I can't help it.

Jude doesn't smile. She wonders what will become of us. In my adolescent daydreams I see us walking back to the highway in a cool rain. Jude steals a car and we disappear into Mexico. The sky is always blue and we have sex three times a day. In a month or so we run out of money and we get bored with sex. Jude suggests a simple bank robbery. But something goes wrong and one of us is killed, probably me. Jude will mourn for two short weeks, then flee to Paris and become a very expensive assassin. I shrug and light another cigarette. There are four left, and I tell myself to leave at least two of them for the boy.

I want to leave in the morning, she says.
 Okay.
 Will we leave together?
 I don't know. Will we?
 Probably not, she says. Then laughs at my expression.
 The shadows are stretching around us as the candles burn down to nothing. Jude's face is now completely in the dark and she easily sinks into it. She's happier not being seen.
 This kid. He breaks your heart, doesn't he?
 No, she says. But he surprises me.
 He's unafraid.
 She smiles. And he makes me laugh.
 You never laugh.
 Anyway, she says. Your kidney would have been wasted on him.
 What do you mean?
 He wants to die, says Jude.

Horatio is still asleep. The light that flickers around him is from the television. I wonder if he's even breathing, if he's slipping away, unnoticed.

This is a good episode, I say.
 I move over to the television and it takes me about five minutes of muttering and fumbling to find the volume control. I tell Jude how Captain Kirk and the lads find this orphaned kid named Charlie on a wrecked ship and he seems like a good kid. He's nervous and shy and anxious to please and he follows everyone around like a cowardly dog but really he's a time bomb. He's tangled up in puberty and flooded with terrifying desires and he's surrounded by women in very short skirts and leather

knee boots. And he also happens to have telekinetic powers that he can't control and in one scene that I can never forget he zaps an anonymous female ensign who has spurned him and she sinks cut in half and rising out of the floor.

I never watch this show, says Jude.

Don't tell me that.

She laughs. I prefer the new one.

Jesus, I say. What is it about that bald Frenchman?

His voice is sexy. And he has a strong nose, like a hawk.

The nose, I say. What do you want with his damn nostrils?

I could think of something, she says.

Horatio mutters, I'm awake. I'm awake.

I remember the boys Lucy used to bring home. They were like pets. She petted them and dressed them up and adored them. She would have eaten this kid alive.

Do you have a girlfriend, I say. A boyfriend?

Horatio stares at me.

What is your favorite sport?

Hush, says Jude.

What will you be when you grow up?

Horatio laughs suddenly, and I think he forgives me.

Jude props several pillows behind the boy's head and gently pulls him to a sitting position. I barely recognize her. She offers him a drink of water and he swallows a few drops. He begs for a cigarette and I light one for him, holding it to his lips each time he has a puff, so the ashes won't fall in his bed.

I have AIDS, he says. Two new kidneys wouldn't save me.

He shrugs and I bite my lip to stop myself from saying, yes, I know.

Jude frowns and I wonder if she would have performed the transplant, if things had gone differently. She could have easily cut herself when her hands were inside him.

It wasn't even sex, says Horatio. I was born with the virus.

I stare at him, stupidly.

My mother gave it to me. He smiles. But she didn't have the same luxury of dying from it.

Jude strokes his pale, waxy hair from his forehead.

Gore isn't your father, she says.

Oh, says Horatio. He claims to be.

Interesting, she says.

But my birth unveiled a thing or two and my mother was dead by my fourth birthday.

Don't tell me she killed herself, I say. Don't.

The cause of death was unclear, he says. He licks his teeth and for a moment I see shadows of his father in him. I wonder if he sees it. The doctors couldn't agree, he says. It was either drowning or a heart attack or a blow to the head. Or it was all three. She was found at the bottom of the swimming pool.

What was she wearing? says Jude.

Horatio looks surprised. Her pajamas.

Murder, she says.

Horatio shrugs. She was dead and my father's little empire began to fall apart. My brother was a pyromaniac. He wet the bed. He tortured animals. My sister protected me like her own child, but she was out of her mind. She was a slut.

Jude smiles dreamily. She had sex with the gardener, she says. With the stable boy. She had three abortions by the time she was sixteen and her womb was ruined.

I know, says Horatio. Childhood trauma is such a bore. It's such television.

But was it a bore when you were six?

No, he says. It was awful.

It's fucking biblical, I say. To be an infant afflicted with HIV.

I do like boys, says Horatio. I just rarely have the opportunity to get out of the house.

Have you never had sex? says Jude.

Once, he says. My sister took me into Dallas. I had a brief and not so horrible encounter with a male prostitute. He wasn't gay, of course. And he was only a year older than me. I told him that I was sick and he said it would cost twice as much, that we would use two condoms. He fucked me in the back of my father's car while Isabel drove in endless circles.

I shudder, thinking of Isabel. Dead in a bathtub, with holes in her feet.

Jude has nothing to say and I wonder if she's in the desert with Felix, the stuttering virgin. He stares at the punishing sun until she has to kill him for a mouthful of water.

My father loves me, says Horatio. I repulse him, but he does. He gave the very last of his money to my brother and packed him off to Colorado to purchase a stolen kidney. I told him to send Isabel, but he said some things are better left to men.

Jude closes one eye. As if she's glaring down a rifle sight.

What a mess, I say. What a fucking mess this is.

I'm used to it, says Horatio.

Still, she says. I think I would like to kill your brother.

He won't come back. He's on a beach somewhere, and the money is nearly gone. He's posing as a race car driver, a retired navy pilot. He's borrowing money from women and children. He's telling outrageous stories, like a monkey performing for free drinks.

Horatio is shrinking. His voice is disappearing. I can barely hear him. He is so quiet, so still. He could be a child that is holding his breath and floating facedown in dark water. He could be pretending to be dead. He could be dreaming of his former, unborn self.

I want to ask you something, he says.

Anything, I say.

I offer him the cigarette and he sucks at it, his lips touching my fingers. He's going to ask me to kill him, to put him to sleep forever. I'm weirdly calm, amazed that he would choose me rather than Jude. I'm happy and shivering and I can kill him as easily as I breathe. I will stare at him until his eyes become Lucy's and I won't hesitate, I won't weaken.

I want to kill him.

Would you kiss me? he says. I haven't been kissed in an age.

Jude laughs, nervously.

I flick off the television and she walks barefoot through the library, humming like a girl. I think she's looking for something to read and I'm curious to see if she will choose poetry or religion. But she merely blows out the drowning candles and I can see the night unfolding before us. The two of us will sit beside his bed without speaking until the sun creeps in and turns everything to ash. Horatio will not wake again, and he won't die.

My face is still marked with Henry's blood and I bend over this boy as if I'm taking a drink from a fountain in the park. I brush his nearly dead lips and they are dry as the back of my hand. His tongue barely touches mine and pulls away like a thief and oh Lucy if you had only asked me for this.

penny dreadful

—Why was the host (victim predestined) sad?
—He wished that a tale of a deed should be told of a deed not by
him should by him not be told.

    —Ulysses, James Joyce

I AM NEAR THE END NOW *and this notebook is falling apart in my hands. Damp, becoming pulp. The pages are swollen together and the ink bleeds. The ink disappears and I am not what I appear to be. I wanted to make that clear from the first, from the beginning. But failed, somehow. I tell myself that nothing has vanished, nothing is lost. The lies are chronological, evolutionary.*

The dead are watching, listening. I wonder what they know.

The thing is that my consciousness drifts and I have forgotten exactly what I look like. I pass my reflection in a blackened window and I may not recognize myself. My reflection is now perceived as a threat, an ugly twin. My reflection is a dark nonperson, a stranger on the street and this is not an identity crisis as I understand the phrase.

Dear Jude. The mutilation of self is normal.

But this is not a suicide note and I don't want you to feel sorry for me. There's no point in that. It has always been in my nature to stare at the sun, to step out into traffic. I am an unlikely suicide but I did want to get a good close look at death, to touch his matted hair and pass him by.

You should know that I am an alien, a stranger. I may ask you for a cigarette, for the time, for spare change. I may suddenly push you down an alley and steal your wallet, cut out your tongue. I may stop you from choking to death on a fishbone and I may have more than one name.

Did you know that your eyes tend to change colors. They slip from yellow to gray and blue and the change is irrelevant to mood, to disposition. The names are something like that. Phineas Poe. Ray Fine. Fred.

I wasn't thinking clearly when I came back to Denver. I followed myself back to Eve's place because I believed I would be safe there. I was equipped only with the small brain of a bird, the heart and bone structure of a chicken. I was a stupid chicken.

I was not quite self-aware.

The strangers in me are easily distracted. They are daydreamers, romantics. And therefore unreliable. They are often drunk and they don't always look out for each other. They pretend not to notice things. It always comes back to this business of drifting and I don't mean the way clouds drift. The way shadows drift behind the sun. It's a geological thing, a tectonic shift. The drift is not so easily noticed, but the impact tends to be profound.

Open your eyes, boy. Your eyes. Open your eyes and no more turn aside and brood.

— from a small blue notebook found on a Denver city bus, apparently the diary of Phineas Poe. This was the final entry.

Thursday

Goo:

The Trembler was young and fair, with red hair and stupid blue eyes and the pale furry limbs of a spider monkey. And shameless. The girl had no shame. She clung to Chrome as if grafted to his hip. Goo rolled her eyes and followed them down a road white with mist. Chrome was her boyfriend, technically. She liked to sleep with him. But she rarely hunted with him. It wasn't her bag. Goo was not a Mariner, and she didn't share his bottomless black hunger for tongue. Nor did she like to watch him go down on others, which Chrome very well knew.

They had found the Trembler under the 17th Street Bridge, crouched near a sewer opening. Alone and mute. She had obviously become separated from her little tribe, her pocket of the game. And when Chrome and Goo had come upon her she had pathetically tried to tremble them, which only made Goo more tired and grumpy.

Chrome, though. He had been unpleasantly cheerful all evening and apparently found the Trembler amusing so he had scooped her up like an injured sparrow. He had muttered something to Goo about having a delicious threesome, a sickening idea. Goo wished he would just take the girl's tongue quickly and cleanly and deposit her in an abandoned car, or behind a trash barrel.

But she could see that he was in no mood for the efficient kill.

The Trembler could be no more than sixteen, thought Goo. She was a newborn, barely an apprentice. Fashionably unclean, barbaric. The girl was dressed as some sort of prehistoric cave dweller, wearing a baby-doll dress of raw suede and no shoes. Her legs were unshaven and she smelled.

Goo spat in disgust. She was an Exquisitor and was therefore expected to be a bit more elegant. She wore brown leather trousers, clean. She wore polished black motorcycle boots and a vest of fine silver chain mail. And Chrome, being a hunter, wore only black. Black jeans tirelessly reconstructed with black tape and rubber patches. Boots that laced up to the knee and a black T-shirt with the sleeves cut off. His head was shaved to black stubble.

Goo watched him drag the unprotesting Trembler along by the elbow, his fingers no doubt raising bruises in her flesh and from a distance he looked just like a boy who had found a lost kitten and was taking it back to his tree house to feed it milk and tuna or possibly cut off its feet and now Goo quickened her step and came up alongside him.

I'm going home, she said.

Nonsense.

I am, she said. I'm gone.

Chrome stopped, flicked his wrist and the Trembler stood upright, quivering.

Have you ever seen such a waif? he said. La jeune fille, exquis.

Yes, said Goo. The girl is exquisite. But I'm bored. I'm hungry and I'm tired and I'm going home.

The girl stared at them, unblinking. She was a wetbrain, thought Goo. She was a ninety-eight-pound victim of the Pale. Chrome growled, impatient.

Come, he said. There's a market ahead. I will buy you a loaf of bread.

They turned down the next street and Goo flinched at the web of bright lights. She didn't like the bright. It reminded her of day. But Chrome did not even look to see if she was following. He merely flowed down the sidewalk, as if he were made of water. The Trembler trailed behind, a balloon on a string, forgotten.

It was near dawn.

Maybe four or five in the morning. Traces of yellow and pink in the sky, like fine hairs. Which made it Thursday. There was a twenty-four-hour Safeway up ahead and Goo sighed. She could get a bite to eat and perhaps distract Chrome from the Trembler. Not that she was sorry for the girl, not in the least. Goo wasn't interested in the girl's fate, near or far. She was tired and she simply didn't want to watch Chrome eat a stranger's tongue.

Through hissing doors into terrible white light. Goo squinted, covered her face.

Chrome grinned, mocking. Le soleil cruel.

Goo hated him. His French was terrible.

But the store was empty, a morgue. She didn't want to flounder alone under the man-made light and so she followed them down a row of canned vegetables, her eyes focused dully on the Trembler's slender but dirty and needle-scarred legs.

The dairy section.

I thought we were buying bread, said Goo.

Chrome shrugged. He opened a glass door and withdrew a brick of Monterey Jack, which he thrust at the Trembler. Hold this between your knees, he said.

The Trembler blinked and Chrome shoved her up against the open door. He bit at her lips until blood ran to her chin and she opened her mouth.

The cheese hit the floor.

Chrome sucked at the girl's dirty face and Goo closed her eyes. She felt sick and reached for something to grab onto, pulling down a row of creamed corn. The dull clatter of heavy metal and she opened her eyes to see the Trembler fall to the black-and-white tile floor as if she were made of lead.

Blood gurgling from her mouth, too much blood.

What did you do? said Goo.

Chrome looked at her, puzzled. I took her tongue.

All of it?

He spat, and something flew from his mouth like a broken tooth.

Nah, he said. The tip is all.

Isn't that a little too much blood? said Goo.

Chrome winked at her, pulling a bit of stained plastic from his teeth.

Blood packet, he said. An ordinary theater prop.

Oh, said Goo.

The Trembler stood up, brushing herself off and smiling meekly. The red ran from her mouth, real and false. Goo wanted to gag but Chrome was watching. He was always watching her. She shrugged and turned to go, as if bored.

I STEPPED OFF THE GREYHOUND FROM WEST TEXAS and looked around at a world shimmering with exhaust and dead air. Denver, unrecognizable. My mouth was full of fucking dust and I was home. Broken glass scattered on a parking lot of black tar.

Dull sunlight.

I stood for a few minutes with the other passengers, waiting stupidly for my luggage. I had no luggage. I had nothing much in my pockets. Two or three cigarettes and a book of matches. Stub of pencil and a useless hotel room key. One dollar and an assortment of coins, most of them pesos. One bright blue pebble that I had picked up on a sidewalk in the French Quarter because I thought it might be lucky. A mysterious coupon for cold medicine. I couldn't remember when I last had a cold.

I started walking and found myself counting my steps. Twenty-seven to the sidewalk, fifty-one to the corner. I needed to focus on something. I needed to find a phone booth and figure out where I was going.

Eve, I thought. I would go see Eve, maybe.

Little help, said a voice.

I looked down, surprised. A hunchbacked homeless man with a bloody nose and no hair squatted against a brick wall. I was nearly standing on his foot. There was a dog beside him, a pale arthritic mutt with a choke chain around its neck. The man worried the end of the chain between his fingers and stared up at me with hope in his eyes.

What do you need? I said.

The man began to cough and I patted my pockets, thinking I could either give him one of my three cigarettes or a handful of Mexican coins.

Lost, said the man. He spoke with a strange lisp.

I looked around. This is 19th Street.

You sure, he said.

Where are you going? I said.

Don't even know my fucking name, said the man.

I stared at him. I know that feeling.

Comfortably numb, he said.

Yeah.

I crouched down, careful not to get too close to the dog. Pulled out my sad pack of cigarettes and found there were only two. I gave him one, and he poked it between blood-stained lips. I lit a match and held it for him. He thanked me and I shook my head. There was only a fine line between us. The guy was younger than he looked, maybe twenty-nine. His finger-nails were clean. His dog wasn't starving and I decided they were newly homeless.

Everything slips, he said. Everything slips away. I had a house and a car and they turned to fucking dust. Disappeared before my eyes.

I shrugged. Life is nasty and it seemed pointless to say so.

The stretch of silence and my knees began to ache. I couldn't help the guy. That cigarette was all I had. The sun slithered out from behind heavy clouds and the man whimpered at the sight. I stood up, dizzy.

Hey, said the man.

I turned. The dog lifted its head now and for a moment was not a dog at all. It looked like some kind of hideous bird.

What? I said.

The man opened his mouth and now I thought he would act like a proper homeless man and ask me for money, or at least offer me a crumb of wisdom. But then his nose started to bleed again and he said nothing at all.

Eve:

She wasn't sure what day it was, Thursday perhaps. Early morning. The sky was a web of gray and blue, as if it might rain even while the sun stared down. The day was otherwise unremarkable until Phineas appeared on her doorstep after thirteen months, his eyes narrow with apologies. He was asleep on his feet. He was dirty and stinking and still he didn't look so bad. The shadows and starvation were gone from his face. There was new muscle in his arms. His hair was long and tangled with fingers of red, as if he had been in the sun.

Words fail.

Her hands felt brittle at the sight of him, but she let him in. A voice in her head said very softly, with a touch of menace and despair: he can't stay here. He can't.

It wasn't her voice and she shook it off.

And he collapsed on the couch and slept while she undressed him, her hands never quite touching his flesh. She was tempted to touch the scar that coiled around his belly, to trace her finger around the dark red rope of alien tissue that had grown there. She stopped herself, she was afraid that she might wake him. The scar must be so cold, like the skin of a fish. There was a knife strapped to his left arm, a slender, pretty thing but very, very sharp. She hid it under a cushion. She pulled his boots off, his torn socks. She unbuttoned his pants and pulled them down, her fingernails trailing through his dark pubic hair. His penis was soft and meek and reminded her of mice sleeping in bits of grass and stolen feathers and she had a sudden peculiar urge to choke it in her fist. As if it were truly a mouse. Then his left hand twitched and slid between his thighs. He was protecting himself, even in sleep. And he should, she thought. He should protect himself from me. The urge was gone, anyway. She shrugged and covered him in a thin blanket and wondered if there was anything but rotten food in the house.

She dragged his clothes down to the basement in a pillowcase stained with pig's blood. The washing machine required quarters, which she did not have. But the coinbox had long been broken. She pried it open with a screwdriver, removed three quarters, then hammered the box shut again. One of her neighbors had left behind a small bottle of fabric softener and she didn't hesitate to steal it. His clothes would need a lot of softening. She stood over the machine for a few minutes, watching the water swirl and become gray.

It was time to go to work. To be fair, she was late and she wasn't so sure she wanted to go. She would love to put on her pajamas and drag the television out of the closet and watch a fuzzy movie, to fold herself in half and lie beside Phineas on the couch.

But she was weak, she was soft.

She could never resist, never. She would chew her leg off before she would stay home.

However. The house felt smaller now and she was changed. But not so much, yet. A wrinkle, a twist of color. Phineas had come back and she had no idea what she might do with him. She wondered what effect he would have on her. She wondered what he hoped to find, what he expected from her. Maybe nothing. Maybe he wanted nothing but a place to sleep for a few days. Then he would move on and would that be so terrible. She hadn't known him so well, really. They were connected though. By blood, by something.

She wanted to think about it and she walked around the small apartment, undressing slowly. There was no music and the ringing silence was a relief. Now she stood over him, naked. Her body was covered in bruises, new and old. She touched one, carefully. Yellow and blue and shaped like a star, a flower. She loved her body, cracked and torn as it had become.

She walked down the hall and dressed before a broken mirror.

Her pale splintered torso. Distended arms and legs, coming apart before her eyes. She watched herself fall and fall through the dark glass. She pulled on a black corset and thigh-high black boots. Hesitated, then chose a yellowed wedding dress that had been crudely altered and was now held together by safety pins and fell in a ragged hem a few inches above the tops of her boots.

Phineas still slept. She folded his clean clothes and left them at his feet. She tried but could not write him a note. Instead she left twenty dollars on the kitchen table with a menu for the Silver Frog, a Chinese place that delivered at all hours.

Down the creaking staircase and outside. Blue and black sky. She would take a cab down to Lodo but first she must walk a few blocks and relax. If she thought about it too much, she might cling to herself. She would be trapped, unable to play. But her breathing soon became easy, fluid. The street narrowed. And almost without apprehension, she transformed. Eve became Goo. And Goo was stronger.

I WAS AWAKE, TECHNICALLY. But I didn't want to open my eyes. I was vaguely aware that someone was watching me. The skin had that familiar creepy tingle and I was naked, it seemed. On what felt like a couch. I was tucked like a dead man under a thin blanket. The material was very soft and smelled of tobacco and rain and skin. I reached between my thighs and gave my testicles a reassuring squeeze and briefly, I was twelve and just waking up in my narrow bunk bed at home with blue-and-white-striped sheets and pale blue walls around me and a whale mobile dangling overhead and my little dick cupped safely in my left hand.

I hoped I was in Eve's apartment.

The couch beneath me felt like velvet. Eve had a velvet couch, dark red velvet. I remembered that much. From before. But I didn't exactly remember arriving here. I must have walked twenty-two blocks from the Greyhound station in a drowsy sort of morphine stupor, even though I had been off that shit for six weeks or so, ever since I separated from Jude in San Francisco. It had been a long walk from the station, and stinking hot. I had decided it must be springtime. April, or possibly May. And who was watching me. It didn't feel like Eve. She must have undressed me, though. I tried to remember her hands. Her thin strong fingers.

I opened my eyes and stared into an unsmiling, androgynous blue-eyed face hovering a few inches from my own. The face sniffed at me.

Human, the face said. And apparently alive.

I sat up and waited calmly for the world to spin around. But the world appeared to be temporarily stable. Maybe this was an exaggeration, but I felt much better than I deserved to. The face grunted, pulled away from me and lit an unfiltered white cigarette.

Can I have one of these? I said.

Il est possible que.

I rubbed my mouth. The face was speaking French, apparently. Languages. I had studied German in high school and been pretty bad at it. I had spent some of the past year in South America and could spit out enough Spanish to ask for breakfast and not get shot. However. I hated the French and their slippery tongue. But I shrugged this away. I had no real reason to hate the French and could barely remember why I did. It had something to do with my grandfather and a prostitute during World War II and a mouthful of stolen gold teeth. Anyway. The unsmiling face before me was fierce and beautiful. It was probably male, I thought. If it were a woman's face I would likely be afraid of it.

Two slender fingers were extended, floating toward me. The fingernails were painted a bright yellow. Horrible, a horrible color. These were the fingers of a corpse, a vampire. A short white cigarette appeared before my eyes like a magician's rabbit. I took it between my lips and allowed the yellow fingers to light it for me. The smoke was bitter and harsh and I coughed painfully into my fist. As usual, I looked for black phlegm or chunks of lung in my hand and was relieved to find nothing.

What the hell is this? I said.

It is a Gitanes, the face said. The finest of French cigarettes.

I'm sure. But it tastes like shit.

The face was unamused. Then return it to me.

Thanks, I said. The tobacco is just a little stale, maybe.

Imagine, said another voice. The human is rude.

Right. I was fucking surrounded, then. I sighed and glanced around. My clothes were tucked beneath my feet. They were folded. I couldn't remember the last time my clothes were folded and somehow this made me feel incredibly lonely. I tried to compose my face but couldn't remember exactly what it was supposed to look like. I only wanted to take a shower. I wanted to be unmolested, unfucked with. But there was a shadow crouched in the window behind me. A boy, or a very small man, in raw brown leather clothes. His hair was long and white and he wore a string of bones around his throat. The room was otherwise empty. Okay, so there were only two of them.

Hello.

The man-boy smiled at me, a ring of sharp teeth in shadow.

I pushed the blanket aside and reached for my clothes. I felt hot, as if my blood was thickening. I pulled on pants and sat there, scratching my chest and not blinking. Trying to be cool, I suppose. As if I woke up on a strange couch with mutants staring at me every day. I wanted a cup of coffee. I wanted these two freaks to give me a little space.

I rubbed at a sore mosquito bite on my left wrist, aware now that my knife was missing. I told myself to wake the fuck up.

The unsmiling pretty face wavered before me, became solid again. A body formed behind it. A black, sleeveless shirt that appeared to be made of soft metal. Hairless, muscular arms with a few unreadable words tattooed on the pale, smooth underside of one bicep. Black pants held together by patches of rubber and electrician's tape and boots stained with mud. The man's hair was black and short and very soft, like the fur of a young black dog. The man was eerily calm and not exactly hostile. He was unpleasantly seductive, though. I guessed him to be about thirty years old. There was a fine web of wrinkles around his blue eyes. And those eyes were now staring obliquely at my chest, my exposed belly.

That is exquisite work, the face said.

What?

The scar, he said. Where did you have it done?

I blinked stupidly at him, smiled. It isn't meant to be ornamental, I said.

How did it happen?

On a lumber crew in Oregon. I stumbled into a tree pulper.

Ah, said the face. The wrath of Pan.

Excuse me. Who are you?

The face sighed. The wrong question, isn't it?

The man-boy began to whisper. A string of curses, or prayers. It sounded like Latin, maybe. One dead tongue or another. What the fuck. They wanted to spook me.

But how did it really happen? said the face.

You wouldn't believe me.

Try me, said the face.

I had an organ stolen, I said. And felt a slight flush. The story embarrassed me, somehow.

The face nodded sagely. Leggers, he said. Happens all the time.

I frowned. This was not the reaction I was used to. Most people looked at me with a peculiar mix of disbelief, horror and amusement. Nausea, basically. One woman actually hit me in the face when I told her about it.

Again, I said. Who are you guys?

I am rather more interested in who you might be, said the face.

Okay. I'm Phineas. A friend of Eve's.

Eve, said the face. I'm sure you mean Goo.

I opened my mouth, then closed it. Yes, I said.

I am Chrome, said the face.

The man-boy still whispered.

How do you know Eve? I said. Or Goo, that is.

I am her paramour.

Okay. I stood up and walked into the kitchen. I was suddenly very thirsty, and wondered how long I had been sleeping. I was shivering a little, claustrophobic. I didn't think I liked my new friends. Perhaps I wasn't meant to. Eve didn't want me here, maybe. And why would she? I barely knew her at all. The last time I saw her, she had just been raped with an assortment of household objects. By someone who was looking for me. She had probably hoped she would never lay eyes on my sorry ass again. Then I showed up on her porch, homeless and unannounced. And after I passed out on her couch she naturally sent these two along to give me a fright.

I opened the refrigerator and peered at its uncertain contents. A few unmarked items wrapped in brown paper. Meat, possibly. But Eve was a vegetarian, or so I thought. She was also a lesbian, the last time I saw her. Now she seemed to have a creepy Goth boyfriend with sharp yellow fingernails. His name was Chrome, for fuck's sake. The paramour. I licked my lips and reached for a jar in the fridge that appeared to contain water. And what the hell did I know. Maybe she was bisexual. Who wasn't a little bisexual at the end of the day, alone with the black fingers of memory and silence? The heart was a frail but curiously stubborn organ. I knew that much. This Chrome person, though. He was a nasty one. And not just dark and dreary. He was a skinny wolf lounging in the sun. The guy was for real. I sniffed at the water and my nostrils burned. It was not fucking water, okay. I leaned over the sink and took a long drink from the tap. Now my mouth felt a little better, but I was lonely.

On the table was a menu and twenty dollars, and I felt my spirits lift a little. Eve wanted to feed me, it seemed. Therefore, she was not trying to kill me. I smiled and licked my teeth, which felt mossy. How long had I been sleeping.

Be nice, I muttered. Be fucking nice.

I wandered back to the living room.

I'm going to order some food, I said. Are you guys hungry?

Chrome sighed. He sat on the couch now, his left boot resting on the blanket I had so recently slept with. And I have to say I was fairly aroused, my senses jangling. I felt sick, too. I concentrated on the fist of hunger in my belly. I stared at Chrome and I was confident that he was well aware of the effect he had on men and women. That he saw other humans as amusing toys. Everyone who ever came near him must want to fuck him or kill him or both. He had dark swollen lips that any supermodel would die for and blue eyes like seawater in the sun. And he smelled like metal, like salt and gasoline.

He was a tease, a torturer. Nothing more, nothing more.

Chrome stared back at me, smiling now.

The man-boy was busily examining the rest of my clothing. He sniffed a boot delicately, then licked the heel. He pressed the socks and shirt to his face.

What do they smell like? I said.

The man-boy grinned. Like a summer breeze, he said. Like chemical detergent.

Chrome spat. I assume Goo laundered them, he said. She is such a woman, sometimes.

I looked at Chrome's throat and wondered where the hell my knife was.

The man-boy grunted. The boots, however, taste of blood and feces. They taste of Louisiana. He glanced up at me. You have come from Louisiana, have you not?

Yes, I said. I was there last week. And I laughed, weirdly pleased by his cleverness. Meanwhile, my bowels felt like they were slowly stretching.

I lived there as a child, said the man-boy. My name is Mingus the Breather.

Well. I rubbed at my eyes and could think of nothing, absolutely nothing wrong with that. It's nice to meet you, I said.

Perhaps you would like us to call you Fred, said Chrome. Because you will be going to see Elvis, soon.

What? I said.

And then we can say: Poor Fred. He was a friend of mine.

That's not true, said Mingus. He won't see Elvis, necessarily.

I'm sorry, said Chrome with a sigh. But the man does not look well.

Nothing has been decided, said Mingus. No one's fate is sealed.

Spare me, said Chrome.

I smiled benevolently. As if I wanted to be nothing more than a gracious host. I picked up the phone and dialed the Silver Frog. My vision was swimming and I calmly ordered mu shu, dumplings, fried rice and eggdrop soup. Then hung up the phone and helped myself to another of Chrome's nasty French cigarettes. I blew a pretty sorry smoke ring and handed the cigarette to Chrome.

Our hands touched. Our eyes slipped over opposing flesh.

I laughed out loud. The tension between us was absurd, cartoonish. I might as well ask the man to choose a weapon.

Chrome merely yawned. Enchantez de faire votre connaissance.

I pulled on my boots and stood there, feeling awkward and clumsy, as if my limbs were suddenly too large for my body. I watched as Mingus patiently repaired a hole in my freshly washed shirt with a needle and a length of black thread. It was a maddeningly slow process, sewing. No wonder I never learned to do it. My mother had been no good at it either and as a boy my socks were always full of holes. Jesus fucking. My mind was about to crash into itself. I chewed at my thumb and wished they would leave. Otherwise I was going to jump out a window any minute now. The silence rose like water, swirling. Chrome stared and stared at me.

Do you like to hunt? said Chrome.

What do you mean. Like ducks? I said.

Yes, said Chrome. Exactly like ducks.

Goo:

She walked along a deserted street through shadows so soft she was tempted to grab at them, to pull them to her face. These were the dark sisters of clouds seen from the window of an airplane, she thought. She giggled like a foolish bird. Goo shook her head as if it were made of rags, disgusted with herself. She was thinking like Eve and she was still weak from the change, the glamour. The street she walked along did exist, she was sure of that. She had bent to touch it countless times. But the street was unnamed, and she could find it on no map of the city. In the end it didn't matter. There was cracked pavement beneath her feet, was there not? And now there were other voices, other bodies. They moved around her, a current. She was not entirely safe, though. Goo was vulnerable still, when out alone. She touched her fingers to her mouth and the soft tip of her own tongue reassured her.

Rain began to fall, a warm mist.

She turned down a tiny alleyway lit by gaslights and entered the Unbecoming Club.

You're late, pet.

Goo flinched. Hello, Theseus.

Theseus the Glove stood behind the bar in a murky green suit with flared lapels and narrow trousers. He looked like a woodland mortician. He did not smile at her. He did not offer her a drink.

The Lady Adore waits for you. And her patience grows thin.

But there is hardly a crowd.

Theseus nodded, staring moodily at the nearly empty club. There were several Mariners in the corner, playing knives and trumps by candlelight. Two lonely Tremblers lounged on a sofa, picking at their loose flesh. And a damp, foul-smelling Redeemer was perched on a stool at the bar, his nose nearly touching the cool yellow liquid in his glass. But there was a guttural swelling in the air outside and Goo could feel it in her fingers, her toes. The club would be full in minutes. The patrons would be hungry for her, for Goo.

And not for the first time she felt a little carsick at the idea.

Goo, she thought. They want Goo, not me.

Her pale splintered torso, coming apart before her eyes and falling through dark glass.

Eve, she thought. You stupid little bitch. She turned to the Redeemer at the bar and wondered what a few words of sympathy would cost her. My God. The man truly smelled. But he was not so pathetic and dirty as he looked at first glance. His hair stood up at freakish angles and was peppered with white. His face was long and sour, wrinkled. He looked like a pale gray prune. The man was old, maybe forty. And this was rare, she knew. The middle-aged were generally too gloomy and stubborn about reality for the game of tongues. The Redeemer looked at her now, his lips twitching into a smile. His eyes were red and scorched but still sharp and he was no wetbrain, she could see that. And he looked very familiar, he looked like someone.

Will you hear me, she said. Will you hear a confession.

The man sighed. As if amused. Why not, he said. I am a Redeemer.

Yes, she said. Do I know you?

No, no. I certainly don't think so.

But you look like someone, she said. What is your name?

Gulliver, he said. His hand was dry, with blunt fingernails.

Hello, she said. My name is Goo.

The Redeemer sipped delicately from his glass of Pale. He wiped at his lips, which were thin and rubbery and morbidly prehensile in appearance. His mouth was ugly but no doubt fantastic when it came to oral sex, she thought. A man could be very popular with lips like that. He nodded and rolled his eyes as if he could hear her thoughts and finally said, Well? What is your problem?

Goo sighed and glanced around, nervous and hating herself. Theseus didn't seem to be listening but she could never be sure. He seemed to be anywhere and everywhere at once. I'm not happy, she said.

Interesting, he said. I don't hear that one often.

Goo whispered, now. Sometimes I want to leave the game.

But why? he said.

I used to have a life, a dayworld life.

The Redeemer raised his furry eyebrows. Do you drink the Pale?

Rarely, she said.

He grunted. Good for you.

I love it here, she said. But I hate it, too.

The Redeemer was gazing at her with pity in his eyes and she wondered if he was thinking of her tongue. His eyes were gentle, perhaps. But the whites of them were laced with blood. Careful, she needed to be careful and now the Redeemer sighed. Who am I speaking to? he said.

Goo, she said. But she knew she sounded doubtful and he just stared at her.

This is getting silly, he said.

What do you mean?

Eve, he said. Don't you know me?

It was hard to swallow, to breathe. She wanted to get away from this man.

It's okay, he said. You can be two people at once.

No, she said. I don't want that.

Disappear, he said softly. Walk outside and disappear from the game.

Her left eyelid began to twitch, to blink uncontrollably. And she felt sick, she felt dizzy because that only happened when Eve was nervous, when she was paranoid and sleepless.

This world isn't real, he said.

My boyfriend would disagree, she said.

Theseus was glaring at them from maybe fifteen feet away and she wondered when he had slithered so close, and how much he had heard. She knew that he disapproved of the Redeemers and tolerated them only because they were necessary.

Her belly was exposed, her weak half.

She couldn't stand to look at him now. She backed away from the bar and dragged herself off to the dressing room, where Adore reclined on a mound of dirty pillows, rigid and bony. She often reminded Goo of a dead praying mantis. Adore had a headache, it seemed. She wore a woven silk ice pouch over her eyes and the room smelled of roses. The only light came from a green lamp that glowed like a fat firefly behind lace. Goo stood in the doorway, feeling like a wayward daughter. Her hair was a wreck and her skin itched as if she were covered in dry white soap. She was short of breath and confused. The Redeemer had not tried to kiss her, to take her tongue. And his advice had been very unorthodox.

No one ever suggested that you leave the game, no one.

Adore made a clucking sound. Gather yourself, girl.

I'm sorry, Lady.

Adore removed her ice pouch and regarded Goo with bloody eyes.

Don't be sorry, girl. You are an Exquisitor.

You flatter me, Lady.

I do not.

Goo cast her eyes away, embarrassed. She was only an apprentice. Adore laughed at her, a delicate and fluttering sound. She held out her hands and Goo moved to help her up.

Shall we take the stage? said Adore.

I FOUND MYSELF SITTING ON THE FLOOR of Eve's empty apartment, eating eggdrop soup in bright, unflinching silence. Eve apparently owned no television, no stereo. The only sound was my own manic slurping. At some point I must have thrown open the windows, praying for a little breeze or the distraction of traffic noise, but I couldn't really remember doing so. It was odd, but Eve didn't seem to have a telephone, either. Though I could have sworn she did have one. I had used it to order the food, hadn't I? And that was an hour ago, maybe two. But now I couldn't find a phone anywhere. It was a little maddening. I looked around and around, my head swiveling like a puppet's. I rubbed my eyes, disgusted. She didn't have a coffeemaker, a toaster. There were no electrical appliances at all. Maybe the food was delivered by fairies. Or else the phone was stolen by them.

I was alone in the apartment. Chrome and Mingus the Breather had apparently taken their leave. Faded from the scene without word or gesture. I could barely remember their faces, now. I wasn't so confident that they were real. They were too similar to the freaks that regularly populated my dreams. But if I closed my eyes, I could see Chrome in distorted flashes as he speared a dumpling with one yellow fingernail and fed it rather graphically to Mingus. There was fried rice scattered on the wood floor, as if I had been feeding imaginary squirrels. There were two untouched bowls of soup on the floor, and two spoons. I was Goldilocks, then. The soup is too hot, too cold. I wanted to write it all off as unexpected weirdness, nothing more. But I was dizzy, numb. As if I had suffered a mild electric shock. Or involuntary contact with two nonhumans. I forced myself to clean up the rice, to wash the bowls. I wiped my hands on my pants and stood staring at a long black wrinkle in my shirt, where Mingus the Breather had been kind enough to sew up a nasty hole in the fabric.

Well, then. They were real enough.

Here we go. I found this little blue notebook in the kitchen and not sure why, but I stole it. Eve had only written a few words on the first page, notes for a class and I couldn't be sure but it looked like Logic 101. And the rest of the book was blank.

I was going to rip that page out and start fresh but decided not to. The disconnected pieces of logic appealed to me, the odd little phrases. They comfort, somehow. And she has such fine crooked handwriting, like bugs crawling out of my head. Anyway. Not sure what I was thinking. It had been months since I wrote anything at all by hand. Not even a postcard to my poor mother. The rare signature maybe, on a bad credit card slip. Oh, yeah. I signed a lot of room service tabs when I was with Jude. She loved fucking room service. But the last thing I would have written by hand was probably an incident report for the department that was dull as a cloudless sky, I'm sure. That shit was deadly.

If I wanted to tell the truth, I would say that I stole Eve's notebook because I wanted to keep a record. And what use this might be is hard to say. I know this much. I can't really trust my memory anymore. Or my perception of what's real. And it's funny to think that I have never done this before. This will be my first diary. If you could even call it that.

Dear Jude. If I knew where you were I might send these notes to you.

But I should tell you that something bothers me and maybe it's nothing, nothing to worry about. I have my share of paranoid tendencies. As you know. Okay. I have been back in Denver for less than a day now and I'm looking over my shoulder like there's a contract out on my narrow ass. I can almost feel the crosshairs on my neck. It's not you, is it? I guess it wouldn't shock me. If you were out there. Following me, watching me from rooftops with the eye of a sniper.

Unless I inform you otherwise, I don't know what day it is. Which is why these notes are not dated. I don't even know the correct time. It seems I sold my watch a few days back. Anyway. It's only been a few hours.

I had to get out of Eve's place. The boyfriend was freaking me out. Did I mention she has a boyfriend, a sick fucker with bad clothes. His name is Chrome and he suggested I change my name to Fred. I'm not kidding. You would want to kill him on sight. He said something funny, though. He asked me if I wanted to go see Elvis and it sounded a lot like a threat. How about that. I'm going to Graceland.

You remember where you were when the news came on the radio that he was dead?

Late summer and stupidly hot and I was at Chloe's house. My first real girl-friend and she was trashy and not very smart and conditioned by her loutish stepfather to flinch when you looked hard at her or moved your arm too suddenly and was therefore happy to suck me off right on the couch whenever I dropped by with cigarettes or ice cream. Which I felt bad about but I was only thirteen and couldn't very well say no when she unzipped my pants and bent over me with the cool silence of a Catholic girl doing a few Hail Marys. We were watching the Stooges, I think. And the couch was covered in dirty laundry and I could smell the stepfather's socks and Chloe's head was busily twisting in my lap when they inter-rupted the broadcast to say that the King was dead. Chloe lifted her face then, her mouth puffy and red. She stared at the television, stricken and pale and she said, oh my mother loves him or she used to, before he got so fat and gross, you know. Then she resumed, she sucked me off like she was born to the task and actually swallowed my gunk. Which inspired me to tell her I loved her. I was thirteen.

Chrome:

He was hungry. Oh, he was violent. He slashed at the air with his long fin-gers and leaned to breathe obscenities into Mingus's left ear.

I want to hunt, he said.

Mingus glanced at the sky. It's raining.

Chrome muttered, not here.

They sat on a circle of grass overlooking the freeway. Chrome was on edge, he was bored. He began to play with Eve's telephone, picking up the receiver and saying: Yes, who's there? He had cut the cord and removed the phone from her apartment on a whim, thinking to confuse and alienate the sickly Phineas, whom he had found distasteful and oddly alluring.

He looked over at Mingus, who still stared like a simpleton down at the freeway. He was fascinated by cars, the poor thing. His favorite was the Saturn. He claimed it was the most graceful and godlike of machines. Chrome had to smile at this notion. He told Mingus that the Saturn was manufactured in Tennessee by unevolved humans.

Mingus was ignoring him, though. Which was not wise. Chrome stared at his own fingers. They were twitching and he realized he could easily kill his little friend. It could happen as suddenly as a violent sneeze, a brief involuntary convulsion. It was disturbing, really.

There's a green one, said Mingus. They are the prettiest, I think.

J'ai faim, Chrome said.

English, said Mingus. Speak English.

I'm hungry, he said.

It isn't safe to hunt by day.

Please, said Chrome. The Freds come and go.

Everyone comes and goes.

But the Freds stay in character.

As do we, said Mingus.

Ah, yes. But I am a bit more self-aware, said Chrome.

Chrome removed a garrote from his boot and twirled it on one finger. The black cord was soft and silky to the touch but strong as piano wire. There was a piece of wood the approximate size of his pinkie at either end, wrapped in leather. He could kill a bear with the thing, if he could only creep up on one.

You twit, he said. That was a Mustang.

My eyes are failing in this light.

How is your nose?

Fine, said Mingus. I can smell you.

Do you not smell meat?

Mingus frowned. A car had drifted to a stop nearby, an ordinary Toyota. It was perhaps a hundred feet away, parked under a little tree. The windows were down and two men sat in the front seat. The angles of their jaws suggested an uneasy discussion of money. Mingus would surely smell sex on them, like salt and fresh earth. Even Chrome could smell it. The sex was coming from them in waves.

We will not hunt a Citizen, said Mingus.

Of course not. You will sniff out an unfortunate Fred who has lost his way.

I WALKED OUT OF EVE'S PLACE and felt better straightaway. The oxygen had been too thin up there, or too pure. And I had been talking to myself in no time, poking at my eyes with restless fingers. I did find my knife, thank God. It was hidden under a sofa cushion. I had tried and failed to write Eve a note. Thank you for the use of the sofa, the money for food. Thanks for washing my clothes. And I love your new friends…and fuck it. I had crumpled these aborted little notes and tossed them at the window. I would see her later, maybe. It looked like she was running around with a lot of freaks but why the hell should I care. She was hardly a proper little girl before, was she. And she was not a child to be looked after.

I had my own bellyful of problems, anyway. No money and nowhere to sleep, no job prospects. If I had three red apples, I might wander downtown and amaze the pedestrians with my juggling. I could gather enough spare change to buy a cup of coffee, maybe hang around a diner all day reading other people's newspapers. I could beg a ballpoint pen off a kindly waitress and use it to mark up the classifieds. A few months ago I had dreamed of a job at a gas station, a video store. I had wanted to change my name and shave my head and write bad poetry.

Yeah.

I rolled my eyes at the sky, at a blanket of gray. I didn't like poetry and I was not a good juggler. And I would first have to steal three red apples. I ducked into a phone booth and realized with some amusement that I bother to dwell on the irony. The call was free, at least. I told the emergency operator that I was a police informant and was in relatively grave danger. The operator was not amused.

This line is for emergency calls only, she said.

I'm going to be dead in five minutes, I said. Is that an emergency?

Your name, she said.

The angry flipper-boy, I said.

Hum of silence.

Phineas Poe, I said. Please tell Detective Moon to come get me.

Theseus the Glove:

The stage was black but for an egg-shaped spot of orange light. One of Goo's bare legs lay stretched there as if cut off at the knee. Her thigh-high boots were nowhere to be seen. Theseus reached under his jacket to pinch his left nipple. He had his doubts about this girl sometimes, doubts about her belief in the game. But she was lovely as a sleeping child when bound and gagged.

A gloved hand entered the egg of orange light.

Goo's leg looked as if it had been discarded, a piece of firewood. The hand began to stroke, or measure, her ankle with blunt, velvet fingers.

Theseus felt wet.

A small wire cage was shoved slowly into the orange light.

The wire cage had two doors. One of them was an ordinary door, with a hinge on one side and a latch on the other. The other opened like a set of flaps, with a semicircle cut out of each side. The gloved hands carefully pulled open these flaps and inserted Goo's bare foot into the cage. The flaps were then closed and the cutout circle fit snugly, if a little tightly, around her ankle.

There was a low, steady grunting from the crowd.

Money. This was silver in his pocket.

Goo's pale, arched foot was trapped in the wire cage. Now the gloved hand opened the rear door and a gray pigeon appeared, as if pulled from a hat. The pigeon was quickly pushed into the cage and the rear door latched. The pigeon crouched there, placid and dumbly staring.

The egg of orange light began to grow.

It widened to expose Goo's hips. Her other leg was crumpled, hidden. The tattered, yellow-white dress lay like dirty snow around her. Her arms were splayed and apparently powerless. She was not restrained, however. She was deliciously passive and Theseus wanted to laugh. The girl was dangerous. Her eyes were shut tight and her ears flattened, feline against her skull. There was a thin pillow beneath her head. The Lady Adore crouched at the edge of the light, near the wire cage. She wore leather pants and no shoes. The coiled black cloth around her torso resembled a bandage more than a shirt. In her gloved hands, she held a bundle of damp gray rags. Adore appeared motionless, barely breathing as the orange light swelled. Adore placed the rags at the rear door of the cage, perhaps six inches from the forlorn pigeon. She lit a match, and the little bundle began to burn. Theseus groaned, sweating.

The pigeon was frantic. It hopped up and down and sideways, like a grasshopper. Adore pulled a straight razor from the cuff of one velvet glove and began to cut and slash briskly at Goo's clothes. The pigeon threw itself against the wires as if it might kill itself, then abruptly stopped. Instead, it attacked Goo's trapped foot. The wedding dress fell away from the razor like paper.

The bird was a mad, thrashing blur. Goo's slim white foot was a web of trickling blood.

The corset was so thick that Adore was forced to hack at it. She peeled it away and Goo's belly was bleeding here and there, from superficial cuts. Her ribs were fine and shadowy. Her breasts were plump, her nipples red. Smoke from the small fire hung over her body. The pigeon was growing weak now, its gray feathers dark with blood. The Lady Adore cut away Goo's underpants and tossed them into the silent crowd. She reached into the cage and cut the pigeon's throat just as the orange light faded to black.

Theseus smiled, pouring drinks all around.

MULTIPLE PERSONALITIES. Don't freak out but I'm pretty sure I have them. Not a clinical thing, not a disease. But a distraction to be sure. There are maybe six or seven pretty concrete versions of myself knocking around in here and I mean it gets fucking crowded when everybody is drunk or talking at once.

And every so often the opportunity arises to assume another identity, to take another name and every time I want to run like hell, I want to run away from Phineas like his ass is on fire. Because I need a little personal space between him and me.

Distance. I need distance from the others.

But the other people I become are never strong enough. Or fast enough. Because Phineas wears them down in the end. He's relentless.

Early morning freak-out. I passed a construction site. Abandoned. Looked like someone was tearing a building down and then ran out of money. Their permit was revoked or something and the building was left half-standing and you could see this exposed brick wall that fifty years ago was an exterior wall but the building had been added onto and the wall was covered. There were old advertisements painted into the bricks, the kind that still said cigarettes were good for you. And rust marks in the wall shaped like the skeleton of a fire escape and windows. A few of the windows were boarded up and plastered over. But the boards were rotten by now. Rotten and the plaster broken through. And through a few of these windows I saw people moving around. Combing their hair and drinking tea and reading the newspaper and these weren't homeless people. They weren't crackheads or squatters. They were just people. They all had that sweet laziness about them, that oblivious air of someone who is watching television alone in a hotel room in his underwear and has no idea he's being watched.

Thought I must be dreaming. Thought I must be deceived by the light but they were in there, I'm sure of it. And you know what? When I see something like that, all the other versions of Phineas scratch their asses and pretend they didn't see a thing.

Fuck them, right. I sat with my feet in the gutter and peered through the iron gate into the black space below, looking for dead birds and lost skate-boards, rotting pumpkins. I scribbled in my notebook and tried not to lament my lack of cleverness. The cars flew past me and I felt more and more like an alien. I was the only creature in sight without a bright, metallic shell. It had occurred to me that Moon might not be so thrilled to see me. But I had no one else to call. Crumb would offer me tea and an amusing story about a guy who came in complaining of stomach pains, who believed he had an ulcer when in fact he was carrying a bullet and was too drunk to recall being shot. I didn't need tea. I needed a job or a place to sleep. I needed a new pair of shoes, I needed a cigarette, and now Moon pulled up in a gray Taurus. The passenger window slid down and Moon stared out at me, his sour mouth twitching with amusement.

Jesus, he said. Get in the car.

Fortunately, Moon had cigarettes. And he seemed more than willing to drive around in forced silence for a while. His radio was broken, or so he claimed. We circled for a while, as if lost. It was a peculiar day. The sky was moody, inconstant. The light seemed to change violently from one block to the next and on one street it was actually raining. I shut my eyes and remembered driving across Nevada maybe ten years earlier. An empty stretch of desert, the highway glittering like a rope of black silver. The sun unblinking and the sky flat and silent as a stone. Peripheral vision fuzzy around the edges. A migraine, I thought. A hawk dropped suddenly from nowhere, swooping over the roof of the car and crashing into the luggage rack. In the rearview mirror I saw a brief windmill tumble of shredded wings, gray and white. As if the bird had exploded. And then nothing but my own face in the mirror and I had been baffled to see myself crying. How are you. How are you. I looked up and now we were sitting at a red light.

How are you, Moon said.

That's a good question. I'm a little confused.

Moon grunted and shifted the car into gear. I examined him. The same clothes, the same meaty face. The eyes vague and expressionless behind glasses but the mouth was vivid, quick. His mouth could be apologetic and menacing at once.

You look healthier, said Moon.

Yeah, well. It's been a year.

Is that all?

I'm broke. I need a place to sleep.

Oh, boy.

What did you expect?

I expected you to be dead by now.

We were driving directly into the sun. It lingered on the horizon, a sullen yellow eye. The sun refused to blink. Every tree and car and lonely pedestrian was skeletal and black, shadows come to life. A wheelchair rolled abruptly across the road, slow and wobbling, as if its passenger were unconscious. I blinked, waiting for Moon to touch the brakes. If anything, he sped up and we narrowly missed crushing the thing. I turned violently in my seat and saw that the wheelchair was in fact empty, drifting safely to the other side. There was no one on the sidewalk who might have pushed it.

What the fuck was what?

What was what, said Moon.

Moon pulled a cell phone from his jacket pocket and smiled sheepishly. He called the station and told someone to take his name off the board. He was taking a mental health day.

I was amused. Are you feeling unstable? I said.

Yeah. I was thinking of you, actually.

I appreciate it. Where are we going?

My place. You can sleep at the foot of my bed, with Shame.

Who the hell is Shame?

My cat.

Curious name, I said.

It was supposed to be Shane, okay. Like the gunslinger.

Oh, yeah. Steve McQueen.

Jesus. It was Lee Marvin.

Whatever.

Steve McQueen was a fine actor, said Moon. But he couldn't have handled Shane. The character was too rich, too complex. McQueen didn't have a true dark side. He was too good-looking, you know. He was a prettyboy. Lee Marvin, though. That motherfucker could act.

I sighed. How did the cat become Shame?

When he was a kitten, I had this girlfriend. And she had a speech defect. Beautiful.

Chrome:

Mingus had a remarkable nose. Chrome was proud of him, truly. He adored the boy. In less than half an hour they had come upon a Fred wandering stupidly down an alley. A thin, starved-looking figure in dirty clothing who meandered along, chewing his thumb and peering into sewer grates and stopping now and again to ponder the contents of a garbage pail.

Chrome rubbed his palms together now, gloating. The alley was narrow and smelled of rot. The shadows were a dark, sinewy green. The shadows were lively. The Fred was perhaps fifty meters ahead of them but Chrome was unconcerned. He happened to know that the alley led to a dead end. And the Fred looked particularly weak, as if his brain had softened well beyond mush. A Mariner's nervous apprentice could bring him down with two fingers.

It was dreary, is what this was.

The best sport was of course a Fred who was self-aware, his nerves jangling with fear and his own new tonguelust. The self-aware would come at you with a piece of pipe, with teeth and boots. The self-aware were dangerous. And much more fun. In a pure hunt, thought Chrome, the hunter and the hunted must be properly entwined. They must be inseparable, of one heart and breath. They must be shadows joined, they must be lovers.

Chrome still twirled the garrote and bit at the air. He glanced at Mingus, who was walking so slowly he might have been asleep. Mingus wasn't happy about this, he knew. It was a violation of the code of tongues to hunt by day. But it was a notion Chrome had been toying with for some time. Hunting in the light and among Citizens would surely increase the danger and thrill, the difficulty. He was bored silly with the stiff parameters of the game, the pious rules. And he was curious to see if anything would come of breaking the code. Besides. He was hungry.

Chrome was always hungry, always.

Mingus was a Breather, and therefore controlled his own tonguelust with the rigor of a celibate, which infuriated Chrome to no end. He spat with disgust as the Fred stumbled ahead and actually walked into a wall and bounced backward with all the grace of a rubber donkey. Fuck it anyway. The wetbrain would be a fast kill.

Mingus now leapt to grab at a fire escape, pulling himself up like a spider.

It will be a boring kill, he said.

Be quiet, said Chrome.

Mingus pulled a brightly colored yo-yo from his pocket, a Duncan. He flicked it down and back with hypnotic ease.

Walk the dog, said Chrome.

You know I can't do any tricks.

I will teach you, said Chrome. After I kill this poor Fred.

MOON'S APARTMENT WAS DARK and relatively damp. He had very little furniture. I found I was not so uncomfortable at all. I had been a little worried that I might be. That we would be two unfamiliar men in a confined space, the smell of one overpowering the other and that any physical contact, skin touching actual skin, would be rare and awkward and tenuous. That we would suffer the crush of ordinary silence.

But I let myself fall easily onto a dusty sofa that was covered in equal parts with brown leather and fuzzy orange stripes. It was a hideous couch and I immediately liked it. I would sleep here, if I would sleep at all. I relaxed for a minute while Moon rattled around in the kitchen, cursing.

What are you doing in there?

I'm cooking, said Moon.

Oh, really.

Well. I'm heating a few cans of soup.

I nodded, gazing at a giant television that was so covered in dust I wondered if anything could ever be seen flickering on its screen. Other than the ghosts of dead baseball players and long unemployed actors. I wondered if Moon was in there mixing together several different and opposing flavors of soup: split pea and clam chowder and beef with barley, for instance. I hoped not. Moon came into the living room and tossed a narrow white box at me. It was a toothbrush, unopened.

Are my teeth green?

Moon shrugged. I went to the dentist the other day. It was free.

Thanks, then.

You shouldn't neglect your gums.

I won't.

Moon stared at me, apparently expecting me to run along and brush my teeth now, rather than later. As if I had a mouthful of dirt. I laughed and got up, thinking I might need to pee anyway. I repaired to Moon's little bathroom, brushed my teeth with Moon's generic toothpaste and poked aimlessly through Moon's medicine cabinet. Foot powder and witch hazel. Razor blades. A variety of pills and fluids that purported to deal with gastrointestinal distress. Generic aspirin. I spat gloomily into the sink, ever watchful for blood. I had a bizarre craving for a tall glass of cherry-red cough syrup with ice and soda water. The toothpaste left my mouth raw and I rinsed it repeatedly.

When I came out of the bathroom Moon was pacing, apparently agitated. I sat on the ugly couch and forced myself to swallow the unidentifiable soup Moon had given me. I wished Moon would sit down. He had taken off his jacket to reveal a blue denim shirt that was torn under one armpit. The sleeves flapped around his wrists, as if the cuffs had no buttons. He violently loosened his tie, his face red and puffing as he did so. He pulled a tiny Swiss army knife from his watch pocket and used the scissors to rapidly clip his nails. A skinny orange cat slinked into the room and came over to inspect me, the new human.

That would be Shame, said Moon.

Poor thing, I said. His name was ruined by a woman and now he looks like you never feed him.

He's just high-strung, said Moon.

I lowered my bowl of soup to the floor and the cat crouched over it, growling.

Moon, I said. You want to sit down, maybe? Relax.

I'm thinking about something. I think on my feet.

Okay. Do you have anything to drink?

Yeah. Next to the sink is a bottle of whiskey.

I went into the kitchen, glad for something to do. There was a mostly full jug of Canadian Mist on the counter. It was covered in dust and I wasn't surprised. The stuff was worse than poison. But I was a beggar, now. I was a jackal. I rinsed two glasses and poured several fat fingers of Mist into each. There were three empty ice trays in the freezer. I cursed and muttered and told myself the stuff would be equally putrid with or without ice. But I compulsively filled the ice trays at the sink.

I came back and gave one glass to Moon, who gulped the Mist in one swallow. Then choked.

Oh, he said. That shit is bad.

Christmas gift? I said.

Yeah. From a guy in Homicide named Tom Gunn.

What did you give him?

Tickets to a Nuggets game.

I guess you're even.

But these were good seats, man.

The fucking Nuggets, though.

Moon laughed. He sat down on a corduroy ottoman with a lurid floral pattern.

What's on your mind? I said.

Save it for later, said Moon. Let's get drunk.

Goo:

Adore smoked a clove cigarette, her eyes glowing red in the mirror like a cat's eyes in the flash of a camera. Goo felt weary, she felt ill and she hated it when Adore sat behind her like that because it was like she was surrounded by her. Adore was behind her and Adore was staring at her in the glass. There were two of them and one of these days she would smash this mirror.

Four walls were enough. In a mirror you had six walls, eight walls.

Goo was bleeding in a dozen places.

A young, nearly invisible girl knelt beside her, silently cleaning her wounds with a cloth diaper that she dipped into a pail of water and alcohol. The cuts were not deep, at least. She would not need stitches, and painful or not she was proud of the work. Goo watched herself smile in the mirror. She was in awe of Adore sometimes, and marked herself fortunate to be her apprentice.

It had been a beautiful piece, The Bird.

The crowd had been tortured into a state of distraction. They had paid good money to see her stripped naked and violated by Adore. But they were undone by their own fascination for blood and couldn't take their eyes off the bird eating from her foot. Then the lights had gone out and they could only sit and listen to the grunts and whispers of what may or may not have been two women sweatily fucking on a dark stage. In fact, Adore had noisily eaten a sandwich while Goo had lain in a blissful stupor. The victims were always shifting in the landscape of the game and now Adore was staring at her.

What? said Goo.

You spoke to a Redeemer, earlier.

She shrugged. Yes, so what?

What did you tell him?

Nothing. I told him that I was having boyfriend troubles.

Be careful, said Adore. You can't trust them.

Who can I trust?

Adore smiled. Are you still seeing that young man, that Mariner?

I suppose. Why?

Adore stubbed out her cigarette, deliberately.

You don't like him, said Goo.

No, said Adore.

The girl had finished with Goo's wounds and now moved silently to brush Adore's hair. Goo leaned back in her chair, still naked. Her clothes had been cut to ribbons, destroyed. It looked like she had been attacked by wolves and emerged remarkably unscathed. She would have to wear something of Adore's if she wanted to go home. That green dress with the gold thread, perhaps.

That's okay, said Goo. I don't always like him, either.

I think it's time for you to design your own piece, said Adore. I will be your victim, of course.

Goo was surprised. Are you sure I'm ready for that?

Adore didn't hear her because Goo's voice had fallen to a whisper. It didn't matter. Because she knew she was ready. She felt a thin, seeping wave of nausea but she was ready. It was Adore who might not be ready to exchange roles. Adore laughed and said don't worry, girl. I'm ready.

My first victim, said Goo.

That is, unless you have another victim in mind, said Adore. A young man, for instance.

Goo stretched her arms and winced at the ribbon of pain across her ribs.

I CLOSE MY EYES AND ALL I SEE IS YOU, JUDE. Your hair is long and wet and you twist it in your hands like a piece of rope. You sleep topless on the balcony with those strange shadows falling across your belly. You have more money than you know what to do with and still you steal fruit from the market. You spend hours shooting green bottles in the desert with your back to the sun.

You ruined me for sex, by the way. I just can't be bothered anymore. I can't be fucked.

I remember something you said about serial killers and how the interesting ones are always very good kissers. I stared at you, stupidly I'm sure. I asked how many serial killers had you kissed and you laughed like the ghost of Lady Macbeth. You kissed me.

Moon was drunk, crashing around his apartment. He breathed wetly. His eyes rolled around, loose from their moorings. He was looking for something to punish, it seemed. He clumsily put his foot through a coffee table, panting. His foot became stuck and he fell heavily to the floor. I scrambled to move lamps and stereo equipment from harm's way. I remember, vaguely, that Moon was not really supposed to drink. There had been incidents in the past, nasty incidents involving borrowed motorcycles and flooded toilets and gouged eyeballs. There had been a rather notorious sword fight maybe ten years ago. But I was never my brother's keeper. The opposite, if anything. I could remember more than one night when Moon had prevented me from doing something stupid or fatal.

Moon now lay sideways on the floor, his foot wedged among the splintered remains of his table. He coughed for several minutes, then demanded angrily to know where Mary had gone.

I was patient. I promised him that I knew no one named Mary and Moon growled, then dropped the subject. I crouched next to him, patting his damp belly as if he were a wounded bear. Moon sighed sleepily and I quickly disarmed him. Moon carried only one weapon, and was known to disapprove of ankle holsters. But this Colt that he had carried at his hip for eleven years and had rarely fired was a regular monster. I hefted it, thinking I could easily kill a car with the fucker. I unloaded it, then slid the big gun under the couch. I currently had no gun, myself. I carried only the knife, and if it came to a knife fight I reckoned I was quicker on my feet than the poor coffee table, which had fared pretty well against Moon.

What happened, said Moon. What happened in Texas goddamn you.

Nothing much, I said. I watched a kid die.

And the woman, said Moon. The fuck happened to that crazy bitch.

I sat cross-legged on the floor. The carpet was dusty, hairy. It was pretty sticky in places. I stared at Moon's heaving chest and belly, at the stains on his white shirt and the limp, smeared tie. The white, hairy stomach flesh that gathered at his waistband. The green canvas military belt with unpolished buckle. The filthy white pants, the white socks. The black shoes with flattened rubber heels. Moon needed a woman in the worst way.

I leaned over and began to extricate Moon's foot from the shards of wood.

Jude, you mean. She's living in Mexico City, last I heard. Married to a nice banker and two months pregnant. She's happy as a clam.

Liar, said Moon. Fuck happened.

Ask me tomorrow.

You shit me.

Sleep, I said. Go to sleep.

Not tired. Let's go up on the roof.

I don't think so.

Fresh air. I can't breathe.

You can't even walk.

Okay. Lemme tell you a story. Moon abruptly began to frisk himself, grabbing at his pockets and crotch. Where the fuck is my gun? My gun, my gun.

I eyed the couch warily, hoping that Moon was too fat and soggy to wiggle over there. It's in the freezer, I said. With your life savings.

Okay. Shut up. Lemme tell you a story.

Yeah. Tell me.

Moon was a lump on the floor. His voice was thick, droning. I lit a cigarette and listened, my own eyes closed.

Thirteen, said Moon. Total of thirteen cops gone missing. But it's gradual. They fade. Not dead exactly. No bodies to speak of. They go undercover for a while and sometimes they come back but when they do they're not right. They're different.

Different how?

Like pod people. And then one day they don't come back at all. These are guys from Narcotics and Vice, mostly. Fuck them, right. But then two guys from Homicide. You remember Jimmy Sky?

Yeah. I never liked him.

Come on. The fucking Skywalker. You never met a cop so cool as him and he slides in dry as ice after a month undercover with a basket full of oatmeal raisin cookies he baked himself. Then he's gone for good. And nobody wants to talk about it.

Who's your chief?

Moon spat violently. Captain Honey, he said.

I laughed.

Moon muttered, the poor bastard is ninety days from retirement and doped up on painkillers. His teeth are no good. He tells me not to worry. Don't worry, he says. Meanwhile he's busy cutting shit out of the newspapers all day: comic strips and "Dear Abby" and coupons for cat food and his horoscope. You walk into his office and Captain Honey says hey, private. What's your sign? He reads you your horoscope and smiles at you like some kind of drunk priest. Then he slips you a coupon for forty-nine cents off Fancy Feast. He says you got a fucking cat, don't you? And the watch commander says there's nothing he can do about it. These guys aren't officially missing. Nobody knows shit. And nobody wants to go undercover, nobody.

A minute or two rattled past. I waited but Moon said nothing else. His voice had disappeared into the powdery air of sleep.

The motherfucker is asleep and maybe I'm jealous. Not sleeping so well lately. Not since I got off the junk. It's like the dark doesn't really find me.

I wait for it. I wait for the velvet, for the warm bottomless silence to come and wrap itself around me but the silence is indifferent and passes me by and I remember the velvet doesn't know me anymore, it doesn't want me.

And I think about other ways to get there. Bleeding to death might work. As long as I didn't cut through a major artery the long slide down to unconsciousness would likely be slow and sweet, something I could savor.

It's a funny thing to dream but sometimes I dream of going flatline. Not sure I would want to go all the way under but for a minute or two it would be pretty nice to take a look around and then swim back to the surface.

Thursday's child has far to go.

Mingus:

Red bricks on all sides. The smell of earth and clay and men sweating. The smoke of a thousand cigarettes. Sunshine and tar. The noise of a bulldozer, loud as fury.

Mingus chomped at his tongue. He was too easily hypnotized by his own sense of smell. The pain in his tongue cleared his head. His legs were asleep and dangling from the iron fire escape. He put away the yo-yo and leaned forward to watch Chrome lazily finish off the Fred. Mingus chewed at his thumbnail, his head still spinning from the scent of Chinese take-out and the strange Citizen they had encountered at Goo's.

That one would bear watching, he thought.

At the end of the alley, Chrome still whispered into the Fred's ear. Mingus stopped himself from summoning the smell of the Fred's damp, fishy hair. He was plagued enough by the real.

The Fred lay curled like a baby in ash and black gravel. He was almost asleep, his hands limp and white. Chrome stroked the back of the Fred's neck, his lips moving softly. He was singing a French nursery rhyme, Mingus was sure of it. Frère Jacques. Chrome was terribly disappointed that he had not been born French. He spoke often of jumping a ship to Paris, of starting their own subterrain there. But it would not be so easy. One did not just withdraw from the game and Chrome's French was hopeless.

He was the cruelest of the Mariners, without question. Chrome garroted the Freds, pulling them down like sick deer. But he didn't kill them straightaway. He calmed and comforted them. He promised not to hurt them and he lulled them to sleep. He made them feel safe in his arms. Then he went for the tongue.

The others were so greedy for tongue that they killed without pause.

The wind rose, flooding Mingus with a sickening spectrum of odors, each of them dense with borrowed memory. Mingus pinched his nostrils between thumb and finger and watched as Chrome knelt beside the Fred, brushing bits of filth from his clothing. He gently buttoned the Fred's jacket to the throat, then patted him on the cheek with the odd, faraway smile of a father who is about to strike.

Mingus closed his eyes because he didn't need to watch, to see.

He could imagine well enough. Chrome would take the man's face in his strong hands and bend forward, as if to kiss the mouth. He would force the jaw open, wide enough to count the Fred's teeth. He would suck the Fred's tongue from his mouth as if it were an oyster, then bite it softly at the pink root and stop himself just short of severing it but still he would draw blood. He would own the Fred's already blurry soul. He would swallow, his eyes flashing silver. Mingus could already hear the Fred screaming, or trying to. His hollow, shrunken voice like the bark of a baby seal.

Mingus opened his eyes and Chrome stood tall over the Fred, skinny and shining. His arms hanging loose. His face and chest were bloody, streaming red and black. Mingus felt cold and rushing dizzy as he saw but couldn't believe what he saw.

The Fred lay motionless, his throat ripped open.

Chrome has killed the man, truly killed him. Mingus coughed, staring. There was a shivering fist in his throat. He felt like he was falling down a brightly lit elevator shaft. This couldn't be. This was a game, a fantasy. The taking of tongues was painful, yes. A little bloody sometimes. But it wasn't real, it wasn't real. What had the motherfucker done. What had he done.

What have you done?

He looked away, then back. This couldn't be what it seemed and now Chrome walked toward him, his face a red mask. He held something shiny in one hand, like a badge.

Mingus, he said. Je me suis égare.

Long shadows. I reached for the jug of Canadian Mist and took a small, bitter swallow. Moon grunted and pulled himself up to an approximate sitting position now, with considerable effort. I ignored him, tried to digest his story. The thing was decomposing in my head and it sounded perfectly fucked up. It sounded like the paranoid tale of some accident-prone crossdresser who had played with himself too much as a boy and his Baptist mother had burned his fingers on the iron when she caught him at it. In a few months or years, Moon would sound like any other twitchy bastard with a theory about how the phone company had started the Gulf War.

But maybe there was something to this. Maybe cops were disappearing and no one cared. Anything was possible.

Anyway.

I had a pretty good idea what Moon was asking for. He wanted me to be a canary, a fragile seeker of bad air. Moon wanted to send me underground, then watch to see if I would come back or disappear. And why not, right? I was a nonperson. I was untouchable. I had no money, no hope. I wasn't officially dead yet, but I was close enough. I knew the terrain, as well. I swallowed another mouthful of Canadian Mist. I had spent more than one day undercover busily deconstructing myself. What was another day, or two? But I couldn't quite see Moon's eyes. I couldn't trust him. I flicked on a reading lamp that I had moved out of Moon's path of destruction an hour ago. It provided a small circle of light that Moon now leaned into.

You can sleep here, he said. For a while. You'll need another address if you go under.

I shrugged, undecided. Yeah.

What do you say?

What is it that you want me to do, exactly?

Moon chewed at his lips, rabid. I want you to find Jimmy Sky.

What about the other twelve guys, I said.

I'll get you a gun, said Moon. A car, maybe. Any equipment you want.

The other guys? I said.

Fuck the other guys.

What's so special about Jimmy Sky?

Moon shrugged. I can scrape some funds out of petty cash. Mad money.

Mad money, I said. Oh, boy.

Yeah, baby. You're gonna have the time of your life.

I nodded, sinking onto the couch. There was one small thing that troubled me. Maybe it was nothing. But I was lying, earlier. I had never heard of a cop named Jimmy Sky. It sounded a lot like the name of a comic book hero, like someone's secret identity. It sounded like a lame superhero, some second-rate character like the Green Lantern. Now there was a pussy if ever there was one. The Green Lantern. A prettyboy with a magic ring.

Goo:

Limping, she was limping. What time was it. The sky had gone red and pink, like an exposed membrane. It couldn't be much past midnight, could it. But it felt like dawn, like the sun was rising. The air against her face had the warm kiss of fever. She crossed the street, barely aware of passing cars.

She told herself to slow down.

It couldn't be morning yet.

When she reached the other side, there was a faraway noise in her head like a hushed whisper, a ghost of fingers in her hair. Goo became Eve. Her apartment building loomed ahead, black. As ever, there was the knife of disappointment. The regret. She didn't want to share herself with Eve.

Eve bore new bruises, fresh cuts.

Her apartment was empty and the air brittle.

She took off her coat and hung it carefully on a hook, then stepped out of Adore's green dress and let it fall to the floor. Her body was numb, as usual. The transition wrecked her sometimes and she would easily sleep for fifteen hours without dreaming. The game was swallowing everything around her with the silent fury of a televised hurricane. Eve had no friends, no family. She had no job anymore and school was a pale, foreign memory. Three classes, she had paid tuition for three classes. Maybe four. One of them was Logic, she thought. Logic, yes. She had chosen it because it satisfied a Math credit, which seemed funny at the time. But she couldn't remember the last time she even went near campus. At least five, maybe six weeks ago. Dizzy. She was a little dizzy. It might not be such a bad idea to withdraw from the game for a while, to catch her breath. Eve glanced over her shoulder. There was no one to hear her disordered thoughts, no one but Goo.

She went into the kitchen and opened a can of tuna. Walked back to the living room and stood in the dark, eating tuna straight from the can. Her face in a black window, looking back at her. The sheen of oil on her lips. She might not want to leave the game, she might not be able to.

What had the Redeemer said? It's okay to be two people, two people.

Bone-white curtains swirled around her and she realized slowly that Phineas was gone. There were crumpled bits of paper on her floor. She picked them up and each one bore her given name.

I WONDERED DIMLY what time it might be. I had reluctantly sold my watch two weeks earlier in Memphis, to a nervous, razor-thin guy named Duke in a downtown pawnshop. Forty bucks for my father's antique diving watch. And Duke had insulted me. He said the watch was barely worth ten dollars, because there was no way it was still waterproof. I was fucking lucky to get forty, according to Duke. There had been a wide, unfriendly silence as I wondered how much the watch was worth to me and how badly I needed to get to Denver. A black fly buzzed past my face, then landed on my wrist. It strolled up my arm, looking for a bite to eat. Duke had stared long and hard at the fly, his head bobbing as I tried in vain to explain that water resistance was really not the point. The watch was a valuable relic, an ode to an earlier age. At which point Duke had wiped his bright red nose and glared at me and said that the forty was about to fucking disappear. Duke had the bright, acidic stink and glow of a meth addict and I had to admit that I could live with forty.

Now I was awake. I was damp and hungry on Moon's couch and I had no useful concept of time. The sky was black through the nearest window but that meant nothing. I had to pee, however. Maybe it was close to morning, maybe not. There was always the chance that God would cancel the day. That God would say fuck this noise and just shut down the whole operation.

I don't believe in God, exactly. I believe in gods. I tend to think there are any number of godlike creatures running around up there and that none of them is all-powerful. None of them is Santa Claus, okay. Most of them have dark intentions, cruel purpose. They want to be wrathful, but they don't quite have the juice. They have good days and bad days. On good days they can lay waste to a fishing village in Honduras or if they're feeling fat and prosperous maybe stop a bus full of kids from diving into a gorge but mostly they just fuck around and stir things up.

Anyway. Take a long look at your own hand. The slender claw, beautiful and cruel. A team of expensive scientists working around the clock couldn't design a more effective piece of machinery. This is what Hamlet was going on about there in Act Two. *Man delights not me, nor woman neither.* Because at the end of the day the hand does what you want it to. It saves the bird with the broken wing from drowning. It snatches the kid out of oncoming traffic and it pulls the trigger that ends the life of someone who deserves it or doesn't. The hand does crosswords and lights cigarettes and feeds the fish and pinches your nipples when it gets bored. The hand is God.

I'm a fool, of course. But in the bright or anyway less shadowy regions of my heart I think I was hoping to come home and find a little space. Which is funny, don't you think. *Home* is a word with such uneasy and fragile and ultimately menacing overtones that anyone else on the planet would have fucking known better.

Moon wants me to find a missing cop named Jimmy Sky and I have a pretty good idea that no such person exists but Moon has been such a faithful protector in the past that I can only nod and say yes.

The queer thing is Moon's tone, his voice. One minute he seems really very worried about the health and welfare of his pal Jimmy Sky and the next he is about to chew his own lip off just talking about him and I catch a vibe that maybe Jimmy was no friend at all and what Moon really wants is for me to find the Skywalker hiding out in some shitty motel room so that Moon can put a bullet between his ears or failing that, maybe find the fucker already dead somewhere so Moon might have the private pleasure of spitting on poor Jimmy's remains.

And I guess it makes no difference to me, as Jimmy Sky is no friend of mine but still I wonder because the whole thing feels slippery and wrong and maybe I'm walking down a road that goes nowhere good.

Imagine you were in my shoes. What would you do, Jude?

Chrome:

He was shivering and wet. The water was so cold. His skin had a faraway brilliance, like he had stuck his bare arm into the snow and left it there. He huddled in the dark mouth of a suburban driveway, using a sleeping citizen's garden hose to wash the blood from his face and hands. He felt absurdly calm. He had done it, he had touched the ghost. He had killed and it wasn't make-believe. The Fred had been a policeman and if he wanted to, Chrome could certainly tell himself and anyone who cared to listen that it was self-defense. The policeman had pulled a gun on him. He had been a threat to all of them, to the game. But that wasn't it at all. The man had been a Fred. He had been passive, a slug. He had barely known what planet he was on. Chrome could have simply bitten the man's tongue and disappeared as he had done countless times. One tongue, taken by force. Two points. Two more points. But the accumulation of points no longer interested him. He had lost count long ago and he had known this would happen one day. And when he nipped the Fred's warm tongue and tasted blood, he had felt everything at once. His skin, bright and tingling as if he could peel it off and give it a shake. The small hairs on his neck. The enamel of his own teeth. He felt like time had folded around him and come to a complete stop. He and the Fred had been trapped together in a window, a bubble. They had fallen into one of those little plastic paperweights filled with water and artificial snow and the Fred's throat had been soft and white and sweetly exposed and Chrome had been unable to think of any reason not to sink his teeth into that skin and simply pull it open. The blood had washed over his face, it had filled him with a sickness and joy that were fleeting. It was like an orgasm, of course. But the comparison was such a cliché it pained him to consider it.

He was a werewolf, a ripper.

He grinned. Très diabolique, non?

Now he took off his shirt, rinsed it and put it back on. He glanced down at the street, where Mingus paced nervously along the sidewalk. The Breather was freaking out, truly. He had looked at Chrome with such horror and disbelief that Chrome had laughed out loud. Mingus had seen what he did. He had seen him kill and Chrome hoped this would not be a problem.

DEAD FACE YAWNING. My own warped face in the mirror. I had acquired the habit of examining it whenever I found myself alone in a bathroom. Otherwise I tended to forget exactly what I looked like. I promised myself this was not such a bad thing, and hardly a clinical condition. I looked like no one and it was nothing to worry about. I pissed confidently into Moon's toilet, then climbed into his shower. The pipes groaned and the water was so immediately hot that I felt a little faint.

Moon had a surprisingly dainty assortment of hair products. Honey and clove shampoo. Conditioner made from dead silkworms, pasteurized goat's milk and raw egg whites. A silicone-gel hair thickener and eucalyptus hair mist. The poor bastard's hair was thinning, wasn't it. It was turning to ash. Moon's hair was vacating. The water crashed down and I dreamed on my feet. I saw Moon through the shower curtain, his hard white belly jutting against the sink and his face moist with sweat. I watched as Moon mournfully tugged another grassy fistful from his skull, then checked his gums for bleeding with a sigh. I watched him give the cat a bowl of dry food and leave the radio on to kill the terrifying emptiness in his apartment and I hoped that he felt a little better when he was out on the street. That he was suffering nothing more than the melancholy dreaminess of a distracted, middle-aged cop. And I wondered, as Moon must, how many years did he have left before he stumbled, before he stepped through the wrong doorway and shuddered from the tug of a bullet never seen, never heard.

Now I pulled on pants and wandered through Moon's apartment, my hair wet and smelling like a field of poppies from Moon's shampoo. The average person has a serious accumulation of shit. Personal shit and sentimental shit. Valuable shit and shit they don't need. But Moon had almost nothing that was his. Nothing to remind him of anything or anyone. He had a couch, a chair, a television. He had a screwed-up cat. He had a broken record player. He had a punching bag, a heavy one. It was covered in a year's worth of dust, though. Dead skin and cat fuzz and pollen. I gave it a passing jab and choked in the sudden, swarming cloud. Moon has a dartboard but no darts that I could find. There were no photographs, no trinkets. There were no books. I remembered that Moon bought one used book at a time and when he was done with it he traded it for another one.

The apartment was just silent. A wide pocket of nothing, a vacuum.

I could feel a mild panic attack coming on and I suddenly wanted to be sure that Moon was not dead or gone. I walked down the hall to the master bedroom and nudged the door open. Moon slept flat on his back, snoring softly. A small television was placed precariously atop a tower of milk crates. A lonely weatherman blinked on the screen, colorless and muted. The crates contained socks, underwear. The orange cat lay coiled around Moon's big bare feet and when I entered the room the beast gave me a look of profound indifference. I allowed myself to sit on the floor, my back to the cold wall. I smoked a single cigarette, dropping the ashes into my cupped hand. The weatherman gestured meaningfully at a swirl of cloud patterns. I stared long and hard at his frosted television hair and finally decided that it must be an expensive toupee. I watched Moon sleep and I had a feeling that he regularly slipped away in the broken light of the weather channel. This pale emptiness is what I had wanted so badly, when I wished my wife would die. It's what I couldn't bear when she did.

There was a clock beside Moon's bed, a pale red digital. Two minutes past five. I hoped the sun would come up quickly. I hoped something interesting would happen on the weather channel. Moon flopped over onto his left side, grunting. I moved closer and stared at his face, at the infinite twitching of his eyelids. His breath was terrible, oozing from his wide nostrils and thick, parted lips. Moon was two or three days past his last shave and I could see the beginnings of gray in his beard. It becomes him, I thought. There was a sudden change in temperature and I jerked back, afraid that Moon might wake to find me leaning over him like a killer. But one window was cracked, and a breath of cold air had merely entered the room. Shame stretched, then leapt from the bed. He glowered at me briefly, his eyes green and yellow. Then stalked out of the room with a lazy flip of the tail.

I wandered after him, stupidly eager for company.

Eve:

A shaft of yellow light in an otherwise dark apartment. Eve crouched in her closet, sifting through papers and discarded shoes. She wore thin black sweatpants and a T-shirt with the sleeves cut off. If she were normal, if she were someone with houseplants and a cat and a nice boyfriend, then she might have just come home from the gym. Her heart still thumping from aerobics. She would be drinking a vitamin-enriched smoothie and her rib cage would not be laced with cuts, she would not be stiff with bandages. Eve wore no underwear and no shoes and she didn't feel at all sexy. Eve was tired, worried. She was annoyed, as well. She was worried about Phineas and she didn't want to be.

As a small child, she had spent hours upon hours in her mother's closet. Trapped, she had imagined herself a spider. She had loved the four walls, the dangling clothes that hung like cheap, shrunken tapestries. Her mother's clothes had always seemed to be moving, touched by an impossible breeze. She would look behind them for a window, a portal. But there was only another wall.

When she was nine, she began to have dizzying nightmares about open space, fields of wheat surrounded by wide gray concrete. Nothing ever pursued her. But the emptiness had been unbearable and she always woke choking, as if she had swallowed half the sky. She would then crawl not to her mother's bed for comfort, but to her mother's cramped closet. Then had slept like a kitten on a heap of dirty laundry that smelled of smoke and fried food.

Now she found what she was looking for. A flat wooden box, taped shut like a cozy little coffin. Eve slit the tape with her thumbnail and removed the bald, naked Barbie doll from her childhood. She had an idea that she might use it for her piece. That Goo might use it. Eve glanced at her watch. She frowned and lifted it to her ear. It had stopped again. A dead piece of metal on her wrist. She tossed it aside and wondered if Phineas was okay, if he was coming back. She noticed there was a strange feeling in her stomach, a peculiar flutter, when she thought of him.

SHAME SWIRLED AROUND THE KITCHEN, murmuring. He twisted himself seductively around my leg. He was clearly hungry and there was no cat food to be found. I dug for a while through Moon's barren cupboards and eventually offered the cat some corn flakes. Shame stared up at me, disgusted.

I shrugged. Aren't you used to this, I said.

There was a crusty jar of peanut butter in the fridge. I scooped out a spoonful and wedged it into a coffee cup, which seemed to satisfy Shame. I knelt, then stretched out on my belly alongside the creature, who made a fairly nasty sucking sound as he worked on the peanut butter. His eyes flickered, warning me not to touch him.

The floor was yellow linoleum, torn and ravaged by Moon's feet, but it felt cool against my skin.

Moon had been drunk last night, raving. But he had offered me a job, sort of. The whole business was borderline craziness. It was nonsense and it wasn't. Moon wanted me to go undercover and look for a few lost cops. As if they were merely trapped on the wrong side of the wardrobe, with the lion and the witch. They could be anywhere and the disappearances could be unrelated. These were cops, though. And cops weren't known to disappear. They went mad, some of them. They got stabbed by their wives. They ruined their livers. But they generally showed up for work.

I watched the cat eat. I thought about it and I tended to think that thirteen missing cops was a case for somebody else, somebody who still had a badge, for instance. If there was any truth to Moon's story, then it was something heavy. It was FBI territory. The kind of case that I was more likely to make worse than better. The kind of case I would be sorry to fuck up. But if Moon really wanted to set me up in a motel room with a pocketful of walking money, then I might as well look into it. I could sniff around.

Why not? I said to Shame.

The cat had finished his breakfast and was now hurriedly cleaning himself. He looked pretty pissed off at me and I decided that the peanut butter was maybe a bad choice. Like glue in those old whiskers. I tried not to laugh, as I was pretty sure that animals didn't much like to be laughed at by ignorant humans. Shame gave his genitals a cursory lick, then glided from the room without a backward glance.

I could not live here, clearly. The cat didn't like me.

Mingus:

Pinched his nostrils between thumb and finger. Breathed through his mouth and stared bleakly at a patch of grass. He had alien memories, images that couldn't possibly be his. A tiny house in the suburbs, painted a dull peach color that had faded to an unpleasant flesh tone. The same color as every home around it. Each house had one sad midget tree in the front yard, a skeletal sapling that would never grow taller than five feet. Trees that provided no shade.

Mingus shuddered as a thin man entered his mind, whistling.

The man wore bright blue suspenders and a torn white shirt. The shirt was tucked carefully into khaki shorts. The man had long, strangely hairless legs. He wore destroyed black penny loafers with no socks. He pushed a lawn mower and sang softly to himself. There was a child in the background, a boy with hair so blond it looked white. The man was familiar, yes. The man was his father. His father. Mingus clutched at his face, his mouth and nose. He'd never had a father.

But he resembled the thin man.

I never had a father, he said.

Chrome punched him in the belly and suddenly he couldn't breathe. Chrome, whose hands were still wet. How does that feel, he said.

Mingus sputtered, unable to speak.

Image of the thin man faded. Boy with white hair was gone. He glanced fearfully at the patch of grass before him and nothing happened. His head was empty, thank god. The bliss of forgetting, of never knowing. He wondered if he would ever control his sense of smell and the terrible rush of images that he could not be sure were his own. The brutal memories that devoured him. He was aware that Chrome was sitting very close to him. He didn't want to look at Chrome for fear of seeing blood. He was reluctant to breathe and he wanted to be careful when he spoke, very careful.

I'm better now, said Mingus finally. Thank you.

My pleasure, said Chrome.

Friday

MANAGED TO BREW A POT of coffee in Moon's wrecked kitchen. There was no milk to be found and the sugar had a few bloated ants crawling drunkenly through it, and more than a few of their cousins that looked to be dead, overdosed on sugar. But what can you do. In some countries, sugared ants are not cheap. The coffee was too thick and black, it was like oil. It tasted of ancient, frozen rubber. I added a fistful of sugar and dead ants and sucked it down.

I attempted to clean up the living room for a while, pushing garbage and dishes and clothes and general debris into various piles but soon lost interest in the project. I ended up just kicking the broken table into a corner. Then I started looking for something to read. The phone book, a dictionary. Even a little junk mail. Bored, restless. But I didn't much feel like venturing into the city. Not sure what I was afraid of. I was feeling shy or something. I didn't want to face the hum and buzz of technology. The drone and clatter of machinery. I was forever hearing false gunshots in the distance.

It crossed my mind that Eve might be worried about me, or rather I hoped she was. I would have called her, but she didn't have a phone. She didn't even have a toaster.

The sun was coming up in a hurry and I contemplated the social order of ghosts. If any of them were still out and about they had better take cover. Because it seemed to me that a stray phantom caught drifting the streets past daybreak looking washed out and pale with less than frightful hair would be tortured by his peers.

I sat with my feet up on a windowsill, my eyes peeled for any interesting neighbors to spy on. I am not a pervert, exactly. If I spotted another human in a compromised position with the shades up I would surely turn away. I was only bored out of my mind and lonely. But there was nothing much to see. An old woman came out with a small bag of garbage and walked to the curb in a painfully slow shuffle, so slow in fact that I was tempted to run downstairs and give her a hand but this would probably just frighten her and I had alternate visions of the poor woman either suffering a heart attack and collapsing at my feet, or beating me senseless with the black leather pocketbook she had curiously chosen to bring with her to the curb.

I smoked the last of Moon's cigarettes and finally gave up on any action from the windows. I made another search of the living room for something to read and came upon a drawer that contained a relative mother lode of unpaid bills and one grimy, water-stained and thoroughly abused leather address book. There were a hundred names and addresses in there, including one heartbreaking entry for Phineas and Lucy Poe that was crossed out with a slash of blue ink. And while almost every other name in Moon's book was that of a cop, not one of them was Jimmy or James Sky.

Chrome:

They sat on a damp beach, waiting for a bus that would never come. Mingus was beside him, hunched over like he had a belly full of angry butterflies. Chrome smiled, or gnashed his teeth. He wanted to tell Mingus to slow down, to taste life and now he whispered it, softly. Taste it, he said. Taste life. But Mingus wouldn't look up. Chrome shrugged and licked his lips. There was a touch of dried blood just beneath his nose, caught in his whiskers like chocolate milk. Everyone loves chocolate milk, he thought. Oh my. How restless he was, how like a child. His arms and legs were bouncing, quivering. As if his molecules were coming loose. He was trembling like a wee little girl. It's just juice, he told himself. It's juice from the kill, from the real. The real.

Oh, yes. He was happy. He wanted to go back to the alley and look at the dead Fred again, to look into his flattened eyes and say thank you. And he realized that true killers always love their victims. They love them. They love them for sharing that last breath. Evolution would never dispense with murder, not if love was involved. Chrome was on fire. He wanted to walk for miles. He wanted to kiss the ground. But he had to think of Mingus. The poor little troll was trembling beside him. He must be exhausted, thought Chrome. And he was visibly upset. He was probably wrestling with his conscience or something. Chrome would have to come down to earth, for his sake. The Breather needed sleep, he needed to feel safe. But what did he need, what did Chrome need? Maybe a little sex would calm him down, a little love. He poked Mingus with a bony finger.

I have blood on my upper lip, he said. It smells like sea salt. It smells like the tiny golden hairs on the back of a woman's neck. It smells like a kid with a sunburn.

You bastard, said Mingus.

I'm sorry. The mind wanders, doesn't it.

Please. I'm a wreck. I need to get inside, to sleep perhaps. To dream.

Are you sure you want to dream? said Chrome.

In my dreams, I have no sense of smell.

Interesting. I am color-blind in mine.

Mingus grabbed at his leg with the small, powerful fingers of a monkey and Chrome jumped.

Let go of my leg, said Chrome. Damn you.

I want to go home.

We don't have a home.

A motel, then. A flop in the subterrain.

Chrome softened. He pried Mingus's fingers loose from his pants with a sigh and now he thought of Goo. She had strong fingers, too. Chrome did need a touch of love. And his friend badly needed sleep. Chrome sighed as it began to rain. He patted Mingus on the head and told him not to fret.

Then he smiled, feeling wicked. Look at the sky, he said. It's purple. Almost the color of a plum. A ripe, sweet-smelling plum. A bruise on the ass of a little child.

Mingus groaned.

Then again, said Chrome. If I were dreaming, I suppose the sky would look sad and gray.

Please, said Mingus.

Chrome still held the little man's hand. Thick callused fingers, with fairly chewed nails. He gave the hand a squeeze and said, come on. Let's get inside.

NOT QUITE SEVEN AND MOON was miraculously awake. If not, there was an angry and very clumsy burglar crashing around in the bathroom and blowing his nose for about five minutes with what seemed to me truly morbid gusto. The toilet was flushed several times. Then more crashing. Moon came into the living room finally, panting. I looked up from the newspaper I had stolen from his neighbor.

The Nuggets won, I said.

Uh. What happened last night?

You killed some furniture.

Moon gazed without recognition at the shattered coffee table. He nodded and stared and I was struck with the uneasy sensation that Moon had no idea who I was. In a minute, the wheels would grind in his head and he would know me for an interloper. Moon would find his strength and leap upon me, beating me about the head and face with extreme prejudice and evicting me from his cage.

You, said Moon. You disarmed me last night.

I nodded. You were something of a menace.

Where is my weapon, please?

The freezer.

Yeah, said Moon. Is there more coffee?

If you want to call it that.

Moon shrugged and ambled away and soon he came back with a cup of the sludge in one hand and his big .45 in the other. The gun looked strange and ghostly, black steel gone smoky with frost.

I blinked. How do your fingers feel?

And after a moment of silence, Moon laughed. Pretty fucking cold.

Don't put it in your mouth, I said.

Don't worry.

Moon settled onto the couch. He wore a fresh pair of white pants, a blue shirt. The familiar fish tie was crisply knotted. His socks appeared to match. His thin hair was slicked back and he looked much like an eccentric football coach. He looked like himself.

Did I tell you a story last night, he said. By any chance?

A wild story, I said.

Moon sat there, nodding at me. I tasted the remains of my own bitter-sweet coffee. Room temperature. The same temperature as my own skin. Tingling. I felt a headache coming on and touched my fingers to my eyes. Maybe it was just loneliness.

Moon is fucking crazy, I thought.

Jimmy Sky is missing, said Moon. I know that much. He raised his frozen gun to his own ear, grinning as he made a hollow popping sound with his tongue. Or dead maybe. He's gone to see Elvis. Poor fucking Jimmy. He was a friend of mine.

What? I said. What did you say?

The bastard, said Moon. I want you to help me find him.

What's this about Elvis?

Moon's eyes were flat and dark. I miss him, he said. I miss Jimmy.

Okay, I said. Okay.

Eve:

Alone in bed, sleepless. The sky beyond her window was the thin, name-less color of thick glass and she felt temporarily trapped between night and morning. She lay on her back, tracing two fingers over the length of her body down from the sensitive throat and hollow place above her collar-bone, tugging at her nipples until they were hard and then moving on to examine the bruises along her rib cage, the tender places where Adore had nicked her flesh and now she pressed one finger into these sores until the pain was fine and bright. She stroked her belly, her hip bones. She trailed the tips of her fingers lightly, lightly along the inner thigh before moving to touch herself through the thin cotton of her sweatpants and with the other hand moved to stroke one breast in small circles close to but not quite touching the nipple and now she was wet and her hips were moving involuntarily and she slipped her hand under the edge of her pants and through the soft patch of pubic hair and the odd half-formed thought that she really needed to trim down there skated in and out of her head without quite being heard and now she had two fingers inside herself moving in slow collapsing circles but soon a shadowy person emerged in her mind, a ghoulish figure who somehow had Adore's thin dark body and long fingers and Chrome's sweet, wet mouth and the cloudy blue eyes of Phineas Poe and still the face belonged to none of them. Eve stopped and her breath came in blunt short gasps that pulled painfully at her bandages. She rolled over, frustrated and cold and her thoughts flying to what Adore had said last night. That it was time for Goo to do a piece of her own, to choose a victim. It wouldn't be easy, for the choice was not about lust or hatred or domination, but a kind of awful tenderness. And the victim must somehow recognize the difference.

I was glad when Moon finally said he might go to work. After a prolonged search that involved a lot of cursing and banging around, Moon produced a spare key and I told him I was going to need some money. Moon snapped his fingers and closed one eye. We were standing in the kitchen, a few feet apart. Hands empty, dangling. Shame brushed past mewling. His fur bright with static.

Money, said Moon. Of course. He grinned too widely.

He opened the cabinet beneath the sink and poked around. Roach killer and empty mason jars and Ivory liquid and one rotting blue sponge. Moon still hummed to himself and the tune was familiar. It was unlikely but I could have sworn this was from the soundtrack for *2001: Space Odyssey*, the opening scene. Two monkeys were fighting over a piece of fruit, or possibly a female. They circle each other, shrieking and spitting. Then it occurs to one of them that he might use a chunk of wood to his advantage. To escalate things. One monkey crushes the skull of another and he is so pleased with himself, with his discovery. He dances around in his enemy's blood and the camera pulls back for a wide view. Dark silhouettes that could be human. Kubrick. He wasn't always subtle but he knew what he was talking about. And now Moon had found what he was looking for: a slightly mildewed cigar box. There was a shadowy, conspiratorial glow in his eyes that I didn't care for. Moon removed a brown envelope from the box and handed it over.

What's this?

Moon didn't smile. We should talk later, he said.

With that, he turned and waddled down the hall to the elevator. His pants were too short and his wide buttocks swung like loose freight. He looked like the fucking white rabbit. He was neurotically cheerful and at least two hours late for work.

I sighed and opened the envelope to find a plastic evidence bag containing maybe an ounce of coke. Maybe less. I was hopeless at eyeballing weights. I shook my head in disgust as my nose began to itch. There was also an array of credit cards and ID under various names. My favorite was Ray Fine. I could be Ray Fine for a while. There was no cash in the envelope, however. Moon seemed to think that I could easily peddle the coke for a little spending money. It was not exactly what I had been hoping to do this morning but I would have to manage. I am so bad with drugs, though. I'm terrible at selling them. I always manage to get myself ripped off and whatever slim profit I come away with is most likely to find its way up my nose. Of course, there was no investment in this case. It was all profit and I should really taste the product before I tried to unload it. What if it was a lot of speed and aspirin and somebody wanted to gut me for burning them? That wouldn't do at all. I merrily chopped out a couple of skinny lines with Ray's platinum Visa card and of course had nothing at all to use as a tube, not a single dollar bill to hoover them with. This was perfect. The lines wiggled on Moon's chipped counter and I was sure that I would sneeze and blow them away before I could find a tube of some kind. I opened my wallet and got out my social security card. It was a little soft and ragged but it did roll up nicely. The coke was pure and fine and now I couldn't feel my own tongue. And what do you know but I decided I was suddenly pretty cheerful and thought a walk was just what I needed.

Besides, the apartment had settled into a mid-morning gloom that I really couldn't bear.

Mingus:

Four doorways and he had come this way before. These were the runnels beneath Los Angeles. Dark, with pockets of burning steam. Land mines. And blackened corpses lay everywhere. Four doors. One of them had the faint red glow of a laser trip wire. Immediate death. As for the other three, well. That was the question. Aliens waited behind two of them. And the fourth held a medkit, possibly a key. He couldn't remember. Okay, okay. He checked his health. A sliver of yellow. He could take one, maybe two shots and he was meat. No problem. He just couldn't afford to choose the wrong door. But if he did, he was by God taking a few aliens out with him. The ugly lizard boys. He checked his weapon. A chaingun, with twenty-nine rounds. Fucking worthless. He could easily waste that firing at shadows and he scrolled through his weapons for something better. Flamethrower: always a lot of fun but unreliable. Shotgun: two useless shells. Nine millimeter: full clip. Rocket launcher: suicidal in such close quarters. The nine it was, then.

Now.

Which door did he like. He closed his eyes for a moment, trying to think.

Pounding, pounding. Someone was pounding on the door.

Mingus opened his eyes and his perspective had changed somewhat. It was still a first-person shooter but he could see more of his body than he should have been able to. His feet, his legs. His abdomen. And his hands, which were empty. They weren't holding a weapon and this wasn't what he thought it was. This wasn't a video game.

This was life, or something like it.

The top of a flight of stairs, a white lightbulb. A single moth darting around it. Chrome was beside him, leaning against chipped gray plaster with a look of mild irritation on his face.

Where are we?

Chrome smiled at him. I'm at Goo's place, he said. Or rather, I'm waiting outside of Goo's place. I'm lurking in the shadows. I don't know where the devil you are.

Yes, I'm sorry. I was in LA, in the sewers. Hunting aliens.

It's nice to have you back, said Chrome.

It was an overload, a crash. A temporary aversion.

Well, then. If you are breathing freely again, why don't you tell me if Goo is in there or not.

Mingus sniffed. She's inside. She's listening to us.

Chrome leaned against the door, his cheek to the wood. Come on, love. Open the door or I will blow it down.

Silence.

Then Goo's voice, muffled. I'm not in the mood, Christian.

Chrome flinched at the sound of his given name, his dead name. Mingus tried and failed to catch his eye. And he realized he was afraid. He stood alongside Chrome with a permanent bellyful of fear and he was getting used to this. This fear wasn't going anywhere. Mingus could smell the girl inside, faintly. She smelled of shampoo and dried sweat and chamomile tea. She smelled vaguely of bitter flowers and Mingus decided she wasn't wearing underpants. The girl smelled like blood. She smelled angry.

Maybe we should go elsewhere, said Mingus.

Chrome shook his head. Open this fucking door, he said. I'm not joking.

Another silence. Long and bright.

Then the door cracked slowly and Goo stood there, barefoot. She held something queer in her right hand, a naked headless Barbie doll.

Mingus held his breath but it was too late. He was in the backseat of a car with a little girl, a sister or cousin. She was small, with dark skin. Nine or ten. She wore a red bathing suit and her legs were long and thin as a deer's. She had no breasts at all and her hair was still damp from swimming and she held a Barbie doll dressed in little tennis whites. The windows were open and the wind crashed through the car. His ears were ringing. His skin was tender, burned. Mingus was choking on something. He has a mouthful of something like sawdust. He glanced at his hands and saw that he held an oatmeal cookie with soft plump raisins staring back at him like dull black eyes.

DEAR JUDE.

I didn't want to leave you but I couldn't sleep anymore. And don't fucking laugh at me, okay.

I'm west of the Mississippi now. Two days, give or take. I remember train stations, rust. Lies. The memory is edited into a knowable body that defies logic. The land between us is dead skin. There are no peacocks, no maneuvers.

There is no invulnerable green.

I was kicking a nice little morphine habit and what did I expect, a soft rosy glow and the soothing hum of furry woodland creatures and one long foot massage to lull me to sleep but that wasn't it. I could handle the withdrawals no problem. They were painful and horrifying and endless but that was pretty much what I expected. As advertised. I would like to sleep in a tin shack with you. Under a tin roof that leaks. What got me in the end was the notion that you were secretly the Dread Pirate Roberts. You know that flick, *The Princess Bride*? The sky is endless, blind, ravenous. Enduring every shade of gray. Hunger. I pray for geometry, for logic. I was the farmboy, Westley. He stupidly believes in true love and is captured by the Dread Pirate Roberts who decides at the last moment not to kill young Westley and instead takes him on as his valet and personal gofer and every night Roberts very cheerfully says to him: Good night, Westley and sleep well. I will most likely kill you in the morning...good night. If I were an archeologist, I would never label my finds. My tender and dusty shards.

Good night, Phineas. And sleep well. I will most likely kill you in the morning.

Chrome:

Eve was annoying him. She was wary, and wouldn't ask them to sit down. Chrome considered this rude, but he decided to ignore it for now. He was reluctant to criticize her, to provoke her. He drifted through her place lazily, as if he might buy it. Mingus stood on one foot, then the other. Chrome saw Eve give him a quick, disappearing smile. She was fond of the poor Breather, Chrome knew. She felt sorry for him.

Chrome rubbed his tongue along the inside of his teeth.

Goo, he said softly. Why are you so unfriendly?

Don't call me that, okay.

She stared at him with cool disregard. That's the real trouble with her, he thought. She wasn't afraid of him. He touched one finger to his left temple, and hoped he would never have to hurt her. She didn't appreciate him. The stupid girl had no idea how exhausting it was, to play the part of a cool and charming psychopath all day. How difficult it could be to stay in character. She had no fucking idea.

He stared at her and saw that she still held the doll in her hand, a headless doll. It was an ugly little thing. The hands and feet appeared to have been mutilated. Then he noticed the tiny pink shaving of plastic on the floor. She had whittled away the hands and feet, sharpened them. He did love her, in a distracted way. He loved the notion that she would carve a doll into a weapon.

What shall I call you, he said.

My name is Eve, she said.

Surely not.

I'm at home, she said. And when I'm home, I'm still Eve.

Chrome took a step toward her. My love, he said.

Her lip curled. Oh, boy.

Chrome laughed. He heard the thin, glassy sound ring from his mouth and he knew he was not faking it. He really was amused, wasn't he. This was fun. This was a truckload of monkeys. Eve took a step back, against the door. He didn't really care if she thought it was any fun.

Are you not my devoted? he said.

Only in the game, she said. Not here.

Oh, no. You wouldn't call our world a game, would you.

Mingus made a chirping sound and ducked away, into the bathroom. Perhaps the closet.

Chrome shook his head sadly. You've frightened him.

What do you want, she said. I'm tired.

Perfect, he said. We, too, are weary. Mingus, especially. He was hoping to sleep on your sofa. And I was hoping to sleep with you.

Funny, she said.

Chrome shrugged. He glanced around the living room at the open windows, at the sunken velvet couch. The scraps of paper on the floor. The bits of Barbie. The menu for the Silver Frog.

Where is your friend? he said.

Eve shook her head. I knew it. You were here, weren't you. What did you do with him?

Nothing, love. We did nothing to the poor man.

Eve chewed her lip, apparently considering whether to believe him or not. It was remarkable, really. When she was Goo, she adored him. She glowed. She couldn't keep her hands off him. But this wretched Eve persona treated him like a diseased dog.

Acceptez-vous les chèques de voyage?

Fuck you, she said.

You love it when I speak French.

She sighed. I really don't. And I think you just asked me if I accept traveler's checks.

Give us a kiss, he said.

No, she said.

What's the trouble, love?

I might want to stop, she said.

What? he said.

The game. I might take a holiday from the game.

Preposterous.

Maybe you should sleep elsewhere, she said.

Chrome growled. He heard himself growl. He lunged at her without thinking. Though he supposed he intended to force her to kiss him. Not a pretty thought. Not for a man of his demeanor. But as he grabbed for her pale throat. Eve raked the headless doll across his face like a knife. He howled and stared dumbly at her. He touched his face and found blood there, a fine mist of red. Oh, he loved her.

NOW WHERE THE FUCK WAS I? The dubious end of Larimer Street, where the economy is based on bail bonds and waste storage and a steady traffic of lost and stolen goods. There are no trees on streets like this and the sun crushes the weal without fail. The sun is bigger out here on the perimeter, it's wider.

Shadows are rare.

I drifted, and allowed myself to consider a few possibilities. I could cut the coke jealously and sell it by the gram. The money would be endless and plentiful but I would of course have nightmares about it. I would have night sweats. I just didn't have the constitution anymore for that sort of thing. I could probably venture into a sex and disco scene tonight and sell it by the nickel to college kids. But that would be too hideous and depressing for words and I would probably fuck it up anyway. I would soon find myself distracted by some shiny little girl with manic blue eyes and plump, unrestrained tits and the cat would run away with the fiddle and I would start giving the coke away. The thing was, no one really did coke anymore. The beautiful people were all dead or pregnant or in grad school. Heroin and meth were cheaper, and more interesting. And crack. Now, that shit was reliable. It would never go out of style. Not as long as the lepers could afford it. The lepers tended to be less fickle. Nobody much wanted coke, nobody. But of course if you had a little coke to spare, then everybody wanted some. Because everyone is sentimental when it comes to drugs. And greedy. The blue-eyed girl I had yet to meet would cling to me like a weightless sloth and I would have a thousand new friends and my own nose would be crusted with blood the next morning, my penis sore and chewed apart. And then Phineas would have no coke, no money. End of discussion. I should really try to sell this bundle in one pop, to some-body who could move it rather painlessly. Or to someone who might spend his weekends throwing money around in Aspen, where coke is still casual. There aren't a lot of ski racks on the cars at this end of Larimer Street, however.

Moon:

Plump, stately Detective Moon hit the street with a mean hard-on for something sweet. Maybe a piece of pie, or sticky bun. His first mistake was turning on his police radio in the car. Bad fucking habit, that was. Another thing he would have to work on. It didn't matter. He could easily turn it off and go about his business. But the first call he picked up was an officer down. He sat in the front seat of his rancid Taurus, dimly registering the details and wondering if he knew the guy. Hungry or not he couldn't very well ignore this.

Let's go.

He put the car in gear and drove south. It looked like it might be a hell of a beautiful day but a cop was dead, or dying. Like a brother. Moon nibbled at his tongue and watched the sky. He spat. He had no brothers, not really. The sky was safe, wasn't it. White and endless with a smackerel of blue tucked into the corners. He made the scene in no time, five minutes or less. Two black and whites blocked the mouth of an alley. Moon eased his car to a stop and sat there. He hadn't lifted a fucking finger and he was already soaked with sweat.

Out of the car, get out.

Through the yellow tape and down the alley, his shoes grinding in dirt and gravel. Red brick walls with ancient fire escapes. Eyes to the front now and there was the body, a lump of black and brown. Moon counted three uniforms and a photographer, the medical examiner and his assistant. And lurking on the edge of the scene like a pale green stork was a Homicide dick he had reluctantly been partnered with lately, a stiff British guy named Lot McDaniel. He gave a long whistling sigh, his throat gurgling like a fucked pipe. Lot McDaniel. Of all the cops he might run into this A.M...son of a whore. How he hated that fucking limey.

And now McDaniel came skittering toward him, all ghoulish and pale.

Moon, old fellow. Don't believe we've seen you in a day or two.

The bastard, thought Moon. He always laid the accent on thick when he wanted to get up your ass.

Yeah, he said. I've been sick.

McDaniel sneered. Oh, my. You aren't sick of police work, we hope.

Shut up, said Moon. What's the story?

Yes, well. Tragic bloody thing. Narcotics officer name of Mulligan. Throat ripped out and he didn't suffer much, as they say. No badge, no gun on his person. Dead since last night at least.

Ripped out how?

Bare hands, old boy. And teeth. The coroner says it was a fair imitation of an animal's kill.

Fucking hell.

McDaniel shrugged. Come on, then. Have a look.

Yeah, said Moon. But his feet weren't so cooperative and it was a moment or two before he could drag himself along behind McDaniel. The uniforms ducked away as they approached, lighting cigarettes and murmuring about hockey. The medical examiner was lazily packing his gear. He nodded at Moon with an empty face. The photographer snapped one last shot, and Moon flinched like a little kid at the sudden flash, the exploding bulb. He crouched down, wheezing. His shirt was dripping. The dead man lay on his side like he was having a nap. Brown hair razored short. Black jeans and a brown leather jacket, buttoned up to the collar. His hands were in his fucking pockets and his throat was a bloody mess. It was pure hamburger. Moon took a long look at the guy's face and saw that he was young, maybe thirty. Thin, sunken cheeks. Black eyes and a crooked nose and this dead man was no one he knew.

Not too healthy, was he? said Moon.

McDaniel coughed. There's been no bloodwork done yet, of course. But he has the look of a user, no question there. An off-duty incident, possibly. Two junkies scrapping for the same bag or something along those lines.

The guy's got his hands in his pockets, said Moon.

McDaniel sniffed. It's only a theory, don't you know.

What's his first name?

Fred, said McDaniel. His name was Fred, I believe.

Fred Mulligan, said Moon. I'm sure he deserved better.

What do you think, McDaniel whispered. Does he look familiar?

No, said Moon. I've never seen him before.

Moon felt hot. His face was sweating now. His face. What kind of god would give him a sweating face. Oh, he was a fucking wreck and he only wanted something sweet for breakfast. There was nothing he could do for dead Fred Mulligan. Nothing he could do and McDaniel was crouched very close to him, too close. His long, white hands hanging from his bent knees like two sleeping doves. McDaniel smelled of rosewater and boiled sugar. Moon stood up, wiping at his damp face with one dirty sleeve.

What about Jimmy Sky, said McDaniel. Do you think Jimmy killed him?

You, said Moon. You motherfucker. Jimmy is no killer.

Jimmy Sky, said McDaniel. His voice dripping scorn. What kind of name is that?

McDaniel stood up now and Moon glared at him for a long twisting moment and maybe his eyes played some kind of trick on him or maybe the clouds were shifting fast up there but something happened to McDaniel's face. His nostrils were suddenly three sizes too big and there was a ridge across his forehead and his skin was like leather and those were fucking fangs jutting up over his lip. He looked like a dog, a dog-man. Then the shadows relaxed and his eyes went normal and McDaniel wore his own thin-lipped pale face.

What do you know about Jimmy Sky? said Moon.

Not much, said McDaniel. I know you won't find him, though.

Moon lunged at him with a vague idea of thumbing the bastard's eyes out and McDaniel snorted, stepping sideways. Moon fell against a rack of garbage pails with an embarrassing crash. He lay there in a heap for two seconds, three. He gazed up at the sky and thought of poor old Charlie Brown and how often the round-headed kid had this very same view of the world. Moon shoved himself back to his feet, panting. McDaniel hopped forward with the dainty footwork of a ballet dancer and punched him in the throat with an elegant, blinding left-handed jab. And Moon went down again, easily.

Take the day off, said McDaniel. You look like shit. You look a lot like our dead Fred, there.

I WALKED IN THE HEART OF DOWNTOWN, where the tall, mirrored buildings gleamed. One of my friends was a lawyer of sorts, with an office in the labyrinth. Griffin, the smiler.

I moodily kicked at a piece of broken glass, spinning it into the street. I wondered if the fucker was still my friend. Maybe not. The last time I saw him was two or three years ago. Griffin had dragged me to some very popular but hateful nightclub that was so packed with mad, happy people that the one unisex bathroom was like a furious game of Twister. People had been living in there, growing rapidly old as they exchanged drugs and money without pause. They had chatted on cell phones, smoking and drinking. And they had noisily fucked each other in the stalls. It was nothing out of the ordinary, right. But that shit gets pretty tedious, after a while. I had finally gone out to get some air, to urinate in peace behind an abandoned car. Griffin followed me, and I clearly remember asking Griffin in a sleepy voice what time it was and Griffin turning to face me, grinning. His eyes like wet black stones.

What time is it, said Griffin.

Menacing.

What the fuck. The fuck.

I had just stared at him, blank and probably smiling. And in a moment of universal weirdness, Griffin pissed all over my legs. He shook his dick at me, then breezily told me to fuck off and walked away. He hailed a cab and left me standing there in damp, stinking pants.

And I had ended up going home with a drunk little bank teller who apparently was equipped with no sense of smell. I apparently collapsed on her kitchen floor without fucking her, which annoyed her. She called the cops on me, then herself went to sleep before they arrived. Two moody beat cops did show up, an hour or so later. They banged on the door until I woke up and let them in. They smirked when I identified myself. The bank teller was by then mostly naked and snoring on the couch. The uniforms looted her fridge and made a big show of checking out her body, cheerfully deriding my lack of taste.

They gave me a ride home and I crawled like a rat into bed with my wife, Lucy. She wasn't dead yet, then. But she was dying pretty efficiently. Cancer and depression were ganging up on her without a bit of mercy.

And I had not seen Griffin again after that. I didn't expect him to have changed much. Nobody changes, really. Griffin would literally pounce on this coke.

Now traffic swelled around me. The noise and shock of overpopulation. Vertigo, nausea.

It was boring to freak out all the time. If I could only remind myself to concentrate, nothing rattled me. I was a cool one at heart, really. Oh, yeah.

If I was dead, maybe. Then I might relax. Downtown always troubled me. I was careful to avoid the pedestrian mall, the gauntlet of gift shops and juice huts along which senior citizens and random tourists gamely refused to buy ugly overpriced T-shirts while sullen kids reclined in the shade, begging for spare change.

Griffin worked in a handsome brown slab of a building. It looked like a coffin standing on end.

I walked into the lobby and was immediately surrounded by mirrors. A security guard leered at me while I patiently checked out my reflection. I wanted to tell him how fucking pitiful it was, how tiresome, this irrational urge to confirm my existence in one mirror after another.

The guard eyeballed me as I walked to the elevators but that was all.

I was obviously no one to worry about.

The elevator was empty and way too big. There was room enough to spare, I reckoned cheerfully, for a dozen commuters plus a nice herd of actual sheep. I stood in the middle and looked at my feet as the box rose slowly, endlessly to the sixteenth floor.

A female receptionist coldly told me to wait.

I waited. I sat on a blue leather loveseat as the woman whispered to Griffin through her headset. There were no magazines in the waiting area. There was one gloomy painting on the wall that could be anything: a gray-and-black landscape of a Scottish moor, a chemically altered examination of a rain cloud. After a few brief moments of study, I concluded that it could only be a giant human brain, floating in a sea of alcohol. I asked the receptionist how much the piece might cost. She looked me carefully up and down, and I knew what she saw. A skinny drifter with ragged clothes and a desert tan, uncombed hair and gray lips still numb from the wind. A paranoid, lonely fucker who badly needed new shoes and who kept rubbing his nose as if it were numb and dripping. A person of dubious means. Not someone who could begin to pay Griffin what must be a very handsome retainer.

Eve:

She lay flat on her back, still wearing sweatpants and a T-shirt. No concept of time. She was like a child and a few minutes could mean anything. Hours were arbitrary. They weren't real. She sighed. It was maybe nine o'clock, or ten. The light had that flat, midmorning quality that she usually hated. She hadn't slept in more than twenty-four hours and she wasn't really tired. She felt a little bit jet lagged, really. Day was night and so on. Boring. Her body was just confused by the sudden shift between worlds. The night before was hazy in her mind.

Adore leaned over her.

The swing and flash of the razor. The frantic wings, the swelling orange light. A Redeemer with the lips of a monkey and now the touch of anxiety when she tried to remember everything that happened and it's only a game, she told herself. It's a game.

She turned her head to look at Christian. He was curled naked on his side, facing her. His limbs were too stiff, unyielding. He was pretending to sleep.

There was a spot of dried blood on his cheek, a splash of rust. She had cut him pretty good. He now had a nasty jagged scratch across the bridge of his nose and one eyelid, like he had tangled with a cat. That eyelid might permanently droop, she thought. Which would either make him look very stupid, insane or sleepy. He wouldn't like it at all. He had blubbered a few meaningless French phrases and accused her of trying to maim him, to blind him. Eve had merely shrugged and reminded him that she didn't like people to grab her. And that she enjoyed fucking with him, with his mind. She couldn't help it.

Christian was sexy, very sexy. Beyond sexy. He was one of those guys that sucked people into his wake, male and female. It was nice to be near him. He smelled good and he was talented in bed. But he was melodramatic when it came to the game of tongues and his face had turned fairly purple when she mentioned that she might just quit. A lovely shade of purple.

But she did feel a little sorry for him, and so she had calmly made up a bed for Mingus on the couch, her heart fluttering foolishly at the sight of an indentation in the crushed velvet that might have been left by Phineas. His head, his bent elbow. His foot. Jesus Christ. She was such a simple girl and all she wanted was a big brother. Mingus thanked her silently and laid himself down, pale as a monk.

Then she had allowed Christian into her bed.

He shed his clothes in a hurry, like she might change her mind.

But there wasn't going to be any sex, she told him.

Oh please, Goo. Give us a break.

She wondered if he was aware that he constantly referred to himself as a collective. If this was merely a peculiar side effect of the game. This apparent splitting, this fragmentation of selves. Because she often thought of herself and Goo as separate but equal.

Meanwhile, Christian had fiddled with his penis until it became hard and red. He showed it to her with creepy, boyish pride, as if he thought she couldn't possibly say no to such a handsome sight. Manifest destiny, or something.

I am not Goo today, she said.

This made him whine.

Eve finally told him to jerk off, if he must. But not to come on her. And not to poke her or prod her with it, or casually try to slip it in while she was asleep. She wasn't kidding. Christian had played with himself for a while, sulking. Then pretended to fall asleep.

That was a half hour ago. Maybe he really was asleep. Eve blew on his eyelids and he didn't flinch. She squeezed his soft penis like it was a peach and she couldn't decide if it was ripe. His penis was pretty long, when hard. About nine inches, he had told her once. He mentioned it casually, as if he were bored by the subject. But he had measured it, of course. Nine thrilling inches. It was too skinny and curved, however. It was what she imagined a dog's penis might be. The way it stabbed painfully into her uterus, sharp and bony.

Christian now began to snore.

She hesitated, then reached out and touched his hair. It was very confusing, this relationship. She didn't know if she liked him at all. But when she was Goo, she loved him. She wanted his children. It was a game, okay.

She was playing a character. Eve stroked his fine black hair and her fingers caught in a funny tangle. His hair was matted with something. She worked her fingers through it and they came away sticky and brown. This was dried blood.

Eve closed her eyes.

GRIFFIN APPEARED THROUGH SLIDING DOORS that literally purred open, cool and silent. It wasn't bad but a really sinister whooshing noise would have been much more effective. He wore a glossy Italian suit the color of blood-wine and it seemed he had begun shaving his head since I last saw him as his skull was now the same pale creamy pink as my own bare ass.

Are you going bald? I said.

I am bald.

Yes. I can see that.

Griffin extended his hand. There was a small tattoo on the inside of his wrist, like a black coin.

Was your hair falling out, though?

Yes, he said. It was like plucking feathers from a dead chicken. He shrugged. I decided to shave it instead. The girls seem to like it.

I'm sure.

Griffin stood there, unbending. His hand still hanging between us like a knife and a knife given as a gift will always bring bad luck. I stood up and shook his hand and the contact was cold but weirdly lacking pressure. Griffin's eyes drifted to focus on my eyebrows and I wondered if that was just a lawyer thing. Or did he truly want to avoid the eyes. I stared back at him, smiling with some reluctance.

Griffin bowed his head slightly and I hesitated, then touched the man's scalp. Oily and hot, almost feverish.

What do you want? said Griffin.

Oh, well. I'm back in town. Thought I would say hello.

Griffin smiled the smile of a gorilla, a chimp. He showed way too many teeth and a ridge of pale gray gums. That's funny, he said. That's a killer.

I shrugged, uneasy. Why is it funny?

Because you don't like me, said Griffin.

No. Not at all.

The receptionist was staring at us throughout this exchange, her lips parted. A bright glow of sweat in the thin blond fuzz along her cheekbones. Eyes glazed and blue, she chewed on her tongue and she looked mesmerized, as if she was home alone, watching a little soft porn on cable. Griffin flicked a finger at her and she abruptly began to type.

Nice, I said.

Let's go in my office, Griffin said. I have champagne, of a kind.

Moon:

Moon was parked on a swiveling stool at Lulu's Dough-nut Shoppe. His throat was killing him, literally. It felt like he had swallowed a mouthful of glass and what the hell happened back there.

He had provoked McDaniel, apparently. The motherfucker had a tight little ass, an irritating accent. Bad teeth. And very fast hands. Moon sighed and shifted his own ass around, trying to get comfortable. His hefty buttocks fairly melted over the sides of his stool. Moon knew what his father would say. Old man Moon would suck on his false teeth and swear that McDaniel would be speaking German right about now if it wasn't for us. And learning to like it. Maybe so, but that does me no good. He wondered if McDaniel was up to something nefarious or just fucking with him. Moon realized he was an easy target these days, what with his poor work habits and his body odor problems. Anyway. Jimmy Sky was nobody's favorite cop, but he didn't kill people. He especially didn't kill other cops.

Moon had a headache. He would worry about it later. And he would watch and wait for a chance to pay McDaniel back for this sore throat. He would wait years, if he had to. One day the motherfucker would fall asleep in the wrong place and wake up with his hat on fire and his hands cuffed to his feet.

Okay, then. He wanted to get drunk and concentrate on his breakfast. He had been coming to Lulu's every morning without fail for years. Lulu was long dead, or never existed. Wiley, a man who claimed to be her husband or stepbrother, ran the place now. He was a grumpy little man who was deadly serious about doughnuts. He wasn't interested in anything else. Wiley always wore strangely colorful clothes. He was a peacock. Today he wore a purple T-Shirt with black-and-white pants and yellow shoes. He was a freak, maybe. But he made the best doughnuts in the city. And he spoke very elegant English in a snotty voice, like a college professor.

Moon had once asked him about the inexplicable hyphen in the word "doughnut."

Wiley had merely shrugged. He said that Lulu had always been too liberal with punctuation, as if this had been an irreversible condition, something he had learned to live with.

Moon stared down at his place. Four fat doughnuts, arranged like the face of a clock. Blueberry at twelve o'clock. Maple swirl at three. Cinnamon at six and honey glazed at nine, to clean the palate. He drank coffee with a splash of bourbon and chased it with concentrated orange juice. He didn't smoke before noon, or he tried not to.

Dead cop with throat ripped out. Like a wolf had done it, a wild dog.

Moon finished his coffee and took a pull of bourbon straight from the pint. He lit a cigarette and noticed that his palms were sweating, they were dripping. It had been quite a while since he had been drunk like this, in public. He felt a stab of something like guilt. What the hell. He had no wife, no therapist to answer to. He was a cop, by God. And he was the only cop in the place. His fellow officers didn't care much for Wiley and his fruity clothes.

Black eyes and crooked nose and a face forgotten already. Hands in his fucking pockets.

Moon wiped his hands with a napkin and fought down a mouthful of bile and he knew he was out of shape, okay. It took a little strength, a little staying power to get drunk so early in the day. Intestinal fortitude. Moon swabbed out his mouth and tongue with the sweaty napkin and tossed it aside in disgust. He had the intestines of a little old lady. He was irregular. He had maybe one successful bowel movement a week, and it was pretty painful. It was rough. The bathroom was his personal torture chamber, lately. It was like he was passing a fucking stone in there.

This was a lot of bullshit, though.

Moon wasn't worried about his bowels, or his own guilt. He could shake off guilt like it was nothing, like a coat of morning dew. Moon would rather have a belly full of guilt than a touch of the flu, any day. But now he was distracting himself from the truth. And the truth was, he was a little worried about Poe. The guy was his friend, yeah. But he was a freak. He was purely section eight. Poe was a delusional fuckup, okay. He had been bounced off the cops for being too schizophrenic and was suspected but never implicated, never charged in connection with the shooting death of his wife.

And most recently he somehow got himself mixed up in the alleged transportation and sale of his own illegally harvested organ. That was a good one, wasn't it. That was a humdinger.

There were sixteen motherfuckers just like Phineas Poe, hanging around the methadone clinic and the homeless shelter right now. Sixteen guys with no money, no cigarettes. Sixteen guys with their brains spilling out of their skulls one teaspoon at a time.

And what did he do first thing this A.M.

Moon rubbed his belly and thought about it.

Oh, well. Nothing much. He gave the bastard a handful of false identities and a lump of confiscated coke and turned him loose on a missing persons case that didn't officially exist. He could only wonder what sort of mayhem would come of that.

Wiley glanced up from his crossword. He cleared his throat politely and licked his lips, as if it was a great effort to speak. What ails you, Sheriff? he said.

Nothing, said Moon. I feel just like a king.

You have hardly touched your doughnuts.

Moon stubbed out his cigarette and plucked the blueberry doughnut from his plate. His stomach heaved momentarily, but he ate the thing in three quick bites.

Jimmy Sky, where was Jimmy Sky.

And five minutes later Moon crashed out of Lulu's, the glass door bending before his bulk and splashing onto the sidewalk. He broke the fucking door, shattered it. He was probably bleeding. There were tiny white fragments of glass on his arms and shoulders. It was in his patch of hair. Fucking hell. He inspected himself for cuts and scratches, cursing the door. The thing must have been defective. He turned to look at Wiley. And Wiley was nonplussed. In fact, he was turning orange about the ears and neck. He looked like one unhappy tangerine.

Hey, said Moon. Hey, Wiley.

Wiley stared at him, disbelieving. You are a menace, he said. A danger to yourself and others.

Moon pulled out his wallet, a bulging chunk of leather that smelled of feet.

He knew that it smelled of feet because he had sniffed it, just the other day. He had been trying to isolate a putrid, cheeselike odor that kept wafting from his body. He was sure it must be coming from his crotch, from the sweat and funk and decay of his package. But he had been sitting at a stoplight at the time and he could hardly bend over far enough to smell himself, what with the steering wheel in the way.

Moon smiled to himself. He couldn't bend over that far if Yoda himself was sitting on his neck, croaking a lot of Jedi nonsense at him. Luminous being we are…yeah. He might be luminous, on a good day. But he wasn't too fucking limber. Then it occurred to him. His wallet was pressed up against his ass all day, absorbing his unpleasant juices, his various gasses. The funk had to be coming from his wallet. And at the next red light, Moon yanked it out and had a good whiff and almost threw up right there.

Now he flipped the stinking thing open, taking care to keep it well away from his face. Sixteen dollars. Hardly enough to replace the door of a dollhouse. And his credit cards were in ashes, lately.

He pondered a moment.

Tell you what, said Moon. I'll write up an armed robbery report and your insurance will cover it, no problem. You could get a better door out of the deal.

Oh, sure. And they won't hesitate to cancel my policy.

Hmm. That's no fucking good.

You're drunk, aren't you. Since when do you indulge on duty?

Moon grunted at him. I'm thinking.

The forecast is for rain, said Wiley. Thunderstorms, you bastard. You have ruined me.

Okay, said Moon. How about this. I broke the door myself.

Wiley frowned, irritated. You did break it.

Yes. But I broke it in the line of duty, you see. In my zealous pursuit of a purse snatcher. You can bill the department. Okay? Tell them it was lead glass, stained glass. Whatever. Tell them it was a five-thousand-dollar door if you want.

GRIFFIN'S OFFICE WAS ABOUT what I would expect. Cool and sterile, with uncomfortable iron furniture. A thick, silent carpet that was such a powdery light blue that it disappeared like the far end of the sky. The sky merging with clouds. Griffin casually uncorked a magnum of something called the Pale. The label looked suspiciously postmodern, with bright ruthless colors.

California? I said.

Not exactly, said Griffin. Then he shrugged. It's two hundred dollars a bottle.

What the fuck. I hate champagne anyway.

Griffin's eyes were flat. You will like this.

I turned away, the glass fizzing in my hand. There were no law books in the office. The walls were gray, with a faint sparkle. The walls were like dirty silver, unadorned by art of any kind. Griffin had an excellent view, however. I stood before his massive window and looked out over downtown Denver. Half of the city seemed to be under construction, deconstruction. This was a sign of prosperity, this effortless ravaging of old, failing stone. A few years ago, Denver had not been looking well. It had been downright ugly, in fact. Emaciated and sickly.

Not anymore, by god. Denver had acquired a baseball team and the city was reborn. If they told you it was beautiful, then it was beautiful.

It's beautiful, I said.

Griffin sneered. Like a postcard.

I sipped at the Pale and it shivered down my throat like mercury, cold and thickly sweet.

What is this? I said.

Wormwood and licorice, said Griffin. With a drop of cyanide. Don't ask.

Absinthe? I said. You are full of shit.

Oh, I stink of it.

I took another drink and the glass felt heavy in my hand. I put it down on the coffee table and smiled. I was a little dreamy, like I had just exhaled a lungful of nitrous oxide. The silver walls rippled nicely. Griffin relaxed on the couch, heels drumming noiselessly on the carpet.

So, he said. What's going on.

Yeah. That's a good question.

Griffin smiled and smiled. His eyes were dilated and I saw him again, turning to spray my legs with urine. With urine.

You pissed on me, I said.

What?

The last time I saw you. You pissed all over my pants, like a dog.

Griffin shrugged. Maybe. Who remembers these things.

It's not something you forget. I fumbled with my zipper. If I emptied my bladder all over that ugly fucking suit right now, would you remember?

What's wrong with this suit?

You look like a big, paranoid grape.

Griffin finished his drink and the smile on his face was elastic.

Okay, I said. I have some coke I want to sell.

Coke, said Griffin. Please tell me you're joking.

I know. It's embarrassing.

Griffin sighed. Let's see the shit.

I pulled out the police evidence bag and Griffin laughed. He clapped his hands.

I have always wanted one of those bags, he said. It would be perfect for my toothbrush and hair gel and shaving gear. I could keep it in my briefcase.

You don't have any hair.

Skull gel then, he said. I like a shiny helmet.

I found myself nodding stupidly. I shrugged, pulled myself together and scooped out a fat bump of coke with one finger and sucked it up my nose. The eyeballs tightened promptly. I licked my finger and offered the bag to Griffin, who tasted it without blinking.

Not half bad, he said.

Do you want it?

Griffin yawned. Four hundred for the shit and two hundred for the evidence bag.

Four hundred? I could cut it up and sell it for five times that.

Good luck, he said.

Give me eight hundred, I said.

See you later, Phineas.

Okay. Okay, I said.

Yeah, he said. The thing is, I don't really want any coke. This is charity. This is like serving soup to the homeless.

Oh, well. I love a good bowl of soup, I said. Three hundred for the bag, then.

I hated myself and Griffin was practically asleep, he was so bored. He shrugged and produced a roll of new bills. He peeled off six or seven hundreds, losing count. He smiled and tossed two more bills on the table.

That's nine, I said.

What's the difference. Have you had lunch?

I watched as Griffin transferred the coke to a gunmetal snuffbox, carelessly. A fine white shadow of spilled cocaine caught the light and Griffin noticed me watching.

Oh, he said. Would you like a last taste?

I hesitated, sniffing. Of course I wanted some. But I shook my head, mute.

Good, he said. That's good.

Griffin dropped the little box into a drawer. He folded the evidence bag into a small square and tucked it into his breast pocket, his eyes fond and bright.

Of course, he said. You're lying.

Yeah, I said. Let's have lunch.

Griffin sniffed, wiping at his nose. I want to show you something, he said.

Okay.

I was a bit clammy, shivering. I thought the air-conditioning was much too cold and I wasn't the least bit hungry and so I just nodded dumbly. Griffin walked over to the big window, his arms and legs hanging weirdly loose. The sun was crashing through the glass like a live thing and Griffin appeared to be held together by thread and I squinted at him through a maddening self-contained haze. I felt like I had wandered onto the set of one of those Roger Rabbit videos where some of the characters are real and some are animated. Griffin was definitely animated. I stared at the big window now, hoping to find myself in the open sky beyond but instead the light shifted and I saw a very peculiar scene in the reflection. I saw myself, standing in about the same position but wearing fairly ridiculous clothing, with a funny gray hat and a slash of white bandage across my face. Griffin looked exactly the same, but was standing on the wrong side of the room with his back to the window and there was a third person in the reflection, a long-legged man with limp yellow hair who wore a three-piece suit of soft brown leather and held a gun in one hand. The gun was aimed at me, at my head.

Do you see him, I said. Do you see him, Griffin.

Griffin turned and smiled, or maybe his reflection did because now the physical Griffin placed both hands on the window and pushed, muttering softly the word *poof*. And I felt my mouth drop open as the entire sheet of glass fell from its frame and floated down toward earth with the lazy, carefree silence of a paper airplane. The glass was crystal-bright and somehow invisible and it swooped and glided back and forth, a pale deadly shadow. And it seemed to fall forever. I leaned out to watch the glass dive into a throng of pedestrians and cut three people in half and now I felt my head bump against the window. I touched it gingerly, with the tips of my fingers. It had never fallen at all. Griffin smiled and smiled.

Eve:

She woke from a drifting sleep and she couldn't breathe. Christian was sitting on her chest, staring at her like she was a bug. He was naked, slim and hairless. She was pretty sure he shaved his chest.

Eve never had a brother. But when she was a kid her best friend was a girl named Minna who had an older brother, a hulking bully named Guy. He had wanted to be a wrestler and his breath always stank of bananas. Guy had been truly manic but never depressed and his fingernails were always chewed to raw, moody shreds. Guy's favorite game had been to sit on his sister's chest, pinning her arms down with his knees. Then he would pinch her nipples and drool yellow spit into her face. Eve and Minna took care of him, eventually. Eve had gotten some codeine tablets after she had a root canal and they saved a few just for Guy. Minna made root beer floats one Friday night and dissolved five of the little white pills into Guy's float. He passed out before ten and they stripped him naked, then soaked his genitals and one eyebrow with Nair, the infamous hair dissolver. Guy woke up with no pubic hair and a painfully sore left eye. The Nair had dripped into his eye, apparently. It ruined his eyelashes and he could have been blinded, probably. But Guy always left them alone after that.

Eve wondered what Christian would use on his chest. Vitamin E and aloe, she decided. And as he was so scornful of technology, he probably used a straight razor. One day, he might lose a nipple.

What are you smiling at? he said.

You, she said. You have a nice chest.

Oh, he said. Now you want to be friendly.

Not really.

Well, said Christian. We don't have time, anyway.

He rolled sideways and off the bed. He stood there, distracted and chewing at his lower lip. Eve realized with some surprise that he actually looked worried. And there was one thing about Christian that he liked: he rarely looked worried.

What's the matter?

Your apartment, he said. It's slipping.

Eve sighed. Fuck you.

She had heard of this, of course. The whispered stories about badly spooked gamers, obsessed tonguelovers who never slept, who stayed in character too long. Their worlds were compromised and their reality began to slip. The idea was that if you lingered in the subterrain for too long, you might never leave. And some claimed to have lost their identities, their jobs. They showed up for work one day and no one remembered them. Their credit cards were suddenly invalid. The explanation for this seemed simple enough to Eve: a lot of gamers and tonguelovers were also computer geeks, hackers. And it would be child's play to tamper with the virtual reality of one of your enemies, thereby erasing his job and identity, his bank account.

Virtual reality was reality. The game of tongues was something else, a peripheral reality.

But it was not so easy to explain the physical slip. A few of these mad gamers claimed that losing one's identity was nothing, it was a joke. The physical slip was the real nightmare. They believed that their apartments and cars had literally become unstable, that they were fading. Disintegrating. Their material possessions actually ceased to exist. The walls around them got fuzzy. They suffered molecular decay.

Eve shrugged when she heard these stories. She scratched her nose. Drugs, she thought. It can only be drugs. Though she was well aware that the elite gamers like Mingus and Christian were pretty clean. They sucked down a lot of coffee and cigarettes and popped a little ephedrine. And the Pale, of course, nearly everyone consumed a mysterious liqueur called the Pale. Everyone but Christian. He never touched it, and he sneered at those gamers who seemed to depend on it.

Come on, said Christian. We'll show you.

Irritated, she slid out of bed. Her feet were bare and cold and she was pretty sure she had been wearing socks when she went to sleep. Christian had a mild foot fetish, or Chrome did. He often slipped her shoes and socks off when she was asleep or otherwise distracted. She didn't mind it so much. Odd as it may sound, she liked the way it felt when he nibbled on her feet. But she was annoyed this time.

Christian, she said.

He pounced on her, knocking her to the floor. His lips were pulled back to show fine white teeth and his eyes were like the blue edge of flame. Those teeth aren't real, she thought. Not real. They must be caps. The dig of pain in her chest and he was hurting her now. His teeth were impossibly white. Erik Estrada. He's got the teeth of Erik Estrada, she thought. What kind of grown man calls himself Ponch?

Thin red shiver of pain as she tried to breathe.

He may have cracked one of her ribs. Punctured a lung. The pain was like a claw, ripping at her from within. Eve took another experimental breath and as she opened her mouth Chrome lowered his mouth to hers. He sucked her tongue out of her mouth and held it between his teeth and his pull was very strong, he could swallow it, he could turn her inside out. He didn't bite her tongue but he owned it for a moment. He owned her. The tongue is the soul, she thought. The soul. The tongue is ugly, vulnerable and not well-hidden.

Chrome released her. Don't call us by that name, he said.

Okay, she said.

He helped her up, his face calm and friendly. As if she had slipped on the wet floor and he were merely bending to her aid. Eve jerked her hand away and looked around for her slippers. Her feet were cold and she felt raw, unclean. She wanted to pull a sheet over her head. Christian briskly pulled on his black jeans and said, come on.

She followed him into the living room, sighing when he told her to avoid a small circle of carpet in the hallway that he had marked with baking powder.

It's unstable, he said.

Eve rolled her eyes. But she stepped around it anyway, then stopped. The carpet did look strange, fuzzy and wavering. She bent to touch it and Christian pulled her away.

Don't, he said. It could be a vortex.

Are you serious?

He didn't answer, but she knew he was disgusted with her. He always treated her like a dim-witted child when it came to the game of tongues. He had no patience for what he called her failure to see what was real. Eve rubbed her eyes, wondered if she was dreaming. This didn't seem possible, logical. But at the same time, she didn't find it so alarming and she felt herself glowing, detaching. She felt like Goo.

Oh, no.

Yes, she said. Her skin was tight and cold.

She was on the verge of becoming Goo, without trying. Horrible and sweet at the same time. Because she loved herself as Goo, really. She forgot that sometimes. Mingus was in the kitchen, pacing back and forth like a nervous uncle. He was waiting for somebody to give birth. He looked at her, briefly. He sniffed her but said nothing. Eve realized from a vague distance that Mingus was reluctant to stand in one place for too long. And it looked like he was keeping his distance from Christian, too. She thought of the dried blood she had found in his hair.

In the living room, Christian pointed to the wall behind her velvet sofa. It looked like gray fog, a curtain of mist. Christian took a coin from his pocket and tossed it at the wall. The coin vanished.

Fleurs du mal, said Christian. We have to get out of here.

Eve stared at the wall, thinking that she would certainly have to move the sofa. That wall wasn't going to keep the rain out, was it?

What? she said.

We want you to get dressed, he said. Quickly. And bring whatever you can carry. We won't be coming back here.

But I have a six-month lease on this place. If I disappear, I lose my deposit.

A small brown bird flew through the wall from the other side and crashed to the floor. It flopped there, dazed. It appeared to be a starling. Christian looked at the bird, then at Eve. He laughed out loud, almost howling. He picked up the bird and snapped its neck.

Believe me, he said. You have already lost your deposit.

GRIFFIN WANTED TO WALK and I really didn't mind. My head was a mess. My head was dusty, full of fuzz and cat hair. I could use the fresh air, no question. I needed a few minutes before I had to sit at a table with my face three feet from Griffin's and his unbending smile.

And I suddenly felt like talking.

Maybe the coke had loosened my wheels, I don't know. Whatever the reason, I told Griffin most of what had happened to me in Texas. I told him all about Jude and how she made me feel like a slug on a razor blade. I told him about the morphine, the lost kidney. I told him about Horatio and how I killed him with a kiss. I told him too much, maybe Griffin didn't say anything, but he did laugh inappropriately a few times.

Griffin took me to a place called Rob Roy's. A dark, silent underground grotto where the waiters were stout, elderly black men who wore bow ties and never smiled. They didn't offer you a menu. And you were clearly a freak if you ordered anything but whiskey and a porterhouse steak. There were no women in the joint, none. A lot of crusty old men, though. They shoveled the bloody meat into their holes like they had never heard of heart disease: they were lawyers, judges, and newspaper writers, and a few drowsy cops.

What year is this? I said.

Griffin looked around, beaming. Nice, isn't it. It's 1955. Hitler is dead and the economy is a house on fire. My dad is sitting over there with Judge Waters, drunk as a fucking pig.

It's freaking me out.

Relax, said Griffin. Drink your martini. Or have another one. I'm buying.

Why are you being so friendly?

Griffin rubbed his naked head, his helmet. He shrugged. The walls of Rob Roy's were dark red and in that burgundy suit he nearly melted into the background. I could only see his eyes and teeth. The soft glow of his skull.

I sank back into the flexible haze of my own head. Griffin and I had gone to the same college, a shitty state school in Memphis. I didn't know him then, not really. But I had heard the stories. Griffin had this little girl-friend, a high school dropout. She was seventeen and after she moved out of her mother's house, Griffin sneaked her into his dorm like she was an illegal pet. He got her pregnant and then went homicidal because she didn't want to have a baby. Meanwhile, the girl did not have such a good reputation. She was a kleptomaniac, she was suicidal. She was white trash, she would give you a blow job if you bought her a milkshake. And she was illiterate. But this was a lot of bullshit. I met her only once and had liked her right away. The girl was sweet and tough, with the voice of a dead jazz singer. She wanted to be a photographer. Her name was Lisa and she was maybe a little too infatuated with Emily Dickinson, but I could forgive that. She was seventeen, right. Then she had a miscarriage and Griffin lost his mind. He knew she had gotten an abortion, he knew it. And so one night he tried to set her on fire, while she slept. Griffin did six months in jail and because he was only nineteen and his daddy was a powerful man in Memphis, his records were sealed. Lisa changed her name and got a job, an apartment. Then Griffin came out of the county farm on good behavior and started hanging around abortion clinics. He started following girls home. And on a rainy day in late April, he knocked on Lisa's door. He was smiling the same punishing smile. He wanted to give her something, he said. He offered her a bloody pillowcase that contained the head of a murdered prostitute. The prostitute, he claimed, was a killer of babies. But Lisa never blinked. She was expecting him, she said. Lisa surprised him, she did. She shocked the hell out of him. Lisa produced a gun and shot him and suddenly Griffin wasn't smiling anymore. There was a hole in his arm the size of a half dollar. Later it was discovered that the pillowcase contained the head of a dressmaker's dummy. Griffin didn't press charges and the case was dropped.

And when I met him ten years later, Griffin was a slick young lawyer in Denver, working in the DA's office. He was arrogant, seductive, ruthless. He was a very good lawyer. I knew he might be a psychopath but what the fuck, right. I struck up a conversation with him anyway. A dark November morning. We were sitting on the courthouse steps, maybe ten feet apart. It was bitterly cold, unpleasantly cold. It was starting to snow. I had come outside to smoke, to get away from the press and the bureau chief and my own lawyer and everything else. Griffin was sitting cross-legged, with an expensive and famously ugly Italian leather coat wrapped around him. He was smoking a cigar. I glanced at his face and saw that he was a little hung over. Maybe a touch of the flu. Anyway, he looked like shit and I didn't feel much better. I had been testifying on a case that involved cops and the secret assassination of a local heroin king who had pretty much deserved to die, and the trial was dragging along like it would never end. Griffin was working an unrelated case, something to do with animal torture. It was boring him to death.

I said to him, didn't you go to school in Memphis?

Griffin had smiled. The smile that made me feel queasy. Like I just stepped on something dead, a bird or mouse bloated from the rain and now I couldn't get its guts off my shoe. But I went out drinking with him that night, and Griffin soon became something for me that every cop needs. Griffin became my ally, my confessor.

Wake the fuck up, said Griffin. Your food is getting cold.

The waiter had come and gone. I looked down. Before me was a wide, metal plate that held the biggest, ugliest lump of meat I had ever seen. Beside it was a deformed brown thing that appeared to be oozing sour cream. I slowly comprehended that this was a baked potato.

Do you have a girlfriend? said Griffin.

What?

Other than the organ thief, I mean.

I ignored him. I poked and prodded at the steak. It was not so bloody at all. In fact, it looked burned.

Your wife is dead, he said. Over a year now.

That's right.

What's your story? said Griffin.

No. I don't have a girlfriend.

Good. Very good.

Why? I said. Why is that good?

Griffin didn't answer. He ripped into his steak, barely looking up for the next five minutes. I stole another glance at my place and was positive that I couldn't eat this piece of meat. My teeth felt fragile, just looking at it. I wondered about Eve. She certainly was not my girlfriend but then I wasn't sure what she was. Whenever I was near her, I felt like I should protect her but such a notion would only make her laugh. She was much more likely to save me, to catch me when I next fall at her feet.

Eve had this dark energy around her, swirling but not quite visible. The ring and shadow of myth. Her voice was ageless. Eve was delicate, childlike. I easily imagined she could be sexy, brutal.

She had the bottomless eyes of someone at war.

penny dreadful

Now where the fuck was my brain taking me. I was slipping down the ugly slope of bad poetry. I must be a little dreamy from that funny drink, the Pale.

Because, said Griffin. If you had a girlfriend, you would lose her before tomorrow comes.

How, exactly?

I wonder. Do you believe in ghosts? said Griffin.

What do you mean, like Casper the friendly?

Griffin delicately wiped a drop of reddish grease from his lip.

No, he said. I'm talking about the underworld, the walking dead.

Yeah, well. I see the walking dead every time I look out the window.

Griffin chewed briefly, staring at me. Listen, he said. You mother-fucker. I'm not talking about urban despair. I'm serious.

Okay. Have you recently seen a ghost?

No, not exactly. But I have seen things that you won't believe.

I lit a cigarette and felt cold, thinking of the ghostly creatures I had seen in the torn-down building. Drinking tea and smoking cigarettes on a forgotten Sunday. *The Lone Ranger* crackling on the radio.

Ghosts. They didn't have a care in the world.

Try me, I said.

Griffin had finished his whiskey and now he growled at the waiter for another one. He looked weirdly angry, confused. I wondered what in the hell he was up to.

Tonight, he said. I want you to come out with me tonight.

Where are we going?

To the other side of darkness.

What is that. A disco?

That's a scream, said Griffin. You fucking kill me.

Moon:

Moon was aimless and hungry, driving around with a big emptiness in his stomach. His stomach was positively echoing. He wished he had brought along those doughnuts. But after taking out Wiley's glass door he had been too embarrassed to go back in and ask for a take-out bag. Almost noon, now. He had sixteen dollars, right. That was enough for a big lunch. Moon had a taste for cow. He wanted a hamburger, a big one. And a milkshake or two. He still hadn't checked in at the station and he was maybe three hours late for his tour. Hey, fuck it. That's cool. He had a thousand sick days lined up like little yellow ducks. And there was one of his favorite burger shacks, straight ahead: Millennium Burgers. He shifted around in his seat, wishing the seat belt didn't have to choke him. There was nowhere to park but that's why he became a cop, right. Unlimited parking. He rolled the Taurus into a loading zone and detached the offending seat belt. He rubbed his throat briefly, then tossed his sunglasses on the dashboard. The seat belt was still tangled around one thigh and he struggled with it a moment, then clambered violently out of the front seat. The seat belt tripped him though, and he nearly landed on his face. Fucking thing wanted to kill him. Moon drifted away from the car, muttering. Then turned back. He wondered if he still had that butterfly knife in his glove box. He leaned into the car, his butt hanging into the wind for the world to admire, and dug around until he came up with a knife. It was a big motherfucker, with maybe a seven-inch blade and a shiny brass handle. The blade was tucked within the handle and the handle was supposed to come apart like wings. Hence the name. If he was slick, he could whip the thing out and the handle would flicker apart like a butterfly in flight. But he wasn't very slick. He couldn't even remember where he'd got the thing. A shakedown, probably. But one of his buddies might have given it to him, as a gift. Cops generally had a pretty bloodless sense of humor and any one of his pals would have hooted at the thought of him trying to flash that knife without cutting off his own nose. Anyway. He opened the knife carefully now and cut the seat belt loose at both ends. Then stabbed the blade into the driver's seat cushion, cutting the beast from belly to throat. Yellow stuffing gaped from the wound and Moon felt better. Much better. He pocketed the butterfly and tossed the dead seat belt into a sewer grate, then proceeded to the Millennium, whistling as he walked.

DEAR JUDE. Something is very wrong with Griffin, I think.

And this is a guy who's never been quite right. He came to the house once when Lucy was in the worst days of chemo and we were watching a baseball game, very casual on an otherwise dead Saturday afternoon and Griffin is eating pistachios. He brought over a sack of them and he's eating them one after the other and tossing the shells into an ashtray and he comes cruising out of the blue and asks Lucy if she's lost a few pounds. And she's sitting in the rocking chair with a blanket pulled over her in the middle of fucking summer and a scarf around her head like a turban and he knows perfectly well she's been sick and he goes on to say that he liked her better with a little meat on her but the way he says it you can't be sure if he's a complete psychopath or he's just living so deep in his own skin that he truly forgot.

I don't know what was in that drink he gave me but it feels familiar. It feels a little too good and I would have to say it's in the narcotic family. But a distant relation. Faint. The way ice tastes when it's been washed in vodka.

Anyway, Griffin paid the tab and instructed me to be at the Paramount around midnight, to catch a swing band called Martha's Dead.

And just as I began sleepily to contemplate whether Martha was involved in a state of being or ownership in relation to the dead, the grinning bastard kicked me under the table and said hey, maybe you can use that little kidney story to get close to some nice pussy.

You know. Milk the girls for a little sympathy, he said.

I stared at him and now it dawned on me that Griffin didn't believe me. He didn't believe a fucking word. It was really too bad that I don't have a few vacation snapshots of Jude sunbathing on a brick patio in an impossibly small bikini, the sky behind her yellow with Texas dust. Jude smoking a cigarette beside a fountain while tourists swarmed around her. Jude throwing money at a beggar. Jude standing in the ocean, hands white and skeletal at her sides. And one shot of Phineas and Jude together, fondling each other in a café. A sweet old lady from Minneapolis took that one. It was a ridiculous story, after all. It was pure tabloid. And why should I care if anyone believed me or not. I walked out with Griffin into gray sunlight and before he turned to go, Griffin touched my arm.

It was a simple thing, a touch.

Like we were friends, like we didn't need words between us. Maybe it was true. I tried to remember how things really were before the urine incident but everything was obscured by smoke and drugs and loud music and faces. Disconnected torsos. The memories disengaged and I was watching a movie on a grainy black-and-white television without sound.

Tomorrow, said Griffin. Tomorrow you will understand.

What? What will I understand?

Griffin shrugged. You will live in another world.

He walked away from me with unfailing arrogance, his legs furious and fluid in those slim purple pants. His smooth, round skull floating at his shoulders. I tried to reconcile this image with the smiling, slithering Griffin who had peed on me with impunity. There were but flashes of his previous selves, of the Griffin who decapitated a mannequin and offered the head to his estranged girlfriend. Of the Griffin who improvised wildly in the courtroom, the Griffin who was at once adored and hated by judges.

Moon:

Now that was fucking better. Moon felt a thousand times better. Nothing like a belly full of undigested meat to set him right. And he loved that bread they used for the buns, fresh sourdough rolls that were never exactly round like those creepy processed buns at McDonald's. Fuck those processed buns. The Millennium buns were properly deformed lumps of bread, often bearing strange tumors. And the Millennium gave a fellow a serious chunk of meat that weighed a quarter of a pound after it was fucking cooked and the fat had dripped away. Then topped with real cheese and fried onions, pickles and jalapeño wedges on the side. Moon had to pass on the waffle fries today. He had been feeling a little bloated of late, and was trying to lay off the starch. But he did soak the burger down with two vanilla shakes. Now he was walking back to the car, laughing at himself a little bit. He had been so hungry that he killed his own seat belt, for fuck's sake.

Droning down the sidewalk, he was on cruise control and feeling good. He was happy, of all fucking things. The hell was wrong with him. Maybe he would go down to the station and poke around, see if there was anything interesting on the board. Hey, now. What the fuck was this? His foot was stuck in something. A wad of green chewing gum that some sociopath spat on the sidewalk. The gum had melted in the sun and was now smeared nicely along the underside of his shoes. Fucking beautiful. Moon sat down on the curb, muttering. The next time he saw a guy, or a little kid even, spitting his gum on the sidewalk…dead. The offender was fucking dead. Moon finally took the shoe off and scraped at it with the handy butterfly knife. Then he heard voices, loud. Maybe two men and a woman, talking at once.

You stupid, stupid fuck.

Listen listen listen.

Whoa, now. I can't breathe with you in my ass.

Tommy, Tommy. Let's go, please.

Moon swiveled around to scope the cracked glass window of a coin-op laundromat. Four or five people were gathered around the change machine, shoving at each other. Okay. This was just what he needed. A random dose of pure foolishness. Moon replaced his sticky shoe and stood up, breathing hard. He walked into the laundromat and everybody froze. He sighed. Did he really look that much like a pig?

What's the trouble?

Everyone was silent and Moon quickly catalogued them. A skinny Latino girl and her white boyfriend, who had the pale, downcast eyes of bystanders. They were already backing away, as if to say: this really isn't our problem. In fact, we were just leaving. Moon shrugged and let them go. He turned to the other three. Black male in mid-thirties, shaved head and nose ring. Wearing blue hooded sweatshirt and sunglasses, black pants and sneakers. He looked angry, sullen. White male in early twenties. Long dirty blond hair and a beard. Filthy bluejeans, no shoes and a torn white T-shirt that read Zippy the Pinhead for President. A small, white female with black hair, braided. Middle twenties and wearing peculiar clothes: soft leather vest that buttoned to the throat, no shirt. Her arms bare and white. She wore a dark red or black skirt, knee-length and made of something like velvet. It was thick and heavy and the colors seemed to shift. A wide belt around her waist, with little beaded pouches dangling from it. Brown leather boots that laced up to her knees. She was staring hard at Moon, as if she knew him. Her eyes were gray as stones, with a touch of blue around the edges.

What's the trouble? he said again.

The woman smiled but said nothing.

This motherfucker, said the black male. He pointed at the white boy. This dumb cracker is trying to get change out of the machine with a piece of lettuce. I need to dry my clothes for work but I can't get some change because of this fool. He's got a pocketful of lettuce, he's got a damn salad in his pants and he wants to try every damn piece of lettuce, one after another. How am I supposed to put up with that?

The white kid grinned, scratched himself. He was a picture of bliss. There were indeed several wilted pieces of lettuce at his feet, and another in his left hand.

Well? said Moon.

Yeah, said the white kid. I'm cool. I'm minding my own shit when this person starts invading my space. Fucking up my head, you know.

Right, said Moon.

He stepped up to examine the machine. The dollar slot was slimy with green and black juices and bits of chewed lettuce. It looked pretty well ruined. Maybe not. He pulled out a dollar and tried to feed it into the machine. The machine promptly rejected it. The machine started blinking, like it was maybe going to explode. Moon sighed and wished his armpits would stop dripping for five seconds. He wanted to help somebody, he really did. He probably had a few quarters in his pockets, but he might need them later. He never knew when he might pass a video arcade. He regarded the fucked machine briefly, wondering how much trouble it would be to smash it open. He had a tire iron in the car, but the idea of going out to get it and coming back to pound on this machine for a while made him weary beyond belief. He did have a gun. But that would be a rather extreme solution, even by his standards. He glanced at the woman.

What's your story? he said.

She shrugged. I'm not involved. But I was curious.

About what?

I wanted to see if the lettuce would work. And I was curious to see which one of these two was going to get stabbed over four quarters.

Nobody's getting stabbed.

The woman sniffed. I smell blood on somebody.

Okay, said Moon.

What about my money, said the black guy.

The machine seems to be broken, said Moon. It won't be accepting any regular money today.

Motherfucker, said the black guy.

Easy, said the white kid. It's all good.

The black guy was rubberband fast. His left fist lashed out and Moon barely registered the shadow of movement, the recoil. But the white kid was already on the floor, bleeding from the nose. The black guy looked at Moon with mild brown eyes.

You gonna arrest me or something? he said. Because I'm gonna be late for work.

Moon shook his head, smiling. He wondered if the black guy could teach him to move like that. It would come in handy the next time he said hello to McDaniel. The white kid was choking, or giggling, at his feet. Moon glanced down at him and the kid was already bobbing his head to some internal hippie music. The kid stared at the blood on his hands and shirt for a moment, then tasted it wondrously, as if it might be raspberry syrup. He clearly didn't remember being punched in the face.

Arrest you for what? said Moon.

The woman tapped the black man on the elbow and he turned, surprised. As if he hadn't noticed her there. She didn't smile, exactly. But her eyes were bright.

I have four quarters you can have, she said.

Thanks, he said. Thank you.

She pulled a handful of coins from one of her little pouches and sorted through them. Flashes of gold and sparkling bits of colored glass. She sells seashells, Moon thought. He couldn't help but stare at her and she was probably used to that. The back of his neck felt clammy just being near her. But that could well be the Millennium burger, or the bourbon. There was a lot of bad juice in his bloodstream. To put it mildly.

The woman separated four quarters and gave them to the man. He offered her a dollar but she shook her head, she turned and walked away.

TIME TO KILL AND MONEY in my pocket and what would I do with myself now. It might be a good idea to go test the waters down at Moon's precinct but I was nervous. I needed a disguise, a wig or some false teeth. I wasn't walking in there as Phineas Poe, that was for goddamn sure. The roof might come down on my head. I wondered idly what Ray Fine might look like. Maybe old Ray could pass for a private eye.

I laughed at myself, now.

Because cops love to talk to private detectives. Oh, they do. They love it. And in five minutes Ray Fine might easily say the wrong thing and find himself in a holding cell with a handful of his own teeth and a dent in his head shaped exactly like the yellow pages.

No shit.

If Ray was going to be a private eye, he would have to dress like he still lived with his mamma, like he might be Norman Bates. He would need a mustache and maybe some ugly glasses that he paid fifty cents for at a yard sale. A carelessly constructed but psychotic geek. A guy that limped.

Okay, okay. This wasn't so bad. I might well enjoy it.

What else.

Ray would have a history of scoliosis and bad feet. His pants should be too short and possibly unzipped, but he would look like a guy who might get violent in a pinch. A guy that you wouldn't want to push into a corner because he might just stab you in the throat with a ballpoint pen, with his keys. Ray should be goofy enough to appear harmless, smart and relentless and creepy enough to get some answers.

That was my plan, such as it was.

I would become Ray Fine and Ray would go talk to Captain Honey and feel him out about my pal Moon and his tale of lost cops.

I started walking and things got slippery, fast. Passed a bus stop and saw four or five women dressed up like vaudeville whores. Leather granny boots covered in dust. Thick skirts that fell to the ground with fur and feathers stitched into the hems. White blouses with complicated hook and eyelet buttons cut low and square across heaving bosoms. Truly. These were tits that laughed at gravity, they fucking sneered at it. These women were each strapped into some kind of corset or bustier that not only aimed their nipples at the sky but gave them eighteen-inch waists as well, right. A wonder they could breathe at all. They carried little paper umbrellas and wore incredible sunbonnets that glittered with beads and colored glass and rose petals. Two of them wore snug little lace pinafores at the waist and the others had black feather boas coiled around their necks. Their faces were painted in terrifying monochrome red and blue and pink and their hair hung in exquisite ringlets and curls. I thought they must be on their way to a costume party and wasn't going to say a word as I was already gawking shamelessly at them but as I passed they commenced to whistle and hoot at me openly. One of them stepped in front of me and gave my arm an exploratory squeeze, you know. Checking the bicep for muscle. Whether she liked the specimen, I can't say. But she sighed and whimpered and asked if I was looking for a good time and her tone was pure Scarlett O'Hara.

Breathless and swooning.

And finally I said, has there been a ripple in time and they just giggled like mad chickens and she said my, isn't he eccentric? And by now they were all pawing at me and blowing into my eyes and touching me and one of them said it was just two dollars a throw. Which meant I could fuck all of them for eight dollars if only I had the strength.

And one of them was actually getting to me. She was small and dark with a mouth the color of fire and her waist was insane, maybe eighteen inches at the most. Pale yellow breasts, heavy and round. The bright smell of mint about her. She had me by the hand and I felt pretty weak, she had me in her grasp and my brain was still chanting two dollars only two dollars but the whole thing was freaking me out and finally I pushed through them like a spooked horse and when I turned to look back, they were gone. One of their bonnets lay on the sidewalk and just as I turned to go back and touch it the wind came up and lifted it up and away and I watched it disappear beyond a dark scaffold of trees.

Moon:

The dark-haired woman lingered on the sidewalk, thin arms crossed over her chest as if she couldn't decide where she was going. Maybe she was waiting for someone. Of course, she might be waiting for her clothes to hit the rinse cycle. Moon hesitated in the doorway of the laundromat, watching her. He liked the way that heavy velvet skirt hung from her small waist, a physical shadow. It caught rays of the sun and spun them away in fragments. She was not waiting for him, for fat sad balding Detective Moon. That much was pretty clear. He was Charlie Brown. Not quite as bald, maybe. But much fatter and clumsier and plagued by nastier and certainly more powerful bodily odors. The little red-haired girls of the world tended to flash past him like flying squirrels. They rarely touched the ground and generally remained unaware of the large, slow-moving and oafish members of his species.

But one never knew.

Maybe she was in some kind of trouble of her own and needed to talk to someone. A sympathetic cop, for instance. Moon shrugged and glanced at his reflection in the window. His fly was at least zipped and his shirt was clean. What more could he ask of himself? He swabbed at his face with the sleeve of his jacket, wiping away any remaining traces of hamburger grease.

Can I help you? he said.

The woman turned. What?

Help, he said. Do you need any help.

She frowned. No, thank you.

Moon fumbled with his car keys, then dropped them. The ring of metal against pavement. Moon poked at the keys with one foot, suddenly reluctant to bend over and not sure what he was afraid of. Take your pick. His pants could easily rip open at the crotch. His body might choose that exact moment to produce some unsavory noise or odor. And he was well aware that he grunted like a pig giving birth whenever he bent to tie his shoes, but he couldn't seem to do anything about it. The woman smiled at him, or allowed her lips to curve slightly in his direction. Moon blinked at her. He showed her his gold shield, casually.

I'm not a pervert, he said. I just thought you might need a ride somewhere. This isn't such a good neighborhood.

Her eyes burned brightly. I live just a block from here.

Oh, well. Moon scratched his head, briefly. Helplessly. His left foot spasmed suddenly and he kicked his own keys into the street.

Your keys, she said.

Yes.

The woman bent quickly, like a bird. Black hair like spilled ink. The long braid swinging lazily around her neck. The twitch of muscle in one bare shoulder. Now the keys jingled in her palm.

She's fluid, he thought. Fluid.

What's your name? he said.

Dizzy, she said. Dizzy Bloom.

Nice, he said.

My great-grandmother was Molly Bloom.

Who?

Now she laughed, softly. Did you not read *Ulysses* in college?

Moon was paralyzed, stupid. Her wide gray eyes tugged at him like gravity and he tried to remember exactly what he had studied in college and came up blank. Sociology, wasn't it? He spent two years reading a lot of depressing German philosophers, then dropped out to join the cops.

Never mind, said Dizzy.

She took a step forward and placed the keys in his left hand. His fingers closed reflexively. The woman sniffed him and the smile vanished from her face.

It's you, she said. The smell of blood comes from you.

What?

Be careful with knives, she said.

Moon felt his head wobbling around on his shoulders, as if it wasn't properly attached. He felt cold. And he had a sudden case of the creeps. He wanted to get away from this freaky bitch. It was too bad, because she had incredible eyes but there was something wrong with her.

I'm sorry, she said.

I HIT A THRIFT STORE FIRST, a cavernous place called Lost Threads.

The stink of mothballs and a rat-faced clerk wearing army fatigues. Pink Floyd seeping like loneliness from hidden or buried speakers. I counted sixteen mannequins, most of them naked and missing crucial limbs. They made the place feel unpleasantly crowded and somber at once. A mirrored disco ball glittered overhead. There were heaps of clothing everywhere, unsorted. Whole families could be burrowed in among these piles armed with sleeping bags and mosquito netting and collapsible stoves, waiting for the apocalypse. I could almost feel their eyes on me, infuriating little needles. The razor whine of imagined voices. I wandered around for a half hour and came up with an armload of clothes that might fit.

The clerk ignored me when I asked if there was a dressing room. But that was okay, really. I wasn't proud. I could blend in with the mannequins. I tried on a few things and finally settled on an outfit that Ray Fine and I could both live with. A pair of black and blue Depression-era pinstriped pants made from an unidentified material that flared slightly at the ankles. These were a good fit, actually. They made me feel taller. A hideous, mostly white rayon shirt with a big floppy collar, a possible blood stain on the left breast, and an incongruous surfer motif: a coiled, naked woman on one sleeve and a big orange sunset on the back. A muddy brown unabomber sweatshirt that zipped up the front. An ugly but weirdly stylish wool blazer, bright pea green in color and equipped with seven mysterious pockets. And topped off by a charcoal gray fedora with grease stains along the brim and a mangy feather stuck in the band. I briefly coveted a pair of silver and green Doc Marten clown shoes but they were much too small. My own cracked and dirty work boots would have to do.

Ninety dollars, said the ratty clerk.

I gave him the money and wondered if there might be something secretly wrong with these clothes. That they might be pox- or lice-ridden, for instance. But at that price, I could live with a little infestation. I had had lice before and I was bound to have them again. It wasn't my problem, anyway. These were Ray's clothes. I asked for a shopping bag or something to carry my old things in, but the clerk ignored me again. I was barely visible, it seemed. I glanced around and spotted a black plastic garbage sack on the floor, bulging with donated clothes. I dumped the contents on the floor and immediately a furious white moth flew into my face. I killed it by reflex, then tossed my old clothes into the bag, tipped my new hat at the ratty clerk and was gone.

Dizzy Bloom:

The smell of cat, of a solitary man. And dust, a lifetime of dust. Boiled tomatoes. Tobacco and whiskey and unwashed socks. Blood, above all. The burned copper stench of blood. She could see the cat now, sniffing at his toes. She could see a television, a twist of leather. And another man, thin and hungry and staring.

Oh, she had a headache. Blue and crushing. A rain of brittle flowers. Her vision shrinking and she was looking through a fish-eye lens and then everything faded and she breathed with relief. She hated this, she did. She never asked for this. She never knew what to do with what she saw.

Dizzy walked through a fine white mist and hoped it wouldn't rain before she made it home.

Yesterday she had touched a woman, a Trembler.

Dizzy took one breath of the woman's ash-white hair and suffered a prolonged vision of her five or ten years into the future, sobbing and ripped apart as she gave birth to a damaged child, a mongoloid with fused spine. But somehow beautiful. It was still a child, a little boy-child and he was amazing and fine when he took his first breath. Even though he wouldn't live more than a year. She couldn't bring herself to tell the Trembler what she saw. It would have accomplished nothing and besides, the Trembler had been heavily drugged. She had been a puppet, a ninety-six-pound ghost. Her flesh had not been her own and her mind was porous.

And besides, it had been Dizzy's choice to tell or not tell. She had owed the Trembler nothing, for the game of tongues described no parameters for the Breathers. They were unbound by the laws that guided the other players, that gave them purpose. For most of them, this was not a problem. They drifted through the game as bystanders, witnesses. They were free to help or ignore the other players as they wished. But Dizzy was the rare Breather who saw not the past, but the future. Fortunately for her, she was not tormented by every breath she took. Thank God for that. She was not plunged into an unknown and possibly terrifying future by every drifting scent. Her visions were rare, unexpected. And so she functioned well enough. The hardest to bear was the unwanted glance into someone's last day. Even with the game, death could be very real and the scent of it left her ill for days. But when she ventured outside the game and into the realm of Citizens, she was at times visited by terrible and confusing visions. She could never be sure if what she saw was real. The Citizens were said to be unaffected, untouched by the game and any visions that swelled from them must therefore be mistaken. But no one within the game could ever agree on this. Only the Gloves knew, and they only smiled when asked for the truth.

The poor policeman. Overweight and lonely and worried about his hair. His blood had seemed real, very real. As if he had been bleeding from an unseen wound along the thigh, the ankle. And perhaps he was not an ordinary Citizen at all. There had been a fading but distinct glow of the glamour about him, the almost visible smell of flowers. He had worn the fuzzy look of the unaware Fred.

Dizzy turned down her street, walking quickly now. She wanted a bath, she wanted bubbles and steam and a small glass of wine. She wanted to shed her clothes and be alone, to sleep. Tonight she would not enter the game, and she would not drink the Pale.

Her mouth was sore but her head was clear, the brittle blue flowers forgotten. The taint of blood was gone. Dizzy sighed and looked to the wide yellow sky and reminded herself that blood was not always the end. It may come of nothing, a cut finger or crushed nose. There were black clouds in the west, seeping into the yellow and she could only hope that the fat policeman suffered nothing more than a mishap with his razor.

Home, she was home.

Dizzy opened the iron gate, started up the flagstone path. Her house was a three-story Victorian with wild roses and creeping vines and a slightly leaky roof left her by her grandmother. She saw the first shadow on her porch, then another. There were three of them and she sighed, but she was not surprised. The game had come to her. She would at least have a bath. But she might not resist the Pale.

The first shadow came down the steps to greet her with empty hands. He bowed to her and she recognized him. Chrome, the Mariner. She didn't know him well, but she had heard rumors of him. That he was a fearsome hunter, collector of a hundred tongues. And that he was a gentleman, a charmer of men and women. Dizzy shrugged. She was not so easily charmed. On the porch behind him was Mingus, a gentle Breather. The third shadow was a young girl, thin and dark and unknown. Chrome introduced her as Goo, apprentice to the Lady Adore.

Welcome, said Dizzy.

DEAR JUDE. DON'T WORRY ABOUT ME. The pain is gone. I can tie my own shoes without whimpering. I have gained a few pounds and people don't stare at me in the street. I don't horrify myself in the shower.

My grandfather had this three-legged dog, a pit bull named Chaucer. And he was a fucked-up animal, he was beyond tragic. Chaucer was a hermaphrodite. I'm serious. Male and female genitalia and neither of them functional. Chaucer was sterile, thank God. A truck ran him down when he was a pup, which is how he lost the leg. And it seemed like that dog would never die. Poor fucker had arthritis, glaucoma. He had bald spots in his fur from a hundred old wounds and most of one ear was missing. He smelled of death, of sewage. He was a sweet old dog but terrible to behold. And if you shoved him into a corner and made him fight he would calmly chew your arm off without blinking because he still had all of his teeth and he just didn't give a fuck. That old dog had no worries. He had already been crushed by a red pickup truck on a partly cloudy Sunday morning and lived. He had a worthless cock and a dried-up pussy and he could never gratify himself but he was still walking around.

That's me, sometimes. That's your Phineas.

And sometimes I think my heart will give out on me. Everything tastes strange and there's a faraway muffled thumping in my ears and I keep looking at the sky, thinking it's thunder. There's a storm coming. But it's not thunder. It's my own stupid blood hammering away and I'm just having a panic attack.

Oh, yeah. You might think you're cool and confident but you live on the narrow, on the hot edge of metal in the sun and you're walking down the street in these clothes that you bought for someone else and you catch a glimpse of yourself in the black windows of a parked car, your reflection is suddenly kicked back in your face and it's not you at all. You're lost, you're lost and here comes the panic.

Here it comes.

Ray Fine:

Don't fucking worry. Stay in character and don't piss anyone off and you will be right as rain. Phineas whispered these last unheard words of advice to his new parallel ego and retreated safely into the shadows to watch and listen. I'm not here, he said. You are on your own.

Ray Fine smiled wetly at everyone he passed. Ray is one of those sad guys who can't quite keep his mouth closed. His lips were forever parted, as if he had a problem with his sinus, as if he were simple. And he limped, as expected. Not terribly, but with enough hobbling and spastic shuffling that he might well crash into a mailbox at any moment. His clothes were very bad. The clothes of someone who might be seen howling prophesies at traffic. He wore a charcoal fedora with a diseased sparrow's feather tucked into the brim. He wore a pea-green jacket and a brown, hooded sweatshirt. A white polyester shirt under this, untucked. Outlandish blue-and-black bell-bottoms that people actually stopped to stare at. He had a ragged mustache that burrowed between his mouth and nose like a pet mouse, and he wore glasses with yellow lenses and black frames held together by a piece of wire. A brand new digital watch with a price tag still dangling that he had purchased for five dollars at a drug store. Ray Fine was another rambling, harmless freak. And he knew it. He limped up the steps to the Ninth Precinct, loudly saying hello and good morning to everyone he saw. A few people even said hello back to him.

Once inside, Ray Fine became mysteriously unobtrusive. He lost the limp for a moment and walked briskly past the desk sergeant, who was busy with someone else and who, if he noticed Ray at all, might have assumed he was an eccentric lawyer. Two rookie uniforms turned to stare at him and he winked at them. Ray Fine knew where he was going. Ray continued down the hallway largely uncontested. Now he muttered to himself and allowed his head to wobble on his shoulders. He was a delirious monkey. He placed one hand over his mouth as if he might vomit. This seemed to help a lot. Now everyone ducked out of his way. Ray turned a corner and resumed his limp.

He smacked his lips and worked his tongue around his mouth, perhaps fishing for debris left over from his lunch. He passed a pretty assistant DA and gave her a friendly thumbs-up, then came to an elevator and merrily pushed the already glowing Up button.

He pushed it five or six times, to be sure.

Two detectives, fat and thin, and a brightly colored secretary stood waiting for the same elevator, and now they turned to peer at him and politely look away. Ray Fine took this opportunity to fart silently and step to one side, his nose twitching. The secretary wrinkled her upper lip and glanced with disapproval at the fat detective. The elevator arrived and Ray graciously climbed aboard last.

Three please, he said loudly. I'm going up to Homicide, you know.

Ray extended his hand. Ray Fine, Special Adjuster #616.

The what?

That's right. There's a problem with the conglomerate eleven two tone appropriation policy. Big problem, big as a fucking house.

The secretary cocked one eyebrow in disbelief. I don't think…

Ray hooted at her. Easy now, little Debbie. You don't want your face to get stuck that way, do you?

The fat detective grinned as the doors opened on the third floor. No one moved a muscle as Ray Fine darted through and turned to give them all a two-fisted thumbs-up just as the doors hissed shut.

Moon:

He was not crazy, not crazy. Sometimes he wanted to get away, sure. To take off his shirt and sprout wings from his humped and painful shoulder blades. His wings would at least be white, he thought. His wings would be deceptively pretty. He wanted to fly high and wide, out across the plains where the high yellow grass would bend and dip in the wind. Moon sucked in his breath, confused. Brief shudder and thump as his head smacked against the roof of his car. He had jumped a fucking curb. Nearly crushed a lightpost. Oh, boy. That's right. He was temporarily without a seat belt. Tufts of yellow stuffing floated up to his face and he tried to grab them with a clumsy paw. He had to get a hold of himself. Maybe he would drop in on the department shrink. The idea made him want to choke up his lunch but what else could he do? He was trashing doughnut shops and making sad eyes at hippie girls in the street and disemboweling his own car. He was killing himself, which he might not mind so much but it could take a while to actually finish himself off. Moon opened the car door, inspected himself for injuries. Nothing to speak of, really. An egg-sized lump on his forehead that would likely be colorful tomorrow, but he could always wear a hat. He stepped back to survey the car. Three wheels on the sidewalk, nose shoved into a wooden post. It was possibly an acceptable parking job, though it might impede pedestrian traffic. He considered moving it, straightening it out a bit, but his throat tightened up at the idea and he had to flail his arms for balance. Fucking wings, for god's sake. He looked up and down the street for moral support and while his might have been the only car on the sidewalk, it did have unexpired tags and a decent paint job and well, fuck it. Moon was a half-block from his building. He would go home, have a cold shower. He would pluck the clumps of dead hair from his bathtub drain. He would brush his teeth and wash his face with witch hazel. Then he would drink a single beer and have a grilled cheese sandwich, with bacon and onions. Maybe Phineas would be there. They could have a good laugh about the lettuce incident and then walk down the street to move his beached car. Right, then. He made sure his doors were locked and turned to go home.

But he hadn't gone ten feet when a shadow fell across his path.

Good day, said the shadow.

A tall man in an overcoat, the sun behind him. Not a breathing shadow. Moon wrenched himself sideways and got a look at the guy's face. Long, wet lips. Fucked-up looking hair, like it was cut by a drunk with a kitchen knife. But at least the guy had some hair to speak of. The guy was about his age, maybe older. Wearing a black raincoat. For about two seconds, Moon thought he was maybe going to flash him.

But the guy just looked at him, his head crooked.

Do I know you? said Moon.

I don't think so, the guy said. My name is Gulliver.

Well, then. What the fuck do you want.

Nothing at all. I was passing by and couldn't help noticing that your head is bleeding.

Moon blinked. There did seem to be a slow leak just north of his left eye, a warm trickle. He grabbed at his skull with one hand and it came away red.

Huh, he said. That little chicken wasn't crazy, I guess.

Excuse me?

Oh, said Moon. I met a very strange girl, earlier today. She said she smelled blood on me.

Interesting.

Anyway. I wrecked my car just now. Must have cracked my nut on the windshield.

The man leaned close, sniffing. I smell nothing, he said.

Moon jerked his face away. Who asked you?

The man shrugged. The girl was a Breather, perhaps.

What?

Don't be thick, man. I can see you're in the game.

Moon took a step back.

It's okay, said the man. I don't want your tongue. But I'm very good with a needle and thread, if you want to stitch that cut.

It's a scratch, said Moon. It needs a Band-Aid, maybe.

I might help you become self-aware.

You're some kind of pervert, right?

The man shook his head. He smiled and his teeth were like bones in the sun, cracked and yellow. Moon was disgusted. He was offended. He didn't feel sorry for people who couldn't take care of their teeth. Maybe it was just a desperate response to the loss of his hair or the foot odor problem but he seemed to brush his teeth about five times a day, lately.

The queers don't usually go for me, said Moon. I'm too butch, or something.

Or something, said the man.

Yeah, said Moon. Thanks, though.

The man sighed. You won't last, he said.

Ray Fine:

They ducked into a restroom, hissing at each other. Pushed and shoved to the sink and ran cold water over their hands, eyeballing the mirror all the while. You want to settle down, or what? You're a maniac, you're out of control. The idea was to be foolish but inoffensive so just settle the fuck down, okay. If you can't be half normal then you're toast. This is my body, right. What's left of it. And if you get the shit kicked out of it then you can go back to living in a cigar box under Moon's sink.

Fucking right.

Then to the urinal for a nervous pee. Ray Fine and Phineas shared a laugh, then Phineas backed off. He gave Ray a final dirty look and let him leave the bathroom in peace to try his own luck with the desk clerk.

She looked like an unforgiving hag. Face like a slab of ham, bright pink and bloated with fat. Thick burgundy hair piled on her head in the shape of a barrel. Ray Fine gritted his teeth and put on a happy face. Behind the hag was a steady hum and bustle of typewriters and telephones and cops going about their business. Phineas felt cold, watching from a distance. He was in the nerve center, such as it was. A trickle of sweat down his back and jangling nerves from skull to fingertips. He hadn't been this close to so many cops in over a year. He didn't like it. He didn't like it at all.

Ray tipped the fedora. Hello, Ma'am.

Flicker of suspicious eyes and a mouthful of gum. Yes?

Yes, well. I need to see Captain Honey right away, posthaste and tout de suite. Life or death and he's expecting me. Ray Fine, from the mayor's office.

The hag shrugged, pushed an intercom button. She bent over it with her pink face. Ray Fine to see you, sir. From the mayor's office.

Long pause, crackling silence.

Phineas squirmed in the dark. Ray Fine grinned confidently.

Nadine, what? The mayor, did you say? Christ on a pony. By all means, send him in. Wait, wait. Ask the poor fellow if he wants a cup of coffee, or a nice danish. Then send him along.

Nadine rolled her eyes. Would you care for a danish? Apple or cream cheese.

Is that real cream cheese?

Hardly.

Ray Fine smiled. Tempting, but no. And don't get up, please. I know the way.

He looked straight ahead as he made his way through an orgy of closely confined odors, of contorted faces. Past the squeals of swiveling chairs, the hiss and purr of fax machines and the groans of his own nervous belly to Honey's office. He looked directly at nothing and no one. Phineas couldn't handle the eye contact and Ray didn't much like it, either.

Captain Honey sat behind his desk in a handsome black wool overcoat. He looked pretty coherent. Freshly shaved, with a single dot of blood on his left cheek. What remained of his hair was combed smartly over his naked scalp. His eyes were blue and clear. He had one foot up on his desk, though, and he seemed to be wearing tennis shorts with no socks. And upon closer inspection, it looked like he was wearing a plaid bathrobe under the wool overcoat. Moon had not lied about the coupons, by the way. The man's desk was littered with coupons. The walls were wildly decorated with old comic strips. Marmaduke. Beetle Bailey. Ziggy. And scarily prominent was the insidious Family Circus. Phineas closed his eyes,

will christopher baer

wished he could go to sleep. Ray Fine smiled and sat down.

Good morning and what can we do for you, private? said Honey.

Ray glanced at his watch, it was nearly five in the evening. Honey was staring at him pretty intently for a confused old guy. Ray Fine stuttered. Oh, well. It's a question of human interest.

How's that? said Honey.

Ray took one rattling breath, smiled, then commenced to babble. The mayor wants to improve the police department image, you know. He wants the people of Denver to feel safe and happy. He wants them to say hello and good morning and God bless you when they pass a cop on the street.

Honey gnawed at a hangnail. I like it, I do. It sounds like a grand idea.

The first order of business is to profile one of your brightest and bravest, to make one special cop look like the guy next door. Our sources say that Detective Jimmy Sky is your finest officer.

Sky, did you say?

That's right.

Oh, dear. I don't think I know him. No, I don't.

He should be attached to this squad, said Ray.

No, no. Jimmy Cliff is a singer. A Jamaican fella, I believe.

Jimmy Sky, said Ray.

Honey thumbed his intercom button. Nadine? Is there a detective named Sky on my squad?

She sighed mightily. No, sir.

Honey smiled. There you go.

Interesting. Let me ask you this, then. Have you had any officers go missing of late?

Honey's eyes darkened, as if a stray cloud had passed before his brain. He leaned forward, one bony finger poling at the air before him. Listen boy, he said. I never leave this office. Except for weekends, that is. I sleep on a fold-out cot like a goddamn soldier. Nadine has all my food brought in by long-haired little shits on bicycles. And I pee right into a mason jar when I need to relieve myself.

Ray took off his hat, ran one hand through his hair. He was sweating.

Believe you me, said Honey. I would know if any of my men were missing.

Of course you would.

Captain Honey closed his eyes and leaned back in his chair. Before long, he was snoring.

Ray Fine sat there a while, nodding. It occurred to him that old Phineas was probably crawling out of his skin right now.

Dizzy Bloom:

Warm inside and dangerously cozy.

The girl called Goo was curled on a nest of pillows by the fireplace. Chrome had gone to take a shower, a cold shower. Dizzy had asked him very politely to save a little hot water for her bath and he gave her a nasty shivering look, saying softly that he took only cold showers. Mingus sat cross-legged in the bay window, his nose shoved defensively into a book of Dorothy Parker's short stories. Dizzy moved in shadows about the room, lighting a few scented candles and turning the radio to a gospel station. She kept looking at Goo. Wondering who she was in real life, how she came to be here and how deep she was in the game. Goo didn't fidget, she noticed. She didn't pick at her fingernails or play with her hair. Her hands were restful, solemn. Dizzy glanced at the ceiling and wondered what Chrome was doing up there. He could be spitting onto every clean towel, he could be masturbating on her bed. He could be using her toothbrush. He could be taking a shower. The pipes were droning but cold water was fairly endless. Dizzy moved to sit beside Goo. The girl smelled of musk and brown sugar, of dried blood and Band-Aids. A rich, intoxicating presence and thank God she threw off no visions.

Are you hungry? said Dizzy.

Goo stretched her thin legs and smiled without speaking. Dizzy looked at her closely now. A short, wild mop of black hair. Dark, soft mouth and gray eyes. Heavy boots. Brown suede jeans and a little black sweater of silk or fine cotton with short sleeves. The sweater didn't quite cover her tummy, and when she moved, it rose a little. Dizzy again smelled dried blood, and she saw the white edge of adhesive tape. The girl had a bruise on her left arm, another on the side of her neck. But this wasn't unusual. She was an Exquisitor's apprentice.

Do you eat meat? said Dizzy.

Goo sighed. Yes. I do now.

What's the matter?

Do you know why we're here?

Dizzy shrugged. One of you is running from something.

My apartment is slipping.

Really?

Yes. It was disappearing before my eyes.

The girl spoke in a clipped, halting monotone. She stared without blinking and Dizzy realized she was in a mild state of shock.

I saw a car disappear once, said Dizzy. It just melted away.

How is that possible?

Physically, it's not. As far as I know.

Physically.

Dizzy grinned. Useless distinction, isn't it.

I want to sleep, said Goo. I want to wake up and be normal.

How long have you been in the game?

The girl hesitated. As if she couldn't quite remember her real life, her past. Then she shivered. A slow flush of color in her cheeks. Not long, she said. A little more than six weeks.

You're just a baby, said Dizzy. You will be okay, eventually.

Dizzy lifted one hand, or allowed it to float sideways. She began to stroke the girl's hair, dragging the soft black curls through her white, crooked fingers. After a minute or two of thick silence, Goo touched her wrist and asked her to stop. Dizzy wasn't offended. Some people don't like to be touched. Dizzy excused herself, slipped away to the kitchen. She tied an old apron around her waist and began to chop onions, thinking she would start with a nice spinach salad. Then perhaps grilled shark steaks.

Excuse me?

Dizzy turned to find Mingus standing in the doorway. Hesitant, as if he was afraid to intrude. Mingus was so strange. Otherworldly, even within the game. It was hard not to like him. He was small, frail. Not more than five feet tall and barely a hundred pounds. He was maybe two pounds heavier than she was when naked and wet. Thin blond hair, almost white and hanging over his dark eyes. He had the sweet face of a boy, soft skin and red lips. He had possibly never been with a woman, although she knew he was about her age. Dizzy was twenty-nine.

Come in, she said.

He moved closer, he moved slowly. He was worried, frightened. Dizzy took a deep breath of him and he was a whirl of scents, most of them not his own. She saw nothing but dark skies.

What is it?

I'm a bit worried, he said.

Dizzy put down the knife, wiped her hands on a towel. Mingus glanced uneasily at the ceiling, then back at her. The shower was still running. The pipes groaned and whistled. Mingus went to the refrigerator and got out a piece of ice. He sucked on it as he spoke.

It's awkward, he said. It's about Chrome, you see. And I don't want to cause alarm without good reason, but he took down a Fred, yesterday. Under the sun. We were not within the game.

Dizzy shrugged. That's risky, of course. But not so unusual.

No, said Mingus. That's not it. He killed the man. Literally, I mean.

An iron skillet fell from Dizzy's hand, crashing to the floor. It barely missed her foot. Mingus stared at her, sucking nervously at the ice.

What? said Dizzy. What did you say?

There was blood, he said. A lot of blood. I don't always trust my eyes but I'm sure it was real. The man's throat was gone and I think Chrome wants to make the game real. Or more so.

Dizzy put one hand over her mouth. Have you ever seen the future?

No, he said. Never.

What about Goo? she said.

Mingus frowned. What about her?

Have you told her this? said Dizzy.

No, he said. Chrome is my friend, my ally.

The girl should know who she sleeps with.

The kitchen was shrinking around them. Pots and pans, a dead wandering Jew. A microwave oven she didn't know how to operate. Crystal champagne glasses that had never once been used. A black-and-white photograph of two strangers, apparently just married. A television that baffled her. She had no idea where it had come from.

Fuck me, said Mingus. I can't deal with this, you know.

And your Glove, she said. Who is your Glove?

Mingus shook his head. I have a Genetics midterm in one week.

Who? said Dizzy.

He sighed. Theseus. You know it's Theseus.

Okay, said Dizzy. Tonight we will talk to him, we will tell him about this.

ON THE STREET AGAIN, my belly ripe with acid and funk. I hated every bend of light. I pulled off the damned mustache that had been tickling my poor nose like a dead thing. Tossed it in the gutter. Fuck that thing. It had been a mortal struggle not to sneeze every five seconds. I removed the glasses, too, but tucked them into my jacket pocket. You never know, I might want them again.

I had intended to meet Griffin at the Paramount as Ray Fine, but there was really no point other than to amuse and confuse. And Ray was not such a reliable persona, was he. Too fucking daffy. I was much better off in my own skin. I would wear Ray's clothes, though. I felt kind of cool in them. I glanced at my new watch, then frowned and plucked off the price tag. It was early and I had plenty of time.

Ducked into a video store with the idea that I might rent a copy of *Shane* and put a smile on Moon's face. We could watch it in the raw sleeping hours past midnight and drink more of that Canadian poison. Funny thing, though. I found the video on the shelf and as my eyes flicked over the credits on the back of the box, I couldn't help noticing that Lee Marvin did not play the lead. It was Alan Ladd, presumably the father of Cheryl and what was in a name, right? Nothing. But it was weird and I decided not to rent the thing after all.

Outside, I hailed a passing cab.

I relaxed in the back and counted my money. I couldn't be wasting too much of it on luxuries like taxis, at least for a while. Was not sure what I was going to tell Moon. That Jimmy Sky doesn't exist and maybe the two of us should take a little vacation down to Florida? A little quiet time, that's all Moon needed. Moon wasn't going to like it at all. He believed in this shit. He believed that cops were disappearing and coming back like zombies. And one of them Jimmy Sky, his friend. Missing or dead. My stomach hurt. I would have to be careful with the old bear. Remember the coffee table, I thought. And then I saw myself smile in the rearview.

Very strange.

Maybe I should take Moon out with me tonight, to see this swing band with Griffin. Those two would get along like a heart attack and a bottle of ether. It would do Moon a world of good, though. Maybe he could hook up with a nice, middle-aged single lady. I would have to keep an eye on him, though, and not let him get so drunk.

Now I glanced out the cab's window. Larimer Street. A few blocks from Moon's place. The cab passed a vacant lot and a length of cyclone fence and then I see a gray Taurus parked crazily on the sidewalk and wedged against a lightpost. Had to be, I said out loud. Had to be Moon's car.

Let me out here.

I passed the cabbie a few bills and walked over to the abandoned Taurus. It wasn't so badly wrecked. The tires were still sound and the front end was maybe a little wrinkled. Nothing to worry about. I touched the hood and it was pretty cold. Peered through the windows and noticed that the driver's seat had been gutted like a goddamn big fish. Yellow stuffing everywhere. Now that was odd. I frowned. There was no blood, at least. Maybe it was nothing. I touched the door handle and what was this? The same unsettling wave of warm dizziness that I felt at Eve's place. Like a plastic bag had been slipped over my head and I couldn't breathe. I didn't like this at all and recoiled, flexing my hand. I looked up and down the street and started walking quickly for Moon's place.

Goo:

Something she needed to do, something important but she couldn't quite remember what because it wasn't her problem, it was Eve's. Never mind, never mind. Hum and holler. It would come to her, or it wouldn't. She sat up and took a good look around. Dizzy Bloom had a nice place. Asian rugs and a thousand books, dried flowers and dark wooden furniture, abstract sculptures and a glowing tank full of exotic fish. How did she maintain all this if she was forever stepping in and out of life? She was a Breather, though. And like Mingus she would be less affected by the Pale, by the lure of tongues. She would have that creepy ability to accept both worlds as real. To let two violent colors merge and become one.

Goo watched her now, as Dizzy laid out a white tablecloth on the floor and arranged dishes and silverware. Dizzy looked so solid, she looked permanent in her flesh. Graceful, silent. Long dark hair and white, white skin almost pink. Leather jerkin buttoned to the throat. Hard to tell if she had breasts or not. Her skirt was full, swirling. But the leather knee boots made her look tough. Dizzy glanced up, saw her looking and Goo could only smile, unashamed.

Mingus cleared his throat and Goo was startled. He was so quiet that she forgot about him sometimes.

What? she said.

Chrome is still in the shower, he said. It's been half an hour.

Goo shrugged. I'll go check on him, if you want.

Please.

Upstairs, she followed the sound of rushing water. Through what appeared to be a guest bedroom with pale green grass cloth on the walls. A queen-sized bed with a puffy white comforter like a small cloud. Roses on the bedside table.

Can't we just live here? she thought.

Eve. That was the sort of thing Eve might wish for. Goo crawled onto the bed, let herself sink into it. She rolled onto her back and felt her body slowly loosen. Her muscles were wound so tight all the time. The shower pounding in the bathroom. His skin would be cold as ice now. Bright with goose bumps. Goo was vaguely aware that Eve hadn't been so nice to

Chrome earlier. She could make up for that, though. She kicked off her boots, slid out of her pants. She dropped the black sweater to the floor and lay back on the bed, naked except for the white bandage taped to her ribs. The sound of water crashing and she touched herself, waiting for him to come out of the bathroom. Two fingers inside her, moving in circles. Okay. She didn't want to wait. She rolled off the bed, tiptoed to the bathroom and pushed it open.

Chrome, she said. Come to bed.

She threw back the shower curtain and no one was there. An empty stall, shower pounding like tiny hammers on porcelain. Goo hesitated, then turned off the water. The bathroom was small, with exposed wooden rafters and a tiny little sink. She felt like she was on a boat. Cold and she wrapped her arms around herself. The window was open and she supposed it was just wide enough for Chrome to wiggle through.

He often disappears, she said. To no one, to herself. It's nothing.

But she remembered the blood in his hair, thick and matted. She looked down and the porcelain tub was white as snow. Goo backed out of the bathroom and dressed quickly.

MOON'S FRONT DOOR was open just a crack, just enough for a sliver of light to escape down the hall. I saw it as I came around the corner and pretty much shrugged. I relaxed. Because I knew something had happened to my friend. Something bad. Moon was dead, maybe. Or else he had gone completely mental. Moon was fucked up. I could feel this in my teeth. If it had already happened, then there was nothing I could do about it. There was no reason to feel bad about it.

My second thought was: I hope Shame hasn't run off.

I edged close to the door, my knife in hand and wishing I had a gun. Eased the door open and the smell was dreadful. The smell of copper and salt. I stepped inside and my heart became a fist. There was no doubt, then. None at all. I moved through the kitchen and into the living room and nearly fell to my knees as if slapped in the head by a giant's meaty hand.

The room was red, now. Dark with blood.

I forget sometimes how much blood a single body can hold. It's astonishing, really. I pinched my nostrils and looked around for the body. Moon must have been bled like a pig. His throat cut, his body hung upside down. But there was no body. As if he had shriveled down to a handful of flesh and the killer just dropped him in his pocket and walked away. I turned in circles, reluctant to walk through Moon's blood. There was little sign of struggle, aside from the smashed coffee table which Moon himself had smashed. Which could mean everything or nothing. Moon knew the killer. Moon had been asleep at the time, or drunk. Moon had put up no fight. The thud of tiny feet and the cat swished past me.

Shame, I said.

The cat was a firecracker of nerves.

I whispered to him, my hand outstretched. I put the knife back in the sheath under my sleeve. Finally, the cat came to me and allowed himself to be held. I cradled him in one arm and stood up. I turned around once more. My eyes full of blood. I took two steps and a tall, thin man in a white hat came out of Moon's bedroom holding a gun in one hand, a half-eaten sandwich in the other. I stopped and stood there, still petting the cat.

Okay, I said. Are you going to shoot me?

Identify your fucking self, the man said.

He had an Irish accent and seemed pretty angry. He was about to chew his own tongue off. The man stepped closer now, the gun held chest-high. The gun was black, an automatic. It was not Moon's gun but that meant nothing. The sandwich looked to be peanut butter and jelly. The hands holding gun and sandwich were gloved in latex and the man's clothes were not bloody at all. Nobody carried latex gloves but cops and cat burglars and medical examiners, and nobody helped himself to peanut butter and jelly from a dead man's pantry but a fucking psychopath. I allowed my brain to skate around this unhappy equation for a moment and decided the man was probably a cop, mainly because he walked like a cop. He was even wearing a white hat. He was Irish, for that matter. And if he was a cop, he might have heard a thing or two about me, about Phineas Poe. And not liked what he heard.

I hesitated, sighed. Ray Fine, I said. My name is Ray Fine.

And what are you doing here, Mr. Fine?

I'm a friend of Moon's.

The man lowered his gun. Hmm, he said. I believe you.

Why?

That cat wouldn't let me touch him. And he fucking knows me, right. I've been here a hundred times. But he seems to love you.

Yeah, well. I fed him this morning. Who are you?

Lot McDaniel, Homicide. I was Moon's partner.

Really. He's never mentioned you.

McDaniel shrugged. I said I was his partner. Not his pal.

Your name is Lot? I said.

That's right, love, Lot. It's a fine, biblical name. Genesis nineteen.

The guy who staggered away from Sodom in disgrace, I said.

McDaniel sniffed. The very same.

Unlucky, don't you think?

How do you mean?

His wife became a pillar of salt.

Exactly. She was unlucky, not him.

Maybe, I said. But your mother must have had a nasty sense of humor.

My mother was a lovely woman.

The Bible is a telephone book of suitable names for a boy, I say. Peter and Paul, for instance. Thomas. John and Michael.

Those fuckers, said McDaniel. They were dreadfully overrated. The apostles in particular. Unemployed fishermen and layabouts, all of them. While poor old Lot never got a fair shake.

I shrugged. I'm pretty sure he had sex with his own daughters.

McDaniel was fuming. Those wee bitches, they got him drunk. They ganged up on him in the dark. And the poor fellow was feeble. Blind in one eye, too.

Whatever, I said. It might explain why the name never caught on.

Numb and sick. I would really rather be standing somewhere else. Anywhere else. Outside, for instance. My eyes were watering now, from the blood. McDaniel was staring at me, his nostrils flared. And he was toying with the gun.

The cat twisted away from me and jumped to the ground.

McDaniel still stared at me.

Something wrong? I said.

A word of warning. I hate that little Americanism, that expression: *whatever*. To my thinking, you may as well just say fuck you and be done with it.

Brief, awkward silence.

I couldn't decide whether I should apologize or run away.

Okay, I said. The smell is making me faint.

McDaniel smiled. Soft in the belly, are you?

I told myself to ignore this. Where's the body?

In the bedroom, said McDaniel. And not what you would call a handsome corpse.

Do you mind if I take a look?

Detective McDaniel smiled and looked at the sandwich in his left hand, the gun in his right. He took a bite from the sandwich, chewing thoughtfully. He put the gun away, then produced an engraved business card. He offered it like a gift and I had no choice but to hold out my hand.

As a matter of fact, said McDaniel. I would mind. I would mind very much. I need to preserve the integrity of this scene. Forensics are on their way, and all that. You've seen your share of police dramas on television, I suppose.

Oh, sure. I used to watch *Barney Miller* all the time.

Then you understand. I can't let you blunder about back there.

No, of course not.

McDaniel pressed the business card into my palm as if he hoped it would lacerate the flesh. I was feeling ill now, very ill and fucked up. I pocketed the card and backed away, hoping I wasn't going to throw up. I couldn't remember ever coming across a cop who carried engraved cards but I would rather not suspect this guy. It was on the tip of my tongue to ask if McDaniel knew anything about Jimmy Sky but now my brain was coughing slowly into action, like a motor with faulty connections. The motherfucker was eating a sandwich. He was a real freak, he was one giant bad vibe and you never saw his badge, never saw his badge. But then you never asked to see it, did you. And so what if the man carried fancy business cards. Maybe he was a little strange. Maybe he came from a snotty family or went to an Ivy League school on a rugby scholarship. Maybe he wasn't Irish at all. Maybe he was fucking British.

Why don't you call me tomorrow, McDaniel said. If you think of anything useful?

Yeah, I said. I'll call you tomorrow.

McDaniel took another bite from his sandwich and stood there chewing and smiling and obviously wishing I would get the hell out. And I didn't want to hang around. Because I was going to be sick any minute. I hurried back through the kitchen, arms wrapped around my stomach and now I could feel it coming. Eggdrop soup and mu shu pork and Canadian Mist and not much else. I threw up patiently in the kitchen sink and remembered something Moon once said: a gentleman never throws up on his shoes.

Yeah.

I bit down on my tongue to stop myself from sobbing and I didn't think I could stand it if McDaniel came in with his white hat and a mouthful of sandwich and dryly handed me a box of tissues. I stood over the sink, bitterly wiping bile and snot from my lips and wishing I hadn't given all of that coke to Griffin. I opened the refrigerator, looking for something to drink. There had been a single grape soda on the top shelf this morning and I was glad to see it was still there.

Next to it, though, was something very odd, something that was not there this morning. A used paperback copy of *Ulysses*.

Chrome:

He was hungry and his lips were parched but this was when he felt most alive. Hunting. His face and hands were painted black and as he passed through a black doorway he knew that only his eyes were visible. He slipped through a crowd of theater-goers and none of them noticed him. A woman with bright orange hair and a string of pearls passed two inches from him, her breath mingling with his and he was sure he could poke his tongue in her ear and duck away and she would turn slowly, she would turn like a cow trapped in mud. She would decide she had imagined it. He could cut her throat and disappear.

The dark was coming on now and this was his favorite time of day, when the sun was nearly gone, when the sun was failing. The sun was too weak to cast shadows and already he could make out faint gaps between the dayworld and the game. He stopped, melted into a doorway. Allowed his eyes to relax so that he might number these gaps: a blurred patch of red bricks, a shimmering pocket of air, a window so purple the glass looked like a pool of spilled ink. If he stepped through any of them, he would likely find a pocket of the game. He was tempted but his intended quarry was out there somewhere, another Fred with a badge. He was perhaps very close. It was a shame he couldn't have brought Mingus along, but the poor Breather was showing himself to be too stiff, too moral to be good company.

THE OBVIOUS SUSPECT is Jimmy Sky, of course. Moon is so hot to find the guy it's like he's got a crotch full of spiders and wham, not twelve hours later Moon's own apartment is washed in blood. A kid could figure it out. So it must not be right.

Anyway. I have yet to confirm that Jimmy Sky is a real person.

It happens all the time, this panic. The worst thing is the urge to dart out into the street like a rabbit. I have to push and prod myself along and find a little corner store where I can buy a carton of milk and maybe a pack of bubble gum. Then outside and find a bench, a patch of grass. I sit down and drink the milk slowly and breathe, breathe until the blood slows down and the milk is gone. Then chew my gum and blow a few bubbles and I'm fine.

On my way to Eve's place now because my head is full of bad voodoo and I want to be sure that everyone I come in contact with does not wind up dead. Because I am not Clint Eastwood, you know. As much as I might like to walk around town and calmly kill every asshole that has ever done me wrong or looked at me funny. A bullet between the eyes and a face full of black tobacco juice and I'm back on my horse.

I'm fucking gone.

But that's not me. I'm not Josey Wales. Maybe something's lacking in me, something is lost.

Oh, yeah. It looks like I'm going to be reading *Ulysses* this weekend. That's right. James fucking Joyce. I've read it before. Or to be correct, I have tried to read it in the past but always failed. I was too stupid, too lazy. I was too drunk. It's a difficult read, no question. But I love it. I love the elasticity of time, the doubtful state of reality. As if reality were a liquid. And you can only imagine my delight when Leopold Bloom trots off to a funeral with a fried kidney in his pocket.

Dear Jude.

Moon is dead. Perished.

I sit on a curb, staring. The blue notebook in one hand, a black felt-tip pen in the other. But every word is a struggle. I watch cars pass with the dull wonder of an animal that wants to cross the road but is so mesmerized by the noise and speed and lights that its ears lay flat and its eyes achieve a glossy sheen and soon the beast has no idea how it ever came to sit beside this road.

Now a bus rattled to a stop. Angry black exhaust and I climbed aboard. I regarded the other passengers with profound suspicion but no one else got on or off. I sat down and waited for the bus to move. But it just sat there, trembling. The driver must have disappeared for a pee or a smoke. I was not fond of buses. I always felt like I had been physically erased when the doors hissed shut and the driver was taking me to hell and I recently spent two horrifying days on a slow-moving Greyhound and fuck it anyway. I could have taken a cab to Eve's place but I was feeling thrifty and altogether too mournful about Moon to hurry anywhere. I pulled out *Ulysses* and opened it to a random page and read: beingless beings. Stop. Throb always without you and the throb always within. Your heart you sing of. I between them. Where? Between two roaring worlds where they swirl, I. Shatter them, one and both. But stun myself too in the blow. Shatter me who you can…oh, that was fine. That was lovely.

Eyes upon me and I lifted my head.

A young man, nineteen or so, was staring at me with the flat cold eyes of a fish. But the boy was not staring at all, I realized. The gaze was unfocused, fixed on a spot above and to the right of my head. The boy was blind. I felt a slight flush and opened my mouth to apologize, but this was unnecessary.

What does your tongue feel like? the boy said.

I hesitated, hoped the boy was speaking to someone else. But of course he wasn't. He was speaking to no one. He was possibly unaware that he had spoken out loud at all.

Silence.

A woman sitting near the boy got up and moved to another seat.

Your tongue, the boy pleaded. What does it feel like?

Excuse me? I said. It feels like an ordinary tongue.

Mine is soft and slimy, said the boy. And warm. Do you think that's right?

Again, silence. The other passengers stared at the boy with the satisfied horror and joy of the unafflicted. The boy stuck out his tongue and flapped it up and down and sideways, tasting the air. I found myself smiling and moved abruptly to sit beside the boy, surprising myself. I was sure that I had made no sound but the boy quivered slightly, as if the small hairs along his arms and neck were so sensitive that he could detect a molecular shift in the air around his body, the slightest change in temperature.

Why do you ask? I said.

Because it's all I think about sometimes. The boy stared straight at me and I was briefly alarmed by the way his face contorted as he spoke, the way he sucked and chomped at his lips. Then I realized that the boy must have never seen himself in a mirror and so his facial muscles were free to wiggle and twist with the unbound chaos of a monkey's.

It's all you think about, I said. How can that be?

The boy nodded violently. Yes, yes. It fills my head, you know. It sleeps there in the dark of my mouth like a beast. Warm and soft. And unpleasantly slimy. And I want to know if that's right.

I might not have chosen the word slimy, I said. But yes. That sounds about right.

The boy seemed relieved and said nothing more. But I was uneasy. I remembered a Charlie Brown comic from childhood in which Linus became aware of his tongue, to the point that he could think of nothing else. And the more he tried not to think about it, the more his tongue conspired to swell in his mouth, to become a limp of oppressive flesh. Lucy listened to this story, sneering as she was wont to do, then walked away. Moments later she was clutching at her throat and cursing her brother, for now she too was aware of her tongue.

I stared straight ahead, consciously licking at my teeth.

Theseus the Glove:
My, my but that was close.

He took one last bite of his sandwich and dropped the crust into Moon's overflowing dustbin. Theseus sighed, wondering if there was anything he needed to tidy up before his fellow officers arrived. It was his own error, of course. Damn his police instincts anyway. He had called this in too quickly, before he had tasted the blood and identified it as cow, not human. Before he had searched the apartment and found no body. On top of which, that idiotic Ray Fine person had blundered in at precisely the wrong moment.

Theseus scanned the living room again. A fine mess, but not extraordinary by Moon's standards. The blood was dreadful of course, but he barely noticed that anymore. He took a deep breath of the pungent air.

It was sweet as milk.

Of course. He rather liked it. But fucking hell. He could only assume that Moon had faked his own death but why he had done so was quite another matter. The man may have simply lost his nut and the real shock was that it hadn't happened sooner. Lord knew the fat bastard had been on the edge. Moon had been literally melting. But perhaps he was only trying to evade the game.

Theseus cursed, now.

He had been so confident that Moon was unaware of his rather unique status within the game of tongues. This was an irritating and unexpected twist, to be sure. Another one. That murdered Fred had been enough for one day, thank you. And unless he was blind as a newborn, the two were connected.

His eyes hurt, just considering it.

Theseus didn't have much time and truly he would rather just disappear, or at the very least give the impression that he was too horrified by the apparent death of his partner to be of any use. Theseus glanced at his watch and calculated that while the coroner would likely realize straight away that this was not human blood at all, he would not be able to confirm it until he got back to the lab.

But this was of little consequence. As a police matter, this scene barely interested him. It was the game that concerned him.

And Ray Fine, also. Ray Fine was a concern. That fellow was certainly not as stupid as he appeared.

Detective McDaniel? said a voice behind him.

Theseus willed his face to become pale and crushed. He should appear to be in shock, after all. His partner was dead, his body apparently stolen for some vile purpose. He rubbed at his eyes and forced a tear and turned to face the uniforms that had arrived.

Yes, he said.

It was easy enough to break into Eve's apartment, what with the door standing wide open. Her things were exposed to the elements. And having just come from Moon's place, my stomach fairly churned at the sight of it. My stomach became a wide black hole and escape velocity was doubtful.

But I wasn't so worried, really.

Somehow I knew she was just gone. Vacated. Most of her clothes and all of her furniture remained, but I could tell she wasn't coming back.

Now I poked through her bedroom with peculiar reluctance, with an older brother's nervous fear and vague arousal that I might stumble onto her diary, her vibrator.

There were clothes, mostly. And shoes.

And a thousand small fragments of Eve: strange little drawings and a collection of pocket knives, polished stones and bottle caps, a few Wonder Woman comic books, chewing gum and nail clippers and ribbons, matchbooks and foreign coins and panties and various girlish items that I couldn't quite name. She had left in a big hurry. I drifted into the living room, sat down on the floor in pretty much the same spot where I had eaten my eggdrop soup yesterday. I told myself not to worry about it. Eve was a tough little bird. She would turn up, undamaged.

Goo Unbecoming:

The candles had burned low and the gospel was nothing but static.

The food that Dizzy had prepared for them lay mostly untouched on the floor and she thought it was a wonder that gamers never starved. They ate like such nervous birds. But the three of them had already gone through half a bottle of the Pale. In an hour or so they would leave the house without comment and drift into the game. Mingus and Dizzy sat on the floor, facing each other but not speaking. They spoke, but not in complete sentences. One of them would produce a word from black depths, an image. The other would then examine the word, taste it and roll it around on the tongue. Then sigh, nodding.

Goo was not terribly worried about Chrome.

She didn't quite love him, not enough to worry. And he was known to disappear. Mingus was worried, though. Obviously. She had seen it in his face when she came downstairs and said Chrome was gone. The way his lips had curled and his hands clutched at nothing. But he wouldn't say why. Goo lit a cigarette and paced around. She felt cold, disconnected. She felt like Eve.

Are you performing tonight, said Dizzy.

Yes.

Have another drop of the Pale.

Goo shrugged. No, thanks. It makes me too clumsy.

What's the matter? said Mingus.

I don't know. I wonder where he's gone, that's all.

He could be anywhere, anywhere.

And you have no idea?

Mingus hesitated. He sniffed and looked at Dizzy, who now pulled uneasily at her hair.

Tell her, said Dizzy. You have to tell her.

Goo felt her throat tighten. A small cold fist inside. Tell me what, she said.

Mingus spoke in a halting monotone. Chrome killed someone yesterday, a Fred.

She smiled. But he does that every day. Twice a day.

No, said Mingus. Not like this.

What are you saying?

He took this one beyond Elvis, said Mingus. It was real.

He killed somebody, said Goo. Dead, you mean.

Dead, said Mingus.

His hair, she said. There was dried blood in his hair today. But I thought it was fake, or cow's blood. I thought it was part of the game oh shit.

Are you okay? said Dizzy.

No, she said. I'm not.

She was not okay. Faint, she felt faint. Her voice seemed to come not from her mouth but from her belly or spine. The words flickered between her lips like moths. This will be the end. The end of the game, thank God. Two candles drowning and the room got a little darker. Goo sat down, or fell. She fell into someone's strong arms. Dizzy, perhaps. Oh, no. Goo was slipping back into Eve's disorderly mind. A velvet couch, a Barbie doll. Shadows and starvation. Thin dark rope, alien tissue. The red skin of a fish and now she remembered. Eve wanted to warn Phineas about the apartment. And for that matter, she had better tell him to watch out for Chrome.

Oh shit, she said softly. This is insane.

Insane, said Mingus. He looked numb, he looked like he was made of wood.

How could he kill someone? she said.

Dizzy shrugged. Easily, she said. I'm sure it came easily for him.

Eve took a couple steps back. She felt like she was dreaming, like she had been dreaming of a birthday party two minutes ago and unwillingly stepped through a window into this other dream. She was lost.

But shouldn't we do something, she said. We should tell someone, report it.

Yes, said Mingus. I'm going to tell Theseus, tonight.

Dizzy nodded. He will take care of it, I'm sure.

But she didn't sound so sure at all. Eve wanted to go back to the birthday party. It was nice in there. Ice cream and cake and funny hats. They had helium balloons and she wanted nothing more than to shrink her voice down to munchkin level.

Do you have a telephone? she said with some effort.

Dizzy blinked. What an odd question. I think so. I have no idea if it works.

THE TELEPHONE RANG and my mouth dropped open. The phone. What fucking phone. There was no phone, I was sure of that.

The phone rang insistently and I followed the noise to the couch. Beneath one cushion was a little portable. I shook my head in disgust and pulled it out.

Hello.

You are there. It's me, she said. Eve.

Hey, I said. Where are you?

She hesitated. I'm at a friend's house.

I nodded, realized she couldn't see me nodding.

Everything okay? I said.

Yes, she said. And no. The apartment isn't…safe.

I glanced around. How's that?

Oh, well. This may sound strange.

This is me, I said. This is Phineas you're talking to.

She laughed. Okay. The apartment isn't stable.

What do you mean, Eve?

Don't ask me how, but it's sort of disintegrating.

I glanced down at my feet and the wood floor appeared normal enough.

Are you okay? I said.

It's hard to explain, she said. But look at the wall behind the couch. It's like…fading. The molecules are breaking down.

Uh-huh.

And there's a hole in the floor, near the bathroom.

Eve, I said. Are you high, or something?

Listen, she said. This is not a joke. Look at the wall.

I lowered the phone and stared at it. Fucking crazy. I felt crazy, like I was really holding an apple in my hand and Eve's voice wasn't real at all and she only existed in my head.

Nevertheless.

I walked back to the couch and hesitated, then reached out to touch the wall. It was pretty ordinary textured Sheetrock, and it felt very solid. It was real. I knocked on it with my fist.

Eve, I said. There's nothing wrong with the wall. Where are you?

I can't tell you, okay. I'm sorry. Please get out of there.

Where are you? I said.

Something else, she said. You met my friend Chrome, yes?

Yeah, I said. He seemed like a really nice guy.

He's dangerous, she said. If you see him, walk away.

Dial tone.

Eve, wait a minute.

Dial tone and I wondered, not for the first time, exactly what sort of research had gone into the selection of that particular sound. The military had been involved, no doubt. The psychological discomfort that the dial tone caused was no accident. The phone company did not want the sound of a dead connection to be pleasing and Eve had hung up on me. I chewed at my lip and nearly tossed the phone at the disintegrating wall, then smiled and star sixty-nined her. I felt very clever for about two seconds, but an automated voice soon told me it was sorry and my call could not be connected as dialed. Please check the number and dial again.

Then I got a fresh dial tone.

I threw the phone against the wall and it shattered pretty convincingly but I didn't feel any better. Eve was in some kind of trouble. Everyone was.

I touched the wall again, almost hoping I would fall through it. But the wall was solid. Then I noticed the damp, brown lump on the floor beside the couch. It looked like a hat, a crumpled sock. I bent to examine it, to touch it. The lump was a dead bird, its neck broken.

Jimmy Sky:

Christ on fire but he was fat. He was large. He caught a glimpse of his tubby profile just now and about lost his lunch. His belly boiled over the edge of his waistband and his thighs rubbed together as if they were in fact connected. It was no wonder he was soaking wet all day. He had no neck at all, really. There was a confounding clump of flesh there between his collar and chin that couldn't be called a neck, not by anybody's standards. And he had tits, okay. That was the big kick in the ass. That was the final straw.

Here was the thing about Jimmy. He only had access to this body on a very limited basis. Detective Moon was tooling around in it most of the time, and abusing it with pure suicidal flair. He was killing himself. Jimmy, though. He tried to eat right and lay off the booze. Jimmy sighed. All of this was going to change, and fucking soon. If he could only shake Moon out of this psychofunk he was wallowing in. Here was the thing. Moon wanted to kill Jimmy. He had asked his sketchy pal Phineas to find him, to find Jimmy. Hilarious, wasn't it. Except for the fact that Moon's intentions were unfriendly. He wanted to wipe him out. He wanted to strip Jimmy of his status as a character. It was annoying, to say the least. Jimmy had been Moon's very reliable undercover identity for two or three years now, an alias is what he had been. Nothing more. Moon had trotted him out now and again for a little police business and Jimmy would make the buy or solicit the blow job or kick the shit out of somebody while Moon took a breather. He had always known that Moon got a laugh out of Jimmy, for Jimmy was a lot cooler and sexier and had no worries about electric bills and taxes. Jimmy was a vacation from himself.

Then Moon got sucked into this game, this game of tongues. Which was interesting for a while. A nice, harmless fantasy ripe with vampires and magic spells, with medieval weirdness and good drugs and a fair amount of nudity. The drugs were a concern, though. Moon had got himself hooked on this sweet narcotic potion called the Pale. Or Jimmy did, as Jimmy Sky was his name within the game. Jimmy was a rare self-aware Fred who was angling to hook himself up as a Redeemer. But Jimmy had a problem, a nasty and fairly frightening problem. Moon and Jimmy were estranged. They barely knew each other anymore. His state of awareness was tenuous at best and he seemed to have no control over how and when he slipped in and out of the game. He would drift into Moon's world without warning and completely forget he had ever been Jimmy. Then he was helpless, he was trapped in daylight with no memory of the game and a powerful ache for the Pale that he didn't understand. And meanwhile, Jimmy was fucking tired of the game and he was mighty tired of being toyed with by Theseus the Glove.

Fuck the game, he said.

He wanted to end it, he wanted to blow it out of the water with a big, big splash and the first order of business had been to put a hit out on old Moon. That's right. He offed the fat bastard himself. He cut his throat and bled him dry. Okay, so he faked it. It looked good, though. It looked real. Beyond that, he had no idea what he was doing. He just wanted to stir things up and see what happened.

DEAR JUDE. THIS SHIT IS WELL OUT OF HAND and there's no reason to think it will change gears and become painless or dull anytime soon. I have to meet Griffin in less than an hour. Oh fucking joy.

Truly, I barely feel like myself. And it's not that I'm afraid of becoming Ray Fine, exactly. There is an ugly new sensation that I can only describe as degeneration. My physical presence is failing.

I am not real, okay.

The reflection that I seek in mirrors and blackened store windows, this is real enough. My reflected image is cruising up the street without a care in the world but I am nowhere to be found and how fucked up is that.

And I thought Eve was crazy. Her apartment was unstable, so what.

Come on you neurotic piece of shit. Take out your knife and poke yourself in the thigh. Your shadowself will hardly bleed, will it. But the mirror version of Phineas will certainly lose its status in the ghostworld if it shows itself to have ordinary bodily fluids so go ahead boy, open up a fat vein.

This was no good, no fucking good.

I was talking to myself and of all my nervous habits, that was one I had never cared for. And I seemed pretty bent on cutting a big hole in my own leg. What a shivering mess I was. I turned around and around, looking for a safe place to roost. A place with normal, friendly humans. There was an open café across the street, yeah. I could have a five-dollar cappuccino and a piece of pie and read a few pages of *Ulysses* and with any luck there would be no mirrors in the place and just maybe that would do the trick.

Nervous bowels or bad coffee or too much sugar. Whatever the cause I was soon camped out in the public toilet with a horrible case of liquid shit. Which always makes me feel like I am probably dying. It just seems inherently bad to spray fluids from that particular hole. The bathroom was not filthy, at least. It was equipped with toilet paper. But the stall had been recently painted and the absence of graffiti was unnerving.

I pulled out *Ulysses* and flipped the pages around. For some reason, I couldn't read it in its proper order and I thought Joyce would forgive this. Why else would he write in such maddening circles.

Metempsychosis. The transmigration of souls.

I was with Molly on that one. Tell us in plain words, as she said. But I got the general idea and maybe this was my own problem. I was transmigrating.

Dear Jude.

I'm sure it's just residual sadness or some kind of projection but I can't read a word about Leopold Bloom without seeing Detective Moon. His round unhappy face. And I hope that doesn't cast me as Dedalus because he was one fucked-up person. He was tormented by memory, by false guilt. He was terrified of water and pregnancy and dogs. He was obsessed with the past, with the death of his mother. He had trouble with women. He had trouble with sex, like the rest of us. Stephen Dedalus was nearsighted and he was forever hallucinating.

He didn't much believe in reality.

Of course. It does sound very familiar.

But I think Dedalus was essentially good. He was frail and tortured and he had his doubts about the origin of sin but he was at least searching for the high ground. He wanted to be pure. He was a tragic hero, whatever that means. I would personally claw the eyes out of anyone who said that shit about me.

Chrome:

Love. He was in love with this one. He had spotted him at one of those automated cash machines where the humans line up like rabbits for a food pellet. Pushing buttons, their faces bright and fearful. They were always so relieved when the cash appeared. They smiled, as if they were chosen.

His target was of medium height, white or Hispanic. Dark eyes and very nice skin. Clean skin was a plus in all new relationships. He appeared to be healthy but not dangerous. And definitely a Fred. It was in the eyes, the emptiness of the Pale. Chrome had watched the man at the money machine, laboring to enter his code correctly. His card kept getting rejected. The Fred's little world was slipping and the machine hatefully spat out his card like a bad seed and he kept pushing it in until the machine finally ate it. The Fred remained placid all the while. He didn't wail at the sky or pull out his hair, he didn't strike the machine. He never blinked. Again, this was the Pale. And when the Fred had first flipped his wallet open to fetch out his card, Chrome saw the flash of a silver badge and felt his pulse jump. Another policeman.

Now. The hunt.

The Fred moved along at a turtle's pace, stopping every so often to obsessively examine his damned shoelaces. As far as Chrome could tell, the man's laces had not come undone yet. It was the very idea that seemed to plague the Fred. And each time the Fred stopped, Chrome was forced to stop as well.

His heart drumming crazily in the shadows. He was sure the Fred would hear it, if he only bothered to listen. But the Fred was busy untying his left shoe now, then tying it again. For the love of Mary. Did every serial killer have to put up with this sort of thing? He doubted that Hannibal Lecter would tolerate such foolishness. It was downright unseemly, is what it was. And he resolved to punish the Fred a little bit extra for the shoelaces.

They were moving east now. Away from downtown. Chrome nibbled at his own tongue and tried to think of ways to make this interesting. Eyes closed, perhaps. Hopping on one foot. Anything to give the Fred a fighting chance. And now the Fred did something that made Chrome smile, that brought the blood to his mouth. The Fred decided to take a shortcut through a graveyard. The ambiance would be divine.

Elvis was waiting.

Major Tom:

Black flies buzzing round and round behind his very eyes and something caught between his teeth, shred of apple skin or a piece of thread. A fingernail, maybe.

He sat at the best available table at the Paramount in his sharpest black suit, sort of a teddy-boy outfit with pants slim as knives and a jacket with no lapels, zip-up boots with squared-off toes perfect for kicking in the face of anyone who made the mistake of fucking with him. Dangling from his shoulder was Kink, his ethereal yet stupid-as-dirt girlfriend. Long dark red hair that looked wet, fine white throat and shoulders. She wore a thin plastic sheath of a bodysuit that appears to be transparent but was not, that stretched around her long muscled limbs like futuristic rubber. He was fascinated by this garment's construction, for there were no visible zippers or snaps and it looked like she had been dipped into the suit while it was still liquid and perhaps would have to be cut out of it later with a sharp knife.

Tom stroked her tight inner thigh with one finger while smoking a thin cigar and chewing a piece of ice and keeping one eye well peeled for the elusive Poe.

Tongue like hot velvet dipping into his ear and he had to fight the urge to turn and bite it.

Careful, he said. Be careful, sweet Kink.

I'm thirsty, she purred.

Wait until my friend arrives.

I can't wait, Tom.

And don't call me that. It will only confuse him.

A cool, long-fingered hand crawled up his leg and stroked his gear through his pants with such delicious carelessness that he shivered and sighed. He wore no underpants with this suit, for the material was so fine and close-fitting that he had to be careful of unsightly panty lines and one consequence of this was that his rig was ultrasensitive from all the incidental rubbing and touching and seemed to live in an ongoing state of half-erection. He pushed the hand away with some reluctance and pondered the chance of missing Poe if he took the dear girl off to the lavatory and screwed her to shreds in an unoccupied stall. He frowned, blowing a long stream of smoke into the glittering crowd. The mysterious Krazy Glue outfit might be a problem, however. For if he was forced to cut or rip it from her body, then she would have nothing at all to wear. He would have to wrap her up in newspapers and deposit her into a passing taxi. And this, he thought, might not be such a bad plan. He had a terrifying erection by this time and it would of course be a lot of fun to cut open her suit and besides, she would only be a nuisance later when he was trying to have an intelligent word or two with Poe. He smiled and smiled, for now the idea struck him that her outfit might well have come equipped with a small, discreet opening at the crotch for just such an occasion. An extra set of lips for the possibility of a good spontaneous public fucking, as it were. And a girl does have to pee, as well. Approximately twenty-nine times per hour, if she was anything like his girl. Right right right. Having settled this bothersome question, Tom was just gathering the strength to take Kink by the cold hand and breathe something vile and daring into her ear and drag her off to the Men's when he saw Poe ducking through the crowd in what at first glance appeared to be a psychotic clown's suit. Tom reminded himself to act more like Griffin and he smiled widely, for Griffin was proud of his fine white teeth and so he smiled with all his fury.

I WAS NOT THE LEAST BIT THRILLED by this scene. Too many disjointed arms and legs in sleek polyester, too much bad hair and too many self-conscious white people dancing badly by far. And I didn't much care for swing music. It was tolerable for about five minutes, amusing even. Then it got old in a hurry. I spotted Griffin now, sitting at a raised table with a not pretty but disturbingly sexy woman dressed like a very slutty version of Catwoman. I glanced down at Ray Fine's noxious clothing and shrugged. But I did take the hat off as I approached the table. I had a little pride left. Griffin didn't get up, but magnanimously pointed at an empty chair with the end of his cigar. I muttered a hello and sat down, lit a cigarette and looked around for a waiter. The catwoman regarded me with supreme disinterest.

Hello, I said.

Poe, said Griffin. I'm glad you could come.

Who's your friend?

This mad goddess? said Griffin. This is Kink, my beloved.

I watched his eyes for cruelty. He was such a good lawyer. He was relatively honest but his words were slick as jelly, veiled in hostility and despair.

Hello, said Kink. Her voice was hoarse.

I wanted to say hello, I wanted to be polite. Instead I just stared at her until she looked away.

What's the matter with you? said Griffin.

Never mind, I said. Then thought about it. What the fuck. I guess it doesn't matter. You were in the DA's office, Griffin. Did you know a Detective Moon, from the Ninth?

Griffin touched his forehead as if he had a sudden migraine. The girl-friend rolled her eyes.

You okay? I said.

If you don't mind, Poe. I would rather not discuss my daytime life, not now.

I didn't care for this answer. Moon got himself killed today, I said.

Please, said Griffin. I'm sorry, of course.

What about Jimmy Sky? Have you ever heard of him?

Griffin brightened. Jimmy Sky, he said. He said it twice, as if the name felt good to his tongue.

Do you know him? I said.

Afraid not, said Griffin. But it's a fine, sexy name.

Uh-huh. I need a drink, I said.

Don't bother looking for the waiter. There isn't one.

Then I'm going to the bar.

Griffin shook his head. That won't be necessary, he said.

He reached under the table to retrieve a bottle wrapped in plain brown paper and Kink promptly began to suck pornographically at her little finger. Her eyes flashing. Griffin removed the paper and I nodded, unsurprised. It was another bottle of the Pale. I had been thinking more along the lines of Jack Daniels, maybe vodka on the rocks with a pint of beer to chase it down, but this Pale stuff was not so bad. A little too sweet for my liking but weirdly potent and now I felt thirsty just looking at the bottle. Griffin reached into the side pockets of his jacket and produced two shot glasses.

I'll drink from the bottle, he said.

Griffin poured out two quivering shots and I swallowed mine before my heart took another beat. My head swam pleasantly. Kink took hers in dainty sips while Griffin had a long, greedy drink from the bottle. I poked my empty glass across the table. Another one, I said.

Griffin poured me another and I sucked it down. It was like drinking air. Another one, I said.

Griffin smiled. Easy, cowboy. We have all night.

Another, I said.

You want to be gentle with this stuff at first.

I took a puff of my forgotten cigarette and smiled. It was maybe the best cigarette I had ever smoked and I knew I was in big fucking trouble. I looked around me. The crowed had faded away and I felt invisible.

The stuff you gave me earlier, I said. It was okay. But this is amazing.

I was having difficulty with my English.

That bottle was mostly water, said Griffin.

And I've had absinthe before, I said. It's not like this.

No, said Griffin.

Kink finished her drink and poured another one. I stared at her, my mouth open like a dummy. She was not so beautiful five minutes ago. Her skin had surely not been shimmering like this. This girl was made of silver and butterfly wings and she seemed to vibrate at some impossible high frequency. As if she might well disappear before my eyes. I was weak, I was a paper torso. I wiped at my mouth with some effort and found that I was drooling and I wanted this girl. I wanted to be inside her, to suck and bite and devour her. More than anything, I wanted to be eaten by her.

Relax, said Griffin. She's a Trembler.

What? I said. She's a what?

Phineas looked down from the ceiling and watched with mild horror as his disconnected body leaned across the table like a puppet with open mouth and splayed hands and he realized that he would do anything to kiss her, anything at all. He could possibly take a kiss by force but he didn't seem to have the strength. He was a worthless beggar and what under the sun did he have to trade her for a kiss? He had his shoes, his goofy hat. He had a few hundred dollars but he didn't want to insult her with an offering so profane.

Griffin poked the girl with a sharp finger. For fuck's sake, Kink. Will you cut it out? he said.

Just a small nibble, she said. Just a taste of his tongue.

Griffin's eyes were boiling now. No, he said.

But he's a Fred, she said. Like any other.

He's a friend, said Griffin softly. Leave him be or I will damage you.

The woman relaxed her gaze and I felt warm, then cold. I slowly regained a little muscular control but my tongue remained unfamiliar. As if it was not my own.

The fuck is going on, I said.

And slimy, my tongue was slimy oh boy.

Griffin nodded, smiling. You want to gather your wits, Poe.

Yeah, I know. Why did she call me Fred?

It's complicated.

My name is not Fred.

Griffin sighed. Have you ever heard of the game of tongues?

The what? I lit another cigarette, fingers shaking slightly.

Are you sure you're okay?

I touched my forehead. It felt like a blood vessel had swollen to almost but not quite bursting, like I should be unconscious now but was not. My vision was extraordinarily clear. I could see through my own skin. The club was dark but I squinted across the table like a traumatized rabbit with pink eyes.

Yeah, I said. Maybe I need a beer, or some regular water.

Griffin glanced at Kink, who pouted briefly then swiveled away.

When you were a kid, said Griffin. Did you ever play *Dungeons & Dragons*?

I shrugged. I was briefly a geek in high school, so what?

Griffin placed his hands flat on the table, palms down, his fingertips drumming the gouged oily surface and I stared at them for a while, unhappily waiting for the table to turn to butter. Meanwhile, Griffin's face and naked skull looked to have been cut from brittle green limestone.

You want to tell me what's in that Pale beverage, now?

Griffin shrugged. It's mostly herbs, vitamins: ginseng and gingko, various algaes and concentrated wheat grass. And the wormwood, of course. It's really pretty good for you.

It's a fucking smart drink? That's what you're saying.

I said mostly herbs. There's also a mild dose of Ecstasy and a touch of synthetic heroin.

That sounds…great, I said. It's just what I need, thanks.

Listen, said Griffin. Forget about the Pale, okay.

I hate Ecstasy, I said. I hate that shit. It makes people feeble and friendly.

Please shut up, said Griffin. The drugs are irrelevant.

I flapped my arms and felt confident that I was in fact made of sticks. I tried not to laugh. I was the stickman.

The Pale is only a means to an end, said Griffin.

Twitch and grin.

I jerked my head up and down like a stupid muppet.

Violent. I wanted to be violent and I was grateful for a concrete concept, for something I could properly wrap my teeth around. Fucking Griffin, though. He just sat there, staring at me. He wouldn't finish the train of thought, the bastard.

Then what is the end? I said, almost shouting.

Griffin smiled. He smiled. The game of tongues, of course.

Major Tom:

Oh, please won't someone give him a bullet. Did he truly not recall what a twisty nervous and altogether paranoid wreck Poe could be?

Fucking Poe. He was exactly like a chick, sometimes.

He wanted to show the old boy a good time and suddenly it was not unlike trying to squeeze a rape confession out of a deaf and dumb schoolteacher. Tom adjusted the knot in his tie and polished his scalp with the heel of his hand. Everything was fine, everything was fine. The first order of business was to get Poe the hell out of this dreadful place. Martha's Dead had begun to warm up, torturously tuning their inexpensive guitars and complaining about the monitors and hammering aimlessly at the drums. And Kink had apparently disappeared into the void, so fuck her. She could catch up with them at the Unbecoming Club. Right right right.

Let's go, he said.

Poe hesitated then bobbed to his feet like a rubber duck.

Tom sighed, watching him screw the moldy fedora down tight onto his head. They would have to do something about his clothes. The poor man was high, of course, but not unforgivingly so. In fact, Poe seemed very cooperative. He didn't ask where they were going and he expressed no concern over abandoning Kink. Tom imagined she was a bit too slithery for Poe's tastes. Poe generally went for women who looked like Catholic schoolgirls but carried a straight razor in their socks. He had always been attracted to false innocence, to girls who looked sweet and pious but might just cut his throat while he slept. He wanted a girl who looked like his sister, a sister who wanted nothing more than to be bound and gagged and fucked in the ass.

Anyway.

Poe stood there, waiting for guidance. Which could be attributed only to the excellence of the Pale. Truly, the game of tongues would not function without the stuff. There would be no new Freds and therefore no new victims. There would be fewer and fewer apprentices. There would be almost no economy, nothing to motivate the lower castes. It would be chaos.

Outside and the air was lovely.

Tom flagged down a cab and shoved Poe into the backseat. He tried to explain a few of these bald truths about the Pale to the pliable Poe, who stared back at him with one unblinking eye and nodded frequently. His other eye was clamped fiercely shut, for some reason, and Tom chose not to ask why. He instructed the cabbie to take them to a particularly isolated spot along Cherry Creek, hoping they would find a small pocket of the game so that he might show Poe the finer points of hunting tongue. Along the way he talked and talked and talked. He could only hope that Poe absorbed some of it.

VIBRATING. I WAS vibrating and for some reason could only see out of one eye. I couldn't really talk, or I didn't want to. Griffin was droning on about something, which was nice. I crawled out of my body and settled into the narrow space below the rear windshield and remembered that when I was a child, my grandmother had owned a Siamese cat that always rode around with her in the car, and the cat had liked to nap in this spot. And I, the young Phineas, had often begged and pleaded for the opportunity to nap there as well. But my granny had always refused. It wasn't safe, she said. It was perfectly safe for the cat, who had superior reflexes and motor skills, but not for a five-year-old boy. And so I would gladly nap there now, or else listen to Griffin's voice if I couldn't sleep.

Where oh where shall I start, said Griffin. Of course you must first understand the caste system, as it's extremely rigid. Movement from one level to another is rare and difficult. But it's really all that the self-aware Freds and Tremblers may hope for, unless they are happy with their lot in life, eh? There is some sideways movement, naturally. Freds may become Tremblers and Tremblers may become Freds, although they surely wouldn't want to. The Freds are usually but not always men, and most of them are unaware that they have even entered the game. These are the most common victims of the hunt. The Mariners pull them down like sheep. The Mariners, mind you, hunt everyone. The Exquisitors too, may take an unaware Fred if they are desperate. They tend to prefer the mutual kill, though. The shared tongue. The Redeemers and Tremblers do not hunt, exactly. They practice various forms of seduction. They also prey on the Freds, and on each other. And the self-aware Freds often hunt each other in small packs. Have I left anyone out? The Breathers, of course. They do not hunt, and claim they don't need to. And the Gloves. They are masters of the game. Each chapter of the game is watched over by a Glove. I don't know if they ever bother to hunt and no one, not even the boldest Mariner, would dare attempt to take the tongue of a Glove.

I was surprised, shocked to see my head turn to the side. I wanted to ask a question, it seemed.

Excuse me. What are you, then? My voice was dull and flat. I hated my voice.

Griffin shrugged. I'm a Mariner. It's the only thing to be.

And...what am I?

Hah, said Griffin. You are technically a Fred, but not for long. Already you are self-aware, and I want you to be my apprentice.

What if I don't want to play?

A brief sweet silence.

I watched the passing cars, lights trailing behind them like honey.

Griffin touched my face. It's too late for that, I'm afraid. Tomorrow you will awake with a mighty thirst for the Pale. And the only way to get it is to play.

The eyes were so heavy.

I pressed my cheek to the cool glass and wished for sleep.

And you will need a name, said Griffin. Everyone within the game has a name, except for the unaware Freds. They are simply Fred.

Okay, I said. I will be Ray Fine.

Ray Fine? said Griffin. It's not very sexy, but I suppose it will do.

Who are you?

Oh, said Griffin. Have we not met? I am Major Tom.

Vibrating. I was vibrating and for some reason could only see out of one eye. I couldn't really talk, or I didn't want to. Griffin was droning on about something, which was nice.

Major Tom:

A wee bit sluggish from the Pale. He stood under a moonless sky and wished his neck did not ache from the various nasty toxins he had consumed this good night. And he wished he had worn underpants as he was nearly to the breaking point with all this rubbing and textile thrashing of his rig. He contemplated, then moodily discarded, the idea of sitting down right here and whipping the thing out for a fast hand job in the wet grass, if only to relieve a little pressure. But he wouldn't want to upset Poe, would he? Although that was not fucking likely. Poe stood alongside him and gazed into the gray and purple sky like he had never noticed it before and he would probably not blink if his pal Griffin commenced to hump a hole in the ground.

Never mind the pain. He would save this stunning erection and its brilliant load of gunk for dear Kink. How sweet it was to love someone, even such a manic ninny as the slippery Kink. Anyway. His bare skull was cold and for a moment he looked with some envy at Poe's crusty fedora. Then laughed softly. Poe turned to him, his face blank as a sleeping dog's and Tom smiled. Don't forget, this was his first apprentice.

Right right.

He pulled at Poe's hand until the poor fellow caught the hint and crouched down beside him. They looked down from a steep embankment of mud and recently transplanted grass at the paltry stretch of water known as Cherry Creek. The creek was dark and silent in its concrete bed and no one ran alongside it at this hour unless he or she was being chased by another.

Do you know where you are? he said.

Poe responded thickly. Denver. This is Denver.

Good. And your muscles, he said. How do they feel?

They feel numb. Not like my own.

Yes, he said. It's the Pale, it saps your strength. If you will be a Mariner you must find ways to overcome its effects, or resist it altogether.

How? said Poe.

Tom sighed. To resist is unpleasant, he said. Of course. But there are always pills and powders to be had that will restore the senses.

He pulled out a little gunmetal snuffbox and passed it to Poe, who took it from him with endearing caution. Poe's face was in shadows but Tom thought he might have seen a flicker of recognition in Poe's one good eye. The mad fucker had the left eye shut tight now, and Tom could have sworn that it was the right eye before. As for the flicker. The box was Griffin's, of course. And Poe had seen it earlier today. It was nothing to worry about. The identities bleed through easily at first. Eventually one learned to suppress them, or to live with them. He watched as Poe opened the box and tipped it with care, spilling a generous amount of cocaine into the palm of his hand. It was easily enough coke to stop his heart, and Tom was curious to see if the old boy was quite dizzy enough to suck it all down. But Poe hesitated, then separated the little pile with his fingernail and inhaled just half of it. Tom was pleased to see this. Poe's speech was rather impaired, but his movements were smooth and fluid and his judgment was sound. It was most common for a new apprentice to blink and stumble about like a defective robot for a few days, until his senses adjusted to the Pale. For physiological reasons that Major Tom did not quite understand, and couldn't be fucked to ponder, women recovered from the Pale much faster than men and were therefore less likely to be cast as Freds. He shrugged and smiled without showing his teeth when Poe offered him his open hand and what remained of the cocaine. Tom bent from the waist and sniffled and soon the little handful of coke was gone. He gently retrieved the box from Poe and checked its contents and felt a rush of the warm and fuzzies upon seeing there was plenty more. He wet his fuck-finger and dipped it into the box, smearing a bit of the sweet powder into his gums. After a moment Poe did the same, then shrugged and said that he was ready. Tom was proud of him, yes.

Let's go, then.

They dropped down to the edge of the creek, silent and shadowy as wolves. Tom took the lead and they walked along the path, a body length between them. Tom chewed softly on his own tongue. His skin might as well have been on fire, what with the raw coke pushing and shoving his blood through his heart as if death itself were on the wing. He had a good feeling about this path, and soon proved himself a clever boy as the creek bent to enter a dark little grotto beneath a viaduct.

Smoke.

Tom smelled smoke and raised his hand for Poe to stop. They crept closer and saw the glow of a small fire. Four shadows around it. Voices. The pulse of music. A droning and distorted bass line. Deathmetal, his very favorite. He turned to Poe and smiled.

Like mice, he whispered. We will approach them like mice.

Three young Freds in various states of awareness. One little Trembler, thin and pretty and not more than nineteen. She was perhaps overmatched by the Freds, who were filthy and starved to the bone, dressed in black motorcycle leathers that no doubt stank of blood and smoke and urine. They wore heavy boots that were surely excellent for stomping and there were ugly chunks of metal driven through their lips, their noses. Probably their tongues as well. On another night Tom would have watched from the shadows to see which of the Freds would be first to take the girl's tongue if she failed to Tremble them. And then of course the Freds would turn on each other and soon he would slither from the dark and say hello.

Tonight was different, however.

He wanted Poe to understand the fever, to taste one or more tongues and to know the fear that the Mariners strike in these others. He wanted Poe to recognize the opposite of love and so he whispered for Poe to follow him, to follow his own heart. Major Tom stepped out of the dark, holding his arms out like wings and for once he wished it were more practical to wear a cape. The drama would be delicious, it would be chocolate and strawberries and his throat was tight just thinking of it. But he would be forever tripping over the thing and therefore useless in a fight. Really, he didn't understand how Batman managed it.

Hello, he said.

THICK HEAD AND TRYING to think was not unlike trying to force a dull blade through overcooked meat while my arms and legs glittered bright with pins and needles from the big spoonful of coke I had just shoved up my snout. I didn't feel quite like myself, but I was trying. God help me. I watched as Griffin, who wanted to be called Major Tom for some reason, approached three punks and a hippie girl who sat looking stoned and fearful around a little campfire. Griffin had become a much more interesting freak than I had ever imagined.

"Major Tom" was the name of a David Bowie song, right? I tried to summon the lyrics but came up empty. Losing your mind, something about losing your mind in outer space. I shook my head and started to feel myself up for a cigarette but stopped in midgrope when Griffin reached into the little fire and pulled out a burning chunk of wood and without warning tossed it in my direction. Motherfucker. But my reflexes surprised me and I actually caught the thing, my right hand easily snatched the end that was not burning without any complicated guidance from my brain. And now I was twirling this chunk of fire around my head like a cheerleader from the bowels of the earth and of course the fire stretched against the dark sky like rippling orange ink and for a moment it was like I was creating fire, I was fire and this was pretty fucking cool. Then my hand was on fire and I wasn't sure if I could feel anything but I could hear the distinct crackle and pop of my own skin and I dropped the piece of wood telling myself not to scream, not to scream.

I peered fearfully at my hand, expecting it to be blackened and crispy or at least bubbled with gruesome blisters but hey, it looked okay. It was only hot, very hot. I looked back to Griffin and the four kids and they were all watching me and maybe the whole fire thing had only lasted two seconds or maybe they all knew I was new to this game or whatever it was so they were patiently waiting for me to stop freaking out and get my shit together and flow.

Then things started to move quickly, very quickly.

One of the punks had a huge silver nosering and oily black hair combed into a ducktail and he looked like Fonzie on acid. He looked pretty tough, or at least he fancied himself tough and he unwisely told Griffin to fuck off and zoom: Griffin was sitting on the sorry fucker's chest. And while I may have been high and my perception of speed and distance were not quite right, I was nonetheless amazed. This new Griffin was some kind of panther, he had reflexes like fucking Spider-Man and I moved closer now, fascinated. But one of the punks screeched at the sight of me and took off, disappearing into the dark and I felt a peculiar tug, like maybe I should chase the guy down and hurt him.

The girl and the other guy cowered together and maybe they were too scared or too stupid to run but maybe not. They clutched and grabbed at each other's clothing with a heavy sexual vibe and I was pretty confident they would have a go right then and there while Griffin and I tortured their pal but suddenly the male, who was probably twenty-two or -three and looked like a mean fucker with a scar on his cheek and long sideburns and a spiderweb tattoo across his throat and surely outweighed the female by fifty pounds, suddenly went all limp in her arms and opened his mouth. The girl leaned over him lazily and gave the guy a deep, penetrating and weirdly violent kiss. She looked like she was trying to suck his tongue right out of his mouth and now I suffered rapid flashes of Griffin's girlfriend leaning toward me in the club with hunger in her eyes.

Meanwhile.

Griffin had his guy by the throat and was flicking the big nosering back and forth with his index finger like he might just pull it out. Then he leaned over and hit the kid's cheek hard enough to draw blood.

Your blood is bitter, said Griffin. What have you been eating?

The guy made a weak choking noise but didn't, or couldn't, answer.

Hey, I said. But I said it too softly because I was curious. Honestly. I wanted to see what would happen.

Open it, said Griffin. Fucking open it.

I glanced over at the girl, who was now casually smoking a cigarette.

Her new boyfriend wasn't moving, though. He looked dead, in fact. But there was no fucking way he was dead from a kiss. The man had to be unconscious or something and as I moved to help him an idiotic voice in my head that sounded a lot like my own voice said maybe what he needs is a little mouth-to-mouth. I kill myself, sometimes. I prodded the stiff with the toe of my boot and was not terribly surprised when he hopped to his feet and looked at us with something like shame and defiance and then turned and ran.

Ray, said Griffin.

Silence.

Then again, loudly. Hey, Ray.

And I turned, remembering dully that this was my name. I was fucking Ray and now I saw that Griffin had forced his guy's jaw open and was crouched over him like a mad dentist. The tip of the guy's tongue was exposed, a small pinkish triangle of meat and I thought of earthworms drowning in the rain.

Come here, said Griffin. His eyes shining.

What?

This Fred will be your first tongue.

I looked at the Fred, whose nosering was slick with snot and blood. It was strange, though. The guy didn't look so terrified. He looked meek and a little furious and yet he lay there with his mouth open, waiting for someone to bite his tongue and temporarily own him. I felt nothing I might call desire. And this is important, I think. I want to be clear about this. It wasn't a moral thing for me. It was an ordinary lack of desire.

I don't think so, I said.

What? said Griffin. His voice thick with disgust.

Let him go, Griffin.

Griffin shrugged. He bent and kissed the Fred, he bit and sucked at the guy's mouth and now I felt aroused. The Fred didn't go limp like the other one. His legs thrashed at the ground and his hips jerked against Griffin's ass. Then it was over. Griffin released him, he smiled and slapped the Fred's belly.

Disappear, he said. And to me he said, don't fucking call me Griffin.

The Fred grunted and clambered to his feet. He brushed himself off and began to fix his hair but Griffin was staring murderously at him and the Fred apparently decided to fuck with his hair later, for he hooted at us and ran away and now a thin, cool voice said, what about me?

I turned my head and the girl was standing very close to me.

Think fast Ray, said Griffin. Do you want her tongue?

What…?

Will you be a wolf, he said. Or a rabbit.

Kill the rabbit, said the girl.

Her breath smelled sweet, like green melon. Long yellow hair that hung in ringlets. A necklace of seashells and bright stones around her long throat. Fantastic eyes, blue with impossible splashes of black. Her lips were dark as berries.

Careful, said Griffin. Be careful, Ray.

I opened my mouth slightly. I did want to kiss this girl and why not, she was adorable and sexy and fresh as a damn flower. And she apparently wanted me to kiss her. I leaned forward dreamily, stupidly while the very paranoid little action figure version of myself was running around in my skull and banging the panic drum, howling don't do it don't do it you dumb motherfucker. The girl's mouth was not two inches from my own and I grabbed her by the face. And she looked pretty surprised.

But I trembled you, she said.

Uh, I said. Not well enough, I guess.

I had her face in my hands and it was ridiculously soft. She had perfect skin and edible lips and now I was not sure what I wanted to do.

You have really nice skin, I said.

Griffin spat. Jesus, Ray.

The girl was staring into my eyes like I was a mannequin. I assumed she was still trying to tremble me, whatever that meant. I let my hands slip to her throat and she rolled her eyes. Impatient, bored. Not afraid.

Are you afraid? I said.

No, she said.

Griffin began to whistle. Raindrops keep falling on my head.

I could hurt you, I said.

The girl shrugged, as if that was very doubtful. A tangible chunk of silence. Then I told her to open her mouth and for a long perilous moment thought that surely she would resist, that she would tell me to fuck off and the spell would break. The moment would shatter like ice. But then she parted her lips.

Tom and Ray, with Phineas:

Oh, brother did he need some love and understanding. This situation was not completely fucked but it was pretty well fucked. Major Tom was worried, very worried and for the first time in recent memory he was suffering an unwanted and completely unforeseen outburst of moisture beneath his armpits.

They had retired to a gas station restroom to clean up and discuss the matter behind a locked door. Tom stood before one of three mirrors, straightening his clothes with brittle fingers and washing the Fred's blood and snot from his hands and face. Ray Fine sat on a toilet with his legs crossed, smoking a cigarette. Tom was sweating because he had perhaps mistakenly lured an outsider into the game who, God knows why, did not want to be a Mariner's apprentice and worse, was too mentally competent to be cast among the hapless Freds. Otherwise, Tom would happily say fuck you, Fred. Have a nice life in the sewers and be careful with your tongue.

You have a problem, said Tom.

Oh? said Ray, as he blew a wobbling smoke ring.

I can only protect you if you're my apprentice.

Ray Fine laughed out loud, the insolent toad.

I'm not joking around, Ray.

What the fuck. Are you gonna protect me from girls who want to French kiss me?

Oh, that's rich. That's a killer.

It's a gift, said Ray. I make people laugh.

Tom wet a paper towel and used it to cool off his skull, watching Ray very closely in the mirror and noticing that while the old boy was making a lot of smart-ass comments, he was looking pale as a ghost.

How was it, by the way?

How was what?

The Trembler, said Tom. Didn't you take her tongue?

Ray shifted his ass around on the toilet and stared back at him. He wasn't so funny now.

Did you bite her tongue?

Maybe, he said. What about it?

Blood. Did you draw blood?

There was a little blood, yeah. Ray flicked his cigarette at one of the sinks.

Tom gave a shadow of a smile. And how was it, Ray?

The sound of water dripping. Ray got up and wandered to the sinks, his blue eyes ghostly and vague. He was clearly drawn to the mirror and seemed to hate his own face at the same time. Tom watched him take one long, reluctant look in the glass and force his eyes away. Then back again.

Fuck me, said Ray Fine. That is an ugly hat.

He could still taste the girl's tongue, the Trembler's. Her blood had been warm and thick and good. And he had felt something he had never expected. He had felt safe.

And how was it, Ray?

The sound of water dripping. He felt dizzy and vague and he wished Griffin would stop calling him Ray. He got up and moved over to the sink, thinking he might wash his hands but there was his pale fucking face in the mirror, floating like a dead thing in still water. He looked like a paper target sometimes. All he needed were black circles around his torso and blood-less tears in the white. Who are you, who are you today. Who do you want to be. He looked away, then back. He was afraid his eyes would be trapped in the mirror.

Fuck me, he said. That is an ugly hat.

He looked away, at a crack in the wall. A long, narrow crack and he flashed to the idle childhood notion that a microscopic universe might well exist in that crack in the wall of a much larger restroom, that there were infinite cracks in the walls of infinite restrooms and here we go, he thought. Here we fucking go. Ray Fine slapped at the electric hand dryer and the white noise snapped him out of it and he found himself staring hard at Major Tom, who stared back without smiling, without breathing. A fat black cockroach scurried out of the dark and Ray heard the crunch of its hard little exoskeleton shattering under Tom's boot heel. The electric dryer died now and they dropped their eyes at once.

It was…very intense, said Ray. It was blinding.

Whoa, said Tom. I guess you're fucked. Have a nice life in the sewer.

Wait a minute.

You're in, man. You're in the game.

Ray stared at him. What is the fucking game?

The tongue is the game, said Tom. The game is tongues.

But isn't there some higher purpose to the game?

Ray was now standing a pubic hair too close to him and Tom felt himself getting edgy, very fucking edgy and he wondered what he wouldn't do for a shot of the Pale and some more attractive surroundings.

What sort of higher purpose, said Tom. He felt like his face was dripping.

Like a quest, said Ray. A noble quest.

Tom stared at him.

You know, said Ray. You could return the magic beans to the Fairy Queen. You could save Christmas. Something along those lines.

Why do you want to insult me, Ray?

Ray appeared to chew at the inside of his mouth and Tom shivered, watching him. He looked away and began to turn the hot water on and off, on and off. Then left it on and held his finger under the stream for as long as he could stand it.

I want you to stop calling me Ray, said Ray.

The tongue is the quest, Tom said softly. And I'm sorry. Your name is Ray.

And so that's it? said Ray. You…you're like a rapist, man.

Tom removed the damp towel from his head and regarded Ray with contempt. He had heard this morbid line of thought before, from soft and puny players of other castes. The Breathers, for instance. He told himself to be patient, to choose his words with great care.

The tongue is a powerful muscle, he said. A thing of beauty. And at the same time, it's weak. The tongue is soft and private and terribly vulnerable, like the genitals.

Unwanted intimacy, said Ray. There's nothing more terrifying, is there?

There's Elvis, said Griffin.

Oh, yeah. Elvis, said Ray. And what the hell does that mean, exactly.

Griffin laughed. To go see Elvis, he said. To die but not die.

Elvis is an imaginary death, said Ray. He nodded. I can live with that.

The taking of tongues is ultimately an act of compassion, said Tom.

Ray laughed. How's that?

Tom leaned close to him, hissing like a woman despite himself. If your tongue is between my teeth, then it's mine to sever. To eat. But I don't.

Why not? said Ray.

Because I'm enlightened.

Now you're a Buddhist, said Ray. This gets better and better.

And what did you do to that girl, the Trembler?

Ray frowned and sullenly twisted his head from side to side until the joints in his neck popped. He took off the hideous fedora and dropped it to the floor. He ran one hand through his matted blond hair, staring at himself in the mirror and finally Tom saw what he saw.

The face of another. One who was not Phineas, was not Ray.

Phineas began to cough, great hacking coughs that would rip him in two. He felt sick and he found himself wondering what Griffin's tongue would taste like. Fuck fuck fuck. He cast his eyes away, at the crack in the wall where another tiny shadow of himself was possibly having a better time. He took off the fedora suddenly and dropped it to the floor. He ran one cold skeletal hand through his hair and glared at himself in the mirror.

That chick wanted to kiss me, he said.

You are so hopelessly hetero, said Griffin.

Oh, really. Phineas smiled. That's odd. Because I'm thinking of your tongue right now. I'm wondering how sweet your breath might be, how your lips would be warm and cold at once.

Ah, yes. I think you will have a future as a Redeemer, said Griffin. The taking of tongues by way of sympathy and charm.

Whatever, man. What sort of thrill do you get from torturing some fucked-up kids?

Griffin rolled his eyes. The Freds are my daily bread. If I want a thrill, then I hunt another Mariner.

I could be a Trembler. I trembled that girl, said Phineas.

A fascinating idea, said Griffin. The male Tremblers do not lead such happy lives, I'm afraid. They are hunted ruthlessly by everyone, and soon they are left with no tongue at all.

Fuck it, then. You can just call me Fred. Or Freddie.

Griffin bent and picked up the fallen hat. He held it between two fingers as if it were a dead thing.

You dropped your hat, Ray.

Motherfucker, thought Phineas. Or did he say that aloud.

He was starting to hate the name Ray, he really was. But he reluctantly took the hat from Griffin.

Thanks, he said. It's not really my hat.

I promise you, said Griffin. You will regret this.

Whatever. Phineas put on the hat and shivered. He was Ray, though. He was Ray Fine. He lit a cigarette and blew smoke at the mirror and said, do you think you could take my tongue?

Now? said Griffin.

Phineas shrugged. Why not.

The sound of water dripping and they stared at each other for a long waxing moment and in a crack in the wall their microscopic shadows likewise stared at each other and Phineas was confident that his little shadow-self would soon pin the shadow Griffin to the floor like a wriggling bug and maybe just rip out his tongue.

Mingus:

He was afraid of Chrome, very afraid. And he wasn't sure the women appreciated that. His poor brain hurt, all the time now. The game was too much for him. It had been days and days since he had slipped outside of it and it was like he could never sleep. He wasn't tired, exactly. But he might be losing his mind. He was beginning to understand that it was dangerous to stay in character all the time. He could not quite remember where he lived, for instance. And he had been fairly shocked to think of that genetics exam, to remember it at all.

It wasn't that he wanted to take the test. Doubtful that he would be able to comprehend the thing at all. The last time he had been to school he had found himself in a microbiology lab with a lot of frightening equipment that he no longer knew how to manipulate. The air had been thin and sterile, with a hateful undertow of chemicals.

Sometimes, though. It might be nice to visit his previous world.

His daylight self made him uncomfortable, however. His name was unimportant but he was a paranoid and sexually nervous computer yuppie who was failing out of med school with alarming speed and grace. He was just over five feet tall and he weighed 110 pounds when wet. He got by with shaving once a month and he had a sticky relationship with his mother. He was boring. He spent most of his time online, cruising the web and playing Doom. He was technically still married, but he and his wife were estranged and she had rarely bothered to sleep with him anyway. It was not a world that he wanted to rush back to, exactly. But sometimes he was curious to see if it had changed at all.

Dizzy's house made him feel safe, though. Familiar and strange, the memories were muted, like beasts held underwater. She kept a lot of candles burning and everything smelled of trees and he saw nothing but soft edges and shadowy landscapes. He sat in a leather chair, barefoot. He worried about Chrome, about what he would say or do if he knew Mingus had betrayed him. He sat with his arms crossed, staring straight ahead. In another hour or two, it would be midnight. It would be time to go out and play. He wondered if he could sit without moving until then, he wondered if he could stop his own breathing.

Goo had gone already.

She had been pacing around ever since he told her that Chrome was a madman. She had been smoking cigarette after cigarette and trying to hide the fact that she had slipped into her Eve persona and failing badly, he had thought. And maybe he should have followed her, he should have kept an eye on her. But she had given him a dirty look when he suggested it. It was funny, really. But little Eve was even more fearless than Goo. Anyhow. She was performing later and had likely gone ahead to prepare.

Change in temperature and the smell of Dizzy Bloom came around a corner. It was an unidentified spice, a color he had never seen. And before he could give it a thorough ponder, she was crouched before him with sweet glowing skin and brief sharp smile and long dark hair falling loose and he felt himself get a little warm. Females rarely came this close to him. He smiled, wondering what she wanted.

Are you okay, she said.

Not so bad. I'm worried, of course.

You're adorable, she said.

What?

Her hands floated to touch his thighs and his breath stopped. His breath shut down pretty efficiently. Dizzy Bloom ran her fingers up to his hips, tugging at his pockets. His brain was gone, long gone. And he let himself slide out of the chair to kneel before her as she stroked his face and whispered to him, kissed him.

Incredible.

Mingus wouldn't have believed another person's lips could be so soft. Dizzy offered him her tongue and he touched it lightly with his own. The room flickered around him as if the house was unstable. Dizzy Bloom shrugged out of her leather jerkin and now her little round breasts were in his cold hands and he felt something like nervous glee, pure shivering foolish glee. And when she slipped his trousers down and exposed his short thick penis to the naked air and lifted her skirt and moved to lower herself onto his lap and gently very gently helped him find his way inside her, well at this point he pretty much blacked out.

CONCRETE AND BARBED WIRE, concrete and barbed wire and I was trying to remember the words to this obscure country song that Jude used to sing when she was washing her hair or painting her nails, something about concrete and barbed wire and how the average state prison was an easily penetrated fortress compared to the human heart.

It was a country song, okay. I didn't say it was poetry.

Griffin or Major Tom was pretty bent on calling me Ray Fine and that was cool. I could walk and talk like Ray. I could be Ray Fine. I had created the poor stuttering bastard, hadn't I? I had purchased Ray's sad clothes and this moldy hat and even perfected the way he limped. Ray was my idea.

Good night, Phineas. I will most likely kill you in the morning.

Dear Jude.

It appeals to me, of course. The shadow world. The ability to slip in and out of the real. A fanciful subterrain where the lord of the rings and bladerunner become one and I can be a mad dwarf for a day, a thief or an assassin. I can be a mercenary with a soft spot for razorgirls and I daydream about this shit all the time, don't you?

When I was fifteen or so it was *Dungeons & Dragons*. A few of my friends had a game that ran for what seemed like forever and we gathered every weekend to play without stopping. We used Mountain Dew and nicotine for fuel because the Dungeon Master was kind of a fascist about drugs. We blacked out the windows but it didn't matter. At sunrise the game always lost its legs. My character was a thief, a halfblood elf named Grim. Don't remember his vital statistics exactly. Dexterity off the chart. Strength and charisma well above average and I wasn't bad looking. No magic skills, though. And I was no good at languages. What else. I was of questionable birth and not terribly stable. And my ethical designation was chaotic/good, which meant I would probably save a young maiden from a pack of orcs but maybe not. There were no promises and you wouldn't want to turn your back on me. I was a thief, after all.

I used to dream of Grim. In my sleep I was Grim. And even years later, long after the game was done, I dreamed of him.

It's easy. You stagger a hundred years forward, a thousand years back. You manufacture a world where the apocalypse has failed to manifest. Urban purgatory. The sun is a joke, a bad memory. The world is dark and wet and waiting to be fucked. The world is a great big pussy. Everything is sex and chaos. Rapidly shrinking human population due to HIV, ebola, mad cow disease. Whatever. The political elite live in orbiting space stations. Mutants born daily. DNA experiments gone wrong. Vampires and goblins. Elves. Werewolves. Androids and common humans. Cyber and weapon technology is at a standstill. Corporations are controlled by artificial intelligence. Evolutionary regression. Past and future merge, or blur. People ride camels and horses alongside landskimmers and hovercrafts. Traveling circus troupes wander nuclear wasteland. The road warrior model. Freak shows, blood sports, theaters of cruelty. Public executions and snuff films dominate the airwaves and pornography is common currency, etc.

Then again, I doubt you would need to daydream. This is pretty much the way you see things on a good day, isn't it?

Major Tom:

Convenience, he thought. Artificial light that made the skin look pasty and green and aisles swollen with bright, fascist packaging. Convenience. Oh, dear. That was rich. That was a regular killer. He stared down at himself from a big curved mirror overhead and tried unsuccessfully not to giggle. Shoplifters in the mirror may be closer than they appear and whoever had dreamed up the phrase "convenience store" was a born torturer.

Tom found himself staring at a long, tubular orange product mysteriously called "Pringles" and his mind began a bitter rhyming game: tingles jingles mingles shingles and what in hell was he looking for? The clerk was staring at him with bright green frog eyes and Ray was waiting outside. Ray, who refused to play the game.

Mouthwash.

Of course. He was on the wrong aisle, clearly. These products were all in the snack family. They were heavy with fat and starches and red dye #2, yellow dye #6. He needed the medicinal aisle, the cleaning creams and powders. He wanted some of that cool blue mouthwash. His tongue was a bit chalky, his tongue was sore and putrid from the mouth of that Fred by the creek and he suddenly wished he had taken a taste of that adorable Trembler. But Ray was a friend, he was a dear old friend and Tom had graciously let him have her without muscling in for even a nibble.

EYES CLOSED AND HAIR WET from the rain. I am surrounded by dark water and the air is different, colder. The air has teeth and it must be winter. A noise like sweet kisses and the low croak of a frog, an old man coughing. I'm different, too. I'm smaller. Thick socks and rubber boots, long underwear. Heavy wool pants and a goosedown vest. Something in my hand, cool and slender. A composite bow. The shallow breathing of another and I'm not alone. Trevor is here, my cousin. A cruel and silent boy four years older than me who holds a shotgun in his steady hands and now I can smell oil and sulfur and bourbon. This is a duckblind and everyone laughed at me when I wanted to hunt ducks with a bow and arrow. And they were right to laugh. I never killed a single bird and check it out: that was a false memory, my first. I never had a cousin named Trevor and I never went duck-hunting as a boy. Pretty cool, huh. Psychological dislocation. Modality of the visible, the tactile. And like Stephen Dedalus I'm walking into eternity along Sandymount Strand.

Nacheinander and *Nebeneinander*. What is real and what is perceived as real.

Protean theory. The real is unstable. The real is self-consuming, like fire. And this seems to be a pretty big deal in *Ulysses*. The real. Stephen Dedalus is tormented by his own belief or disbelief in what he can see and hear and the way I understand it, *Nacheinander* refers to physical reality as it is perceived in linear time, to objects or events that occur once after another. While *Nebeneinander* is a spatial reality. Objects that exist on the same plane, or side by side.

Okay. What the fuck, right. But everything Dedalus sees is tangled up with memories real and false and reconstructed images. There's no separation.

Meanwhile, his own thoughts are more coherent and more immediate than the noise around him and so it all blurs into this terrible internal monologue that shifts and changes and licks at the air like fire. Stephen Dedalus exists on four or five levels of reality at once.

Which seems to be what's happening to me.

The creepy little hunting scene might have happened to someone I know, or I might have pieced it together from a book or movie. It doesn't matter. I stepped in a puddle or heard a migrating duck cry in the distance. I smelled damp wool or brandy and the whole false memory was triggered. For five seconds it was real.

Dear Jude.

I'm freaking out, yeah. But it's a lot of fun.

Chrome:

Now this was quite the fucking pickle. He couldn't be certain but it seemed that he was bleeding very badly and his left arm may as well have been attached to someone else. His left arm was unresponsive. He could see it there, extending from his shoulder and resting in wet yellow grass tipped with frost, but he couldn't feel it at all. He couldn't feel it.

Shot. The Fred had shot him.

Chrome sat with his back to a modest pink marble headstone that read: Lucinda Sweet, faithful wife and sister. His math was spotty but she seemed to have died just a few months ago, at twenty-nine. Chrome himself was twenty-nine. He was long in the tooth and slipping into winter.

S'il vous plaît, aidez-moi avec mes bagages.

Christian's favorite movie was *La Femme Nikita*, the original. The American version with Bridget Fonda was vile, it was beyond putrid. The producers of that shitty mess should be lined up and gutted like dogs. They weren't worth the bullets. He had heard from someone that Nikita was now a very hot blond starring in her own television series on cable and the show wasn't half bad, but Christian didn't own a television. He had sold it to his brother. His brother. He had not thought of his brother in months. What the hell was this. Chrome was slipping, he was actually slipping. His brother's name was Anthony. Two years younger and slightly better looking. Anthony had those killer green eyes and a perfect scar on his chin. It made him look tough and he liked to tell people it was from a fight but Christian knew it was a chicken pox scar and now Chrome bit his own tongue, hard. He was allowing the defunct Christian to poison his dying thoughts.

He would have to be careful, very careful.

Ironic, perhaps. But it was his own blood that was keeping him warm. It was like sitting in a hot bath. This was an illusion, though. He would catch a nasty chill if he didn't move along soon. But he was curious about the nature of the wound and he sent his good right hand on a casual scouting mission across bloodwet skin to get a clear notion of the damage. He had a cartoonish idea that the hole would be clean and round, the size of his fist. And as soon as the blood dried up his friends and lovers would be able to peek through it like a window. Those round windows they have on boats, he loved those windows and the bullet had struck him somewhere on the left side, obviously. The chest or shoulder. It had spun him around like a toy soldier hit by a stone. It had made him angry, very angry. And before the shock and pain had dropped him to his knees, he had managed to crush the Fred's skull with a handy chunk of concrete and then to eat out most of his tongue, like it was sushi. The tongue had been sweet as a nice cut of raw tuna and Chrome now sat with his boots resting on the Fred's soggy torso because he had always believed it was proper to elevate the legs when injured but he would definitely need to get inside, and soon.

Please, he said. Won't somebody help me with my luggage?

I SMOKED A CIGARETTE and waited for Griffin, who had stepped into a convenience store to buy mouthwash, of all things. Time was unreliable, as ever. Griffin had been gone five minutes, or half the night. I stood on one foot, the left. Because Ray had a bad right knee, from an old basketball injury. The knee ached on these rainy nights. I smiled into the dark as Griffin walked toward me, sipping from a travel-sized bottle of Scope.

Docile.

I became docile. I allowed myself to be led on a crisscrossing and seem-ingly nonsensical path across town that threaded the inner eye and dipped in and out of memory and dream. That was it. If I had been dreaming and some person from a strange land had asked me to draw a map of Denver, it would have resembled the city that Griffin dragged me across. I couldn't have sketched it in two dimensions, however. It would require impossible three- or four-sided paper and the bright textured pop-ups of a children's book. There was a remote pain in my legs and Griffin seemed to be moving along at a fast trot, a jogging pace that I could never have maintained on an ordinary evening.

I followed Griffin along bright, crowded sidewalks without touching anyone, without making eye contact. Through damp, black tunnels and across scorched vacant lots and before long I was climbing. I was climbing a cold metal fire escape and never realized it until we had ascended a rooftop.

The Pale.

That shit was magical. Tar and gravel underfoot. Griffin's steady breathing in the dark. I looked around and around and the sky was curved around me, it was a hollow black dome bright with needles. My God it's full of stars. Laughing, someone was laughing. The soft and fearful laughter of a paranoid. I was laughing. Phineas was laughing. A voice hissed at me to shut the fuck up and now Griffin leapt to the next roof without a backward glance, rolled to his feet and grinned like a monkey and said, come on Ray, pull yourself together. It was five and a half feet across, maybe. The length of your average dead body. No problem. I sucked at my tongue and looked own. We were high enough that the ground below was invisible, the ground was purely speculative and I did a fast inventory of personal phobias. The fear of heights did not seem to be among them and while I couldn't speak for Ray Fine, I jumped easily across the narrow chasm.

Faith.

Eve, Not Goo:

How did she feel and oh God but that was a stupid question, so stupid and she hated herself for thinking this way. Unglued. She felt like she was in a dentist's chair waiting for him to cut into her gums and realizing that the painkiller had not taken hold and she wanted to tell someone but her mouth was full of cotton and mirrors and that sick little device they used to suck out your saliva. It was fear. The kind that bubbled up from deep in the tissues and paralyzed you. She wanted to run away but her arms and legs were so tight and she felt herself curling inward, tucking herself in crash position and she wasn't sure if this conflict of the senses was panic or rage or despair. Or nothing. She was bursting out of her skin, she was molting and she didn't want anyone to see or touch her.

One thing was clear. She was not Goo, not at the moment.

Eve was backstage at the Unbecoming Club and she was going on in like ten minutes and she wasn't ready. Or was she. Eve could do this, she could do this. And maybe this was her chance to get out. To get out of the game. An hour had passed since she learned that her boyfriend was a murderer and she was numb and stupid with goose bumps even though it wasn't cold at all. It was hot in here, the air was thick as soup but in her head she was walking along the top of a very high cliff, a place where she could stop and see for miles and miles on a clear day but the sun was much too bright and the wind was pulling at her, she was contemplating the plunge and it just didn't seem real. But this was enough, wasn't it. This was it. Christian had killed someone and that was reason enough to disappear. She wanted to go back to the world where your boyfriend was a bad driver or an asshole, a hypochondriac, a compulsive shoplifter. Or married. The daylight world was depressing but safe and predictable and she could at least relate. She could see for miles on a clear day. Her boyfriend was a killer, though. It was so melodramatic, so Hollywood. My boyfriend killed a guy, yeah. That's right. Fucking killed him. And I'm Courtney Love. Tap tap tapping. She sat on a circular green sofa that smelled of pee and her foot was nervously bouncing on the dirty stone floor and she remembered that she wasn't alone. Goo was here somewhere.

No, she said. Goo wasn't going to make it. But Adore was here.

Adore was ten feet away, talking in a hushed, conspiratorial tone with Theseus. One ghoul talking to another, oh God. Theseus was dressed in white, all white. Fine white linen suit, white shoes and hat. But his clothes were stylishly frayed and crusted with grime and mold. He looked more or less like Mr. Roark's corpse, freshly dug from the grave. Adore was dressed in pretty straightforward *Aeon Flux* gear: three banded leather straps across her chest that managed to cover some but not all of her muscular breasts. Obscenely tight, shiny green vinyl pants and black motorcycle boots. And Eve might have been seeing things but Adore appeared to be wearing a prosthetic penis tonight. She had a plastic banana or something shoved down her crotch. Adore had quite a package.

Eve hopped up now, jittery. She felt weirdly like a grasshopper.

The bathroom. She needed to pee, she needed to be alone and she skittered along the dark hall backstage, her legs were full of juice and she was trying not to hop. She was trying, God help her. She should never have shared the Pale with those guys. In the bathroom she got a look at her clothes and she looked fairly mild by Exquisitor standards. Dark suede jeans and a little black sweater that would probably better fit a twelve-year-old. It was thin and snug as a glove and her nipples looked like they were trying to escape but Adore would say she was much too conservative for this crowd of rubber and latex and aluminum clothing and she could always alter that before she took the stage, or not. Never mind that. Her hair was a fucking fright. Black tendrils, unwashed. Her hair stood on its ends as if she had just licked her finger and jabbed it into a socket. Eyes sunken, buried in hideous dark circles. White vampire skin and too-red lips. She pressed one finger to the big artery in her neck and measured her pulse. Fast and furious, her heart was violent. She was apparently terrified.

Eve peed.

Fuck it, oh fuck it.

A HAZE OF BLUE smoke and endless, untethered shadows. The flicker of gas lamps. It was an old warehouse space with a gray stone floor and scattered sawdust and I briefly imagined I could smell the raw meat that had once been packed here. There was movement in the dark and I saw that maybe a hundred people were drifting, scurrying through the place. They slithered about like ghosts. Long fingernails and pale makeup. Bone and silver jewelry, tattooed flesh. Leather and silk and rubber, in relatively Goth colors. Black and black. In the far corners of the dark I caught the random mottled flash of naked skin jerking and grinding but there was altogether more fear than sex in the air and most of these freaks were just kids. They sat huddled in small groups, sharing unmarked bottles of the Pale.

I give you the Unbecoming Club, said Griffin. I give you beauty and chaos.

Paranoid murmurs. No one trusted the others.

It's a happy place, I said.

Hush, said Griffin.

A bar had been hammered together in one corner out of misshapen scraps of metal and wood. There was a large unfinished stage in the center of the space which was empty but for a curious pair of steel hoops under a single muted spotlight. There was an upright piano against one wall and there was a truly odd assortment of furniture: church pews and cast-iron tables and chairs that might have been salvaged from the dump. There were several torn and weathered sofas, water-damaged leather armchairs that might have once looked nice in a bank lobby. Rocking chairs and one bright blue La-Z-Boy recliner. Even a few wheelchairs. There was a terrifying fan mounted in one wall, the eye of Cyclops with seven-foot blades.

Griffin's face was glowing.

He clearly loved it here and I could only wonder if he saw this crowd as one big family or a lot of potential victims. And what was the difference. I sat down in an empty wheelchair and began to spin myself in slow circles. Now a sinewy, silver creature detached herself from a semiconscious cluster of trolls and came over to give Griffin a long, lurid kiss on the mouth and when she came up for air she turned to look at me and I recognized her. The creepy girlfriend, Kink. Who had wanted to eat my tongue. I was doubtful that she could hypnotize me a second time but one never knew. I would be careful with her.

Hello, she said.

I ignored her. I decided that if Griffin ever went to the bathroom I just might try to Tremble her myself, for kicks. Her tongue was probably nine inches long. I lit a cigarette and looked around and everyone seemed to be waiting for something to happen. And while some of the patrons had the pallor and attitude of zombies, there were plenty of others who looked like Griffin. Hungry and watchful.

So. What are we doing here? I said.

Hmmm. Do you want a drink? said Griffin.

That depends. Do they have anything but that Pale shit?

Griffin shook his head. Please, Ray. Will you keep your voice down?

I think there is some kind of sweet wine at the bar, said Kink.

Yes, said Griffin. There is usually a barrel of port.

Fantastic, I said. I'll see you later.

Griffin blinked at me and didn't smile. He obviously didn't think it was a good idea for me to wander off alone and unsupervised. What the fuck. That was as good a reason as any.

Wait a minute, Ray.

I rolled through blue smoke and although it did cross my mind that handicapped folks would probably be pretty unamused to see a guy with two good legs zipping around in a wheelchair like it was some sort of toy, I have to say it was a gas. And lately I hadn't been having much fun and I would have to take it wherever I found it. I rolled over to the bar and was about to ask somebody what kind of currency was accepted here, brass buttons or seashells or actual dollars, when I found myself staring into a familiar face. Long and gloomy and washed of color. The same self-admin-istered haircut, the mental patient special. Crumb, of all people. And why not. Crumb would naturally gravitate to any underworld scene that fea-tured drugs and regular nudity.

You son of a bitch, I said.

My God, said Crumb. As soon as you think the day is wasted you get a nice surprise.

Never fails, does it.

You're alive, said Crumb.

Pretty much.

Did you take a bullet in the spine?

What?

The wheelchair, said Crumb. Are you a paraplegic?

No, man. I'm just fucking around.

What are you doing here?

I'm looking for a drink that isn't laced with methadone.

Fancy that, said Crumb. You don't care for the Pale.

Not really.

I would have thought it was exactly your speed.

Yeah, well. Once upon a time.

I stood up and was so stupidly glad to see Crumb that I threw my arms around the old fucker and he still smelled like he never bathed. I lit a cigarette and wiped at my eyes. Fucking hell. I was lonely, wasn't I? Two days in the city and I had briefly touched three friends, with mixed results. Eve had promptly disappeared. Moon was dead. And Griffin was out of his fucking mind.

It's good to see you, I said.

Now I turned to the bartender and asked for a jar of the port, a request that was met with mild disgust and a trace of fear. For God's sake.

People are suspicious of nonconverts, said Crumb.

I shrugged and paid two dollars for a tall glass. It was strong and sickly sweet.

What about you, I said. Do you drink that shit?

The Pale? said Crumb. I take a drop, now and then. Purely medicinal.

Uh-huh. And are you involved in the game?

Crumb licked his gray lips. I am Gulliver, he said. The Redeemer.

Perfect, I said. I'm Ray Fine.

And have you chosen a caste?

I'm a Fred, I suppose. I'm self-aware.

Crumb grinned. He scratched at his dark, unshaven jaw. The harsh whisper of sandpaper against stone and I was surprised to find my senses were still unusually heightened.

Eve:

Out of the bathroom and right away she saw Dizzy Bloom and Mingus standing in an uneasy circle with Adore and Theseus and without even thinking about what they must be discussing she hopped over to them and was glad when Dizzy smiled and pulled her close. Eve needed that, didn't she. She needed someone to protect her, someone to tell her she was okay, to love her. Because everything was coming apart and Theseus was already spitting electricity.

What will we do, said Mingus.

Nothing, said Theseus. You will do nothing.

But Chrome is dangerous, isn't he. This is real, it's too real.

Adore scowled. What do you propose, little one?

I don't know. The police?

Theseus laughed richly. The police, he said. What an idea.

He should be severed, said Adore.

Yes, said Theseus. Amputated from the game like an infected limb.

You're going to kill him, said Dizzy.

Don't worry, pet. Chrome won't be harmed. The dear boy. I will take care of it and none of you will be the wiser. Chrome will simply disappear for a time.

Eve didn't want to say anything but she couldn't stop herself. Her voice was escaping whether she liked it or not, her voice was a desperate little air bubble.

Excuse me, she said.

They all looked at her and she tried to focus, to remember what she wanted to say but she couldn't help noticing something different about Mingus. He was not so pale and amorphous. He didn't look like you could just put your hand right through him. There was a touch of new metal in his eyes. Oh, well. This was obviously sex. He had finally fucked or been fucked by Dizzy and Eve wanted to give him a squeeze and say she was happy for him. It was about time.

Adore was staring at her. What do you have to say, dear?

His name was Christian, said Eve. He has parents somewhere, and a brother. He has a master's degree in French lit and he works in a video store. Or he used to.

Brief, unpleasant silence.

He loves movies, she said.

Theseus and Adore looked at each other, smoke trailing from their noses. Eve had hoped that Adore would be on her side but that was just silly.

I don't believe my fucking ears, Theseus said.

Maybe she's right, said Dizzy.

But she took a half-step back and Mingus grabbed for her hand as Adore extended one bony fingernail and traced a slow, hypnotic figure eight in the air before tucking a loose strand of hair behind Dizzy's ear. Mingus looked like he might faint but Dizzy never flinched.

Adore licked her lips and said, I detest Breathers.

Eve felt calm. Her blood was still furious beneath her skin but she was calm.

Open hunting, said Theseus. He smiled. I will spread the word among the Mariners that the three of you are to be hunted like dogs if I hear another word about the police. And it will get very bloody if I hear any silly rumors about a fictional person named Christian with a master's degree.

Adore turned to Eve. Are you performing tonight?

Eve stepped close to her and said softly, yes. I think so.

Adore smiled, showing two jagged rows of bright yellow teeth and Eve wondered how much the sick bitch had paid to have her incisors sharpened. Or had she done it herself, with a file.

I'm glad, said Adore. And what piece would you like to do?

The Scavenger's Daughter, said Eve.

How yummy. Who will be the victim?

They stared at each other for a perilously elastic moment and Eve wanted nothing more than to drop her eyes and look away but somehow she borrowed the guts from Goo to lazily grab Adore by the crotch and give her little make-believe cock a fierce, familiar squeeze. Theseus coughed, apparently embarrassed.

I will, said Eve. I will be the victim.

Tenth Plague:

The blades of the giant fan had begun to move. The blue haze fell away and

Phineas gratefully reclined on a lemon-yellow couch in the darkest corner of the space. He sat close to Crumb, his head lowered like a thief. Crumb was talking philosophy, however.

It's all about obliteration of self, said Crumb. The utter loss of self. I have failed at the game personally. It amuses me to be Gulliver for a day or two but I'm still Crumb.

And what about these others. Do they know their own names?

I'm never sure, said Crumb. Everyone lies to me, which is peculiar. I'm a Redeemer, a confessor. And still they lie. But a lot of them have day jobs so they must be able to come in and out.

Brief silence. Phineas thought about the fact that he would really have to find a job soon, or starve. It was a surreal notion.

Who did you come here with? said Crumb.

Friend of mine, a lawyer. He called himself Major Tom.

He's a Mariner?

Yeah, said Phineas. I took a girl's tongue with him this evening.

Disturbing?

A little.

The intimacy is fantastic, said Crumb. Obviously. But the transaction is strangely antisexual in the end.

It's fucking creepy. And I don't quite understand it.

What? said Crumb.

The tongue. The temptation.

Crumb smiled. It's not so complicated, he said.

You obviously have a theory.

Have you ever had a good look at hieroglyphs, said Crumb.

The sideways people? said Phineas.

The sideways people, said Crumb. They have very large mouths.

Okay.

Think about it, said Crumb. In religious art and literature, the mouth and tongue are always big symbols. They carry serious voodoo. The tongue is the spoken word, the tongue is Creation. Then you have the chaos of Babylon, the scattering of tongues.

Crumb paused, grinning. Phineas lit a cigarette because he knew

Crumb didn't want his opinion, not yet. Crumb was only warming up.

But that's not really what this is about, said Crumb. The mouth is often fearsome, a source of destruction. The mouth devours, after all. And the most hideous beasts in medieval literature always breathe fire, right. The tongue of fire.

Phineas regarded the stoned kids around him.

The powers of fire and speech, said Crumb. The two skills that set us apart from the lower animals. Creativity and destruction are thereby intertwined in man.

No shit.

Have you read the *Upanishads*?

What do you think? said Phineas.

I suppose not, he said. But if you had, you might know that the mouth is said to represent an integral consciousness in the context of sleep. The mouth is the door between real and unreal worlds, between reason and madness. And if one is unlucky and sleeps too long without waking, then the soul must escape through the mouth.

But look at these people, said Phineas. They don't have a clue about that shit.

That's irrelevant, said Crumb.

And he was right. A child may not be able to explain how or why he is affected by the symbolism of a dream, but he knows he is affected. He can feel it in his skin. He is instinctively afraid of spiders, rats. He is charmed by beauty. He is moved to do things he doesn't understand. Phineas sipped his port and watched Crumb, who was now smoking a leisurely cigarette.

Do you know a guy named Jimmy Sky? said Phineas.

Crumb shrugged. He's a player, I believe. A Fred of some kind but I don't know him.

He's an undercover cop, said Phineas.

That's beautiful, said Crumb. Does he know what he's gotten himself into?

No, said Phineas. I don't think so.

And you want to save him?

Phineas laughed. I'm not sure, really. I think I'm looking to kill him.

Theseus stood by the bar, immaculate and white.

His lips were wet as he surveyed the crowd, his jaw clicking. A young Mariner named Peter Quince appeared at his elbow, whispering that there was a telephone call for him. Theseus frowned. He did not like to use the telephone at the Unbecoming Club. It intruded upon his dreams. But Peter Quince was a fine fellow, very discreet. He never touched the Pale and Theseus often used him for difficult errands. The call must be important.

Theseus turned and walked into the dark and through a doorway and into a sparse, box-shaped room with office furniture. He sat down at the desk, picked up the telephone and looked at it with distaste. Hello, he said. Hello.

Silence on the line. Theseus lit a cigarette and put one white shoe on the desk with dull thud of rubber against wood.

I can hear you breathing, he said. You fool. You sound like a dying bloody horse. Come on, then. Who am I speaking to?

He blew smoke and waited.

Theseus flared his nostrils and was about to hang up when a man cleared his voice on the line and said, this is Jimmy Sky.

Jimmy, he said. It's good to hear your voice.

Did you hear about Moon? said Jimmy.

Yes, yes. Such a shame. How kind of you to hold onto his cell phone, though. In case he needs it on a rainy day.

Fuck you, said Jimmy.

No, don't hang up. Long pause. I'm sorry, said Theseus.

Oh, yeah. I bet you are, said Jimmy. Please make a donation to the Negro College Fund in lieu of flowers.

Ha. That's very funny. What do you want, Jimmy?

Pause.

I want self-awareness.

Theseus smiled. Is that all?

The dead cops, said Jimmy. Are they Freds?

Of course.

Who's killing them?

You are, Jimmy. You are.

Motherfucker.

I'm joking of course. But then you did kill Moon.

Who is it?

A talented young Mariner, said Theseus. He's known as Chrome but his given name is Christian Wells.

Where can I find him? said Jimmy.

He's a houseguest of Dizzy Bloom.

The address, you fucker.

Look in the telephone book. It's her real name.

If I kill him, will Moon be self-aware?

It's possible, said Theseus. But not likely.

I hate you, said Jimmy.

Oh, by the way. It might interest you to know that Captain Honey suspects someone else entirely. I think you know him.

Who?

Theseus shrugged. An unstable person by the name of Ray Fine.

One face bleeding into the next and Tom had what he might best describe as an ice-cream headache. The slow rush of dirty skin. Twisting hair and scar tissue and pockmarks. Terrible eyes sleepless and drugged, bright and searching. A handful of men and women before him on a ratty Oriental rug in various postures of despair, some of them nodding in junk stupors while others twitched and vibrated and muttered about the intricacies of the rug's design. One girl of about seventeen lay with her cheek pressed hard to the floor as if she were listening to the earth. A single strand of oily brown hair fell over her visible eye and every five seconds or so she laboriously moved her bruised right hand to brush it away and not more than two feet from her, Kink was violently kissing a barefoot peasant girl with blond hair who could have been the first girl's twin. And at the center of the rug, where the design came to an angry climax of flowers and geometry, Major Tom soon found exactly what he was looking for. A beautiful man with black dreadlocks and dark chocolate eyes. The unspoiled face of a new Fred. Tom sighed. He contemplated the tongue.

Dizzy was loath to admit it, but she was happy. Mingus sat beside her on a slick black sofa, holding her hand. Their faces were pushed together, not kissing but close enough to share the same air.

Tell me about your parents, said Mingus.

I don't remember them.

What do you remember?

I grew up with my grandmother, Millicent Bloom Devine.

Tell me about her, said Mingus.

Why, though?

Because I have no memories of my own. None that I can trust. I see a man in the suburbs cutting grass. A thin man in bad clothes. A father. I see a sister, a little girl in a red bathing suit. But they aren't mine.

What else?

I remember walking through a silent green jungle armed with two 9-millimeter pistols and a box of flares. Terrible and beautiful at once. The foliage is so thick it's as if the sky is green. A tiger jumps at me and I shoot it five, six times. The chatter of unseen monkeys. I climb over a stone wall and jump across a pit filled with cobras. Then avoid the quicksand and enter a catacomb of ruins. And I'm a woman. I have tremendous breasts and a British accent.

That's not real, then.

I think it's a computer game called *Tomb Raider*.

Okay, said Dizzy. It's okay.

Tell me about your grandmother, said Mingus.

Dizzy smiled. I called her Grandma Milly. She was the firstborn daughter of Molly and Leopold Bloom.

And who were they?

They lived in Dublin, long ago. Leopold was a pervert, a Christ figure. And he was a kind of grifter, a complicated man. But very well-educated. Molly was crazy, I think. And she was a little slutty, or so they say. A prolific adulteress. I prefer to think that she was looking for true love.

What happened to her?

Chrome entered, bloody.

One arm cradled and useless. The other held out sideways for balance. His face white as death. Whispers from the slippery crowd. Oohs and aahhs. One kid with the furry hands and feet of a hobbit floated by on a skateboard and insolently patted Chrome on the back and murmured very real, brother. Very real. Chrome took one step. Then another. He was going to fall over any minute and there was nothing he could do about it. Mingus appeared, seemingly from nowhere.

Run away, said Mingus. You aren't safe here.

Mingus, Mingus. I'm hurt.

I can see that. What happened?

Shot, apparently.

Chrome fell forward and Mingus caught him.

You haven't heard me.

What? What…so tired.

Theseus knows. He knows about the kill.

You, said Chrome. You betrayed me?

Helpless. Mingus shook his head.

Not possible.

Yes. I told Goo, and Dizzy.

Why?

You have to get out of here.

But I should be safe here, I live here.

No. They want to remove you, to cut you off.

Help me. Je suis malade, s'il vous plait.

Mingus smiled as if he might weep. Chrome was leaking blood like a hatful of water and he wanted to tell the Breather not to worry but his strength was gone.

Je suis malade.

Dizzy came out of the throng and took Chrome's good arm. She threw it over her small shoulders like a wrap. Mingus held the bloody arm and together they led him away, his feet dragging between them.

Chrome relaxed. He would not die alone, at least.

Eyes dry and staring. Too much sugar in his system. Phineas watched as a
very young girl sat down at the piano and began to hit random, discordant
keys. Electric lights came up and a low hum and cry ran like a current
through the crowd. Crumb nudged him and pointed to the main stage.
The small spotlight was abruptly killed and now the only lights came up
from the floor.

White fingers.

Eve walked onto the stage and Phineas opened his mouth, then closed it.

I should have warned you, said Crumb.

Another woman took the stage. Motorcycle boots, hot green pants and
leather straps across her torso. Eyes hidden behind black mask. In one
careless hand she held a long slender metal rod that most resembled a car's
radio antenna.

Who is that? said Phineas.

Lady Adore, said Crumb. The Exquisitor.

Eve wore only white underpants and a black sweater with the sleeves
hacked off. Her pale arms extending yellow and thin from ragged, gaping
holes and now she pulled the sweater over her head in an abrupt, non-
sexual motion. She walked to center stage and crouched to pick up the
joined metal hoops, which she examined briefly before handing over to
Adore without comment.

The hoops were approximately fourteen inches in diameter and held
together by a steel clasp. Phineas didn't feel well, looking at them. Lady
Adore separated them and dropped one to the floor, where it spun briefly
like a coin.

Eve fell to her knees, as if to pray. Expressionless, staring. She sat with
back straight and buttocks resting on heels. Thighs pressed together. Arms
loose, palms upright. Lady Adore circled her with the single detached hoop
in one fist. Now she whipped at the air with the antenna and Phineas
looked away, to the crowd.

They were hushed, gathered close.

Phineas stood up, stricken. One hand touching his mouth.

What is this? he said. What is this?

Performance torture, said Crumb.

Phineas watched as Lady Adore crouched beside Eve and pulled the first hoop over her bended knees, then worked it slowly and with much effort up over Eve's thighs so that the metal rim circled her hips at one edge and the tops of her feet at the other.

Eve's face was sickening. Colorless, beaded with sweat.

Adore now placed one hand on Eve's head and forced her to bow until her nose was nearly touching the floor. Eve's arms remained at her sides as the second hoop was pushed down over her head, then forced over her shoulders and down to the small of her back. Now the two hoops were touching and Adore clasped them together.

Eve was fetal. Dark red streaks, a web of blood extending beneath her skin.

The hoops formed a terrible figure eight around her body.

Adore took a step back and turned a slow circle, slicing at the air with the antenna and grinding her hips suggestively. Then turned and uncocked her long left leg, touched the toe of her boot to Eve's trembling shoulder and gave just a tiny push. Eve flopped onto her side, she was a fish and she was bleeding from the mouth and nose. Adore raised the antenna above her head and when the crowd groaned, she hesitated, smiled. Adore dropped to one knee and kissed Eve on the mouth, then rolled away and bouncing to her feet lashed her twice across the back with the antenna.

Phineas pushed through the crowd. Sick and feverish.

He threw his elbows against unseen flesh and vaulted onto the stage. It was four or five feet off the ground and he shrugged, as if surprised at his own agility.

Adore turned to face him, visibly disgusted.

You, she said. You are the victim.

He was speechless, dreaming. And she whipped him across the face with the antenna, opening a long cut that extended from the corner of his mouth to just below the ear.

Fuck, he said.

Adore swung at him again and he tried stupidly to catch or block the flashing antenna with his left hand. Now his fingers were bleeding and he took two quick steps forward, striking Adore in the nose with the heel of his right hand and she went down, the nose likely broken. Phineas kicked her in the stomach, not terribly hard but hard enough to be sure that she stayed down, then turned to Eve and hesitated to touch her, for she was so white and her face was stretched like a drum and running with sweat.

Eve, he said. Oh, fuck.

Theseus leaned on one elbow, sipping a pale yellow drink from a martini glass. He was relatively serene, gazing at the stage with gross indifference until Ray Fine chose to interrupt the program. Theseus shrugged and looked away, scanning the crowd. He left his unfinished drink at the bar and sauntered into a throng of bodies. Angry. He was fucking angry and soon came to the rug of triangles and flowers and crouched to mutter furiously in Major Tom's ear.

Do you know that man? he said.

Major Tom turned, wary. Then smiled the smile of a lotus eater.

Phineas slipped one hand between Eve's thighs and belly, fumbled for one agonizing moment then managed to release the clasp and slip the first hoop from around her legs.

The metal surprised him, slipping so easily over her wet flesh.

He straightened her legs carefully, gently. He removed the second hoop and rolled her onto her back, checked her pulse. Eve was breathing but she was shaking, she was in shock. Phineas rubbed her arms and legs for a long moment, hoping to restore circulation. All the while he was talking to himself, to her. It didn't matter what he said to her. Anything, anything. He wrapped her in Ray Fine's wool jacket and carried her to the edge of the stage and stood there for a moment, the floor lights throwing shadows across his bloody face and he realized that he couldn't jump down while holding her, that he might drop her and so he laid her down and now the crowd began to grumble. Phineas jumped to the floor and faced them.

Who has a car, he said. Who has a fucking car.

There was no response and he picked up a wrought iron chair and hurled it into the dark with the crash and clatter of iron against wood and a fleshy thud as it struck a body. A car, he said. Come on. Who has a car?

Crumb came from the shadows, his hands held out wide as if to show that he was unarmed.

Take it easy, he said. I have a car.

DEAR JUDE.

You can say what you like about me. I have a tender fascination for the obvious and I'm slow to process violent stimuli but I tend to think that men are much softer than women, more sentimental. They cry at the movies and pretend not to. The male of the species is weak. He doesn't tolerate pain well, he is quick to break down under interrogation.

And while two mostly naked women spanking each other under bright lights sounds like a good idea the reality is something else.

Perhaps if they had been strangers. Then I could have shut down, I could have relaxed properly. I could have tolerated open flesh wounds and crushed feet and eyes burned with bleach. I could have imagined fucking them, hurting them. I could have been shamed and abused to the point of massive and paralyzing despair.

And I suppose this is what the torturer meant, when she said I was the victim. Because while Eve was visibly suffering it was I who cried out first.

Funny because I remember something you said to me once. That I had an unfortunate tendency to fall in love with the victims. And you were right.

But who am I in love with now? Eve, do you think?

By the way. I am not a particularly stupid man, right? But when it comes to literary theory and existential philosophy, well. I am stupid. I'm thick. Crumb had to give me the lowdown on a lot of that protean theory in *Ulysses*. The business of realism is a favorite topic of his but you have to be careful with Crumb. If he's had too much to drink he can easily chew your ear off about the Greeks. And according to Crumb, Aristotle had it all figured out two thousand years ago. The universe, the big nasty. Human existence. God and consciousness and death. The serious shit. Aristotle was on top of it all and his Poetics and Ethics were like very detailed instruction manuals that the average human is too fucking stupid or lazy to sit down and read.

Yeah. When Crumb gets going in that vein, he doesn't smoke cigarettes. He's so worked up he eats them.

You never met Crumb, did you. He patched me together after you relieved me of my kidney. Wait, that's not true. They took care of that at the hospital. He made sure I wasn't dying, though. And he gave me the first shot of morphine, which I suppose made things that much easier for you. He's a friend and I don't have many.

A friend is like anything else. A dog, a plant. You ignore them and they tend to die on you.

Chrome:
Not quite conscious.

The taste of aluminum and a slow downward spiral. He was close to Elvis, too close. Floating like a scrap of wood in high water. The floating was a trick, an illusion. Loss of blood and so on. He was in fact being carried and dragged along by Mingus and a female Breather whose name he could not remember at the moment. His toes dragged and he wished he could lift them, raise them up. For the dragging sensation caused his teeth to ache. Where. Where were they going. He might have asked this. But there was no answer. The pace began to slow and he wondered distantly if he was heavy. No, surely he was not. Chrome was slender, so slender. He was a reed and he took pride in his narrow waist.

Headlights. The grumble of a motor.

Slam of a car door. Mingus speaking softly to someone, someone else.

Horizontal now and soft tissue under his head. The female's thighs.

His head must have been cushioned in her lap but he could smell nothing but his own blood. Hum of rubber on wet pavement. This was the backseat of a car, a hired taxi. Fingers in his hair. The female. Hospital. They were taking him to a hospital and he believed this was not a good idea. Dangerous. He was shot, gun shot. And the hospital was the very very last place he should go, even if dying. The police would find him.

Mingus, he said. Mingus.

The little dwarf's worried face soon loomed into view and Chrome realized he had been unaware that his eyes were even open. He had mistaken the black vinyl seat before him for the inside of his head.

Hush, said Mingus. You have lost a lot of blood.

Don't, he said. Don't take me to the hospital.

You need a doctor.

The police will kill me.

Christian, said Mingus. I'm not sure if I can deal with this.

He groaned. Then stop the car and let me out.

No, said the female. We can take him to my house.

Who is that?

It's Dizzy.

Yes. Take me to Dizzy's house.

You're dying.

Then I can fucking well die there.

DARK SKIES AND BITTER RELIEF to be outside again. The air was wet and if I opened my mouth I could soothe the tongue. Eve had stopped shaking pretty much but had not said a word and I wondered if this was pain or shame or what. She couldn't be that injured, could she. Those joined hoops had been like something out of the Inquisition, though. And the thing about torture was that the victim always confessed or died.

Always.

They didn't put you on the rack for a day and a half and then decide you were innocent. Eve wasn't guilty of anything but she might well have suffered internal damage. Those hoops were evil. The way her nose was bleeding had scared the shit out of me and I was sure she might have had a blood vessel or two burst in her brain. On the other hand, I have a fucked-up imagination and an irrational but profound fear of embolisms and brain tumors and maybe I was projecting.

And I was still flying high with adrenaline.

My mouth was bleeding pretty freely where the dominator had cut me with her metal whip and it struck me that I would probably need stitches. I would have a handsome faceful of thread and it was too bad I couldn't pass that little problem off on Ray Fine.

Truly. What else was an alterego good for.

Eve relaxed her arms now and moved her head, brushing my cheek with her lips.

Put me down, Phineas.

Are you sure?

I'm not hurt, she said.

I put her down and she stood there, barefoot on the wet sidewalk. She fastened the buttons of Ray Fine's wool jacket up to the throat and suddenly she looked about fourteen. Thin white legs and bruised, angry face. The sleeves were too long for her and she used them to wipe the blood from her nose. I lit a cigarette and gave it to her.

Thanks, she said. And I'm sorry about your jacket.

Don't be, I said.

She crouched down on the curb and smoked hungrily.

Hey, she said. How are you? We haven't really gotten a chance to talk.

Yeah. I'm fine.

How was Mexico?

Eve, I said.

Did you get to see a bullfight? she said. I've always wanted to see one.

You're in shock, I said.

But I think I would cry when the bull was killed.

Eve, I said.

It's cruel, don't you think?

Do you want me to call you Goo? I said.

She choked back a laugh or sob and I thought, here it comes. The embolism.

No, she said. Please don't.

I sat beside her and she passed me the cigarette.

I'm out of it now, she said. I'm out of the game.

Oh, I said. How do you know?

Because that was me up there. That was Eve.

Yes, I said.

What are we waiting for? she said.

Crumb, I said. Crumb went to get his car.

Who? she said.

And before I could remind her that she had known Crumb for years, that she used to work for him for God's sake, I saw the headlights of Crumb's car, a rusted yellow Rambler with what sounded like a rotten muffler. The car choked out an angry cloud of black exhaust and I found it disturbing to think that this ugly piece of metal had probably rolled off the line a few years before Eve was born.

Crumb didn't get out of the car. He just sat there, revving the engine.

I smiled and my mouth felt white with pain.

The Rambler would probably die if Crumb took his foot off the gas. Oh, this would be a fantastic ride. Crumb was notorious for getting lost and I was still confused by the madman's map of Denver that Griffin had spawned in my head. The car had a wide bench seat in front so the three of us could ride cozily. Eve slid into the middle, tugging at the jacket to cover the white triangle of her underpants. Now she turned to Crumb and looked at him for a moment.

But you're Gulliver, she said.

Crumb sighed. Yes.

I didn't like this at all. Eve seemed to know who she was, and who I was. But she was still so entangled in the game that she didn't know Crumb from Gulliver.

Do you know where you are? I said.

Denver, she said with a trace of disgust.

Meanwhile, Crumb put the car into gear and we lurched forward. He found the Rolling Stones on the radio: "19th Nervous Breakdown." It was appropriate, I suppose. Though it generally alarms me when life has a soundtrack. I tried to relax and let the street outside become a blur. After a few minutes I turned to Eve and whispered, do you know Jimmy Sky?

No, she said. I don't mingle with the Freds.

Then how do you know he's a Fred?

Where am I going? said Crumb.

Don't know, I said. Eve's place, I suppose.

No, she said.

You need some clothes.

My place is slipping, she said. It's not safe.

Ah, said Crumb. The slip. Very nasty.

Shut up, I said.

He's right, said Eve.

Two minutes ago you said you were out of the game.

Eve stared at me. That doesn't mean it isn't real.

Oh, fuck. Will you please listen to yourself?

By the way, said Crumb. Your face is a mess, boy.

I touched my mouth. I know. It feels like hamburger.

Then let's go down to the shop. I can sew that up and we'll all have a cup of tea and a nice talk.

Jimmy Sky:

He was back, baby. He was back.

Jimmy Sky walked around and around the house, stomping on rosebushes and cursing the thorns. He was looking for easy access. It was such a cute little house, very Victorian and all that and he would hate to break a window. But that was not to say that he wouldn't.

Now.

Jimmy was well aware that Theseus was giving him some sort of happy fuck-around. On one level, anyway. But there wasn't much he could do about it just yet. He wanted to find this Mariner, what was his name again. Aluminum foil or magnesium boy or ironhead. He chuckled. Chrome, it was Chrome. And according to Theseus, the kid was taking tongues from cops who were dizzy and fucked from the Pale and leaving them dead and somehow, his fictional friend Ray Fine was the prime suspect. And that made Jimmy fucking grumpy.

Theseus. He would deal with that fancy boy later.

Okay. His feet were muddy and he was pretty well sick of walking around this house so he ambled up the back steps and used his formidable girth to huff and puff and kick down the door. It wasn't so easy. It took three tries and on the second he found himself flat on his ass.

But the door was only wood, and wood splinters in the end. It gives.

Jimmy Sky crashed through and found himself in a kitchen. Flicked on a light and commenced to explore. A lot of knives in here. He opened the fridge and found a leftover carton of moo goo gai pan, barely touched. Excellent. He grabbed a fork and walked into the living room, shoveling the stuff into his wide gob.

Nice fucking place.

The Breather who was said to live here was obviously thick with silver.

Jimmy stomped upstairs and took a cursory look in each of the bedrooms, his eyes peeled for human shadows. Everything was fine and white and fairy-tale clean and he was sorely tempted to take a long yellow piss on one of the sheepskin rugs but then couldn't be bothered. He couldn't be fucked.

However. He did need to pee and of course whenever he found himself alone in a stranger's house, one of Jimmy's favorite tasks was to find the nearest bathroom and root through the medicine cabinet for prescription drugs. But then he supposed everyone was this way. He shrugged and soon located the bathroom. Thankfully emptied his bladder and polished off the moo goo gai pan as he did so. Jimmy sighed to see it go and tossed the empty carton into a wastebasket, then hurriedly washed his hands. He opened the medicine cabinet and whistled at its contents. He had found the mother lode, hadn't he? And the little Breather who lived here was mad as could be.

Decisions.

Well, now. There were plenty of vitamins and expensive herbal smart-pills and a wild rainbow of antidepressants that didn't much interest him. But there were also quite a few muscle relaxers and painkillers and amphetamines that were exactly to his taste, and he thought a couple of

Demerol tabs would go down nicely with a diet pill or two. He rolled four or five pills around in his mouth as he walked back down the hall because he always preferred to taste whatever he was consuming and so he favored the dry swallow. But now his mouth seemed to be full of chalk and his tongue was a bitter ashen lump so he rapidly steered himself back to the kitchen and took a pitcher of what he incorrectly assumed to be lemonade from the fridge and had a big unfortunate gulp of the stuff.

Grapefruit juice.

Which might as well be poison, in his book. And not only did it burn his sore gums and torture his glottis, but the juice did not integrate well with the moo goo gai pan and before he could say howdy doody Jimmy Sky was vomiting all over his shirt. And what a fucking mess. His shirt was foul beyond belief and he was standing in partially chewed noodles and bits of gray matter that upon closer inspection were not necessarily meat nor vegetable and to top it off, the pills he had just taken were gleaming like tiny extra buttons down his chest.

Now then.

He could have gone back to the bathroom and gotten a few more tabs of the Demerol but these little guys on his shirtfront were hardly dissolved and what was the difference anyway. Waste not, yeah. Jimmy Sky plucked the little buttons between thumb and ring finger and swallowed rather more carefully this time, washing his mouth out with water from the kitchen sink.

And he paused, thoughtful.

Jimmy Sky was a practical man. But this sort of behavior, the consumption of partially digested pills, that was pure Moon. Ah, well.

Bang.

Metal against metal.

Bang, bang and his ears perked up like an old dog's. That sounded a lot like the front gate.

FAMILIAR AND SAD, he back room of the Witch's Teat.

The whorehouse décor and somber lighting. The whistling kettle. The peculiar smells. Crumb peddled inexpensive sex toys, used records and relatively legitimate drug paraphernalia out the front door, and in the back room wielded his untrained medical skills on the mad souls who wanted or needed to avoid regular hospitals. Crumb was no butcher, and he would rarely reach for a scalpel when drunk. But his education was spotty. His run at college had been disastrous, from what I could gather, and irrelevant besides. Crumb had been a theology major. He had picked up a little medicine while working in a tattoo parlor, and later was apprenticed to a back-alley abortionist for a year or two. And beyond that, Crumb was self-taught. He subscribed to the *New England Journal of Medicine* and he kept an expensive video library of the medical dramas on TV. He swore by *St. Elsewhere* and complained that *Quincy*, while entertaining, was medically unsound. *Quincy* was a menace, he said. Crumb read every textbook he could get hold of and had faithfully practiced his surgical skills on rubber dummies, dead dogs and a few comatose friends. His specialty was extractions: bullets and other foreign objects, bad teeth, unwanted fetuses. Crumb could remove things from the body. And he was pretty good with a needle and thread. I had come to him quite a few times over the years, with minor lacerations and other flesh wounds that I might not have wanted to report to the department.

Crumb had acquired a dentist's chair in the year or so since I last needed his services. It faced the television and gleamed darkly in a corner by the sink. There was a Batman cartoon on the box, the sound muted. I stared at the screen for a moment, my brain clicking. It was so obvious, and kind of sad. But all superheroes had pretty much the same problem. Batman was flash and sexy compared to Bruce Wayne and even Robin the Boy Wonder was a lot cooler than Dick Grayson. As for Superman, well. It was a fucking miracle that Clark Kent had never committed suicide. I glanced at Eve, who was pacing around the little room as if she couldn't stay and she couldn't go. Obsessively twirling one finger in her hair, around and around.

Crumb steered me toward the dentist's chair and tottered off to scrub his hands.

No thanks, I said.

What's the matter? said Crumb.

Nothing. I've got torture on my mind, though.

So?

A dentist's chair?

It's perfect. I can clean your teeth while I'm at it.

Fuck that. My teeth are fine.

I'm joking, of course. But I do have a tank of nitrous, if that helps.

I had to admit that nitrous would help.

And five minutes later I was strapped into the chair with a mask over my nose and I could feel the needle tugging at my skin as if it wasn't skin at all, but a plastic sheath that I wore around my head. I could feel Crumb's fingers resting heavily on my face and I could see Crumb's eyes, round and never blinking bug's eyes. Crumb had bumped up the volume on the TV before he started, saying it helped him to relax and that if I didn't want my ear sewn onto my forehead not to complain and so now I listened as Batman exchanged dark nihilistic metaphors with the Joker and I smiled warmly with drool running down my chin.

Eve leaned over me, slow and sudden at once. It was stupid, she said. What you did was stupid.

I gurgled at her. Tried to smile but I felt vague about who she was. The dreambrain identified her as a conglomerate. My mother was in there, the sister I never had. My dead wife and a long line of forgotten lovers and characters from books and movies that I might have fantasized about.

I'm a creature of comfort, said the Joker.

I'm glad, though. I'm glad you were there, she said.

And I was pretty sure the needle would pull my face off. My poor skin could only stretch so far and no farther before it slipped from my knob like a wet bathing suit. It's terrible, isn't it. The way your skin clings to you.

Mingus:

He could hardly credit it but Mingus was losing his sense of smell. Overload or temporary freakout or some kind of total shutdown. Because he should have been able to taste Christian's blood by now. The stuff was all over him.

He glanced over at Dizzy Bloom and was struck with worry and nausea, a queer star-shaped feeling blossoming in his throat for her. What visions must she be suffering, he wondered. Dizzy Bloom was strong, though. She had borne her half of Christian's weight without a whimper. Maybe she was holding her breath. Dizzy Bloom was an alien, a beautiful creature, and he supposed the star-shaped sensation creeping up from his belly was love or something like it. This was unforeseen and perhaps a little frightening but he was too worried about his lost sense of smell to give it a lot of thought. He could see nothing behind his own eyes and he had no memories true or false. He had nothing.

Mingus took a deep breath as they lowered Christian onto Dizzy's porch swing but there was still nothing. He watched as Dizzy dug through what seemed like a thousand pockets for her house key. He closed his eyes. He breathed.

Wait.

Rotten chocolate, thick and pungent and it wasn't chocolate at all, it was the smell of fresh earth, of death. And as fast as it came it was gone and Christian was falling off the porch swing. Mingus crouched beside him, hugging his friend's cool damp body and waiting for Dizzy to unlock the front door.

Isthmus cerebri, said Mingus. Vena ascendens.

The door swung open and Dizzy turned to help him with Christian.

Tunica elastica. Quadratus menti. Corpus callosum. Sympathetic plexus and vitreus humor.

What? said Dizzy.

Mingus blinked. He was only remotely aware that he had been muttering these phrases aloud.

Medical terminology, said Christian. His voice like the faraway croak of a frog. Our friend Mingus, he said. He often quotes from *Gray's Anatomy* when nervous.

Mingus blushed, hoping that Dizzy would smile at him in the dark.

Christian, he said. Be quiet.

Why, said Christian. Why do you call me that?

Because you're failing.

Dizzy sniffed the air and stopped short and the three of them nearly tumbled into her living room.

There's someone here, she said.

Mingus felt the prickle of goose bumps along his arms. Fearful.

Theseus? he said.

No, she said. It's the smell of sick.

The overhead light was flicked on and a stout, balding man in vomit-streaked clothes stood before them, a gun in his right hand. He touched his own forehead with the barrel as if scratching an itch.

Fuck me, he said. You call yourself a Breather. A little kid could walk in here and smell puke.

You, said Dizzy. I know you.

Christian was slumping to the floor and Mingus moaned, holding him close. And as he always had, he felt safer with Christian beside him. Even like this.

No, said the man. You don't know me.

You're a policeman, she said.

Not tonight, sister. The man waved his gun and nearly fell over. I'm no cop.

Who are you? said Mingus. He had found his voice, it seemed.

I'm Elvis, said the man. I'm king of the fucking Freds. I'm Jimmy Sky.

Dizzy's face was white, her lips flatline. Our friend is hurt, she said. What do you want?

The man guffawed. I want him, of course.

What do you want with him? said Mingus.

That depends. His name is Chrome, yes? The Mariner.

Mingus hesitated. Yes, he said.

And the man who called himself king of the Freds stepped forward, he swaggered close with his gun held crooked. He swung his arm around, breathing crazily. He faltered, mumbled an obscenity or two and glanced upward as if looking for the sun. Then poked the end of the gunbarrel at Christian's mouth.

Chrome, he said. You have made the game real.

Mingus watched the man's chubby index finger tighten around the trigger, he watched the tiny creases in the skin of Jimmy Sky's finger turn white and he could already feel the hot spray of Christian's blood but there was a pause, a heaviness in the air. And Jimmy leaned close enough.

Don't you find it curious? he said. That I don't want your tongue.

Christian straightened, his cheeks deathly. Mingus knew that he wanted to be proud but he couldn't stand alone. There was no strength left in him. Dizzy said softly, wait. And the man never heard her, he never did. But he was staring at Christian with the sudden horror of recognition in his eyes.

I know you, he said. You work at the Video Hound. I rented *Star Trek* from you, just a few weeks ago. *The Undiscovered Country*. Last month. Last fucking month. Jimmy lowered the gun. Oh, he said. This is...unexpected. This is fucking strange. And look at you, he said. Look at you. Someone has already killed you.

Please, said Dizzy. Let's talk about this. I can make some coffee.

Coffee, said the man. Fuck that shit. Your friend doesn't need coffee.

Mingus made a rare, free-falling decision. He decided to say fuck it and he stuck out his left hand and took the gun away from Jimmy Sky. It was easy, really. The fat policeman yawned at him, unconcerned. Mingus turned the gun over and over in his hands, wondering how one might unload it and at that precise moment, Christian's knees buckled and he fell forward, pulling Dizzy down with him.

Oh, this is pretty. This is gorgeous, said Jimmy Sky.

The room collapsed into the glass eye of a fish.

The room curved inward and Mingus twisted the gun this way and that, careful to keep it pointed at the floor. He could not fathom how the bullets went into it and he cursed himself for never learning such things as a boy.

In warped space he could see Dizzy shoving at Christian, rolling him over onto his back and bending to breathe into his mouth and behind her the fat policeman was lazily removing his jacket and tie, his shirt. Dropping them to the floor like soiled rags then fumbling to release his belt buckle. This seemed terribly inappropriate and Mingus lifted the gun. The man's pants sagged but did not fall down and Jimmy Sky shrugged. He lifted one heavy foot and began to hop around in a circle, trying in vain to yank off his shoe.

The gun was unsteady and Mingus felt sure that it would go off any moment.

Dizzy breathed into Christian's slack lips. One of Jimmy Sky's shoes hit the floor, followed by a dirty white tube sock. Mingus fumbled with the gun and now Jimmy Sky sat down, cursing because his other shoe would not come off. There was a knot in the laces. Mingus lowered the gun. Dizzy was beautiful, he thought. Dizzy was silent and mournful and her eyes never left Christian's face as she offered him her breath. The gun was heavy, warm and heavy and suddenly Mingus darted back outside into the dark and grunted as he threw the thing onto the roof. And he stood there a long moment, waiting to see if it would fall back to his feet.

Silence.

The gun didn't fall and soon Jimmy Sky came outside, barefoot and eerily peaceful. His great white belly jiggling.

Horrorshow.

Mingus stared at him, unafraid now.

Nice fucking night, said Jimmy.

Yes, said Mingus. They stared at each other for another moment and Jimmy burped wetly, then gave a great sigh. He tottered down the steps and Mingus slowly turned and went back inside, his head full of noise. Dizzy looked up at him and he knew everything was bad. It was real.

We have to do something, she said.

There was bad air in his mouth and he didn't know what to say.

What? he said.

I don't know, okay. But there's a bullet in him and he's almost dead. If we get the bullet out, maybe he won't die.

His tongue felt thick. That seems naïve, he said.

Dizzy glared at him. Isn't he your friend?

Oh, God. Mingus touched his eyes and they were dry. Of course, he said. Yes, he said. And I keep expecting him to sit up. To laugh at me and say: quelle heure est-il?

Huh?

What time is it. Christian wishes that he were French, you know.

Why won't you call him Chrome?

Because Chrome wouldn't be dying.

Dizzy shook her head. Please, she said.

I didn't think you liked him.

Dizzy shrugged. I don't like him. But it's part of the game, Mingus.

No, he said. No, it's not.

She stood up. Help me move him into the kitchen.

Mingus helped her. He could hardly say no, could he. And it was grue-some, the way Christian's body slid across the floor. They dragged him into the kitchen and the blood became a muddy streak across black-and-white tile.

Bright overhead light.

Mingus sat beside the body, his fingers pressed to Christian's throat and there was perhaps a faint pulse but he knew that if he touched the floor or the leg of a chair he would likely feel the same faint, faraway beating. Dizzy was opening one drawer after another and he realized she was looking for tools.

Do you have a knife in your pocket? she said.

No, he said.

Take this, she said. And she handed him a blunt little knife, the sort of knife one might use to cut cheese at a party. A soft cheese like Brie.

I want you to cut open his shirt, she said.

Mingus nodded. He stared at Christian's torso, at the fine silver mesh shirt. The gentle curve of pectoral muscles unmoving. He shifted his eyes to the brightly defined collarbone below Christian's throat.

Blood, the blood there was nearly dry.

Mingus slipped the point of the blade in at the neck of the shirt and sawed through the thin material and he was disgusted to hear himself grunting. The shirt fell away and Christian's chest was black with blood. Mingus reflexively pinched his nose but he needn't have bothered. There was no smell, not for him. Dizzy sat down across from him and he took one look at her and almost laughed because she knew it was inappropriate but he wanted to kiss her. There was a nice glow of sweat and urgency about her face and her lips seemed darker, almost brown and her hair fell in heavy black braids that touched the floor. The little muscles jumped in her arms. He saw that she held another knife with a black handle and serrated blade, an ice pick and a small sharpened spoon that he thought must have been intended for pitting olives. She laid these on a white linen napkin and together they gazed at the wound.

Which was not so bad, really. Torn flesh.

It was more of a rupture than a hole but they needed something to clean it with, alcohol or something. He mentioned this and she said, I looked. I don't have anything.

The Pale, he said.

There's none to spare.

He sighed and realized that he was only calm because his tiny reptile brain believed none of this was happening. This was a very intense video game, a first-person shooter from hell.

What about cough syrup, he said. Some of them have alcohol.

Yes, she said. Yes. I have NyQuil.

What color? he said. And it didn't matter, it didn't matter. Christian was dead.

Green, she said. I hope.

Yes.

Dizzy said she would be right back.

Okay, said Mingus.

He stared at the knife, at the funny little spoon. He wondered what in God's name would she do with the ice pick. And in a moment Dizzy came back, another linen napkin in hand. She stained it green and began to wipe the blood from Christian's chest and soon his chest was green, as if his blood were green.

This isn't necessary, said Mingus.

What? she said.

He touched her wrist, he grabbed it. There's no one around, he said. We could drop out of the game for five minutes.

You can't be serious.

Mingus sighed. He wanted her to call him by his proper name. He wanted her to kiss him again, he wanted to talk about tomorrow and beyond. They had a lot to talk about. But Dizzy was unwavering when it came to the game.

Look at him, said Mingus. He's dead.

Are you sure?

No.

Aren't you a medical student? she said. In the daylight, I mean.

You know I am, he said. And I'm on academic probation.

Dizzy shrugged. I don't care. We have to try, at least.

That six-fingered claw in his belly was love, he was sure of it. But when she offered him the serrated knife, he shook his head. He couldn't do it and he didn't want her to do it but she bent over Christian and felt for the bullet with her finger. She couldn't seem to find it and he heard her suck in a deep unsteady breath as she lowered the sunshiny little blade to cut at the flesh around the hole in Christian's dead chest. And Mingus was calm, he was far away. Dizzy made an opening the length of her finger above Christian's left nipple and stopped. She looked like she might faint and now Mingus took the little sharpened spoon away from her.

Fuck, he said. Oh, fuck.

He wished he could dig around in the area of Christian's heart and find the bullet, if only to give it to Dizzy so she could breathe again. But he couldn't.

Dead, he said. He's dead, Dizzy.

Yes.

Dizzy leaned forward and felt around in Christian's pockets until she found a packet of cigarettes, then sat back against a cupboard and lit one.

The gray sunken cunt of the world, she said.

Mingus took the cigarette from her.

What? he said. What did you say?

My great-grandfather, she said. Leopold Bloom. He called death the gray sunken cunt of the world and I never understood what he meant until now.

Mingus blew smoke at the ceiling and thought what a beautiful freak she was.

Dizzy, he said. Leopold Bloom is a fictional character. He was never real.

Oh, she said. I don't know about that.

Long silence. Mingus wondered about tomorrow.

J'ai faim.

Dizzy Bloom smiled. What?

I'm hungry.

THE FACE WAS NUMB and I couldn't smile.

But I liked to think that smiling was unnecessary and now I looked down with mild effort to see that I was still strapped into a dentist's chair, hands flecked with the blood of Phineas and folded piously in my lap. I released the seat belt and maneuvered my legs into standing position and this was not so bad.

Breathed. The air was still and I supposed it must be approaching dawn. I spied a clock that claimed it was slightly past three. Technically it was Saturday. No sign of life but for a vaguely humanoid lump on the couch and I doubted they would have just left me in the chair because I might have had a seizure and thrashed myself to death but Crumb had always been one to fade before first light and Eve, well. She was not quite herself.

Jesus.

Eve was freaking me out. She looked about thirteen sometimes but she was fierce, she was stoic. I would have been crippled and sobbing after two minutes in those rings.

Found her in brightly lit bathroom. Narrow.

A mirror directly to my left, I could feel it there. Eve sat on the toilet with the lid down. I was sick of fucking mirrors and I stared straight at Eve. She was so tiny. Her feet barely touched the floor. Her legs were crossed, one foot bouncing. She was reading a glossy magazine.

Crumb? I said.

Asleep, she said.

That lump on the couch, you mean.

Yeah.

What are you reading?

People, she said. It's very strange.

I nodded. Yes.

These celebrities, she said. They all look terrified.

I could feel the mirror beside me, a pale reflecting skin. I told myself not to look at it.

They are terrified, I said. They have lost themselves.

Eve touched finger to tongue, flipped another page.

Those cannibals are right, she said.

Breathe. One two three four five.

What cannibals?

The ones that claim the camera steals your soul.

Without a conscious thought I pulled an aluminum towel rack off the wall with a brief sparkling shower of white dust and turned and smashed the mirror beside me in one long circular motion.

Do you feel better? she said.

No.

But the spiderweb of glass that obliterated what would have been my face was a fair beginning.

Let's get out of here, she said.

How?

She rattled Crumb's car keys.

You want to steal his car, I said.

Eve shook her head. He gave them to me. I think he wants us to leave.

Saturday

The Scavenger's Daughter:

SHE HATED HERSELF and she could not sit still.

Eve squirmed like a worm on a hook and tried to whistle. She tried to whistle something pleasant like merrily, merrily your life is but a dream or maybe the theme to a Burger King commercial, something safe and normal. Have it your way. You can have it your way. But she was a poor whistler, she always had been. Eve was much better at spitting. And so she shifted around behind the wheel of Gulliver's yellow Rambler like she had sand in her pants, or spiders.

It's Crumb, she told herself. Crumb, not Gulliver.

Why was that so hard. She had known Crumb for like three years. And she, or Goo, had only encountered Gulliver a few brief times. The whole thing made her dizzy and she was glad to be out of it. But she was squirming because Phineas was sitting beside her, because he was looking at her. He hadn't said more than two words since they left and his mouth was probably sore with those stitches.

God.

When did he come back, anyway. Three or four days ago. Or was it a week?

Eve tried to remember how she had felt when she saw him on her doorstep. When she laid eyes on him. Warm. As if she had just swallowed a mouthful of brandy. She had felt like she was fifteen and she had a stupid, hopeless crush on her best friend's brother who had just come home from college and whose legs had rubbed briefly, innocently against hers beneath the dinner table.

Warm.

But the brandy fingers had been fleeting. They had flown away like five small birds and she wondered why she hadn't simply asked him to get her out of the game, to rescue her or something. But fuck that. She wasn't anyone's little sister. Of course. He had rescued her, in the end. He had pulled her from the Scavenger's Daughter even though she never asked him to.

If she had a therapist and she wanted to analyze it, she might say that she had been daring Goo to stop her, to save her. Or maybe she had been curious to see how long she could stand it. How long before she passed out. Or failing that, she might have hoped that Chrome would lift a finger, but he hadn't ever been there. Anyway, she didn't want to analyze it.

Where are we going? said Phineas.

To Dizzy's place, she said.

What is that, another club?

Laughing. Dizzy is a friend.

Phineas lit a cigarette, which he smoked out of the corner of his injured mouth.

You know what? he said. I think I've had enough of your sick friends. Let's go to your place.

Eve sighed. I told you. It isn't safe there.

Brief silence, tender.

Eve, he said. There's nothing wrong with your apartment.

And besides, she said. Dizzy isn't sick at all. She's nice.

Whatever you say. He blew a line of crooked smoke from the side of his mouth.

It's my life, she said.

I'm sure it is.

But she thought about it, she tried to see it from his angle. And somehow her life was not hers. It was a loose thread, a plot twist. It was a situation and situations get fucked up. Three months ago she was reasonably normal and enrolled in college and now she was bloody and bruised and anorexic and squirming behind the wheel of a borrowed Rambler.

Okay. It was fucked up, she could see that.

But she liked to think that once in a while the sun was meant to shine only for her. Eve squinted as she drove and it occurred to her that she wasn't wearing any pants. She carried no identification, no proof of her existence at all. She wouldn't want to get pulled over but she smiled and thought, if she was pulled over she could pretend she was a prostitute, she could let Phineas do the talking and she would love to hear what he had to say. It was still dark but the sun was shining somewhere, it was shining for her benefit and here was Dizzy's house. She slowed and let the Rambler drift to a stop.

This is it, she said.

Phineas frowned. Who is this Dizzy person?

I told you. A friend.

Right, he said. And is she in the game?

She's a Breather, said Eve.

Oh, good. I like Breathers.

They got out of the car and walked up to the house. Eve didn't flinch when he took her hand. The front door stood open, a crack of light. Phineas dropped her hand and eased through like he was made of smoke and shadows and she remembered that he used to be a cop.

Irrational, but she felt safe with him.

Discarded clothes on the floor. As if someone had undressed while drunk. White pants, green military belt. Blue shirt and blazer and wide yellow tie. Phineas picked up the tie, twirled it between his fingers and she wondered what he was thinking.

There was blood on the floor, a long brownish streak.

Phineas followed it into the kitchen and she followed him and they found Dizzy Bloom and Mingus sitting on the floor with Chrome's body stiff as a canoe between them. Blood and streaked with something sticky and green. Dizzy and Mingus were eating chocolate pudding cups and drinking ginger ale mixed with the Pale. They whispered to each other like kids drunk on sex and Phineas ignored them, bending to examine Chrome. Eve stopped in the doorway, a wide blank space forming in her head.

Goo, said Mingus. He tried to stand up but failed.

Eve looked at the blood, at the wound on Chrome's chest. Christian, she thought. Oh, my.

What happened? said Phineas.

He was shot, said Dizzy.

Yes, said Phineas. Who shot him?

A Fred, said Mingus. It seems.

It was a policeman, said Dizzy. I think.

Phineas blinked. Did you say a cop shot him?

He was hunting, said Eve. He was hunting and he went too far. Again.

Again? said Phineas.

Chrome killed a Fred yesterday, she said. Or was it the day before? Eve touched her fingers to her mouth, to her tongue. She didn't feel much of anything at all and Dizzy Bloom was looking at her, worried.

Goo, she said.

You have chocolate on your nose, said Eve.

Dizzy shivered like a scrap of fine cloth in the open air and after a bottomless silence she wiped her nose.

Phineas looked ill. The yellow tie clutched in his left hand. The stitches like black flies crawling out of his mouth. He leaned against the fridge and Eve watched as he fumbled through his pockets. He pulled out a cigarette and looked around.

You must be Dizzy, he said.

Dizzy shrugged and held out her hand, palm down. Eve felt the air turn stiff and she saw everything at once. The ice pick, the sharp little spoon. The linen napkins. The pudding packs. The blood, the green streaks of what she now saw was cough syrup.

Christian was dead.

His smooth pretty chest marred by a black and muddy patch of flesh over the left breast. Eve saw herself as Goo. She was in bed in another, much darker room, another pocket of time and she was kissing, sucking at his nipples. She was counting his ribs and marveling at his stomach muscles and still she didn't feel anything. Now she looked at Mingus, who was pale and blushing and confused. She wished he would get up and explain this scene to her. She wanted to know what her character should be thinking.

Hello. Do you mind if I smoke? said Phineas.

Please, said Dizzy.

Eve stood in the doorway. She looked at Phineas, but he was looking at Dizzy and so she tugged at him with her eyes, she tried to pull his skin apart with her thoughts and now he looked back at her, he held out one hand.

Are you okay? he said.

Yes, she said and suddenly she didn't want him to comfort her. She couldn't stand it.

Phineas turned back to the others. How do you know it was a cop who shot him?

Oh, well.

We don't, said Dizzy.

The two of them started talking at once and Eve smiled. Or you could call it a smile. Her lips slipped apart and she felt air on her teeth. They already sounded like lovers, she thought. Interrupting each other. Their words tangling together. Eve sighed. She looked at Chrome and didn't recognize him.

Hungry.

She stepped over his body and touched Phineas on the shoulder with one finger. He moved aside and she poked through Dizzy's fridge until she found a jar of dill pickles. Now she sat down and began to munch on a huge sour pickle, the jar between her legs in case she needed another one.

What should we do? she said.

Dizzy and Mingus looked at her. They shrugged as if joined at the hip and she remembered how irritating two people can be when they adore each other. Phineas coughed. He ground out his cigarette and fingered the yellow tie, he picked at a stain on the thin material. They all looked at him, waiting. Because he would know what to do. He was the adult.

Obviously, he said. We need to get rid of the body. Unless you want to tell this fantastic story to the cops.

No, said Dizzy. I don't.

Okay, he said. I can help you. But I want to know whose tie this is.

Dizzy sighed. Wow. I almost forgot about him.

Who?

He said his name was Jimmy Sky.

Phineas laughed out loud and now he sounded a little fragile, Eve thought. He sounded like there was a big handful of mad laughter in his stomach and he could only let it out a little bit at a time because if he laughed it all out at once he would go fucking crazy. Eve licked her fingers and took another pickle from the jar. She watched as Phineas tied the yellow tie in a crooked knot around his neck. He was smiling a thin, bitter smile and it occurred to her that he might not want to be the adult.

No, he said. This isn't high school and I'm not your big brother. I can make this body disappear but you can't just go to bed and forget about it.

Who is Jimmy Sky? said Eve.

He's no one, said Phineas. He used to be a friend of mine.

Well, she said. What did he want?

I think he came here to kill Christian, said Mingus.

And? said Phineas.

Mingus shrugged. Christian was already dying.

Jesus Christ. Phineas looked around the room as if he might be dreaming.

Dizzy touched his leg. What? she said.

I'm sick, he said. I feel sick.

It's okay, she said. Everything is okay.

Have you ever had someone die in your kitchen? he said.

Dizzy hugged her knees. No, she said. Never.

You're a Breather, right? he said.

Dizzy nodded. Yes.

And that means what? he said. That you're clairvoyant? That you can smell my clothes or fondle my keys and see my past, my future?

Sometimes, she said. Only sometimes.

Mingus got up suddenly, nervously. He climbed onto the kitchen counter and sat there like a very tired boy and began to take off his shoes. Eve was empty, she felt empty. The pickles were making her ill and her boyfriend, who was not really her boyfriend, was dead. His body was two feet away. It was too much, really. She tried to put on a new face. A cheerful face. That's what her mother would suggest and now she put a fist to her lips, trying not to laugh. Phineas pulled a fat paperback book out of his jacket pocket and Eve saw that it was a copy of *Ulysses*. He placed it on Christian's chest and Eve flinched.

His body isn't a coffee table, she said.

No, said Phineas.

He picked up the book and offered it to Dizzy, who received it gingerly, fearfully. As if it were made of lead.

That was Jimmy's book, said Phineas.

Dizzy opened the book and read aloud: tired I feel now. Will I get up? O wait. Drained all the manhood out of me, little wretch. She kissed me. My youth. Never again. Only once it comes.

Phineas stared at her. Fantastic. But where is Jimmy Sky?

Dizzy closed the book and stroked the smooth, worn cover with the tip of her ring finger, then lifted the book to her mouth and kissed the spine, licked it. But she did not smell it.

I don't know where he is, she said. I can't see him clearly. But he's cold, he's shivering.

Phineas rolled his eyes. Do you think so? His clothes are all over your fucking living room.

Eve laughed, she giggled. Oh, she tried not to but it came spilling out of her.

I'm sorry, said Dizzy. That's all I see.

I love this game, said Phineas. I love it.

Please stop, said Mingus. I want to stop.

Eve looked up and she felt bad for him. Mingus looked exhausted, he looked thin. Dark circles under his eyes. His hands trembling. Christian's dried blood on his clothes. Eve wanted to close her eyes, to sleep. She heard Dizzy exhale heavily, as if she had been holding her breath. Eve wondered what Goo would do if this was but another scene from the game. And she had no idea, no idea. All she could do was put the pickles away and wait.

Dizzy hesitated, then returned the book to Phineas.

His face was pale, apologetic. Eve hated it when he said he was sorry and she hoped he wouldn't do so.

I'm sorry, he said.

Dizzy stood up and she looked unsteady on her legs. She backed away from Phineas, from Christian's body. She was really beautiful, Eve thought. She was dirty and speckled with blood and her braids were falling apart but she was beautiful. Her arms were thin and muscular and she had nice hands and Eve realized that she was attracted to her, to Dizzy.

Her mouth felt dry.

Dizzy held out her hand and Eve wanted to take it but she didn't move. The hand was not reaching for her. Mingus hopped down from the counter. He kissed Dizzy's neck and Eve shrugged. They did seem happy together, safe together.

Flesh was flesh and bodies needed other bodies.

Eve looked at Christian and she could admit to herself that a thin far-away part of her was glad that he was gone. Chrome was dead and Goo would have no one to come back to. She looked at Phineas and wondered what she would do with him. What did she feel. She stared at his sick blue eyes. At his thin, hard mouth. His unshaven jaw and bright crooked teeth. And she thought of the way he had taken her hand in his as they had approached this house.

Flutter. She felt the flutter.

It's late, said Dizzy. It's very late and I'm going to bed.

Okay, said Mingus.

Dizzy tried to smile but it was like the muscles in her face were rotten. Eve smiled back.

It's not okay, said Dizzy.

No, she said. It isn't.

You can sleep here, said Dizzy. If you want. There are several spare beds.

Do you have any paint thinner, said Phineas. Or bleach?

His voice was dry, unflinching. Eve felt something twitch in her spine. Her breath slipped away from her. Paint thinner, she thought. This seemed like such a gruesome question but Dizzy was fairly untouchable, she was cool and weightless as a sparrow. She glanced down at the body and nodded.

Look under the sink, she said.

The two Breathers retreated from the room and Eve was left alone with Phineas and the body. Phineas went to the sink and began to dig through the cabinet. Eve stared down at Christian and told herself to touch him, to say good-bye. To feel something. His eyes were closed, thank god. He had such long, black eyelashes and she wondered how many times she had watched him sleep and felt invisible beside him, completely invisible. How many times she had curled up beside him like a little frog changing colors and wished one of them was dead.

Funny, though.

Because she never thought it would feel quite like this. Empty and cold and sick from lack of sleep, with the taste of pickles in her mouth. Christian's eyes were weirdly asymmetrical and she realized now that the left one was still swollen from the scratch that reached down the side of his jaw, where she had cut him with the sharpened doll. She touched the swollen eye, lightly. It felt rubbery and strange, it felt like a misplaced testicle and she was a little hysterical, perhaps. Can you see me, she said. Can you see me now.

Hand on her shoulder.

I need your help, said Phineas.

Her muscles were light and feathery. Yes, she said. I can help you.

Eve stood up and he handed her a metal jug of turpentine. Which made strange little echoes, like splashes at the bottom of a well. She watched as Phineas lifted Christian onto his shoulders, grunting with the effort.

He gave her dead lover the hug of a fireman.

Heavy footsteps. Out the back door, across Dizzy Bloom's dark, wet grass.

Brick patio, then more grass. Eve looked up at the sky and wished they could sit down to identify their favorite stars. The jug of paint thinner against her knees. Jack and Jill went up the hill. She opened the back gate and held it open for him. To fetch a pail of water. Parked cars and stretch of gravel. It was too bright and she realized how bad it would be if they were seen. Eve took the lead. Jack fell down and broke his crown. She didn't ask Phineas where he wanted to go.

Instinct.

She turned between a little red house and a vacant lot, she followed her feet along a dusty little path that might have struck her as charming under other conditions. Jill came tumbling after. The path curved through a gang of bushes and dumped them in a parking lot behind a fast-food place. Happy meals, she loved happy meals. Child-sized portions and always a prize. Every meal should include a prize. Two big blue Dumpsters like sleeping whales and she veered toward them without a thought. Is this far enough, she wondered. Is this far enough from the house and she could hear Phineas breathing hard and fast through his teeth. Between the Dumpsters and her eyes squeezed themselves shut as he shrugged Christian's body down like a sack of gravel.

Now, he said. Breathing.

He took the turpentine from her and she had to ask.

What is it for? she said.

Fingerprints, he said. Hair and fibers. Don't you watch television?

Not lately, she said.

Phineas sighed, hesitated. Then slowly and without ceremony, he dumped turpentine over the whole of her ex-boyfriend's body.

Goo's ex-boyfriend.

Her nostrils burned and Eve sat down abruptly on a wooden box that stank of tomatoes. She looked around and around. The air was bright and gray, the air was the color of metal under the pale winter sun. Phineas carefully wiped down the sides and handle of the empty jug, then tossed it into one of the Dumpsters.

That's it, she said. Do you want to say anything?

Eve looked at the body. Christian was deflated, he was much smaller than before. He was wet.

I can't, she said.

Phineas reached into his pocket and pulled out a handful of tobacco shreds and lint and coins and scraps of paper. He picked through and selected two dimes, which he placed on Christian's eyelids.

The dead suffer no laughter, he said.

What does that mean, exactly?

Phineas shrugged. Tell him a joke, if you can think of one.

Okay, she said. How many serial killers does it take to change a light-bulb?

Unwavering silence and shards of color now in the sky.

How many? he said finally.

One, she said. But it takes him a long time.

Phineas looked at Christian, then at her. Why?

Because he first has to dismember the old one, she said. Then masturbate on its remains.

Phineas nodded and she laughed to herself, brief and manic. He held
out his hand and she took it and they walked back across the parking lot
and along the twisting path, through the gate across Dizzy's dark garden.
Phineas steered her around to the front of the house so they might avoid
the kitchen and she was glad, she was warm. As they climbed the front
steps she caught a flash of pink movement above. Thought she saw a fat
pale gargoyle on the roof and was amazed that she had not noticed it
before. Now she blinked, looked again.

But the gargoyle was gone.

Through the front door and Phineas still held her hand. He didn't say
anything and he didn't once try to let go of her hand. He glanced around
at the crumpled clothes on the floor and took a long shuddering breath.
Eve lowered her eyes, she frowned at her own wet feet. There were bits of
yellow grass between her toes and she wasn't going to let go of him. Of
Phineas. She took him up the stairs and down the hall to the guest bedroom with the cloudlike white comforter.

Dead gray morning light.

But it was dark enough that his mouth and eyes were vague and
shadowy as unfinished sketches and Eve wasn't quite breathing. The pillows were cool and grotesquely soft and she slapped at them, half
expecting them to disappear. Phineas took off his hooded jacket and sat
down on the bed, slowly took off his boots. He unbuckled his belt and he
seemed terribly calm. He opened his mouth but Eve didn't want to talk and
she pushed him down onto his back. And she pulled his socks off, his
pants. Her fingers never quite touched his skin but she was sure that she
could hear his heartbeat. Or her own. Eve dropped the wool jacket to the
floor and now wore only underpants. White underpants and she wondered
how white her skin must be. How thin she was. Her breasts felt heavy and
cold and too large which was funny and unfamiliar but she folded her
arms across them and when she moved she felt the deep bruise from the

Scavenger's Daughter that circled her back and thighs and belly, an endless figure eight in her flesh. It would be purple tomorrow. Phineas still wore his shirt, a white polyester shirt with a red stain on the chest and a woman in a bikini down one sleeve. The faint smell of mothballs and he was naked from the waist down, he was apparently speechless but unashamed and she could see he had an erection. And she lowered her arms, she unbuttoned his shirt and lay on top of his chest with her legs drawn up like a grasshopper and at first thought that she only wanted his skin against hers but soon she was kissing him, she was kissing him. His tongue was slow and shy and she was absurdly wet but it was a long time before his cock was inside her, before he entered her. And when he did, he just held her. His face was pressed to her throat and she wondered if he could even breathe, his arms were heavy around her and he didn't rock or pound or thrust at her. They barely moved at all and after what seemed like an hour she began to rise and fall against him and over his shoulder she again saw the face of a fat pink gargoyle peeking at her through blackened window but that was impossible and she closed her eyes as Phineas said her name once or twice in a sweet faraway disbelieving voice and now he seemed to get bigger inside her and she began to shake and come apart and vaguely hating herself she kissed his ear and said please, don't come inside me.

DEAR JUDE. THE TRUTH IS I DON'T KNOW WHAT I'M DOING.

It might look like I'm trying to save somebody from something but I'm not. How can you save anybody when everything is reflex, everything is a muscular spasm. I saw a movie once where two guys are standing at the end of a tunnel, two guys named Frank and Joe. Frank is very cool, he's James Bond with long hair. He gets all the women and he can disarm a bomb while hanging upside down. He quotes poetry ever so casual. Frank is a gourmet cook, in fact. And Joe is a fuck-up. Every friendship has one. Joe is Barney Fife on speed. He shuts his hand in the car door and ejaculates prematurely and prefers cheap American beer. Meanwhile. There's a bad guy with a gun at the other end of the tunnel and I don't remember why he wants to kill Frank and Joe but that's not the point. At the precise moment that the bad guy pulls the trigger, Joe flinches. He lunges side-ways, he throws himself between Frank and the gun and takes one in the shoulder. Frank is amazed. The audience is amazed. Because Joe was trying to save his life or something. But upon closer examination, the bullet was a ricochet and if Joe had never moved, the bullet would have missed them both. Joe couldn't deny it and he didn't want to. He wasn't thinking about Frank, he wasn't thinking anything at all. He just jumped. And that's what I'm talking about.

Now I stole my first sour breath. Eve beside me, soft naked thin with a sur-real childish glow to her cheeks but then she was just twenty, still a girl. I had a feeling she would laugh at me if I let myself feel bad about fucking her. She would laugh and laugh. My eyes were not yet open. Yesterday I had felt like her brother, her big clumsy brother. But what had I really wanted.

I had wanted to adore her, to protect her.

Which was funny, wasn't it. I was so poisoned by Hollywood. I would open my eyes, soon.

Saturday.

Thank God. Friday had been too fucking long by far. When I opened my eyes there would be daylight, deadlight. Eve smelled good, she smelled like fire and spilled ink and bright cold glass and she was all angles beside me, she was bent knees and sweet sharp elbows and collarbones I could drink from and I need to get hold of myself.

Eyes still closed and I let my fingers flutter up one of her thighs.

I would open my eyes and the morning light would be thick and color-less, there would be no discernible shadows and I would blink and rub my sore blue mouth and look around for reckoning and resolution but resolu-tion was a daydream, a phantom construct. My fingers now fell upon her hipbone and drifted down the hollow slope between her belly and pubic hair and for the first time I wondered what time it was and part of me wanted to slip out of bed and disappear but I remembered what she had said in the dark, her breath cold and urgent as she said please, don't come inside me and I had tried not to, I had come everywhere else, on belly sheets and hair and part of me wanted to wake her now and make slow hungover love to her by daylight and without hesitation, I wanted to eat her alive but my teeth were sore from grinding and this was it. I was taking control.

There would be no one else's point of view, no one else's voice. I was going to end this and I couldn't deal with the drift anymore. I could no longer filter the thoughts of other characters. The sinister bend, the false angles of a body held underwater. The secrets. I never said I wanted to be a filter and I was pretty sure I was not good at it. I dragged my hand away from Eve's sleeping body and sat up, I opened my eyes. It was late morning and everything was faintly, unpleasantly yellow.

Okay.

I felt sick. This was a lot like a hangover but not. There was something wrong with my bones and my stomach felt inside out. I had what felt like a mouthful of rust, of bloodorange metal flakes. There was a small bathroom five, maybe ten feet away and I pushed myself away from the bed with relative arrogance then crawled the last few feet to the toilet, where I vomited quietly, painlessly. The contents of my belly were clear, gelatinous, nonthreatening. It was a pure morning. I sat cross-legged on a fuzzy white bathmat and regarded my bruised genitals from what felt like a terrifying distance.

Nausea.

I had a fantastic erection but now I doubted that Eve wanted to be molested this morning by me or anyone else and anyway my skin felt weirdly rigid, my body was fragile and unfamiliar and it would probably take forever to successfully masturbate and what I really wanted was to gather my clothes and go downstairs, I wanted to smell the air and figure out where the fuck I was.

Griffin was right. I had an uncanny craving for a shot of the Pale.

Muscles. It was a good thing they operated on their own, most of the time. I reclaimed my clothes and managed to dress myself without too much horror or difficulty. I kissed Eve on the lips and wondered briefly if either of us had tried to take the other's tongue last night and was happy to realize this was irrelevant.

Downstairs.

I was amazed to find cigarettes in one pocket, unsmashed. The night came back to me in funky disconnected flashes and it seemed I had been pretty high and still there was no lost time that I was aware of. False memory was possible but I didn't detect the lingering scent of overripe oranges, I didn't feel the reverse tug in my arms and legs that signified the artificial.

This was Dizzy Bloom's house, I knew that.

Dizzy was twenty-two or maybe twenty-nine, she was dark and small and pretty and possibly fictional but I believed she was real and I found her in the kitchen. It was bright and hot and Dizzy was on her hands and knees, she was scrubbing the floor in a wrinkled white dress, her nipples protruding through the material like little brown beans and I felt a sudden headache that seemed to originate in my mouth at the sight of her but then she seemed to be one of those women who was really not trying to fuck with your mind by not wearing a bra but simply wanted to be comfortable. I hung in the doorway for a moment, watching her. My jaw hurt and I suspected this was more a consequence of worry and stress than of drugs and the fragmentation of my senses.

Hello, I said.

Dizzy Bloom looked up and suddenly I knew why she had reached for my copy of *Ulysses* with such sadness last night. Today she was sober and damp with sweat and red-faced. She was irritated and a little fearful of the unknown but I clearly saw Molly Bloom in her. Dizzy was skinny but she had a dislocated heaviness about her, there was a fat unshaven woman in her who wanted to lounge too long in bed eating sweets, who had not yet found the love she wanted.

Hello, she said. Did you sleep well?

Too well.

I was fucking thirsty, I was made of sand. It was on the tip of my tongue to ask if there was any of the Pale but I squashed this question like an ugly green bug. Then shrugged.

Is there any of the Pale?

Dizzy gave me a certain look. The look of one addict who knows another and I tried to smile. I tried to show her all my teeth because while I instinctively wanted her to like me and trust me, I didn't much give a fuck. This wasn't a narcotics anonymous meeting.

Yes, she said. In the freezer.

I walked to the fridge and slung open the freezer door. One unmarked bottle of honey-white liquid, thick but not frozen. I looked at it but did not drink.

Okay, I said. Do you want to talk about what happened last night?

Not yet, she said.

I chomped at my tongue. I wanted to smoke five cigarettes at once.

Are you hungry? she said.

I stared at her, at her dark lips and mild, forgiving eyes. She still held a yellow sponge in one hand. The floor was glowing wet, rubbed to a spotless black and white. Her hands, though. Her hands were stained red from squeezing blood out of the sponge. My stomach twitched and I looked around at her kitchen. Two windows. A fishbowl with no fish and a lot of cookbooks. There were no modern appliances but there was a fond array of expensive knives and fine pots and pans that gleamed like silver. Dizzy Bloom was apparently childless and unmarried, a Breather who had somehow shorn herself of any real identity. I gazed at her now, my brain sore and dull. She probably had a trust fund and a degree from a posh university and was no doubt much smarter than me.

Who are you? I said.

Dizzy Bloom, she said. We met last night.

I know. But who are you?

What an archaic question.

No, I said. I'm not hungry.

Well, she said. There's a naked man on the roof.

A what?

The man who left his clothes in my living room, she said. Jimmy Sky.

Oh, I said. Oh, fuck.

I glanced down at myself, at my rumpled Ray Fine clothes. I hoped Jimmy would recognize me. I hoped someone would. Dizzy Bloom dipped her yellow sponge into a bucket of soapy water, she crushed it in her fist and resumed scrubbing the floor. I watched her and tried to think.

Well.

I had found Jimmy Sky without really trying and maybe the two of us should have a nice talk. I listened for Dizzy to murmur or sigh as I took the half-empty bottle of the Pale from the freezer. But she was silent, preoccupied with vanishing bloodstains. The cold bottle bit at my hands and I left the kitchen, intending to go outside. But instead veered down the hall, instinctively seeking a bathroom. I had been too busy throwing up earlier to give my psyche a proper shakedown. Now I locked the door behind me and peed, then turned to the mirror and stared. I didn't look much like myself and there was nothing I could do about Ray Fine's goofy clothes so I opened the medicine cabinet and saw that Dizzy had quite a few problems. She had a borderline personality, she had sleeplessness, she had seizures and a fuck of a lot of stress. She had bad dreams and psychotic episodes and while this was all very interesting I couldn't give it a lot of thought and for once I didn't want to drug myself. I wanted something more immediate and a pair of scissors jumped out at me. I breathed and thought about it and yes, I needed a haircut. I took one small sip of the Pale and stared cutting. The hair fell like dead leaves, random. I grabbed chunks of hair and cut them away without thinking of symmetry or logic, I slashed at my hair until the shape of my head pleased me and now I felt like myself.

I took the Pale and went outside. It was a nice day, sort of. It had the atmospheric freak show of seasons changing too close to the mountains. Green leaves winking back at me. Premature rosebuds and the possibility of a late snow made the sky appear farther away, a thin hostile blue. I walked backward over wet slick grass and scanned the roof and there, hunched next to a little brick chimney, was Detective Moon or Jimmy Sky, pink and shivering. Facing the sun with eyes closed.

I lifted the bottle of the Pale to my lips and drank but didn't swallow. I rinsed my mouth and spat into the grass, trying to decide how best to climb onto the roof. The one tree that stood alongside the house had long frail branches that extended to touch the rain gutters but that tree looked pretty dead. That tree was dead, boy. There were holes drilled into the bark where someone had poisoned it, probably because its roots were fucking with the foundation of the house. Those upper branches would hardly support a child. I was inclined to holler at Moon and ask how exactly he had gotten up there or even chuck a rock at him and bring him tumbling down but I doubted that I would be able to put him back together again if he shattered into a thousand bits of Moon. Again, I rinsed my mouth with the Pale, allowing myself to swallow a few drops. I stared up at Moon, who had begun to rock back and forth like an autistic kid.

Poor fucker needed help.

I walked around to the side of the house, looking for a ladder or some of that handy white scaffolding that young lovers always use to sneak in and out of bedrooms in the movies. I moved to the back of the house and saw an upstairs window that seemed to open onto a sloping lip of the roof and now I remembered Eve saying something as she was falling asleep about a strange gargoyle at our window.

Quickly back inside.

I stopped in the front room to grab Moon's crumpled pants and jacket. Took the cell phone from one pocket and patted down the others. Found a butterfly knife but nothing else: no wallet, no keys, no gun. I hoped Moon was not armed and told myself that naked guys are almost never armed because they have no pockets. But then again, I hadn't seen Moon's gun lying around anywhere, had I? Nothing I could do about it anyway. I slung Moon's pants over one shoulder like a scarf.

Eve was no longer in bed and I wondered if she was okay. If she had doubts about me. If she was standing now under the hot blast of a shower, scrubbing the stink of Phineas from her skin. I couldn't worry about it. The window wouldn't open so I calmly put my heel through it and tapped the remaining bits of glass from the frame, then stuck my head out and looked around.

The roof was steep with slick, balding shingles and I bent to unlace my boots. I slipped out of my socks and briefly considered stripping off all my clothes as Moon might feel more comfortable if we were both naked, but decided against it. I tucked the bottle of the Pale into my pants before climbing onto the roof. My bare toes gripped the rough surface and I

leaned sideways, scrambled to the peak and over. I angled up to Moon slow
and very joe casual, as if I had just happened along this way and maybe we
could wait for the bus together. I pulled the bottle from my crotch and sat
down beside the naked man without a word. We shared a moment of
silence. Dizzy Bloom had a pretty nice view and I felt like I could see three
sides of Denver.

I removed the pants from around my neck, dropped them in Moon's
lap.

Moon glanced sideways. Get away from me, Poe.

Put them on, I said. You will feel better with pants on.

Bright cold air. The tops of trees against blue. The side of Moon's
unsmiling face.

What did you do with that kid's body? he said.

Nothing. I just relocated it.

Why?

Why not?

He was killing cops, said Moon.

I shrugged the artificial cool. Part of the game, wasn't it.

He worked in a video store, said Moon. I knew him. I knew him. I
probably had fifty conversations with him. The kid knew a lot about
movies.

Moon made no movement to put his pants on but he did straighten
his legs briefly as he scratched an itch and I saw the barrel of his big .45
clutched between his thighs.

Hey, I said. You want to give me the gun?

The coo of stupid pigeons.

No, said Moon.

Who am I speaking to, by the way?

Moon hesitated, smiled. It was a wide, shit-eating smile that I didn't
recognize or like.

Jimmy? I said.

Moon shrugged. Yeah. We're both here, I guess.

I found you.

I didn't want to be found.

It wasn't hard, I said. Half the city can see your white ass.

What were you going to do when you found Jimmy Sky?

I don't know. I thought you wanted me to kill him.

Yeah.

Long cold breath and my lungs hurt. My ass was going to sleep and I really didn't want to wrestle Moon for the gun, not on this roof. I took a small sip of the Pale and offered it to Moon, who took it and held it up against the sky. He gazed at the liquid behind glass for a few heartbeats and I relaxed, reached for a cigarette, thinking: if Jimmy was high, he might be easier to deal with. But Moon upended the bottle and poured it out and I saw that his doglike brown eyes had become black in the last of the winter sun. The Pale was so thick it seemed to bead up and dart down the roof like a pack of silverfish.

Fuck, I said.

You're better off, said Moon.

For a moment, I saw myself scrambling down to the roof's edge. I saw myself trying to scoop up the disappearing Pale with my bare hands and I blinked as Moon smiled and swung the bottle at me in a slow flashing arc and I just managed to jerk my head down like a turtle and the bottle glanced off the top of my head and shattered against the chimney with a sudden white sparkle of raining glass and my eyes flickered shut again, involuntarily. I opened them and now had a good close look at Moon's big gun.

What are you doing, Moon? What are you doing? I said.

There was glass in my hair, down my shirt.

Moon sighed. I've been watching the birds. It's what rooftops are for, right. And these birds, they're just shitty brown city birds, sparrows or starlings or who the fuck knows and I keep hearing these doves but I can't see them. Anyway, I love the way these brown birds seem to vibrate, like their hearts are beating so hard and fast they might explode. And they don't even know it. They don't realize, they have no concept of self-destruction.

I nodded because I wanted to be friendly. I didn't much want to hear a schizophrenic birdman rant on the subject of what separates us from the beasts but Moon had the terrible glow in his eyes that said there was no stopping him.

The coolest thing, said Moon. The coolest thing is flight of course. To fly, right. Everyone wants to fly and I'm not going to jump if that's what you're thinking. I don't want two shattered legs, okay. I want to sleep. If anything, I want to sleep alone. But it's the way they float, they ride the currents. The thermals. They catch an updraft of warm air and just coast up to the sky and it's so effortless it's like they coexist with the fucking air. Can you imagine?

Meaning what? I said. That you want to coexist with yourself?

Moon swore softly and adjusted his crotch and I wished he would put his pants on. It would make this whole scene a little easier to take, I was sure.

I tried that, said Moon. I tried and tried.

Listen, I said. Let's go. Let's get off this roof, okay. Have some breakfast. Let's get out the yellow pages and find someone you can talk to, a private shrink or someone. Someone you can trust.

Is there some reason I shouldn't trust you?

No. I didn't say that.

Whatever. Do you like birds?

Whatever, I said. You know, I met someone yesterday who just about bit my head off for saying that word to him. Your partner, Lot McDaniel.

Moon clenched his fists. My partner.

Yeah. A dapper English guy.

You don't have a clue, do you.

What?

That fucker is running the game. He's the man behind the curtain.

Really. I swiped at my forehead, amazed that I was sweating in the cold.

Yeah, really. His name is Theseus the Glove.

I did think he was a trifle strange.

I've been meaning to kill him, said Moon. Or at least scare him. But he's evasive. He's smarter than me, he's smarter than Jimmy and what can I do. I'm just a Fred.

Let's go talk to him, I said. Fix his wagon.

Fuck you. You just want me down off this roof.

I shrugged.

And why? Why do you want me down and don't say it's because you care about me.

I worked my jaw, took a long look at the trees and sky. Okay, I said.

Thank you, said Moon. Because we both know it's bullshit. No one saves anyone else because they care so much. It's all about avoiding a mess.

Yes, I said. Your dead fat naked body would be a big mess in Dizzy's yard and I already dumped one body behind the Burger King so I can't go back there.

Dizzy, said Moon dreamily. He sighed. She's a peach, isn't she? She inspired me to buy a book, if you can believe that. A fat book with no guns or horses and so far I have only read a few pages. It's not something you can skate through while sitting on the toilet. I mean, it's not exactly a western even though Buck Mulligan sounds like the name of a deputy marshall.

Ulysses, I said.

You know it?

Vaguely.

Her great-grandmother is the main character, or something.

Not exactly, I said. But she does have a sexy monologue in the end.

Moon nodded. I met Dizzy Bloom yesterday and she looked right through me. She's a real honey.

A honey, I said. And she's in the kitchen right now, she's cleaning up blood.

I saw her last night, said Moon. She didn't recognize me and besides, she seemed pretty sweet on that little elfboy, that Breather.

Let's go inside, I said. Inside, okay.

Hey, fuck you. I saw you last night, said Moon. You were slipping it to that other little chick, that torturer. Did you tell her your real name?

I nodded. That was Eve, I said. She knows me.

Remember when you were a kid, said Moon. You always wished you were someone else: Tom Sawyer or Billy the Kid or Pistol Pete Maravich or even some cooler smarter faster kid you knew in school.

Yeah. I wanted to be Han Solo.

It's fun to be someone else, said Moon. Until you can't stop being them.

I held my breath and released it slowly through my teeth and I don't know. I think what I felt was sympathy. It was all I had.

I know, I said. Everything gets fucked up in the end.

Fucked up. Moon laughed.

Uh-huh. Why don't you give me the gun?

Moon shook his head. Get off this roof, Poe. Unless you want to get shot.

Nobody broke your heart, I said.

He smiled. I know. I broke it myself so why don't you fuck off. Disappear.

What are you going to do?

I don't know. I'm gonna have a little heart to heart with myself, I guess.

Moon or Jimmy laughed and rolled his eyes, rubbing his belly with the free hand. I felt like my eyeballs were sweating. I was staring at Moon's unsteady trigger finger. His whole hand seemed to be vibrating and the gun was going to go off, soon. I backed away as carefully as I had come.

Okay, I said. Do you mind if I call for an ambulance?

Moon shrugged. Go ahead.

I continued to edge backward, dropping to my belly now.

Do me a favor, I said.

What's that, said Moon.

Put your pants on, please.

Moon grinned and fired a single shot into the air. I bit the side of my cheek and tasted blood. If one of the neighbors hadn't called the cops already, they would surely do so now. I slithered wormlike down the other side of the roof and back through the window. Breathing, I counted to ten. I sat on the edge of Dizzy Bloom's big cozy guest bed and put my boots back on. I sniffed the air. It did smell like Eve had taken a shower. Her clothes were gone and the bed was made. I couldn't remember if it had still been disheveled before I went out to talk to the mad birdman and I just wished she was near me. Really the worst thing about being alone was that there was never anyone to turn to and say: hey that was fucking weird, wasn't it? I took out Moon's cell phone and turned it on.

Wonders never ceased for the battery still held a charge.

I found the cream-colored and very nicely engraved business card that McDaniel had given me the day before. The snotty bastard answered on the tenth ring, his voice dry and very British.

Cough. McDaniel.

Hello, sir. Detective McDaniel?

Yes.

This is Ray Fine. We met yesterday.

Forced warmth. I remember.

You said for me to call you tomorrow and here it is, tomorrow.

Pause. Crackle and hum.

Indeed, it does look like tomorrow. What can I do for you Mr. Fine?

I have some information for you about Moon, or about who might have killed him. I guess there's a nut running around out there killing cops.

Oh, well. Yawn. Anything you can tell me would help.

The killer's name is Theseus, I said. I don't know if that's his first name or last name or what but I figure he's a Greek guy. Doesn't that sound Greek to you?

I suppose so, said McDaniel.

Is there a Greek Mafia in this town, that you know of?

No, he said.

His voice was getting pretty frosty and I smiled.

Whatever, I said. He's definitely your guy.

Hmmm. Where did you come by this information?

Very reliable source. A fellow named Jimmy Sky.

McDaniel snorted. Jimmy Sky, did you say?

That's right.

And where is this person? I might like to ask him a few questions.

He's outside. Having a smoke.

Do you think you could entice him to come downtown?

Maybe. Will you buy us breakfast?

But of course.

You might regret that, I said. I can eat a stack of pancakes the size of your head.

I'm sure you can.

Do you have an expense account?

No, I don't.

Are you dirty? I said. Because dirty cops on TV always get free breakfast.

Mr. Fine, please. Let me give you an address. Do you have something to write on?

I have the back of my hand, I said.

And I managed not to flinch when McDaniel gave me the address. I didn't have to write it down. I knew it already. Griffin's office.

Have you got that, then?

Perfectly, I said.

Very good. I shall see you in oh, a half-hour or so.

Cheerio.

McDaniel grunted and hung up. I exhaled. There was something wrong with me and I couldn't seem to stop smiling. Maybe the universe was okay. I hesitated, then reluctantly dialed 911. Again, I identified myself as Ray Fine. I told the female operator that I had a friend on the roof suffering a psychotic episode. Dangerous to himself and others. The operator said not to worry, they had already received three reports of a naked sniper and the cops were on their way. I choked back an obscenity and told her calmly that he was no sniper. I told her the cops would only spook him and asked her to send an ambulance, a fire truck.

I knew they would send a carload of cops, no matter what I said.

But I told the operator five times that the subject was a cop, that he was armed and he would very likely resist. I suggested that they bring a net, maybe a tranquilizer gun. The operator told me not to worry and I said I would give it a try. I hung up and glanced at the clock by the bed. The average response time was nine minutes but it was early. It was Saturday morning. I would give them six and I hoped to god I was gone before they showed.

Moon, I said. I'm sorry about this.

Downstairs and I barely recognized anyone. It was like the mothership had touched down in my absence and reclaimed the pods. Dizzy Bloom had tangled her hair into a complicated bun. Her face was different, too. Dark lipstick and round little steel-framed glasses. They were much nicer than Ray's glasses. She wore jeans and a black cardigan sweater and she was reading a newspaper, a cup of tea or coffee in her left hand. The swirl of steam around her face. There was a plate of bagels on the table and now she put down her coffee and reached for the cream cheese. A young man with a very serious posture sat across from her, smoking an unfiltered cigarette and staring intently at the screen of a laptop computer. Thin blond hair pulled into a severe ponytail and no jewelry. Expensive white dress shirt with cuffs buttoned, dark green twill pants and black shoes. If I was not mistaken, this was Mingus. His eyes were bright and not the least bit psychotic as he smiled and held out his hand.

Hello, said Mingus. I don't think we've met. I'm Matthew Roar.

Okay, I said. I'm Phineas.

We shook hands and I looked as far as I could into the man's face, his mouth and eyes. There was no hint that this was part of the game.

And you know my wife, I believe. Dizzy Bloom, he said.

You two are married, I said.

Dizzy smiled, a cruel flash. I kept my maiden name, she said.

Uh-huh.

I looked sideways and saw Eve. And I knew her, I recognized her. I had seen her in multiple incarnations and this was but another one. She wore black boots and white stockings and a silky black skirt with a thin blue sweater that she must have borrowed from Dizzy because the skirt was sexy but much too collegiate and the sweater was a little too small. There was a white line of flesh at her hips between sweater and skirt and the sleeves were too short. Her hair was tucked behind her ears and she held a coffee mug in both hands. She was blowing on it with pale puckered lips, staring at me.

You look nice, I said.

She flinched. Thanks.

I went to the stove and poured myself a cup of coffee that was hot and black as death and smelled of cinnamon and chicory. I sipped it carefully as Dizzy picked up a pencil and began to examine the crossword. Matthew was bent over his laptop, which now made a happy chirping sound to indicate that he had mail. I nodded. Dizzy and Matthew were not fucking kidding about this game of tongues. Their characters were so divorced from their real identities that they were probably going slowly but surely clinical. But I had a feeling they knew it was over. They must. Their friend had died in their kitchen last night and they were calmly eating bagels and cream cheese and they were probably sorry they had no smoked salmon to offer us but their worlds were going to crash soon. The cops were coming and I was tempted not to warn them. Eve came over to stand next to me.

Do you have a cigarette, she said.

I gave her one. I want you to come downtown with me, I said.

Okay. Why?

I have an errand to run. And I don't think you want to be here.

She lit her cigarette at the stove, careful not to set her hair on fire.

Why? she said.

Because the cops are coming.

Dizzy Bloom looked up. Do you know a six-letter word for "dark"?

Opaque, I said.

Thank you.

Did you hear me?

What? she said.

The cops are on the way. Two minutes, maybe three and they're in your living room.

What do they want?

I shrugged. Madman on your roof.

Dizzy smiled and nodded. Of course.

I felt hot, irritable. I poured the rest of my coffee down the sink and yes, I wished there was more of the Pale. The others were so fucking unflustered, like robots. Something was very wrong with them. They were all supposed to be junkies, right. Confused. Out of touch with reality. I looked at them and thought maybe they weren't real, maybe they were only pretending to be normal people for my benefit. I wiped at my face and told myself I had one minute left.

Eve and I are going, I said.

Will you be back for lunch?

No. I don't think so.

Matthew looked up and there was a trace of something like sadness around his mouth. I hesitated. The sun was coming through the windows and I could hear sirens in the distance and I realized I was going to miss the little Breather. I bit at my tongue and wondered when Chrome would walk in wearing a T-shirt and sweatpants, hungover and slack-jawed with ordinary life and carrying a basketball under one arm.

Do you want to shoot some hoops, he would say.

Dear Jude.

I have no soul inside, only gray matter.

I think *Ulysses* is finally getting to me. I jumped ahead to the end, to Molly Bloom's melancholy monologue and after two pages of somber cock-sucking and the philosophy behind the mixing of urine and menstrual blood, I was freaking out. The physical details are heavy of course but pretty casual by modern standards. The consumptive nature of her voice, though. It's like cancer. Her voice is relentless and unwavering as a slow-burning fire. I can't read that shit anymore. Okay. I understand that Joyce was trying to re-create the random sound and fury of a human mind at work but I'm not sure why he would want to.

Painful and blinding. Trapped in the wheels of another's thoughts.

And moreover I'm not sure why Dizzy would choose such a tragic character to be her number one ancestor. Molly Bloom suffers a lot of weird and profound indignities as the object of her husband's whim. Leopold asks her to walk barefoot in horseshit as a kind of demented foreplay and when she is fat with milk he begs her to let him squeeze a few drops into his tea. And he torments her in the end with the seemingly innocent request for breakfast in bed which now strikes me as a truly frightening though nonaggresive act of marital sadism and I wonder if Dizzy truly hates Matthew Roar for being weak and virtuous and kind to her and maybe she wishes for a physically grotesque man like Leopold Bloom. If she wishes for someone like Moon, like Jimmy Sky.

A horse named Throwaway, I said. Throwaway.

Are you okay, said Eve.

No.

The belly wail of sirens were close and getting closer and they might as well have been inside my head. I grabbed Eve by her small hand and squeezed it, the bones moving beneath her skin fragile and rubbery like the ribs of a bird and I only hoped she wanted to come with me. That she wouldn't resist or pull away because I needed her and was not sure how or why, but I did. It wasn't that I was particularly afraid but I had no plan, no idea what I would say to McDaniel. Maybe she could help me there. She apparently had some higher knowledge of torture and not to change the subject but part of me was happy, I was happy that Goo had not slept with Ray Fine, for instance. Although that might have been the least frightening and strange of all the possible combinations.

Outside and I pulled her across the backyard. Jimmy might have become sweaty and agitated by the sound of the sirens and I imagined he was up there flapping his naked arms like an angry crow and I didn't want him taking any potshots at us. One of the more annoying voices in my skull proclaimed that we should stick around and see him through this but I disagreed. Because you can only save yourself, right.

Yourself.

Running. Wet grass.

I told myself not to crush Eve's fingers because she wasn't resisting, she was light as a shadowpuppet and she followed me without a word through the back gate and across a curve of gravel and suddenly I knew that I wanted to have another look at Chrome's body because after that little scene in Dizzy's kitchen it seemed more and more likely that his death was just a crooked line in the script, a typographical error.

He's dead, said Eve. Her voice was sharp.

What?

Christian, she said. You're wondering if he's really dead.

Come on, I said.

I pulled her across the vacant lot, ignoring the little path. I was pretty sure by now that he would be reclining beside one of those blue Dumpsters, that he would be a blood-stained but unusually handsome homeless man. He would be scratching his jaw and dazedly contemplating his ruined clothes and wondering what exactly he had been up to last night. I pulled her across the parking lot, slower now.

The only footsteps were our own.

The parking lot stretched before us like the sky and suddenly we were upon him. His body was where we had left it, stiff and gathering flies.

Eve sucked in her breath.

I didn't need that, she said.

Oh, fuck.

Yeah.

It was a stupid idea, of course. I had carried him here just a few hours earlier and he had been cold and dead in my arms, he could have been a posterboy for death but dream and game and daylight had seemed so readily interchangeable that anything should have been possible. Eve backed away, one hand over her nose.

He stinks, she said.

That's the garbage, I said.

But that was a fucking lie and why did I want to lie to her.

Yeah, I said. He stinks.

Eve wrinkled her nose and I saw how pretty and young she was without Goo's face tangled up around her own. It would be inappropriate to kiss her now, standing over her dead boyfriend's body like this. The air ripe with his gasses. But I wanted to kiss her.

Let's move him into the Dumpster, she said.

Why? I said.

The cops will want to ask me a lot of questions. Won't they?

Probably. You're the girlfriend.

If we move him, maybe they won't find him today.

I stood there nodding like a dummy and it wasn't that I disagreed with her. Eve was right, of course. I had no idea why I had left him exposed like this. He should be moved and there wasn't a lot of time to stand around talking about it but I wasn't sure I wanted to touch him again.

He had such a pretty face, pale and puffy even as it was in death.

I made sure the Dumpster was not padlocked and threw open its jaws with a screech of metal that would send the rats running for shelter. I hoped that a pimply kid in Burger King brown wasn't on his way out with an armload of rotten buns and meat even though I could probably use his help.

The dead are heavy, after all.

I lit a cigarette and took two quick puffs, then gave it to Eve. I stepped over the body and without pausing to let myself freak out or feel sorry for him, bent down and sunk my hands into the soft fleshy pockets of his armpits. I dragged him up to a rubbery standing position and danced him over to the blue Dumpster and his knees dipped and buckled comically as I slipped one hand between his legs and got a firm grip on his crotch. I lifted and tried to throw him over the side of the Dumpster but I was too short or he was too heavy or something because he tumbled down on top of me and favored me with a damp, gruesome embrace.

Eve didn't laugh and for that I thought she was pretty cool.

Help me, I said.

And she didn't balk or hesitate at all. Eve locked her teeth together and held her breath as she lifted one end of the body. She was grim and almost smiling as she held him by the feet and I wondered how many times she had watched him tie the laces of those boots. Together we managed to sling him up and over and into the Dumpster and two minutes later while she crouched in the shadows wondering if she was going to vomit, I climbed in and covered her boyfriend's body with trash.

But first I patted him down for cigarettes, money, weapons.

Eve finished retching, or gave up trying. Now she walked quickly away from me, across the parking lot. I climbed out of the Dumpster feeling about as clever as a drunk raccoon. The stink of French fries in my clothes and hair. I followed her, glad to see she was not walking back to Dizzy's house.

Jimmy was on the roof, naked and angry.

I hoped the paramedics would be able to talk him down. I hoped we wouldn't hear screams or gunfire. I hoped we wouldn't hear the deadening silence that meant he had fallen. I followed Eve to a little plastic igloo that housed a pale green bench with the names of a hundred assholes gouged in the wood. I sat two or three feet away from her. I hoped there was a bus coming.

Do you want to talk about it? I said.

About what, she said. About Christian being dead, or last night?

I shoved my hands in my pockets to stop myself from scratching at my skin.

Either, I said.

No. I don't know.

Across the street a young man with a bullet-shaped head leaned out of a window and yelled at a barking dog. I looked up and down the street for something to focus on, something to talk about that wasn't dripping with realism.

Eve was an arm's length away, her hands restless on her knees. Her face pale and sober. She tugged at the hem of her borrowed skirt, as if it wasn't quite comfortable. I wanted to comfort her but I was too clumsy. And I felt like I was fading, I was blurry and unreliable. I was suffering a transporter malfunction, a pixel error. Every inch of my skin was shimmering. I wanted to take off my shirt and ask her to scratch a maddening itch down the middle of my back but I told myself the itch was not real.

The itch was not real.

I'm sure he deserved it, she said. And I didn't love him, if that's what you think.

Empty hands.

No, I said. I don't think that. But what's the difference?

I liked having sex with him, she said. Or my character did. But I think that when someone you love dies, you should feel something unbearable. You should feel crushed and lost and you shouldn't be able to breathe.

The bullet-shaped head came through the window and yelled at the barking dog to shut the fuck up.

And how do you feel, I said.

I need a bath, she said. And I think I have food poisoning.

That's bad enough.

I can breathe, she said. How do you feel?

Unpleasantly awake. Frustrated, empty. I want to get high.

You were a cop, she said.

Not a very good one, I said. And it was a long time ago. It was an alternate universe.

That Fred, she said. He said Christian was killing cops.

I stared at her. And?

Isn't that supposed to make you insane?

I shrugged. This isn't television, right. No one likes their coworkers to get killed and obviously it's scary when someone shoots a cop because it means they are much crazier than the average crazy person but I never swallowed that Hollywood notion that a cop's life is worth more to me than a bike messenger's or a drug dealer's or a homosexual dogwalker's. A lot of cops are bitter assholes and they can't wait to fuck you, to rob you blind and shit on you. And so are a lot of bike messengers. I don't know any dog walkers but they can't all be nice people. Meanwhile a lot of drug dealers are just guys who like cartoons and fast food and they have kids and dogs and student loans and they're basically harmless so the answer must be no, I don't particularly give a fuck.

No, I said. I don't give a fuck.

And what about last night? she said.

A bird flashed across the horizon of my brain, a speckled brown blur of words too raw and strange to be spoken aloud.

It was fantastic, I said. It scared the shit out of me.

I don't think it was real, she said.

Eve was chewing at her lip and the muscles in her throat were killing me. Her nipples were visibly hard and her thighs were long and slim and perfect in those white stockings. I felt like Humbert. I rubbed at my eyes, disgusted. I leaned close enough to kiss her but she turned and my lips brushed her cheek like a brother's. I am a suicidal romantic, or I was at that moment. I wanted to tell her it's never real.

Doubt, I said. It's everywhere, it's all around us. You can't see it or smell it but it's there.

Yeah, she said sourly. Like oxygen.

Do you want to try again? I said.

Eve's mouth was crooked and sweet, her eyes cloudy. She didn't have to say anything. I knew the answer was yes, she wanted to. But we wouldn't.

Here comes a bus, she said.

Yeah. Where's it going, though?

Dead cops meant nothing to me. I didn't know them and so they were just names, faces. They were characters in a movie that I wasn't watching. I was eleven years old when *Star Wars* came out and I have rarely been more shocked and heartbroken than when Obi-Wan Kenobi was killed but I had the distinct feeling that she wanted to get off the subject so I stood up as the big silver bus approached, rattling and heaving. The brakes moaned with the familiar whispering metallic sigh that echoed too long and always made me think there were people being tortured in the bowels of the thing. It was going downtown, at least. I wondered if I would see that blind guy again, the one that was tormented by his tongue. I fucking hoped not, because he did seem like the sort who rode the bus for days and days without stopping, from one end of the line to another. Eve took my hand and climbed aboard first, then turned to look at me with eyes wrinkled and amused.

No money, she said.

Oh. I forgot about money.

I dug around in Ray Fine's pockets and came up with a sticky wad of bills. The driver extracted two singles and gravely told me to take a seat.

The bus was mostly empty and we found seats near the middle, near the center of gravity. I wanted to tell Eve that I have black-and-white night-mares about buses and I think they have something to do with the movie *Metropolis*. I have this recurring vision that I will wake up one day to find myself standing in a long line of black-faced men and women in dark, con-servative clothes waiting to board an unmarked bus that will take us to hell and when I first pass the driver he seems normal enough but when he turns around his face is a skull with patches of raw skin and empty holes where the eyes should be and when the doors hiss shut I know they will never open again, not until we arrive in the first ring of hell.

I sat beside Eve, our legs touching. I liked the way she pressed her knees together, the way she picked restlessly at the thin stockings she wore under her borrowed skirt. I didn't know what to do with my hands, either. I wanted a cigarette, of course. Eve took my right hand and held it in her lap, she trapped it there like a nervous kitten and I laughed.

You're manic, she said.

The shakes, I said. But no worries.

Yeah.

Eve shrugged and turned to look out the window. I nodded, admiring the harsh line of her jaw. The uneven color of her cheeks. I met her a little over a year ago, when she was nineteen, when she was so unpleasantly sexy it left me stupid and weak.

If you saw her in a grocery store, stalking through the dairy section in jeans and army boots and a T-shirt that said she was tough and fragile and fully capable of fucking you to tears, you would sigh and clutch your belly as if kicked and duck down the frozen foods aisle. Because you would want to follow her, you would want to see what she was buying and you would want to get another good look at her in the odd shadowless supermarket light but you really couldn't stand it and instead you would buy ice cream that you didn't need. Eve was a year older now and she didn't quite para-lyze me. Don't get me wrong. My jaw ached a little yet, looking at her. But I was a year older, too. I was relatively unchanged. I was a year closer to dying of lung cancer. The bus wheezed to a stop but no one got off. There was a tickle along the back of my neck and I looked up. The driver was peering at someone on the sidewalk.

Well, he said. You getting on or not?

There was no answer and the driver moved to shut the doors.

Hold it, chief.

I recognized that voice and could only stare as Jimmy Sky's round head heaved into view. Moon but not Moon. He stood alongside the driver, swaying slightly as he dug through his pockets and managed to come up with a dollar bill, which he pressed flat against his chest before surrendering. Jimmy was shirtless, barefoot. His belly jutting over the waistband of the white pants.

I glanced at Eve, who didn't blink.

Money, she said. It's something you forget about, in the game.

Yeah, I said. I imagine a lot of things are like that.

Jimmy ambled heavily down the aisle, staggering as the bus lurched forward. He caught hold of a safety bar overhead and hung there a moment, panting. I tried to catch his eye but he stared through me.

Your head is screwed on wrong, said Eve. Everything looks strange. The stuff that seems so important to your other self, your daylight self, is just funny. You wonder how you ever believed in anything. But then your character starts to run wild and you get almost homesick for reality.

Jimmy Sky regained his balance and continued down the aisle. His eyes were calm but his breathing was so loud it seemed deafening to me. Wind through dead trees. Moon might have been a giant talking frog and he would have looked just as strange to me. Now he passed without a flicker.

You feel like you're disappearing, said Eve. Your daylight self is like a little kid who fell down a well. You can hear her voice down there in the dark but it seems faraway and weak and you don't know how to get her out. You want to throw her a rope but you can't be bothered or something.

I glanced over my shoulder to see that Jimmy had found a seat in the very last row. He was wedged between two sinewy black men who wore gang colors and had the feral eyes of dogs that kill their own. They were somehow unoffended by Jimmy and I shook my head, thinking, but he must smell like death. How can they tolerate him?

Eve poked me. Are you listening, she said.

My thoughts flailed. I am…yes. What is she like? I said.

Who?

Goo, I said.

She's a lot like me, said Eve. Only better. Goo has no morals, no inhibitions. She can step outside herself and use her body like it's a piece of machinery.

How is that better?

Eve shrugged and said, Goo is an Exquisitor.

Which means what, I said. Exactly.

It means that she can extract emotions from people that they don't realize they possess.

Isn't that what happened last night?

Eve frowned. Goo isn't nearly as selfish or paranoid as I am. And she's still here. She's not going to just go to sleep and disappear.

Really, I said. That's…comforting.

Eve breathed into my right ear and I flinched as if bitten.

What about you, she said. Did you have a character in the game?

Oh, yeah. I was a Fred named Ray. For about eight hours, anyway.

What was he like?

Ray? I said. He was a great fucking fool, a fearless idiot. He was a lot like me.

Eve giggled. And what happened to him?

Nothing happened to him. I made fun of his hair and stole his clothes and treated him like dirt and he just fucked off after a while.

I like his clothes, she said.

Aren't these nice?

You should be doing magic tricks for spare change.

I don't know any tricks.

Everybody's dying, she said. Just pick a disease.

I wasn't sure what she meant by that, but I liked the idea. I resisted the urge to glance back at Jimmy. I couldn't protect him and I doubted that he wanted me to. I doubted that he knew my name. I let my eyes flutter shut and soon I disappeared and daydreamed. I tried and failed to synchronize my breathing with the seasick rumble and drone of the bus.

Eve squeezed my thigh. Be careful, she said. You don't want to fall asleep.

Why not?

You might wake up and not know who you are.

Imagine that.

It isn't funny, she said.

Okay. Tell me about Mingus and Dizzy, I said.

What about them?

Are they really married, for instance?

They're separated, said Eve. But that's her real name.

Oh, well. That explains everything.

Today was a big day for them, she said. Those two never step out of character. And why would they want to. Look at them. Mingus and Dizzy are much more fun to be with than Matthew and Dizzy.

This was making my head hurt.

You truly become someone else, she said. You lose your previous self. You amputate it. I know a few gamers who have faked their own deaths and never gone back.

Moon. The poor bastard. I glanced over my shoulder and saw that Jimmy was staring straight ahead, grinning. The two black men had abandoned their seats and now stood in the aisle, their faces watchful and distressed. Jimmy had spooked them, apparently. I turned to Eve.

And then what happens? I said.

Eve shrugged. You live in the game. You gather tongues and drink the Pale. You act out complicated plots scripted by your Glove. You accumulate points.

But what do the points mean? I said. What do you get in the end?

Nothing, really. I suppose you can improve your power and status but the class system within the game is so rigid that mostly you try to stay alive. If your tongue is taken sixteen times, then your character dies. You become a wetbrain, a shadowfred.

A shadowfred?

Eve nodded. A dead character. You're too weak and disoriented to reenter the game and too fucked-up to go back to reality. It's really very sad. The Mariners hunt the wetbrains for sport, even though their tongues are worthless.

Whose tongue is the most valuable?

A Glove's, obviously. But no one would try to take one.

Why not?

Punishment, she said. The punishment would be severe.

The bus shivered but did not stop. I wanted a cigarette. If the bus didn't stop soon I might put my hand through the window.

Of course, I said. How is the game different from life, then?

Eve laughed, uneasily. I held onto her hand.

The city was two-dimensional behind shatterproof glass. It flattened out like stock footage that's been used one too many times. I wanted off the fucking bus. The *Metropolis* dream was twisting around in my little brain and I was having difficulty breathing but eventually we came to a stop downtown that was within walking distance of Griffin's office. It did occur to me that I didn't have to go there at all. Eve and I could go have breakfast and talk about tomorrow and maybe go over to her apartment and check the walls for unwanted portals. But I had a feeling that it wouldn't matter which direction we took when we stepped from the bus. We could walk north or south and we would still arrive at Griffin's building.

The bus stopped and the doors whooshed open.

This is it, I said. This is our stop.

Eve stood up to go but I just sat there.

Are you sure? she said.

Yeah, I said finally.

I followed her down the aisle and hesitated at the steps. Jimmy would get off with us, surely. But when I looked back, he was reading a newspaper.

Oblivion, I thought. The destruction of self. I imagine it feels good.

Eve and I didn't hold hands on the sidewalk. There was no one about and the air fairly buzzed with silence. It was early, I guess. Or maybe it was just one of those lost Saturdays, one of those blank days where the color of light never changes from morning until dusk. The sky was on hold. Time and weather were nonexistent and it was like half the city was unconscious.

Griffin's building soon loomed against the empty sky and as we approached the dark reflecting glass doors, I wondered what we would do if they were locked. But the doors weren't locked and I stupidly told myself not to be surprised that the lawyers and other pinstripe types who had offices here would be working on the sixth day. How else would they get ahead. I held the door open for Eve and let her go in first, which meant she was between me and McDaniel when he stepped out from behind a big artificial plant with a gun in hand.

Theseus, she said. Her voice brittle.

If it isn't little Goo, he said. I love your disguise.

Her shoulders went stiff. What's that supposed to mean?

Nothing, pet. Nothing at all. I'm sure you have made quite the victim of this one.

Oh, shut the fuck up.

Ouch, he said.

And by the way, she said. My name is Eve and Goo is as good as dead.

McDaniel was glowing, he was so smug. And he looked very elegant in what appeared to be a deerskin suit. I don't know. It could have been human skin. He wore a tiny ruby stud in his left ear and his teeth were obnoxiously crooked and white when he smiled. I looked around for the security guard who had eyeballed me so nastily the other day but the lobby was white and silent as the moon.

McDaniel coughed. I relieved him of duty, he said. Official police business.

Thank God.

He shrugged and pulled a square key on a brass ring from his breast pocket. One eye on us and the gun held high, he inserted the key into a lock on the wall and turned. I could only assume the doors we had just come through were now electronically locked and the alarm system activated.

Where is Mr. Sky? he said.

Indisposed.

His teeth flashed. A poor choice, he said.

I shrugged. Eve was furious and I was very sorry that I hadn't told her who we were coming to see.

McDaniel waved the gun impatiently. Come along, then.

Eve shrugged and threw me a shivering glance that said she wasn't afraid, exactly. But she wasn't too thrilled about this. And without waiting for me to blink she turned on her heel and walked to the elevators. McDaniel frisked me quickly and seemed unsurprised to find that I wasn't carrying a gun. He took away my knife though, and Moon's copy of *Ulysses*, which he tossed sideways with a snarl of disgust. The book hit the marble floor with a tremendous echoing crash and slid to rest against an emergency exit door. He left me with the blue notebook, a pack of ciga-rettes, what little cash I had and Ray Fine's yellow-tinted glasses. There was no reason for him to prod me along with the gun at my ribs, and so we walked to the elevators side by side, like friends. McDaniel was a few inches taller than me and he smelled sweet as a clump of freshly killed flowers.

Eve had already pressed the Up button and she fidgeted against the wall, looking much like a restless and sullen teenager. The slash of her dark eyes and hair hanging forward. All she needed was a mouthful of gum to pull into a pink tangle between her fingers and lips and whatever McDaniel was thinking, I wanted nothing more than to let her go home. Eve was tired, she had done nothing to deserve this. The elevator would be there any minute and if I was going to do something it would have to be quick and very fucking fancy. McDaniel stood two or three feet to my left, his body at a slight angle so that he could watch both of us. The gun dangled in his right hand, against his thigh. I looked at his eyes and he was completely focused on Eve; on her slim white thighs and the line of exposed flesh at her narrow waist; on her firm little tits. The motherfucker. He was no weakling but he was tall and thin and likely had a poor sense of balance and I thought I could probably kick his legs out from under him and drop him like a scarecrow made of rubber bands and sticks, but if he didn't drop the gun he would easily shoot me in the face as I tried to jump on him and gouge out his eyes. And he looked like he had a fair grip on the gun. I glanced at Eve and as strong as she was I thought she was too far away to help much. What I wanted to do was kick the gun out of his hand and hit him in the throat with some kind of karate chop, or bite it off. As long as he dropped the gun, and Eve came up with it, everything would be cool. I would have a mouthful of blood but Eve could go home and take a bath or check into a hotel, order room service and figure out how to pay for it later. And she could seek a little psychological help. The two of us could even check into rehab together. A day and a half on the Pale and my own morphine problem had developed new legs.

Anyway.

All of this nonsense flickered through my head in the space of two seconds and as I was sucking in a deep breath and getting myself ready to launch a sideways boot at his gun, McDaniel turned and raised his right hand and I was looking down the thing's dark steel nostril. McDaniel smiled and a soft bell chimed to indicate that the elevator had arrived.

I backed away from him, into the mirrored chamber. Eve beside me, silent. McDaniel stepped through the doors and told me to push the button for the sixteenth floor. I resisted a smart-ass temptation to push every button, as I was reluctant to annoy him in such close quarters.

The box began its ascent.

You aren't very clever, he said. Are you?

No, I said.

McDaniel produced a set of handcuffs and gave them to me.

Who are these for?

He grinned. They're for her, he said.

I didn't move. What's up?

McDaniel hit me in the ear with the barrel of his gun, not so hard. But hard enough that I found myself on one knee with butterflies and ringing telephones in my head. Four or five crumpled helpless reflections of myself in the mirrors around me. The elevator abruptly stopped in midair and hung there like a bomb waiting to fall and I guessed that he had slapped the red emergency button, which might well account for some of the ringing noise. Eve's face hovered into view and the chickenshit voice that does a lot of the talking in my skull at times like these began to howl and cry the word *bait*.

This was a trap and Eve was the bait.

Oh, me.

Eve pulled me to my feet and held one finger before my eyes.

One, I said. I could still count, by God.

She smiled and moved the finger back and forth and I suppose my eyes were still tracking because she looked relieved. The handcuffs were heavy in my left hand and I was ready to drop them when McDaniel told me to look sharp and cuff her to the handrail. In the far corner, away from the fucking buttons.

Both hands, please.

I sighed and felt my skin turn gray with rage and I wondered if he would actually shoot us if I refused but Eve suddenly pecked at my cheek, a sweet dry kiss and two whispered words.

It's okay, she said.

And so I clamped one metal ring around her right wrist and pulled the second one up and under the rail and locked the other wrist so that her hands were behind her back.

Perfect, said McDaniel.

What are you going to do? said Eve.

I don't know, said McDaniel. I really don't know.

He stepped close to me and pressed his mouth to my cheek in almost exactly the same spot where she had just kissed me and I wondered if he could taste her on my skin.

Don't worry, he said. After I've finished with your friend, I will come back for you. And I might amuse myself with you further, or I might just take you home. I might take you to Lady Adore and let her punish you in a really interesting way.

I'm not going back, said Eve. I'm finished, Goo was finished.

McDaniel chortled. Quite right, he said.

Adore will let me run, she said.

He shook his head. You don't know her very well.

I was anxious. And growling, I realized. I sounded exactly like a para-noid dog and so I lit a cigarette, reasoning that it might calm my nerves and that it would certainly be to our advantage if a fire alarm went off. McDaniel was not stupid, however. He slapped the butt from my mouth and crushed it under his heel. He stroked my cheek with the barrel of his gun and I flinched. The pain was irrelevant and I wouldn't mind so much if he hit me again but I was afraid I would be unable to stand up if I suffered any more damage to my inner ear.

You like her, he said. Don't you?

I didn't move or speak. I had a bad feeling.

Why not give her a kiss, he said. On the mouth.

I hesitated, then stepped close and kissed Eve's lips.

Very nice, said McDaniel. But quite dull.

Fuck you, I whispered.

Yes, he said. Later, perhaps. But now I want you to slip your right hand up her skirt and give her box a squeeze. And don't let go.

I turned in circles and the mirrors were bright. There were bits and pieces of me in every corner.

Quickly now, he said.

Four or five versions of myself. I slipped my hand under Eve's skirt and cupped her pussy like a peach that I would hate to bruise and she was hot, in fact. She was wet. I stared into her face and told myself to think of garbage and black flies, dead fish and horseshit. I told myself not to get hard, not to get hard because an erection would only rob my brain of useful blood and make me dumber than ever. If that was possible. Eve's mouth twitched slightly and she moved her hips to push against my hand and I was hard as can be.

And now with the other hand, said McDaniel. Tickle her titties.

That's enough, I said. Motherfucker.

McDaniel sighed. Oh, all right. This is just for fun. But I do want you to kiss her again, and this time please force her mouth open and take her tongue.

He doesn't need to take it, said Eve.

Take it, said McDaniel.

My reflection was in fragments and part of me was enjoying this. If I had to come back from the dead to hurt McDaniel for this, I would try. But for now I bent and kissed her again, my mouth open. Eve allowed me to bite her tongue, and I offered my tongue to her. She bit it just enough to draw blood. I felt dizzy and realized my hand was still tucked against her crotch like a glove and the fingers were moving. I pulled away and McDaniel laughed, apparently satisfied. He hit the red button and we continued up to the sixteenth floor. I kissed Eve once more, for luck. I wanted to promise her I would come back for her but was afraid it would sound false and much too dramatic.

I hope you aren't claustrophobic, said McDaniel.

Not at all, she said.

McDaniel motioned for me to remove myself from the elevator. I backed away from Eve and stood between the doors to stop them from closing. McDaniel placed the gun against Eve's head to keep me from getting any funny ideas, then pinched her nose shut between his thumb and finger until she stuck out her tongue but he didn't try to bite it. He laughed, and told her not to worry. He promised that he would be back for her. Eve closed her eyes and I threw my thoughts at her like furious hail. Don't worry, don't worry, don't worry.

I almost laughed.

Because one of us would be back and I was the only one armed with a blue notebook. But I did remember her telling me once that she had nightmares about open spaces, that in fact she loved to feel trapped. McDaniel roughly touched her ribs and belly with long white fingers, he was tickling her with unpleasant intimacy and now she lunged and squirmed away from his touch like an angry daughter. And before he disembarked the elevator, the fucker happily pressed all twenty-nine buttons.

Now he shoved me down the long yellow hallway, through the little waiting room and past the desk where the freakish and overtly sexual receptionist was not sitting, past the dark landscape of a drowning human brain and through the hissing doors to Griffin's pale white lair. And Griffin, or more likely Major Tom, was napping restlessly on the black leather sofa where just the day before he and I had shared some very nice coke. I could use some of that shit now. My reflexes were fucking poor, my reflexes were impoverished and now McDaniel pushed me toward the sofa where Griffin lay sleeping.

Wake him, he said.

I kneeled beside the couch and looked into Griffin's face. At first I thought he must be dead but his lips were much too rubbery and slick with drool. He wasn't easy to wake up, though. I thumped his nose with the blackened nail of my middle finger. I spat into my hand and palmed his bare skull like a basketball. I tugged open one eyelid and blew hot air onto his naked eyeball and still he snored until McDaniel grew weary of this and kicked the glass coffee table over, shattering it. Griffin sat up with a foolish grin on his face while I rolled into a nearby corner to pick small bits of glass out of my skin.

Theseus, said Griffin. Welcome, welcome.

McDaniel rolled his eyes and gave a mock bow. He stalked the length of the office with the cool inner fury of a stage villain whose head is so ripe with mischief that he can't begin to begin.

What can I get you, said Griffin. A drink, a cigar?

I would like a moist towel, I said.

Griffin sneered. Hello, Ray. Ever the prole, aren't you?

The what? I said.

Proletariat, he said. The dull, wage-earning class. Haven't you read *1984*?

No. I did see the movie, though. David Bowie, wasn't it?

William Hurt, you troll. McDaniel fairly snarled.

Whatever, I said. And I said it slowly, letting the word roll lavishly over my lips.

Excuse me? he said. His eyes like pinpricks.

Fuck you, I said. Fuck you, okay.

Griffin coughed and threw a pillow at me. Wipe your face, Ray. You're a fright.

Thank you.

Griffin stood up, then. His arms out wide and his posture grossly servile. He moved close to McDaniel and began to grovel and kiss his hands and virtually lick at his genitals in such a way that might have been fashionable two hundred years ago, in a surreal French courtyard full of bursting flowers and castrated male servants. McDaniel primped and preened throughout and I had to wonder what I was doing with these two mad fuckers while Eve was handcuffed to herself in an elevator.

Let's get this over with, I said.

Griffin literally purred as he helped McDaniel out of his jacket. He hung it up, careful not to crease it, and turned to look at me with disdain.

Your tone of voice is offensive, he said.

Offensive, I said. Are you serious?

Terribly.

I am not offended, said McDaniel. Yet.

Well, then. Who wants a cocktail? said Griffin. I have a pint of the Pale here somewhere.

I wasn't sure if Griffin was high or just acting high. McDaniel exhaled through his nose and murmured that he was not thirsty. I did want a drink, however. I wanted two fingers of dead memories, served over ice with a wedge of lime and a splash of tonic, chased with a fat line of coke that would leave my jaw numb and heavy. I told myself to change the subject.

McDaniel cocked his gun now, and uncocked it.

I smiled as my education finally kicked in. *A Midsummer Night's Dream*, I said. Isn't that right? Theseus was the Duke of Athens.

McDaniel squinted at me. Very good. You are not quite the oaf I imagined.

I shrugged.

But did you know that the character of Theseus is generally played by the same actor who portrays Oberon, King of the Fairies? Both men are grand manipulators.

I scratched a phantom itch along the side of my neck and thought it small consolation that McDaniel had taken his name from a comedy.

No. I didn't know that.

And what is your given name? he said to me.

Phineas Poe.

I thought so, he said. The wife-killer from Internal Affairs.

The blood does not actually boil. It's a useful, if somewhat exaggerated expression. My skin was not even hot but I was sick of cool good-byes and reluctant eyes and while I would let this comment pass for the moment I was pretty fucking sick of this nursery-rhyme explanation for my wife's death.

McDaniel held the gun on me and I bit at my tongue.

Griffin himself looked fairly sickened. He sucked air through his teeth and I wondered if he now was my friend or McDaniel's toady.

McDaniel grinned at me. What is your intention? he said.

Excuse me?

You called me this morning, he said. Do you remember?

I don't know, I said. I'm making this up as I go along.

As am I, he said. But why did you not bring Jimmy Sky?

Jimmy was naked and suicidal on somebody's roof this morning, I said. He's probably in the hospital by now. If he's lucky.

McDaniel sniffed the fingers of his left hand.

Did you hear me, I said.

What does your hand smell like, he said.

What? I said.

I wonder if it smells like Goo, he said. I imagine she has a stinky package.

I sighed. He was definitely going to have to shoot me before I would discuss the smell of Eve's panties. Griffin went over to his desk and began to fiddle with the controls of a police scanner. He reached for a set of head-phones.

Moon was a friend of mine, I said.

McDaniel waved the gun. Detective Moon was officially dead yesterday, he said.

Tired. I was tired of his face, of his snotty accent.

You fucker, I said.

I created Jimmy Sky, he said. And just when I have a good role for him, he's gone mad.

What role was that?

His eyes flickered yellow. Two cops have been found dead and mutilated in the past two days. Three, if you count Moon. I was planning to package Jimmy as the killer. Major Tom there was going to tidy up the legal side. But then you came along and confused things.

I confused things, I said. That's hilarious.

When did you arrive in town? he said.

I nodded. Two days ago.

Perhaps you would like to be the killer.

I would love to help you, I said. But your killer is already turning green in a Dumpster behind a Burger King on West 17th. He was just a guy named Christian.

McDaniel either didn't believe me or didn't care. He raised the gun.

Whoa, I said.

On your knees, he said.

Griffin turned off the scanner. A naked gunman was shot and killed by police an hour ago, he said. Identified on the scene as Detective Walter Moon.

That can't be, I said. That can't be right. Moon is riding the crosstown bus with no shirt. He's on the bus. In fact, I'm expecting him to walk in here any minute and start taking names.

McDaniel smiled a crooked smile and even Griffin looked as if he felt sorry for me, because I was so ignorant. And I chose that moment, for good or ill, to pick up a little straight-backed chair made of steel and chrome that looked very uncomfortable and throw it at McDaniel. He ducked under it easily and the chair bounced off the massive window behind him like it was made of rubber. The same window that I had seen fall from its frame and glide down to earth the other day like the hand of God. The chair landed almost at my feet and McDaniel grinned like a cat, his lips turning purple. He took a step forward and I knew he was going to shoot me.

Easy, said Griffin. Everybody take it easy. This carpet is Egyptian silk and cotton, okay. And it's white. It cost two thousand dollars per square foot.

McDaniel snarled out of the side of his mouth and the veins in his forehead bulged nicely. He had a very long nose, I noticed. He looked like a pale, sickly dog-man. Half man and half dog and not quite civilized. He turned now and stared intently at Griffin, as if he might just shoot him for practice. He stared and stared and the air between them became elastic. I touched my forehead and found my skin cold, rubbery. The skin of a frog. I had a hangover, I think. This was withdrawal or something. I wanted a shot of the Pale and I was operating on fumes.

Griffin sat down abruptly, on the floor. He was trembling.

Don't look at me, he said. Don't look at me like that.

McDaniel stared at him.

I was beginning to wonder if I might just slip away when Goo walked into the room. She wasn't Eve. I knew this without quite understanding it. Her face was different, colder. Her eyes were far away. She wore nothing but a black bra and underpants. There was a smear of blood across her stomach and she held the rest of her clothes away from her body as if they stank.

These aren't mine, she said.

No, I said. Dumbly. They're Dizzy's.

She didn't know me. She looked at me without comprehension. But she veered toward me and dropped the clothes at my feet and I saw that her hands were bloody. I reflexively kicked the clothes away from me, as if they were diseased.

McDaniel beamed at her like a proud papa and I knew he was thrilled by this little distraction, because he wouldn't have to think for a few minutes.

But then, neither would I.

Meanwhile. Griffin still sat on the floor, his face blank as a scarecrow's. He was having a private little meltdown, an identity crisis. He had chosen the worst possible moment to crack apart and to be honest, I was tempted to sit down beside him but now Goo was drifting around the room in a slow, disintegrating figure eight, her bloody wrists held out away from her body. She had wriggled out of the handcuffs, somehow. I wasn't terribly surprised, when I thought about what she had been doing for a living the past few months. But I knew how tightly I had cuffed her. She held her hands out like a child, like she was shocked by the blood. But that wasn't it. Her hands were fucked up, I saw. I stepped in front of her and took her by the wrists, gently.

Jesus, I said.

She had broken both her thumbs and ripped away a handful of skin to get free of the handcuffs. Her eyes were glassy. Eve was not okay. I had thought she would be okay in the elevator, but she wasn't. Goo had come along and ruined her pretty hands and now she needed medical attention. She needed a shot of Thorazine.

I looked at McDaniel. I'm taking her to a hospital, I said.

No, he said. You're not.

I want to go home, she said. Home.

McDaniel aimed the gun at her. Torture us, he said. Entertain us and I will take you home.

No, I said. Fuck that.

Goo hesitated and I saw nothing familiar in her eyes. She had become a stranger again and now she pulled away from me. She lifted her arms over her head with the horrible elegance of a prisoner who has been told to dance for her supper or be killed. I will never know what she was going to do but I like to think that she was going to hypnotize him and eat his tongue and pretty much rescue us all from this game but I never found out because McDaniel relaxed at that moment, watching her, and I chose to end things differently. I bent and picked up the chair again and this time swung it like a tennis racket and caught him in the face with one of the legs and although the gun went off harmlessly as he went down, he was down and that was all I wanted and his face was like a burst tomato.

Fucked, howled Griffin. The carpet is fucked.

The gun was on the floor and I scooped it up. It felt good in my hand. I kicked McDaniel in the ribs, hard. He seemed to be unconscious and I kicked him again.

How much did the carpet really cost? I said.

Two hundred a foot, said Griffin. But two thousand sounds better.

Nervous laugh.

I was still on edge. Legs like water and I was hearing things. There is a noise that people make when they can't breathe, a noise that isn't a noise at all but is the opposite of noise because without oxygen there is no sound and now I heard, or imagined such a noise and turned around to see that Eve was on her back. The bullet from McDaniel's gun had gone through her throat.

This was the result of my choice. I picked up a chair and five seconds later Eve was dying at my feet. Planetary alignment was irrelevant. I knelt beside her and pressed my hands to her wound but it was hopeless. Eyes hot and staring. The dark, bloody mess of her throat. Her pulse was a flicker and I held my hands there until it stopped. Blood in her black hair and I rocked back and forth beside her. I was humming. Eve was dead. Her eyes were closed and I wonder if she would have recognized me if the bullet had strayed six inches to the left and buried itself in a wall. Black cotton bra and underpants. Fine white skin flecked with blood and broken thumbs. I rocked back and forth. She had fallen awkwardly and lay twisted, her left leg was crumpled under her body and I saw for the first time how many bruises she had. She was a rainbow and I fell away from her.

I sat against the wall for a while. Five minutes maybe. Griffin stood up and began to pace around.

This is serious, he said. This is serious shit, Ray.

I ignored him. I covered Eve's body with my coat and turned my attention to McDaniel. He was still out and I hoped he was dying. I sat on his chest. I felt his pulse and it was strong, it was thumping like a drum and he would be awake soon.

This is bad, said Griffin. I don't know if I can fix this.

Here's your big chance, I said.

Griffin rubbed his bald head, frantic. My chance for what, Ray?

Fuck, I said. Will you not call me that anymore?

Yeah, he said. I'm sorry. This is just a little intense. I slipped out of character, back there.

When?

When he said that shit about your wife.

I spat. That's fucking great. And who are you now?

Griffin stared at me. My name is Griffin.

Yeah, I said. Do you want his tongue?

The room seemed to swell and shrink around us of its own accord, like a great beast breathing. The two of us were in its belly. The air was thin and Eve was outside somewhere. She was gone.

Do you want this man's tongue? I said again.

My god, he said. No, I don't. I want to wake up with both legs tomorrow.

Right, then.

I stuck the gun down my pants because I would need both hands. I retrieved my knife from McDaniel's breast pocket. The blade was sleek, bright, warm. It was comforting. I reached for his mouth, pushed his lips apart and ran my fingers over the sharp ridge of his teeth. I massaged his jaw briefly and his mouth opened. Took a breath and poked two fingers into the dark hole, fishing for his tongue. This was foul beyond belief. I don't know how dentists do it. The mouths of strangers are forbidding, grotesque. I touched his tongue and knew I couldn't do it. I looked at Eve's body and told myself I had to do something to him, something bad. I remember her scrawled logic notes that had spawned my diary and bit at my tongue softly. It was warm and familiar. My own tongue was not grotesque. It was not the source of horror that the blind kid had described on the bus.

I needed to hurt McDaniel.

The gun in my pants was pretty ordinary, a Smith & Wesson .38 Special with black rubber grip. It held five shots but I wouldn't need them all. I had noticed earlier that McDaniel was wearing very expensive Italian boots that came up to barely kiss the ankles and fastened on the sides with a chrome buckle. The boots were composed of a soft, glossy black leather and the soles were heavy lug rubber. They would look fine with a tuxedo. They would not slow you down if you wanted to climb a tree. The footwear of dreams. My own boots, meanwhile, had been killing my feet lately and his looked to be about my size. I removed them, fumbled with the buckles like a novice shoe salesman and left McDaniel in his stocking feet. I tried the boots on and they were perfect. I wanted to walk around in them and admire them but was afraid he would wake up soon and I needed to finish this before I freaked out and ran away without doing anything.

McDaniel lay on his back in the center of Griffin's nice white carpet.

Half of his body was obscured by shadows. Of course it was. I took a few steps back and without hesitating or stopping to think, raised the pistol and aimed at McDaniel's left foot and Griffin may have shouted at me, I don't know. I never heard him. I pulled the trigger and McDaniel's foot pretty much exploded. The bones in the foot are complex and fine and his would never be put back together. He would probably be up and around on a prosthetic in a year or so, but he would certainly need a cane and I imagined that if the game survived he would get one that doubled as a sword.

My head was ringing, my head was full of crashing waves.

I stared down at McDaniel and he appeared to regain consciousness for a moment. His eyes found mine before rolling back into his head and I doubted that he would ever forget me. I took a shallow breath and laughed, a brief glittering laugh. That first shot had been easy.

I lifted the gun again and calmly destroyed his other foot.

Griffin was sitting on the floor against the wall, his hands covering his ears. I glanced at the big unforgiving window where I had seen the three of us before and perhaps it was because of the clouds or the angle but there was nothing, no one reflected in the glass now. There was only a curved gray sky, and for a brief horrible moment it seemed to have no top or bottom and it looked very much like the inside of my head. I was sick, I was filled with vertigo and loss. I thought of the wall behind Eve's couch, the dead bird on her floor. I wondered if I could walk through that wall of glass, if there was another reality there that might sustain me. I was slipping. I turned and vomited into Griffin's wastepaper basket, which was of course made of black wire and did not hold liquids very well. The white carpet was truly fucked, now. It was time to go. I crouched beside Griffin and touched his face. I needed him to act like a lawyer and I guess he was finally thinking the same thing.

He took the gun from me and said, go. Get out of here.

I cast one last look at Eve, at Goo. I wanted to touch her, to say something meaningful but that was Hollywood. Her face and chest were hidden
in my dirty coat and her naked legs stuck out at odd angles. She had the
discolored plastic limbs of a life-sized doll.

My feet were heavy and unfamiliar in my enemy's shoes. Dragged myself
back through the waiting room and this time I didn't look at the brain
landscape. I found my strength and ran back down the yellow hallway and
pushed the Down button. I practiced breathing. Thirty seconds passed,
ninety. The doors opened and I stepped inside. The handcuffs dangled
from the brass rail, unopened.

Blood on the metal, smeared and nearly dry. Fragments of torn skin like
pink threads.

The elevator took me down to the lobby and I barely glanced at the mirrors on the way down. I hurried to the emergency exit door and picked up
my copy of *Ulysses*. The fire alarm tripped when I opened the door and no
one was waiting for me.

I stood in an alley surrounded by white stone and it was like the sky had
simply fallen. There were sirens in the distance and I walked away from the
exit at what I hoped was a normal pace. I came out of the alley and was
facing a street.

Pedestrians, traffic. I looked at my hands, at the tips of my fingers. They
were untrembling but still numb from pulling the trigger.

The sidewalk was new, freshly hardened concrete. There were no cracks in
it at all, no impurities or scars. It was a little eerie and after a while I crossed
over to the other side. I walked and walked and when I grew weary, I
drifted to a bus stop. The thought of another bus ride fairly horrified me,

but on a cellular level it seemed that I couldn't resist. I got on the first bus that came along.

The liquid sigh of the doors shutting behind me. The driver, gruff and unsmiling.

I paid and made my way along to a seat that looked safe.

Red, torn vinyl.

I scanned the faces of the other passengers but none of them was Jimmy Sky and none of them was the blind kid with the maddening tongue and my loved ones were all cartoon characters in the end. I pulled out the blue notebook and found that I had lost my pen.

Open windows and blank faces. Strangers all.

Dear Jude.

There is nothing but the greedy suck and churn of the engine beneath my feet and I feel serene. There is no motion sickness. I borrow a black ballpoint from a little old woman who smiles and coughs and tells me to keep it. I close my eyes and wait for Stephen Dedalus to come sit down beside me. I have saved no one but myself and now I watch for the other universe to unravel in my skull, for the sky to become my own skin and fill with stars.

hell's half acre

*Let a pair be introduced and increase slowly, from many
enemies, so as often to intermarry—
who will dare say what result?*

—Darwin, *Notebooks on Transmutation*

one.

PINK AND GRAY SKY, THE COLOR OF MUSCLE. The truck screams past and its exhaust drifts into dark flowers that hang on the air and fade away like I'm staring through a mirror stained with my own fingerprints. I saved a guy's life just now and I think it was a mistake. I didn't recognize him, not at first. I jerked him back from the edge by pure thoughtless reflex, like I was saying god bless you to the stranger sneezing beside me on a bus. Then I got a shiver-fast scope of his face and in a far corner of my brain came a sunspot flare of recognition, like glancing up at a passing cloud and thinking wow, that cloud looks exactly like a girl on a bicycle. Blink, and the flare is gone. Even now the particulars of the guy's face are dissolving into a thousand others, but I remember he had dirty blond hair and mercury eyes. The slow spin of echoes and I realize I know this man, and I believe him to be a monster. I think he is one of my own monsters come home.

This is how it begins.

I was crouched on the side of the curb at Geary and Jones, waiting for a dive named Mao's to open. A dead dog lay stretched along the curb beside me, gold and black fur busy with flies. I kept thinking that if I picked up a stick, maybe that dog would get up and run. I had a touch of the dry mouth and dark clouds were forming around the periphery of my vision. These were the first indicators that a seizure was on the way and soon the air would commence to accelerate and pulse, like a bird was attacking me.

I would suffer the imaginary rush of wings furious around my head, and I wasn't in the mood for it.

And just then a man came running from a narrow dark gap between buildings. He staggered and turned toward me, confused. He didn't realize he was in the middle of the street. I shook off the phantom wings and glanced left to see a delivery truck hurl around the corner way too fast. For my money, it was about to crush him to the pavement and burst his skull into nasty wet chunks, just like your average melon. I came to my feet and ran toward him as the truck heaved up close. I grabbed the guy and spun him out of the way and the truck squealed past, missing us by maybe a foot, the exhaust hot as god's own breath. The man was an inch or so shorter than me and had liquid gray eyes. Blood down the front of his shirt, a lot of it. He stank to heaven of gin and there was something about him that screamed bad voodoo and at this point I suffered that flare of recognition, like I had seen this guy before. I just couldn't say where I knew him from. A lot of faces have flashed by me over the years.

He grabbed my shirt in both fists and by habit or reflex I picked his pocket. My hand darted into his jacket pocket cat-quick and came out with his wallet and he never had a clue. This was a talent I'd picked up in the last few years as a means of survival. There was a wavering moment between us as the last splintered rays of the sun fell on our faces and I sort of froze in disbelief. I thought he might laugh or hug me or punch me in the face and all of a sudden I felt a hot wave of regret, like I might have just saved somebody who couldn't wait to go home and kick the shit out of his dog and beat up his wife or worse, and maybe I ought to follow him. And maybe he didn't want me to follow him because when he let go of my shirt he without so much as blinking slugged me in the mouth.

The guy had a heavy fist and I went down to one knee dizzy, while he sprinted up the street and disappeared. The bastard was gone and I was crumpled in the street with blood on my hands, on my shirt. Funny thing was, he may have done me a favor. Hitting me in the jaw had eighty-sixed that seizure I felt coming. A car horn sounded and I looked up. A woman in a gray BMW was honking at me, and giving me a dirty look through her windshield. I staggered up and out of the way and for half a tick I was just happy to be packing the same number of teeth. Then I glimmered the thin shadow mouth of the alley my possible monster had come running from and wondered why the dude was running and who from.

I walked into that dark mouth.

At the farthest end of the alley there was a shrinking egg of light. A man and woman were fighting in that sphere, fighting furiously. They were each of them expert fighters and crazy fast. Their hands and feet moved like insects attacking in mid-air. But the man was hurt, shifting his weight and trying to protect his left side. And as I approached, the woman spun and landed the kill shot, a knife to the throat. He went down so suddenly it was like pulling the plug on a computer. The guy just went dark.

Now the woman crouched low, looking at the body of the dead man on the ground. She didn't see me, and I didn't yet recognize her because the shadows were so thick and purple. I walked toward her slowly through the dark. I had no urge to hurry. I don't know exactly what I was feeling. I had just pulled a guy out of traffic and my skin was humming. But there was still that echo of recognition and the slow forming notion that he was a demon from my yesterdays, an idea that was like the taste of sick in my mouth.

The woman never saw me coming. She crouched there not moving, not breathing. Long arms resting on her knees. Blood on her hands. She didn't touch the man on the ground, not at first. She was hunkered over him like a wolf over prey. She made no effort to help him and something told me he was beyond help. I couldn't be sure if she was waiting for him to hurry up and die, or if she was mourning his passing.

Black hair falling like spilled ink to her jaw. This was unmistakably Jude.

I almost stopped breathing.

Jude and I had wounded each other deeply, and we had not parted well. But still I had spent going on five years looking for her.

I was not close enough to see the stars around her eyes but I could see that the corner of her pale mouth had gone flatline, and by her posture she looked more than a little freaked out and furious but by no stretch did she look scared. She wore heavy boots and black military trousers and a thin pale blue summery wisp of a shirt mottled with blood. I could see the muscles jumping in her arms and I had a glimmer that her every molecule was on fire, her body caught in the slow whirl between shock and adrenaline. She was so still she might have been painted there. And now she moved. She wiped the knife on her thigh. She took the man's head in her hands and, using the tip of the blade, made two fast flicking motions with her wrist. I couldn't quite see what she'd done, but I had an idea.

Then she got freaky.

With no hint of ceremony or theater, Jude took a fistful of the dead man's hair in her left fist and pulled it back like a clutch of dead flowers. She put the edge of her knife to his forehead, just below the hairline, and began cutting. She made a near perfect circle around his head, then twisted his hair in a truly violent motion. I was fifty feet away but still I heard the man's scalp rip away from his skull. She flung the bloodsoaked mass of hair and skin into the shadows. She fucking scalped him. I knew why she'd done it, and as well as I knew her, I couldn't quite believe it. My left boot touched a bottle and the sound of glass on stone shimmered like a bell. She came alive now and ran from me, never looking back. At the far end of the alley she hopped onto a stripped-down silver racing bike that looked like a pterodactyl on wheels, which I reckoned was a Ducati. She yanked a black helmet down over her head, roared the bike to life, and rocketed away.

Fine by me.

I knew where she was holed up, and anyway I wasn't ready to talk to her.

I came to the body and knelt beside him. There was a wide black puddle of blood around him that ran to the brick walls in either direction. The guy was in his early thirties, handsome. That is, he had been. Pale and feral. He had a patchy gold beard and a girl's rosy lips. I assumed his hair, too, had been the color of dirty gold. I couldn't be certain, as the top of his head now was a horrorshow of seeping blood, wrecked tissue, and exposed bone. And he had no eyes. His eyes were gone. She'd scooped them out with the tip of her knife. I glanced around and saw one of them, a bloody knot glistening in the dark.

And like the guy with ghost eyes in the street, this man was familiar. I knew where I'd seen them. Even mutilated, the likeness was easily apparent. The men were brothers. I had laid eyes on them once before in the flesh, in New Orleans. And I'd dreamed of them many times since. Thinking about it made my skin crawl. I felt nothing much, but I was glad this one was dead.

He was thin, wearing a faded jean jacket. The knees of my pants were soaked through with his blood. I could see that his carotid artery had been severed and he was about as dead as anybody can be. I bent over him and sniffed at his mouth anyway, an unorthodox little habit that I picked up somewhere along the way. I don't know what this is about, but I could always tell the living from the dead with one whiff and the air that seeped from this guy's hole was pure graveyard. I touched two fingers to his throat for form's sake. There was no pulse to speak of.

I slapped at the guy's pockets and found a fat ziploc baggie that contained small individual balloons of what looked to be generous dimes of heroin. I stared at them a moment, tempted sore. Then hissed at myself and threw the lot violently into the far shadows. I found a cell phone in his jacket pocket and dialed 911. The operator came on and I muttered the words dead man at Geary and Jones, then dropped the phone on the guy's chest. I wiped my bloody hands on his pants and stood up. I wanted to make myself scarce before the cops showed, and besides I had an appointment with an old flame that was long overdue.

Here's what happened. I arrived in San Francisco five days ago, having tracked Jude to California after losing her in New Orleans some five years back. I have been on the road so long I've about lost myself. For the past nine months I've been crisscrossing the southwest, eyeballing the sun like it was my blood enemy. By the by, saying I tracked Jude anywhere is generous as hell. I'm not much of a hunter, never was. And most of the time I was wandering around on foot, as the seizures and false visions have got progressively worse of late, making it dangerous for me to drive. I do know how Jude's mind works, however, and I've had some okay luck just following my nose.

Anyway. Two weeks ago, I was laid up in a shitty motel in Bakersfield, where Jude's trail had run cold. The only evidence that she had even been there were the busted collarbone of a bartender in Flagstaff named Rabbit and the severed hamstring of his buddy Steve, a bouncer by trade and former kickboxing champ who was never gonna walk right again. Rabbit and Steve told me they had run afoul of Jude a month or so prior when she blew into town and began sniffing around for two guys, brothers named Shane and Sugar Finch. These names meant nothing to me, but they did mean something to Rabbit and Steve, who told me between shots of whiskey that they had been best pals with Shane and Sugar since they were all still wetting the bed. Shane and Sugar had moved on years ago, they said, having graduated from freelance thugs to mercenary killers. But they were still practically family, Rabbit said, and when Jude showed up looking for them, Rabbit and Steve got nervous, and rightly so.

The woman they described had identified herself as Jesse Redd, and they had taken her to be a professional bounty hunter. They said she had a body that knocked you out at first glimmer, but when you examined her up close she was pure muscle and hard as cut glass with a scar at the corner of her mouth and long devastating legs and hair so black it looked wet, skin somewhere between yellow and pale coffee, and eyes shaped like almonds. They said she was wearing desert boots and army fatigues that fit her ass snug as a bug and a scuffed black motorcycle racing jacket and a little white T-shirt underneath so thin and tight you could see her nipples plain as day.

That freaked me out, said Rabbit. She caught me looking at those high beams and she stared through me so hard I caught a chill.

No shit, said Steve. It was her eyes freaked me out.

How so? I asked.

She didn't seem to blink, for one thing. For another, she has this long white scar that starts just above the left eye and disappears into her hair, like somebody tried to damn near cut off the top of her head. And around the other eye, she's got three small black tattoos, three stars, like her own little constellation.

This was Jude, without question. The physical description was dead on, and I had known her to use the name Jesse Redd when we were on the run in Mexico. Jude had fake passports in a dozen different names. Wendy Sweet. Emma Frye. She liked names that sounded like superhero secret identities. As for the scar above her left eye, she'd acquired that in New Orleans, the same night I came by the massive blow to the head that caused a goodly knot of scar tissue to form in my brain, which may or may not account for the seizures and false visions that developed slow but sure over the past years. And while I'd known Jude to have several tattoos, an eye between her shoulder blades, a Greek symbol on her forearm, and a small dragon on her hip, the stars around her eyes were new. Apparently she's acquired more ink since I lost her.

The long and short of Rabbit and Steve's story was about what I expected. Jude was looking for info on the possible whereabouts of their childhood buddies, Shane and Sugar Finch. She was asking nicely, at first. Everybody was getting along. And then Rabbit got a little too fresh with her, and maybe Steve gave her some static about hassling their friends. At which point she handed their asses to them, in exchange for the information that Sugar, which they swore upside down and sideways was his real name as shown on his birth certificate, used to have a girlfriend named Maggie who slung cocktails at a tittie bar called the Painted Lady, in Bakersfield.

two.

I HEADED FOR BAKERSFIELD THAT SAME NIGHT, where I learned that the Painted Lady had burned to the ground almost a year ago. Nobody knew anything about a waitress named Maggie, so I checked into a motel with a bottle of rum and a notion to get drunk and take a three-day nap before I contemplated my next move. I stretched out on the bed with a plastic cup of rum on my belly and stared at my boots. The heels were worn down to nothing.

I flipped on the TV, realizing I couldn't remember when I last watched a baseball game, the news, or a stupid movie with explosions and chase scenes. I was barely aware who was even president these days, or who we were currently at war with. I surfed around until I came to CNN, which was airing footage of some political block party in Berkeley, where some guy in a suit was giving a speech. His name was MacDonald Cody, and after a while I gathered that he was a senator, recently elected, the prodigal son of a former California governor, Anderson Cody. This younger Cody was talking about jobs, healthcare, the environment, family values; he was covering all the bases. He had a smoke-and-gravel voice and rugged movie-star looks, with a glint of the rogue sparkle in his eye, silver blond hair, nice tan, healthy American teeth, and he looked vaguely familiar to me in that way that a lot of people on the box do. But then he raised his left arm to emphasize a point and I saw that he wore a prosthetic hand, and I popped upright like a half-drunk jack-in-the-box, my stomach in my mouth.

It's a small world and getting smaller, but the source of my shock was as
follows. Not quite six years ago in a brightly lit motel room in Mexico City,
I held a sponge and bucket while Jude surgically removed MacDonald
Cody's left hand with an electric saw for twenty-five thousand dollars, paid
in advance. We had no idea who he was, at the time. First names were dis-
couraged in such transactions, and for all we knew he was just another
sick, rich fuck from the States who'd come south of the border to satisfy his
amputation fetish anonymously. Jude had performed a half dozen similar
procedures in the space of four months, and this one was nothing special.
She wore a clear plastic raincoat while she worked. She cranked up *London
Calling* on a boombox to drown out the noise as she took his hand.

Then, a year or so later. Jude and I had made our way back to the States
and landed in New Orleans, and were uneasily adjusting to our re-entry
into the atmosphere. One day Jude came home with a funny look on her
face. I asked her what was up and she said she had run smack into one of
our former customers from Mexico, one of our flipper boys.

Which one? I said.

She shrugged. The handsome one.

That narrows it down.

She poured a glass of wine. As I recall, there were only two I would
have called handsome. This one looked like an ex-quarterback.

Did he recognize you?

I think so, yeah. But what difference could it make?

And I had to agree. It was a funny coincidence but one that seemed
not to matter. We weren't going to bother the guy, and it seemed unlikely
that he would bother us.

Two days later, four men wearing masks entered our rented French
Quarter flat. Jude had gone down to the market to buy limes and salt. She
wanted to make margaritas. I was taking a bubble bath, of all things. I was
thumbing through a *Rolling Stone* magazine and smoking a cigarette. I
remember the ashes fell into the bubbles like little black snowflakes. I

heard the front door open. I heard footsteps that weren't Jude's. Voices, low and dangerous. We didn't have any guns in the apartment, having ditched our gear before flying into Miami, and we hadn't gotten around to picking up new shit. I got out of the bath, wrapped a towel around my waist. There wasn't much in the bathroom that could pass for a weapon but the lid of the toilet tank. I picked it up and eased the bathroom door open. I could see two of them, lean fuckers in black masks, with their backs to me. One of them had pushed his mask up over his forehead and was sniffing a pink thong of Jude's that had been laying on the coffee table since the night before. I swung the heavy tank lid like a baseball bat and hammered the panty sniffer in the small of the spine hard enough to break it. He went down and I thought okay, he's done. I caught a sideways flash of dark hair and bright eyes, but I was in a hurry and didn't really study his face. I dropped the tank lid as his partner spun around roaring at me, and I swung what I thought was a pretty nasty punch at his throat, a shot that never hit its target. Instead I felt what I took to be the heavy talons of a massive bird sink into my back, above the shoulder blade, and I went down like a sack of bones. At which point they commenced to kicking me in the head with their boots, and were still kicking me when Jude came home.

I was barely conscious by then, with a fast-seeping hematoma on the brain so profound the doctors later told me it ought to have killed me. I was also bleeding pretty good from the wound in my back, which as it turned out came not from a giant bird, but from the claw end of a hammer. The guy had sunk it in me about as deep as it would go. Anyway, I was dead to the world when Jude returned. I didn't see anything for a while. And when I started to come out of it, my vision and awareness coming back in splintered flashes, I was strapped into a chair. I reckon they figured they would have plenty of time to kill me later.

Jude was tied to the bed, her clothes bloody and torn to ribbons. I still don't know how they got the drop on her. And yes, there were three of them, as my guy was down for the count with what I hoped was a shattered tailbone, but I had seen Jude take on three guys at once on more than one occasion. The average hired muscle stood no chance against her, weapons notwithstanding. Jude had been in the Army, special forces. She had spent two years training with an Israeli death squad and she could throttle a mountain lion in a fair fight. But somehow these humps took her down.

She would barely talk about it, later.

They were pros, she said. They were very fast, and very good.

I pieced it together from what she didn't say, and what little I could remember. The way I figured it, the guy I nailed with the tank lid was the crew leader, and since he was down, the others decided to have some fun with Jude before they killed her. They took off their masks and arrogantly allowed her to see their faces. Two of them were feral white guys with dirty blond hair, thin hard guys built like welterweights who could have been brothers. The other was a silent, muscular black man with shaved head. They tied her facedown on the bed and tortured her, and they took their sweet time about it. They sniffed out that she had a thing for knives, so they cut her. They cut up her feet. They opened up her left arm. They made shallow cuts on her back that I think were meant to look like wings, and they gave her that long curved wound that Rabbit and Steve described, that begins above her eye and wraps halfway around her head.

Then one of the white guys backed off, lit a cigarette. He waved his hand like he was bored with this shit. And his buddy then did the worst thing I could imagine, he did something worse to Jude than just rape her. He knelt on the floor like he was receiving the sacrament and went down on her. He took his sweet time about it, then took off his pants and fucked her proper, grunting as he did so. Jude was silent throughout. She just lay there on her belly, eyes streaming with blood and tears, glittering like two pieces of glass on the beach. When he was finished, his buddy stepped in to have a go. I struggled in my chair, hopeless, slipping in and out of consciousness. These men had come there to kill us, no mistake. You don't rape and torture somebody like that unless you mean to kill them. And even with a concussion it wasn't hard to glimmer that they were hired to erase us and thereby protect the identity of the man Jude saw downtown, the one she said looked like an aging quarterback.

Shudder and sigh, five years later.

I was crouched on a rented bed in a shitty motel with a bottle of rum between my knees, and that quarterback was on television, giving a speech. I wondered how his people had spun the story of that prosthetic hand. A wild tale of Mexican banditos, perhaps, a story so wild it had to be true. He had rescued a servant girl from certain death and lost his hand in the process. The brave, sympathetic hero. The shy, handsome California boy who would be king. A story that would start to stink fast if there were even murmurs about amputation as a sexual kick. The Codys had been a proud California family since the gold rush days, boasting a long line of congressmen, state reps, and two governors. And according to the CNN commentator, this MacDonald Cody was now on the short list to be running mate to the Democratic frontrunner for president. Good god, I thought. No wonder they had come for us in New Orleans. And as the camera panned the crowd for reaction shots, I saw her for just a second.

Jude.

She wore rose-colored wraparound sunglasses and a stylish white designer suit. The jacket was cropped short and the pants rode just a little low on her hips. She looked like a very expensive prostitute or runway model who had borrowed or stolen a trendy lawyer's clothes for the day. She was watching the handsome senator with the cool detachment of a spider, and just as the camera paused to linger on her she seemed to feel it like the sun on her skin and she turned away.

The next morning, I headed for the nearby Denny's to get a bite and some coffee while I waited for the next Greyhound north. I took a stab and asked my waitress if she had ever known a girl named Maggie, who used to work at the Painted Lady.

Sure, she said. I know Maggie. She went up to San Francisco after the Lady burned down, got a job at some little bar. She sent me a couple postcards.

That's nice. Do you remember the name of the bar?

The waitress grinned. It was called Mao's, like the Chinese dictator. I remember because I used to love those Andy Warhol paintings.

three.

I'M STARING AT THE BACK OF A CAB DRIVER'S NECK. The thing is, I'm not used to being around people. I have been living on the edge of nowhere too long. I've been asleep for years, it feels like. My sunburned hands twitch like birds. I crush them together, force them to be still.

This is heavy traffic and nothing more.

Downtown San Francisco, or thereabout. I don't know the city well, but it looks to be composed of wrong angles. It's one of those cities where two streets may run parallel for a few blocks, then cross each other. The streets are not to be trusted. I need to relax. I'm an ordinary passenger in an ordinary yellow cab, waiting in traffic. I'm on my way to a hotel called the King James. Upon arriving in San Francisco, I experienced a rare moment of trouble-shooting cool and called a dozen hotels asking for a guest named Jesse Redd until I got a hit. The receptionist who answered the phone was a young girl named Holly, apparently new on the job, and I had managed to flirt with her just enough to wrangle Jesse Redd's room number out of her.

The mind wanders, forward and back. Jude was never my girlfriend in any conventional sense of the word. I met her in a hotel bar in Denver almost seven years ago, less than a week before Christmas. I had just been released from a state hospital with my head shaved and my emotional infrastructure rewired. I was an ex-cop but my judgment was poor. I mistook Jude for a prostitute and invited her up to my room. She relieved me of all my cash and didn't give me so much as a handjob in return. I barely copped a feel before the horse tranq she'd slipped me robbed me of my senses. I woke up some twenty-four hours later in a bathtub full of ice, and one of my kidneys was gone. She'd targeted me before I ever walked out of Fort Logan, having helped herself to my med records and shaky psych profile.

It sounds complicated but it amounts to boy meets girl and girl steals his kidney. Boy wants his kidney back. Boy wants to kill girl. Boy catches up with girl and decides he likes her. He just might love her. And so he doesn't kill her. He becomes her partner, and pretty soon boy and girl get along like two ducks flying high in a washed blue sky. I called her that sometimes, when I was feeling daffy.

Give us a kiss, I'd say. Give us a kiss, duck.

It annoyed the hell out of her. She reached for sharp objects. And eventually those two ducks fell to earth and I found myself in a world of shit, a world where I didn't think twice about holding sponge and bucket while she amputated a future senator's hand. Jude and I were together for just over a year.

I remember the strangest things about her. I remember she played with matches when she was nervous or bored, lighting one after another until she burned her fingers. She favored a black raincoat on cloudy days, and wore nothing under it. She liked to flash me in elevators. She trimmed her pubic hair into a narrow, shadowy wing. She had a tendency to bite but never broke the skin. She was a trained killer but still she was afraid of spiders. She brought me ice cream when I was sick, and she spent a lot of money on fantastic hats. Jude never did anything lightly. She could be washing the dishes, making spaghetti sauce, playing a video game, or painting the bathroom red. Or fighting a guy twice her size. She did everything with the same delirious gum-chewing mania. In the bedroom she was reckless, she was all over the map. The sex was exhausting, hilarious, fragile, and scary. And sometimes, as I closed my eyes at night I wondered if she would kill me in my sleep.

I last saw her in New Orleans. Late morning and Jude was brushing her teeth. Blue around the lips. The drone of pipes and ultraviolet light. Her back against the sink. The shadow of wet hair in the mirror, black with traces of chemical red. One arm dangling, she wore a blue shirt unbuttoned. Thighs and belly bright with oil and sun. Trickle of blood down one knee where she had cut herself shaving. Dead flowers in a teacup on the television behind me. I stood in the doorway, on the threshold. I was holding her suitcase, which I'd found in the living room, in one hand. It felt heavy.

What's this? I said.

Hazy silence. She turned her head, so I could see the pink scar.

I'm leaving you, she said.

Where will you go? I said.

Don't follow me, she said.

Why?

Flicker of hurt in her eyes, like moth's wings.

You, she said. You disappeared long ago.

The yellow cab heaves to a stop. The slow turn of the driver's face, white and sickly.

Twenty-two fifty, he says.

What?

This is it, man. The King James Hotel.

I turn to the window, my nose against glass. I am still in San Francisco. The mad shamble of downtown humans. Towers of glass and stone and fingernails of sky, blue and white. Long shadows and swirl of dust and trash. The driver begins to cough and choke without stopping. The slushy noise of ruined lungs. He has emphysema and this actually makes me crave a cigarette, maybe two.

Don't follow me.

Bittersweet, yes. Pale with sorrow and heartbreak and soft light. Also complete and utter bullshit. That tender farewell bathroom scene is a load of something stinky, it's bad fiction. The other version, the truthful one, has me living for weeks in the attic above our rented flat in the Quarter. I was busy talking to myself and slowly going bugshit crazy. I was a busy little toad. I was plotting the murder of three men whose proper names I didn't even know, whose whereabouts were impossible to say. I barely knew what they looked like and I was so far from finding them they might as well have been living on the other side of the sun.

Thoughts of revenge will eat the brain away sure as cancer.

I should have just been happy we were alive. It was a small miracle, really. Four men had entered our apartment. One of them lay crippled on the floor, groaning. The two white guys had raped my woman, savagely. They had finished in under an hour, and now they lounged about, smoking cigarettes. One of them was raiding our liquor cabinet, the other had flopped down on the sofa to watch TV. The black dude was taking off his pants, stopping to fold them carefully. These guys were taking too long, and being very stupid, and I knew that a window was opening. I just wasn't sure how to climb through that window. I kept blacking out, which scared the shit out of me, because dimly I was aware that I was sporting a serious concussion, and I could feel the blood seeping inside my skull. Each time I blacked out could be my last. And I was tied down so securely, I could barely wiggle my fucking toes. I hoped Jude had an idea about that window. The black man put aside his pants. He rubbed his gleaming skull for luck and lowered himself onto the bed.

Jude opened her eyes. She managed to smile.

Let me use my hands, she said. It will be so much nicer for you.

I was in the hospital for a week. My doctor told me I would have blurred vision for a while. He said that the bleeding around my brain had stopped, that scar tissue would soon form, and that I would likely have headaches the rest of my life. Otherwise, I would recover. He asked if I could identify my attackers, did I want to file a police report. I declined. I asked about Jude, but he shook his head. He knew nothing about the woman who brought me to the ER, only that she had paid my medical tab in full. I went home in a taxi.

The apartment bore no evidence of the attack, not a drop of blood. But then Jude had always been meticulous about cleaning up a crime scene.

Jude was locked in the bedroom. She refused to come out.

I'm going to take the door off the hinges, I said.

Jude didn't answer me. I went to the kitchen and came back with a hammer and screwdriver. The apartment was ancient and the hinges on the doors had been painted over probably a dozen times. I was starting to knock the pin loose from the bottom hinge when Jude spoke up. She said in a cold voice that I would be sorry if I did that.

Jude, please. Just come out.

Tomorrow, she said. Maybe tomorrow.

But tomorrow came and went and Jude didn't come out. She wasn't starving herself or anything. She was just avoiding me. Now and then I found a bowl in the sink, a spoon.

Okay, I thought.

Jude didn't want to be seen and she didn't want to talk. She didn't want to be loved or touched or comforted. I could have tried. I should have. But guilt is a terrible bedfellow and maybe I was afraid to look at her. I told myself she would come to me when she wanted comfort. I shut myself in the attic room with a laptop and searched the Net for three men who may well not have existed, and for the flipper boy who'd hired them.

Three men.

I searched for just three men, because the black man with shaved skull had unwisely succumbed to Jude's offer, perhaps thinking he would get a blowjob out of the deal, and untied her hands. Maybe he was just stupid. Maybe he didn't know how dangerous she was. Whatever the reason, he had complied and Jude had run her hands seductively up his chest as she kissed him, pulling him close. She promptly bit off most of his nose and upper lip, wrenching her jaws so violently that I actually heard the flesh rip from his face. Then she snapped his neck. The two white guys looked at each other and said fuck this, and disappeared like vapor, while Jude was untying her feet. She could have easily killed their crew leader, the one I'd disabled with the toilet lid, but didn't. She barely looked at him, in fact. She stepped gingerly around the man, almost as if she were afraid of him, and came to me.

Maybe she was in a hurry to cut me loose and take me to the hospital. Either way, the chance was lost, because when she returned, he was gone. The white guys had come back for their leader, apparently, because the faceless body of the black dude was gone as well.

Pretty soon I was on a shitload of painkillers and I had started using crystal meth to stay awake and for me it was always too easy to go mad. It was like rolling out of bed. I didn't speak to Jude for days, maybe weeks, and anyway she never came out of her room. I saw her a few times, though. I saw her reflection in the window, a dusty flash of her in the glass. I saw her behind me on the stairs once, naked and descending like a wraith but when I turned to look for her she wasn't there. The speed was getting to me and my brain wasn't right. The phone was long dead but I ripped the cords out of the walls anyway. I removed the bulbs from all the lamps. I carried the screwdriver everywhere I went. I didn't eat or sleep and before you could say Howdy Doody, I had gone over the wall to crazy land. I was limping around the apartment at night, pouring sweat and muttering.

One morning, the bedroom door was open. I went in to ask Jude if she was hungry but she was gone. The bed was stripped bare and there was a splash of red in the center of the mattress. It wasn't a lot of blood at all but it scared me. I thought she had killed herself and started looking around for her body. I came out of the bedroom and there she was, sitting at the kitchen table. Jude wore sweatpants and a jean jacket buttoned to the throat even though it was not cold. Her posture was very straight. I sat down across from her and put the screwdriver on the table. I could smell myself and it wasn't a good smell. I was wearing white pants for some reason, and nothing else. I was hungry and I felt like I was coming back to the world.

Hey, I said.

I just came from the clinic, she said.

Are you okay?

No. I'm pregnant.

Oh. Shit.

Shit, she said.

How pregnant?

Eight weeks. She lit a cigarette and immediately put it out.

Bad for the baby, she muttered. Her hand was trembling and she made a fist. I wanted to say that everything was okay, that we were together and everything was okay but it was almost impossible to conceive of Jude pregnant, Jude a mother, and finally my brain kicked in like a radio that only works on rainy days because rats have been chewing the wires. That blood on the bed was something to worry about yes but there was something else, wasn't there. But I couldn't bring myself to say anything.

The attack was exactly eight weeks ago, she said.

And we, I said. We had sex that morning, and the night before. I remember because the phone kept ringing and you threw the portable out the window.

Jude half smiled. That's right.

We didn't use a condom, I said.

No, she said. But you withdrew.

And they didn't, I said. Did they?

Jude sighed. She said that she was tired.

Look, I said. It's okay. We're gonna be okay.

Jude shook her head. No, we're not.

She went to take a nap and when I went to check on her, she said she wanted to be alone. I tried to pull myself together. I got myself cleaned up and went to the grocery store, numbly thinking that she would need things like chicken soup and milk and ice cream and bottled water because even if she was going to get an abortion she would need to eat. I wasn't too rational. I hadn't been out of the apartment in almost a month and my vision was still blurry and when I came back to the apartment Jude was gone. She was just gone. I went out and bought a shotgun, and waited as long as I could stand it, maybe a month. I was hoping the men would come back to finish the job. But they never did and I realized Jude was probably hunting them, and maybe she'd already found them, and after a while the silence of the apartment and the springtime stink of the Quarter had driven me half crazy, and I decided Jude wasn't coming back. I got on a bus and headed back to Denver, where I plunged myself into an altogether different nightmare. But that's another story.

I'm still sitting in a yellow cab outside the King James Hotel. The driver is waiting for his money. I reach into my pocket and find the wallet I took off the dead man in the alley. I flip it open to find a wad of small bills, maybe ninety bucks. No credit cards. Driver's licenses from five states. The same blond hair and silvery eyes with five different names, and if the IDs are fakes, they are well crafted. I study his face for half a tick. Thin, intelligent, fierce, hard as the underside of your boot. The Nevada license, expired, is the only one that bears his Christian name, Sugar Jefferson Finch. This was one of the dogs Jude was hunting. This was one of the men who attacked us in New Orleans, one of the savage fucks who raped her, and I saved his life today. I wonder if he was the one who took me down with that hammer, and I feel sick.

Furious and sick.

The dead man in the alley was presumably his kid brother, also known as Shane. Tucked into Sugar's wallet is a book of matches from the Alamo Hotel, with a phone number scribbled on the inside. Might be a long shot, might be an easy ground ball, hit right at me. The cab's radio crackles with the dispatcher's voice, and now my driver turns around to favor me with his gray fleshy face, mottled with a pink rash.

What's it gonna be, pal? In or out.

You know a place called the Alamo?

The driver grunts. Big drop-off from the James to the Alamo.

That's cool. Is it far?

The Alamo is strictly Section Eight. Peeling paint and the stink of mildew and a humming death vibe. The lobby is a narrow brown tomb, the walls painted the color of shit. I hate to generalize, but if I was looking to kill myself in a cheap coldwater garret where none of my neighbors are gonna say boo, this is the place. The receptionist is a guy watching TV behind a chickenwire cage. The house rates are scrawled on a blackboard behind his head, which is shaved smooth as my ass and covered in fine, intricate tattoos. I step up to the cage and the guy growls at me, jerks his fascinating skull at the blackboard. I glance at the board just long enough to register the notion that a bed in this shithole may be rented by the hour for the kingly ransom of ten dollars.

I'm not interested in a room, I say.

You a cop?

I'm looking for a buddy of mine, Sugar Finch.

The skull gives me a long look, and apparently decides I am just unsavory enough to indeed be pals with a piece of shit like this Sugar Finch.

He's in room 39, third floor.

You know if he's in?

Think I saw him, yeah.

Don't buzz him, okay. I want to surprise him.

Buzz him? Shit man, you think we got phones in the rooms?

I take the gummy wet stairs up to the third floor, my steps echoing soft. The fire door opens onto a long windowless hallway with rancid gray carpet and gray walls streaked with water damage. The air is funky in the Alamo. I cruise silent down the hall and find the door marked 39, keep going. Communal toilet at the opposite end, which accounts for some of the funk. I retrace my steps to the fire door. On the wall to my left is a fuse box. I flip it open and take out my knife; what I aim to do deserves the cover of darkness.

I shove my knife into the control panel and twist. The hall lights blink once, and go black. It's just like being inside my head. Dark, with lingering echoes and the faint stink of mildew. I touch one hand to the wall and stealth-walk along to 39. Trouble is I'm not much of a killer. The fact is, I've never killed anybody, not on purpose. I've wanted to, plenty of times, but always stopped short. It's just not part of my wiring. Now I'm in a dark hallway, maybe twenty-five feet from one of the men who raped Jude, and I don't quite know what I'm going to do. I may suffer mind-ripping headaches all the time, and with them apocalyptic visions, but I can't discern the future.

The best I can imagine is disappearing into the shadows along the wall. In a minute, Sugar Finch will come out of the room nervous and freaked by the power failure. It would be the easiest thing in the world to sweep his legs out from under him, to fall like a cat onto his chest, to slash open his throat before he even cries out. Easy as cake to imagine, damn near impossible to see myself doing it. Now the door to 39 opens cool as a whisper and I fade against the wall.

four.

THE KING JAMES HOTEL IS STRICTLY OLD WORLD. I limp into the lobby, still shaken. A silent valet in an elegant green uniform comes forward to take my bag, a shapeless leather pouch that holds my toothbrush and what remains of my wardrobe. I shake my head and mutter that I'm not feeble. The valet tips his cap, flashes me a ghostly smile. I give him five dollars, because I believe in big tips and because I don't necessarily want him to notice that I've just had my ass kicked good and proper.

The valet is young and thin with dark circles under blue eyes.

What's your name? I say.

Jeremy, sir. I'm here until midnight.

I have a bad hangover, Jeremy. What do you recommend?

He shrugs. Vanilla milkshake with a shot of espresso and splash of brandy.

That sounds perfect.

Your room number, sir?

I glance at the scrap of paper on which I've written Jude's room number.

My name is Poe. I'm in room 1221.

The kid blushes at the mention of this number and I gather he's met Jude. This makes me smile. Jude was always very sweet to grocery clerks and postmen. I give the kid another five and he says the milkshake is already on its way.

The elevator rises slow and dreamy. I use the time to pull myself together. Take a few deep breaths to slow the pulse, examine the shoes for dog shit. Look in the mirror, check my face for spattered blood. Polish the teeth with my shirtsleeve and hope my breath is not too poisonous. I slap my face for a touch of color. Drag the fingers through my hair and sniff the clothes. Tobacco and vodka and unwashed Phineas. I stare at my hands, which tremble. I tell myself that everything is right as rain. Only now do I allow the video drone in my head to replay the unhappy meeting I just had with Sugar Finch.

On the third floor of the Alamo I had disappeared into the shadows, soft and velvet. A fire alarm sounded, a low-pressure slow burning grind that hit you in the spine and made every molecule in you beg to get the fuck out of there. I waited, though. I was gonna kill this guy. I didn't know how. I imagined he would be running when he came out of the room and I was going to sweep his legs, take him down the way Jude taught me. Then disable him with a punch to the throat and figure out how to stop his heart beating. Maybe I would ram my thumbs into his eyes and just keep digging until I struck gold, until I scooped out brain matter. But when he came out of room 39, Sugar Finch wasn't running. He was walking, right at me. Like he knew I was there, like the motherfucker could see me plain as day. I went low and tried to sweep his legs but it was a joke. He was way too fast and he jumped right at me. He was on top of me like a spider on a moth, his hand on my throat.

He leaned close and said, I remember you. You saved my life today. I won't forget that. But come to my house even once more and you won't walk again.

He stood up, yanking me to my feet. I could barely breathe.

I remember your girl too, he said. That pussy tasted just like sunshine. He grinned, and licked his teeth. I should have kissed you goodbye that day, you could have tasted her on my mouth.

Then he was gone, blowing away easy as smoke.

Now the elevator groans and the doors open on the twelfth floor of the King James.

The hallway before me is silent. Blue and comforting. The light is soft and there are no shadows. Hum of a faraway ice machine. Lush carpet under-foot, dark as midnight with random flowers and triangles of pink and gold. And so soft that my footsteps are a whisper. I could fall over dead and the carpet would swallow the noise and this is why I love hotels. Two a.m. and two p.m. are interchangeable. The light is ever gentle. There is always ice to be had and a body may hit the floor without disturbing anyone. The room numbers descend to the left and I move along in search of 1221, the fingers of my right hand trailing down the wall behind me. The hall twists and turns and intersects itself more than I feel is necessary, and I wonder if the rooms come in unusual shapes and sizes. I am soon lost down a narrow tributary and the numbers are pissing me off. They irrationally grow larger on one side and smaller on the other. I pass 1217, 1219 and stop. Blue midnight stretches before and behind me. Traces of pink and gold and the underwater light of dreams.

The door to 1221 is cracked open. Not a mistake Jude would generally make, not in this life or the next. I push it open ever so gentle, and still there is a soft hiss of escaping air, as if I have just opened the hatch of a spaceship. The room is five degrees colder than the hallway and completely fucking dark. The door closes softly behind me and I'm blind as an under-ground beast.

Exhale and wonder.

The brain of your average human male is damp and slippery and the descent into adolescent fantasy is as casual as falling off a log. I turn on the light and Jude is naked and blue on the bathroom floor, a plastic bag over her head. I turn on the light and Jude is lounging on a puffy white bed in black leather pants and nothing else. Tangle of wet black hair on white pil-lows twisting like snakes and the pants are so tight they will have to be peeled from her skin. I turn on the light and Jude stands an arm's length away, a straight razor in one hand. She wears dark sunglasses and a glossy red raincoat that won't show blood.

I turn on the light and the room is empty.

Make a fast sweep through the entire space, which is big enough to house a small army, to be sure. I take a pass through the bathroom. Nightmares and bad blood be damned. Black tile and three walls of mirrors. The shower is a dark chamber behind pale green glass, empty. The tub is sunken into the floor. There is a bidet, which pleases me somehow and I smile into three mirrors at once. There is an antique cosmetics bag on the edge of the marble sink, black leather with silver clasp. The only other sign of her presence is a fine black streak of fecal matter on the slope of the toilet bowl.

Taped to the bathroom wall are three photographs, bright color shots taken with a telephoto, blown up to eight by ten. By the angles, I'd guess she shot these from high above. I see Jude on a rooftop, crouched like a sniper and wonder why she didn't just kill them when she had them in her sights. And a voice in my head says, because that wouldn't have been so up close and personal as an intimate scalping. I focus on the three faces, three monsters. Two of them are Shane and Sugar Finch. Their names, birthdates, Socials, tattoos, and distinctive marks are written in fine black ink along the borders, like delicate marginalia. The third photo is a guy with dark hair and blue eyes flecked with black, like turquoise in the sun. The name is John Ransom Miller. Five foot nine, one seventy. No Social, no distinguishing marks. D.O.B. is 11.02.59. Blink and I'm back in our flat in the Quarter. I see John Ransom Miller sprawled on the floor. This is the guy I crippled with that toilet tank lid. I wonder if he's up and walking again. Maybe he's in a chair.

Scrawled on the mirror above the sink, in brown lipstick, are five words. *The velvet warms and binds.*
   Velvet.
   The trouble is I don't know the frame of reference, the context.
   Velvet.
   Jude always loved the word. She tossed it around like spare change and it had more than one meaning to her. In friendly conversation, the velvet may simply be defined as twilight. The gloaming. The velvet was telephone code for heroin. I had often heard Jude refer to her pussy as the velvet. And

the velvet was used metaphysically to refer to the subconscious, to childhood memories. For Jude, velvet was the lost time of alien abductions.
Velvet was euphoria and dread. Velvet was a perfectly good word, but one
that always troubled me.

To my mind, the velvet is best translated as the sleep that resembles
death. Velvet is the sleep that becomes death.

Outside of the bathroom proper is a vanity area with mirror and sink that
serves as the bar. I reach for an open bottle of Jack Daniels and take small
contemplative sips from it as I survey the room. The windows are blotted
out by heavy curtains the color of smoke that fall from ceiling to floor. The
sun may as well not exist. The sun has no hope in this room, and again it
could be day or night. The television and refrigerator are tastefully housed
inside an armoire. The carpet is the pale fleshy pink of a monster's tongue
and the walls are painted red.

Two queen beds, one of them stripped bare.

The exposed mattress is yellow with pale gray stripes and a bright red
bloom near the middle that looks like fresh blood but is actually a pair of
red silk underpants and now I feel a faraway surge of nausea tinged with
memory. My head is fucking with me. The other bed is covered in a white
quilt with splashes of blue flowers and looks as if it has not been touched
since the housekeepers left it.

Along the far wall are two Beowulf chairs and a curved glass coffee
table the shape of a teardrop, beneath which are two curious blue sneakers
with orange stripes. Jude does not wear sneakers, as far as I know. I try to
imagine her jogging along a bike path in sweatpants and sports bra and it
just doesn't work for me.

The cracked leather pouch still hangs around my neck as if I'm afraid
someone might steal my toothbrush. I shrug it to the floor and kick it into
a corner. I lift the bottle to my lips and commence to take another, longer
drink of whiskey.

Jude blows softly on the back of my neck as she walks past and I nearly jump
out of my skin.

Drinking from the bottle, she says. What would your mother think?

I choke and spit and manage not to bite off a mouthful of glass. I turn around slow as blood clotting, my eyes shut tight. Five years since the attack and in my head her face is still terribly swollen and bruised. The skin is black in some places and her left eye is drifting loose in the socket. I open my eyes and her face is perfect but for the pale narrow scar that nearly blinded her, that left a notch in her right eyebrow and now runs almost parallel with the worry lines in her forehead and disappears into her gold and brown hair.

Jesus, I say. Have a little mercy.

Mercy, she says. Mercy?

Compassion, I say.

Huh, she says. Any relation to the word merchandise?

The same Latin root, I say. I will give you this fine pig and ten sacks of grain if you spare my miserable life.

I thought you liked being miserable, she says.

Her hair is damp and longer than I remember. Her mouth is unchanged, the round lush lips with a tiny scar at one corner, where her boyfriend hit her with a rock as a kid. She wears a tight lime green shirt with no sleeves. The shadow and distraction of ribs and muscle and nipple. She's had her bellybutton pierced since I last saw her. She wears blue jeans too big for her, that hang well below the hip. Barefoot, she is perhaps two inches shorter than I am but it's hard to be sure because she rarely stands still. I'm dizzy, looking at her. The air between us is bright with sparks, like there's static electricity coming from her skin. I have an urge to back away from her and I tell myself not to be silly.

She reaches to touch my face and I flinch away.

There is a brief, heavy silence. Jude stares at me, not smiling.

I open my mouth and she leaps on me like a cat. I drop the bottle and we fall to the bed, struggling. Jude was always very strong and she enjoyed violent foreplay but she's not laughing, her eyes are shining with something that resembles desire but isn't and when I try to kiss her, she moves her head and sinks her teeth lightly into my throat. I throw her to the floor and roll away. My hand goes to my neck and I am fairly surprised to see that she has actually drawn blood.

Jude breathes heavily, grinning at me.

What the fuck, Jude?

Her eyes are wild and manic, pupils big as marbles. Jude rarely touched drugs when we were together but I can see she is extremely high, almost vibrating. She shrugs and picks up the fallen bottle of Jack, most of which has seeped into the fleshy carpet. She takes a highball glass from the dresser and empties the bottle into it.

Mind if we share? she says. It's the only clean glass.

five.

I AM SITTING ON THE NAKED YELLOW MATTRESS, numb and staring at Jude with my mouth open like a mental patient in front of the television. My throat is bleeding and I think maybe I should look at it. I go to the sink and run cold water over a washcloth, cocking my head sideways to examine the wound. The skin is broken and there will be a bruise but it's not bleeding so badly. Jude paces back and forth and now she appears in the mirror behind me. I notice that she is grinding her teeth, sucking at her tongue. The voice in my head keeps muttering that she's high, that I have no idea what's been happening to her these years, that I should be gentle with her.

What are you on, baby?

Nothing, she says. I'm happy.

I saw you today, I say. In the alley.

That was you?

Jude backs away from me. Her eyes fall on the mirror and she spins away from it, lifts the whiskey to her mouth. I can hear her teeth chattering against the glass. I stand and take the drink from her. I could put my arms around her. I could try. I remember lying in bed with her like it was yesterday. Her flesh sticking together with mine in a hot room and white sheets flung to the floor. Jude always wanted to be touched. But now she's volatile, untouchable. Jude has become an unknown compound.

Whoa, I say. Don't freak.

How did you find me? she says.

Doesn't matter, does it?

How?

I've been tracking you, feels like forever. Finally landed in Flagstaff, where I talked to a couple guys named Rabbit and Steve.

Her eyes flicker dark. How were they?

Pretty crippled.

She nods. I felt bad about that.

Really?

I'm not the same, she says. Not the same as you knew me.

What's different?

She scowls. Everything, my heart. My head.

Come on, I say. From the look of that guy in the alley, his eyes gouged out and missing his hair, I'd say you've reverted perfectly to form.

It's impossible, isn't it? For a man to imagine what it's like.

I've tried, Jude. I've spent five years trying.

And you'll never get it.

There is a soft knock at the door and Jude has a gun in her hand before I can blink.

Expecting someone? she says.

I ordered a milkshake, I say.

Rustle and sigh and dead leaves falling.

How boyish, she says.

Jude bends close to me and slips the gun under the mattress, the back of her hand just touching my leg. Our eyes crash together.

What have you become? I say.

Very careful, she says.

Jude goes to the door and I am alone for a moment. Breathe and release. Two minutes in this room and she is well under my skin. That's the trouble with the human body. My ex-girlfriend is armed and dangerous, and I have an erection. This is how people wind up on afternoon talk shows. Blood rush and I stand up, cross the room on stiff legs. I pick up one of the blue sneakers and turn it over in my hands. Size 9, a man's shoe. Jude wears a woman's 7. I lift the sneaker to my face and it smells new. I turn around as Jude returns with a silver room service tray. Thick milkshake in tall glass and stainless steel beaker. She places the tray on the coffee table and crouches there, not smiling. I watch as she lifts the milkshake to her mouth, then swabs the white cream from her dark lips.

How is it? I say.

Yummy.

I sink into one of the Beowulf chairs and let the sneaker fall from my hand.

Who is the runner?

Jude stares. Friend of mine, she says.

Does he have a name?

Jude sips the whiskey.

I tell myself not to push. I watch her throat move. She sits on the bed beside me, our hands not quite touching. The yellow mattress is a dirty lemon sky between us. Jude sinks back into that sky, her hair dark as seaweed. She balances the drink on her tummy and a lazy smile drifts across her face and disappears as if chased away by memory. I hesitate, then lie down beside her. Together we stare at the ceiling like two kids looking for reptiles in the clouds. We are surrounded by the sky.

I'm glad to see you, I say.

I'm not ready to have sex with you, she says.

Who said anything about sex?

I just want to be clear, she says.

Okay.

Okay, she says.

This is a nice room, I say.

Jude looks around. It's obscene, she says.

How are you paying for it?

Don't be rude, she says.

What are we doing here, then?

There is a long silence.

Jude swallows the last of the whiskey and allows her arm to fall lifeless on the bed. She closes her eyes and stops breathing for a moment and I remember a fetish of hers that I never much cared for. Once in a while, Jude liked to pretend she was dead while I fucked her, a beautiful dead girl.

The glass rolls out of her hand and across the mattress. She sits up and slowly turns her doll's head around to stare at me. Her eyes are glowing and suddenly I don't recognize her at all. I feel my body go tense.

I found them, she says. The three of them.

Yes. I saw the photos in the bathroom.

She sits up and lights a smoke. Handsome, aren't they?

Now there are two, I say.

Yes, she says.

What will we do with them?

Kill them, she says. Slow and careful.

The silence in the room is like copper in my mouth.

I followed the brother, I say. Today, after that scene in the alley.

Sugar Finch? she says.

Yeah, I say.

Don't you love that name? she says, bitterly.

I love it.

Where to? she says.

A hotel called the Alamo.

What happened?

I had him. Then lost him. He's dangerous.

That's okay, she says. It will be nicer to kill him together.

I hope so, I say.

Jude glances at her watch and sucks in her breath.

We're gonna be late, she says.

The fuck. Late for what?

Jude doesn't look at me.

Where are we going?

She touches her mouth with two fingers barely trembling and I remember how she used to sink into these funky silences just before she was about to lie to me.

Shopping, she says. I need a new pair of shoes.

I stare at her, wondering if she knows how psychotic she sounds.

Jude smiles. Come on. Your baby needs a new pair of shoes.

There follows a strange hazy almost domestic moment as Jude and I gather ourselves and prepare to go out. She touches up her makeup. I give my shoes a fast polish with spit and a washcloth. I brush my teeth, washing away the taste of booze and smoke. Jude examines my face the way she used to, checking my skin for blemishes. Our faces close together, sharing the same air. I can almost taste her smoky lips. I can feel the burn of her eyes as she takes care of a blackhead for me, and all the while the words your baby ring in the air.

I have to ask, Jude.

What?

Did you have the baby?

She kisses my left eye. What do you think?

six.

DOWN TO THE SURFACE IN A HUMMING BOX and the elevator game resumes between us as if we have not been apart more than a day. Jude stands on the far side of the box, rocking slightly back and forth and cleaning her fingernails with the edge of a key. She is the only woman I know who can clean her nails and give the impression that she is stripping down an assault rifle. I slouch on the far wall and stare rudely at her. The elevator game has two rules: Jude and I are strangers and we must stand on opposite sides of the box, no matter how crowded. Otherwise we are free to stare and flirt openly, to speak or not speak.

The elevator shivers and stops on the ninth floor.

A man and woman get on, a married couple in their sixties. The man has gray hair almost blue. Black wool overcoat. The woman wears a string of pearls and her face is stretched and glossy with Botox and plastic surgery. I imagine she has a poodle at home, and a hired dogwalker. The two of them smile and nod and move to the back wall but I can't acknowledge them because I am staring at Jude, who stands with her eyes closed and her arms crossed over her breasts. She is trembling slightly. Her eyes seem brighter, perhaps because her face has gone pale. I don't know if this is arousal or anger or what and I think it might be terrifying if there were a blackout right now and the elevator stopped between floors.

I would not be afraid for myself, but for them. Because I have a feeling that Jude might do something well north of freaky.

What the fuck are you staring at? Jude says softly, to me.

The old woman with altered face is so visibly uncomfortable I'm afraid she might pee on herself.

Nothing, I say. I'm sorry.

The game is over when one of us apologizes. Jude comes close to me and I can smell her. Oranges and musk. I am intensely aware of her every bone and muscle, her small round breasts. Her long, volatile throat and dark eyes. The old guy to my left is making damp, fleshy noises in his throat and shifting on his feet. Jude looks at him, smiles sweetly.

This world, she says. Then the fireworks.

Dead silence.

Pardon? the old man says.

Jude turns to me.

Empty your pockets, she says.

Ah, says the old man. Excuse me.

Jude's left hand snakes out and touches the emergency stop button. The elevator heaves mightily and stops between floors.

What's going on?

Impromptu theater, she says.

Let these people go. They don't need to be here.

No one is going anywhere, she says.

Please, says the old woman. Please. I have asthma.

Jude pokes her index finger into her mouth and slowly withdraws it, staring at me with lazy eyes.

Asthma, says the woman.

Her husband makes a clucking sound and she slumps against him. He puts his arm around her and pats her shoulder.

Well? says Jude.

I thought you weren't ready for sex, I say.

Jude grunts. A blowjob is not sex. It's a favor, a service.

That's great. Let them go.

No, she says. Empty your fucking pockets.

The old guy sniffs. Think you better empty your pockets, son.

I crouch and empty my pockets onto the floor. There isn't much. A clump of money, two hundred dollars or so. A half pack of cigarettes, a book of matches. Pocket knife. The key to Jude's hotel room. Sugar Finch's wallet, thin and useless. Jude takes it all, putting everything in her bag. She counts the money, then puts it away too.

Having fun? I say.

Not yet, she says.

The growl of a zipper and now Jude gives me something in return. The gun she was waving about before, the little black automatic, a Walther P22.

What is this? I say.

It's a gun, sweetie. Do you like it?

I turn it over and over in my hands. Black steel under fluorescent light. The gun fits nicely in my palm. To my left, the old woman is breathing like a wounded horse and I think she's going to have a heart attack. I run a hand through my hair and it comes away wet.

Do you like it? says Jude.

Yes, I say. It's very nice. Why are you giving it to me?

Jude shrugs. Would you rather lie around that hotel room and wait for the world to end?

I stare at her. Would I rather lie around the hotel room waiting for the world to end than what?

This is about the old man, she whispers.

What about him?

He's a molester.

Please, I say.

Look at him, she says. Look at him.

I glance to my left and imagine the old guy down on his knees. Eyes pink and streaming. The old man has manicured hands, immaculate clothes. He doesn't look like a molester but then they never do. I see a hole in his forehead the size of a quarter.

What are you looking at, sir? says the old man in a quavering voice.

Do you have an erection? Jude says, to me.

Jesus. This isn't funny, Jude.

Do you? she says.

I touch myself. This level of public intimacy is like waking up covered in sweat.

Well? she says.

Like a dead bird, I say.

Jude sighs. Maybe you should consider therapy.

Maybe.

Are you going to shoot the old man? she says.

He's not a molester, I say.

There's no way of knowing that, she says. Maybe the wife knows.

The old woman begins to weep. Jude folds her arms across her chest and stares at me.

And if I say no?

Then I might just kiss you goodbye, she says. You could find yourself walking out of here with the clothes you are wearing, a pack of cigarettes and a gun. I imagine you are resourceful enough to find your way home.

I don't have a home.

Jude sighs. It's a figure of speech.

The old woman continues to weep. The sound is like that of a radio stuck between two stations. I look at the gun in my hand. I wouldn't care to hitchhike back to Flagstaff. There is a lot of desert between here and there and the sun would be unfriendly. I could possibly carjack a tourist and rob a few convenience stores for cash and food. But I would most likely get shot by a kid with pimples and a plastic name-tag and besides, I just got here. I lift the gun. I touch it to Jude's head, gently. The old man groans.

I want my money back, I say.

Jude yawns. What?

The money. I'm going to need it for incidentals.

Incidentals? she says.

Taxicabs, I say. Food and drink. More than one drink.

No, she says. I want this to be difficult for you.

Believe me. It hasn't been easy so far.

Jude shrugs. She hits the emergency button and the elevator resumes its slow fall, stopping again on the fifth floor. The old man and his wife get off without a word. No one gets on. I slump against the wall with the gun in my hand. I am soaked with sweat.

Jude nods at the gun. You might want to put that away.

What was that shit about fireworks?

It's a short story by Jim Thompson, she says. It's about incest.

Outside and everything is pale and strange. I stand on the sidewalk, blinking. The gun is heavy in my pocket. It seems like forever ago, but Jude gave me two fat lines of coke before we left the room and my skull feels stretched thin. I breathe air that doesn't stink of fear. Jude walks away and I'm not ready to follow just yet. Jeremy the doorman watches me, a withered smile on his face. He comes over and offers me a cigarette.

Thanks, I say.

Familiarity breeds contempt, he says. Am I right?

What?

Your wife there, he says. She's pure hell on wheels, no shit. But sometimes a man needs a change of scenery.

I sigh, weary. She's not my wife. And get the fuck away from me.

He shrugs and slips me a card. The Paradise, he says. You won't recognize your own dick when you come out of there.

Jude is disappearing in the distance. I look at Jeremy. He smiles at me, as if he's my buddy. My new pal. I can see the traffic and bobbing faces around us but there is an internal vacuum, an absence of noise. The sunlight is rosy. The sunlight is meaty, bloody. This is the moment before the gunfight in a movie. I tend to get squeamish in crowds but everyone is fluid, perfect. Everyone cruises along in his or her own bubble and I wonder if today is a holiday. I take the gun out of my pocket and Jeremy takes a step back. I try to imagine how his face would change if a bullet ripped through his abdomen.

I can't see it, yet.

Jude pushes through the heavy glass doors of Nieman Marcus. I follow her and regret it immediately. The ceiling is fifty feet above the floor and composed of elaborate gold and white stained glass, like the roof of a cathedral. I tell myself not to look up again, unless I want to vomit in public.

These posh fucking stores.

They always have a grinning torturer standing just inside the doors, a guy whose job it is to greet you with white teeth and cool, appraising eyes. I am about to dodge away from him but Jude gives him a mercurial nod and he just melts away. She glides to the first exhibit and pretends to examine an array of hairy sweaters. I come up behind her, breathing like a pervert. I violate her space.

Dead cats, I say. They look like dead cats.

Jude doesn't look at me, she doesn't even tilt her head.

Keep walking, she says. Pretend you don't know me and whatever you do, do not call me Jude.

What should I call you?

I'm going to count to three, says Jude.

I touch her shoulder and she spins around.

You will fucking talk to me, I say.

She smiles, harshly. What's the matter?

Everything, I say. Why did you run that scene in the elevator?

Instinct, she says. It felt right.

What was it about them?

You saw that woman, didn't you? Her face, her plastic fucking face. She went under the knife for him because she wasn't pretty anymore.

Jesus, I whisper. That was about your face?

Keep walking, she says. Pretend you don't know me or I will start screaming.

I try to be cool. I try not to blink but I have a bad mixture of junk and fear and confusion in me. I try to imagine how Jude feels, how it would feel to be a woman raped and mutilated. She is still stupidly beautiful, to my mind. Men and women alike still turn to look at her on the street, but that curved white scar above her eyes may be the only thing she sees when she looks in the mirror. Try as I might, though, I can't feel what she feels. The bitter shame, the hatred of self. Irrational or not. My brain is heavy with bad water and my heart is actually chirping. I've got crickets in there. That coke she gave me was some kind of uncut Bolivian rock, nasty stuff. I don't know where her money is coming from but she apparently has plenty of it.

Anyway, she told me to be cool and I don't feel cool at all.

I mutter something incoherent and totter off to look at a display case of men's watches, as if I might buy a Rolex. And when I look around, she's gone.

Freak out. Phineas gonna freak out.

I don't function so well in these high-dollar department stores. The problem is comprehension, identity, sensory deprivation. I have muddy vision. Brown beige gray black. Everyone in the store is narrowly focused on some unseen prize. Everyone is looking for salvation. If they find the right pair of shoes or the perfect new raincoat they will be saved for an hour, for a day. I can't see the big picture and so I walk in circles. I get lost. I'm fearful of the salespeople. They lean against marble columns, mute and faceless, pods recharging and when they lay eyes on me they will detach themselves from their stations and come forward with teeth bared.

Can I help you can I help you? Are you okay? they say.

No, I say. I'm only looking. I'm looking for something but I don't know what.

I don't understand the layout of the fucking store. The clothes are arranged without regard to season or function. The prices are hidden from sight and it's certainly shameful to ask. There are too many shoes by far and the suits just frighten me. I contemplate a new pair of pants but can't bear to try them on. I'm afraid someone will come to the dressing room door while I'm wriggling out of my old pants, sweating, fumbling with a knot in my shoelaces.

The polite knock, the hushed voice. Are you quite all right in there, sir?

It's brutal. The dressing rooms have become these new world torture chambers. I like to ride the escalators, though. The slow freefall, the mirrors. The escalators go up and down, up and down. I have these childlike fantasies that I am secretly a rubber-limbed superhero who can slide through keyholes and I don't have to get off the escalator, that I can disappear in the crack between escalator and marble floor and get a brief glimpse of the afterlife below that resembles the dark, stinking hold of a slave ship. I try not to stare at anyone and I successfully disembark before security decides I'm a nutbag.

Eventually I break down and ask someone where women's shoes might be.

seven.

JUDE SITS IN A BLACK LEATHER CHAIR WITH CHROME ARMRESTS. Legs crossed.
She is thin as a spider and she has taken her boots off, her socks. Her naked
left foot bouncing. I see a yellow flower in the rain. I lean against a far wall
between opposing racks of jackets and watch her. She flashes from psychotic to fragile so fast it's like watching a strobe light. I don't know what
to do about her, honestly.

Follow her, play the game.

Or walk away and pretend I don't know her. Tell myself I never loved
her.

I stare at her like I want to take her skull off. I put out a fearsome
sexual vibe but she doesn't seem to notice. A salesman with red bow-tie
and receding hair approaches her, his face faintly flushed. Four shoeboxes
in hand. He kneels like a zealot and takes her foot in his hand. Jude's lips
move but I can't read them. The salesman touches the curve of her foot,
the instep. Her eyebrows twitch and from across the room I can see the
man's hands are shaking. I imagine she has said something innocent about
male pattern baldness, about men who wear bowties in public and how
such men secretly want to be whipped by a woman in leather. She may
have said something about his chapped lips or the sorry hygiene of his fingernails. She may have offered to suck his cock. Whatever it was, she
touched a bone. Jude loves to touch a bone. The salesman fits her with a
pair of green velvet stilettos and Jude stands, she turns a circle and takes a

few experimental steps. She's looking for a mirror and she walks right past me, her right hand brushing against my thigh. I close my eyes and now I hear a man's voice, a voice full of smoke and money.

Very nice, he says. You have beautiful feet.

I open my eyes. Jude is standing before one of those low mirrors, her legs cut off at the knee. Her legs float away from her body and the green shoes seem to sparkle. She does have beautiful feet and a lifetime ago, I spent a lot of time biting and sucking at them. Jude ignores the man who spoke to her but I take a good long look at him. White male, thoroughbred. Expensive education, manicured face and hands. He holds a long black umbrella in his right hand. He has an arrogant mouth and I'm sure his teeth are perfect. Probably in his middle forties and he looks better than me. He wears a charcoal suit, elegantly cut. Dark gray shirt buttoned to the throat and no tie. Fine black hair shining like metal. Bright blue eyes. I saw this guy's photo on Jude's bathroom wall just an hour ago. According to Jude's notes, this is John Ransom Miller.

Jude ignores him. His lips curve and he blows softly on her hair.

My stomach makes a funny noise and I chew my lip. I feel strange, jealous. On one hand I am positive that this man is about to die, that Jude is about to turn and just gut him where he stands. But on the other, I don't think so. Jude is acting not like herself and I can see this guy has some hefty mojo, some bad juice about him, and I wonder briefly does he have some hold over my girl.

You are very pretty, the man says. Are you a model, perhaps?

I recoil, unnoticed. I can't tell if he's fucking with her, or if he simply cannot see the left side of her face from his vantage point.

Jude turns, slowly, and shows him her whole face. That's not funny.

His expression doesn't waver. I don't mean to be funny.

I'm an actress, she says. Or I used to be.

Really. The man smiles. I'm sure you were very talented.

Oh, my. I don't know about that, she says. But thank you.

This new Jude is packing a mean bag of tricks and now she whips out an otherworldly mixture of nubile self-consciousness and predatory voodoo. She is suddenly leaning toward the man, her lips slightly parted and I'm irritated to realize I'm getting an erection. The man looks more than a little bothered himself.

Would you like to have dinner with me tonight?

I would, says Jude. I really would. But I have a prior entanglement.

Are you sure? he says.

Yes, she says. I'm afraid so.

Oh, well. That's too bad.

Jude licks her lips. Too bad, yes.

The man stares at her and I fancy there's a trickle of sweat along his jaw. But he's a tough cookie, I think. He reaches into his breast pocket and produces a business card. On the ring finger of his right hand he wears a heavy fraternity ring with a dark red stone. I hear myself exhale. Jude takes the card from him as if it's a long-stemmed rose.

You should call me, the man says. I have a friend or two in Hollywood.

Lucky you, says Jude.

Are you a spiritual person? he says.

No, she says. Not anymore.

He smiles. I'm a Buddhist, myself.

Jude nods, considering. You must have a great capacity for suffering, she says.

You have no idea, he says.

Tempting, she says. Maybe I will call you, after all.

Yes, the man says. He stands there, rocking back on his heels as if he needs more oxygen.

Goodbye, says Jude.

The man stares at her, mute. Then turns to go. Jude glances down at the card he gave her.

Wait, she says.

The man keeps walking, his back to her.

This is just a phone number, she says. Who shall I ask for?

He grins at this. My name is John Miller, he says. Then steps onto the escalator and disappears.

Jude doesn't look at me, not yet.

The salesman sits patiently in one of the leather chairs, his head bowed. She touches his sleeve. I love these shoes, she says. Will you box up my boots, please?

The salesman nods, his face turning pink. Then he scurries away. I walk toward Jude, my head buzzing. The locusts in my head are getting ready to descend, and my brain is a field of wheat. Jude is glowing like she just swallowed a fistful of stardust. She stands with hands on her hips, pelvis thrust out.

Did you not recognize him? she says.

I stare into the mirror and see the photos in her bathroom again. I see a sideways flash of dark hair, of blue and black eyes. John Ransom Miller was one of the masked men who'd come to see us in New Orleans. He was the panty sniffer, the one I'd hammered to the floor with the toilet lid. He had lain crumpled on his side the entire time, watching as the others raped her. He barely looked at me, that day.

Yeah. I recognized him.

Well? she says.

This is why you gave me the gun? I say. You want me to kill him.

Jude shrugs. Perhaps you should rethink your ideas about fate.

The gun is heavy in my pocket.

Yeah, I say. Perhaps I should.

Don't kill him, she says. Not yet.

Why?

Because we need him to get to the quarterback.

Senator Cody, I say.

Yeah. She points at the mirror. If not for him, I'm not looking at this face.

What then? You want me to make friends with this guy?

If you want to hurt him, she says, bring me his finger. The one with that hideous ring.

I stare at her.

Go, she says. You're going to lose him.

I take the escalator down to menswear. Jude stands at the top of the escalator, hands on her hips and a crooked little smile on her face. I'm going to hell, of course. I turn around to face the descent and when I look back she's gone. The escalator nears the bottom and I wait for my feet to touch solid ground. Five seconds, four. Time enough to contemplate my situation. Jude wants me to follow this man, but I am not to kill him. Thank god for that. I had an opportunity to kill Sugar Finch earlier today, and fucked it up like a rock star. I tell myself that if I love her, I will not fail her again.

Five years have passed since Jude and I were together. The years just slip away. I take off my shoes and pause to examine my toes and two days disappear. I wander into the bathroom to brush my teeth and a week is gone. I pour myself a cup of coffee and a month floats past. The years tumble past you like bits of paper on the street and you may not even feel the breeze at your back but then something catches your eye, a twist of black hair or a dog leaping to catch a tennis ball. The splintered chorus of a stupid pop song. You turn around and another chunk of your life drifts by like unrecognized trash and it was never yours to begin with.

But look at it this way. Jude and I had a fight once, way back when. The apartment was expanding, warping. The rooms were gelatinous and everything was curved. Our bedroom was taking the shape of an egg. The room was freaking me out and drugs were involved. They usually are. This is a natural law, like the one about gravity. If a body has physical mass, then it will fall to earth. If your hotel room is transforming into a metaphysical bubble, then drugs are probably involved.

Anyway.

Jude was completely nonverbal and I was crouched high atop an armoire, stuck there. I was suddenly terrified of heights. And of her, probably. I watched Jude crawl around on the floor with a knife in one hand, a long bright red dildo in the other. Jude was trying to speak. She was grunting, snorting. I was pretty sure she wanted to kill me, she wanted to fuck me to death. Her shoulders were slick with blood and snot and black grime and her brain was so shredded by coke she would not have blinked if I had spontaneously burst into flames. But that's just another drug story, a psycho love story. The real Jude lay curled up like a cat beside me less than twenty-four hours later asking me what color she should paint her toenails. She wanted to drink cheap white wine and eat chocolate for breakfast. She wanted me to stay in bed all day and watch MTV with her. Jude put her head in my lap and asked me in a destroyed voice if I still liked her. Jude is composed of claws and teeth and unblinking eyes but she is vulnerable, perhaps now more than ever. She is a wolf but like anybody else she's afraid to grow old, she's afraid that one day she will walk into a room and no one will look at her.

I touched her hair and whispered yes, I like you.

There is an obscure musical instrument called the theremin that produces sound without ever being touched. The player moves his hands in a slow circular motion between twin antennae thin as ghosts, calling forth eerie underwater noises akin to whalespeak. Brian Wilson was particularly fond of the theremin. He used it sparingly on the *Pet Sounds* album, I believe. Anyway, Jude and I have always managed to extract sound from each other, without ever touching the skin. And I think that's love, or something like it.

John Ransom Miller is nowhere to be seen and I hear Jude's voice in my head.

Do you believe in fate, she says. Or not?

I want to go back to that hotel room and I might need to bring her a strange man's severed finger to gain entry. It sounds like a bad joke but now I'm anxious that I've lost him. I have lost the owner of the finger and I hurry through a demilitarized zone of postmodern Italian shoes. Gucci and friends. A green and black spaceman's boot catches my eye and I pick it up by the laces and let it dangle. Prada. Nine hundred dollars and I laugh out loud, nervous. I don't want to hunt this man and I don't want to lose him, either. I want to go back to the obscene hotel room. I want to get good and drunk. I twirl the boot and stare at it until mesmerized. I feel like a monkey confronted by the miracle of a yo-yo. A salesman glares at me and I put the boot down as Miller walks right past me.

I follow him. What the hell, right.

John Ransom Miller doesn't drift and meander the way I do. He knows where he's going and he obviously expects people to get the hell out of his way. He takes the escalator two steps at a time and bullies his way past a throng of Japanese tourists, then outside. This no-nonsense attitude of his gives me a sense of purpose and I hit the street at a cool ten yards behind him. There's a nasty wind coming off the bay and I button my coat against it. I light a cigarette and wonder grimly if I will have to ration them, as I have no cash on me. Then I start to worry that Miller will hop into a yellow cab and leave me standing on the sidewalk, a scarecrow equipped with useless skin and teeth.

Options.

If he does get into a cab, then I could get into the next cab and tell the driver to follow him. This maneuver probably doesn't work outside of the movies, but who knows. I might get a driver who has seen a lot of movies and secretly wishes his life was more interesting and I can always show him my gun when the subject of money comes up. But I don't like this plan. It has been my experience that big-city cabdrivers are not to be fucked with and you never know when you will meet the one who has his backseat boobytrapped with poison gas and spring-loaded spikes and is in fact driving around all day just hoping to encounter someone like me, a stupid asshole with a gun.

I keep one eye glued to the back of Miller's head and scan the street with the other. A half block away I see a stout, middle-aged guy buying coffee at an outdoor espresso hut. The guy wears gray pants, a dark blue blazer. Bright red suspenders under the jacket, white shirt. He wears glasses and his hair is long and wispy. The man is distracted and soft. I watch as he pays for the coffee and receives his change.

He puts his wallet into the left breast pocket of his jacket and proceeds toward me. I take a breath. I have done this more times than I can count, with mixed results. But this guy looks like an easy mark. He takes a drink of his coffee and cringes as if he has burned his tongue. He's perfect. I look ahead to be sure that Miller is still in sight, then lower my head and stumble directly into the guy with red suspenders and that hot coffee pretty much explodes all over his white shirt and now I see that it's not actually coffee but some kind of giant mocha with whipped cream, which of course not only burns him but makes a fine mess. The poor bastard yelps and nearly falls over, which is not at all what I want. A good pickpocket is fluid and graceful and easily forgotten. He doesn't cause a scene.

Jesus, I say. I am so fucking sorry.

The guy is sputtering and I catch him by the lapels, as if to help him up. The mocha is dripping down the front of his pants in little chocolate rivulets and the guy moans in despair. No one pays us any attention and I glance up the street to see that Miller is disappearing around a corner. I apologize loudly and use my right hand to smear the whipped cream around on my guy's chest and slip my left hand into his breast pocket, palming his wallet.

My favorite shirt, the guy says. My favorite shirt is ruined.

It's not ruined, I say. Take it to your dry cleaner and it's good as new.

I can't, he says. I'm a communist.

What?

I don't believe in dry cleaners. They are servants of the ruling class.

How about that. I just mugged a communist and I will eat my hat if his wallet is not empty. The last time I looked at a newspaper, the Russian government was running vodka into Canada and selling used office furniture for pennies. This guy has probably got moths in his pockets. I give his collar a brutal tug and he flails weakly at me. He is so mournful that I'm tempted to slap him around but I don't have time for such indulgences.

You motherfucker. What kind of communist drinks a mocha with whipped cream?

The guy moans. I can't help it, he says. I'm a victim of advertising. I walk past a Starbucks and I become a robot. Their mochas are divine.

The gods are laughing at me. I can hear them up there.

You're a class traitor, I say.

The communist goes limp in my arms and I drop him like a sack of compost. He immediately curls up on the sidewalk and I imagine he will lie there until the stormtroopers come for him.

eight.

I RUN LIKE THE HEADLESS HORSEMAN IS BEHIND ME and come around the corner in time to see Miller walk into a drugstore maybe a block away. I take a breather and fade into the shadowy mouth of an alley to inspect the comrade's sticky wallet.

Two dollars.

The wallet holds three yellowed clippings from a communist newsletter, two sad dollars and one expired library card. Leonard Brown, 2112 Valencia. I regard the dollars with a gassy sigh and lean back against a wall of red bricks to contemplate life. One man is soft in the belly and clumsy. He is confused. He drops three of his last five dollars on a capitalist mocha and is allowed a brief moment to savor the hot, bittersweet chocolate. Then another man, thin and hungry and only slightly less confused, comes out of nowhere and uses that mocha to fuck up the first man's favorite shirt and thereby ruin his day.

For two useless dollars.

I could buy a pack of gum and god knows gum will be handy when I run out of cigarettes. I won't go insane and I will have fresh breath and this shit should be funny. Jude will surely think so, tomorrow. John Ransom Miller might think so. I leave the two dollars untouched and dart across the street to drop Leonard's wallet into a mailbox.

What to do.

I can't grab another wallet. My skull is still tingling from the first. I stare at the dark windows of the drugstore and wonder what the hell Miller is doing in there. I could use the gun to rob the store and maybe take him out in the crossfire, thus solving two problems at once. I could empty the cash register, then chop off his finger and hustle back to the King James. Then I would have plenty of time to get good and drunk before dark.

I feel a headache coming on. My vision goes black around the edges. Blackbird on the wing. I'm tired of walking. I'm tired of stink and vapors. I'm tired of California already. Winter is gone, a torn wing. The horror of Christmas lights in the month of May. The swab of yellow glimpsed through trees is nothing to fear, the yellow is nothing but the sun. I have to keep walking. But when did you last eat something, when did you become sick. Such a simple thing, to ruin the body from within. Child's play, chutes and ladders. Easy to poison the blood, to wither the precious organs. The nervous system is consumed by Phineas and already the sense of smell is gone. Perhaps it's time to kill yourself and soon, before madness sets in. The fingers and toes will be first to fall from the host. The shadow that walks beside you is neither man nor woman. The shadow is a friend, the shadow is your beloved. The shadow beside you is death.

Come on, boy. Don't you know me.

Death is always on the wing.

Lucy. Henry. Eve. Moon. These are my dead. They died on my watch, all of them an arm's reach away. The beautiful dead flutter beside me always, torn clothes I can never take off.

John Ransom Miller exits the drugstore, a small white paper bag in hand. Prescription drugs, maybe. I hope he has some good stuff, something I can steal from him later. He heads up the street and I follow him, still penniless. Three blocks pass and I start to wonder if the bastard is just walking home. Now he's entered a BART station. I follow, wondering how far two dollars might have taken me. The machine that dispenses tickets informs me that for two dollars one can gain entry on BART, but not necessarily return. I am weirdly cheerful as I hop the turnstiles like the scumbag I never wanted to be and luckily the guard is off taking a crap somewhere, or shining his shoes.

The train isn't crowded.

Windows streaked with fingerprints. Smoke blue carpet. There are so many empty seats that I feel indecisive and find myself standing across from Miller. He is too restless to sit. He stands with his feet wide apart and his hands in his pockets. The train lurches forward and as I reach for the bright steel safety bar, a smile edges across his face.

The smile disappears without recoil and maybe I imagined it.

I feel warm, though.

John Ransom Miller is staring at me, or through me. His eyes are unfocused and this is but the etiquette of trains. I tell myself to let my own eyes glaze over, to look at the flashing windows. I tell myself to close my eyes but I'm stubborn. I can't help but stare at him. I am thinking of killing this man, unlikely as it sounds. His name is John Ransom Miller and he is the force behind a lot of evil doings in the velvet. I tell myself that if I kill him, none of what follows will come to pass.

I want to remember his face and at first glance, he is near perfect. He looks like a movie star. Upon close inspection though, he is not so perfect. He leans hard on the umbrella. His black, square-toed boots are fairly ruined. The leather is gouged in places and streaked with brown and yellow grime. He recently stomped through some nasty shit. His pale charcoal suit is a fine Italian wool and silk blend and probably cost five thousand dollars. But the jacket is soiled and wrinkled, as if he slept in it. The trousers are flecked with curious stains and his gray shirt is missing a button. He licks his lips once, then stops himself. His lips are red and cracked, as if he's dehydrated. His left eye is bloodshot beneath the drooping eyelid, which makes the right eye appear very white in contrast. There is black stubble along his chin and upper lip.

John Ransom Miller played rough last night, obviously.

He slept on someone's floor and went to work without changing clothes. He slept in the trunk of someone's car. He's having a nervous breakdown, or his marriage is fucked up. Or none of the above. He continues to stare through me and one thing is clear. He doesn't look vulnerable.

Ten minutes pass, pushing twenty. I relax. And then two white guys come hopping down the rabbit trail and my heart begins to wiggle around like a spider caught in its own web because the headache ratchets up a notch and I have a vision of what's going to happen, real or false. I know what's going to happen.

Dirty clothes and expensive tennis shoes and fierce rabbit faces. They have the look of those Nazi rabbits in *Watership Down*, the ones that shredded the ears of their enemies. Those rabbits were tough motherfuckers but they were still rabbits, and they ran like rabbits when that big black dog showed up to eat them in the end. They died like rabbits and now I watch these two human rabbits approach us from the rear of the car and I am not surprised when Miller moves his hips to force a little unnecessary physical contact with them.

John Ransom Miller is a black dog at heart.

The first rabbit is muscular and rubbery, with red hair that falls in greasy shanks. He stumbles into his friend, a bald skeletal kid with metal studs through his eyebrows and blackened lips. The two of them turn to stare at Miller with the splintered flashes of hate and love that usually mean violence is on the wing. The adrenaline kicks in and I feel the muscles tremble in my arms.

This is a scene from the dark side of my skull. This is a product of one of my seizures but it can't be. This is random. This isn't my drama and I tell myself to back off, to relax and let it happen. As if I'm watching television.

Miller smiles. How clumsy of me, he says.

His voice is a soft, metallic monotone. His voice is computer-generated and I believe these rabbits are fucked. The bald one wobbles a step back and glances fearfully at me. He knows it too, perhaps. I look at him without emotion. I don't know him and I don't care if he lives or dies. I truly don't give a shit. The rubbery rabbit-boy sneers and tosses his red hair out of his eyes.

Every motherfucking day, he says. Every day I pass your narrow ass on this train and every day you bump me.

I know, says Miller. It's weird, don't you think?

You a faggot, says the rubbery guy. Or what.

He wants to be mean and dangerous, a human razor. He looks the part but his lips tremble slightly as he says these words. His little bald pal shifts from one foot to the next and the tension is like jelly. I'm thinking I might as well stick out my finger and taste this jelly as the rubbery redhead smiles and leans forward and Miller steps into him, bringing his forearm around like the butt of a shotgun. A great purple scarf of blood billows from the redhead's nose and hangs in the air like comic book art. He buries his face in his hands as the train rattles to a stop.

Miller shrugs. Excuse me, he says. But this is my stop.

The redhead is bent over, bleeding onto his own shoes. His little bald friend has already bolted from the train. The redhead tries to speak but his voice is far away, underwater. He is gurgling and I wonder if he is swallowing his own blood.

Miller nods. His throat is full of blood, he says.

I stare at him, unblinking. That doesn't seem good. Does it?

It probably won't kill him.

The redhead chokes and spits blood. I shoot a glance at the doors and they remain open, for now. The air shimmers between train and platform. The redhead will soon be blowing bubbles with blood and I wonder if I should just get off. John Ransom Miller is looking more and more like a psycho and maybe I don't want him to think I'm following him but the doors will surely close soon and I can see myself standing on the wrong side of them if I get off too quickly and Miller decides to hang around and torture the rabbit some more. I shove my hands into my pockets, gaze up at a snarl of graffiti where someone has written you are beautiful in black ink. Beneath it, someone else has written or else you're dead.

I scratch my head.

The doors have been open forever. John Ransom Miller crouches down to face the bleeding redhead, who is still hunched over with his face in his hands. Miller smiles warmly, tenderly.

My skin crawls.

Miller reaches into his breast pocket and the redhead flinches. Miller laughs and hands him a gray silk handkerchief. The redhead stares at it as if he's never seen a handkerchief before, as if this might be some kind of trick. Miller shoves it into the rabbit's hand and says softly that no one ever died from a nosebleed. The redhead gurgles back at him and John Ransom Miller shrugs.

He nods at me. Are you coming?

nine.

I'M GETTING COZY WITH THE IDEA THAT TIME IS CIRCULAR, that lost time will come back.

Behold.

I find myself outside in the final minutes before dark falls over California and I am confronted by an apocalyptic sunset. The odds of this happening today and not tomorrow seem astronomical or anyway too staggering for my small brain to contemplate right now. The hills before me are splattered with some kind of freak sunlight that appears to exist on a physical plane but is forever shifting from one form to another and is therefore impossible to contain. If only I had an instant camera, then I would never need step outside again. I despise cameras, though. They butcher your memories and anyway when you're an old man drooling yellow shit down the front of your pajamas and your eyes are long gone, what good is a boxful of shitty snapshots that have turned green with age.

Nothing is real to me anymore. The world around me has been systematically reconceived through digital imaging and computer animation until every flower and raindrop is pure and flawless as the flowers and raindrops of the book of Genesis. The new world is brought to life in high-density pixels and is then transferred to human memory. The digital sunset always looks better than the real thing, always. Because a sunset generated by the basic package of yellow sun and blue sky is unreliable. Today it may be stunning, hypnotic. Tomorrow it may be lifeless and dull, a white sky scorched with yellow. Tomorrow the sky will be velvet.

Beautiful or not, it disappears. The sky goes dark and what are you left with.

The image stored in my head suffers rapid decay and within hours I will be unable to describe the sunset that I have just witnessed without accessing the false but technically perfect sunsets that I've seen on a thousand television and computer screens. I have no personal memories that are untainted by media and marketing and I often suspect that I am dead but still functioning. My heart is raw and pink, a package of ground beef wrapped in plastic. My body is composed of shatterproof glass and fluoride and vitamins and sheep hormones and recycled copper wires. There is no poetry in such a being but neither is there fear. I tumble easily into the void and I am safe as a kitten in the bony confines of my own skull. If I can afford the proper software, then I can download anything imaginable. The physical world is getting less and less realistic by the minute and eventually I will learn to pay it no mind.

Twilight, now.

John Ransom Miller and I have been walking for nearly an hour, most of the way uphill, not talking. I am chewing a hole in my lip. Miller is much too cool and friendly and unconcerned about my sudden presence in his life. The silence is heavy between us, but not terribly unpleasant.

What's your name? he says.

First names are dangerous, I say.

Why, he says.

The intimacy, I say.

My legs are heavy and I hope Miller doesn't try to run away. The BART station is a long, long way down. He won't run, though. John Ransom Miller could not be any less afraid of me. But he might like to fuck with me. I would probably fuck with him, if our positions were reversed. Miller nods and again I have the sticky feeling that he can hear my thoughts.

Yes, he says. Intimacy is a tricky thing. I would think it's hard to kill somebody if you are in the habit of calling them by their first name.

I whistle through my teeth, irritated. Why don't you have a car? I say.

Miller shrugs. I have two cars. Three, actually. I had a driver for a while, a guy who wore one of those fucking sailor hats. I don't know. I started to hate the cars after a while. I would sit in traffic, listening to Mozart and drinking bottled water and it was like my soul was trapped in a Mason jar.

The hole in my lip is getting bigger. It will bleed, soon.

I like cars, I say. I believe in cars.

What about the soul, he says. Do you believe in the human soul?

No. But I think mine would be perfectly safe in a Mason jar.

Miller stares at me, unblinking. You might want to punch holes in the lid, he says.

Okay, I say. What makes you think I'm going to kill you?

He laughs. You would be wise to kill me, that's why. You would save a few lives and probably your own sanity. But you won't kill me. You won't even try.

That's a good answer, I say. Damn good.

By the way, he says. You can call me Miller for now.

His voice trails away from his mouth, exhaled like smoke. There is a narcotic quality about it, as if it comes from inside my head and now a feeble smile drifts unwanted across my face, a polite muscle spasm. Which bugs the shit out of me. This is my face, right. This is my fucking face and I will be one sorry meatpuppet if I ever lose control over who sees me smile. When and where and so on. I keep shining my crippled smile at this man and I may as well piss myself on a crowded bus. I may as well be a whore with a weak bladder. I abruptly take the gun from my pocket and Miller doesn't blink. I wave the gun at a low stone wall that creeps along the side of the road and tell him to just sit the fuck down. He shrugs and sits down, crossing his legs and fiddling with the crease in his trousers.

Are you okay? he says. You look green.

Miller is one of those rare fuckers with a psychic sense of smell. He takes one sniff and he knows you. He knows things about you, things you might not want him to know. He should have been a cop, probably. The funny thing is I am starting to like him, and this idea makes me feel slightly car-sick. I tell him to get up and we keep walking. I put the gun away and try to relax.

Pretty sunset, I say. Don't you think?

Miller shrugs. I saw a peculiar story on the news the other day. A news-paper in China confessed that they've been falsifying their weather reports for the past twenty years.

What do you mean?

They would claim that it was sunny yesterday when in fact it rained.

Revisionist weather, I say. That's brilliant.

Isn't it?

What the fuck, I say. It's nice to meet you, Miller.

Miller yawns. You never know when that person will come along, the person you have been waiting for.

Yeah. What is that supposed to mean, exactly?

Life, he says. It's often a dull dream.

I scratch my head and suddenly I hear something like the manic hum of locusts but it's only the drone of rubber tires on blacktop as two boys cruise by on mountain bikes.

They look like brothers, I say.

Miller and I turn to watch as the boys disappear over the next hill.

Poof, says Miller.

Like they just fell off the edge of the earth, I say.

Amazing, says Miller. How easily a child can vanish.

Miller takes a sheaf of mail from a bright metal box on the side of the road. The box looks new. The surface is shiny as a silver dollar and unblemished by bird shit, but there is a nice round bullet hole in the thing's belly. The hole is black around the edges and I poke two fingers in there without lubrication. It was a big bullet.

You have enemies? I say.

No, he says. The neighborhood kids. I love it, though. I love it when the kids have spirit.

I finger the hole. That's some fucking spirit.

Miller might be a liar. He might not be. He has the eyes of a sleepy blackjack dealer and why should I care if he wants to lie about a misplaced bullet. I lie all the time, to myself and others. I lie whenever it feels right. I'm a cheap rug. I am not very good at lying, however. Jude can always sniff out a lie before I take another breath. Then again, she's a woman. Jude says that if a woman has ever fucked a guy and studied the ugly contortions of his face, the face that he wants to hide from sight, then she knows the machinery behind his mouth and eyes and thereafter she always knows when he's lying.

Anyway.

I shot up a few mailboxes when I was a kid, with a pellet gun and later a .22, a rifle meant for shooting squirrels. This hole came from a big gun, a serious gun. Miller has got Dirty Harry shooting at his mailbox and it's none of my business.

Not yet, says Miller.

What? I say.

It's none of your business, he says. Yet.

It is still not quite dark but the air is the color of blue plums. A black Mercedes rolls past with headlights off, eerily silent. It looks like a tank on a night mission. A white moth flickers past my face and I wave it away, distracted.

Do you want to come in? says Miller. Have a drink?

I sigh. Are you going to be doing a lot of that?

What? he says.

Oh, you know. Reading my mind and that sort of thing.

Miller laughs. I can't read your mind, man. I pretend that I can.

Uh huh.

It's easy, he says. People aren't very complex. You take a stab at what somebody is thinking. Then politely spit it out like a piece of gristle. And even if you're wrong, it makes people nervous. There's no better way to fuck with a snotty waiter, or a salesman. Try it sometime.

Interesting, I say. Do I look like a salesman to you?

Why, he says. Are you nervous?

Miller pushes open the iron gate that opens onto a downward drive lined with gravel and heavy flat stones the color of cigarette ash. The front yard is a hillside, wild and dark with twisting rose bushes and exposed roots. The house is barely visible from the road. The white moth returns to strafe my face and I wonder if I'm glowing. I try to catch it in my fist, to kill it. But the little bastard is too fast for me and I clutch at the air like a spastic. I lower my head before it decides to fly down my throat. Miller starts down the slope and I follow him.

The house of Miller is bewildering, and much larger than it looks from the outside. He gives me a rapid tour of the lower level, telling me there are nineteen rooms in all. The house is primarily constructed of stone, but some of the walls are made of glass. The house is cold and dark and I imagine it is cold and bright by day. There are three floors, or levels. The house is not vertical, but staggered. It clings to the hillside like a giant spider. Two massive trees come up through the back of it, like twin spines. A complex series of wood platforms is built around these trees, with rope ladders connecting the various levels. The kitchen door opens onto level two. I stand in the doorway, a goofy smile on my face.

It's like something out of a fairy tale, I say.

Miller is pouring tall glasses of bourbon and soda.

Yeah, he says. I think the guy who designed it was out of his mind, however.

How's that?

Miller shrugs. You can feel it. There's madness in the walls.

Ah, yes. Madness in the walls. I hate it when that happens.

Miller stirs our drinks with what appears to be a bright blue chopstick.

Do you live alone? I say.

Not exactly. He hands me a drink, very strong.

The kitchen is black tile and bright steel. Harsh white light. Functional, cold, a surgical theater. I imagine myself laid out on the island with a mask over my face and tubes running in and out of my belly, surrounded by a crew of silent men in dark red gowns. I doubt there's anything in the refrigerator but olives and French mustard and spare plasma.

Come on, says Miller. Let's go to the lizard room.

A long, windowless room that glows from the light of twenty-two terrariums. These contain lizards, iguanas, chameleons, and various snakes. Obviously. I walk the perimeter and look them over. I am fond of reptiles, generally. Because they can sit on a rock for two days without moving. Because they are untroubled by the loss of a limb and more than likely will grow another one. Because they methodically seek out sources of heat, but will not necessarily perish without it. Their chances of survival on this planet seem so much better than ours and I think Miller is wise to be friendly with them. The last terrarium along one wall houses a very large boa constrictor, coiled and sleeping. I stare at him for a while and I think I would like to hold him, to close my eyes and wonder at his strength.

It's too bad you didn't come yesterday, says Miller.

Why is that?

It was feeding day, he says. The boa put on quite a show.

Does he have a name?

I'm sure he does, says Miller. But I don't know it.

There are two black leather chairs at the far end of the room. Miller sits in one of them, his legs stretched out and his feet up on a round coffee table of solid, roughly cut glass that looks like a block of ice. The wood floor is stained the color of black cherries and down the middle of the room runs a narrow Turkish rug, green and gold. The rug comes to an end under the glass table and the colors melt and magnify. The walls are painted a dark, faintly metallic green.

Miller tells me to sit down. He doesn't sound like he's asking.

I take a sip of whiskey and suddenly feel strange, almost happy. This place smells of Dr. Moreau's island and there may be much mischief in store for me, but I don't care. Miller is an excellent host and I like it here. I am wary of telling him so, however, and I have to remind myself who he is and what he did to Jude. I have to steel myself against his charm. The house feels empty but for the reptiles and ourselves. The house has been utterly silent since we entered but now I imagine that I hear music, the soft lament of a solitary cello. The same few notes over and over, stretched and groaning.

They stop and start, as if there is someone practicing upstairs. It's a mournful tune and the only explanation for this sort of thing is that my brain is full of poison. I sink into the chair across from Miller and put my feet up.

He smiles at me and promptly the cello resumes, urgent now.

Okay, I say. Do I hear music? Or am I fucking nuts.

The cello stops. Miller lights a cigarette.

Beethoven, he says. Piano Trio number 4, in D Major. The love song for Anna Marie.

Who is playing, though?

I don't hear anything, he says. Perhaps you're nuts.

Uh huh. Give me a cigarette, please?

Miller pushes a pack of Dunhills across the glass table. I light one and we blow smoke and stare at each other. I wait for the cello to resume but it never does. The player is self-conscious, maybe. He heard us talking about him.

I feel like I've seen you before, says Miller.

I have that kind of face.

It's a good face, he says. Not too handsome, but interesting.

Thanks, I guess.

Miller leans forward, pours two fingers of whiskey into my glass.

Have you ever tried acting? he says.

The whiskey burns my tongue. I light another cigarette, vaguely uneasy. Miller smiles at me and I wait for him to tell me what I'm thinking. But he doesn't.

I can become someone else, I say. If that's what you mean.

Interesting, he says. I'm talking about regular drama, however.

Only as a child, I say. In the fourth grade I had a non-speaking role in *Great Expectations*. I was beggar number nine. And one Christmas I was an anonymous shepherd in the nativity scene.

Miller laughs.

Why do you ask?

I'm interested in making a film, says Miller.

I am a thousand miles from home and once in a while I have to remind myself that I have no home. This is California and on any given Thursday there could be a nuclear sunset. And it's earthquake country. The earth could come apart beneath my feet, any day now. Jude is waiting for me in a hotel room but I am prepared for the possibility that she may not be there when I return.

I won't like it.

But I will sit down on the bed and take off my shoes. I will breathe the recycled air that may or may not smell of her hair. I will read the newspaper and smoke a few cigarettes and eventually I might take a nap. There will be no one to hear me if I speak in my sleep.

What sort of film? I say.

I finish off my bourbon and consider shooting Miller.

Do you know anything about snuff films? he says.

Urban legend, I say. But probably true.

Why do you say that?

Anything you can imagine is probably true. And the worst you can imagine is probably worth money.

How philosophical, he says.

Fuck you. People tend to kill people. And they do it every twenty-nine seconds. In the time it takes me to smoke this cigarette, eleven people will be murdered in this country.

Where do you get these statistics?

I make them up.

Excellent, he says. What else?

Everything is on videotape. Vacations, weddings, birthdays, dogs and cats doing tricks. Every time you go to a cash machine or mail a letter or purchase a quart of milk, you're on tape. If you get murdered, you're probably on tape and somebody somewhere on the Internet is going to masturbate while watching it. Reality is in the business of killing off fiction.

I like you, says Miller.

Okay.

There is a brief silence. Miller picks up a remote control and aims it at what I thought was a giant mirror on the wall behind me. The mirror flickers to life, a television. He mutes the sound and flips through the channels until he finds a baseball game, the Mariners and A's.

Why do you ask? I say.

Because I want to make one, he says.

A snuff film?

Yes.

I take the gun out of my jacket pocket and point it at him, politely.

Take off your fucking ring, I say.

Why?

I'm leaving now. And I need proof that I killed you.

Art, he says. It's going to be a quality piece of film, a masterpiece of blood porn. Literary, mysterious. The kind of thing you can screen at Sundance.

Mysterious? I say.

Miller smiles richly. That's the beauty of it, the suspense factor. Because I have not yet finished the script, the victim will be uncertain until the end. It could turn out to be me or you. Or someone else. Perhaps an innocent will die. It will be called *The Velvet*.

Oh, fuck you, I say. You've been talking to Jude.

Miller picks up the remote control and my eyes go to the television, where the Oakland game rolls silently. Ichiro has just stolen third base for the Mariners and the cameras cut away to the crowd for reaction shots. The fans are not pleased. They boo and hiss. They bang drums. There is a close-up of a bearded man with a massive naked belly and a plastic jug of beer sloshing in each hand, dancing like a drunken god. The camera zooms on his face, then cuts to a luxury box where the fans are a bit more sedate. Miller pushes a button and the picture goes to slow-motion. And there is a lingering shot of MacDonald Cody, senator and tapped to be president one day, sitting next to a small blond-haired boy with the same dark eyes. The boy looks to be about five years old. He laughs and claps his hands with the kind of glee that most adults can barely remember and now someone who sits outside the frame leans over and gently touches his hair. The shot widens and I see that the man who touched the kid's hair is

Miller.

Motherfucker, I say. This is a tape?

Sort of a home movie, says Miller. His voice has slipped into that narcotic tone.

What the hell does that mean?

Miller presses another button, freezing the tape. The kid with dark eyes stares out at me. He is no longer smiling and like his eyes, his lips are dark and just slightly too big for his face and now they are pressed together and he looks very serious, almost somber. He looks sleepy.

Beautiful kid, isn't he? says Miller. Those eyes could break your heart.

Yeah, I say. He looks just like his father.

I suppose you recognize him? says Miller.

MacDonald Cody, I say. The senator.

Miller stares at the TV, then looks at me.

But you've met him, am I right? He says.

Turn it off, I say.

Look at the kid, he says. The camera loves him.

I'm gone, I say. I'm fucking gone. It was a real thrill to meet you and everything.

Look at the kid, he says. You wouldn't want anything to happen to him, would you?

Fuck you, I say.

Whatever you say.

I stand up and Miller lazily tells me to hang on a minute. He tugs at the big ruby ring, but it won't come off. He slips his finger into his mouth and sucks on it for a moment. The ring slips off easily and Miller offers it to me, red and wet as a bloody eye. I hesitate, trembling. The gun still in my hand, forgotten. I should just put a bullet in his skull. I should. I should. I should. I should put the motherfucker to sleep forever and maybe Jude and I could rest easy tonight. But I have never killed anyone, outside my dreams. It's not an easy thing to shoot a man who has done nothing but talk to you, a man who sits in a leather armchair smiling. Miller smiles at me and I take the ring from him. I drop it into my pocket and now it occurs to me that I need cash for cigarettes and the train back to San Francisco. I hit Miller up for fifty dollars and he gives it to me without a word.

ten.

THERE ARE FOUR CHAMBERS IN THE HEART, four rooms. I stumble through the house of Miller and my chest is full of terrible echoes.

Through the kitchen and a woman is there. Blue jeans and a white tank-top. Pale blond hair, wispy. She stands with her back to me, staring into the open refrigerator. Her shoulders are narrow and bare and I don't want to frighten her.

Excuse me, I say.

The woman turns around, slow. Honey brown eyes with dark circles. Thin lips, silent and moving. As if she is whispering to herself. Or praying.

I thought I heard voices, she says. She shrugs. I wondered if we had company.

Exhale. Sorry if I startled you, I say.

Molly, she says. My name is Molly Jones.

Phineas, I say.

Her lips begin to move again and I think of Franny Glass. Her mouth silent and ever moving to form the words Jesus Christ have mercy on me in not quite perfect time with her heartbeat as she slowly came to pieces in a snotty restaurant while the ivy league boyfriend yawned and explained that Flaubert was ultimately a mediocre talent because he had no testicles. Franny Glass was my first love. Hopeless and somehow appropriate that at the age of sixteen I was in love with a fictional woman.

Your lips are moving, I say.

Oh, she says. I'm sorry.

Prayer?

It's a short monologue that I'm having trouble with.

What do you mean?

I'm sort of an actor, she says. I'm a theater major at Berkeley.

And the monologue?

I'm playing May in a production of *Fool for Love*, she says.

Sam Shepard, I say.

Do you know the play?

Hell, it's the story of my life. Do you want to practice on me?

Molly smiles, takes a breath.

I don't understand my feelings, she says softly. Her face goes pale, as if she's banished the blood from her skin. I really don't, she says. I just don't understand how I could hate you so much after so much time. How… No matter how much I'd like to not hate you, I hate you even more. It grows. All I see is a picture of you. Of you and her. I don't even know if the picture is real anymore. I don't even care. It's make believe. It invades my head. The two of you. And this picture stings even more than if I'd actually seen you with her. It cuts me. It cuts me so deep. I will never get over it, never. And I can't get rid of the picture. It just comes, uninvited. Like a little uninvited torture. And I blame you for this torture. I blame you.

I stare at her. I feel hot, almost guilty. Molly shrugs and her face returns to normal. I'm having trouble with the tone, she says. How did it sound to you?

Very cold. A little psychotic.

I know, she says. It needs to be more vulnerable.

Heartbroken and weary, I say.

Molly bites her lip, thinking. Yes.

Think of your mother, I say.

What do you know about my mother?

I shrug. Mothers. They are often heartbroken, weary.

She nods, staring. Do you want a sandwich?

A sandwich?

Yes. I was going to make a tomato sandwich.

Okay.

You have a gun in your hand, she says.

What?

Is that a prop, she says. Or is it real?

Uh. I believe it's real.

I am so fucking stupid. I know that. The gun hangs at my thigh. I slip it into my jacket pocket and mutter an aborted apology. Molly shrugs and turns back to the fridge. She takes out mayonnaise and a brick of white cheese, then leans over the sink to get a red tomato from the windowsill. She opens a drawer and takes out a long sharp knife.

Echoes, footsteps. Miller is nowhere to be seen.

Molly wears scuffed brown cowboy boots. I look around. The kitchen is not so cold and frightening as before. The lights are different and I never noticed the tomatoes in the window.

It's okay, she says. But would you mind leaving the gun on the island, where I can see it?

I hesitate, watching her slice the tomato on a round wooden cutting board.

Please, she says. Humor me.

I take out the Walther and remove the clip, then place the gun on the bright steel surface between us. I am tempted to give it a spin, to see who the gun favors.

Thank you, she says.

Oh. You're welcome.

Long pretty hands, unpainted nails.

Molly cuts the sandwich in half and wipes off the knife. Takes two red paper napkins from a drawer and gives me half the sandwich. White sourdough bread, red tomato that drips onto my fingers and white cheese. Molly leans against the island while she eats, holding the sandwich in two hands.

I realize how hungry I am.

John refuses to get barstools, she says. He thinks they reveal a profound lack of taste.

I nod, dumbly. Molly takes small, fierce bites of bread and tomato. She murmurs softly as she swallows. I contemplate the aesthetic of barstools. I watch the muscles in her throat ripple.

The corner of your mouth, I say. You have a bit of mayonnaise there.

She touches the red napkin to her lips and says thank you.

I should be going.

No, she says. Don't go.

The soft flash of honey eyes. That monologue got to me, the way her lips moved. It tore me up. I tell myself to be careful.

Miller is your husband? I say.

Molly frowns. Did he tell you that?

I stare at her and realize she has likely not read Miller's script.

He has gotten so weird, she says. I can barely talk to him.

Yeah. He seems a little preoccupied with…baseball.

You're going to work on the film with us? she says.

I don't know, I say. I haven't decided.

You have a beautiful face, she says. Your cheekbones would look good in black and white.

Have you read the script? I say.

Molly sighs. Only bits and pieces. John is very secretive with it.

I'm sure he is.

Molly has finished her sandwich and now she takes out a red and white pack of gum and pulls one stick out. She offers it to me and I shake my head. She slowly peels away the cellophane and folds the stick into her mouth. I reach for the gun between us and at the same time her hand drifts down and brushes mine. She is reaching to touch the gun, to touch my hand. I don't know which. But her touch is soft and maddening, the touch of someone in a dream soon forgotten. Then she pulls her hand away and her face is slightly red. The blood comes and goes in her face. Molly is sensitive to barometric pressure. I put the gun away and hesitate, then offer her my empty hand. Molly doesn't smile. Her lips come apart and I can see her teeth. Now she takes my hand and I feel her pulse with the tip of my middle finger and this is not what anyone would call a handshake because our hands are not moving but holding each other and our skin is the same temperature and after a long silence one of us lets go.

Dark outside and moonless. I stand in the middle of Miller's road, staring at his mailbox. Bullet hole in bright metal. I wonder if there are phantoms out tonight. Neighborhood kids with spirit. I touch my hand to my mouth and wonder if Jude will smell Molly on me. It doesn't matter. Jude pushed me at these people and now there's a small body of water between me and the King James Hotel. I should go east but I won't.

Fool for Love. I know that play, yeah. Three people in a room, two of them lovers. Tortured, forbidden. The third is an old man who may or may not be real. Then another man enters, the hapless blind date, who one might suppose represents the unsuspecting audience because the two lovers proceed to fuck with him without mercy. I have never seen a live production but I have seen the movie with Kim Basinger and Harry Dean Stanton a few times. It's a tight, claustrophobic picture. One long act, relentless. Four people in a room, crashing into walls. Four people turning inside out. Four people in a room and the whole time you're wondering which one of them is going to get killed.

Down the black, winding hill. Lost and then not. I wander along Telegraph a while. Faces bright and searching. The infinite flow of tourists and junkies and homeless guys and skate rats and lost hippies and spare changers and vendors and privileged boys and girls. This is the sweet hate machine of human chaos and no one wants to be noticed, no one wants to be saved. My brain is a rattling trap and I think it would not be easy to live here. I have a low tolerance for the culture of emptiness. I buy cigarettes and a green slushy drink at a convenience store. Brief overhead view of myself through the store's surveillance camera. Black and white. I'm looking through the eye of a fish. The subject is a white male, late thirties. Medium height and thin. Dark circles under pale eyes, unshaven. Dirty blond hair. Brown leather coat and blue jeans and black T-shirt. He is not a student, not a thief but possibly an English professor, which makes me laugh at myself.

I walk until I come to the BART station. The machine that dispenses tickets is complex and unforgiving, but I manage to buy a ticket without causing a scene. The platform is crowded with people who don't look at each other. I want a cigarette but the use of tobacco is prohibited in California, everywhere it seems.

I crouch against a wall and wait.

Drunk white guy shambles up and down the platform. He wears torn gray pants stained with bodily fluids and he's looking for someone to talk to. Young black girl sits on a bench, reading a book. Drunk white guy sits down next to her and everyone on the platform takes a breath.

I love to eat out a girl's asshole, he shouts.

Oh, boy.

Humming silence.

I love to eat asshole, he says again.

The drunk is going to touch her any minute and she's going to freak out. I have a gun in my pocket. I could show it to him, if he touches her. Everyone is watching but no one has moved. The drunk reaches for her hair with one trembling hand but the black girl doesn't freak out. She laughs and the drunk's hand falls as if it suddenly became too heavy for him to carry. He wanders away.

Lonely.

I almost miss John Ransom Miller. He was a freak but at least I had a sense of purpose when I was following him. And he would have loved the drunk guy, the asshole eater. I take out his ruby ring and slip it onto my finger. Rumble and sigh and here comes the train. I wonder what time it is. Every other car is packed with flesh but mine is ghostly, quiet. I turn my face to black windows and no one pays me any mind.

Downtown. I retrace my steps past Nieman Marcus and back to the King James. There is a different doorman on duty. This guy is massive, maybe a foot taller than me. His arms are the size of my thighs and his face is like a

fat gray melon, with small dark eyes sunk into gray skin. Thin cruel
mouth. He shrugs and opens the door with a grunt.

What happened to Jeremy? I say.

Don't know, he says. Punk called in sick.

Too bad.

Why? he says.

I shake my head. No reason.

There's nothing Jeremy can get what I can't get. You need a whore?

Not yet.

eleven.

THROUGH THE MEDIEVAL LOBBY. Empty as before. The elevator, the isolation chamber. I chew at a fingernail and find myself thinking of Molly. The way her color rose and fell. She made me a sandwich and I am so stupid that only now does it occur to me that she was the phantom cello player. The love song for Anna Marie that haunted us down in the Lizard Room. I wonder if she was just fucking with us.

I come to room 1221 and remember that Jude has stripped me of my key. This irritates me, now. I feel like a delivery boy, a chump. I knock on the door and after a long suffering silence I get the ticklish sensation that someone is breathing on the other side, eyeballing me through the peephole.

Jude. What the fuck.

The door opens slowly and the temperature changes. Jeremy the doorman stands there.

Hey, he says. The smile melting across his face.

Jeremy is not wearing a shirt. He wears pale blue jeans. He is barefoot. I glance down at my boots. I am technically still in the hallway. I am outside the room. Jeremy leans against the open door, against the flat of his hand. He looks comfortable. He has an underwear model's body, muscular. Tattoo of a monkey's head above the left nipple. Jeremy has a washboard stomach but my teeth are better than his. He's got a mouthful of crooked, fucked-up choppers that indicate poor breeding.

Jeremy, I say.

Jude's in the bathroom, he says.

Yeah?

Jeremy shrugs and lets go of the door. It swings toward me, silent as a puff of smoke. Jeremy drifts back into the room. I catch the door and stand there a moment. Rapid heartbeat and a basket of snakes in my skull.

Here we go. Things get complicated.

I follow Jeremy into the room. Pause to glance at the bathroom door. Slash of yellow light at the floor. Listen and breathe and stare at the door until it pulses and for a moment I expect to hear Jude's thoughts, her voice in my head. I wonder if I love her. I wonder if it's relevant. Two hours ago, I touched another woman's hand. I felt her pulse and I wanted her. It was a physiological reaction, molecular. People crash into each other and things get interesting. Jude may have fucked this guy and she may not have and maybe she's in the bathtub right now, washing his juices from her body.

Jeremy sits on the floor, smoking a cigarette. I go to the vanity sink and pour myself a glass of gin. The sink is a nightmare of ashtrays and Chinese take-out. In the heart of the mess is a blue plate flecked with cocaine. Beside it is a big fat hunting knife, like a small sword. I remember the stiletto Jude used to carry. It was a nasty weapon and she wielded it like it was part of her, like a talon freakishly evolved. I taste the gin and it might as well be water. I find myself staring at Jeremy's bare feet.

What size shoes do you wear?

Nine, he says.

Those would be your running shoes, then.

Jeremy glances over at the glass coffee table, where the blue and yellow sneakers fairly glow.

Yeah, he says.

Why are you here, Jeremy?

I'm waiting.

For what?

You should talk to Jude about that. I'm not in charge.

Imagine.

Jeremy shrugs. How did you like that magic milkshake?

Delicious, I say.

He blows smoke at me, thin and blue. I put down the glass of gin and pick up the knife.

I'm glad you liked it, he says.

Yeah. Why don't you put your shoes on.

Jeremy smiles and closes his eyes and I take two, three steps forward to crouch beside him with the knife. He flinches away and I grab him by the hair. His eyes are wide open, now.

I'm not going to cut you, I say.

Okay, he says.

Did you fuck her?

He hesitates. No.

I don't care if you fucked her. That's her business.

The hair, he says. Please, man. Let go of the hair.

Jeremy, I say. You may have fucked Jude today, or been fucked by her. Listen, man.

You may fuck her in the future. It doesn't matter. But you are a guest in this room, a visitor. You are an employee of this hotel and I don't like it when you smile at me.

Okay, he says.

Pick a body part, any body part.

Why?

I changed my mind. I'm going to cut you after all.

Then silence. I wonder if Jude is listening to this sorry episode of male theater. My knees are trembling and I will have to stand up soon.

The arm, says Jeremy. The left arm, if you don't mind.

You want me to cut your left arm?

He grunts at me, his face red. This is enough for me. I don't feel better, exactly. I feel different and now I let go of his hair and he falls away from the knife. I stand up slowly, legs still trembling.

You're not going to cut me?

Not today.

Jeremy grins. I think a knife scar might look cool, actually.

Yeah, I say. Put your shoes on.

I want to stay.

Whatever. I just don't want to look at your naked fucking feet.

The bathroom door is not locked. I knock softly, then push it open. Jude wears snug leopard pants and a black T-shirt too big for her. That's my shirt. She is leaning into the mirror as if to kiss it. She is doing something to her eyes, her eyelashes.

She is barefoot, like Jeremy.

You're wearing my shirt, I say.

I hope you don't mind, she says.

No. I don't mind.

Are you okay, honey? she says. You're stuttering.

What's happening here, Jude.

Be specific, please.

I slip Miller's ruby ring from my finger and drop it into the sink. Bright and clattering red against hard white porcelain then disappearing down the open drain.

Jude frowns. I hope he didn't want that back, she says.

Fuck him. The guy's a freak.

He's a wealthy freak, she says.

I light a cigarette and Jude extends her left hand. She wants to share. I ignore her for a moment. Then pass her the cigarette.

He wants to make a snuff film, I say.

Yeah, she says. He's just a tiny bit nuts.

No shit.

Jude shrugs. He's sitting on a pile of money.

That's nice.

What's the problem?

Where the fuck should I start?

Do you have to swear constantly?

Are you fucking kidding?

Please, she says. I'm so tired of that word.

Fuck fuck fuck, I say. Fucking fuck. When did you get so fucking sensitive?

Are you finished?

Listen to me, please. I just spent four very scary hours with the man. If we make this film with him, somebody is going to die.

Maybe, she says. Maybe not. The most interesting art is a little dangerous.

Oh, please. Don't give me that shit.

Her voice goes cold. Take a good look at my face and tell me about danger.

I'm sorry.

And don't sulk, she says. It's not attractive.

Look, I say. By definition, you can't make a snuff film without a victim.

She shrugs. Some victims are predestined.

I suppose you're too clever to get waxed, I say.

Jude smiles and blows smoke at her reflection.

What about me? I say. I'm not so clever.

Phineas is only stupid when he's drunk, she says.

Maybe, I say. But I tend to drink a lot, when I'm with you.

Jude shrugs. I will keep an eye on you, then.

That's comforting.

Jude finishes reconstructing her eyes and turns to look at me. What do you think? she says.

I stare at her. I can't tell the difference.

Jude sighs. What do you think about the film, she says.

I have my doubts about the concept, I say. The genre seems…played.

Listen, she says. Miller is going to give us a million dollars and deliver us MacDonald Cody on a silver plate. I don't care if he wants to shoot a remake of *Old Yeller* with fucking Muppets.

Travis? I say. Where you going with that gun in your hand?

Jude smiles. That poor boy.

Did you ever see that snuff film flick with Nicolas Cage?

Yawn, she says. And I love Nicolas Cage. I would watch him eat soup. But after two hours of him looking worried and morally compromised... I was ready to scream.

What kind of soup?

Jude stares at me. Campbell's tomato.

Long silence. I watch her in the mirror. I flush the toilet, restless.

This bathroom needs a sofa, I say.

Miller called, she says. Just now. He said you were quite taken with Molly.

I chew at my lip. Yeah.

Well, she says. You wouldn't want her to be the victim, would you.

Oh, you bitch. That's why you wanted me to follow him home.

Perhaps.

Jude sits on the edge of the tub and turns on the hot water.

Okay. Let's talk about Jeremy, then.

Who? she says.

The half-naked boy watching TV in our bed.

Oh, she says. Jeremy wants to make movies when he grows up, just like everyone else on this sad fucking planet. He's very clever with a camera. And we need someone behind the camera.

How old is Jeremy?

The room slowly fills with steam. Jude pulls the black shirt over her head. Leopard print bra and yellow skin. Today, she is a cat.

Jeremy? Twenty-two, she says. Adorable, isn't he?

Umm, yes. Why is he here?

He quit his day job, she says. I told him he could stay here until we begin the shoot.

That was nice of you.

Phineas. Are you jealous?

I don't get jealous. Shit, two hours ago I wanted to fuck Molly.

Jude rolls her eyes. Why does this bother you, then?

I don't like surprises. I want some privacy with you. I don't want a stranger in the cocoon.

Please. The cocoon is an illusion.

Where will he sleep?

I don't know, she says. There are two beds.

And three of us.

Jude turns off the water and the silence is sudden. Dripping.

Yes, she says. There are three of us. I like him and I imagine you like him. Maybe you would like to explore some of your multicultural urges.

The steam is thick and I can barely see her now.

I don't think Jeremy is interested in me, I say. I took a knife to him just now.

Jude is a ghost, gray and faceless in the steam. I imagine she drops the leopard rags to the floor and slips slowly, carefully into the burning water with a sigh and moan.

Try, she says. Try to be friendly.

How long have you and Miller been cooking this thing up?

Jude shrugs. A week or so.

Give me some back story.

Simple, she says. I arrived on his door one day, looking to kill him. He offered up the Finch brothers, but I already had them. He said he would give me Cody, if I played nice. And only if I did this film with him. He already had Jeremy and Molly in the fold.

I need air, I say.

Whatever, baby.

I come out of the bathroom and crash around for a minute, ignoring Jeremy. The sound of pay-per-view porn from the television.

Jude sinks underwater in my head, her flesh slippery.

What do I want?

I want anonymous flesh and unconsciousness. I want to cut my head off and use it as a strawberry planter. I scrape together a skinny line of coke from the ashy remains on the blue plate.

Unspeakable dialogue and electronic music. Heavy breathing and I tell myself to be friendly.

Get out, I say.

What? says Jeremy.

Get the fuck out, boy. I need to talk to my girl.

twelve.

LONG SHADOW OF A NAKED WOMAN becoming man with green skin. The velvet surrounds us, keeps us. Two bodies in the dark. The only light comes from television and bathroom in fever pitch of dream and mirrors. Otherwise dark. I separate from her in dreams and go belowground to hunt blind silverfish, bony creatures that are more frog than fish but taste of spider. Other travelers pass me in the dark and I offer to trade my silverfish if they can answer a riddle.

What is the shadow with green skin that is not man, not woman?

The mind wanders, as it will.

At one point, there was a digital clock in this room. It gave off fine green numbers that floated in the dark like fireflies until the clock met with a sudden misfortune. Jude took it apart in a cocaine fury several hours or days ago and now there are bits and pieces of clock in the bed and on the floor, plastic bread crumbs scattered for terrible birds. Because it was humming, she said. Humming. The internal clock says this is morning and backs it up with the big morning penis that comes out of nowhere, wandering and discontent. The penis that wants a piece of chocolate cake and won't be fucked with.

Jude is asleep, however. Or pretending to be.

I grope through the tangle of sheets and find under my pillow a small tube of Astroglide, a substance originally designed for the slippery purpose of getting astronauts in and out of their spacesuits. To my mind, space travel is an accurate but ultimately gruesome metaphor for fucking. There is no air pressure in space, no gravity. For one breathless moment you are a feather in the void and the brain is on holiday. The dead weight of soul and ego are cast adrift and you are nothing but blood. Then you achieve orgasm. You notice the tiny hole in your spacesuit and now your guts are spilling out of your ears like pudding.

Curious George, I say. It all goes back to the man in the yellow hat.

Jude pushes two fingers into my mouth and tells me to shut up. Her fingers taste of salt. I nibble at them and the bed heaves and she is on her feet, breathing like a fighter. The shadow bends, as if to kiss me. Her hands find my throat and I tell myself not to fight and abruptly she kisses me. The taste of her mouth is like chewing on rose petals sweet with mint, with poison and I want to kiss her again but she dodges away and now one of her hands slithers over my ribs and across my belly and down. I try not to think of monkeys and in another minute I'm inside her.

Arms and legs thrashing. The hammer of blood and so on.

It's okay, she says. I'm right here.

But I can't see you.

Violence and whispered apologies. Detachment of self. The eyes wander and drift, as if searching for something never seen, something that hides in the dark under bone.

What's wrong with my eyes?

Hush, she says. Nothing is wrong with your eyes.

How long? I say.

How long what? she says.

How long have we been crashing around in the dark.

Two days, she says. Maybe three.

Jude and I have returned effortlessly to form. Immediately after I evicted Jeremy from the room, Jude broke out a large quantity of the excellent pink cocaine. Together, we snorted enough of it to kill a small horse. My face was completely numb. Jude picked up the phone and called John

Ransom Miller. She told him that we needed some time to get reac-
quainted. She also told him I needed time to get into character, which
made me laugh like a goddamn crazy person. Then she hung up the phone
and turned off the lights, one by one. She told me to take off my clothes.

The skin between us is destroyed, unrecognized. Dead and dying tissue
between us. Visible wounds that move from one to the other and back.
There's a nasty gash down my right shoulder in the shape of California but
backwards, gouged by Jude with a corkscrew. The wound is much worse
than she intended. Oozing and slow to heal and soon it will be impossible
to lift my arm. And perhaps was not Jude at all. Perhaps was inflicted on
self. I remember how awkward the cut had been to make, how unlike the
cut of a knife. The flesh unyielding, slow to give. And it happened not long
ago because an echo of the pain lingers in my arm now even though the
skin appears to be smooth and good as new, the wound is gone without
trace but this is not possible and I worry for Jude, I worry for the body that
moves with me now as if through water. I have mistaken her breathing for
my own and it seems that she pushes me along even as I push at her and I
have the idea that neither of us can swim and if one us fails to push then
both will drown. I am aware too that I should stop thinking, that conscious
thought will surely fuck things up between us but I am worried about her
shoulder, I want to examine her shoulder for a wound in the shape of California and already I am losing her and now she swims ahead and it
appears that if anyone is going to drown it will be me.

Arms and legs thrashing. The hammer of blood.

I'm coming, says Jude.

And holds her breath. Orgasm is brief, nonviolent.

What color? I say.

Devastating blue, she says. The pale blue eyes of a murdered boy.

Very nice.

You remembered, she says.

Jude comes in colors. How could I forget. Trembling blond orgasms
that seem to piss her off and rare pink orgasms that never end. Chemical
red orgasms that fill her with guilt and perfect orgasms black as fresh

earth. Orgasms shadowy and gray that may or may not cause her to weep and orgasms the color of bruised skin, orgasms that fade from purple to yellow and remain visible for days.

I want to turn on the lights.

Please, she says. I prefer the dark.

But the dark is making me insane.

You're not insane, she says.

Thanks, I say. How do you know?

Because insane people never think they are insane.

I'm tired, Jude. I'm tired of sitting in the dark.

You remind me of Pinocchio, she says.

Before or after he became a real boy? I say.

Did you hate your father? she says.

No, I say. I don't think so.

Jude blows air through her teeth. Then it was your mother who fucked you up.

Fuck you. What's this bullshit about Pinocchio?

I think it's obvious, she says. He hated his father.

That's nonsense.

One of her hands slips into my lap, cold. I flinch and she laughs.

I could eat you, she says. Truly. I could eat your skin from the bone.

Geppetto wouldn't hurt a mouse and the boy adored him.

Whatever, she says. Pinocchio was a freak. He was the little wooden Elephant Man and he would never have existed if the old man hadn't carved him. Gepetto was like any other punchdrunk god who thinks he's doing you a favor and then just completely shits on you.

Then silence.

Which is it? I say. Pinocchio or the Elephant Man.

Jude shrugs. Both.

Well. I can see the Pinocchio bit, I say. The donkey's head, for instance. And his problem with telling the truth. The Elephant Man, though. He was a sweetheart. Hideous to look at and you wouldn't want to touch him, but he was probably a nicer guy than me.

Who do you think of? she says. When you fuck me?

I close my eyes and try to think of a normal, well-adjusted response. My mind does tend to wander during sex. I suffer strange, inappropriate visions. I often think of Jenny, a neurotic border collie I used to have. Jenny had wings. That dog could catch a Frisbee no matter how high or far I threw it. The trouble with Jenny was that she would never give the Frisbee back unless I threatened her. Jenny would run from me, she would hide in a patch of tall grass and chew and suck at the Frisbee in a way that was manic and eerily sexual. And she could destroy a good Frisbee in five minutes.

Do you see whores from your past? says Jude. Pale pubescent girls? Waitresses with bad skin or small hairless men?

What was the third choice? I say.

Jude bites my ear, hard enough to draw blood. I push her away from me.

You haven't come yet, she says. It's been three days. Three days of sex and not a trickle. I try not to worry about it. I tell myself that you're a freak. That it's because of the drugs. That it's not my problem.

But you're a liar, I say.

Yes, she says. I need to make you come.

What does my come taste like?

Aluminum, she says.

The taste of fear, I say.

Exactly, she says.

I grope the walls and flip the lights. The room is a horror and my dick is soft, very soft. It sleeps, meek and fleshy against my thigh and I'm sure that a soft penis is what death looks like. Loose skin and a thousand wrinkles, gray and wasted.

I offer this comparison and Jude doesn't smile. I offer to go down on her.

She squints at me. Your eyes are the same blue. But exactly.

Don't look at them, I say.

We have been in the dark too long. I have acquired the blue eyes of a murdered boy and I want to go outside.

Irrational or not, the horror of space travel goes back to Curious George and his sinister companion, the man in the yellow hat. That guy was obviously not right and I instinctively hated him as a boy. I see his face whenever I hear the word pedophile and as it happens, the only Curious George story that stuck in my head is the one in which the man in the yellow hat blackmails poor George into outer space. And there you go. If my mother had reached for a different book, I might have manifested a sexual fear of bicycles or kites.

Four hours later, give or take.

I wake up and the bed is empty. Jude is in the bathroom, naked and sitting on the edge of the tub, head cocked like a praying mantis and her hair falling in a mad tangle over her left shoulder. A vanity mirror between her thighs and she's probing herself with two fingers. She looks too crazy and hostile to be masturbating and I know she hates stupid questions so I decide to pee and say nothing.

I have an itch, says Jude.

What kind of itch?

A maddening itch.

I glance over my shoulder, sympathetic but obviously trying to pee.

There was no itch yesterday, she says.

I'm not awake yet and to my mind yesterday is still happening. I stare at the ceiling and wonder if she'll freak out if I mention the word imagination. There is water damage on the ceiling, a warped and dripping stain in the shape of Bob Dylan's head. Imagination is never a popular word in these domestic situations and at four in the morning it might be deadly. The only solution is to back away from the toilet and change the subject.

Water damage, I say. The ceiling is fucked.

What? she says.

It may not be safe in here, I say.

Her eyes narrow. If you say this is my imagination, or even think it.

Imagination? I say.

The feet, she says. I will do something terrible to your feet.

Do you think I afflicted you with something?

Maybe, she says. Maybe not.

I scratch my head, helpless. Do you want me to look at it?

No, she says.

Maybe it's a spider bite.

Jude stares at me. A spider?

Maybe.

What would a spider be doing in there?

I chew on my lip.

Careful, she says.

Oh yes. I want to be careful with this question. I promptly discard the notion that the spider was looking for food. I like the sound of gravitational weirdness but this is perhaps too vague, too unscientific. Jude sighs, staring at the little mirror. I slide close enough to touch her shoulder, to breathe her air.

Eucalyptus. Dandelions and salt. Opium and rainforest.

I have no idea what her scent is called, or where it comes from. Jude uses a lot of mysterious oils and lotions and it could be any of them, none of them. It could be her blood, her internal juices coming to the surface. Her smell is always on my skin and always fading. Jude turns the mirror sideways, squinting.

Fancy, she says.

What? I say.

It looks like a tiny deformed heart, she says. From a certain angle.

I count to five. What time is it, do you think?

Jude puts the mirror aside. Two o'clock, she says.

Come back to bed.

Why? she says.

We should get some sleep.

It's two in the afternoon, she says.

We could have sex, I say.

Jude stares at me.

Or not. What about a drink, then?

Please. With just a drop of vodka.

I hold out my hand and she allows me to lead her back to the bed.

There are two empty bottles of vodka at the vanity sink. A jug of ginger ale, a fifth of Jack that we've barely touched. There is a carton of milk, unopened and no doubt very sour. The ice is gone and the sink is foul with gray water and mutilated limes. The refrigerator is stuffed full of drugs and cash. When Jude checked into the room, she apparently removed all of the overpriced cheeses and chocolates and white macadamia nuts and miniature bottles of liquor and Snapple and put them in the hall and told the first maid who came along that we didn't want that shit and that she would personally hurt anyone who tried to restock the fridge. Jude can be very convincing when she promises to hurt someone and the maids have barely peeked in here since. They leave fresh linens and soap outside the door every morning but I don't think we have changed the sheets even once.

The vodka is gone, I say.

Jack and ginger then, she says.

The crushed pulp of limes. My eyes water. I consider opening the drawer to my left but don't. I mix the drinks like a robot. Jude is watching me in the vanity mirror.

You have a nice body, she says. For a junkie.

I stare back at her, wary. Thank you.

It's not hairy, she says. And it's almost perfectly symmetrical.

I regard myself in the mirror and decide that I am malnourished and freakishly pale, considering that I spent the last few years living on the edge of my imaginary desert. I'm no ghost but three days in this room and I have started to fade rapidly, to disappear. Jude is brown as deerskin.

Fuck it.

I move out of her line of sight, then open the drawer to my left. There is a brief, contemplative silence. I turn on the cold water tap and hope that Jude will think I am brushing my teeth, that she will not register the sound of an otherwise intelligent man snorting a bump of cheap brown heroin that may or may not be poison. Jude has forbidden me to touch it because yesterday, when she was taking an endless bubble bath I got restless and snorted too much of it. Jude came out of the bathroom with a towel around her head and found me nodding and drooling and grunting like a monkey that can't decide where he wants to lie down and die and soon I was feverish and hallucinating and spewing a grim yellow substance from my mouth and ass.

The heroin has turned me into jelly. I carefully give Jude her drink, then float backwards into a chair and spill my own drink all over myself. It feels nice, actually.

Bananafish, I say. Let's go fishing for bananafish.

Jude sips her drink, staring at me. Her eyes are sharp as nails and I can feel them poking through to the back of my head.

You opened the drawer, she says.

Oh that's true.

She stands on the bed, naked and very tall. I peer up at her from my sunken position, Jack and ginger pooling in my bellybutton. She drains her glass and I watch as her face shrinks through the bottom of it. I'm sure I have a stupid expression on my face but there's nothing I can do about it and now Jude throws the glass over my head. She throws it sidearm like a shortstop and it curves slowly past my line of sight to crash into the wall.

I told you to stay out of that drawer for a while.

Ummm.

Jude pulls on underpants, staring at me. She takes a big black gun from beneath her pillow, one I had not known was there. Looks to be a Glock 37, a serious fucking weapon. I wonder how many guns she's got hidden around this room like deadly Easter eggs and now that I think about it, I've lost track of that Walther she gave me the other day. I've a bad habit of mis-placing weapons when I'm high. Jude checks the clip, glances down the sight at me. I'm fairly confident that she won't shoot me because our rela-tionship has evolved. Now she hops on the bed and bounces up and down, rising like a dead leaf caught in a warm updraft. The room has low gravity.

You need to get dressed, she says.

Why?

Because we have a meeting.

I don't understand.

A meeting, she says. It's when two or more humans sit down together and talk.

Oh, I say. That sounds horrible.

Too bad, she says. It's been three days and Miller is getting clinical. I told him we would meet him for cocktails at six.

What does he want?

What do you think he wants? To discuss the film.

I shake my head, violently. Fuck that, I say.

Please, she says. Pull yourself together.

No, I say. Not gonna do it.

I want her to stop bouncing and I'm about to say so when she springs across the gap between bed and chair and lands in my lap. Jude is very light on her feet and somehow I don't start hemorrhaging upon impact. Now she sinks her teeth into my nose and my peripheral vision disappears.

Get dressed, she says.

Yes. Why not.

A walk sounds fine. The legs are functioning like never before. Brilliant glowing hole where my face used to be but that's no trouble. Personal supernova. I rumble around the room, negotiating with my clothes. Black jeans and black T shirt and brown leather jacket. Feeling colorful, yes. I dress myself without difficulty and I'm confident it's a pretty rapid process but when I finish lacing my boots, Jude is smoking maybe her ninth cigarette and gazing at me with disgust. I see that she is wearing a much more complicated outfit than mine. Pale silver boots that buckle up to the knees and a black skirt with steel zippers up the sides, a transparent orange shirt and some kind of black nylon vest that looks to be painted on. She has applied immaculate lipstick and she still holds that gun, I notice.

On your feet, she says.

She takes my outstretched hand and drags me over to the vanity area. Taps the mirror with a short blunt fingernail. The mirror ripples like water but does not break.

Look, she says.

I look in the mirror and I see what she sees. My hair is dirty but not so short and frightening now that I have stopped cutting it myself. I could use a shave, but none of my clothes are inside out. Probably I have looked worse in the past, a lot worse. Jude looks great, though. She looks like she should be with some other guy, someone much younger and cooler and altogether more hygienic than me.

You're staring, she says.

I like to look at you.

Jude hands me a pink CD jewel case that previously held a mysterious software called Darkstar. Jude has a slick new laptop and lately she likes to disappear online when I become dull or impotent. I was sure she would spend most of her time hitting porn sites but was somehow not surprised to learn that she is in fact a compulsive day trader. Jude has changed since I saw her last. She has become infinitely more competent and dangerous than even before. There are two fat lines of coke chopped onto the pink plastic case. I reach for a red cocktail straw and snort them without hesitation.

Phineas has a dubious policy about cocaine: When it's offered him, he tends to do a lot of it.

I rub a little into my teeth and suddenly I look much better in the mirror.

I'm a handsome motherfucker, I say.

Jude opens the drawer that contains the stash of bad heroin. She removes the foil lump and shows it to me. Her left eyebrow goes up.

Are you paying attention?

I nod and follow her into the bathroom and watch as she flushes the little package down the toilet without comment.

There's still plenty of cocaine, I say.

Jude turns. You're not that handsome.

I smile provocatively at her, then turn and vomit into the sink.

thirteen.

INTERNAL DISTORTION, OVERLOAD. Too many conflicting desires and anxieties and I walk five blocks without thinking about where I'm going.

Flesh, perhaps. Inexpensive flesh.

Jude was pretty irritated about the vomiting. She said some very nasty things that I'm sure she didn't mean, then went to meet Miller without me. I took a couple of Vicodin and went to sleep.

That was yesterday.

I woke up the next morning and she hadn't come back. I took a bath and called room service for some breakfast. I needed a drink and thought solid food would be an interesting plot twist but I found the bacon too crunchy and alarming and the Western omelet downright objectionable. I drank the bloody mary and went back to sleep. There was no sign of Jude when I woke up and I formed the theory that she was busy fucking Miller to death and taking her sweet time about it.

I want to lose myself for a while. I want the anonymous touch of a whore. The streets are fuzzy. The hiss of traffic on wet blacktop sounds like analog, like vinyl. I'm angry and not sure why. I vaguely remember telling Jude that I don't get jealous but now I'm thinking that was a lie. The swirl of cigarette smoke and ruined voices around the corner. I come upon two women with thick, muscled shoulders and narrow hips, heavy thighs. Terrible mouths and the bodies of men. I ask them to point me in the direction of the Tenderloin and they commence to hoot and holler. They ask me what I'm looking for.

Gratification, sympathy. False intimacy.

I don't know, I say. Maybe a massage.

Honey, says one. I know just what you need.

Lord yes, says the other. Four hands better than one. You come along with Sorrow and me and we gonna take care of you. You think you gone to heaven.

Sorrow? I say.

That's right, says the first one. My name is Sorrow and this my sister, Milky Way.

Temptation.

I am briefly tempted by the horror of another rented room. The sour sheets. The stink of boiled skin, the heavy perfume. The flicker of dying light. The panic and grind of Latin pop music. The raw, foreign hands of two transvestites with such unlikely names.

Invasion, humiliation.

I could easily lose myself, I think.

No, thanks. I'm looking for a regular girl.

Oh, honey. Now that's rude.

I believe you want to apologize, sucker.

I'm sorry. I'm looking for a different girl.

Uh huh. You sorry as can be.

What kind of girl?

I don't know. Foreign.

They laugh and screech like mad chickens and Milky Way finally tells me to go fuck myself.

Jude and I are two people, not one. Funny but I have to remind myself of that sometimes. The velvet warms and binds but I don't really know her. I don't know what's in her heart. I am safe with her for one day, two. The cocoon is temporary and what do I want. Obliteration. The ability to fly.

I tell myself to shut up, to keep walking. I have four hundred dollars. Enough to take me back to Flagstaff, to a mattress on the floor. Dishwater skin and bourbon in a jelly jar and a window with an unbroken view of the sky. The edge of the desert. I can listen to public radio and daydream about Atlantis and I can satisfy my physical hunger with my own two hands. I can destroy myself, if necessary. I stop in the middle of the street and look down at my open hands. The little finger of my left hand has twice been broken, and is now crooked. Otherwise they are ordinary hands with but one visible scar between them. Twenty-nine stitches on the palm of my right hand that effectively wiped out my life line. I tell people that it happened in a knife fight but the truth is that I was the only one involved. The wail of a car horn and someone yells at me to get the Christ out of the road.

I keep walking, keep walking.

This is the wrong way.

I am moving slowly uphill and I have a feeling that the Tenderloin should be down from here. I should be moving in a downward spiral. But perhaps this is metaphorical thinking. Or would that be irony, symbolism. These things are vaguely defined in our culture. This is San Francisco and eventually I will find whatever it is I'm looking for.

The Paradise Spa on Hemlock, a nasty little alley off Van Ness. Tanning and oriental massage. The very same establishment recommended me by young Jeremy. The sign is barely visible from the street and I might have easily walked by it. Blue neon, pale and wispy. Tucked in along a doughnut shop, a Vietnamese grocery. The Paradise Spa is open until midnight. Because you never know. You never know when you might suffer a pinched nerve, or when you might want to do a little maintenance on that tan. I wonder if they even have tanning beds.

The front door needs a coat of paint.

Open it and step inside and I'm facing a steel mesh door, locked. Dark red curtain behind it. To the right of the door is a small black sign with white lettering that tells me a half hour massage is fifty dollars. A whole hour is very economical at eighty dollars. Tanning is twenty bucks for twenty minutes but who gives a shit. To the left of the door is a buzzer. Press it with my thumb, briefly.

The red curtain is pulled aside and the face of a troll appears, shriveled and brown as a peach pit with black eyes bright. The eyes study me a long moment. Troll apparently decides I am neither cop nor psycho because the door is unlocked.

Come, she says.

Troll takes me by the wrist with little claw, pulls me inside.

Come. You ever be here before?

No.

You want half hour?

I want to be agreeable. Yes, I say. The half hour.

Come.

Warm, soft light. Japanese prints on the walls of the hallway. The furniture is cheap, simple. The kind of shit you find in a Holiday Inn. Troll leads me down the hall past several closed doors, her sandals flapping softly on tile floor. I hear whispers.

Then grunting, man or pig.

Pulse quickening now. Troll shows me to a tiny room with bed and chair. The bed is covered with white towels. On the wall above the bed is a shelf with yellow lamp and radio, a box of tissues, and various oils and lotions. The radio is tuned to soft jazz, elevator-style. Troll holds out her hand, impatient. The money, yes. Fumble in pockets and produce fifty dollars.

You need shower, she says.

What?

Take shower. You wash.

No. I'm clean.

Troll makes a nasty smacking sound with her leather tongue, stares at me. I stare back at her, hoping she doesn't insist on the shower. I feel relatively cozy in the confines of this room and I just want her to close the door, to go away. I don't like this idea of a shower at all. I would be vulnerable, paranoid under bright lights. I would be slippery and exposed and I don't want my asshole inspected.

I don't want a shower.

Troll stares at me and I decide she wants an explanation.

I'm afraid someone will steal my shoes.

Troll frowns and sighs. Undress, she says. Lie on bed.

The door closes behind her and I sit down in the chair. Unlace my boots with fingers numb, unresponsive. Wonder how it is that my hands fall asleep in my pockets. I flex them a few times. Touch left thumb to throat and find my pulse is racing. I shove the boots and socks under the chair and out of sight. Pull off the rest of my clothes and try to fold them but I'm incompetent and finally heap them on the chair. I stand naked beside the bed a moment, staring at the radio. The soft jazz is maddening and I flick at the tuning knob until I find Patsy Cline and stop. I turn around in a manic circle because country stations are tricky. Patsy may be followed by Kenny Rogers or worse. I tell myself to lie down. There's a laminated notice on the wall above the radio that lists the house rules of Paradise Spa, with a lot of misplaced apostrophes and inappropriate italics. The thing is framed, like a diploma. Translation: no alcohol, no illegal drugs, no weapons, no violence. No solicitation and no sexual acts of any kind because the Paradise is a wholesome place.

Patsy Cline falls to pieces. The bed smells like disinfectant, with a hint of breezy fabric softener. Bounce, I mutter to myself. Downy. I flop on the mattress, belly down. Then wiggle around like a nervous cockroach and clumsily cover my ass with a towel. Take deep breaths, meditative. I wish my heart would stop pounding and I wonder what Jude is doing to young Jeremy and abruptly Patsy is muscled aside by Kenny Rogers. "The Gambler." I want to laugh but I can't.

The door opens with the coo of a dove. Hello.

Open my eyes and at first I think there is some mistake. The girl is barely five feet tall in a little plastic white dress that clings to her like wet tissue.

Her hair is a massive, fizzy black nightmare. She has arms and legs thin as sticks and surely this is illegal. The girl is maybe fourteen. I roll over and try to sit up but she pushes me down with a cool hand and now I see her face. Tiny wrinkles around her eyes and mouth. And her breasts are surreal, too large for her body and perfectly round and defined by the clean hard edges of the surgically enhanced. Her breasts swell above her ribcage as if they might float away.

What's your name? she says.

Um. Fred, I say.

Please. On your tummy, Fred.

And what's your name? I say.

I am Veronica, she says.

A slight accent but her English is not bad. Better than the troll's and no doubt better than your average American's. I think she is Vietnamese but then I am only slightly less stupid than the next white guy when it comes to distinguishing one East Asian group from another. Veronica runs a hand up my thigh and pulls the little white towel aside. I don't have an erection yet but I can feel the blood gathering. She smiles faintly and I feel a gentle twitch of nausea. I roll over onto my stomach and close my eyes.

Veronica has great hands.

This is not a massage, however. It's foreplay. It's like being tickled by silk feathers, by the tiny velvet fingers of dolls. Her hands roam up and down my legs, stroking my ass and thighs and feet with the sweet lazy touch of a lover and now one hand sinks shivering between my legs to lightly touch my penis.

What's this? she says.

I don't like this hide and seek shit, usually. But it's nice to close my eyes and pretend I'm twelve and playing doctor with the girl next door. I don't remember her name but she has dirty blond hair and crooked teeth and she smells like strawberry lip gloss and maybe, just maybe she has a fucking Band-Aid on her knee, oh my.

What do you want? she whispers.

I open my eyes and roll over. Veronica massages my chest and belly and leans close to me, rubbing her hard round tits against my arm. What do you want. What do you want. I want her to do whatever she wants to do. I want her to be professional. I want her to touch me for money.

You want to make love, she says.

Love. The word seems grotesque.

I don't think so.

Veronica shoves one finger into her mouth and sucks at it. You want? Why not?

You will give me nice tip, she says.

Of course.

Veronica is already bored with me. She sighs and mechanically lowers the straps of her dress and her cartoon tits bounce into my hands. She allows me to fondle her nipples for approximately ninety seconds, then pushes my hand away. Veronica straddles my torso, her ass in my face. The white plastic dress is short and quickly rides up over her hips and under it she's wearing a black lace thong that is too small for her and her shaved red pussy is two inches from my face and I am tempted to lift my head and bite her, to rip at the thong with my teeth but now she is nibbling and kissing at my rock-hard dick and briefly I am confronted with an image of Jude wearing the same black thong and she's laughing or crying and Miller stands over her and just as Veronica sticks her pinky in my ass I grab her by the shoulders and push her ravenous mouth away.

Stop, I say. I'm sorry, but just stop.

And with that, the transaction is finished. Veronica hops off me and quickly straightens her dress. She adjusts her mass of hair and I see now that it's a wig. She leaves the room and I lounge there, a frog waiting to be dissected. I have been injected with that shit that makes the blood purple and gelatinous and still I feel empty as hell. I just want to get the fuck out of here. I reach for a tissue and swab at my package but it's pretty gory down there, still rock hard, now marked with red lipstick. I won't wash her mouth away without a nice long bath. The door opens again and Veronica slips through, smiling. She holds a Diet Pepsi in one hand and a warm washcloth in the other. She hands me the soda and I sit there like a soiled child while she wipes down my gear with the washcloth. And when she's finished, she holds out her hand. I give her the Diet Pepsi and she frowns. I reach for my pants and pull out three twenties. Veronica rolls her eyes and I pull out another one and now she smiles and nods and the money disappears into her shoe. Veronica asks if I am not thirsty and I say no, thanks. She shrugs and leaves me to dress myself and when I open the door, Troll is waiting to escort me out.

I could kill myself sometimes. I am cast adrift in California and though I may appear to be easily confused, I know exactly what I'm doing. Through the filter, removed. One angle black and white fuzzy with no sound. I am talking to myself on a wet sidewalk tainted with yellow then red of traffic lights in a strange city and I'm not wearing a watch but I imagine it's been less than an hour since I left the hotel room. I have just had my cock effectively gobbled by a stranger and I am feeling no pain and now I am aware of blue neon behind me, the fading signature of a ghost.

fourteen.

I LEAVE THE PARADISE SPA and walk up Geary to Jones. Enter the bar called Mao's that is empty but not. The walls are painted with black and white murals of old world film actors. Charlie Chaplin. Fatty Arbuckle. Laurel and Hardy. They stare and stare and I feel surrounded. I go to the bar and an old guy with silver hair and little round eyeglasses comes over, puts a napkin in front of me. The empty barstools to my left and right are too perfectly aligned and a little creepy. I ask for ice water and two shots of whiskey but I am really tempted to demand a glass of hydrogen peroxide because my mouth feels wrong. It feels like it's full of fucking cigarette ash. I suck down the water in a long furious swallow, drooling. The bartender has a lazy brown eye that wanders around loose as a marble while the other stares straight through me.

That's gonna be eight dollars, he says.

I give him a twenty and tell him to go ahead and bring another shot.

Long day? he says.

Endless, I say.

The bartender shrugs and glances up at one of the overhead televisions. There are seven of them, I notice. On two screens are the same silent baseball game, the Dodgers and Braves. Three of the others are running old movies. Bette Davis howling and bug-eyed and completely nuts on the left. Jimmy Stewart peeping at his freaky neighbors to the right. And Laurence Olivier tediously dying straight ahead. The last two screens are gray and blank.

Are you Mao? I say.

Professionally speaking, yes, the bartender says.

Interesting name for a bar.

It's all about mind control, he says. Propaganda, baby. The customers come in here like suicidal sheep and the televisions mesmerize them. The old movies make people melancholy and therefore thirsty. The baseball keeps them sedated. Think about it. Television and advertising and the power of mass hypnosis were completely unrealized before Mao and Hitler showed us a thing or two. Of course, it would be financial suicide to name a bar after Hitler.

I stare at him and he laughs, low and rasping.

The place is kind of empty, I say.

Yeah, he says. What the fuck do I know?

What about soft porn, I say.

Nah. He waves a hand. Don't want the wrong element in here.

I shrug and swallow the first whiskey.

Pull up a stool, boy. You might as well stay a while.

I sit down and take slow, cautious sips of the second whiskey. I would hate to get drunk. I grin to myself and look up at the Dodgers game and see that the Braves are methodically destroying them. The players on the Dodger bench are serene, peaceful. The camera moves in on one young black player, a rookie who wears silver wraparound sunglasses even though it's a night game. He stares out at the field as if he's sitting in church and his face is frozen, cut from stone. The camera lingers and now I detect the faint twitch of artery or muscle below his jaw.

You said that the customers are suicidal, I say. The sheep.

The bartender nods. Yeah.

What do you mean by that, exactly.

Huh, he says. I'm not a goddamn psychologist and wouldn't want to be. But it seems to me that anybody comes into a bar and sits by himself and sinks five or six cocktails one after another and never says boo to another soul well he's got a gun to his head. He's just taking his time about it.

I regard my own row of drinks.

Don't take offense, he says.

I wouldn't.

The bartender grins. Like I said previously. I don't know shit.

You ever think about it, Mao?

Pull my own plug?

Yeah.

Once or twice a day, in the morning especially.

The morning?

What the hell. I'm sixty-four years old. I got arthritis. I try to jerk off and all I get is a fucking cramp in my neck. Thinking about suicide is the next best thing.

Right.

You want another? says Mao.

I shake my head.

Well, then. When are you going to eat a bullet?

The third whiskey sits before me, untouched. My stomach is gurgling for lack of food and the bartender is a madman. I think he should have called this place The Faustus. I think my skull is full of black ice. Mao begins to wipe down the bar with a rancid yellow towel. The stink of mildew. That lazy eye drifts by, unfocused. The fucking thing is making me seasick and I try to ignore it.

Were you ever married? I say.

Mao jabs one finger at the lazy eye. No, he says.

I shiver, unsurprised. That eye would be hard to deal with.

You? he says.

A long time ago, yeah. But she killed herself. Blew herself to bits.

Mao looks up. You serious?

Yes.

Then I apologize to you. That was some insensitive shit to say.

I tell him not to worry about it. I tell him that it was a long time ago, another lifetime. Mao nods and murmurs and graciously tilts his head to the left so that I don't have to face the lazy eye. I tell him she was very brave, my wife. That she killed herself only out of the desire to sidestep a slow death. I am tempted to tell him that I don't have arthritis, that I spend a lot more time daydreaming about various gruesome ways to kill myself than I do actually bothering to masturbate. I'm not quite sure if this is true, however. And while it has a nice ring to it, I don't think such a confession would exactly put a smile on Mao's face. Anyway. I am trying to cut back on these incidents of drive-by intimacy. I stand up and tell him thanks and realize I am a trifle unsteady. I am wobbling. The third whiskey remains untouched and I ask him to please raise a toast to the next suicide that walks through the door.

Outside and yes, noticeably drunk. I have no sense of direction, no sense of time. I am wobbling on a street corner in downtown San Francisco. Vision is unreliable and after six, seven blocks, I am fast approaching blackout but not yet illiterate and the street signs that loom fuzzy black and white along my periphery identify this corner as 6th and Mission and danger is everywhere. Don't laugh but I think I'm being followed. I hear footsteps, echoes. I take a few steps and I hear the scrape of leather against stone behind me. I stop walking and the echo is gone and I know this is the paranoia of bad movies.

The nostrils twitch and I smell feces.

Cut away to handheld camera, delirium tremens.

I swing left and right now full circle and find the shitter, a runaway white girl sixteen maybe seventeen, a poor little crackhead crouched in blue doorway with bright yellow miniskirt bunched around her waist, leaving a wet black steaming coil of shit on someone's stoop.

Daffy.

This could be a clip from *20/20*. Lost children etc.

Probably her condition should trouble me, it should offend me or move me somehow. But I am too drunk and blind and preoccupied with my own problems to care about the public health and anyway it's not my doorway. The girl has to poop somewhere and even now her lips curl into a yellow snarl because I am staring at her. From her point of view, I am a stupid drunk middle-aged pervert and I'm staring at her, I'm invading her personal space. And if I breathe a word to her, if I offer to help this girl or give her money or a word of advice she will surely bite me.

I stand with my back to her a moment. Drunk but not unaware. The shitting girl is exactly the sort of lost soul that normally I would be compelled to help. I have a touch of Travis Bickle in me, says Jude. The watcher, the idiot avenger. But I'm not half the psychotic cracker that Travis was and I like to think my social skills are better by a mile or two. Anyway, something possesses me to turn around and ask the girl if she needs help. She has finished shitting by now and I can smell it. Her face is cracked and yellow and what's left of her brown hair is thin and stringy. Her eyes are black holes but I notice with a kind of horror how shapely her legs are.

This girl was once a beauty.

Five dollars, she says. Give me five dollars.

I fumble with my money and locate a five dollar bill. I don't want to think about what manner of service she might provide for five dollars. And when she sees the money, her small teeth flash.

Hey, mister. Let's go. I'll make you feel alright.

I shake my head, confused. Because this isn't going to help her and I don't know what will. I try to think what Jude would want me to do. She'd want me to be kind to this girl. Take her to IHOP and feed her pancakes with blueberry syrup, then coax her life's story out of her. Then go out and kill the father or brother or boyfriend who made her like this. But I can only imagine that. I can only give her the five dollars and turn away from her but she grabs at my arm, her nails raking the skin along my wrist.

I raise my hand to hit her, to drive her away, but stop myself. She falls against the wall, screeching.

Jude would not want me to hit this girl, I don't think.

The death shuffle. I walk a mile, or so it feels. And I have no fucking idea where the hotel is. I mutter to myself about milk and fallen angels and pretty polly and the glory of Ludwig Van in a terrible British accent because in the adolescent reptile portion of my brain I want to be Malcolm McDowell when I'm drunk but I am generally not so clever or elegant. I am stupid and cruel and violent and lonely and aching and maybe it would be best to take a cab out to Berkeley and curl up between Jude and John Ransom Miller like a lost sibling and worry about my intentions tomorrow but I am drunk and like any droog what is full of piss and lacking the common sense to lay down his head and sleep or die, I want to fight or fuck someone.

I want to fight John Ransom Miller.

Dear Jude, where are you. I want to be perfect just like you.

I can hear the freeway, the rush and hiss of a thousand cars. The edge, I am coming to the edge of something and I wonder if I am near the ocean and now I raise my eyes to see the curved freeway overpass like the massive spinal column of conjoined twins and glowing against black sky are the big green signs that provide blunt directions to Chinatown and North Beach and suddenly I am scared of the government and I want to get inside. I want to get inside and in the distance a shadowy line of people waits against the white wall of a building below the freeway. Three vertical black words against the wall over their heads, with a crude black arrow pointing to the heavens. It takes me a minute to make out the words but soon I form them silently with rubber tongue. The End Up.

Fate, baby. This is my new destination.

Melt into the line outside the End Up. Become a falling leaf brown and gold falling anonymous to earth with thousands of others. Infinity is mine, for two seconds. Then spot a mesmerizing blond girl with wide brown eyes and sharp features, hip bones jutting through thin nylon skirt. Belly button and nipples and goosebump arms and meathead boyfriend. Wobble like a duck. I gaze up the length of the line, where two very muscular bouncers with gold jewelry and black baseball caps are methodically patting people down before they go inside. They are looking for drugs, probably. But this is no problem, as I'm not holding. I forget for the moment that I am carrying a gun.

I turn to the nearest person, a Latin kid with blue hair. What is this place? I say.

He regards me with pity, scorn. It's like a rave, man. But better.

Wow.

The kid edges away from me, as if I have the pox. You better straighten up, he says.

What's the rumpus?

You're drunk, he says. And you smell like almonds.

I sniff myself, lifting one arm to my face. The kid is not wrong. I stink of almonds and I am about to say so but the lifting of my arm has apparently caused an unfort ate redistribution of personal mass which throws me off just slightly and I fall sideways into the blond girl with goosebump skin. She recoils in disgust and says loudly, oh gross and now the boyfriend leaps on me, beating me in the face and chest with stony fists and I am knocked backward, flopping into the crowd like an inflatable man and now fists come hammering down on me from all sides. Monkey in the middle. Something hits me in the eye that feels like a rock. Claustrophobia, numb panic. My cheek is gouged open by a sharp ring and the blood runs into my mouth and now someone lands a heavy fist in the back of my neck. This drops me to my knees. I'm trying to decide if I care for a fight and really I don't. I'm too sleepy and my arms and legs are like boiled noodles but I can fight if necessary and so I try to push myself upright as a heavy boot sails into my ribs, maybe six inches north of the hole Jude left in me so many years ago and I roll heavily over the curb. I flop into the gutter on my back like an old dog that wants his belly scratched.

The commotion draws the attention of the bouncers and one of them stomps down the sidewalk, muttering into a headset. For one truly stupid moment, I think he's coming to save me.

He's not.

The bouncer crouches over me, cursing. He says some unkind shit to me. Then frisks me with big, unforgiving hands. He gives my testicles a brutal squeeze and I nearly vomit in his fucking face. He takes my money, all of it. He puts it into his own pocket, which seems grossly unfair.

But then I'm drunk, yes.

I am really very drunk and a drunk is not quite human. I have therefore forfeited my civil rights. I mumble at him to please fuck off anyway and he laughs. He finds the gun. He grunts with purely sexual satisfaction and leans down close and whispers, the cops are coming you piece of shit and I hope you sleep like a baby. Then unceremoniously bashes me between the eyes with the butt of my own gun.

fifteen.

AND I WAKE UP ON A RUBBER MAT. Bright light overhead and fine powder of broken glass in my eyes. Force them shut and extend one hand to examine my environment. There's maybe an inch of water on the floor, cold water and I can hear the steady drizzle of a burst pipe. My hand splashes around in the water a while, blind and weak. My hand is a drowning rat. Unsanitary perhaps, but I use my wet fingers to soothe my eyes. I sit up and look around. The cell is five feet by seven. Overflowing toilet and two bunks tricked out with rubber mats. An inch of standing water on the floor and now I comprehend that I touched my sore eyes with toilet water. Brilliant. I'm alone in the cell. I was violent and they wanted to isolate me. I was comatose and they wanted to keep the crazies in the drunk tank from eating me alive. I'm wearing an orange jumpsuit and my bootlaces are gone. I was suicidal, maybe.

The memory is fucked, full of holes. Handcuffs chewing into my wrists. Crumpled in the backseat and my view of the world is sideways, upside down. The back of a cop's head through steel mesh. Fuzzy blond hair. He wears no hat and I am muttering a lot of nonsense about Nazis. He ignores me but when we arrive at the station he drags me out of the car in such a way that my skull smacks into the doorframe with a lovely hollow thud. The booking process is hazy. But I can imagine it. I have been arrested before and I always fuck up the fingerprinting. They tell me to relax and I immediately go tense. The prints smear every time and it pisses them off no end. I was carrying no identification and I wonder what name I gave them. Ray Fine. Fred, or maybe Jack. That would have been beautiful. I might have slipped into my role of Jack the retard. The cops would not likely be amused by Tourette's. They would probably beat a guy pretty severely if he was barking obscenities and repeating everything they said.

Oh, god.

I seem to remember a gloved finger wiggling around in my asshole, but maybe I was dreaming of Jude just now. I remember the sudden flash of the camera. That mugshot is a rare beauty, I'm sure.

I sit up and stare at the toilet. The water is churning up over the sides like there is big trouble underground. The water looks clear enough, for now. But as soon as I use the toilet then I will have my own nasty fluids rippling around me. I may as well take a shit on the floor.

I wonder if they gave me a phone call. That phone call shit in the movies is nonsense. The scene where some poor bastard is moaning about his rights. I know my rights, he says. I want my phone call. The phone call is not a constitutional right, as far as I know. Thomas Jefferson and the rest of his crew didn't have telephones, and anyway they sure as hell didn't give a shit about any drunk asshole's rights. And the word asshole is crucial. If you get arrested for public drunkenness, it's because you're an asshole. You walk in the door and you're already an asshole. You're an asshole. I'm an asshole. Everyone in here is an asshole. The cops can wait three days to charge you if they feel like it. And if you're an asshole with no manners, well. You may as well forget about your fucking phone call for a while.

But I appear to be on suicide watch. And this means that somebody will come by to rattle my cage before long. They have to be sure I don't eat my own tongue or gouge out my eyes. They have to at least pretend to care. I slosh over to the door like I'm going duck hunting and man I am none too steady. Drunk as a bishop even now and when did I last eat something. The tomato sandwich that Molly made for me. I wonder how she would like me now. I lean against the steel door and I hope my neighbor is friendly. I put my mouth close to the little window, pressing my lips against the cool mesh.

Hey, I say. Anybody out there?

Long hollow silence and for a few horrifying moments I imagine I'm the only one. Like something out of a science fiction movie. All of the prisoners have died of some horrible virus. The guards have fled and the prison is functioning on computer autopilot. But that can't be.

Hey, I say.

Shut the fuck up, says one thin voice.

Then another, dry and torn. What's up, cousin?

Confused, I say.

About what? says the voice. You're in the pokey.

Yeah, I get that. Are we on suicide, though?

Damn straight, he says.

Fuck me, I say.

I always go suicide, says the voice. Always. Like flying first class. I got to have my privacy.

Yeah. But they hold you for seventy-two, I say.

Nothing wrong with that, cousin. Three days peace and quiet.

I close my eyes. Three days drifting on a rubber mat in a pool of my own urine. And no cigarettes. I will probably die without cigarettes.

How long since the sheriff last came by?

Don't have a watch, cousin. But I'd say a half hour. At least.

The thin voice pipes up. Bullshit. It was ten minutes ago.

You shut your hole, says the torn voice. You got no concept of time.

Hey. You want to come suck my fucking dick?

Laughter, wheezing. What dick?

Thanks, I say. Thanks anyway.

I flop down on my little rubber lifeboat and wait for the next head count. I chew my lip for the residual taste of tobacco. I stare up at the bright fluorescent tube of light and wonder if it is day or night. I would sleep, if I could. I would dream.

Come footsteps. The rattle and echo of a billybat against one steel door after another. Then a chorus of voices, the music of hollow bones. I can't be sure if they are coming from within or without. To hell with boys creeping up slowly. I'm hungry, hungry. And a man may fish with a worm that hath eat of a king and then eat of the fish that fed on the worm and around and around you go. Through the guts of a beggar and I don't like ice cream.

On my feet and to the door.

The face of a young black guard appears at my window. The whites of his eyes like porcelain. He thumps the door and asks if I'm okay.

Yeah. Thanks for asking.

He grunts and starts to move on.

Excuse me?

Yes? His eyes narrow.

I hesitate. I need to sound sane and I'm not sure my voice is reliable. What do you want?

I need to speak to someone. I'm not sure I belong here.

The other prisoners begin to wheeze and cackle like a gang of chickens.

I'm not suicidal.

The guard peers at me. What's your name?

Poe, I say.

He consults a clipboard. Yeah, he says. The ex-cop.

I'm not a cop. I'm just a regular asshole, now.

Says here you're an ex-cop.

Furious whispers from left and right. Long slow, creeping shadows at the edge of my vision.

I sigh. Yeah. What am I charged with?

Assault, he says. Public drunk. Vagrant. Resisting arrest. And oh, shit. You won the lottery. Looks like you're up for murder.

Did you say murder? That doesn't sound right.

Tell it to the detectives, he says. They'll be wanting to talk to you, now you're awake.

He moves along to the next door and my neighbor says that he doesn't belong here either. That he's not crazy. He wants a phone call, a lawyer. He knows his fucking rights. Then he lowers his voice and confides to the guard that the fallen prophet Jeremiah has in fact been creeping around in his cell all night with his guts leaking out between his fingers and the motherfucker won't shut up. Jeremiah is pissed off at God and he won't let the rest of us sleep. The guard laughs and moves along.

I squat in the center of my cell with eyes closed. Murder, huh. That wasn't part of my plan for this night, I know that much. I try to remember what happened. There was a sad fucked-up scene with an Asian whore. Then stumbling drunk. I was offensive. There was some sort of slapstick confrontation with a bouncer outside a nightclub that might have got messy, but murder seems a bit extreme.

I open my eyes now and a funny thing happens. I look around and for two seconds maybe three, this is no jail cell. I see fake wood paneling and molded furniture, avocado green. I see a stained mattress with faded blue stripes and I see an open doorway and miles and miles of yellow earth and this is home. This is my trailer back in Arizona.

I believe I would trade my soul for a cigarette.

The mad jangle of voices, farther away now. The drip of my toilet like a soft summer rain.

The thin voice. Hey, man. What the fuck? You five-oh, or what?

Long time ago, I say.

Once a cop, he says. Always a cop.

Fuck you, kid.

You talk like a cop.

Then laughter, like glass breaking apart.

Hours pass, maybe days.

My neighbor with the torn voice tells me that they never turn off the lights, that time is therefore elastic and that if I am not insane now, then surely I will be soon.

The young black guard returns and says the detectives are ready to interview me. I am led down the hall in shackles. My unlaced boots loose and flopping.

Voices.

Hey killer what you got in that bag is it my true love's head?

I don't listen. I maintain a straight face. I keep my expression straight and true, like a well-groomed garden. I want to get out of here and I need to look right.

The guard is silent.

A security check-point and we wait to be buzzed through. Something stinks of sweat and vomit and I have a pretty good idea it's me. Now I catch a muddy glimpse of myself in a bank of plexiglass and baby I'm a fright. Bruises and black streaks on my face and scarecrow hair. I touch my face and remember lying in the street, bloated and damp and I have to say my hat's off to that bouncer. He bounced me good.

The guard deposits me in another small, windowless room. He tells me to shut up and wait, as if I have a choice. I sit at a scarred wooden table and flash back to the interrogation room back at the Denver P.D., not to mention a thousand and one poorly drawn rooms from the movies and television. I have been on both sides of the table and I know that interrogation is a pretty simple game of rhetorical hide and seek. The results are written in advance, like the streaming threads of fate, but however you arrive there the scene is bound to be ugly, and numbingly tedious, poorly designed and self-consciously acted.

Even so. I didn't kill anyone and I want to see the sun today. I want a cigarette. There are right answers and wrong answers. The right answers will get me out of here. The right answers will put me on the street with the other humans. The wrong answers will get me a shot of Thorazine. I think of my neighbor, the one tormented by Jeremiah and I wonder if I should present myself as a paranoid Christian. A lot of good it's done my neighbor.

The first cop is a short white guy, heavy and morose, with a bad mustache. It droops down over his lip and his tongue darts in and out as if to taste it. He adjusts his belt and gun and crotch and belly and heaves himself into the chair across from me, sighing. The second cop is small and pale. He doesn't look like he weighs more than 140 or so and his hair and skin are the same pale beige color and basically he has a lot to overcompensate for and I have a feeling he's as mean as he can be. He stands against the back wall, silent and staring.

Name? says the first cop.

Phineas Poe.

Middle initial?

None.

Interesting.

Is it?

Phineas Poe, he says. Formerly of the Denver P.D., Internal Affairs Division. He spits out these last eight syllables like bad meat.

Long time ago, I say. Hell of a long time.

Do you know why you're here?

What's your name? I say.

He stares at me. He stares at me for a while and I wonder if he's counting to ten. His tongue darts out again, pink and terrible. That mustache truly bothers me and I try not to look at it. I realize that I have made a mistake. Questions will only make these guys angry. Your lines are already written so just spit them out in the proper order and everything will be fine. I tell myself to sit up straight. I try to indicate by my expression that I'm an okay guy. I'm intelligent and cooperative and respectful and all that shit but I don't really think my face can handle so much at once. I glance at his pale little partner and he's licking his lips, as if he just can't wait for me to say the wrong thing.

Where are my manners, says the first cop. My name is Captain Kangaroo.

I tell myself to shut up, shut the fuck up. Don't breathe.

But it's like I have a manic little butterfly in my mouth, dying to get out. I shoot a glance at the pale little cop and I say it. I just say it.

I guess that makes you Mr. Green Jeans, I say.

He smiles at me and his teeth are the same shade of beige as his hair and skin.

Again, says Captain Kangaroo. Why are you here?

Because of a misunderstanding?

A misunderstanding.

That's right.

I see. What did you do tonight?

Nothing interesting, I say.

He yawns. Tell us anyway.

I had a couple of drinks at a place called Mao's. Then I wandered down the street and immediately got my ass handed to me by a very unfriendly bouncer. Then I woke up here.

I guess you're harmless, says Captain Kangaroo. I guess we should let you go.

The two of them stare at me and I just feel weary.

I know that I have a role to play here, I say. But I just can't do it.

What? he says.

Why do we have to dance around this fucking bush? I say. The guard told me I'm charged with murder. Why don't we talk about that?

Are you suicidal? says the pale cop.

I don't think so.

Do you ever entertain suicidal thoughts?

Of course.

How often?

I entertain such thoughts every day. Don't you?

No.

I think it's normal.

It's not normal.

Define normal, I say.

The pale little cop begins to whistle tunelessly. His partner sighs and looks at his watch. The pale cop sits down for a moment and takes off his left boot, which is an imitation leather Teddy boy boot that zips up over the ankle. He comes around the table, still whistling and walking funny because he only has the one shoe on. He smiles and shows me the boot, like a salesman. I look at it politely. Then he bashes me in the head with the heel of the boot and I feel something in my neck pop.

Normal, he says. There's no such thing.

No such thing, says the Captain. He speaks in a numbing monotone.

That's why we have crime in this country, says the pale cop. Because nobody feels normal and nobody wants to be normal.

There's blood in my mouth. I swallow it.

Philosophy, I say. To be normal is to be dead.

Exactly, he says. And you're about one smart answer away from another bump on the head.

You call that a bump?

Okay, says the Captain. This is boring the shit out of me.

He tosses an envelope on the table. The envelope contains crime scene photographs. I look at them one by one and they're pretty bad. There's so much blood I don't recognize the girl at first. But it's the yellow-faced girl I saw shitting on the street. Dead from every angle. Her skirt up around her waist and her pretty legs spread wide. It looks like her head was just about cut off. The last photo is a grim shot of her blackened fingers clutching what looks like a bloody five-dollar bill. I stare at her fingers until the scratches she left on my wrist begin to throb. There is something different about her and I realize it's her hair. The girl shitting in the street had stringy brown hair like she was already dead, but in these photos she's wearing a frizzy black wig.

That's odd, I say. It sounds terrible as soon as it comes out of my mouth.

Odd? says the pale cop. I take it you've seen her before?

She's wearing a wig, I say.

The pale cop shrugs. Her natural hair was falling out.

Captain Kangaroo tosses another photo on the table, a Polaroid. I reach for it, then pull my hand back. I can see from where I'm sitting it's a picture of a Japanese fighting knife that's been dipped in blood and looks a lot like mine. I look at the Captain. He yawns and his tongue flicks out to taste the mustache.

I guess I want a lawyer, I say.

The pale cop flashes his brown teeth. I'm sure one will be provided for you, he says.

Another guard comes to take me back to my cell. He informs me that I can see my lawyer in the morning, before I'm arraigned. His words sound so strange. I wonder exactly how many courtroom movies and television dramas I have seen in my lifetime. I sit on my rubber mat and watch the water rise around me. I wonder if anyone has ever died by drowning in jail. My neighbors have become moody and silent, which makes me lonely. I contemplate my situation and it seems pretty clear to me that I'm fucked. The girl in the street was apparently killed with my knife. The medical examiner will find bits of me under her fingernails. The black wig she was wearing will turn out to be Veronica's, the whore from the Paradise Spa, and even though I never came, the wig will no doubt have traces of my semen in it. What else. That's enough, isn't it. They don't need much else.

Phineas is fucked.

I crush my eyes with the heels of my hands until I see stars but I am not transported back to my trailer in the desert or anywhere else. I wonder who it was, who set me up. John Ransom Miller. Molly. Jude. Jeremy, the spurned doorman. Veronica had no discernible motive but then motive is the biggest crock of shit in legal and literary terminology. Consider the waitress with a hacking cough who serves you hashed browns at five a.m., what the hell motivates her. The guy outside the diner, waiting for a bus with a hole in his shoe. The guy who drives the fucking bus, for that matter. What motivates them. What motivates any of us but money and sex and basic survival. Veronica had arms like winter twigs but she might well have been stronger than she looked. She had intimate access to that wig and if someone offered her a thousand dollars, who the hell knows, she might have been happy to shank a common street whore. How the hell do I know. I had my cock in her mouth for about ninety seconds but I didn't get to know what was in her heart. I can't help but laugh. I love this society we live in. I don't know. I don't know who rang my bell and it really doesn't matter. It could have been any one of them. It wasn't me, anyway. I was drunk as a lord but not drunk enough to kill.

I am left to decompose for a few hours.

At what feels like two in the morning, the new guard arrives with a gloomy kid in medical scrubs who takes samples of my blood and urine. Then at dawn I am served a meal of processed meat on white bread, half of a canned peach in sticky syrup, and a small paper cup of grape Kool-Aid. The meat is slimy, the bread damp. The peaches are gray and the Kool-Aid is grape only in name and color. I need my strength, though, and I consume the food mechanically, masticating with a dull efficiency that pleases me.

Along about five, not long before the first pink fingers of dawn, I get another surprise. The guards bring me a cellmate. A white guy, cat thin and lined with tattoos. The hard leather arms of a welterweight. Dirty blond hair and eyes like smoke, a scruff of beard. His name is Sugar Finch, and when he sees me, he just grins. He grins like his mouth is full of locusts.

sixteen.

AND THE GUARDS TAKE HIS BODY AWAY AT NOON. I never get breakfast or lunch. I expect them to move me into another cell, an isolation unit, but they never do. I expect them to come beat me half to death, but they never do. I expect the detectives to send for me, so they can tell me just how badly I have fucked myself, but they never do.

I dragged Sugar Finch into the corner, where the water was up to my ankles, and killed him with my hands before dawn. Impaled his eye sockets with my thumbs, just as I'd imagined. I skull-fucked him with my fingers and the blood spilled up my arms, all the way to my elbows. I don't want to talk about it, not yet. I may never want to speak of it. It was the worst thing I've ever had to do. This little cell is now the perfect crime scene. I expect dire consequences, but none seem to be in the offing. No one says boo to me.

Come six or seven next evening and my head is a pocket of rage. Tunnel vision. The angry flap of blackbird wings, just out of reach. I am crawling with imaginary bugs. My skin is slick with sweat and I'm cold. This is one of my usual headaches, with a touch of the delirium tremens thrown in. I reckon my body has designated this as happy hour and now it wants a fucking cocktail. And here comes the guard, just like that. Wonders never, so they say.

Phineas Poe, he says. Time to see the judge.

I don't understand. They wouldn't take me directly to be arraigned, not after I'd killed my bunkmate, would they. I would expect another round of questioning, maybe even a beating.

The guard leads me down a long corridor with flickering lights. My hands remain shackled together but I consider myself lucky. I am told to wait in line with about twenty prisoners to be transported to court and several of the poor bastards are wearing those leg and crotch shackles that make them walk like angry ducks.

The courtroom is fairly disappointing. The walls are a pale pea green and the floor is carpeted. The lights are fluorescent and everyone's skin looks faintly orange. There are no shadows. I am taken in by the bailiff and led over to the defendant's table where John Ransom Miller is waiting for me. He wears a black suit with black shirt and black tie. He has recently shaved and smells vaguely of licorice.

You. You're my fucking lawyer.

He hisses at me to be quiet and sit down.

This is just great.

Quiet.

Maybe I have something to say.

Later, he says. You can talk later.

I curse inwardly at him and sit down in a wobbly wooden chair. It seems to me that the state could step up and provide chairs that didn't wobble but then maybe they have other fish to fry. Miller sits beside me and shuffles papers. I find my nostrils twitching every time I catch a whiff of licorice.

The whole thing plays out with very little drama. The bailiff coughs and tells everyone to rise and there is great, unceremonious shuffling of bodies as a middle-aged white man with a shiny bald skull comes in wearing the standard dark robe. My name is called and the charges are read. The judge barely glances up through the whole thing, which takes about ninety seconds. He asks how we plead and I flinch as it occurs to me that Miller and

I didn't exactly discuss that. But he says not guilty and no one is surprised. The assistant prosecutor makes a fairly convincing statement about the horrific nature of the crime and claims that I am a vagrant and therefore a flight risk and should be held without bail. Miller says nothing, which pisses me off. He stares at his fingernails, bored, as if he knows the outcome already. Then the judge whacks the gavel and says that the prisoner will appear before the grand jury in one week and bail is set at two hundred thousand dollars and that's that. The prosecutor mutters a few sweet nothings to herself and the bailiff comes to take me away. Miller informs me that because the police are holding my clothes as evidence, he brought me a suit to wear and he hopes it fits.

He says he will be waiting for me outside.

The process of being released from lock-up involves a lot of waiting on benches with three or four other gloomy fuckers who smell bad and look sorry as hell. I am given a small, grimy envelope that holds a mashed pack of cigarettes and ninety dollars. I had no wallet, of course. I had no identification and no jewelry. There is blood in my hair and I stink to heaven, so I ask to be allowed to shower but the guards ignore me and it seems like a good idea not to push it as I wouldn't want anyone to get the bright idea to delouse me or something. Then I am given a new Hugo Boss suit in a sort of chocolate brown color and stylishly cut with narrow legs and wide lapels. The material is a wool and silk blend and light as a feather. There is a pale pink shirt to go with it and no tie, and I must say I look fucking sharp. I particularly like the way the bloodstains on my motorcycle boots complete the outfit and I start to snort and giggle like a mental patient.

Then outside, flinching away from the sun like a rat. Miller waits for me on the steps. He asks me how I'm doing and his tone is casual, as if we are meeting for lunch.

I'm a peach. Where is Jude?

Detained, he says.

How did you know I was arrested?

He shrugs. Heard it on the scanner, actually.

Cool, I say.

Yes. He sniffs me.

I know. I stink.

You're deadly, he says.

I assume you paid my bail.

He smiles. It was the least I could do.

Thanks. I take it you're a good lawyer.

The best, he says. And very expensive.

Of course.

I nod and he nods and the two of us stand there, nodding. I extract a bent cigarette from my pack and Miller hands me a gold lighter. I fire the thing up and it's probably the best cigarette I ever had. The smoke drifts hazy in the sunlight and if I close my eyes, the traffic sounds like the ocean.

You killed that girl, I say. Or arranged for someone else to kill her.

Miller raises an eyebrow. I glanced at the evidence, he says. And it looks like you killed her.

Oh, yeah. The evidence.

Pretty damning, he says with a sigh.

I agree. I am living in agreement. But doesn't it strike you as a fat freakish fucking coincidence that just when you get tangled up with Jude and you want to cast me in a sensitive snuff film that you can screen at Sundance, I get charged with murdering a junkie on the street and then you happen to be a lawyer with the necessary juice to bribe a judge.

I didn't bribe him. But I could easily see to it that this goes badly for you.

What about Sugar Finch? How did you arrange for him to be placed in my cell?

My gift to you, he says. Did you like that?

I loved it.

Tell me about it, he says, Don't leave anything out.

Fuck you, Miller.

My pleasure, he says.

The DA was right, you know. I am a flight risk.

You won't run, he says.

How do you know?

Because you're a nice guy. Molly thinks so, anyway.

Please. Why not just let me rot in jail?

Jude, he says. Jude won't do the film unless you're involved.

I don't deserve such faith.

Miller whispers. Maybe…she wants you to protect her from me?

I flick my cigarette away and sparks tumble down the steps. And as if this were a signal, a reporter appears out of nowhere with a cameraman.

For god's sake.

Miller grins at me. I think you might want to take this seriously.

He steps between me and the reporter and I feel almost grateful. Don't get me wrong because part of me wants to turn and run like hell from him. But part of me wants to do this. The idea of shooting a snuff film with a crazy stranger and his beautiful girlfriend is weirdly appealing. It makes sense to me. And maybe I want to find out what happens. I want to know who the victim will be. Miller is right about one thing, sort of. Phineas is an arrogant fool, sometimes. Because I believe that somehow I can control what's going to happen, that I can protect Jude and Molly and whoever else drifts into his path.

Miller dispenses with the reporter and turns to me. Are you ready to go, he says.

Yeah. I'm ready.

Excellent. I have a car waiting.

When he says he has a car waiting I foolishly imagine a limousine with somber driver and a fully stocked wet bar with shimmering mirrors. But it's just a simple yellow cab with a fat bald driver who smells of Old Spice. The radio is tuned to the Giants game and the driver sighs mightily whenever the Giants do something stupid. He sighs frequently. Miller takes a silver flask from his breast pocket and mentions that I have the look of a man who wants a drink.

No shit.

I badly want a drink. I need one. I might trade my left foot for a long greedy swallow of whatever is in that flask. But I really want to straighten up, to see clearly for one night at least. I shake my head and he puts the flask away without comment.

Where are we going?

To meet Molly and Jude for dinner.

Bullshit.

Hardly.

Where?

Miller shrugs. A hideous little place in the Mission. Very trendy.

Good god.

You will love it, he says.

An endless red light and pocket of silence. I catch an unexpected whiff of myself and it's a complex bouquet. Blood and general funk. Essence of urine and something in the vicious chemical family. I remember being dizzy and I wonder if the cops gave me a splash of pepper spray.

Maybe I should shower. Or something.

He smiles, or bares his teeth. Actually, I would rather you didn't.

I smell like urine. Unless that's the cab.

The driver turns around slowly, his eyes raw and poached. What did you say, convict?

Nothing.

My cab don't freaking smell like urine.

Of course not. I was joking.

And I don't like comedians, says the driver.

Miller smiles. I will give you a twenty-dollar tip if you turn around and shut up.

The driver stares at him. And if I don't.

Miller shrugs. Then I will break your jaw.

I try to indicate by my blank, universally friendly expression that Miller is not serious but the driver is already fairly pale and now the light is green and he turns to face the front without another word. I glance over at Miller. His hands are carved and white, resting easy on his knees. His eyes are nearly closed and his face is meditative but for a faint movement in his cheek that suggests he is chewing at his tongue and I have the distinct feeling that he wishes the driver had not shut up.

The remainder of the drive is somewhat uncomfortable.

But Miller is true to his word. He gives the man a twenty-dollar tip as soon as we are deposited safely in front of the restaurant.

Exterior, night. The façade of the restaurant is pale with ghostly lights. Twenty or so very beautiful people wait around in little clusters, smoking cigarettes and talking in murmurs. I'm not quite ready to go inside yet. There's surely no smoking allowed inside. I am learning to hate California. The veneer of humanity is stretched impossibly fine and no one seems to care. I stand on the sidewalk, sucking at a cigarette. I recently went eighteen hours without one and I feel like I owe it to my body to get the nicotine count up. Miller is a few feet away from me. He doesn't want a cigarette. He wants to taste the air, he says.

Uh-huh.

What's the matter?

Nothing. Did you really need to threaten the driver?

Miller smiles. I know a few things about you.

Yeah?

Of course. I looked into your past, when Jude suggested I use you for this role.

And what did you find?

I found that you tend to be morally ambiguous.

Again, fuck you.

Am I wrong?

I didn't say that.

Then what's your problem?

No problem. It's not about morals. But if you walk around randomly fucking with everyone who comes into your peripheral vision, you will eventually be sorry.

Miller nods. Interesting theory.

Take it or leave it.

Relax, he says. You're right. There was no reason to threaten the driver. But I get irritated sometimes. I get irritated when confronted with stupid, brutish people. I have been trained by society to apologize, to pacify such people. To avoid trouble. And this irritates me.

I toss my cigarette in the street. And for once, I smile.

Why are you smiling?

Because I know exactly what you mean. And because I think you're fucking dangerous.

He steps close to me. Are you afraid of me?

No.

You will be, I think.

Maybe.

I don't usually like it when people stand so close to me. It makes me think they might want to stab me or kiss me or something. I don't think I'm paranoid or overly sensitive but I really prefer a little cushion between me and the other mutants. But I don't want to back away from him because I think this would please him. I breathe through my mouth.

Jude says you're going to pay us a half million each to do this film with you.

That's right.

What kind of lawyer are you?

He waves a hand. I represent a very large, very old and powerful corporation that is responsible for the use of asbestos in hundreds of schools, hospitals, and government buildings. My job is to fend off the class action suits and generally drag things out until the plaintiffs either give up or die.

How nice.

Yes. Very Hollywood, isn't it?

I shrug. It pays well, yeah.

Absurdly well. But it's very, very boring.

The ghost lights flicker around us and Miller glances at his watch.

Let's go inside, he says. I'd hate to keep the girls waiting.

I follow him inside, a half step behind. Down a long dark tunnel, my thoughts buzzing. Miller is a bored and wealthy sociopath, which makes him the best kind of friend to have. It also makes him the worst kind. He pauses to exchange cool whispers with the hostess, who is typically thin and pale and at first glance rather beautiful but somehow ugly in a fierce ravenous way and wearing a glittering black sheath that grimly reveals every bone in her body, and it occurs to me that the one word I would not use to describe Jude lately is girl.

seventeen.

THIS WAY, GENTLEMEN.

Our waiter is a male model in a perfect white shirt. He leads us through a shadowy dining room to an outdoor grotto where smoking, by God, is allowed. Small miracles keep me afloat. Jude and Molly sit at a table in the back. Two women, dark and fair. They sit across from each other, drinking red wine. Their heads rise and fall at opposing angles like two predatory birds warily feeding on the same kill. Miller moves to greet them. I hesitate, confused because there is a movie playing silently on the brick wall behind them. Unsettling because no one else pays it any mind and so I assume that only I can see it. *Cool Hand Luke.* Paul Newman is coming out of the box in a white nightgown. He looks like an angel with a hangover. Molly smiles when she see us and stands up to brush Miller's mouth with her lips. His expression remains neutral. Molly wears dark suede jeans and a white shirt, open at the throat. Behind her, Paul Newman is ten feet tall, as he should be.

Jude does not stand, but she looks at me in that way that tugs at my belly. Assimilation, husbandry. Her eyes glitter like wet green glass and her scar is a bright white line across her face. I realize how glad I am that she doesn't try to hide it. I jerk my head at Molly and mutter hello as I sit down next to Jude, who immediately puts her hand on my thigh. I am very pleased to see her. I tend to be uncomfortable in these social situations and somehow she puts me at ease. Because she is familiar, because she smells like memory. She smells like my own disordered thoughts. Paul Newman is running through the swamp. The dogs are on his ass. Jude wears a slim green dress and a black leather motorcycle jacket, zipped to the throat. Her hair is loose and I remember dimly that the reason I left the hotel room and got so drunk and subsequently was arrested for murder was that I was angry at her.

They put him in the box because his mother died, because they thought he would run.

Jude's breath is a hot whisper in my ear. You did it, baby.

What?

Sugar Finch, she says.

It wasn't easy.

Thank you.

Jude kisses me and I feel like our heads will come screaming off. I feel like every fucked-up thing I've ever done has been worth it, worth this kiss. Miller smokes his cigar, meanwhile, and Molly watches us with the unblinking eyes of a cat.

Cocktails? says the waiter. He speaks to Miller in a dry, civilized voice.

Miller orders a whiskey sour and nods at me.

What is this place? I say.

Foreign Cinema, says Miller.

What the fuck does that mean?

It's the name of the restaurant.

And they show American movies on the wall, I say.

Miller glances over his shoulder. Brilliant, isn't it.

Indeed.

Would you like a drink…sir? The waiter is staring at me with pure hatred.

Yes. I want a glass of water.

The waiter sighs and turns on his heel.

Dot com, says Miller. This place is filthy with dot com dollars.

What?

Dot com, baby.

Is that an adjective or a noun? I say.

He grunts. I believe it's an obscenity.

Molly smiles at me. I don't think the waiter likes you.

They never do, I say.

Why not? says Molly.

Look around, says Miller. This place is thick with the privileged, the chosen. Handsome educated white people with tasteful hair and clothes. Phineas is not one of them.

I shrug. I went to college.

But you understand that you are dying, yes?

Of course, I say.

Most of these people are not yet thirty, he says. And they believe they will never die. They believe the world is a giant yellow peach waiting to be eaten.

Jude snorts. Did not Al Pacino teach us that the world is a giant pussy?

Miller smiles at her. And one should not eat pussy unless invited.

The two of them should write greeting cards. Then the other psychopaths would have something nice to send their mothers on holidays. Molly turns to watch the movie. Paul Newman is bruised and weary and the man with no eyes stands over him with a rifle. The sun is low and fierce, throwing razor blades off those mirrored shades. Molly twists a strand of hair around and around with the little finger of her left hand. Her ears are small as a child's. Her throat is long and fine. Jude strokes my thigh and whispers, how pretty she is. I glance at Miller, who is studying the menu.

Have you fucked him? I say softly.

Jude hums, studying her menu.

Miller looks up. Do you know what you want?

I'm not sure, I say.

Jude leans close to me, bites my ear. Puritan, she says.

The lamb is generally good, he says.

I jerk my head away from Jude, dizzy and irritated.

And by the way, says Miller. The answer is not yet.

What? says Molly.

The waiter returns, scowling. Are you ready to order?

I will have the lamb, says Jude.

Miller nods. The same.

The steak, I say. Medium.

Molly politely orders the chicken, and the waiter goes away. I take a drink of my water and decide to ask for a big glass of gin as soon as the bastard comes back. Jude has not fucked Miller, yet. I pat my psyche down, wondering if I care. Molly is staring at me.

How long have you two been together? she says.

Oh, I say. We're not really together.

What does that mean?

Yes. What does that mean? says Jude.

Molly leans forward, her elbows on the table. Her mouth is red with wine and falling slightly open and I can just see the tip of her tongue. Her gray eyes are sharp and I wonder if she ever tortures Miller, if she ever fucks with his mind. I wonder if he ever thrashes awake beside her, his arms wild and twisting in the dark because he is unable to breathe and when he tries to pull her small strong hands away from his throat there's nothing there, if she then kisses him and tells him that he's only dreaming. I wonder if he ever wakes in the morning to find her naked and crouched beside him, studying him in the first blue breath of light as if he were not her lover but a strange new insect that crawled into her bed.

We aren't married, I say.

Molly shrugs. That hardly matters.

I wonder if he ever feels like an insect she may or may not impale on a slab of foam.

And we have been separated for…a while.

Why'd you split up?

You ask a lot of questions.

Does it bother you? says Miller.

Why did we split up? says Jude. I would like to know.

I slouch low in my chair. The three of them are like wolves and it occurs to me that evolution is a funny business. I don't particularly want to tell the kidney story. It never goes over well and anyway it's not nice dinner conversation. Paul Newman is getting his ass kicked good and proper. The waiter hovers at the edge of my peripheral vision and I turn to face him with what I hope is a friendly smile.

I would like a large glass of gin, please.

Excellent choice, he says. Would you like that mixed with something?

No. Thank you.

Jude smiles at the waiter, apologetically.

Anything else? he says.

Champagne, says Molly.

The waiter fucks off and I turn to Jude.

What was that?

What, she says.

That look. The look that says my poor stepbrother is retarded.

You are so paranoid.

He wants to change the subject, says Miller.

Paul Newman is digging his own grave in the prison yard and in a minute one of the guards will tell him to fill it again and start over.

Answer the question, says Jude.

I smile at her. I despise couples who fight in public, I say. You know that. But in about two minutes I'm going to politely tell you to shut the fuck up.

I look at Molly and she smiles, as if to encourage me. Molly seems very relaxed and I wonder if she's not drifting on a private little ocean of prescription tranquilizers. Now the waiter arrives with my gin and I decide he's not such a bad guy. I have four inches of gin in what looks like an actual jelly jar, a big one. I take a drink and watch as he tries to open the champagne. He looks uneasy, our waiter. His upper lips is damp with sweat. He's having a spot of trouble with that bottle. The four of us are staring holes through him and I imagine the vibes coming from this table are nasty. After what seems like forever he pops the cork and slithers away and I feel relieved for him.

I raise my jar.

To the truth, says Miller.

Which truth?

Come on. Tell us how it is to live with Jude.

I stare at him. It gets weird sometimes. One day she drags me into a public bathroom and hands me a gun. I ask her what the gun is for and she tells me to kill the man in the blue suit and meet her outside in five minutes. Then she asks if I want to get a latte.

Miller nods, sympathetic.

And for my birthday one year, she took me to Mexico City for the weekend. What a sick time that was. Our second day in the city, she turned to me on the street and gave me a mask. What is the mask for? I said. Didn't I tell you? she said. We're going to rob this bank. And then we're inside the bank and everybody is freaking out and I don't know what to do because I never robbed a bank before and I don't speak Spanish. And then Jude shoots the little blind bank teller because she won't stop screaming.

What the hell are you babbling about? says Jude.

Huh?

That was a bad dream you had, she says. You were sleeping right next to me. I remember the night you dreamed that.

Well. That is peculiar.

You and I never robbed a bank together, says Jude.

False memory. I got hit in the head a while back.

Interesting, says Miller. The artificial flashback. A feeble attempt by the subconscious to cover something more painful.

I wonder would anyone notice if I went ahead and bit off a chunk of my jelly jar and swallowed it whole. On the wall above us, Paul Newman is a wreck. He's in worse shape than me, anyway. He's crawling before the guards like a dog, begging them not to hit him anymore and I think, what we have here is a failure to communicate.

eighteen.

TWO HOURS LATER WE ARE FLYING ACROSS THE BRIDGE in a silver Mustang and I am glad it's not a convertible because sometimes the elements are just too much to bear. Not quite midnight and there is very little traffic. Jude is leaning against me, her head on my shoulder. I don't think she's sleeping but I have this funny idea that she is happy, or possibly nervous. But surely she is not nervous because this is what she wants. Molly drives with the cold manic fury of a girl who grew up in a household full of boys. I am tempted to ask her about her childhood but I stop myself. I don't want to talk to her in front of Jude. There is no music in the car, no conversation. Miller is silent in the passenger seat and I imagine he is contemplating the velvet.

Over the bridge and through the hills. We are going to Miller's house.

By the by. The remainder of our dinner party passed without relevant incident. Or nearly so. I knocked over a bottle of champagne around the time Paul Newman was shot in the throat, but Jude managed to make the waiter feel so hot and guilty about it that he gave us another one on the house. None of us got particularly drunk and no one asked me any more difficult questions, and I refrained from demanding another jelly jar of gin. Jude kept trying to talk about the film, but Miller wasn't having it. He wanted to wait until we got home.

Home.

I was informed over crème brûlée and coffee that Jude and I would be staying with them for the duration of the project. Our things had been transferred from the King James to Miller's house while we were at dinner and for some reason I imagined a little team of munchkins, ferrying our stuff across the bay on the backs of winged monkeys. This image pleased me and I was about to share it with Jude, but when I turned around I saw something in her face that I didn't like. Jude looked scared. Jude had obviously not known about this move.

The Mustang glides down the dark driveway. Miller holds the car door open for us and Molly darts ahead to unlock the house. She's a little too happy, to my mind, and I wonder if it's the champagne. Jude holds my hand as we go up the steps, then stops and whirls around to kiss me, a long kiss. Her tongue is sweet in my mouth and something is wrong. This is the sort of kiss that resembles love.

What's the matter? I say.

Nothing.

Uh huh. Why are you being so affectionate?

She jerks her hand away and hisses at me to fuck off, then.

There you go, I say. Doesn't that feel better?

I wonder if she is feeling guilty about something. Jeremy, perhaps. The meeting for cocktails with Miller that inexplicably lasted a day and a half. It's always possible that she missed me while I was falsely incarcerated. But somehow I don't think so.

Inside and the house is warm with soft, rosy light. Jude and I pass through a shadowy entryway that feels very small, as if I should duck my head. Then we come into a large open room, the living room. The furniture is elegant, minimal. Dark wood and leather and red velvet the color of freshly spilled blood. The floors are hardwood. Molly is curled barefoot at one end of the bloody sofa. Her shirt is loose and unbuttoned to the waist, revealing a nearly transparent camisole of white gauze. Molly is small and curvy and probably doesn't weigh much more than a hundred pounds but I notice her breasts are bigger and rounder than Jude's, who glances at me with a cold little smile. I shrug in response, but I am not stupid. Jude is five foot five. She weighs one hundred twenty pounds and doesn't have a shred of fat on her body. She has the muscles of a snake. I wrestle with her sometimes and I cannot hold her down. She is too slippery, too fast. Too strong. Her breasts are very small but I have always thought that large ones would only annoy her.

I wonder where Miller is. Jude sits down in a leather chair and slowly pulls off her boots, dropping them to the floor with one distinct crash, then another. I remain standing. There is another armchair, but it is way the hell across the room next to a bay window. I am reluctant to move it and the most logical place for me to sit would be at the other end of the sofa, next to Molly. But I am still conscious of the way I smell and I have a feeling she would promptly put her small white feet in my lap, and she has very nice feet. Jude watches me and I can tell she's pleased by my confusion. She takes off her leather jacket and tosses it on the floor. The green dress has long tight sleeves and small green buttons all the way down the front and the dress fits her so snugly that I can see the muscles in her arms and stomach. Jude isn't wearing a bra and her nipples are pretty much always hard.

Do you want to sit down? says Molly.

I have a headache, actually. I see things that aren't there.

Molly frowns because this is not really an answer but it's the best I can give her. I have a headache and I wish I'd not stopped at one glass of gin. If there's one thing I understand, it's my own fucked-up biochemistry. I wander over to the bar, where I find a set of beautiful highball glasses. They weigh about two pounds each and it would be easy as falling out of bed to kill somebody with one of them. I find ice and a bottle of Bombay and I feel better already. I wouldn't mind so much if Molly put her feet in my lap. I have a thing for feet, sometimes. And maybe my sense of smell is out of sorts and this is all a lot of misguided body language but something tells me that Jude or Miller or both of them are setting me up to fall for Molly.

What are you babbling about over there? says Jude.

I ignore her. I pour myself a sensible shot of gin and tell myself to be careful, for once.

Miller comes limping out of the dark carrying a black ceramic tray in both hands, and I remember smashing him in the back with that toilet tank lid, and at the same time I remember him not limping the other day. Apparently, I didn't damage him so badly as I'd thought, and wonder if he's faking it for my benefit. He has changed clothes. He has undressed, basically. He now wears old, torn blue jeans and nothing else. Miller is dark and hairless. He has a belly but it looks okay on him. It suits him. He passes very close to me, close enough for me to touch him. On the tray is a stack of papers, a pot of espresso and four small cups, a woman's antique hand mirror and a big, friendly lump of coke chopped up very fine.

Here we go.

Miller places the tray on a short wooden table at one end of the sofa.

I thought some of you might be tired and I want to talk.

He moves across the room with the maddening ease and comfort of a panther at the zoo. You can see him back there in the shadows but he doesn't want to come out into the light. He moves back and forth in the dark recesses of his habitat. He's not hungry and he's not sleepy and you know he's conscious of you. He just doesn't want the humans to look upon him. Miller slowly drags a chair over to the circle, the same chair I was reluctant to move.

I stand by the bar, sipping my gin.

Jude and Molly have moved to crouch beside the tray, whispering and giggling and probably plotting something. I love the way women will become temporary allies, even when they don't like each other. Jude lights a cigarette. Molly takes it from her fingers and has a puff. Jude pours out four small cups of espresso. Molly gives her back the cigarette, then begins to cut up lines with a small pocketknife that she takes from her pocket. Jude rolls up a bill and gives it to Molly, who bends delicately over the mirror. Her fine blond hair falling over her eyes like silk. Jude moves on her hands and knees to give Miller a cup of espresso. I have never seen her quite like this. Molly does another line, then climbs back onto the sofa with Jude's cigarette between two fingers.

I stand by the bar, sipping at my gin.

Poe, says Miller. Come and sit down.

I'm okay.

I would rather you sat down, he says. He points at the sofa.

I finish my gin and pour another, smaller shot. I don't move for two breaths, three. Then I walk across the room. I bend over the tray and touch the coke with the tip of my finger, which I rub slowly over my teeth. Miller points at the sofa and I sit down. Molly sighs and stretches her suede legs. She puts her white feet in my lap, curved and serene as two porcelain doves. I don't touch them but look at Jude, who kneels on the floor. Her dress has slipped up nearly to her hips and I can see that she wears tiny yellow underpants. She holds a cup of espresso in both hands. I wonder if she's carrying a gun or anything. She seems to be armed all the time, lately.

I begin to rub Molly's feet.

Now, says Miller. I want to talk about *The Velvet*.

Finally.

Jude flashes her eyes at me and I'm not sure if she said this or I did. Miller blows thin blue smoke rings. He drinks his espresso like it's water but I notice he hasn't done any coke. I want some, though. I want a nice fat line but I don't want him to know it.

Morality, he says. It's a morality play like any other.

My favorite, I say.

Jude stands up and I can tell she's getting anxious. She thinks I'm fucking with Miller and she doesn't like it. She walks around to the far side of the sofa. She leans over the red velvet edge and places one hand flat on Molly's stomach. Molly closes her eyes and begins to rub her feet together in my lap. I pull my hands away and watch Jude's face, her eyes. She is staring at me, at me. Her eyes are narrow and dark, then slipping away. I know that look. She might be seducing me, she might be threatening me. It's a familiar and useful look. I begin to touch Molly's feet again. Molly lies perfectly motionless, as if asleep or dead. But she is obviously not asleep. Her face changes like the ocean at the slightest touch. Jude's finger trails slowly down to her bellybutton then moves away. She remains standing, though. Jude sways slightly from the hip, staring now at Miller. This pleases me, because she is more menacing when she's moving. Miller coughs. He is becoming rather pissed off, it seems to me. Jude smiles at me, a secret smile that the others don't see.

Please continue, she says.

Well, says Miller. My vision of this film is old world. It has just a touch of *The Turn of the Screw,* very Henry James, but with an edge.

Henry fucking James? I say. With an edge?

Phineas, says Jude. Be nice.

Molly sighs. You still haven't told us what the film is about, John.

He nods at the stack of papers on the tray. Those rough pages comprise the first act, he says. If anyone wants to have a look.

The room becomes a vacuum and I hold my breath. Everyone wants to have a look at the script, of course. But no one wants to show it. I stroke Molly's feet and she runs her hand along my thigh in response. I have an erection and I wonder if she notices. I wonder if Jude notices. I wonder if anyone gives a goddamn.

It's pretty much a Joe Blow story, says Miller.

Joe Blow, says Jude.

That's right. Joe Blow in a world of shit.

Okay, says Molly.

Think about it, says Miller. The books that really get under your skin and the movies that are worth two hours of your time are always about Joe Blow.

Jude is pacing around as we talk, a nervous beast in strange quarters. She has no doubt heard this Joe Blow theory before and maybe she is less than mesmerized. She stops and does another line and I think maybe we should put that shit away. My hands soon move up Molly's legs, to her knees. The suede is so soft, it's like touching her bare flesh.

Give us an example, I say.

Miller shrugs and begins to rattle them off. Odysseus was the original Joe Blow, he says. Then you have Moses and half the poor fuckers in the Bible. If you think about it, pretty much everybody in the Bible was Joe Blow, they were all walking headfirst into a world of shit, except Jesus. He was the only one who had any idea about what he was getting into. After that, the list is endless. Hamlet. Ishmael. Tom Joad. Huck Finn. Philip Marlowe. Nick Carraway and Holden Caulfield and on down the line. Luke Skywalker is probably the Joe Blow to end all because that boy was dumb as a post and it was really a miracle that he survived.

Molly pulls one foot away from me and curls onto her side, fetal. The other foot remains in my crotch, pressing against my dick as if it lives there.

And what about the world of shit? says Jude.

She drifts in the dark somewhere behind me, as if she doesn't want to be seen.

The world of shit, says Miller, is composed of three acts. And yes I know Shakespeare did most of his work in five acts but he was fucking Shakespeare. He could do whatever he wanted. But the second and fourth acts were transitional anyway. Are you guys even interested in this?

I shrug. Miller seems calm but I notice a muscle jump in his jaw.

I am, says Molly.

Anyway, says Miller. You introduce Joe Blow in act one and casually let it slip that he's terrified of heights. Then you encourage him to climb a tree from which he cannot get down. In act two, you surround the tree with dogs and maybe set the woods on fire. Then you start throwing rocks at Joe. And in the third act, Joe either falls from the tree and shatters his spine, or he gets over his fear and climbs down. Maybe his girlfriend or his faithful buddy comes along to help him or maybe he just stays in the tree until he dies of exposure.

Jude moves around the couch, sparks flickering from her body. Her legs are long, curved, and yellow. The dusty yellow of flowers, of butter-flies, the yellow that disappears when you touch it. I must be high.

And who is Joe Blow in your movie? I say.

Miller smiles. Any of us could be. But I think your odds are best.

I reach for a cigarette. No doubt. I am certainly in a world of shit.

Let's talk about the characters, says Jude.

Please, says Miller. This is the fun part.

Don't tell me, I say. I get to play a dwarf?

Miller takes Jude's knife from the table, lifts it to his mouth and takes his time licking coke from the blade. I am dying for some of that shit. I look at Jude, and she looks away from me.

No, says Miller. Much better. You will be Molly's husband.

Molly takes a breath. What?

Miller shrugs. Swing, baby.

Jude does another line of coke, then leans over me with a generous bump on the end of the knife. I think she's offering it to me but I'm wrong. Molly sits up and presses a finger to the side of her nose and she's very trusting. I'm not sure I would let Jude hold a knife to my face like that. Miller slips from his chair and crawls across the floor. He removes mirror and knife from the tray and sits crosslegged, arranging lines. He passes the mirror to Jude and she leans over it like an animal bending to drink. I am beginning to feel a bit claustrophobic. I push Molly's leg away and she makes a soft noise in her throat. I stand up and light a cigarette. I am tempted to light three or four at once.

I look around the room and everyone is sky high.

Jude is crouched on the floor near the wall, twisting her hair into pigtails. Her movements are feverish and precise and I know she knows that I think pigtails are terribly sexy. I am sitting on the sofa, in a low humpbacked position that makes me feel like a troll. Miller is like a dead man. He lies on the floor at my feet, his head cradled in his hands. Molly is on the far side of the room. She is dancing, I think. Molly is floating on air. But there is no music. I am becoming painfully aware of the fact that there is no music in this house, which is just creepy. I am about to say so when Miller beats me to it.

There's no music, says Miller. Because I want you to get used to functioning without.

What do you mean?

Molly will play the cello over the credit sequences but otherwise there will be no music on the set, no music in the film.

Why not? says Jude.

Because music manipulates the emotions.

And what about silence, I say. Does it not manipulate the emotions?

Maybe. But it's more organic, says Miller. And I want it to be creepy.

I smile and smile like a madman because I'm tired of talking to John Ransom Miller. I'm tired of listening to him think out loud. I'm tired of him reading my mind like it's nothing and I am fast coming to the conclusion that, like cab drivers who secretly want to be writers, lawyers who want to be filmmakers are often dangerous assholes.

Excuse me, I say.

What?

Where is the bathroom? I desperately need a bath.

Yes, he says. You do need a bath. But I thought we might have a conversation.

About what?

About sleeping arrangements. About personal philosophies.

The fuck do you mean.

Monogamy, he says.

I reach for the gin. I change my mind and reach for the plate of coke. Monogamy, I say. What about it?

Do you believe in it?

I look at Jude. She's crouched against the wall, angry. Her arms and legs are pulled close to her body and she looks like a beautiful, yellow spider monkey. I'm not sure what she's angry about. But I see her as a whole, a composite. I see her ankles and feet. I see the tiny white scar on her left knee, the big scar over her eye that she hates. I see the long shadows of muscle in her bent thighs. I see her dark green torso and I suppose I regard her body as mine in some way, simply because I know it so well. Every curve and hollow. I close my eyes and I can see her fingers, furiously twisting in her hair. I see her face, the long sharp cheekbones. Her lush wet lips. Her dark yellow eyes. I don't particularly want her to fuck another but I know she will if she wants to and ultimately I don't care if she does. She is not mine but on some molecular level I feel like I am hers, if only temporarily.

No, I say. I don't necessarily believe in monogamy.

Excellent, he says.

I like Miller, really. He's an interesting person. But he is beginning to irritate me. I want him to stop using that word. Excellent. It bugs the fuck out of me.

What about you? he says, looking at Molly.

She stares at him and I get the feeling they have had this discussion before.

Yes, she says. I believe. You know I do. I want to believe and I want love to work. I may be romantic and stupid and puritan but I believe that monogamy is possible. And I expect to find it, with the right person. I am with you now, but I don't want to be yours.

That's enough, says Miller. That's more than enough.

He turns to Jude but she withers him with such a look that even I feel pale.

Never mind, says Miller.

Where is the bathroom? I say.

The nearest one is upstairs. Down the hall to the left.

nineteen.

THE UPSTAIRS BATHROOM IS LARGE and relatively spartan with a black-and-white tile floor and a white clawfoot bathtub. Toilet and sink and shower with smoky glass door. Black towels. The closet is empty. In the shower are expensive shampoo and conditioner and black soap. I have brought my glass of gin with me. I am smoking a cigarette. I drop my clothes to the floor and consider the bath. I don't much like baths. I don't care to sit in a pool of my own filth but I have always loved the clawfoot bathtub, as an abstract concept. And it reminds me of my mother's house. I stand there, naked and smoking. It is everything I can do to stop from looking in the mirror. The coke is causing a nasty rattle in my skull and I don't want to descend into any prolonged examination of self. I have an unfortunate tendency to cut my hair in these situations, to somehow mangle myself. There are knife scars on my arms and chest that no one can account for. I drop my cigarette into the toilet and crank up the hot water in the shower.

I scrub myself fiercely with the black soap. It smells of opium, of wormwood. There is something visually disturbing about black soap and somehow this appeals to me. I wash my genitals with curious fanaticism. I let the water pound down on my head. I am obliterated by needles and I am slowly disappearing into the smoke of irrational shame. If not for the night in jail and a fear of parasites, I'd probably not bother to wash my hair. The shampoo is also black. I dump a small amount of it into my hand and drag it through my hair, then rinse. I sink into the corner of the shower with glass of gin in hand and breathe the hot steam.

Jude opens the shower door and stands there, looking at me. I am crouched in the corner, rubbery and wet and dizzy from the heat and under her gaze I feel like Gollum with my empty glass in hand. I have lost my precious. I want to ask her a riddle. What is the shadow with green skin that is not man and not woman, the shadow that stretches before us and becomes another.

It's not fair to ask us what it's got in its nasty pockets.

Jude still wears that green dress.

She mutters something that I can't hear.

What? I say.

She smiles and steps into the shower with me. The water crashes down on us and soon her hair is wet and hanging like black ribbons in her face. Her dress is soaked, a dark green secondary flesh. Jude kisses my neck, my chest and belly. I am thirsty and I want her. I reach for her but I am clumsy and my muscles are atrophied from the heat. I am briefly detached from my arms and legs. I want to drink her, to eat her wet eucalyptus skin. I want to rip the green dress from her body but I am floating somewhere above her and I have a magnificent almost distended erection. I pull Jude close to me and lift the wet green dress up over her waist and slip inside her and she is so wet and my thoughts are so splintered that it is hard to say where either of us begins or ends but soon the noise of our breathing is like the rattle and hiss of new fire.

I read somewhere that more than half of all household accidents take place in the shower and I am not surprised. It's very slippery and dangerous in there, what with your arms and legs wet and twisted into rubber doll parts that don't quite belong to you. Your mouth is full of hair and you can't breathe and you can't talk and within five minutes I come inside her, which is exactly what she wanted. Because I have been unable to come lately. And because it makes her feel pretty when I come inside her, or so she says.

Are you joking? I say.

But she just smiles at me. If I were her shrink, I would probably say it has to do with power. I would speculate that she was anorexic as a girl. I would root around in her skull for some barely remembered incident of childhood fondling or worse. But I'm not her shrink and wouldn't want to be. I would rather eat my own eyeballs with a spoon than wiggle around in that head for money. As for birth control, well. Jude told me a few nights ago, in bed at the King James, that she doesn't bother about birth control anymore because she had her tubes tangled sometime after the unwanted pregnancy in New Orleans.

Ten minutes later we sit on the black-and-white floor. The air is white with mist and we pass a damp cigarette back and forth. I've put my borrowed pants back on and Jude has wrapped herself in a massive blue towel. She's wrapped in a chunk of sky and only her feet poke out. Her feet are beautiful, but not so pretty as Molly's. I shut my eyes. I have a sudden urge to grind the cigarette out on my arm.

What are we doing here? I say.

Jude blows smoke at me. Don't, she says.

What?

Don't think about it so much. And don't try to suck me into some philosophical debate.

Okay.

Brief silence while I wonder who is going to die.

What shall I think about?

Jude shrugs. The sleeping arrangements, she says.

What about them?

You're sleeping with Molly tonight.

Jude is not kidding, it seems. She gives me that look of stone and I can't tell what she's thinking. She lets the blue towel fall to the floor and stands there a minute, naked and foreboding. Now she gives her hair a shake. The water flies from her in tiny rays of broken light.

You're kidding, I say.

I'm not kidding.

Jesus.

What's the problem, she says. You want her, don't you?

Maybe. But I might rather make that choice on my own.

Jude shrugs. I don't see how it makes a difference.

And where are you sleeping?

Wherever I want to, she says. With menace.

With Miller, you mean.

I have to get into character, she says. We both do.

Give me a fucking break, Jude.

Listen, she says. We are shooting this goddamn movie with Miller. When it's done, he will bring Cody to me. Until then, we cooperate.

I watch as she takes a robe from the back of the door, a man's robe. Black with green checks. She pulls it tight around her and she doesn't look like any of this bothers her much.

And this doesn't bother you? I say.

Weren't you listening? says Jude. Monogamy is hopelessly antiquated. And therefore defunct.

You want me to sleep with her.

Jude stares, never flinching. Yes. Tonight, I want you to sleep with Molly.

I just nod. All right, I say. Anything for you, baby.

I walk down a hallway of muted yellow light. Molly is waiting for me behind door number three and I feel flushed, nervous. Like I'm on a blind date. And Jude is right, sort of. Monogamy is defunct, an antiquated concept that never held much water. I had tried to educate myself while I wandered the desert, chasing Jude's shadow, and one of the books I slogged through was Darwin's *The Origin of Species*, or one of its sequels. I wouldn't call it a page-turner but one thing was pretty clear: Darwin was a maniacal old fucker half-addled by cocaine but the man was no dummy and he wouldn't have bet a nickel on monogamy hanging around as long as it has.

Monogamy doesn't work unless it rises up from the bones. Because it promises nothing but fear and tension when forced on you. It fills you up with despair where there might be joy. It shoves guilt and paranoia and self-loathing down your throat, if you don't truly want it. Jude and I were monogamous when we were together, for the most part. And monogamy was a fucking drag. It seemed like a social obligation, an arbitrary puritanical construct, and after a while we started lying to each other. When I was with Jude, I pretended to know what I wanted, and with a hellish quickness my face became a jackal's mask. Then I took a bubble bath one night and a gang of psychos ruined her face before we figured the shit out.

I used to watch her sometimes, when she was painting her toenails or brushing her teeth or yawning on the floor in her underwear, flicking through a glossy woman's magazine. I loved her. I didn't love her. Once, I watched her take the television apart in the middle of the night because she was bored. I watched her reduce the television to a scrap heap of apparently ruined fuses and wires. Then I watched her put the television back together and was not surprised when the reception was improved. I thought I loved her, then. I watched her smash the same television to bits two days later because she didn't like some snotty actress and in that moment, I thought I loved her. But there was fear between us, truly. There is always fear but when two artists, two liars, or two killers occupy the same house and sleep in the same bed, rage runs rampant and becomes entangled with mistrust and doubt and alcoholic despair. The love between them isn't safe in the bones, the marrow.

Jude doesn't belong to me and never did. I don't belong to her because our love is unsafe in the marrow.

Therefore, Jude and I are each set free with the flickering hope that we may come back to each other and the knowledge that we may not. And in the meantime we may as well fuck other people and we may as well be casual and nihilistic about it. It doesn't mean anything because we don't belong to each other, at least, not now. One day, though. One day. I might just come around a corner and stumble into the version of Jude that I belong to. And when I find her, I just hope I have the good sense to give myself to her.

This is the moment when the blood throttles up to eleven and everything else slows down. The air around me glimmers and I can see the world a little too clearly. I can see the imperfections in the wood and brick and I can see the fine threads in the carpet under my feet. I can hear Miller breathing downstairs. I imagine Jude tying him up, whispering sweet nothings in his ear. The door at the end of the hall is a little black square that from six seven eight feet away looks much too small for me to pass through. It's just large enough for a little British girl or a fat white rabbit and I love it when pop culture bleeds through to the cellular level. The endless memories that are not my own.

I stop at the door and listen.

She's got a razor sadness about her, nothing a hundred dollars won't fix. Tom Waits is playing softly in Molly's room. *Rain Dogs.* Bob Frost is a good egg. This is encouraging, I think. Any woman who likes Tom Waits is bound to have sweetness in her heart. I open the door without knocking. Molly sits cross-legged on the bed, her hair hangs yellow and loose. The room is softly lit and eerily windowless. There's a green armchair in one corner. The red walls are lined with bookshelves. Two silver curtains shaped like angel's wings hang over a doorway opposite. The bed is small and puffy, with an iron frame. I'm sure it would make a hellish commotion during even the most careful sexual activity.

Molly's feet are still bare. Hello, she says.

This is awkward and I wait for her to say Can I help you? But she smiles and shrugs slightly and I take it that she is expecting me.

This is awkward, I say.

No, she says. I like you. And we don't have to do anything.

Oh. Thank god.

But you have to be nice to me.

I stare at her. It's not a request I'm used to hearing.

Molly picks up a book and curls into a pool of lamplight. The bathroom is there, through the curtains, she says. If you want to brush your teeth.

Thanks. Do you mind if I smoke in here?

Molly shrugs and I sit down on the end of the bed. I dig out matches.

By the green chair, she says. There's an ashtray.

I move to sit in the green chair. I smoke and watch her read for a while. It's peaceful but weird, and I realize I'm unaccustomed to peace. Jude and I are rarely so quiet together.

What are you reading?

The Lover, she says. Margurite Duras. Have you read it?

No.

It's pretty sexy, she says. And depressing. But it reads like film.

What's it about?

She stares at me and I wonder if she suspects the truth, that I've seen the movie twice and, for perverse reasons of my own, don't want to admit it. Molly smiles and before she can tell me what the book is about, I commence to babble at her.

It's about obsession, I say. It's about a French girl living in the Philippines. She wears a man's fedora, which probably has to do with the fact that her father is dead or missing from the scene. I don't remember which. Her mother is crazy and her brother is crazy and they have no money. Then she meets a very wealthy Chinese man and becomes his child lover and pretty soon she's extracting money from him.

You've seen the movie, she says.

Yeah.

Why did you pretend to know nothing about it?

Because there's something wrong with me.

Molly kneels on the bed, eyes bright. Her shirt hangs open as a promise. Throat and collarbone exposed. Her nipples are shadows behind pale camisole and I wonder what her hair smells like, what her skin tastes like.

You didn't say a word about love, she says.

What about it?

Do you think she loved him, the Chinaman?

No. I think she loved the sex. She loved being the object of desire. But then, I haven't read the book. I may be ignorant.

Are you in love with Jude?

Whoa.

I'm sorry, she says. Too personal?

No. But kind of sudden.

I'm sorry, she says. Anyway. Are you?

Fuck. You're one of those people, I say.

I light another cigarette, still jumpy from that coke. Molly seems serene, though.

Which people? she says.

The relentless question people.

I'm just curious. And I think it's relevant to the project.

Okay, then. I don't know.

Why?

Jude and I have been apart for too long, I say. And when we were together, we went through some hairy shit, old-fashioned psycho-ward shit. And I don't think we trusted each other, which is a problem. The sex was good, is good, but it has a lot more to do with domination and pain than actual tenderness.

You believe, though. You believe in love.

I have to believe in something.

Molly shrugs. Good answer.

Thanks, I say. I want to brush my teeth.

Okay, she says. There's a spare toothbrush on the sink. Or you can use mine, the blue one. And there's Valium in the medicine cabinet if you want it.

Valium, yes. I could use some of that.

She nods. You look a little…uneasy.

What about you, I say. Do you love Miller?

Molly sinks onto the bed, gazes up at the ceiling. He doesn't love me, she says. He never loved me.

That isn't what I asked you.

No, she says.

I wait for her to finish the thought but there's no more coming. Her eyes are closed tight but she's staring hard at something unseen.

I get up and walk through the silver wings. I lean on the sink with both hands and give myself a good long stare. I just wish I had a reliable smile. The sort of smile that flashes out of reflex, the smile that puts other humans at ease. I work on it for a minute but it's just no good. I still look like Travis Bickle when I smile. I look like a young Robert De Niro with a bellyful of maggots and a ticklish hair up his ass. Best not to smile at all. But it will come in handy when I want to become Joe Blow and I might as well take care of my teeth. On the edge of the sink is a toothbrush still in the package. The kind the dentist gives you after he's done fucking up your day. I flick at it with my finger and it spins slowly. Then I reach for the blue one in the pewter cup. Molly's toothbrush, still wet. I have a feeling we're going to be intimate.

When I come out of the bathroom the room is dark but for a guttering candle. Molly is tucked beneath the covers, shadowy and feline. I hesitate. This is a peculiar situation. I am about to crawl into bed with a woman I don't really know. And yeah. I have done that before, numerous times. But I was typically a lot more fucked up on those occasions and there was a different energy in those rooms, with those nameless and faceless women. There was that underlying vibe of desperation and self-destruction, that slow aching psychological suicide by a thousand cuts that comes with meaningless sex. But I feel none of that now. Molly is just another human, with warm blood and fragile skin and a skull filled with her own angels and insects and childhood shadows. She wants nothing from me but kindness. I take off my clothes and blow out the candle, then creep into bed next to her.

She sleeps with her back to me. I move close enough to smell her hair but not close enough to poke her with my erection. Because that would be rude, I think. Molly wears a long white nightgown, silk with thin spaghetti straps. Her hair smells like the wind when there's a storm coming. Her shoulders are pale and smooth as eggshells. She sighs, or growls. Then moves close to me. Molly presses herself against me and I realize that she wants to spoon, which seems bizarre to me, freakish.

But I know good and well who's the freak in this bed. I'm just not used to this sort of thing. I can adjust, though. I tuck my penis out of the way so that it presses innocently against her thigh, then slip an arm under her neck and without really thinking about it, I find myself holding one of her breasts in my hand. As if someone just handed me a ripe melon and said with a sly smile, are you hungry old boy? I move my hand away and tell myself not to grope or fondle her again. I position my arms so that one hand is flat against her stomach and the other is resting on her shoulder. Molly is smaller, softer than Jude. Her bones are arranged differently and somehow her body is a better fit against mine. This feels absurdly good and it occurs to me that it is easier to find someone on this planet you want to fuck than someone you might really want to sleep next to.

In a city like San Francisco, you can throw a rock out your front door and hit someone with a nice ass and pretty brown eyes. But to find someone you want to fall asleep with, someone you want to breathe and dream next to, is terribly rare.

I kiss her softly on the back of the neck, just once. Good night, Molly.

I wear yellow gloves, yellow gloves stained with blood. I'm in a motel room with bright orange carpet the color of dull fire under plastic sheets. There's a single naked light bulb above casting shadows like manic fingers. The bed is stripped of linens and covered in thick plastic. A tall pale handsome white man, early forties, is handcuffed to the bed. Jude stands over him and in this particular dream, her name is Jesse Redd. She wears a white raincoat, sprayed with blood, and holds an electric bone saw in gloved hands. I stand across from her holding bucket and sponge. Jude takes a breath, then resumes the task of hacking off this pale man's left hand just above the wrist. I look at the man's face, twisted and white with endorphins and sheer masochistic joy. He looks like a Heisman quarterback gone gray and this man is not a victim, but a client. He is paying us twenty-five thousand American dollars for this service. He has a profound amputee fetish, and he wants to become one. The handcuffs were his idea and he declined the use of ether. Jude is a field surgeon but this work requires very little skill. It requires steady hands and a belly of stone, which

I lack. The one time I tried to wield the saw, I threw up a muddy puddle of beans and rice and tequila and I've been relegated to sponge duty since then.

This is the last one, I say.

What are you talking about?

I'm not kidding. I'd rather just kill people.

You'd rather kill people than what?

I'd rather kill people than mop up another drop of this motherfucker's blood.

Wake up, she says.

I'm not kidding, Jude.

Wake up, says Molly. I am not Jude.

I pull myself out of a motel room that exists only in my own damaged head and false visions. Molly is beside me. The smell of wind and thin strong arms around me. I am covered in sweat and shivering, cold. Delirium tremens, my favorite new affliction. Molly tells me to hold on. She slips away from me and goes to the bathroom, returns with a warm washcloth and a small bottle of brandy. I reach for the bottle and she tells me to take small sips. Molly kisses my cheek, a cool dry kiss. She puts the washcloth on my forehead and gives me a cigarette.

Tell me, she says. Tell me about the dream.

And for an hour or so, Molly and I sit in the dark. I tell her a nasty bedtime story and she is so polite she never says a word about my tendency to cast Jude as a psycho in my dreams.

twenty.

AGORAPHOBIC YES, AND WEIRDLY HAPPY. I wake up alone. The room is dark, muted but it feels like morning. The sound of water falling behind silver wings. Molly is in the shower. I can see her standing with eyes closed and head lowered as if praying. The blades of her shoulders, the fine ridge of her spine. The bed is very comfortable and I might like to lie here and smoke a cigarette and daydream for a while but I don't think I'm ready to see Molly just yet, what with the aftershock of new intimacy and bloody bedtime stories between us. There's always the possibility of a sudden freakout when you get to know someone a little too well, too soon.

Therefore. I drag my intimate ass out of bed. I'm looking around for my pants when I notice there are no shadows in the room and I remember how Peter Pan misplaced his shadow and Wendy was kind enough to sew it back on for him and this makes me think of Molly and I tell myself to be very fucking careful with this line of thought. And besides. I always hated Peter Pan. The Lost Boys were pretty cool of course but Pan himself was a complete wanker, a fancyboy. Peter Pan was a racist sexist little fuckhole in green tights. He was shitty to the Indians and mean to Tinkerbell. I wouldn't mind seeing a remake directed by John Woo in which Captain Hook kills off the Lost Boys one by one, gutting them like rabbits, after which he feeds Pan's liver to the ticking crocodile and puts his impish head on a stick, and then gets into some serious bondage with wee Wendy. Now that would be edgy.

The shower still hums.

I make the bed, or rather I jerk at the bedding until it looks present-able. I am tempted to leave Molly a note or something, a few words. But I don't have a pen on me and anyway I don't know what I would say. Thanks for keeping me warm last night, and thanks for not being horrified by me.

Fuck it. I'm going downstairs.

I find Miller in the kitchen, standing at the counter. He wears the black and green bathrobe that Jude was wearing last night and his dark hair is slick with gel, combed into a skullcap. He's eating a bowl of Fruity Pebbles and reading the *Wall Street Journal.* The windows are open and the air swirls, tugging gently at his newspaper. I glance at the sky, white with clouds.

Poe, says Miller. How goes?

I light a cigarette. Is there any coffee?

He shrugs. French press by the sink. But I think it's gone cold.

That's fine. I ramble around the kitchen as if I live here, opening and closing cabinets until I find what I want. I pour lukewarm but very black coffee into a tall glass, then add ice and milk and sugar. I take a long drink and feel better right away.

How's Molly? says Miller.

What do you mean?

He smiles at me over the stock page. How did she fare last night? he says. How did you fare. How do you like her. How does she like you? That kind of thing.

Molly is fine, I say.

Miller squints at me, amused. That's your answer?

Yeah. Molly is fine.

Do you have another cigarette? he says.

I give him one and we stare at each other.

How is Jude? I say.

Ahh, he says, blowing smoke. Here it comes.

I shake my head. Never mind.

He grins. Molly is sweet, isn't she?

Yeah, I say. She is. What the hell is wrong with you?

Listen, he says. You ignorant Philistine. There is nothing wrong with me. I am simply trying to expand my horizons, and yours.

By letting me fuck your girlfriend.

Did you? he says.

What?

Did you fuck her?

No, I didn't.

He laughs. Jude was right. You're soft around the edges.

Fuck you.

Have you ever been married? he says.

Yeah.

How did you like it?

My wife is dead, I say. I wouldn't insult her.

Miller leans forward and his robe falls open. He scratches his chest lazily and smiles at me, shaking his head and rolling his eyes as if he feels sorry for me and I remember practicing my crippled smile in the bathroom mirror, my deathly grimace. He picks up his spoon and wipes it down with his tongue, then tosses it into the sink with a clatter. Molly said that he doesn't love her, that he never loved her and I wonder if he has ever hurt her. I wonder what his head would look like in a box.

Your sense of loyalty is fascinating, man.

Fuck you, Miller. Where is Jude?

She took one of the cars and went into the city.

Why?

He shrugs. To get some equipment.

What kind of equipment?

Lights, cameras. Nothing special.

Be warned, man. If you put her in danger, you will be crawling around on prosthetic limbs.

Miller shrugs and concentrates on his cereal.

What are you doing today? I say.

I thought I'd get started on the storyboards.

Yeah, I say. Regarding the script…I wonder if I could get a look at it.

Miller slurps his milk and grins. Had your chance the other night, he says.

Then what the fuck, right?

Why do you want to see it? he says.

Because I'd like to know what I'm getting into.

Oh, says Miller. You're in well over your head.

Long humming silence.

Speaking of fuck-ups, I say. Have you given any thought to my case?

The murder charges?

Yeah. Those.

Pretty cut and dried. They have you by the short hairs and all. But I think with a little slick lawyering, I can get you down to manslaughter.

Thanks for that.

Enter Molly, agitated.

I'm late, she says. I'm so fucking late.

Her hair is still wet. She wears a white cotton sundress and the destroyed brown cowboy boots she was wearing when I met her. She touches the back of my head as she passes, a soft cool touch.

The whispering breath of fairies.

A voice in my head says she smells like sunflowers but upon reflection I have no idea what sunflowers smell like. Molly acknowledges Miller with a smile, a cool shrug. Then goes to the refrigerator and takes out a container of strawberry yogurt. She rips it open and uses her finger as a spoon.

Miller sighs, opens a drawer. He removes a bright silver spoon and hands it to her.

What are you late for? he says.

Rehearsal, she says. *Fool for Love.*

He snorts rudely.

Molly smiles at me. John doesn't much care for Sam Shepard.

Why not?

He's a minor playwright, says Miller. And a redneck, besides.

Ignore him, says Molly. She touches my arm. Do you want to come?

I follow Molly to the garage, glad to get away from Miller. The garage is cavernous, cold, and smells of chemicals. I see several red plastic gas cans. Miller strikes me as the sort of cat who's prepared for the end times, and as I look around I see he's laid in a six-month supply of water, batteries, first aid gear, canned goods, emergency flares, camping equipment, and more. He's got all manner of fishing and deep sea gear: wet suits, surfboards, spear guns, oxygen tanks. Mounted on one wall are two small sharks he presumably murdered himself. As for vehicles he's got jet-skis and a speedboat named *Jezebel* and several cars. An old white Jaguar XJ6, the silver Mustang, a dusty green Jeep, an ancient but gleaming convertible Mercedes coupe. I wonder what sort of ride Jude is tooling around in. A black Range Rover, probably, with black windows and a cloaking device and hidden gun turrets. Two motorcycles, Ducati Monsters, skeletal street bikes silver and black. They look like birds of prey on two wheels, and now I remember that Jude was riding a black Ducati the day I watched her scalp Shane Finch.

Let's take the silver one, I say.

Molly tosses me the keys and a black helmet. She grins at me and pulls her own helmet on. This is trust, baby. I haven't been on a motorcycle in years and anyone who knows me would say that's a good thing. I tend to fly too close to the sun, when given half the chance. I tend to get distracted. I have smashed up more than my share of vehicles while daydreaming, and lately I have the headaches and blackbird visions to worry about. But my skull feels clean and clear and sometimes you have to say fuck it. The bike purrs to life and Molly climbs on behind me. Her arms slip around my waist like they belong there. I take it easy up the long driveway and I'm about to glance around and ask her which way am I going when she tells me that she's not really so late and maybe we should just ride a while.

It's a fine day for it, she says.

The sweetest decline is always voluntary. I cruise through the hills above Berkeley, slow and winding, and soon I'm wondering how fast this bike is and how long it would take me to kill myself on an open road. I begin to descend, with no idea where I'm going. The wind and sun are sweet narcotics and I imagine Molly's dress whipping about her thighs and now she slips one hand under my shirt to touch my chest, and oh, the galaxies in my head. The way she kissed me last night. The way she held me when I was shaking. I was covered in sweat and she didn't pull away from me. The pulse of sorrow and loneliness between us. The mad babble of imagined friends. The dizzy smell of her hair. I woke beside her twice in the night, drunk and still dreaming and I wanted to just eat her cold white skin. I remember how she said the bellybutton is terribly sensitive, how death is always on the wing. But I must have dreamed these things. I must have been dreaming. My skull begins to ache and my vision shimmers. Deathly, the crash preconceived. The earth forever pulls at you, gravity and all. It pulls you down. I suffer random, grasshopper thoughts. The subconscious fancy that I will lose Jude in this, that she will never be mine. That tomorrow is possibly unkind. Tomorrow is unknown and one of us may die in traffic today and I have to wake up before tomorrow comes.

The inside of my own head is a half acre of hell.

I run through a red light and the blast of a truck's horn rips a nasty hole in my internal sky and I nearly lay the bike down.

Jesus. Are you okay?

I bring us to a shivering stop under a grove of lemon trees. My heart is hopping around in my chest. Molly yanks her helmet off and her yellow hair is wild around her face and I taste the guilt, the sour guilt of nearly killing someone I barely know and prematurely adore.

I'm fine, she says. What happened back there?

Dreaming, I say. I was dreaming.

About what?

I open my mouth and realize the answer is foolish, romantic but foolish.

Never mind, I say. I'll tell you later.

It doesn't matter, she says. Are you okay?

Yeah.

Molly smiles, then takes one of my cold hands in hers.

You're none too steady, she says.

That's normal.

If you say so.

Torn shadows and silence under the lemon trees. The motorcycle warm, ticking.

twenty-one.

THE HOWL AND SWARM OF TELEGRAPH AND HASTE. The hyper mingling of pretty little Asian girls and junk-ravaged homeless guys, gutter punks and skater kids, wealth and despair. I park the bike between a polished black Saab convertible and a snot-colored VW bus where two white guys with dreadlocks are cooking what look like seaweed burgers on a hibachi. The sun is too hot and everything is razor bright. The smell of curry and gasoline, of clove cigarettes and patchouli. There is a sign in a shop window that declares this block to be a nuclear-free zone.

Molly sighs. I hate Berkeley.

I stand on the sidewalk, smoking. She says she's thirsty and wanders into a little café. I toss the cigarette and follow her.

Aren't you going to be late? I say.

No, she says. I'm getting a soda. Do you want anything?

I shrug. Espresso, a double.

The girl behind the counter looks familiar. Nineteen or twenty, with short black hair falling out of a baseball cap worn backwards. Dark almond eyes and lush lips. Very thin, with big round breasts compressed into a red sports bra. She's maybe Vietnamese.

Do I know you? I say.

Her lip curls. I doubt it.

What's your name?

Daphne.

Scooby Doo, I say. Where are you?

Funny, she says. You owe me six dollars.

Molly is watching me closely, pale hair around her face like a hood of light. I shrug and reach for my money.

We sit at a table outside and watch the world drift by. I realize why Berkeley is so strange to me. It feels like a miniature town, like a kid's model train set. I mention this to Molly but she doesn't smile or respond. She drinks a lemon and vanilla Italian soda, her jaw working as she slowly chews a piece of ice. I finish off my espresso and light a cigarette. Molly takes one but does not light it. She begins to pull the cigarette apart.

Are you nervous? I say.

I have to tell you something, she says. Two things.

What?

I don't have rehearsal today. I quit the play, in fact.

Why? I say.

Why did I quit the play? Or why did I lie?

Either, I say.

Molly stares at the sky behind me, shredding her cigarette.

I quit the play because it was a conflict. When we begin shooting the film, there won't be space for anything else.

Are you sure you want to do this film? I say.

Yes, she says.

How old are you?

Twenty-seven. I know what I'm doing.

That's not what I meant.

What did you mean?

I watch a guy across the street in yellow clown pants, juggling apples. I blow smoke.

Aren't you afraid of dying? I say.

Of course. But not terribly so.

I have lost people, I say. And think of Henry. Eve. Moon. Their faces boil in my head. I tell her it rips a part of you away that you don't get back.

Molly shrugs. I want to do this movie. And I don't think I will be the victim.

No one thinks they will, I say. That's the genius of this thing. Put three people in a lifeboat, tell them that a storm is coming and that one of them will be dead by nightfall, and they all think it will be one of the others.

Brief, complicated silence.

Then maybe we shouldn't get attached to each other, she says.

I mash my cigarette out and stare at her. I remember the day I found her in the kitchen. Blue eyes dark with circles and thin lips moving, as if in prayer. I thought she was Franny Glass come to life and she's right. If I am attached to nothing, then I have nothing to lose.

Too late, she says. Isn't it?

Jude's voice. John says you were quite taken with Molly.

Maybe. Why did you lie about the rehearsal?

John, she says. He wanted me to get you out of the house for a while.

I don't like the sound of that. I look over my shoulder, then back at her.

Why? I say.

Molly hesitates. *The Velvet*, she says. It may not be exactly the film you think it is. It's a little more complicated.

How so?

I haven't read the whole script, she says. Only bits and pieces.

How? I say. How is it more complicated?

Molly never answers me. Her eyes roll away white. A vein jumps in her throat and her left arm twitches once, twice. Then clutches at nothing. For one regrettable moment I think she is playing around, fucking with me. Then she slips out of her chair and begins to jerk around on the sidewalk like a fish.

Okay. Molly is having a seizure.

I come out of my chair and fall to my knees beside her. I reach for her hand, my thoughts rattling. The cries of distant birds. Her face is so pale. The traffic noise dies and everyone on the sidewalk disappears. I've suffered a dozen seizures in the past five years, but I have no memory of them.

What the hell do you do when someone has a seizure?

I wish Jude were here. She knows about these things. I remember being on a ferry on the Panama Canal with her when a German tourist suffered a violent grand mal. Everyone got out of the way and eyed him with horror and disgust and someone screamed that he was swallowing his tongue, his tongue oh god but Jude said that was nonsense. She said that a seizure victim might bite his tongue, but he doesn't swallow it. She pushed everyone out of the way and gently held the German tourist's head until he stopped thrashing, to prevent him cracking his skull, she said.

Molly seizes beside me and I can't do anything for her but put my hands under her head.

One minute, maybe two.

Then it's over and she goes fetal. The baby, she says. What about the baby?

I pull my hand away from her as if she's burning up. I tell myself that she doesn't know what she's saying, that a seizure is like fireworks on the brain.

You're okay, I say. You're okay.

But I have no idea. I have no idea what I'm talking about.

Molly comes around pretty quick. She sits up and her eyes dart this way and that. Bright blue, with pupils like needles. I hold up three fingers and she says three in a cold, faraway voice. Her voice is angry and I think I understand. I have had seizures, blackouts and whenever I come out of one I am angry and paranoid. I can't remember anything and I don't know who has been watching me. I carry her inside and the girl named Daphne brings over a glass of water. Molly says thank you and Daphne smiles and perhaps I'm imagining it, but a look seems to pass between them and I wonder if they know each other.

I called an ambulance, Daphne says.

No, says Molly. I don't want to go to the hospital.

Daphne shrugs. I don't care what you do. Just don't die in here.

Milk, says Molly. Will you bring me a glass of milk.

Whole or nonfat? Says Daphne.

What the fuck kind of question is that? I say.

Daphne glares at me. This is a coffee shop.

Whole milk, says Molly.

Anything for you?

No, I say. Thank you.

I take Molly's hand. Her skin is a little warm but not unusually so. I find her pulse and glance at the clock on the wall. Thirty seconds crawl by. Her heart beats thirty-three times.

You sure you're okay? I say.

I'm fine, she says. Fine.

Molly is slouched low in her chair, staring at me mournfully.

I don't quite believe you.

I'm sorry.

What was the other thing you were going to tell me?

Molly smiles, a thin bright smile. That I have seizures, sometimes.

Molly drinks her milk slowly and the color returns to her face. It seems unwise for her to get back on the motorcycle anytime soon and she shrugs when I say so. But she doesn't resist when I take her outside. Molly stands beside me, silent and docile and possibly embarrassed. I tell her not to worry but she just stares at me, forgotten helmet in hand. I hail a cab and help her into it. Molly recites the address and the driver shrugs, says it might be twenty bucks. I give him forty and tell him to make sure she gets there. The cab disappears into slow, maddening traffic. I get on the bike and just sit there a moment. Molly never answered my question. The film is more complicated than Miller gave us to believe. What the hell does that mean. I cruise around Berkley in low gear until I come to a sporting goods store. I go inside and purchase a set of compact, high-powered binoculars, then head for the hills.

I approach the house of Miller from above. I leave the bike on the road and walk until I come to a reasonable vantage point, creep into the neighbor's yard and climb his tree. If trespassing is the only law I break today then it's a good day. I am not directly above Miller's house, but at such an angle that affords me a view of eleven windows. I am less than a hundred yards away.

I scan the windows for signs of life and nothing is doing. It occurs to me that Miller might very well be performing animal sacrifice in one of the rooms I can't see, but I tell myself that that which I cannot see does not concern me. It doesn't exist. I settle into the crooked arms of the tree and light a cigarette. I contemplate a nap. I don't sleep, however. I don't care to wake up with a broken neck. Twenty minutes pass, slowly. I am bored silly and my ass is sore. I would give my left arm for a pint of whiskey. I smoke cigarettes and watch the house.

The yellow cab rolls up and deposits Molly in the driveway and it does seem like she should have gotten home long before now. She carries a package wrapped in plain brown paper, entering through the kitchen doors. Miller appears and they talk for a minute. Their conversation is relatively subdued, their body language wary. They appear to disagree for a moment. Miller tries to kiss her, but she withdraws. Molly moves into a part of the house that I can't see. Miller goes into the living room and flops down on the couch. He puts one foot up on the coffee table and does not move again.

A black Range Rover arrives with a U-Haul trailer in tow and I bring the binoculars up. The first to get out is Jude. She wears jeans and boots and a white leather jacket. Her hair is loose and she wears no sunglasses. Now the other doors are thrown open. Two men and a woman get out. One of the men is Jeremy. He wears black jeans and a black T-shirt under a black vest. The other man I have not seen before. He is large, slow and burly, with a red beard and a wild head of red hair. He wears brown coveralls and boots. The woman looks tiny beside him. She wears black sweats that hang loose from narrow hips and a red tank top. There is a camera bag slung over her left shoulder. Now she turns slowly in my direction, as if regarding the sky. Daphne, from the café. She no longer wears the baseball cap and it hits me. I know where I've seen her before. Two nights ago, her name was Veronica. She gave me a grim blow job for ninety bucks. She stares in my direction for another minute, then bends to remove a video camera from her bag.

This is getting interesting.

Jeremy and his burly pal begin to unload equipment from the trailer. I watch them for a moment, glad I am not home. That shit looks heavy. I check the windows of the house and see that Miller has not moved, but now he is wearing a straw hat. He looks like a coke dealer. I find Molly in one of the bedrooms. She wears a black leotard and appears to be practicing yoga. One long white leg is perpendicular to the floor. This is very sexy but I don't have time for casual peeping. I return to the scene out front. Jude is standing at the back of the truck. The hatch is open and I can't see her face but I get the feeling she is talking to someone.

Jude leans into the truck and helps a small boy climb out.

He is five or six years old, with a shock of blond hair. He wears green pants and a green T-shirt with a big yellow Nike swoosh across the front. The boy is shivering and so am I. I've seen him before. His mouth is covered in duct tape and he is blindfolded but I recognize him straight away. He's the kid from the videotape, the kid from the baseball game. He is the first-born son of MacDonald Cody.

Jude is gentle with the boy but he looks fucking terrified.

Legs cramped and bright with needles. I stumble, running for the bike.

twenty-two.

FADE IN.

Exterior, house of Miller. Day.

Wide angle of yard. Long shadows stretch across a gravel driveway. Two white men, fat and thin, struggle under the weight of a large, black metal case. The thin man is Jeremy, 22, recently employed as a doorman at the King James Hotel in downtown San Francisco. Jeremy is an aspiring film-maker born in Mississippi. He has lived in San Francisco for seven years, surviving alternately as a bike messenger, meth dealer, male prostitute and busboy. The fat man is Huck, 29, originally from Los Angeles. Huck is a guitar player who supplements his income by running lights and sound for small-budget films, primarily in pornography.

> Huck- Get your end up. Get the whore up.
> Jeremy- Fuck you. I've got my end.
> Huck- Just hang on to it. I'd hate to lose a toe.
> Jeremy- Take it easy. This is the last one.

The roar of a motorcycle as a rider in black helmet comes down the hill, too fast. The bike spins out of control and the rider lays it down on its side. The rider yanks off his helmet and tosses it to the ground, where it twirls for a moment before coming to rest. The rider is Phineas Poe, white male, 39. Disgraced and severely disturbed ex-cop, with a history of drug and alcohol problems. He is prone to petit mal seizures accompanied by apocalyptic visions. He wears a brown leather coat, jeans, and black shirt unbuttoned at the throat. He approaches Jeremy and Huck, his face pale with anger. He stops just short of Jeremy and puts one hand on the metal case.

Poe- What the hell is going on, Jeremy?

Jeremy- You need to talk to your girl. She's in charge.

Poe- Were you with her when she grabbed that kid?

Jeremy- I don't know anything about the kid. He was in the truck when she picked me up.

Huck- Hey, man. This box is heavy. You mind getting the fuck out the way.

Poe- The box is heavy?

Poe shoves Jeremy and the box falls to the ground, spilling open.

Huck- Motherfucker. That is some expensive gear in there.

Poe- Do you think I give a shit?

Huck- Jeremy, who is this asshole?

Poe- I'm Joe Blow. Who the fuck are you?

Huck- The name is Huck. I'm running sound and lights on this picture.

Poe- I hope somebody is paying you well.

Huck- None of your business but yeah, they are.

Poe- You're an accomplice to kidnapping already.

Jeremy- Listen, brother. We're on the clock, okay. Why don't you let us do our job and you can take this up with Jude directly.

Poe turns his head to the right and looks directly at the camera. Now he glances back at Jeremy.

Poe- If you call me brother again, I will eat your fucking heart.
Huck- Oh, man. This is gonna be fun.

Poe approaches the camera. In the background, Jeremy and Huck can be seen picking up the box and carrying it to the house. Poe comes closer now and his face fills the frame.

Poe- What's your name? Daphne or Veronica.

He puts his hand over the lens. Dark, with slivers of light. The sound of breathing.

Poe- Put it down. Put the fucking camera down.
Daphne- Miller wants everything on tape. Everything.

Poe knocks the camera to the ground and there is a prolonged, blurry shot of dust and green leaves.

Poe- What is your name?
Daphne- My real name is Jennifer. But you can call me Daphne.
Poe- What about the other night?
Daphne- That was like…an audition.
Poe- Jesus…

The crunch of gravel as Poe walks away. The camera is picked up and now there is a shot of his back as he approaches the house. The camera follows him inside.

Interior, the house of Miller. Day.

The living room. The camera swings around Poe as he enters, then slowly pans room. The room is bright with sunlight. High ceilings and massive windows. The window frames splinter the room with shadows in the shape of crosses. The décor is gloomy, futuristic. Bright blue sofa, kidney shaped.

Metallic chairs without arms. A chrome loveseat and a coffee table of bubbled volcanic glass. There are a number of kitchen appliances scattered
about, broken or taken apart. There is a puddle of red paint on the hardwood floor beneath a bay window. The small, uneven footprints of a child
lead away from the puddle and stop near the center of the room, where a
number of broken toys lie.

John Ransom Miller reclines on the sofa. White male, 42, dead or sleeping. He
wears white linen pants and a straw hat and nothing else. Miller is a homicidal Zen Buddhist with a degree in criminal law, originally from Florida.

Enter Molly Jones. White female, 27. Miller's girlfriend. She came to California from Tennessee six years ago, hoping to become an actress, and is
currently a student at Berkeley studying theater. Molly is epileptic. She
wears a white cotton sundress and brown cowboy boots. Her blond hair is
pulled into a ponytail. She glances at Poe, who stands in the doorway, then
averts her eyes. Molly sits down on the edge of the coffee table before Miller.

Zoom slow on Poe. He scratches his head, scowls at the camera.

> Poe- What's happening, Molly?
> Molly- Phineas…you're here. Thank god.
> Poe- What?
> Molly- It's begun.
> Poe- I can see that. Where the hell is Jude?

Enter Jude, white female, 35. Last name and place of birth unknown.
Estranged girlfriend of Phineas Poe. Jude is a professional killer, formerly
of the Army's special forces, who honed her skills with an Israeli death
squad. She has a long white scar on the left side of her face. Black hair,
unkempt. Jude wears red velvet jeans and a white tank top, black motorcycle boots and no jewelry. She crosses the room and sits down on the sofa
beside Miller.

Poe- What's going on, Jude?

Jude- I just heard the funniest joke. I almost died.

Poe- You brought a kid in here, just now. I saw you.

Jude- Are you sure about that?

Molly- There's a kid in the house?

Poe- A little boy.

Molly- I don't understand. Where did he come from?

Poe- They snatched him, apparently.

Molly- They?

Poe- My girlfriend, there. And your husband.

Molly- He's not my husband.

Poe- Whatever. Hey, Miller. Wake up.

Jude- Do you want to hear it?

Poe- What?

Jude- The joke.

Poe- (glaring at Miller) What the hell is wrong with him?

Molly- I know. He looks dead.

Jude- He's depressed, maybe. He's afraid you don't like him.

Poe- I don't. I don't like him.

Molly- He looks dead.

Poe- Are you high?

Jude- He's not dead.

Molly- But he's not breathing.

Jude- It's a Buddhist thing.

Poe- That would explain the funny hat.

Jude- Anyway, the joke concerns Billy the Kid…

Poe- Enough of this shit. Where is the boy?

Jude- Do you want to hear this joke, or not?

Poe- Please. Tell us a fucking joke.

Jude- Billy the Kid was in a shootout with his pal Charlie. Billy shot Charlie in the throat, but didn't kill him. Charlie fell in the dirt and started rolling around like he was drowning in yellow dust. He was taking forever to die. While he was thrashing, a chicken waddled over to Charlie where he lay and grabbed hold of this exposed vein in his neck, grabbed it up in his beak and just yanked it out like a purple rope, then tugged and tugged until it was like ten feet long. And what do you think Charlie said?

Molly- I don't...I don't know.

Jude- Get away from me yer stupid chicken.

Molly- That's not a joke.

Jude- No. It's kind of a poem, by Michael Ondaatje. He wrote the *English Patient.*

Poe and Molly exchange glances.

Jude- Come on. You can't tell me that's not funny.

Molly- I hated that movie.

Jude- Don't even think of fucking with me, honey.

Molly- Yeah, well. I just kept wishing the English guy would die, already.

Poe- Where is the boy, Jude?

Jude- I can't tell you.

Jude begins to laugh. Molly chews a thumbnail, worried. As Poe exits the room, Miller opens his eyes and draws a finger across his throat.

Cut to black-and-white overhead surveillance cameras and follow Poe as he searches the house. He moves from one room to the next but finds nothing. In the basement, he comes upon Jeremy and Huck, who are surrounded by an array of sound and video equipment. The three of them stare at one another.

Huck- You. You fucked up my boom mike.

Poe- Unreal. This is unreal.

He stalks around the room and comes upon a large box marked props. He throws open the box and methodically digs through it, tossing aside cell phones and wristwatches and eyeglasses and a prosthetic arm until he finds what he's looking for: A small snub-nosed pistol, a .32.

Jeremy- You're wasting your time, man. Blanks in it.

Poe- I don't want to kill anyone, yet.

He glances up, suddenly aware of the tiny camera in the corner. He gets up and stares into the lens, then wearily smashes it with the pistol. The picture goes to snow for a moment.

Fade to interior, living room. Day.

Miller sits on the sofa with Jude. Their heads are bent together, as if sharing a secret. Jude smokes a cigarette, reading from a page of the script. Miller has a red pencil in his mouth. There are more pages of script on coffee table and floor. Molly paces around the room, turning now and then to glare at the camera.

Molly- Does the camera have to be on for this?

Miller- The making of the film and the film itself will overlap and become one.

Molly- It's self-indulgence. It's bullshit.

Miller- Maybe. But I think the making of the film might ultimately be more interesting than the film itself. And more frightening.

Jude- What's with this scene between me and Poe?

Miller- Which scene?

Jude- This sex scene on page 36. It says here that I make his nose bleed without touching him.

Miller- Yeah. I'm thinking you have telekinetic powers, or something. I haven't sorted that out, yet.

Molly- What sex scene?

Jude- Don't tell me you're jealous.

Enter Poe, holding the gun. He looks at Molly, then down at the child's footprints. He bends to touch the paint and his finger comes away red. He shakes his head, disgusted. He kicks the glass coffee table sideways with his boot. The loose pages of script fly into the air. Poe points the gun at Miller.

741

Miller- Improv. I love it.

Poe- This is going to hurt, I'm afraid.

Miller- Please...you must be joking.

Poe- Where is the boy?

Miller- The boy?

Poe- Don't do that. Don't fucking echo me.

Miller- The script does mention a boy. But I haven't decided what to do with him. Child actors can be such a nightmare.

Poe- I saw Jude bring the boy in here.

Jude- He's imagining things.

Molly- What about these footprints?

Poe stares directly at the camera again.

Miller- I wish you wouldn't do that. I hate it when actors address the camera.

Poe- What are you afraid of?

Miller doesn't answer and without warning, Poe swings around and fires the gun at him. The shot is loud, deafening. Everyone jumps.

Miller- Missed. He missed me, by god.

Poe- I missed on purpose. For effect.

Molly- What about these footprints?

Jude- I can't stand the smell of this fucking place. Did you ever notice how every family has its own terrible smell?

Pan to Molly, who stands on far side of the room, in the puddle of red paint. She has removed her cowboy boots and her feet are smeared red. Now she unbuttons her sundress as Jude reads aloud from the script.

Jude- The smell of furniture polish and dead flowers, the smell of shampoo and dirty boots. The smell of ashtrays and garlic and spilled gin.

Molly steps out of her dress and throws it aside. The dress flutters toward Poe, who catches it. His face is blank. Molly stands in red paint, wearing white underpants and bra. The camera moves closer and closer.

Jude- Every family has its own smell and if you're not careful that smell will attach itself to you, it will sink into your skin and wipe out your own smell. It will become your smell. And ever after you will smell like a family.

Molly sits down on the chrome loveseat and buries her face in her hands. Poe goes to her. He stands over her but does not touch her.

Miller- Beautiful. Print it.

twenty-three.

I SIT DOWN ON THE CHROME LOVESEAT beside Molly, who wears just a thin white bra and panties. Her feet are stained, red. I have a gun in one hand and her crumpled sundress in the other. I offer the dress to her and she takes it, holding it in both hands as if she doesn't quite recognize it. I look around the room and Jude is at the bar, mixing drinks. Her hair falls shadowy around her face. The muscles jump in her brown arms and I can see that she's glowing.

Jude loves this shit.

Miller is bent over the coffee table, making notes on the script. I look over his shoulder and my eye catches on a random line of dialogue, attributed to me: Who is the shadow that walks beside you? It sounds like something I might say when drunk. It seems like this should disturb me but I don't much care. Daphne has opened a window and now sits on the ledge, smoking a joint.

Will somebody please tell me what's happening?

Miller peers at me, confused. Jude brings me a margarita on the rocks.

I would like some of that weed, says Molly.

You might want to get dressed, says Jude.

Oh, says Molly. You're right.

When did you change the furniture? I say.

Molly touches my thigh. While we were out, this morning.

Do you like it? says Miller. I think it makes for a nice set.

Molly gets up and pulls her dress over her head and buttons it slowly, her bra and panties exposed in flashes. The monologue, I think. She got a charge out of Jude's psycho monologue. Molly reaches back and pulls her ponytail apart, shakes her hair as if wet. She glides across the room and takes the joint from Daphne. They whisper to each other briefly, like two thieves. Daphne yawns and stretches lazily and announces that she wants to take a dinner break.

Okay, says Miller. But don't be long. We'll be shooting tonight.

Daphne nods. Do you mind if I take one of the cars?

Take the Mustang, says Molly. The keys are in the kitchen.

Daphne exits, pausing to pluck a dead yellow flower from a vase.

I take it you know her, I say.

Molly nods. Daphne goes to school with me.

I can't trust you, can I?

Why do you say that?

Did you fake that seizure today?

No, she says. No.

Please, I say. Button your fucking dress.

Molly looks at me, hurt.

I'm sorry. I'm an asshole, I say.

This is breaking my heart, says Jude.

You love this, I say. Don't you.

What do you mean?

I mean you're a compulsive liar.

Everybody shut the fuck up, says Miller. We need to talk.

The whine of a power saw from downstairs.

Hammering, grinding. I wonder what the hell Huck and Jeremy are up to. Molly comes over and hands me the joint. I take a long, grateful drag. I stare at Jude, who lounges on the edge of the couch, stroking herself like she wants to fuck somebody.

The boy, I say. I want to know about the boy.

You're wondering how he will fare in the film, says Miller.

Exactly.

The fundamentals of *The Velvet* are simple, he says. One of us in this room will die. That has not changed. But relationships can be tedious, I think. This is not a comedy, after all. It's a postmodern horror. And so now we are making a film about four people who have kidnapped a small boy to finance an independent film about four people who have kidnapped a small boy. Or something like that. The boy will be the focal point of the conflict between these four characters. The sexual relationships will be secondary.

You like to throw that word around, I say. Postmodern. You realize it doesn't mean anything?

Miller shrugs. I like the way it sounds.

Where is the boy?

Upstairs, says Jude. Downstairs. In a secret room.

Did you know about this? I say to Molly.

No, she says. Of course not.

I want to see him.

Jude shrugs. And if I say no?

Don't fuck with me, Jude.

She lays one hand flat on her stomach and thrusts her hips once, twice. But it's so much fun, she says.

I know this is a bad idea but I walk toward her, my hands out wide to show her that I am unarmed. I shuffle my feet, as if I want to dance with her. Jude raises her arms over her head and pumps her hips faster now, fucking the air. I am a terrible dancer but I'm not shy and I drift close to her, shaking my ass like a fool. I close my eyes for a moment and I see her in a Mexico City motel room, an electric bone saw dripping blood in one hand and a pint of vodka in the other. Her raincoat is covered in blood and she sways back and forth, slowly grinding her pelvis against mine. I look down and her boots are slick with blood, she's dancing in blood and now I open my eyes and throw my right fist at Jude's head, a short compact swing that should knock her flat on her ass but she vanishes, she ducks under my fist and when she rematerializes she is to my left and slightly behind me and she hits me with a jab in the side of the throat, then casually sweeps my feet out from under me. I go down like a sack of fertilizer and now Jude is squatting on my chest with a scowl on her face. I am having difficulty breathing and I will be eating nothing but ice cream for a while. I take shallow, gasping breaths, my hands at my throat and I have a feeling she pulled that punch, that she could have crushed my fucking esophagus, that she could have killed me if only she wanted to.

Wow, says Miller. I wish we'd got that on tape.

Are you okay? says Jude.

I see a dark and thorny bramble of emotions in her face. Worried that she has really hurt me, scared but angry as well. Jude bends to kiss me softly on the side of the mouth and I know she loves me, she hates me.

Don't speak, she says. It's going to hurt for a while.

Get away from him.

This comes from Molly, who stands a few feet away, a baseball bat in her hands. She has a nice, relaxed grip on it and I believe she knows how to use it. But she doesn't know Jude very well.

I'm serious, says Molly.

Jude sighs. Honey, I could take that away from you with my eyes closed. I could make you suck it.

Easy, baby, says Miller.

The word baby rings in my head like hammer on stone.

But I won't, says Jude. I'm done fighting for the moment. I'm tired and I have to pee.

She heaves a theatrical sigh and stands up. She stands over me for a moment and I get a nice view of her crotch. The velvet pants fit her perfectly and her package looks like a ripe red plum. Jude looks good from this angle and she knows it. Now she walks away and Molly bends over me.

Are you okay?

No, not really. My voice is gone, a ragged whisper. I sound like I have laryngitis.

Why did you do that?

I try to smile. I want to tell her it's complicated. Molly helps me up and I don't really mean to, but I push her away. I don't want her to touch me, or something. I don't want her to help me, to be tender with me. And I like Molly. I think I'm falling for her but right now I need to go talk to Jude. I glance at Miller and by the expression on his face I can see that he is very pleased with things so far.

It's a waste of breath, I know. But I ask him anyway. Where is the boy?

Sorry, he says. The kid is Jude's project.

I stagger down the hallway to the bathroom. The door is locked.

Jude, I croak. Let me in.

There is a brief, calculated silence.

The stink of melodrama, sweet and acidic. Then she opens the door, turning aside as she does so. I kick the door shut behind me and go to the sink. My face in the mirror is relatively purple and I don't know if this is shame or anger or internal bleeding, in which case I'm dead in the morning and none of this shit matters. I take a long sloppy drink from the tap. Water runs down my chin onto my shirt. Jude climbs into the clawfoot tub and sits with her knees drawn up to her chest.

I'm really fucking mad at you, she says.

Oh yeah? I hadn't noticed. I was too busy choking to death.

That's hilarious.

Okay, I say. Enlighten me. Why are you mad at me? Because I didn't fuck Molly last night, or because I wanted to?

You asshole. You ignorant asshole.

What?

I don't care what you do with that wet bitch. I could not care less.

You're lying.

Phineas, she says. You and I are never going to be happy. We are never going to be an attractive couple with a dog and a kid and a house in the hills. We are never going to file a joint fucking tax return.

Do you even pay taxes?

That's hardly the point.

Tell me, then. Why are you mad at me.

Because you're stupid. You're so stupid. Because you don't trust me anymore. Because you tried to hit me just now. And because you seem determined to fuck up this project.

This project is a nightmare, I say.

It's barely begun, she says.

You should have told me.

I couldn't tell you.

Why not?

Because I knew you would freak out, just like this.

Then it did cross your mind that I might not be up for an actual kidnapping.

Trust me, she says. You have to believe that I know what I'm doing. And it doesn't matter because you're already involved.

I stare at her. The only sound is the dripping tap and it suddenly occurs to me that we are probably on camera right now.

Is this fucking scripted? I say. Did Miller write this scene?

What. Why do you say that?

It's just a little late in the game to talk about trust.

That hurts, she says.

Answer the question, Jude.

No, she says. This exchange was not scripted. But yes, the cameras are everywhere. Anything we say or do may end up in the film.

I smile because suddenly I have to take a tremendous shit and I feel just a little self-conscious.

What's so funny?

Nothing, I say.

You don't have to love me, she says. But trust me and you will walk out of here alive, with half a million dollars in an offshore bank account.

If you want me to trust you, then let me see the kid.

Jude sighs. Fine.

I follow her upstairs and through the kitchen. Molly stands by the stove, stirring a cup of tea. Jude growls at her and I understand that I need to keep an eye on them, that I should never leave them alone together. I smile at Molly, or try to. I tell her everything is under control and Jude laughs like a mad bird. I follow her down the hall and there are voices coming from the Lizard Room. Miller is in there and at first I think he must be talking to Jeremy but then I realize that one of those voices is mine.

Hang on, I say. What the fuck?

Miller is sitting in one of the black leather armchairs, his legs slung over the side. He wears thin cotton pants and no shirt. He is barefoot. He is smoking a cigar and lazily stroking his chest and watching five televisions at once and my handsome face is on every one of them.

Black and white video, poor quality. Fisheye perspective. I am in a room full of mirrors. Television number one features me and Jude in a stalled elevator with two very frightened senior citizens. Jude is so sexy it's disturbing, and she clearly knows where the camera is. I look diseased, next to her. We are talking about money and blowjobs and whether or not I should kill the old man and pretty soon I am holding the gun to her head.

Motherfucker, I say.

On television number two, I am having my cock munched by Daphne at the Paradise Spa in grainy black and white, poorly lit. Miller chuckles and freezes the picture. I have to admit, the expression on my face is priceless. I look as if I've just seen God in the flesh and at the same time realized that I am terribly constipated.

Oh, honey. That's special, mutters Jude.

On the third screen, I am stretched out in the gutter, getting bitch-slapped with my own gun by a fatass bouncer outside the End Up. Miller is kind enough to rewind that one a few times, so we can view it in slow motion. On television number four, I am crouched in an alley talking to an emaciated junkie who wears a yellow miniskirt. I give her money, then pull back my hand as if to strike her.

And finally I am in bed with Molly, trembling like a kid. She bends to kiss my forehead and there is a lingering, shadowy shot down the front of her nightgown.

Dynamite, says Miller.

Huh?

The way she comforts you when you have a scary dream. I wish you wouldn't mumble so much, though. I can't always make out what you're saying.

I stare at him. I just don't know what to say.

Maybe later, he says.

Miller eases out of the armchair, rubbing his belly. It occurs to me that he's really a lot like Captain Kirk. His chest is completely hairless and he's packing a nice set of love handles and he's way too smug and pleased with himself all the time. He walks over to the entertainment console and fiddles briefly with the controls, then slips in another tape.

Fade in. The living room, day. The furniture is as it was before Miller redecorated. Jude sits on the couch in a black dress with slits up either side. Her bare legs are stretched across Miller's lap. He stares at her legs but does not touch them. Jude leans close to him and begins to whisper or blow into his left ear. Miller pushes her away. Jude smiles as he removes a black Magic Marker from his pocket. Miller slowly, deliberately scrawls the word Mother on one pale thigh and Repent on the other.

Is that permanent ink? says Jude.

He shrugs. It's as permanent as your skin. It will disappear in five, maybe seven days.

Jude climbs into his lap. She squats over him as if she is about to pee in the woods.

What do you want? she says.

Dominate me, says Miller. His voice is sarcastic.

I'm no good at domination, says Jude. That's why I'm such a terrible mother.

Funny, says Miller. Very funny.

Jude kisses him, roughly. They wrestle for a moment, panting. Miller tugs at his belt buckle and she tries to pull away.

No, she says. I'm not in the mood.

Miller holds her by the wrists and she just sits there, glaring at him. I wait for her to headbutt him or something but she just sits there on his lap.

Honey, he says.

Don't fucking call me honey. I hate that.

Miller's eyes become slits. His nostrils flare. He slowly begins to twist Jude's arms and she sucks in her breath as if in pain.

Are your wings broken? he says.

Fuck you, she whispers.

Fly away, he says. Fly away, Jesse.

Jude struggles with him but he is too strong for her. I assume she's taking a dive for the video, but it looks very real. I glance at her now and her face is stony, watching. I look back to the screen as Miller relaxes his grip and Jude yanks her hands away. She stands over him now and her eyes are terrible with fear and anger. I can't remember ever seeing fear in her eyes, real or not.

Miller yawns on the screen. Fly away, he says.

And beside me he whispers, fly away.

Jude slowly pulls her underpants down from under her dress, standing on one leg, then the other as she slips the panties over her feet and drops them to the floor. She raises both arms over her head and twirls a slow, seductive circle. Her eyes to the floor,. Jude twirls once more and now she begins to spin, faster and faster, so that her dress rises and falls and the curve of her white ass flashes the camera like a blinking light and finally she stops spinning, dizzy and breathing hard.

I'm Mary Tyler Moore, says Jude. I can make it anywhere.

But you will always come back to me, says Miller.

Zoom on her face, then fade to Miller sitting on the edge of the coffee table, naked. Jude is crouched sideways on the couch, legs folded under her like a grasshopper. Her back is to the camera and I can't see her face, but her hair is damp and tangled and she makes no effort to fix it. She still wears the black dress, now wet and barely recognizable, ripped open down her spine. There are new bruises along her back, dark plum bruises the size and approximate shape of a man's hand. Miller lights a cigarette. He offers one to Jude but she doesn't respond. She doesn't look at him. Miller reaches for her and she flinches away.

Easy, he says. Take it easy.

Miller leans forward and strokes Jude's legs with one finger, barely touching her. Jude shivers, or trembles. Then slowly Miller begins to pull at her legs, unfolding them. Jude doesn't resist, but shifts her weight and allows him to extend her left leg so that her foot is in his lap. Now he massages her foot, rubbing it softly with both hands. He might be an affectionate guy whose girlfriend has just had a long day at work except that she is bruised and trembling and he is naked and sweating and has a cigarette hanging from his lips with more than an inch of white ash.

You have beautiful feet, says Miller.

Jude says nothing and he continues to rub her foot.

It's too bad, he says.

Why? she says. Why is it too bad?

Miller removes the cigarette from his mouth and impossibly, the ash does not fall.

Because one day I will cut off your arms and legs.

The picture abruptly goes to snow, then blue.

Beside me, the physically present Miller sighs as if bored. I look around and see that all of the screens have gone blue. Miller flicks the televisions off one by one. He moves over to the bar, stopping to whisper something to the big boa constrictor. Then he chuckles, as if the snake said something clever in return. I look at Jude and her face is completely blank. She could be waiting for a bus or making up a grocery list in her head. But I notice that she is flexing and unflexing her hands.

Who shot that video? I say. And when?

Jeremy shot it, says Jude.

When? I say.

Miller pours whiskey into a glass. Anyone want a drink?

When? I say. Your hair is much longer now.

I think we should go see the kid, says Jude. Before I change my mind.

Excellent idea, says Miller.

Jude turns and walks out of the room.

I stand there a minute like a dummy, staring at the blank television.

Miller raises his glass in my direction. Cheers, he says.

twenty-four.

THIS PLACE IS A LABYRINTH. And it seems to me that most of the people who went into the labyrinth were killed by the Minotaur. I mention as much to Jude and she grunts at me. Jude doesn't want to talk, it seems. She is stomping along in a mild fury and I reckon she wants to inflict some physical harm on somebody or something. I'm curious as hell about that video but tell myself to save it for later.

She leads me through a series of forgotten, unfurnished rooms and narrow passageways. The house is much larger than I imagined and I am forming the notion that it simply expands whenever necessary, like a house in a cartoon. I follow her along a hall that I have not been down before. Bare wood floors, unlit. The smell of dust. I have a feeling this part of the house is never used, possibly haunted. I follow her around a corner and into a library. Thousands of books, from floor to ceiling. Persian rugs, faded with age. Bright splashes of the sun from skylights above. I take a deep breath and release it slowly.

The room is awesome, the kind of room you whisper in whether you want to or not.

Jude doesn't blink, of course. She acts like she owns the place, and I have a bright strange vision of her when she was nineteen, sailing through here on a skateboard.

What are you staring at? she says softly.

I love her briefly, for whispering.

Don't, she says. Don't stare at me.

There is something wrong with her. The girl on the skateboard disappears and now I am looking at the woman who made a very creepy video with Miller, weeks or even months ago and never mentioned it and now her voice sounds almost fragile, torn. Her face is still a mask but slipping at the edges.

Do you want to talk about that video?

Jude folds both arms across her chest. What do you think?

I think your voice sounds strange.

And how does it sound strange, exactly?

Torn, I say.

Don't fuck with me, she says.

I take a step toward her and Jude does something I never expected. She takes a step backward, into a box of sunlight so bright she appears to glow. She stands very still and for a moment I think she is vibrating, humming. And then she abruptly sits down on the floor, as if standing before me was becoming a nasty chore and she needed to rest or die.

What's wrong with you? I say.

Nothing. I don't want to talk about it.

Jude moves away from the sun to slouch against a wall of books. I sit down beside her and we share a cigarette. I won't ask her any more questions, not now. After a few minutes of silence, she brings herself to lay her head briefly on my shoulder, but that is all the comforting she will allow.

Then she stands up.

Do you want to see the kid or not?

Jude removes a copy of *Treasure Island* from the fifth shelf. The sound of gears and hinges groaning and then a wall of books on the other side of the room swings open to reveal a hidden door.

You must be joking, I say.

Don't you love it, she says.

Oh, I love it.

It was designed by a magician named The Fantastic Marco, fifty years ago.

Behind the secret door is a spiral staircase that disappears into the darkness below. Jude produces a small flashlight and says, I hope you're not afraid of the dark. At the bottom of the staircase is another door. Jude takes two plastic white masks from a box on the floor and instructs me to put one on.

I don't want to scare the boy.

Do you want him to memorize your face?

The mask has two round eyeholes and a narrow gash at the mouth and I've seen this mask before, at the movies.

Jason? I say.

Michael, she says. I wanted something from the movies. I wanted something simple but menacing.

Of course.

Are you ready? she says.

Yeah.

Don't go soft on me.

Jude unlocks the door and I push it open slowly. The room is small, with dark wood floors and walls like a little ski lodge. There is a lamp in one corner and the soft yellow light is warm, almost cozy. There is a small refrigerator in one corner, the kind you might find in a college dorm room. In the opposite corner is a toilet and sink. There is a television on, the sound turned low. And then there's the boy. He's silent, tiny. He's lying curled on his side on a narrow futon, his back to us. He is not bound or gagged and he is not blindfolded. Jude and I stand in the doorway and he doesn't notice us at first. He is watching *Tom & Jerry*. The boy is transfixed, numb. He holds the remote control in his left hand. His face is dirty and his hair needs to be brushed. I am glad to see that Jude has provided him with the Cartoon Network and a Gameboy to play with and two pillows and a puffy comforter and even a fat stuffed bear for the bed but even so I feel sick to my stomach.

Hey, little man.

At the sound of my voice the boy scrambles into the corner near the toilet. Dark feral brown eyes, so dark it's like he has no pupils. Or maybe his eyes are completely dilated with fear.

It's okay, I say.

He shakes his head violently. His whole body is shaking. I take my mask off and drop it to the floor. Jude makes a noise in her throat and I have a feeling she is not amused. I glance up at the ceiling and find the video camera in the corner above the television. Miller is in the Lizard Room, watching us. I can feel his eyes on me. I stare at the camera with pure sweet hatred and slowly mouth the words fuck you.

I turn to Jude. I want to be alone with him, I say.

She stares at me, disgusted. But then she shrugs and walks out.

I sit down on the edge of the futon and pick up the stuffed bear. The boy still crouches by the toilet.

My name is Phineas.

The boy peers at me. I will never hear the end of it from Jude but I tell him my real name. I look at the television and see that Tom has a giant, swollen red paw. He's hopping around like a maniac and Jerry is laughing at him, hammer in hand. The boy follows my eyes. He stares hard at *Tom & Jerry* for a minute, then back at me. I wish he would laugh. I want to ask him his name but I reckon it's best not to push him. We watch *Tom & Jerry* for ten minutes or so, until it gives way to *Dexter's Laboratory*. I'm not familiar with Dexter but I notice the kid's eyes light up. During a commercial I go over to the little fridge and check out the contents. It seems to me that the boy is more likely to freak out if I stand up, so I crawl over to the fridge on my hands and knees. Jude wants people to believe that her heart is made of stone but she's not so bad. The refrigerator is stocked with juice boxes and pudding packs and pickles and individually wrapped American cheese and grapes and yogurt and baby carrots and animal crackers and a big plastic jug of chocolate milk. On top of the fridge is a green plastic cup, brown at the bottom with the dregs of chocolate milk.

Whoa. It's the mother lode in here.

The kid just looks at me. I might be babbling in Greek, as far as the kid is concerned. But I notice he is no longer crouched by the toilet. He has moved maybe two or three feet closer to the futon.

Do you want some more of this chocolate milk?

He stares at me.

I'm gonna have a juice box, I say. You want one?

The kid doesn't answer. He manages to shake his head and nod at the same time. I get out two juice boxes anyway, and the bowl of grapes. I crawl back to the futon and I'm near enough to touch him. He doesn't move away, which seems like a good sign. We watch Dexter for a while. I drink my juice box, slurping at the straw and making appreciative noises now and then. I leave the extra juice box on the floor by my foot. I eat a few grapes and the boy looks at me a few times, like he wants a grape but doesn't want to ask for one.

How old are you? he says.

I'm thirty-nine.

The kid nods, as if calculating.

How old are you?

Five and a half, he says.

Damn good, I say. Damn good age to be.

That's a bad word, he says.

You're right. It is a bad word.

My dad says that word when he's mad. Are you mad?

This just about breaks me.

No, I say. I'm not mad.

He looks at me. Can I have my juice box now?

Yeah, I say. Of course.

I pick up the juice box and hold it out to him. He comes over and takes it from me and I offer to help him with the straw but he says he knows how to do it. The boy has a serious little face and he frowns, working on the straw. But he gets it in the hole eventually and sighs, pleased with himself. I imagine the juice tastes pretty good. He sits down on the futon, a couple feet away from me.

Do you want a grape? I say.

Yes, he says. Yes…please.

What about some of those animal crackers?

The boy shrugs one shoulder. Okay.

I get out the animal crackers and we sit there munching them a while. Pretty soon, Dexter gets himself into some kind of terrible jam with a time machine that keeps coughing smoke and sending Dexter sideways in time, and then a noisy girl appears, who keeps yelling at him. The boy explains that this is Dexter's sister, Deedee.

Oh, I say.

Do you like this show? he says.

Yeah. It's good, I say.

It's pretty good, he says. *Johnny Bravo* is my favorite, though.

When does that come on?

It's coming up next, he says.

What's your name? I say.

Sam, he says. My whole name is Samwise. Samwise Cody.

Samwise, I say. Your mom and dad must have liked *The Lord of the Rings*.

The boy's face lights up. Yeah, he says. Except I don't have a mom. But my dad reads me that book, sometimes. When I go to bed. How did you know?

I read that book when I was a boy. It was one of my favorites.

He nods. It's my favorite, too.

Your dad's name is MacDonald Cody? I say.

Yeah, he says. Most people call him Mac.

I nod. Your dad seems like a good guy.

The boy gazes at me, hopeful. Are you a friend of my Dad's?

No. I've never met him. But I've seen him on TV.

The boy nods sagely, and I figure he's used to hearing people say that. After all, his father is a senator from California. He plays one on TV.

I sit with Sam for another half hour or so. We watch *Johnny Bravo* together, and he laughs a time or two. Or he laughs when I laugh, that is. The kid has a sweet voice, soft and a little hoarse. I ask him what kind of toys he likes to play with because I notice there are no toys in the room except for the stuffed bear. He says he likes action figures, mostly. I tell him I'll look into getting him some, and then I say it's time for me to go. He looks so heartbroken that I am tempted to just sleep down here with him, but I have a feeling that Jude wouldn't stand for that. But I promise him I will be back soon. I tell him to stay up as late as he wants and to watch cartoons until he's sick.

The boy looks concerned. Do cartoons make you sick? he says.

No, I say. They never made me sick.

Jude is waiting for me in the library. She sits high atop one of the shelves, still reading about Jim Hawkins. When I come through the secret door she drops to the floor like a cat.

What is wrong with you? she says.

What do you mean?

You let the kid see your fucking face. And then you hang out with him for over an hour. What were you doing down there?

I shrug. We were watching cartoons and eating animal crackers.

Motherfucker. You were bonding with him.

He's five, Jude.

Jude begins to pace back and forth.

He's five, I say. Five.

I know how fucking old he is.

The kid is scared, I say.

I suppose you told him your name, as well.

I shrug. He broke me down.

I'm so glad you were thinking straight.

That's funny, I say. The only thing worse than a sociopath is a funny sociopath.

Fuck you, Phineas.

And how much do you suppose the kid is worth? I say.

Jude stops, her eyes narrow. A million, easy. Maybe five.

His father is the senator, MacDonald Cody.

Jude shrugs. How did you figure that out?

I've seen the kid before.

Where?

One of Miller's creepy video tapes.

Jude nods. He does enjoy the home video.

What the fuck is going on between you and him? I say.

I told you. I don't want to talk about Miller.

What makes you think Cody has five million lying around?

He's a politician. Fat cats pay a thousand dollars a head to have dinner with him. He's got more dough in his war chest than your average third world country.

I light a cigarette.

Okay, I say. Here's the way I see it. If I try to fuck this up and return the kid to his family before we collect the ransom, you will…what? You'll kill me?

Jude shrugs. Maybe.

That's nice.

Nothing about this is nice, she says.

I shake my head. No shit. Have you read Miller's script?

No, she says. Not really.

Molly has. She read the first draft, I say.

So what? Jude says.

So, she says the kid dies in the second act. He dies, Jude.

He's not going to die.

Then he might as well be comfortable, I say.

How comfortable?

Cozy, I say. I'm going to hit Toys-R-Us, get him some action figures to play with. I'm going to make sure he eats once in a while and I'm going to hang out with him in the afternoons, when we're not shooting this goddamn film.

That sounds like an unhealthy level of attachment, Jude says.

Why don't you come with me? I'll buy you something pretty and pink.

Jude smiles, a glimmer of affection in her eyes.

It might be fun, I say.

Miller owns us, baby. Best not to aggravate him.

I grab her hands. Let's just kill the crazy fucker and get lost.

Jude pulls away, cold. It's not half that easy.

Why not?

Jude takes the cigarette from me and takes a fierce puff. She crosses her arms, backs away from me, her face so miserable I don't recognize her.

Because, she says. I'm kind of married to him.

Bullshit. That's not even funny.

I'm not kidding, she says.

Jude and I sit in silence in the library for almost five minutes. A long time to go flatline with a person who's got your heart in their fist. Miller's library is plush as hell, and I could think of worse places to torture myself. There's a nicely stocked liquor cabinet along one wall, for instance. I pour myself a glass of gin, retreat into a corner and crawl into a leather armchair and smoke one cigarette, then another. Jude's face is very pale. She drifts around the library a minute and I think she's looking for something to hit, really. I shake my head. She is so pretty it's stupid. She climbs the ladder and dives back into *Treasure Island.* One long leg dangling, a curved blade. I watch her turn the pages. Her hands are amazing, I think. Very strong, and elegant as twin birds of prey. A stray lock of hair keeps falling down over her eyes and she brushes it back with a long finger. I stand up and Jude snaps the book shut.

Explain this to me, I say. When, for instance?

Nine years ago, says Jude. After I left the Army. I met him at a casino in Morocco. He was…well, you've seen him. He was powerful, mysterious, he was rich as God. He was the most arrogant man I'd ever met. And he had…certain appetites that appealed to me.

Fucking hell, I say. What are you doing to me?

Back off, she says. You were married once, too. Your wife died under mysterious circumstances and have I ever fucked with you about that?

This shuts me up like a charm. I sip my drink.

Anyway, says Jude. I liked the twisted shit, for a while. And then I got tired of him. I got tired of his lifestyle. Everything was protected by his money. I wanted to get outside and get dirty. I had spent my whole life training to be…what I am. I wanted to work, you know. Miller just wanted me to eat room service and go shopping and be his little psycho playmate, his windup fuck buddy. So, one night when he went to the opera with a client, I got spontaneous and disappeared myself.

twenty-five.

WHAT WAS AND WHAT WILL NEVER BE ARE NOTHING TO ME. My head and heart are upside down. Jude is a married woman. She's married to John Ransom Miller. The way she explained it to me, she got bored with him. She left him but never got around to divorcing him. Why would she bother, she asked. A divorce required paperwork, and paperwork creates a trail. She had simply disappeared, erasing her identity behind her. Jude had been expensively trained by the government to become a fucking shadow in the rain. People generally did not find Jude unless she found them first, and the people she found were generally sorry.

But it's a small world, and six degrees of separation are like a ticking clock. She had never told me about him, and I suppose that should hurt me somehow. Maybe there's something wrong with me but everything I feel right now can be gathered into one cupped hand. I feel the fading rush of being surprised, the stupidity of not knowing, which tastes a little like dogshit in my mouth. The most clear and present thing I feel is the residual echo of Jude's shame and self-hatred. And I am not one to judge. I had been married before I met her too, and I had rarely spoken to her of Lucy. The only difference was that Lucy was dead.

Jude had a sniper's brain, though. She lived in a world that was defined by mathematical probabilities, and I'm sure that in her mind Miller had been as good as dead. The version of her that had been married to him was therefore dead, too. But still, Miller represented a massive loose end, and

Jude did not tolerate loose ends, which made me think she was afraid of him.

The way she told it was flat, unemotional.

She had vanished into the ether and begun freelancing. She had done a few contract hits, but mainly she'd been a hired seeker. If you had wealth and you wanted to recover something that was impossible to find, a stolen Van Gogh, a rare religious artifact, or a military document that didn't officially exist, you hired Jude. She had done very well, living a shadow existence free of relationships, sleeping in posh hotels, working only when she needed to, or when a job appealed to her. Miller had rarely, if ever, crossed her mind. She knew that her husband worked for the Cody family, but she'd never met any of them, never given them any thought. They were public people whose activities were generally aboveboard, and they weren't the kind of people who had occasion to employ her. But one day an obscenely rich drug and weapons trafficker in Texas had hired Jude to find a kidney of an uncommon blood type, and that was how she found me and fell into a relationship. The relationship took her to South America on the run, where she had needed to make money. She had been trained as a field surgeon in the army, and she learned early on that there was good money to be had doing procedures that regular doctors would not do, so she set up shop in Mexico City. I knew this story, of course. I was there, holding the bucket. She performed a couple of expensive fetish amputations for rich Americans who recommended her to their friends, and eventually a very disturbed man who looked like a quarterback gone soft had come to us and paid Jude twenty-five grand to cut off his left hand. That man, as it turned out, happened to be MacDonald Cody, and when he saw Jude on the street in New Orleans he was being groomed by his family to make a run at the senate, and it had been only days before Miller found us.

I find Molly in her bedroom, reading. She has changed into black leather pants and an impossibly small, transparent T-shirt that says pornstar across the tits. I stare at her.

What? she says.

I don't like those pants. You look like Jude.

Why don't you suck my dick?

That's nice. Now you sound like her.

I'm sorry, she says. I'm just trying to get a handle on my character. I don't want her to be too passive.

Uh-huh.

What do you think? she says.

About what?

My character, she says. Do you think she's tough enough?

I close my eyes. Do I think Molly is tough enough? No, not really. Molly is too neurotic and fragile. Molly is sweet but there's something ghostly about her and you get the feeling she's not gonna make it.

Molly stares at me.

I'm sorry, I say. This thing with the kid is making me...uneasy.

Did you see him?

Yes.

How is he?

He's a nice kid. His name is Sam.

Is he okay, though?

He's scared. What the hell do you think?

Molly hesitates. I think he would break my heart.

There is an incessant grinding noise coming from down the hall and suddenly I don't want to talk about the kid anymore. I have a powerful urge to rip off my own head. Or Molly's head. The grinding noise is slowly but surely eating into my spine. I have a beauty of a headache, a whopper. I push through the silver wings to the bathroom and commence to root around in Molly's medicine cabinet for pills. The grinding noise is louder in the bathroom. It's coming through the pipes, it's echoing. I want a muscle relaxer, something in the narcotic family. I want a big glass of whiskey but I don't care to wander around the house anymore so I eat a Valium and two aspirins and chase them with a chewable vitamin C.

What the fuck is that noise? I say.

What noise?

That grinding noise down the hall.

Oh, she says. Huck and Jeremy are constructing something in the dining room. We're shooting the dinner party scene in a few hours.

Fabulous. I sit in the green chair and close my eyes. Then open them. What dinner party scene?

Molly frowns. I think it's one of the new scenes John added to the script.

Brief, awkward silence. What color would they be? says Molly.

I hold my head. What color would what be? I say.

Those Nazi lampshades. Do you think they would be pink or yellow? What?

You know. The Nazis made lampshades from the skin of death camp victims, supposedly.

I stare at her, helpless. What the fuck are you talking about?

It's a line from a Sylvia Plath poem.

Okay.

Do you like poetry? she says.

No. I don't like poetry.

Why not?

I don't know. Because I'm empty inside. Because I have a headache.

But you're such a good kisser.

Have you been talking to Jude?

No, she says. Why?

Because Jude has a funny theory about murderers and poets being the best kissers and now I wonder if you and she are only pretending to dislike each other.

Molly stares at me. Are you a murderer?

I have never kissed you, I say.

Anyway, she says. Pink or yellow?

I don't understand this conversation.

Molly rolls over and stares at me. I'm reading lines from the script. You and I have a scene later where we discuss Sylvia Plath.

Oh, I say. Of course.

Molly smiles at me and she looks so sweet and normal I feel insane. I cover my eyes with my hands. I try to crush my eyes into my skull.

Are you okay? she says.

No, I don't think so.

Molly sighs. I think John just wants us to go mad and kill each other.

Long beat.

He's succeeding, I say. And those lampshades would definitely be yellow.

The grinding noise stops, mercifully. Then immediately resumes. I light a cigarette and notice that my hands are twitching.

I don't know, says Molly. I think they would be pink.

Molly, I say. I have to get out of the house.

The grinding?

The grinding.

Let's go somewhere, she says.

Do you want to go shopping with me?

Where? she says.

I explain that I want to get the boy some action figures, that if he has his own little army of five-inch superheroes to wreak imaginary mayhem with, maybe he won't be lonely. Molly kisses me, a quick darting kiss on the mouth and I remember something my redneck baseball coach once told me, perverse but true. Be kind to dogs and children, he said. Women love that shit.

And so we take the motorcycle across town to a Toys-R-Us.

It's an American afternoon, by god.

The parking lot is a shiny wasteland of family cars and minivans and I wish the sun were not so bright. I wish the sun would fuck off for a while. The statistics claim that people in the Northwest kill themselves at a much higher rate than those in any other region, presumably because of the endless rainfall. But it seems to me that the opposite should be true, that the unfortunate souls who are confronted day after day by the glaring sun would be the ones most likely to reach for the sleeping pills. The sun is neither flattering nor sympathetic. The average American is afflicted with some combination of bad skin and bad hair, bad posture and bad shoes. Bad habits and bad genes and bad taste and bad fucking luck and the sun seeks out such flaws with the cool, detached efficiency of a sniper.

Just ramble down to the beach on Labor Day weekend. Take a good look around.

Once inside the store, I relax a bit. There is music in the air—the theme song from the recent Winnie-the-Pooh movie featuring Tigger, a happy wacky little tune about the semi-charmed life that is just perfect for bouncing and therefore perfect for Tigger. But the lyrics are not so cheerful, however. I may be ignorant about contemporary poetry, but it seems to me that the song is about the perilous highs and lows of being a crystal meth addict. And this puts a smile on my face. I turn to Molly and she too is smiling. It is one of those goofy moments that needs no words and I feel like my head will soon be in a box.

I take Molly's hand and we literally scamper through the place. Down the gloomy aisle of stuffed animals waiting to be loved and past the freakishly pink Barbie aisle, then past the brightly colored plastic swing sets and sandboxes shaped like turtles and bumble bees. Past the gleaming rows of bicycles and tricycles and red wagons and midget electric cars. Turn a corner and come upon the action figure aisle. I stop and suck in my breath with reverence. This is a kid's promised land.

Molly laughs at the expression on my face.

I reach for a shopping cart and start loading up on little role models. Explaining to Molly as I go that Batman is indispensable. The Dark Knight, baby. Spider-Man is a nerd and talks a lot of trash but he has the coolest powers. Wolverine is your ultimate psycho and what kid doesn't want adamantine claws. The Silver Surfer is the mad philosopher, the cursed poet, Hamlet on a magic surfboard. And then there's Ghost Rider. Obscure as hell but I was always partial to him because he has a flaming skull and he's not always a nice guy. Ghost Rider is sometimes a bad guy, and this is an important lesson for a kid to learn. I pass over Superman because he was such a bore. He was like the president of the student council. And he hung out with Aquaman, over there in the Justice League. Now there was a worthless ninny if ever there was one. Aquaman talked to the fishes. He was handy during an oil spill or a tropical storm, maybe. But if somebody was robbing a bank, where the fuck was Aquaman?

Women, says Molly. What about some women?

Of course. I immediately reach for Catwoman.

Catwoman? says Molly. The femme fatale from hell?

Or heaven, I say. It's just a matter of perspective.

How so?

If she's handing your lunch to you, then maybe you don't like Catwoman. And rightly so. But if she's giving you a superfreaky blowjob in the back of the Batmobile, then she's your best friend.

Uh huh. Does the Batmobile even have a backseat? says Molly.

I scratch my head.

And does a five-year-old need to contemplate such things?

No. I guess not.

Now we argue about female superheroes, briefly and with a fair amount of giggling. I am not wavering on Catwoman so Molly insists on Jean Grey, on the grounds that she's essentially the opposite of Catwoman.

Jean Grey is an intellectual, says Molly. And she doesn't generally flash her tits.

Okay, I say. Wolverine likes her, anyway.

I throw in a sweet Batmobile with a lot of high-tech gear and a few villains, explaining to Molly that superheroes tend to lose their will to live without bad guys to tangle with. And then we are on our way to the cash registers when I am temporarily mesmerized by the Hot Wheels aisle and I flash back to the elaborate, multileveled, and structurally unsound metropolis that I constructed from those plastic orange tracks as a boy.

The silence of snow falling outside.

The oppressive smell of garlic and mushrooms and red pepper. There was spaghetti for dinner and now my mother and father linger in the kitchen to finish a bottle of wine. Their voices rise and fall and slip easily from flirtatious to hostile and back to tender and estranged and all the while it is impossible to say whether or not they are happy.

And here comes Carly Simon on the record player, her voice hoarse and splintered by static and fine scratches in the vinyl. You're so vain, I bet you think this song is about you.

This song was the soundtrack of my childhood, and I often wonder about its long-term effects.

You're so vain.

I am maybe seven years old, sitting on the floor of my room in cowboy pajamas. I am surrounded by the small orange universe of my own design and even though I lack the necessary vocabulary, I am no doubt contemplating the laws of physics, the inevitability of inertia and gravity. I place a very small turtle on one of the orange tracks, the kind of turtle that cost ten cents at the pet store and usually died within a week. I select one of my fastest cars, a blue Corvette. I position the car at the top of the track and hold it there a moment, watching the turtle wiggle along the track. I release the blue Corvette and it drops straight down, as if falling down the sheer edge of a cliff, and crashes into the turtle with a nice meaty thud.

The turtle is knocked from the track and is dazed but not killed.

My parents are arguing now, or maybe not. Maybe one of them is seducing the other.

I return the turtle to the track and reach for another car. I reach for a glossy black Aston Martin and I am stupidly pleased to see that the cars are still exactly the same, composed not of plastic but actual metal and perfect to the tiny detail. The packaging has not changed and the Hot Wheels logo has not changed and a single car costs just a dollar, which seems to me a reasonable level of inflation over so many years.

Vertigo, dislocation. You're so fucking vain.

Hey, says Molly. You okay?

What?

She takes the little car from me.

Don't I look okay?

No, she says. You look like you're going to cry, or throw up.

I'm not sure how to explain what happens next, but I reckon my head is still halfway morphed into the inarticulate seven-year-old cowboy-pajama-wearing version of Phineas and the only reasonable way that a boy can show a girl how much he likes her is to hurt her somehow.

Boy pokes girl, pinches girl, pulls girl's hair.

Boy makes girl cry and everyone says oh, well. He just likes you. And how many battered wives and girlfriends soon to be murdered will stare at you with puffy, blackened white marble eyes and insist that their abusers love them. The words like slush from their mouths, because their lips are blackened.

Anyway. I regard Molly for a moment, then hit her.

What the fuck?

Molly backs away, her hand touching lightly the place just above her heart where my fist struck her. The blow was not terribly hard. But it was not gentle. And just as I am about to apologize, to attempt some lame explanation about Carly Simon and Hot Wheels, she hits me back. Her fist catches me like a hammer below the eye and I'm going to have a ripe blue shiner come morning. Molly holds her fist out away from her body and looks at it, fairly horrified.

Oh, my god. Oh god, she says. I'm sorry.

No, I say. That was the perfect thing to do.

I hold my arms out wide. It seems like the perfect moment for a slow, zooming close-up.

twenty-six.

INTERIOR, HOUSE OF MILLER. NIGHT.

Bright lights come up on the dining room. Jude sits at the head of a long, carved black table that has been placed on a raised stage of rough, unfinished wood. The table is polished and bare except for a single unlit candle in the center. Jude's hands lie flat on the black surface before her and she stares straight ahead. She wears a white, sheer blouse with elaborate ruffles around a plunging neckline. Her hair is loose. I stand in the doorway where she can't see me.

Pan the room, slowly. There is no furniture other than the table and chairs and the skeletal light stands. The windows have been covered with heavy black shades. Huck is crouched in a corner. He wears a tool belt and appears to be repairing or modifying an electrical outlet. He glances briefly at me and winks.

Jude is now standing. She sighs, impatient. She takes a book of matches from her pants pocket. The table is so long and wide that she cannot easily reach the candle and so she crawls slowly across it to light the candle and then remains there, stretched on her belly and staring at the flame.

My skin tingles and Molly appears at my shoulder, dressed as before.

Are you ready? she says.

No.

It's okay, she says. It will be okay.

We enter together, then separate and go to sit at opposite sides of the table. Jude lies between us, still staring at the candle. She doesn't speak or acknowledge us. I am restless and soon light a cigarette, flicking my ashes on the wooden stage. Molly leans back in her chair and puts her feet up, crossing one leg over the other, the heels of her boots striking the table like hammers.

What's on the menu, then? I say.

I don't know, says Jude. You should ask the lady of the house.

Who is the lady of this house? says Molly.

That's become rather unclear, says Jude. Hasn't it.

Everyone shut up, please. This from Miller, entering.

He wears a gray wool suit and tie and an incongruous black top hat. In one hand he carries a flat cardboard box. In the other, what appears to be a small birdcage covered with a black hood. He stares for a moment at Jude, who remains on the table. She yawns, as if sleepy. Miller sits down and opens the box to remove a stack of bound, photocopied scripts. He tosses them around the table. Molly takes a copy and begins flipping through it. I pick up my script but I don't open it.

This is the final draft? says Molly.

For now, yes.

Then you must know which of us is going to die.

The final scene has been removed from your copies, he says.

Of course, says Jude. Her voice very dry, like salt.

What's in the cage? I say.

It's a surprise, he says.

I don't see a dinner party scene, says Molly.

Ah, says Miller. That's because there isn't one.

What's going on, John? says Jude.

Tonight's shoot has been cancelled, he says.

Why? she says.

Jude, he says. Get off the table. You look like a tramp.

Jude scowls at him, then slithers slowly to the other end and takes her seat.

She stares at Miller for a beat, then lowers her eyes and sullenly picks up her script. One copy remains on the table. Jeremy is behind me. I can feel him back there and I have a feeling the camera is pointed directly at my head, like a gun. I would love to see a swinging, upside down shot of the room that slides out of focus and returns to focus on the back of my head before cutting away. Miller laughs softly and turns to look at the door as Daphne enters, leading Samwise by the hand. The boy wears blue and white striped pajamas. He is frightened, numb.

What's going on? I say.

You fucking psycho, says Jude. You've let him see my face.

You're his mother, says Miller. He's got to see your face.

Jude is seething. I am not his mother.

Who's the father? says Jeremy.

Miller frowns. That's not your line, boy.

Molly reads from the script, irritated. Who's the father?

I am, says Miller. Or I might have been.

This is a scene? I say.

I thought we weren't shooting tonight, says Molly.

Fuck this, I say. I'm not playing this game.

The boy needs you, says Miller, softly.

The boy, I say. The boy needs to go home. He needs to sleep in his own bed.

Why are you doing this? says Jude.

Miller shrugs. I have a theory that actors need to be surprised now and then. Besides, the boy has to get used to being in front of the camera.

The boy is terrified, says Molly.

What's your point?

John, for god's sake. You can't make a kidnapped boy memorize dialogue.

Of course not, says Miller. He will be allowed to improvise.

How is that going to work? I say.

Witness, he says.

Miller removes the black hood from the cage to reveal a small brown rabbit. Now he takes off his top hat and places it on the table, upside down.

Do you believe in magic, Sam?

The boy looks at me and I shake my head, fiercely.

No, he says.

Interesting, says Miller. I thought all little boys believed in magic. Would you like to see this rabbit disappear?

The boy shrugs one shoulder. Then nods. Daphne reaches down and strokes the hair out of his eyes. Miller takes the rabbit from the cage and places it inside the hat. He waves his right hand slowly over the hat, muttering incoherently. Everyone watches him, curious to see what will happen. Miller counts to five, then turns the hat over. The rabbit falls out of the hat and crouches on the table, shaking.

Tharn, I say. The rabbit is tharn.

Miller feigns surprise, waving his hands.

I know what he's going to do before he does it, but I can't stop him. I sit frozen, my hands like stones on the table. Miller picks up the rabbit with both hands and strokes its head once, twice. Then without changing his expression, tries and fails to break the rabbit's neck. Blood sprays from its nose, and the rabbit begins to scream like nothing I have ever heard.

Molly cries out loud, incoherent.

Goddamn it, says Jude. Goddamn it, John.

She picks up the crippled, screeching rabbit and takes it out of frame, to the kitchen. The screaming abruptly stops. Sam still clings to Daphne's hand. His face is so white he looks as if he will faint. A puddle of urine appears at his feet.

Motherfucker, I say.

I come out of my chair and hurry to the boy, growling at Daphne to get the hell away from him. I lift the boy up by his armpits and hold him close to my chest.

I whisper to him, my voice low. Okay, you're okay.

Jeremy moves in with the camera, a slow zoom.

I look up and Miller has taken a gun from his breast pocket. His face still bloody.

What are you doing, Poe? he says.

I stare at Miller. I pray God strikes him with boils.

This gun contains live rounds, says Miller. If you're interested in such matters.

Are we done? I say. Are we done with this scene?

The boy is heavy, so heavy he could crush you but at the same time he weighs nothing. I take him down the hall to the bathroom. He's trembling, a little. His face pressed against my neck. His pajamas are wet and now my shirt is wet but I don't want him to think I notice. I hold him close. I tell him he's cool.

You're cool, little man. You're okay.

Into the bathroom and I close the door. The same black-and- white tiles. The light over my head is bright as the sun on snow and I wonder where the camera is.

The camera. The camera is obscure.

I ease the boy down onto the fuzzy black bathmat. He doesn't look up. He doesn't look into my eyes. His hands on my shoulders. He stands with his feet wide apart and I notice how small his feet are, smaller than my hands. His feet just about kill me. He doesn't look up. I can hear him breathing.

Do you want to take a bath? I say.

He doesn't answer at first. Then nods, fiercely.

He doesn't want to let go of my shoulders so I pull him over to the clawfoot tub with me. I turn the hot and cold taps until the water feels warm but not too warm. There is a bottle of cucumber-flavored bubble bath on a little shelf next to the tub and I dump some of that in.

The water turns pleasantly green.

Does your dad ever call you Sam I am?

The boy nods again.

Would you, I say. Would you could you in a box?

He stands there, breathing.

Not with a fox, he says. Not in a box.

The tub fills slowly and the room is white with steam. The boy and I are quoting everything we can remember from *Green Eggs and Ham,* and making up new ones. Not in a boat, not with a goat. Not on a slippery slope. Not at the end of a rope. Not on a train by god, and never in the rain. Not in the house of pain. I ask him if he wants to take his bath now. I know it won't kill him but I hate for him to stand around in pajamas soaked with urine. I have been in those shoes. I have stood in my own piss and it's not cool. The boy nods and says he needs some privacy.

Yeah, I say. That's right. Everybody needs privacy sometimes.

Sam looks up at me now and I see how red his eyes are, how dirty his face is. I want to wash his face but I don't know if he will let me.

The action figures. The action figures are in Molly's room.

Hey, I say. Do you want some friends to play with in the tub?

Sam nods. Okay, he says. What kind of friends.

How about some good guys, I say.

He shakes his head. I don't want any bad guys.

I leave him to undress and go down the hall to Molly's room. She is sitting on the bed, smoking a cigarette and agitated as hell. I ignore her. The toys are in the green chair. I dropped them there, before we went into the dining room. I dig through the bag and come up with Batman and the Silver Surfer. D.C. and Marvel and therefore not of the same universe but a fine combination nonetheless. Vengeance and poetry, the stuff of life. What else is there. I rip the packages open, careful not to drop Batman's grappling hook. I wonder if the Surfer's little surfboard will float and now I notice that Molly is staring at me.

Molly is staring bullets at me.

What?

I don't know.

How is he? I say.

Yeah, she says.

He pissed himself. He's not happy.

Molly wraps her arms around herself. She's pretty, so pretty. I wonder what it's like to be pretty. If it gives you strength. If it pulls you under the surface, somehow. Molly begins to rock back and forth and I know she needs me to talk to her, to sit on the bed with her and make sense of things but she's going to have to wait.

Wait, I say.

Back down the hall and I have a feeling that Jude is lurking, waiting for me in the shadows. Jude will soon jump out at me and stick her tongue in my ear and say something freaky. Jude is always lurking somewhere, lately. But there's no sign of her. I can't smell her and instead I run into Huck. He's crouched in the hall, a beer in each hand.

Hey, he says. Hey, man.

I stop and stare down at him. Huck is a big man but he manages to shrink into the shadows. He lifts one of the beers to his mouth and drinks. Then wipes his mouth on his sleeve.

Hey, I say. Are you okay?

No, he says. I'm about two thousand miles from okay.

Where is Jeremy?

The fuck I know. He went off with Jude somewhere, and Daphne.

Nice, I say. That gives me something nasty to think about.

Huck shivers. Uh-huh.

What about Miller?

The fucking Lizard Room, he says. Feeding another rabbit to his snakes, probably.

He's watching us.

Fuck him. You want a beer?

No, I say. Thanks. The kid is waiting for me.

Huck crumples the empty beer can into a jagged knot and tosses it into a potted plant. He shakes his head and says, you tell that boy to keep the faith.

The boy is swimming in the bathtub when I return, the bubbles around him like fallen clouds. His head comes out of the water and he is slick and dark as a seal. I offer him the action figures and he takes them from me, murmuring. Batman he's familiar with. But I have to give him the historical lowdown on the Silver Surfer. He listens intently, nodding. He frowns when I tell him how lost and heartbroken the Surfer was and there is a brief, contemplative silence between us.

Does his surfboard float? he says.

I smile. That's the question, isn't it?

Sam doesn't want to wash his hair or his face but I figure he's wallowing in enough cucumber bubblewater to purify a pig, so I leave him alone. He asks me to stay in the bathroom with him until he's done with his bath. I tell him not to worry. I'm not going anywhere. I sit on the floor with my back against the wall, watching him play with Batman and the Surfer.

The surfboard does float.

It tends to fall over when the Surfer is actually standing on it, but the boy doesn't mind. He's got Batman hanging upside down from one of the taps, his legs tangled up in the cord of his own grappling hook. The boy is narrating.

Help me, says Batman.

I'm too sad to help you, says the Surfer.

Help me. I'm drowning over here.

Okay, okay.

I smoke a cigarette, dropping ashes into the toilet. I know that I shouldn't smoke around him but this has been a long fucking day and I'm waiting for the boy to ask me about the rabbit. I want to tell him the rabbit wasn't real. It was a fake rabbit and I know it looked real and maybe that's why it was so disturbing but I know this is bullshit.

If you lie to a child, he will smell it.

He will smell the untruth coming from your skin like the sweet smell of rot and he may accept it or he may not, but he won't thank you for it.

Footsteps and there's a knock at the door, soft. The boy is spooked and disappears underwater. I figure it's Molly at the door, come to tell me something. But when I open the door it's Jude and I guess she sees my face change. She hands me a glass of scotch and a clean T-shirt for the boy. Her lips move to form the words I'm sorry and she touches my hand before turning away. I shake my head. Her talent for slipping and sliding between evil and kindness is extraordinary. I tell myself that everyone is this way, that most people are just very clumsy about it. I take a small, medicinal swallow of the scotch and it feels good, it goes down like liquid smoke and I am surprised to realize this is my first drink of the day. I thump the side of the tub with my knuckles and smile, remembering how I used to lie underwater with my eyes shut tight, the faraway echoes stretching in my skull.

Knock, knock.

The boy comes up for air and I tell him it's time for bed.

He convinces me to let him stay in the bath for five more minutes. Five more minutes. He says it like a mantra and I imagine he has had this conversation with his father a thousand times.

Five minutes, ten.

I am not too concerned about bedtime, you know. What difference does it make. The boy is a hostage. It's not like he has a soccer game tomorrow. And after a while, he tells me that the water is cold, that his skin is getting a million wrinkles. I pull him out of the tub and wrap him in one of the big black towels. I offer to help him with his T-shirt but he says he doesn't need any help because he's five and a half.

I'm big, he says.

Okay, I say.

I watch him wrestle with the T-shirt. He has a little trouble negotiating the second armhole but he sticks with it. The shirt is on backwards but he doesn't care. His hair is sticking up all over the place and he looks like a little madman and when he smiles at me, I am tempted to take him to bed with Molly and me but I'm not sure this is a good idea and I know that Jude wouldn't like it.

I take him through the library and down the stairs, taking care not to clue him in to the workings of the secret passage. This has to do with instinct, or respect for Jude. I tuck Sam into bed and he promptly burrows into the corner with the stuffed bear. He arranges the pillows around himself, like a fort. He's got Batman in one hand, the Silver Surfer in the other. Vengeance and poetry. There are no books to read and I wonder if I should go up to the library and look for a copy of *The Lord of The Rings,* but the boy's eyes are heavy already and I don't want to leave him. I flip on the television, thinking cartoons will give him pleasant dreams, colorful and two-dimensional and easily resolved. If he was my son, I might lie down next to him and let the sound of my heartbeat ease his mind. But he's not my son and I am reluctant to get too close. I don't want to freak him out so I sit down on the floor beside his bed and halfway through *Johnny Quest* the boy is asleep and snoring softly.

twenty-seven.

MOLLY'S ROOM, NIGHT.

I lie on her puffy white bed, smoking a cigarette. I wear filthy blue jeans and nothing else. I am exhausted and pissed off about the rabbit, but I could be worse. I have a fresh glass of scotch balanced on my chest, my third of the evening. I am staring dumbly at the little television across the room. The sound is low but I can just make out the numbing dialogue of a sitcom involving a gang of attractive white people and their innocuous homosexual black pal. I flip around until I land on CNN, hoping to find something about Sam.

On the bed beside me is Miller's script. *The Velvet.*

Yeah.

I don't know what I think of that title. Too oblique, too nihilistic, or too esoteric or something but it's not my problem. *The Velvet* is Miller's baby. Molly has left the room, to get into character. She wants to run a scene with me and of course she already has her lines down. I have agreed to cooperate, but I'm going to read my lines from the script in a voice composed of discarded feathers and broken glass.

Molly enters, wearing white underpants and a little white tank top. Her hair is wet. She's carrying an open bottle of red wine and an orange. She tosses the orange on the bed beside me. Takes a drink of wine and wipes her mouth on her wrist. She offers the bottle to me and I shake my head. I put the glass of scotch aside and sit up, the script in hand.

What's the orange for, I say.
    I have a vitamin deficiency, she says. I'm getting rickets.
    That would be scurvy.
    What?
    You're getting scurvy. And deaf, too.
    Oh, shut up.
    Have you seen a doctor?

I toss the script aside because I remember how it goes. This scene is based on an actual conversation between Jude and me, so long ago that I feel sick with loss. I take a shallow breath, realizing that Jude must have at some point collaborated with Miller on this thing. Molly ignores me, bends to pick up a shirt from the floor. She smells it, apparently decides it's relatively clean and begins to rub her hair dry with it. I watch her for a while.

Isn't that my shirt? I say.
    Yeah, she says. I already used my shirt to dry my poor body.
    Oh.
    Why don't you buy some towels? Your houseguests might appreciate it.
    I take the shirt from her. I rub her head gently with it.
    What houseguests? I don't have houseguests.
    You have me.
    Well. I don't know where they sell towels.
    They? she says. Who would they be?
    You know. The household luxuries people.
    Molly laughs. Phineas…towels are not luxuries.
    They are if you don't have them.
    You have sheets, she says. You have nice, clean sheets.
    Yeah, well. My girlfriend bought the sheets. Before, all I had was a dusty mattress and a sleeping bag. She said I would never get laid unless I had real sheets.

Molly's hair is dry. I toss the shirt aside and lean over, reaching for my scotch. Molly bites me on the shoulder. Then we wrestle for a minute and I let her pin me to the bed, or so it goes in the script. Molly is wiry and strong, though. She doesn't need a lot of mercy from me.

Your girlfriend was right, she says. Wasn't she?

There is a long silence, which Molly interprets as me being lost. I am lost, but not in the way she thinks. Molly sighs and takes a drink of wine and her lips come away dark as berries.

I don't know, I say. This was a nice sleeping bag, a mummy bag.

She rolls her eyes. Why don't you ask this girlfriend to buy you some dishes, too. Wine glasses, for instance.

I have coffee cups, I say.

Two coffee cups. One of them is dirty. The other one has a plant growing in it.

At this point, the script calls for Molly to nonchalantly remove her tank top. I am weirdly nervous about this. Because while Molly and I have been slowly, painfully seducing each other for days now, and it seems reasonable to assume that any day she might in fact remove her top, there is a sense of detachment and hostility between us that seems to arise directly from the script. Anyway, after slight pause, Molly shrugs and pulls the tank top over her head and she is exposed to me.

The script now suggests that I fondle one of her breasts as if I'm preoccupied, distracted. I am supposed to randomly tweak and pinch her nipple between thumb and finger as if fiddling with the tuning dial on a car radio. This seems rude but I give it a whirl. Her nipples are hard. She tolerates my affection for a minute, then slaps my hand away.

What is that, she says. Foreplay?

I shove her off me, gently. Then pick up the orange and begin to peel it.

Why do you have a vitamin deficiency?

Because I never eat vegetables, she says. Because I'm anemic.

Yeah, I say. Maybe you should lay off the coke.

Phineas, she says. Don't...

I feed her a fleshy chunk of orange.

Okay, I say. What kind of towels should I buy?

Thick ones, she says.

What color?

Dark colors. Something that won't show blood.

Of course.

Then you will be the perfect man.

I feed her more of the orange. Molly nibbles at my fingers and I notice a flicker of electricity in my chest.

By your definition, I say. The perfect man is one who has clean sheets and plenty of nice, thick towels that don't show blood.

That's right, says Molly.

She begins to giggle. I feed her the last of the orange and juice runs to my wrist. Molly licks at it, then kisses my hand, sucks at my fingers. Her mouth moves to my throat.

Jesus, I say.

What's this girlfriend of yours like?

I glance at the script, suddenly uncomfortable...She's like a hummingbird, I say.

Does she drink sugar water?

She vibrates, I say. She moves so fast you can barely see her.

And should I be jealous of her? she says.

You, I say. You're a blur. You're already gone.

This is the end of the scene but I slip my hands under her ass and lift her onto my lap again. Molly fumbles with the buttons of my jeans and I think I'm going to come any minute. I touch her through her panties and she's wet, she's melting. Molly pulls my cock loose and begins to run her hand up and down, barely touching me. I push her panties to the side and slip my fingers inside her and now she moves her hips, pushing her pubic bone against my hand and one of us is groaning and then suddenly we pull away from each other.

Whoa. What the hell was that?

Drama, she says. Her voice is bitter.

What's wrong with you?

You, she says. You still haven't kissed me.

Bright pocket of silence.

That dialogue, I say. What a load of shit.

I think it's romantic, she says. Or it would be, if it were real.

It's embarrassing, I say. It's pap.

What is pap, exactly? she says.

I stare at her and realize I am not sure. Pap is a sticky, sweet mucus type substance the color of pus. Jesus, I don't know. Pap is fucking pap.

Well, she says. I think he sounds like you. Your character sounds just like you.

Molly folds her arms across her chest. I shove myself back into my pants, rather grimly. I sit beside her, listening to my rapid heart. I want to scream. I lean over the side of the bed for the bottle of wine. I take a long, greedy drink and pass her the bottle. She lifts it to her mouth and stops, staring at the television.

Oh fuck, she says.

There is a picture of Sam on the screen.

…Samwise Cody, five years old…presumed to be kidnapped… blond hair, brown eyes. Forty-nine pounds, with no identifiable scars or birthmarks…missing two days now.

The camera cuts away from photo of Sam to footage of his father at a press conference. Distraught, unshaven. He appears to be unable to speak.

…is the son of MacDonald Cody, popular U.S. senator from California and one of the power players in the Democratic party, figures to be a factor in the next presidential election…. There has been no ransom demand, no contact from kidnappers at all.

I look at Molly. The bottle of wine still tucked between her legs, forgotten. One hand over her mouth. Her hair still wet and she is naked, lovely. But I feel nothing resembling desire. I feel nothing much at all.

This is wrong, I say. So fucking wrong.

It will be over soon, says Molly.

I sink back and yes there is rage in me but not enough. Pale rain clouds far-away and they may not get here anytime soon. They may pass by, they may fade away. I remember nothing but ailments. Impatience, affliction, and morbid restlessness. I cut my hair last night and saw your face. I saw the uselessness of the organism, the sequence of maladies. Disorder of the stomach and love letters amount to threads. The imperfection. The diffi-culty in forming ordinary vowel sounds. The sleeve of the female engages threads of the male. This is the hum of empty space. This is a photograph of a boy no longer a boy. Please, don't. Don't interrupt me. Badly drawn stick figures and the voice of another is like a forgotten blue T-shirt on the floor. He came inside me and said he didn't mean to. This room has such poor light. Why did you buy an orchid of all things. Because you were not home. Because the phone just rings.

The light touch of rose petals on my shoulder.

I am asleep, or nearly so. I'm dreaming in my own voice. This can't be good for anybody. Molly has turned the light off and she lies half-naked beside me, not quite touching me. But I can feel her breath on my skin and the rose petals might have been her lips. The television is still on and I am grateful, because the silence can be too much to bear. I might have been dreaming but I thought I heard the rest of the news. The sports, the weather. Partly cloudy tomorrow. Partly, partly. Uncommonly hot. A train wreck, brutal traffic. Power lines down. Forest fires and earthquake weather. Fol-lowed by a story about a monkey. A monkey has apparently escaped from the Oakland Zoo. A three-year-old ring-tailed lemur by the name of Casper.

And then in the dark hours, the following conversation. Awake or dreaming. Drunk and still dreaming and who is speaking I can't say.

He could be mine. He's the right age, anyway. And he does look like me.

Are you talking to yourself?

But a lot of guys look like me. I have an ordinary face and god knows who else she was fucking.

Who.

The whore with the ruined face.

Jude, you mean.

You're not the father. You're dreaming.

I'm not dreaming.

Wake up. Please wake up.

I could teach him to ride a bike, to throw a baseball. I could buy a new car, a family car. I could buy a big American car with airbags and we could take him fishing. I can see the three of us in a little boat, laughing and eating sandwiches on white bread.

Three people in a family car doesn't make a family.

But it looks real. It looks like a family.

Do you even know how to fish?

Hah. I could teach him to be a fisher of men.

Who am I speaking to?

Disconnected. Drunk and still dreaming.

I wake up and my chest is slick with sweat. Molly snores softly beside me and there's no way I'm going back to sleep right now. I get up and pull on a pair of jeans. The clock says four a.m. but that means nothing. It would be useful, though, to explore the house a little during the wee hours. Maybe I can find something to eat in the kitchen.

I check on the boy first. He sleeps in a fierce ball, one corner of his pillow clutched in his fist. His face is peaceful, his cheeks rosy. I can see his eyes flickering behind their almost transparent lids. I touch his hair and move on.

I turn the corner into the kitchen and stop when I hear voices. Jeremy and Daphne are in there, making out like teenagers. Which they are, basically. Jeremy sits in a wooden chair and she straddles his lap. Her tank top is pushed up and I catch a very brief glimpse of her breasts by moonlight and they are still amazing. Jeremy is whispering sweetly into her ear and she is stroking his hair. I slip away without them noticing me and I find myself smiling. For some reason, I feel like the world might still be okay.

I drift down to the Lizard Room and just being in there gives me the creeps. The televisions are blank and lifeless and I am tempted to screw around with the controls to see if I can find anything on the monitors. But this idea makes me uncomfortable, like the smell of vomit. And I know that I would fuck something up and then Miller would know I was in here. Then I notice a flicker of green lights coming from a cabinet door that hangs open. I shrug and take a look inside to find stereo equipment. The green light is coming from the digital meter that indicates the recording levels. I don't hear anything, though. I adjust the volume and fiddle with various controls and I get nothing. I find a pair of small headphones and put them on and Jude's voice fills my head. I sink into crash position, hands over my ears.

Jude- Don't fucking touch me. I don't want to be touched right now.

Miller- You're pathetic. You must be the only narcissist on the planet with a face that would make children run away screaming.

Jude- You can't hurt me. You can't hurt me.

Miller- I don't want to.

Jude- You're such a liar.

Miller- What do you think Poe is doing downstairs, with Molly? Do you think he's fucked her yet?

Jude- Doesn't matter. His heart is his problem.

Miller- For now, anyway.

Jude- He won't let you do it, you know.

Miller- What?

Jude- He won't let you kill that boy.

Miller- I'm writing this picture. He's got no control.

Jude- Believe me or not. I don't care.

Miller- What about you? Do you think he will let me kill you?

Jude- I don't know. He might have no choice.

Miller- Because I will, baby. I will break you in half.

Forever, it seems. I wait in the dark forever but she never answers him.

twenty-eight.

MORNING FINDS YOU, NEVER FAILS. I sit on the porch with a mug of black coffee laced with Irish whiskey. Miller may be a bastard, but he keeps a very respectable liquor cabinet. It's early yet and the sky is white with fine threads of pink, like quartz. I light a cigarette and turn my attention to the scene unfolding in the driveway before me.

Jeremy and Daphne are in the back seat of the silver Mustang. Jeremy is naked. Daphne wears a bright red bra, and from what I can tell, nothing else. They are fighting, or fucking. It's violent, whatever you choose to call it. The car is trembling. Huck is crouched low on the driver's side, filming them through the open window.

I can see my reflection in the car window, the white sky endless behind me and superimposed upon my reflection hangs one of Daphne's skinny legs, a pale yellow question mark dangling over the front seat. Jeremy's dark shoulders, lunging. Now the sound of masculine grunting and a low, whining scream that must be Daphne achieving orgasm. Or Daphne's dramatic portrayal of Daphne achieving orgasm.

Miller comes out onto the porch, his face sliced open by a hard little smile.
    Do you mind telling me what's going on? he says.
    I glance at him, amused. Looks like Jeremy and Daphne are shooting

a love scene.

Was this your idea?

Nah. I came out to have a cigarette and Jeremy said he needs me to be his brother. His character just got out of jail or something. And I'm not too happy to see him.

His character? says Miller.

Yeah. Jeremy says it will crank the tension up a notch.

This character of his, says Miller. He's meant to be your brother?

I know. He doesn't look much like me, I say.

Miller scowls. Yeah. He's too good-looking.

That's true, I say.

And Jeremy wrote this scene?

He conceived it. The dialogue will be improvised, apparently.

Miller is so irritated that his mouth opens and his lips twist speechless in the breeze and this amuses the hell out of me but I don't get a chance to enjoy it as there is a sudden flash of gray and black fur cutting across my peripheral vision and out of nowhere there is a monkey crouched on the hood of the Mustang, a ring-tailed lemur idly chewing on one long black finger. This can only be Casper, the fugitive monkey. I open my mouth, then close it. My only coherent thought is that the monkey is probably not safe here.

I'm a son of a bitch, says Miller. That's great video.

Huck turns to get a shot of the monkey.

It's a Disney moment, I think. Everyone loves God's noble creatures.

The monkey screams and leaps away as Daphne's head comes splashing through the Mustang's passenger side rear window with a rain of sparkling glass. It seems like it takes forever for the glass to stop falling and Daphne's head flops hard against the side of the car.

Thrilled. I can see by Miller's face that he's weirdly thrilled, and so am I.

But I need to be angry. I prepare to improvise. Daphne's head is bleeding but I don't move. Huck is coming around the car to get a close-up of Daphne through the broken window but then he is distracted by me. He zooms on my face. He wants a shot of my reaction.

What is my reaction?

Vaguely horrified, now. I scroll through my consciousness and there is little else. Detached spontaneous compassion, perhaps. The thrill is gone. I pollute my lungs with smoke and contemplate how my behavior is affected by the presence of the camera, how I am holding the cigarette the way I imagine James Dean might hold it, if he were hungover. But upon reflection I decide I am more interested in Casper the monkey than Daphne's bleeding head. Daphne's not going to die and anyway she agreed to this shit, yeah. But head wounds are tricky. The blood is running freely down her neck and her hair is thick with it and she will probably need stitches but I have a feeling it's just a minor laceration.

Anyway.

Huck cuts away from me, to the interior of the car. Miller stands behind me, cursing.

Did you see the monkey? says Jeremy.

Daphne touches the back of her head and her hand comes away red.

Did you? he says.

Daphne scrambles into a ball against the rear door, away from him. She makes herself as small as possible. Jeremy hops out of the driver's side, humming to himself. He is naked and evidently pleased with himself. He comes around to the front of the Mustang and peers closely at the hood.

Monkey footprints, he says. How fucking cool is that?

He cocks his right hand into an imaginary gun and fires several shots into the sky, then raises both hands over his head. He does a manic little dance and stops suddenly, his face shining.

Children everywhere will weep tonight, he cries. For Curious George must die.

Jeremy shrugs happily and cruises around to the passenger side. Huck backs away from him. Jeremy opens the rear door and extends a gallant hand. Daphne hesitates, then allows him help her out. By now she has pulled on a pair of black silk pants and she stands in the driveway in black pants and bra, the blood still wet on her face and shoulders.

Daphne is obviously confused. What with loss of blood and so forth.

I glance at Miller, who stares at the sky as if he despises the sun.

Thanks, says Daphne.

No worries, says Jeremy.

He stands there, nodding. Then turns and begins to knock the remaining shards of glass from the broken window frame. He glances at Daphne.

You might want to go inside, he says. You're bleeding pretty good.

Daphne stares at him. You're a fucking psycho.

Jeremy smiles, pleased. Have a nice day, he says.

Daphne hurries up the steps and now my humanity kicks in and I have half a mind to ask if she's okay, if she wants me to look at that head wound, but according to Jeremy's brief instructions, Poe had too much to drink last night and it's got him in a bad mood, so he must leer at her instead.

I barely notice that Miller has stepped into the shadows.

Daphne's breasts are fantastic. Unreal, but fantastic. The red bra barely contains them and she is so skinny that her belly is concave. Daphne doesn't look so healthy, when I think about it. Daphne looks like a starved junkie with a boob job. She looks like your average Hollywood actress. It may be inappropriate but I can't help remembering that hypnotic massage she dropped on me at the Paradise.

Despair, alienation. Loneliness and hatred, oh boy.

There were visible threads of each of these between us but still she had the hands and mouth of a fallen angel. In that brief moment before I punked out, Daphne was divine. She could have turned my friends into pigs. But a hired blowjob is no way to start a friendship and now Daphne brushes past me, slamming the door. I finish my coffee and wait for Jeremy, who is whistling as he removes a pair of jeans from the trunk of the Mustang. I watch as he hops around the driveway, pulling his pants on over skinny legs.

He approaches me, now.

Big brother, he says. How goes?

Uh-huh. When did you get out? I say.

Yesterday. He stands on the bottom step, grinning at me.

That's a nice car.

Umm, he says. It's stolen.

Bad luck about the window.

Tragic, he says. Fucking tragic.

Who's the girl?

Whore, he says. Asian, isn't she. There's nothing like yellow pussy in my book.

Sure, I say.

Anyway, he says. She doesn't speak English. Don't pay her any mind.

I just heard her call you a psycho, I say. In perfectly good English.

That's strange, he says.

It irritates me to realize that this scene isn't half bad. And the monkey carried it.

You can't stay here, I say.

Why not?

I shrug, tired of the conversation. It's not safe.

Jeremy grins. Did you see the monkey?

Jingle, jangle.

Miller steps out of the shadows, coins jingling in his left fist, and Jeremy stops laughing as if his cord were yanked from the wall. He peers up at Miller like a kid sweating for approval, glowing and nervous at once. Miller wipes at his mouth and I see that he's drooling slightly, he's losing his cool and he's losing it in a slow, dangerous boil. His eyes seem to shrink and the white trickle of drool reappears at the corner of his mouth. His face turns gray and cloudy and a single vein stands out in his forehead.

Jeremy looks nervous.

But not nervous enough, I think. He stands too close to Miller, smiling now and puffing out his chest stupidly.

You nasty boy, says Miller. You nasty little pup.

Take it easy, says Jeremy. Take a pill. You're going to pop a blood vessel.

Easy, says Miller.

What did you think? says Jeremy, softly.

Miller stares at him, his jaw bulging. I think we have a failure to communicate.

But the scene, says Jeremy. What about the scene?

The scene, says Miller. The scene was ill-advised.

I'm trying to help, says Jeremy. I thought another character or two would add depth, man.

Miller is spitting, now. This is my project, my fucking project.

Jeremy frowns. Phineas said it was okay with him.

Oh, is that right?

I shrug and smile and say nothing, looking from one to the other. I wouldn't mind seeing Miller throw a massive hissy fit, personally. I think I would enjoy it quite a lot. I also think it would be best to push his buttons carefully.

Don't get waxy, says Jeremy.

Miller smiles, a horrible gray smile. There is a long, shimmering silence. I light another cigarette and wonder if I should say something to ease the tension, or something to aggravate it.

I loved the monkey, I say. That was a nice touch.

It was a pure moment, says Jeremy. And purely coincidental.

That monkey saved your life today, says Miller. He turns and walks inside.

Jeremy looks at me. What did you think?

It was a hell of a nice scene, I say. But apparently not appreciated.

Yeah, he says. The old man is mental.

Maybe. But I would be careful with him.

Jeremy shrugs. It's boring to be careful all the time.

He strolls inside, humming. I flick my cigarette and follow, slowly. Huck with the camera is a shadow behind us. The wheels are turning in my head. Miller is vulnerable. Daphne is stretched out on the stainless steel island in the kitchen under bright, white lights. Jude crouches over her. She is sewing up the cuts in Daphne's head and face with black thread. Daphne has a big loopy smile on her face.

Miller stands behind her, his face recomposed.

Oops, says Jeremy. I'm sorry but I just sewed your eye shut....

Jude gives him a dark look but says nothing. Jeremy opens the refrigerator, still humming. He tells Huck to get some close-up footage of Jude
sewing up Daphne. Jude regards him with her sleepy, assassin's eyes.

What happened out there? says Jude.

Miller and Jeremy exchange glances but neither of them says boo.

Jude looks at me. Well? she says.

My brother got a little…extreme with his affections.

Do we have any ice cream? says Jeremy.

Jude looks at Miller. I didn't realize there was a brother in the picture.

There's not, says Miller. He makes a throat-slashing gesture to Huck,
who promptly lowers the camera. Jeremy is cheerfully preparing a peanut
butter and jelly sandwich.

You've made an error of judgment, says Miller.

What's your problem? says Jeremy.

People skills, says Miller. I have poor people skills.

Jeremy shrugs. You know what this picture really needs?

What? he says.

Dwarfs, says Jeremy.

Miller takes a deep breath, apparently deciding to ignore him. He leans
over to get a better look at Daphne, who remains blissful as Jude patches
her face together.

How is she? he says.

Minor cuts, she says. But a lot of them. Her face is a mess.

This reminds me that I have a lovely black eye. It looks like I was in a
bar fight and no one has even mentioned it. What's the world coming to.

Dwarfs on motorcycles, says Jeremy. Doing stunts and such.

Molly mutters at him to shut up. He winks at me, his mouth full of
peanut butter.

Are you high? I say.

Miller sighs. He tells us to ignore him. Jeremy just wants attention, he
says.

Jeremy, I say. I want you to apologize to John.

Jeremy laughs, insolently. Miller turns to look at him, a gruesome
smile grafted to his face. Jeremy shrugs and offers him a bite of his sand-

wich and Miller punches him hard, in the stomach. Jeremy is caught completely off guard and goes down in a spastic wheezing heap. Everyone is distracted and I take the opportunity to fuck off. I grab the bread and peanut butter and head downstairs to look in on the boy.

twenty-nine.

THE BOY IS ASLEEP, or appears to be. I crouch beside the bed. His eyes flicker. Long dark lashes that remind me of the wings of a dying moth. There is a spot of blood on his pillow, as if he's had a nosebleed. I ask him if he feels okay and he doesn't seem to hear me. There's a slow trickle of yellow liquid laced with blood coming from his left ear. I touch his face and his skin is so hot. His breathing is shallow and I can barely find his pulse. I pick him up and take the stairs two at a time, yelling for Jude.

I carry the boy into the futuristic living room. The stage lights are blinding. I lay the boy down gingerly on the chrome loveseat. He wears new brown corduroys and a white T-shirt that says there's no escape from New York. He wears black Chuck Taylors, new and unlaced. His face is pale and the chrome beneath him is polished so bright he looks like he's asleep on a bed of glass. I chew my fingernails a minute, staring at his shoes. I need to tie those laces before he steps on them and takes a spill. I need to tie those suckers into double knots. I drag my hand through my hair and it comes away dripping with sweat. I holler for Jude, again. I murder her name with my voice and just when I'm about to snap, she appears out of nowhere.

Relax, she says. You would think you're the father.

What's wrong with him?

How do I know? she says.

Jude eyes the child as if he is a piece of muddy firewood and she's reluctant to touch him. But perhaps her ability to remain detached is for the best. She takes a breath, then bends to press her ear to his chest, listening to his lungs.

What is it?

Jude ignores me. Fucking stoic, she is. Now she uses a penlight to examine his eyes, to look into his ears. One by one, the others drift into the room. Molly sits close to me, but not too close. Her face is an unfamiliar mask. Her eyes are black with mascara, her lips painted red. Otherwise, she wears jeans and a T-shirt. Her face is disconcerting. Miller is muttering softly. It sounds like he is calculating figures, running numbers. But then I might be imagining that. Jeremy and Daphne barely pay any attention to us. They are at the bar, arguing in whispers about the proper ingredients for a margarita. Daphne looks like she was in a car wreck and I guess she was. The white bandages on her face are proof that she was chosen by the gods, that she was given one more day to live. Jude is peering into Sam's little brown eyes as if they are a deep, dark wishing well and she is wondering just how much cash is down there.

Jude, I say. Talk to me.

I may be wrong, she says. He seems to have an ear infection, which is causing the fever.

The shit oozing from his ear, I say. That's normal?

Drainage, she says. He probably burst his eardrum.

That's bad, right? That's bad.

It's not the end of the world.

I stare at her. He needs his eardrum, I say.

The eardrum will repair itself.

He's barely breathing.

Jude nods. I'm not sure what's causing that. Maybe an allergic reaction.

I shake my head. The boy's eyeball could be hanging out of his skull by a fucking bloody thread and butter wouldn't melt on your tongue.

There's no reason to get nasty.

No, I say. What are you going to do?

Jude stands up as if to go.

What are you doing? I say.

I'm going to the bathroom, she says. Will you please fucking relax. Have a drink, or something.

I would love a drink. I wish someone would bring me one.

Molly slips away and everything seems to go on autopilot until she returns. She hands me a glass of vodka, with ice.

Thank you, I say.

He watches too much television, says Molly. That's what it is. When my baby comes, I won't let her watch so much TV.

I glance at Molly and I feel like I just swallowed a bug.

You aren't really pregnant, I say. You know that, right?

She stares at me for a moment too long. Of course, she says.

The boy is pale and catatonic against chrome. His breath comes thin and slow. The grim hiss of air seeping in and out of his lungs.

Does anyone have a cigarette, says Jude.

She stands over us, a small bottle of liquid Benadryl in one hand and a blue can of Pepsi in the other. There's a white plastic eyedropper stuck between her lips like a cigar.

I can't wait to hear your plan, I say.

Trust me, she says.

Jeremy brings over a glowing tray of margaritas. He gives Jude a ciga-rette and lights it for her. I try to meet his eye and now it occurs to me that there is a shadowy area of my mind that has somehow accepted him as a brother. I don't like this idea and I remind myself to harden my heart against the script.

I have an overwhelming urge to get outside. To get the fuck away.

But I look around and the boy remains on the chrome loveseat, feverish and barely breathing. Molly is a ghost at the edge of my vision, her mouth so small and dark it might be a scar. Her hands fidgeting, fidgeting. I get the feeling she wants to hold my hand but is reluctant to do so, maybe because Jude is watching. Maybe because I just suggested that she's nuts. Miller appears and reappears across from me, his eyes closed. Jeremy is whispering something apparently pornographic to Daphne and she is laughing, covering her wet mouth with her fist. I drain my vodka and place it carefully on the floor, then take one of the margaritas from Jeremy's tray. There is thick salt around the mouth of the glass and I lick at it, hungry.

Jude lifts the boy into her lap and holds him so that he's sitting up. She twice fills the eyedropper with liquid Benadryl and pushes it between Sam's pale lips.

Jude looks at me. The antihistamine, she says. It will reduce the swelling in his ears.

And the Pepsi?

I don't know, she says. The sugar and caffeine should give his heart a jumpstart and maybe that will help his breathing.

I nod, silent. It makes as much sense as anything.

Jude frowns. He needs antibiotics, probably.

He needs to see a doctor.

But we can't take him to a doctor, says Jude. Her voice is slow and gentle, as if I am the child.

Jude begins to funnel Pepsi into the boy's mouth, her eyes downcast and lips pursed. She blows softly on his face. He coughs and Pepsi dribbles between his open lips. She wipes it away with the back of her hand. How tender she is. I don't quite recognize her.

Sam wakes up, now. The boy is disoriented and unhappy. He doesn't like the idea that everyone is looking at him. I can sympathize. He turns his head and I don't think he knows where he is. He doesn't seem to recognize any of us and he does not come to me for comfort. He allows Jude to hold him, to wrap her arms around him. He rests his head on her shoulder, his eyes flat and glassy. Jude blows softly on his hair and whispers to him in a way that angers me. Because lately I want her to be the villain. I want her to be the one who dies in the end.

But the boy apparently feels safe with her. In another moment he is asleep again and I don't know what to make of this. I put my hand on Jude's thigh and I am confused, vaguely queasy. I don't know if this is guilt or love. Her mouth twitches and now I think it's a little bit of both. She glances down at my hand and I slowly withdraw it.

Miller is staring at Jude as if she has just grown a spotted tail. I reckon he thinks she's gone soft on him. Jude stares back at him with eyes narrow and feral and I have a happy image of Miller waking up with his intestines spilling out of him in a rich steaming mass. I sip my margarita and look from one to the other. It occurs to me that I have been ignoring them lately and now I realize that I have no idea what manner of nastiness transpires between them in the dark. Jude stares and stares and Miller never turns his eyes away from her and after two or three minutes of savory, textured silence during which Jeremy and Daphne drift uneasily from the room, presumably to have sex without bloodshed, Jude passes the boy to Molly, who glows upon receiving him.

Do you see something green? she says to Miller.

He shrugs. Repent, he says. Repent, mother.

Molly walks slowly around the room, hugging young Sam to her chest. She sways back and forth, instinct kicking in. She begins to sing, softly. Momma's gonna buy you a diamond ring. Her face is shadowy and blissful and I shake my head. Molly too is falling for the boy and I believe we are fucked, all of us. The boy is definitely getting to her. There are black streaks on her face.

Molly, I say. Your eyes are dripping.

What?

I take the boy from her. You've got black shit running down your face.

The mascara, she says. I forgot. We were getting ready to shoot a scene.

What scene?

You're not in it, says Miller. Only the girls.

That reminds me, says Molly. I want to talk about the nudity.

What about it?

The script says that Jude and I are sitting around the bedroom, right. We're drinking wine and smoking cigarettes and having a raunchy conversation about sex.

Yeah? says Miller.

Jude is topless in the scene, says Molly. Which seems unrealistic, frankly. And I'm supposed to be bottomless.

Bottomless? I say.

Jude laughs. She takes the margarita from my hand and finishes it off.

Two girls getting drunk and friendly, says Miller. A prelude to sex.

Maybe, says Jude. But nobody sits around bottomless and chatting.

Would it be more realistic if there was a pillow fight?

This is hopeless, says Molly.

Okay, I say. How about we talk about reality for a while?

What did you have in mind? says Miller.

The ransom, I say. I think we should make the ransom demand today.

No, he says. That's impossible.

Why?

Because we have just begun shooting *The Velvet*.

Jesus. The film is a farce. It makes no fucking sense and we should end it now.

Miller stares at me, his eyes mild. Whatever you say.

The boy is sick, I say. He needs a doctor.

He frowns. Don't you have faith in Jude?

Jude strokes my thigh, her hand venturing close to my crotch. Molly turns away and goes to the bar. The sound of ice in a glass. I shift the boy in my arms. He's heavy. Miller lights a cigarette and watches my face. Blue smoke whispers between us. Jude strokes my thigh and I stare into the distance. I stare into the past, into the future. I consider the word faith.

Miller shrugs. Neither here nor there. We will make the ransom demand when I say so.

And if he dies in your basement?

Then it gets more interesting, doesn't it?

thirty.

BACK THROUGH THE RABBIT HOLE and down the stairs. I tuck the boy into bed and arrange his pillows around him. Sam is breathing well now. But his body is too warm and the hair at the back of his neck is damp. I settle onto the floor with the remote control and flick on the television. I watch cartoons for a while but they depress me for some reason. I surf away and come upon a rerun of *Starsky & Hutch* squatting on some channel ominously called TV Land. The implications of such a channel are too brutal to wrap my noodle around and anyway Huggy Bear is giving a wildly animated, hopelessly rhetorical, and truly surreal speech about human rights. He's wearing a maroon suit and a pink tie and a big straw hat and his eyes are bugging out of his tiny head. I'm good for about five minutes of this before I freak out and am forced to flee TV Land. I cruise the TV universe until I find a ball game, the Red Sox and Yankees.

This has potential tragedy written all over it and I promptly mute the sound.

I am tempted to skulk upstairs and get a beer and a sandwich but I'm in no mood to run into any of the others. I don't want to know what they're up to and besides, beer would only make me want a cigarette and I would rather not smoke around the boy. I fetch a juice box from the little fridge and settle in to watch the Yankees massacre the Sox.

Baseball slows the vital functions and in no time I am dreamy, contemplative.

I contemplate the boy. He is approximately forty-nine pounds of flesh and bone. Blond hair and big brown eyes nearly black. He has eyes that could swallow you. His nose is the size of a button, the size of my thumbnail. His unflawed skin is somewhere between pink and pale yellow, the flesh of a peach. His hands are devastating. His hands could make a monster weep. He smells like the sun, like the fine sparkle of dust swimming in a burst of sunlight. He smells like a color you can't name.

He breathes, in and out. Five years of life, barely a ripple.

But there is some serious voodoo packed into his small body and it's not just him, but all children. There is nothing on the planet quite like a sick or injured child, a frightened child. Jude is a cool hand and usually nothing touches her, nothing moves her. But I could see the boy tugging freely at her cold, broken heart.

This is something that fills my head, sometimes. The idea that I broke her heart somehow.

I fall asleep next to the boy and dream that we are lost in the woods together. Sam is unchanged. He is five years old, with long blond hair. I am nine, his brother. The trees are dense and twisted, with thin black branches that hang just above our heads and tangle together like terrible hair, blotting out the sky. Unseen wolves howling in the dark, their voices ghostly.

Sam is brave, though.

He pushes ahead and I follow him and when we come to a house of gingerbread and licorice, I know that the house is not safe. It's not safe but I have no control over my limbs and I stroll directly up to the door and hammer on it while Sam helps himself to a tasty chunk of cinnamon rain gutter. The woman who comes to the door is no crusty hag, however. She is maybe thirty, with hair black as tar. She wears raw leather pants stained with what looks like blood and a vest made of fine silver chain. The woman smiles when she sees us and her teeth glitter white as needles. I don't trust her but Sam shouts hooray when she asks if we like sugar cookies. He trots inside and I follow him, helpless. The woman strokes my face and her fingers are cold and bony, with long black nails. She purrs that it's a shame but I am too old for her table, that my skin will be tough and gamey. But my brother is still soft and plump and if killed properly and marinated in butter and blackberry wine he will make a delicious stew. The woman asks me to gather wood for her fire and I comply.

I am not stupid, however.

I am only vaguely aware that this is a dream and I can't seem to wake myself up but I know this woman. I would know her anywhere. I shiver myself awake and Sam is sitting on his haunches like a little stone frog beside me, staring at my face with profound curiosity.

My head hurts, he says.

I know, I say. Mine does, too.

You were talking, he says.

What was I saying?

You said you weren't hungry. Then you said the boy is my brother.

Jesus.

Am I the boy?

Yes.

You were having a dream, he says. A bad dream, huh.

Very bad, I say.

What was it about?

His face is pale and fine, his lips still rosy with fever. He is so close to me that I can smell his breath when he exhales. The air coming from him is sour. The smell of sick.

How do you feel? I say.

He thinks for a minute. Okay, he says. But not my arm. My arms hurts.

What's wrong with your arm?

I don't know, he says.

Show me where it hurts.

He pulls his sleeve up over the elbow and I see it right away. On the pale underside of his biceps, there is small white mark surrounded by red flesh. It could be a puncture. It could be an insect bite. I take a deep breath and remind myself that kids get nervous when adults freak out.

That doesn't look bad, I say. Do you remember feeling sick today?

Yeah, he says.

When did you feel sick?

Today, he says. A little while ago.

He bobs his head up and down and sideways and shrugs one shoulder and I remember that he's five and therefore has no real sense of time.

Uh-huh. What were you doing?

I was sitting on the floor, he says. I was playing with the guys you got me. Wolverine and the guy with fire on his head. They were fighting.

Ghost Rider, I say.

Huh?

The guy with fire on his head is Ghost Rider.

Oh, yeah.

Who was winning?

Wolverine, mostly.

That makes sense. What else were you doing?

Nothing, he says. I was only watching TV…. I was watching *Sailor Moon* and I was having some chocolate milk. That's all.

Chocolate milk, huh.

He nods, vigorously. I like chocolate milk. I love it.

The trees are dense and twisted, with thin black branches that hang just above our heads and tangle together like terrible hair, blotting out the sky. Unseen wolves howling in the dark, their voices ghostly.

The boy is brave.

I don't even have to think about it. The chocolate milk is bad, poisoned. I haul it out of the fridge and look at it carefully. The boy is watching me and it occurs to me that children, like animals, generally have a keen nose for madness. I don't want to scare him, so I whistle softly as I examine the chocolate milk.

Paranoid people don't whistle, surely.

What I'm looking at is an ordinary plastic milk jug with a white, screw-on top. Brown and white paper label with a bar code and the words chocolate milk two percent and Sunny Fields Dairy in bright, cheerful script followed by your average nutritional bullshit in small print. The jug is half empty. Or half full, if you're a positive thinker like me. I unscrew the top and sniff it, then the contents of the jug. It smells like chocolate milk. But that's too easy.

Do you want some? says the boy. He's looking at me.

No, I say. I'm not thirsty.

Oh, he says.

He doesn't say anything else but I can see the little-kid wheels turning in his head. Why are you sniffing it, then?

I think this chocolate milk is bad, I say.

It's good, he says. I think it's good.

Yeah. But sometimes milk just goes bad, when you least expect it.

Can I smell it? he says.

Of course.

He hops up and comes over to me. I crouch down so he can reach it and he inhales deeply, frowning as he does so.

Trust me, I say.

The boy nods, gravely. As if he knows the world to be a mysterious, often nonsensical place and is therefore willing to accept the notion that chocolate milk, while it may smell good and taste good, may in fact be bad.

What have you had to eat today?

He tells me that the lady brought him some chicken nuggets earlier.

Which lady?

I don't know, he says. The lady who wears a mask and doesn't talk to me.

The lady who wears a mask and doesn't talk to me. That sounds familiar, doesn't it. I head upstairs, taking the chocolate milk with me. I cruise through the kitchen, the living room and dining room. I peek into the Lizard Room and no one is about. The house is endless and silent. They could be anywhere, and I begin to go from room to room.

I find them in Molly's room. I open the door and everybody is packed in there under white, hot lights. The air feels thick, almost humid.

Molly sits in a wooden chair, crying. She wears white underpants and bra. Jude is behind her with scissors in hand, bright steel blades that look very sharp. She is apparently cutting Molly's hair. There are yellow tufts of it like a ring of feathers at their feet. There is a nasty bruise on Jude's face, puckered and bloody. It looks like a bite mark. Her shirt is torn at the throat. Miller lies naked on the bed behind them, staring at the ceiling. Huck stands in one corner with a camera, Daphne in the other. They don't look too comfortable. Jeremy sits in the green chair, out of the shot. By the expression on his face, I would say he has an erection.

Why are you crying? I say.

I'm okay, says Molly. I'm okay.

Jude, your face. What happened to your face?

She doesn't answer. She snips at Molly's hair and Molly winces at the sound.

Miller looks at me. What do you want, Poe?

Where should I start? I want to know why you're naked. I want to know why Molly's crying and I want to know what happened to Jude's face. I want to know what's in this fucking chocolate milk.

Jeremy giggles.

You. You're in my chair, I say.

Jeremy stands up, shifting his gear to hide that inconvenient wood. He looks around but there's nowhere else to sit. I brandish the jug of chocolate milk like it's a weapon. I approach him, menacing but feeling ultimately goofy.

Have a drink, I say.

No, thanks. He scratches his head, confused.

Jesus. Just sit down, I say.

Meanwhile, tufts of yellow hair fall slowly to the floor. I find myself staring at them. The hair falls so slowly. It floats.

Dreamy, isn't it? says Miller.

I look at him on the bed and he is lying on his side, playing idly with his flaccid penis.

What? I say.

Haven't you ever noticed that our eyes, our very brains have been programmed to register certain images in slow motion?

I shrug. I have noticed that, yeah.

Television and film have been around for what, a hundred years? he says.

That sounds about right.

In less than a hundred years, our brains have mutated. We don't process visual information the way our great-grandparents did.

What's your point, Miller?

You walk into a room and you see the following things. Two attractive women in their underwear. One is crying. The other has a bruised face. You see a naked man on a bed. You see two minor characters in the shadows, holding cameras. You see a young, handsome boy who will soon be dead, sitting in a green chair.

What is your fucking point? I shout.

What do you see?

In the green chair, Jeremy croaks like a frog. I'll be dead soon?

Jude, I say. What happened to your face?

Molly bit me.

Okay. That makes sense.

She stares at me like she has a thousand times before. Her eyes open in such a way that I know she actually sees me. The scissors gleam in her hand and her face is temporarily ruined. Her hair is braided into pigtails so that her face is fully exposed, as if she had planned for this.

What's in the milk, Jude?

Chocolate, she says. It's chocolate milk.

Where did it come from?

Who knows. A brown cow, I suppose.

Are you poisoning that boy?

What? she says.

There's a mark on his arm, like the mark of a needle.

Miller scoffs. It's probably a spider bite.

Taste it, says Jude. Taste the fucking milk.

Molly wipes her face and stands up. Everyone, she says. Everyone get the fuck out of my room. Everyone, please.

Her voice is silent and roaring at once. Her voice is mildly terrifying, like driving into an ice storm. The silence ripples and after a brief pause, everyone begins to come alive. I stand in the doorway, wondering if she wants me to go. Or just the others. Jude puts down the scissors and walks toward me. I step aside to let her pass, which she does without quite looking at me. Miller flops off of the bed and comes toward me, naked and hairless. He scratches his chest, grinning. He doesn't say a word. Jeremy, Huck, and Daphne troop past me, their heads lowered. Molly stands in the center of the room, arms folded across her chest. I tell her it's okay, we're off camera. She stares down at the yellow hair at her feet and mutters a response I don't understand and, with two fingers, gently pushes the wooden chair over backward so that it falls with a dull crash. She turns to the bed and violently strips the sheets from the bed, throwing them to the floor.

What did you say?

Molly turns her doll's head around slowly to look at me, her blue eyes unblinking.

What did you say just now?

Dead flowers, she says. My hair looks like dead flowers on the floor.

Molly crawls onto the bare mattress and crawls slowly across it and for a moment it's like she's crawling across an endless table, blue and white. There's a bowl of porridge at the far end and she just wants to taste it. She huddles in the corner against the wall, arms wrapped around her legs. She looks like a kid on a boat and she's afraid the waves will take her away. Her hair is short and wispy but it doesn't look bad. Jude could have butchered her, if she had wanted to. She could have cut her ear off or something. I expected her to, really. Molly looks cold and I crawl across the mattress to give her a sweater. I sit next to her, not touching her. The air in the room has a silver, post-apocalyptic glimmer, a strange fairy dust quality that I associate with dinner parties and domestic violence.

You're still here.

Yeah.

She lowers her head to rest on my lap, and I stroke her new hair.

What do you think? she says.

You look like a boy. But not bad.

Molly sighs.

What happened? I say.

The scene, she says. We were shooting the scene. Jude and I were lying on the bed, talking about you and John. We were sharing a cigarette. We were talking about sex and drinking vodka and Jude was touching my arm, just lightly touching it, you know. It felt nice and I kissed her, I kissed her cheek and then she kissed me on the mouth and we started sort of making out and it was weird because everyone was in the room but I think it was a nice scene. The lights were soft and there were good shadows and it felt natural, it felt pretty. Jude was touching me, touching me and I was spinning or falling like I was going to come. And then suddenly John was on the bed, he was naked and he stank and he started kissing Jude, grunting and groping at her and she pushed him away and I started to sort of panic. I wanted John to go away. I wanted everyone to go away but John was trying to get Jude's clothes off and she was telling him to stop, just stop but he jerked her pants down and he was trying to get inside her and she was crying and the three of us were tangled together and suddenly it was hot, I couldn't breathe and it was like I had these extra arms and legs and too much skin and Jude was kissing me, her mouth was all over me, her mouth on me and John's eyes were so black and the light started to turn green around the edges and I was slipping, disappearing. I had a seizure and I was gone for a minute and when I came out of it Jude was holding her face and there was blood in my mouth.

Jesus.

By now she has climbed on top of me. Molly is as small as she can make herself, crouching like a bug on my chest. I wrap my arms around her, carefully. I don't want her to feel trapped but maybe it's what she wants. Molly is no longer shaking but her arms and legs are so cold. Her skin feels like she's been outside in winter. I have an erection but I ignore it.

And then what?

Then John told Jude to cut my hair, to punish me. He told her to make me ugly.

What did Jude say?

Molly shivers. She didn't want to do it but I think she's afraid of John.

I think so, too. It worries the hell out of me but I don't say so and then I forget about it because Molly is aware of my erection. Her hand drifts down into my crotch to give me a squeeze. It seems like the wrong time for this but I groan and she unbuckles my belt and slips her hand into my pants. Molly kisses my ears and throat and chest but she avoids my face and mouth, as if she is reluctant to let me see her. She unbuttons my shirt without looking at me.

A ring of yellow hair on the floor.

Lost feathers, dead flowers.

I make love to Molly on her bare mattress and the sex between us is grim, tender, wordless.

thirty-one.

MOLLY SLEEPS BESIDE ME, snoring softly. I'm wide awake and staring at nothing in muddy underwater light. The gloaming, baby. Panic attack, delirium tremens. Headache and shrinking vision. Blackbirds on the wing. I can't tell the difference between panic and sickness but my body is begging for a drink. My arms and legs are numb, naked and tangled with Molly's. The separation between us is vague. I slip out from under her and she mumbles nonsense at me but does not wake. I gather my clothes and creep into the hall to get dressed. The clock chimes four times and for a moment I have no idea whether it's afternoon or morning.

Jude is in the kitchen, drinking coffee. She holds the cup with both hands and sits with her back very straight. She stares through me and says nothing. The mark on her face is purple and swollen. I take a bottle of vodka from the freezer, then fetch a glass and pour myself a generous shot over ice.

Happy hour? she says.

I grunt and light a cigarette.

Your hands are shaking, she says.

It's a new feature. I don't want to talk about it.

Jude sighs. You are dying before my eyes.

How's your face?

It hurts. But it's no one's fault.

What about Miller?

What about him?

Molly said he forced himself on you.

Jude flinches, slightly. That's not true.

What is the truth?

He wanted to make love to me, she says. I wasn't interested.

I don't understand.

What, she says. What don't you understand?

I don't understand why you don't cut his wee willie off and feed it to him.

Jude takes a cigarette from my pack, fumbles with the matches.

Are you afraid of him?

Jude strikes a match and lets it burn down to her fingers without lighting her cigarette. She strikes another and watches it burn. I push the glass of vodka across the table but she shakes her head. I reach for her hand but she pulls it away and now Miller crashes into the room. He wears black jeans and a black military-style sweater with patches on the shoulders. He tosses my jacket at me.

On your horse, Poe. We're out of here.

Where are we going?

Baseball game, he says. The Giants are playing the Reds.

Oh, yeah. Who's going?

Miller winks at Jude. The boys, he says. Just the boys.

I finish my drink but make no move to get up.

Don't tell me you're not interested, says Miller. These are dream seats, behind third base.

I look at Jude, who nods and lights another match.

Yeah. I'm interested.

Excellent choice, he says. I'll meet you out by the truck.

Outside and the sun is fierce in a white sky. Jeremy and Huck wait beside the Range Rover and I have a sudden, surreal vision of the four of us at the ballpark. The crowd like an ocean around us, roaring. The smell of peanuts and big plastic cups of warm beer. Miller waving a big puffy hand. Huck grimly shoving fistfuls of cotton candy into his mouth. Jeremy flirting with a red-haired girl behind us. I can see it like it already happened but there's a tracking problem and the back of my neck has gone cold. Huck sits on the hood of the truck, smoking one of Miller's cigars. His hands are filthy and he looks tired. Jeremy crouches in the driveway, tossing pebbles at an empty wine bottle. His eyes are narrow and red and he regards me warily as I approach.

I crouch next to him and pick up a rock. I whip it at the bottle but miss.

What's up, I say. You look like shit.

Jeremy shrugs. Nervous. I'm nervous.

Why?

You heard what the man said. I'm gonna be dead soon.

He's fucking with you.

Oh, yeah? Why don't you ask brother Huck what he's been doing this afternoon.

I glance up at Huck. Well?

Digging, he says.

Digging what?

A very deep fucking hole.

It's a grave, says Jeremy. The man had him digging my grave.

Where?

It's a sweet little spot, says Huck. Around the east side of the house. Jeremy's going to be tucked in between a fig tree and a chunk of limestone.

I glance at the house. What the hell is Miller doing in there?

Fuck him, says Jeremy. Let's take a look at my final resting place.

The three of us drift around to the side of the house and Huck's hole indeed resembles a shallow grave. Four or five feet deep and the approximate length of a body. I drop down into the hole and lie down. The sky is white framed in black. The tops of trees. Huck and Jeremy peering over the edge.

It's cold, I say.

Get out of there, says Jeremy. You're giving me the creeps.

The two of them pull me out and we sit at the graveside, smoking.

Why are you guys doing this? I say.

I want the dough, says Huck. But I'm done. That little rape scene today was the end for me.

What do you mean? says Jeremy.

Huck shrugs. I'm gonna run. When we get to the ballpark, I'm gone. It might help if one of you wants to keep the psycho occupied.

Jeremy, I say. You should run, too.

No, he says. I want to do this.

Why?

Jeremy sighs. I don't want to go into the whole tear jerking poor little orphan routine, but my life has not exactly been rosy, you know. Miller hooked me up with that doorman job and I feel like I owe him. Before that I was selling meth to college students and freaks on the club scene. Before that I was sucking cocks for twenty bucks a throw in the Castro. And before that…did you know I was born in a halfway house. Did you know that? I was actually born in a fucking halfway house. My mom was sixteen, a junkie runaway. She was living in a shelter for teenage heroin addicts when she popped me out and she was gone before I could sit up. I've been in the system ever since. Foster homes, group homes, jail. I just want to be in the movies. I want to have a normal life.

There's no such thing, says Huck. And nothing resembling it in California.

Jeremy scowls, stubborn. Well, anyway. I aim to find it.

You shouldn't have done that scene, says Huck. That scene where you put Daphne's head through the car window. All you did was aggravate him.

But I was good, says Jeremy. I was good wasn't I?

Yeah, I say. You were good.

I had a funky dream last night, says Jeremy. I dreamed that I killed that monkey. I bashed his head in with a rock. I cut him open and there was a white bird where his guts were supposed to be and it just flew away, easy as you please. I felt its wings brush my face.

Blackbirds, I say. I always dream of blackbirds.

You guys are freaking me out, says Huck.

What do you think it means? says Jeremy.

I don't know, I say. It seems to me the white bird is lucky.

The sky is changing colors and Huck says we should probably head back to the truck before Miller gets cranky.

That scene today, I say. In Molly's room. He raped her?

Damn near, says Huck. Near enough.

And neither of you did anything?

Jude told us to back off, says Jeremy.

I wish to god she would just kill him, I say.

Jeremy exhales loudly. You don't know shit, do you?

What do you mean?

He looks at me with eyes dead as coins. What god has joined, he says, let no man put asunder.

Yeah, I say. That's right.

Miller is waiting by the truck. He holds an aluminum briefcase in one hand, a black flight bag in the other. He wears a black jacket and a black knit cap pulled tight on his skull. He doesn't look like he's going to a ball-game, but my head is full of noise and juice and I've got a monster headache on the periphery and so I don't give his outfit too much thought. Miller tosses the keys at Huck and tells him to drive. Jeremy climbs into the front passenger seat. I get in the back with Miller, who lights a joint and passes me a silver thermos.

Have a martini, he says.

Thanks.

What were you doing in the woods with Heckle and Jeckle? he says.

Gathering flowers, I say.

Uh huh.

What time is the game? I say.

We aren't going to the game.

I didn't think so. Where are we going?

To get cigarettes, he says.

I have cigarettes, actually. I offer him my pack.

He shakes his head. I prefer a different brand.

The truck winds down out of the hills and Miller tells Huck to take a left. I am sitting with my back against the door, my feet up on the seat. The thermos between my legs, unopened. I take the joint from Miller and allow myself one puff, to calm my nerves. I am watching him closely, every movement of his face. Every tick and flicker. The way his eyes go narrow and dark when he's thinking. The way he licks his lips and the way his nostrils flare. I'm looking for a family resemblance and now I see it, now I don't. The power of suggestion. I could ask him, I suppose. But I'm starting to hate him and I don't want to see him smile at me.

After a beat, Miller instructs Huck to pull into the parking lot of a 7-11 that squats on the edge of a ravine. Huck obediently kills the engine and the four of us sit there, eyeballing each other.

Jesus, says Jeremy. Pass me that joint before I scream.

Miller gives it to him and he sucks at it with almost sexual intensity. I look out the window and watch as a guy and a girl get out of a red Toyota and go into the store. There are two other cars parked in front, but I can't see more than three people inside. The sun has not yet gone down but the fluorescent lights have come up in the parking lot and the result is a bright haze that hovers over the 7-Eleven like a solar cloud. Miller opens the flight bag and removes four rubber masks. The shriveled faces of dead celebrities. John Wayne, Marilyn Monroe, and Alfred Hitchcock. Woody Allen, who is perhaps not actually dead. He gives the John Wayne mask to Huck and tells him to put it on. He gives me the Marilyn Monroe mask, then smiles and apparently changes his mind and gives Marilyn to Jeremy. He takes Hitchcock for himself and gives me the Woody mask. The rubber is cold. I hold it in my lap like a dead fish. In the front seat, Jeremy and Huck are doing startlingly accurate impersonations of John Wayne and Marilyn Monroe.

What are we doing?

We are shooting an action sequence, says Miller.

I shake my head. Tell me we're not going to rob the store.

Ah, well. I need cigarettes, like I said.

This is unwise, I say.

Nonsense.

It's a pointless risk.

You are just like my wife, he says. Always worrying.

Oh. Do you want to talk about your wife?

Miller pushes the mask up over his eyes so that it looks like a deflated Alfred Hitchcock is chewing at his hair. He grins at Jeremy. What have you been telling him? he says.

Nothing, says Jeremy. I don't know anything.

Miller, I say. This is stupid.

Do you know why the boy is sick? he says.

Why.

It's not the chocolate milk, he says.

I close my eyes and I can see Miller naked and grunting on top of Jude. It was an image I could live with this morning and now it's all I can do to stay calm because I want to gouge out his eyes with my thumbs and eat them. I can taste them already, warm and salty as sheep testicles. I keep my voice low, my teeth together.

What are you doing to him? I say.

I need cigarettes, he says. Then perhaps we can discuss the boy.

Have you contacted Cody yet, about the ransom? I say.

No, he says. And I'm not going to.

What?

Miller grins.

Don't smile at me, motherfucker.

Hear me, says Miller. Jude can do whatever she wants with that kid, but she is kidding herself if she thinks I'm gonna hand her Senator Cody on a plate.

For thirty ticks that stretch and pop like dry wood in a fire, Miller and I are alone in a bubble, and I understand that he has the power. And he is abusing it. He is playing Jude like a kid's guitar, something I would have thought impossible. I think it's time for me to do something. I pull the mask over my head and I'm Woody Allen. Miller removes a small digital camera from the flight bag and gives it to Huck, who receives it reluctantly.

Oh and by the way, says Miller. Don't try to run.

No, says Huck. Why would I do that?

I don't know, says Miller. I really don't. But I would be more comfortable if you let me hold onto the car keys.

Huck hands over the keys, which Miller deposits in the breast pocket of his jacket. He now opens the briefcase and takes out three identical handguns. He gives one to Jeremy and one to me, and keeps one for himself, selecting them seemingly at random. Huck does not get one, apparently. I examine my gun, which is a .40 caliber Sig Sauer Pro, matte black, a nice gun. I feel fairly certain mine and Jeremy's are loaded with blanks, if at all. But I refrain from checking the magazine. Finally, he passes out latex gloves.

Now, he says. Let's play.

The four of us cross the parking lot slowly under a pale electric haze, walking abreast as if we're going to a gunfight. Miller is a step or two ahead of me and I point my gun at the back of his head.

Pow, I say.

Miller reaches the door and hesitates, his breath ragged through Hitchcock's mouth. The plan is simple enough. Jeremy will hold a gun on the clerk. I will control the customers and watch the door. Miller will roam the store, amusing himself. And Huck will get it all on film. He throws the door open and I go in first, thinking that if I'm careful, I can stop him from killing anyone.

This is a hold-up, I say.

The music in the store is loud, Sonic Youth. No one hears me. No one pays me any mind and I reckon people in Woody Allen masks walk in here every day. Hitchcock comes in behind me and fires one shot into the ceiling. There is a spray of falling white plaster and now everyone is paying attention. Marilyn Monroe comes in and goes directly to the counter with his gun held chest high. The clerk is a ratty white kid, mid twenties. He has a long dirty blond ponytail dangling from a black baseball cap. He's chewing gum, the muscles jumping in his face. He watches Marilyn closely.

I count four customers. In the back is a white girl in motorcycle leathers with a stud through her nose and blue hair, maybe twenty. She was stirring cream into her coffee when we came in and now stands very still, staring at me. Near the counter is a crusty old white guy wearing a T-shirt that says Jesus Freak. He holds a quart of beer in one hand, a package of beef jerky in the other. And near the Slurpee machine are the guy and girl who got out of the Toyota. They are attractive in a blue jeans ad, immediately forgettable way, twin models with blond hair and perfect teeth. The girl has a sweet smile but the guy is an arrogant bastard, probably abusive, you can tell by the way he talks to her. It's not fair but I decide that if anyone in this scene gets shot, it will be him.

It helps to have a ready sacrifice in mind.

This is a hold-up, I say. Everybody be cool.

John Wayne cruises around the store, camera in hand. I stand by the door, one eye watching the parking lot. Hitchcock is amusing himself, as he said he would. He is tearing up the store, knocking displays over and throwing bags of chips and cookies and Hostess goodies into the air. He comes up behind Marilyn and tosses the flight bag at the clerk.

The money from the register, he growls. All of it. And throw in the latest issue of Playboy and a few cartons of cigarettes.

What brand? the clerk says.

Whatever.

This irritates me. I tell the clerk to give us Camels.

He begins to stuff money into the bag and I shake my head in disgust. There will be two hundred dollars in that bag, at most. Hitchcock continues to destroy the store and the candy falls like hail. John Wayne is getting a close-up of the girl in leather. Marilyn is watching the clerk and I notice that his body is vibrating. He's going to pull the trigger any minute.

And at that moment, Hitchcock yells, hey Marilyn.

Marilyn turns his head, confused. And as he looks away, the ratty clerk drops the flight bag and reaches under the counter. I scream at Jeremy to turn around as the clerk comes up with a shotgun and blows Marilyn backward into a rack of cold medicine. The shot rings and rings in my head and it takes me forever to cross the store. I slide on my knees through blood and candy and come to rest beside my fallen false brother. The hole in his chest is the size of a basketball. I could put my head in there. I pull the Marilyn mask from his face and he is obviously dead, eyes rolled back and a crooked little smile frozen on his mouth. Out of the corner of my eye, I see the Jesus Freak running across the parking lot with a quart of beer in one hand, beef jerky in the other and I don't care. I'm happy for him. But it won't do to let the customers flee just yet. The blond girl with perfect teeth is screaming and screaming and it seems that she will never stop. I stand up in time to see Hitchcock hit her in the face with the barrel of his gun and she goes down hard, crashing into the Slurpee machine, her jaw no doubt broken. I turn to face the ratty clerk, expecting another blast from the shotgun.

But he has put the gun down and resumed filling the flight bag with cigarettes.

What the fuck? I point my gun at him.

The clerk squints at me as if he doesn't understand English.

You kill my brother and now you want to cooperate? I say.

He was your brother?

No, I say. He was just a fucked-up kid.

The clerk looks at Hitchcock, who comes over to the counter with an armload of ice cream and potato chips that he apparently wants to take with him.

We had an arrangement, the clerk says.

Indeed, says Hitchcock. And you have fulfilled your end marvelously.

The clerk flashes a mouthful of yellow teeth. Do you want a bag for those groceries?

What kind of arrangement?

The clerk shrugs. I'm bagging groceries, dude.

Hitchcock looks at Jeremy on the floor, then at the clerk.

What kind of arrangement? I say.

Two thousand dollars to kill Marilyn, says Hitchcock.

Jesus…

It was a hell of a bargain, says the clerk. Damn good.

He stands behind the counter, beaming at us. Yellow teeth like a neon sign. I glance around the store and see that no one has moved. The blond guy kneels on the floor, cradling his girlfriend's ruined face in his lap. John Wayne stands over Jeremy. He has stopped filming. The motorcycle girl is leaning against the far wall, holding her coffee.

Do you like her, Poe?

What?

Hitchcock points his gun at the motorcycle girl and she drops down behind a glass case of hot dogs. Hitchcock shrugs. He swings around and shoots the ratty clerk in the forehead.

Wow, he says. That felt good.

His voice is on fire and through the mask his eyes glow like he's about to embark on a full-scale killing spree. This is out of control. I figure we have been in the store almost five minutes. Two people are dead and the cops will be here soon. I don't know what good it will do but I raise my gun and point it at Hitchcock's head. I shout his name and he turns, grinning. He raises his own gun and does a little dance, like a jig. We are perhaps five feet apart, Alfred Hitchcock and Woody Allen.

Wayne, says Hitchcock. Look alive, pilgrim. This is great stuff.

Fuck you.

Miller, I say. Put the gun down.

Unlikely, he says.

Are you going to shoot me?

Pull the trigger, he says. Pull it, baby.

I shrug and pull the trigger and I see his face twist in surprise. The gun jerks in his right hand but I have already hit the floor and rolled sideways. Everything slows down and I expect to see the cotton wadding from my gun bounce harmlessly off his mask. But there is no cotton wadding and Hitchcock goes down on one knee, groping at his mask and yanking it off. Blood spurts from his left eye and he howls like a monkey. I look at my gun in surprise.

What did you load this with?

He groans. Wax bullets, non-lethal.

But very painful if you take one in the eye, I say.

Miller groans. The blood seeping between his fingers. Giving me wax bullets was a mistake I would not have made. I scoop up Miller's fallen weapon and turn to face the customers.

Everyone get out, I say. Run.

The blond guy drags his now less than perfect girlfriend out first. The motorcycle girl drifts over to the door, grabbing a pack of cigarettes and smiling at me as she passes the counter. Huck yanks off his mask and takes a long look at me, then nods and backs out the door. Once outside, he throws the digital camera high into the air and when it comes down, it splinters into a thousand shiny pieces. I grab a handful of Miller's hair and jerk his head up so he can see me.

You got your fucking snuff film, I say. Two dead.

Minor characters, he says. Insignificant.

I bring the butt of his gun down on the top of his head and he collapses in a heap. I toss the Woody mask and tell myself I have one minute to find the store surveillance tape. I hop over the counter and unfortunately step on the ratty clerk's face with my boot. There is a nasty squishing sound. I mutter an apology and look around, frantic. There is nothing resembling a VCR back here. For some reason, I grab the fallen flight bag and Miller's absurd bag of groceries and toss them in his direction. I head for the back, the door marked Employees Only. The door is locked and I fire two shots, then kick it open. I tell myself to be careful. I am breathing like a maniac and now there are sirens in the distance. The tiny office smells like the bright orange nacho cheese sauce dispensed from those nasty machines. And messy as hell. Desk and chair and file cabinet, time clock and safe and VCR hooked up to the surveillance cameras. I grab the tape and rip it apart as I run back to the front of the store.

Miller is gone.

Fuck, I say.

The flight bag is gone, also the groceries. I push open the doors and the Range Rover is gone. I forgot to take the keys from him. The sun has fallen, now. The sky is dark and getting darker and the sirens are so close they might as well be up my ass. I wish I could take Jeremy's body with me and bury him properly somewhere but I can't. He won't be decomposing in a shallow grave next to Miller's house, anyway. Goodbye kid, I say. Good luck in the next world. Then turn to run back through the store. I crash through the emergency exit doors and an alarm begins to whoop. Without hesitating I drop over the edge of the ravine.

thirty-two.

IT TAKES ME OVER AN HOUR TO LIMP BACK TO THE HOUSE. I am torn to pieces.
There is blood on my hands and my left ankle is fucked up. The cops are
cruising, slow and watchful, the sky splashed with search lights. I skulk
through back yards, avoiding dogs. I breathe through my nose and maybe
I've cooked my noodle with poison and drink over the past week, but I've
never felt better.

The house of Miller is dark.

The Range Rover is parked crazily, on top of a bush. I smile, thinking
of Hitchcock with one ruined eye. He must have been cursing at the sky
like a mad sailor. I rest on my haunches, out of sight, watching the house.
There is no sign of life and suddenly I have this horrible idea that Miller
came home and slaughtered everyone.

I limp through the living room, the kitchen. No one is about. I look in on
Molly and she's sleeping peacefully. I pick up a bottle of whiskey and head
for the library. Jude is downstairs with a magazine, watching over the boy.
She wears cowboy boots and a thin, sleeveless white dress. Her hair is loose
and she's not wearing the hockey mask. The bite mark has begun to fade.

What do you think? she says. I borrowed some of Molly's clothes.

You look like a nice college girl.

Don't be nasty.

I'm sorry. Your face looks much better.

The mask seemed pointless, at this point. And it frightened him.

How is he? I say.

She frowns. He's not good.

I go to the bed and touch his face. Sam is feverish, breathing too fast.

His lips, I say. They feel like sandpaper.

He's dehydrated, she says. I gave him some Gatorade earlier but he couldn't keep it down. I gave him milk and crackers, more Benadryl. I gave him children's Tylenol. But his fever won't break.

Miller is doing something to him, I say.

What?

I don't know. He wouldn't tell me.

Jude looks at her watch, worried. I don't know what he needs.

He needs a doctor.

Yes, she says. He won't get one tonight.

Where is Miller?

I'm not sure. He's somewhere in the house, watching.

Jeremy is dead, I say.

I know. He told me.

How is the bastard's eye?

Jude smiles. It's fucked. I'm afraid John doesn't like you anymore.

That's too bad, I say.

What happened out there? she says.

I am seething. Nothing. We jacked a convenience store.

How many dead, besides Jeremy?

The clerk. Miller shot him in the head.

Jude sighs. He's cracking. This will be over soon.

Oh, for fuck's sake.

What? she says.

Are we on camera now, I say.

What do you take me for?

He's playing you, Jude. He's never gonna serve up Cody, okay. This whole thing is just a game of chicken designed to make you his bitch.

Jude stares past me, blank. I can see she's already arrived at this conclusion.

I'm nobody's bitch, she says.

You have to deal with him, Jude. Deal with him, or I will.

I will, she says softly. I will.

I want to ask her again if it's true, if she is truly married to the man. But her face is so ashen, her hands so unsure of themselves. It must be true and it must not be and either way I feel like it would be rude to ask her. Miller is her nightmare and Jude will talk about it if she wants to.

Jude, I say. I'm going to take Molly and the boy and get out of here.

No, she says. You don't know where John is. And he's got a lot of fire-power.

What do you suggest?

Tomorrow, she says. I will take care of it tomorrow.

Jude wants her voice to be cold, detached. She sighs and glances at her watch as if we are discussing the time and place for a lunch date tomorrow. But her voice is tinged with rust and her hand trembles.

Are you sure?

The art of hunger. Jude kisses me, a long penetrating kiss that pushes me to the edge of hunger and leaves me dizzy.

I'm going to kill him, she says.

Are you sure? I say.

I will find a way to get him alone, she says. To distract him. And when I give you a look, you'll know it's time to get Molly and the boy and run.

What kind of look? I say.

I don't know, she says. A look that passes between us that only you can recognize.

The boy sleeps, barely. He is breathing so fast that he seems to rest on a fragile plane between unconsciousness and death. He sleeps in the velvet. My headache is soaring like a high-pitched sonic whistle that only dogs can hear. Blackbirds crash at the edge of my vision. Jude says that she wants to stay with him for the night and I agree.

I resolve not to sleep this night. I want to watch the house and I would sorely hate to be surprised by Miller. I am bitterly tired, though. I need something to keep me awake and I slip into Molly's room, remembering that she has a stash of pot and coke in her underwear drawer. I touch her lightly on the shoulder and she moans, dreaming. I open the underwear drawer and search it silently, stopping once to press something fine and silky to my face. The smell of rain, of a storm coming. I find a short plastic straw and a little yellow envelope of coke, a gram or so. I glide through the silver wings and merrily chop out four fat lines on the back of the toilet. I am in a dangerously good mood, for some reason. It was that kiss, maybe. Jude can tear my head off with a kiss, sometimes. I pause, considering. Four lines is too many, perhaps. Perhaps perhaps. I hoover two of them, then wash my face with cold water. I bend over the toilet with the straw and snort the third line.

Phineas?

Molly's voice. It sounds like she's talking in her sleep.

Phineas. I'm bleeding.

I push through the silver wings, my head a rage of white noise. I go to the bed and touch her. She's wet, the bed is wet. This can't be blood. There's too much of it. I fumble madly for the lights and they snap on with a yellow hum. Molly sits up in bed, her face pale. I don't believe what I'm seeing. Her nightgown is bloody from the waist down and the sheets are soaked red, almost black. The mattress is a river of blood. I bend over her but she is not wounded and soon I have blood up to my elbows.

Where, I say. Where is it coming from?

From me, she says. It's coming from me.

I fly downstairs to get Jude. I don't know what else to do. The blood is too much for me. It takes me back to the amputees in Mexico City. The swinging shadows, the raw white light. The bloody plastic under my feet. The sponge in my hand, the bucket of blood. Jude in a white raincoat, wiping blood from her goggles.

I hover behind the silver wings with a glass of whiskey while Jude checks Molly out. I am tempted to smash the mirror but I don't want to make things worse. After what seems like an hour, Jude pokes her head into the bathroom.

I need your help, she says.

Molly lies naked on the terrible bed, bloody and unconscious. Her short yellow hair is like a ring of pale fire around her face and she looks like Ophelia, dead and floating on her back. There are several towels on the floor, red with blood. Jude's hands are bloody.

Don't tell me she's dead.

Not yet.

What happened? I say.

I need to get her cleaned up, says Jude. And I'm afraid if we put her in the bathtub, she'll start bleeding again.

Who did this to her?

Jude frowns. I think she's done it to herself.

What the fuck do you mean?

It may have been a miscarriage, she says. But there's so much blood. It's unlikely she would hemorrhage like this, with an early miscarriage. I think she might have given herself some sort of coat-hanger abortion.

You're saying that Molly was pregnant.

Apparently.

It was John, croaks Molly.

She can't open her eyes or lift her head but twice she whispers that it was Miller who did this to her, no mistake. My skull is ringing, ringing. Peripheral vision all but gone and I feel like my spine is twitching. I can't wait to kill the motherfucker, and it makes me happy to think of it. But I have a feeling I may have to defer to Jude on that particular job. She calmly reaches for the whiskey and I go to the bathroom to soak washcloths. Together, we wipe the blood from Molly's arms and legs and belly and wrap her in a clean sheet. I carry her out to the living room and stand there in the dark, holding her while Jude arranges a bed of pillows in the bay window. I lay Molly down and she looks ghostly in the moonlight.

Okay, says Jude. I'm going downstairs.

Her voice is weary. I reach for her and she lets me hold her for a moment and I don't need her to tell me this might be the last time we will touch each other like lovers.

The night is endless. I sit at the head of the dining room table, smoking cigarettes and occasionally snorting a bump of cocaine. I can see Molly in the living room, a sleeping corpse swathed in white. I can see most of the kitchen and I can see the front yard, the driveway. I can't see the Lizard Room. The night ripples and hums around me and I remember a line from an old spaghetti western. A running man with a sharp knife may cut a hundred throats before the sun comes up. I smoke one cigarette after another and wait in vain for Miller to appear. Jude comes to me, though. I open my eyes and she is sitting next to me. Everything is different. The room, the chair I'm sitting in. Her hair is different and her face is bandaged. This is our apartment back in New Orleans. The high ceilings and burnt orange walls and dirty hardwood floors and the smell of paint thinner. Jude sits beside me and touches my arm.

I have to tell you something, she says. I didn't get the abortion.

My head swivels around so slowly it feels like it's on wires.

You had the baby? I say.

Yes.

I open my mouth to ask a shitty question, and clamp it shut so fast my teeth hurt.

Jude nods. You want to know if he's yours?

Sorry, baby. I can't help it.

That's okay. It's an animal response, Darwinian.

Jude takes a cigarette from my pack. She ghosts across the room, touching books and small strange pieces of art and arranging flowers and examining the furniture for flaws. She touches the things in this room as if she owns them and of course, in another lifetime she did. Whenever I'm with Jude, I realize, I watch her hands. I always watch her hands and I wonder what this is about. Her hands are painfully pretty, the way two predatory yellow birds might be pretty, and while I like pretty things, I have a feeling I watch because I don't quite trust those hands. Jude looks at me, her lips trailing blue smoke.

Did you say...he? I say, finally.

Jude nods, glowing. We had a boy, she says.

He's mine?

She smiles. I did the blood test myself.

Jesus Christ, baby. Why didn't you tell me before?

I wasn't ready, she says. I'm working, for one thing. And I wanted to… observe you for a while.

What's his name?

Everson Poe, she says. For your brother.

You remembered my brother's name? I say.

Jude shrugs. I remember everything, she says. Every word you say.

I am so happy I'm on fire. I forget where we are and what we're doing. Because I have a son. Jude and I have a son.

Where is he? I say. I want to see him.

He's in Toronto for now, says Jude. With my sister.

thirty-three.

BLINK AND MORNING IS UPON ME. I am staring, unhinged. I feel like I'm waking from a dream. But that was no dream. Jude and I have a child, a boy named Everson. He's with Jude's sister, and who the hell would have thought Jude had a sister? I always figured she was harvested in a lab, with all the other genetically enhanced ninjas. She named our son after my brother, whom I mentioned to her exactly once, the brother I haven't seen in a thousand years. There is a cigarette in my left hand, burned down to the filter. Ashes on the table, dirty snow. The sound of a tea kettle. I look around the corner and see that Daphne is in the kitchen, wearing snug little boy shorts and a sleeveless T-shirt ripped in half. I don't want to talk to her. I hold my breath until she takes her tea and goes outside. I want coffee, now. My muscles make unpleasant popping noises when I stand.

I have one complex objective now.

Jude and I must get out of this place, alive. I want to meet my son. But I have to get Sam out too, and Molly. I may have to kill Miller to accomplish this. I'm uneasy because the last time I saw him, some twelve hours ago, I shot him in the eye and he's bound to be angry about it.

It's early, maybe seven.

I start a pot of coffee and go to check on Molly. Her face is pale yet from the loss of blood, but her pulse is strong and she's breathing normally. Blood is strange. Donate a pint of it to the Red Cross and you go home lightheaded but otherwise feeling fine. The nurses give you a cookie. But you spill that same pint into somebody's bed and it's a fucking freakshow. I fetch myself a cup of black coffee and return to the window. I'm not feeling so insane as last night and I want to sit with Molly. I want to watch her sleep. Irrational, no doubt. Drug related. But I am weirdly cheerful. I feel like a guy who's on his way to the airport, like a guy who's going home. I feel high. Molly sleeps.

I find myself floating around the house, peering aimlessly out the windows. On the west side of the house there's a little Japanese rock garden overgrown with weeds and yellow wildflowers. There are a couple of wrought-iron chairs and a hammock. It looks like a nice place to think and I am about to go try out that hammock when Daphne walks into frame, carrying her tea. I immediately hunker down to watch her from the window. Daphne eyes the hammock, but I figure she's afraid she will spill her tea because she sits in one of the chairs instead. She now wears the same gauze white dress she wore at the Paradise, thin and translucent and it clings to her in such a way that it could cause madness. I take a shivering breath and tell myself to banish evil thoughts.

But it won't hurt to watch her. I light a cigarette and make myself comfortable.

Daphne isn't doing anything interesting, though. Daphne is drinking her tea and daydreaming about the past, maybe the future. Daphne is smiling, watching a few birds hop around the garden and I am about to go back to the living room when Miller walks into view, carrying one of the spear guns I saw in the garage. He wears a patch over his left eye. The hair on my neck tingles but somehow I just sit there. I just sit there. I don't know what I'm thinking. I tell myself he's on his way to see me, to put an aluminum spear in my heart, and he's just stopping to say hello to Daphne and after a few pleasantries, he'll move along. Daphne stands up and her lips part in the shape of hello. Miller smiles and bows and she offers him her hand and now Miller moves very close to her. He violates her space. He kisses her hand and she laughs, as if he's being silly. Miller says something to her but

I can only see the side of his face and I probably couldn't read his lips anyway. Daphne stands with the teacup in one hand, Miller holding the other. Daphne is smiling but the smile is fading, slowly fading. Miller shows her the spear gun and Daphne's brow furrows politely, as if she is thinking yes, that is a very nice spear gun but why are you showing it to me. At which point Miller shrugs and shoots her in chest. The spear plunges deep enough to come out the back and the sound it makes is like smashing a pumpkin with a hammer and even as I run for the door I imagine I can hear the air and fluids hissing from her body.

Through the kitchen and out the back door, running blind. Feet hammering like mad on the wooden deck and from the sound of it you would think there were three of me. I still have Miller's gun, with two real bullets in it, and I would love to shoot him with one. I swing myself over the handrail to the ground below and because I'm high and deprived of sleep and something of a fool, I come down on that fucked-up left ankle from last night. The pain is electric and I roll into a fetal position. But not for long. I don't want to be found like this.

I pull myself together and come limping around the side of the house, gun in hand, listening for him, sniffing the air for Miller and automatically my eyes go to Daphne's body. Twisted, unrecognizable, her body is contorted so that at first glance she appears to have one leg and two broken arms and no head. Her white dress is black with blood and now I see that the spear indeed stabbed though her just below the ribcage and came out the other side, and the words pig in a poke flash helplessly through my head. I stare at her for a long breathless moment, and then there is the crunch of gravel behind me and a baseball bat hits me in the right shoulder hard enough to break me.

Oh, the way the brain functions.

Because even while getting my ass kicked, my brain is happy to do some fast calculations and let me know exactly how Miller got the drop on me. He heard me coming. He knew I was watching, and killed Daphne for my benefit.

Or maybe not.

He has the bloodlust, no question, and maybe he killed her purely for the giggles but he probably heard me crashing through the kitchen and out onto the deck. He certainly heard me moaning and cursing over my fucked ankle, and so he went around the house to get behind me, stopping in the garage to grab his Louisville Slugger.

Meanwhile.

The right arm is crippled but somehow I'm still holding that gun and a kid could tell you I'm gonna shoot myself in the foot, any minute now. I try to transfer it to my left hand but Miller just shrugs and hits me with some kind of karate kick that spins me around like a toy soldier. The gun sails away and disappears into a yellow and brown carpet of fallen leaves.

Fucked. Phineas is fucked.

Miller is hellish pleased with himself. He dances away from me, bouncing on his toes. He sends another kick my way, this time at my head. I hobble sideways and manage to take it on the side of the head, instead of directly between the eyes. He seems annoyed that I haven't fallen down yet, and frankly I'm surprised. He doesn't say anything though, and I thank him for that. I hate guys who make a lot of wisecracks while they're pounding on you.

I back away from him, breathing hard. My vision is screwy and everything is on a diagonal. Miller hops toward me, grinning. And I move to his left, his blind side. He is not used to the eye patch and this gives me an opening to hit him square in the face with a little jab that causes his nose to bleed and pisses him off something awful, and Miller promptly hits me in the chest with one of those karate punches that I understand conceptually but don't know how to throw, the punch that aims for a spot somewhere beyond the point of initial impact so that the fist punches through you like a lead ball and reaches maximum density somewhere behind you, knocking you four maybe five feet backward and in the meantime sucking all of the air out of your body. Then he follows it up with another savage kick to the head and baby I am down.

The fight is over and I want to tell him to finish it. If your guy is down you don't stick around for anger management. You snap his neck and move on.

But Miller is just getting started. He has issues, and he wants to work them out. He kicks me mercilessly, again and again. I wish I could tell him that he's wasting his time, that I can't feel anything because I'm slipping into shock and one section of my brain is already experiencing a tasty in-flight movie in which Michelle Pfeiffer exposes some righteous flesh. And after a while, he just gets tired of kicking me. He picks up the baseball bat and takes a few swings, but his breathing is labored and apparently he doesn't want to kill me just yet, because he suddenly loses interest and tosses the bat aside. Then he crouches down and sticks his vile tongue in my ear.

The indignity. I'm going to kill him for that, if I ever walk again.

I'm slipping down a black tunnel and the last thing I see is Miller, upside down and sideways and stuffing Daphne's body into a red, white, and blue duffel bag and dragging her out of sight, presumably to deposit her in the grave dug by Huck and I reckon it's handy to have a grave dug in advance.

I wake on hard, cold wood, a damp T-shirt wadded into a pillow under my head. Bright cruel needles of sunlight and now there is a face looming over me, Molly's face.

Are you okay?

Uh. I don't know.

Don't try to move, yet.

I give her a feeble smile and run a fast systems check on the body. The fingers and toes are responding, which bodes well. The ankle is still sore but less noticeable now, what with all the other bruised and broken body parts howling for a little attention. The skull is a bit tender and I allow for the possibility of fluid on the brain. The right arm is numb and sore but unbroken. I can move the fucker, anyway. The face has that tight leather feel that I personally associate with dried blood. That would be from the previously mentioned head wound. I estimate maybe four broken ribs and that's all for today.

I'm a peach.

Jude's face heaves into view and she looks worried. For her, she looks very worried. Jude is biting her lip and her pupils are so dilated they swallow her eyes and I have a feeling she's worried about more than just Phineas and his talent for getting the shit kicked out of him. Her nerves look to me to be utterly jangled. She holds up her finger and moves it back and forth and tells me to follow it with my eyes. After a minute she sighs, apparently satisfied.

What's up? I say.

You have a concussion. Don't go to sleep tonight.

Okay.

This is it, she says.

Huh?

She hisses at me, please. Please.

I'm here, baby.

When you get out, she says. Burn it down.

Burn it, I say.

Do you understand?

Yes.

Jude nods, and slips away.

Where am I?

Molly strokes my forehead. I need you to get up.

You look pretty, I say. How does it feel to be pretty?

Phineas, please.

I know. I need to get up.

Molly gives me her hand.

Don't help me, please.

I pull myself upright and allow myself a fuzzy look around. This is a room I've not yet seen. High, vaulted ceilings with exposed rafters. The hardwood floor. Tall windows and bright morning sun. There is no furniture but a shitty-looking mattress on the floor, with no sheets. Miller sits naked on the mattress, grinning. Jude stands on the other side, unbuttoning her dress, the same sleeveless white dress. Dizzy and I wobble sideways into Molly, who holds me up.

Help me, I say.

I'm here, she says.

I have to talk to Jude, I say. I have to ask her something.

You can't, says Molly. Not now.

Why not?

Hush…please.

Where am I?

This is John's room, she whispers.

It's…nice.

I'm a son of a bitch, says Miller. You're a tough cookie, Poe.

Thanks. What are we doing?

He shrugs. Just getting ready to shoot a little sex scene.

The crew is dead, I say. You killed the crew.

I know, he says. Nasty business, isn't it.

Jude is a shadow behind him.

Nasty, I say. Yes.

Anyway, he says. Looks like I need you behind the camera today, Poe.

Lucky, I say. Lucky thing you didn't kill me.

Miller nods, staring at me. He touches himself. Behind him, Jude removes a knife from her boot and slips it under the mattress.

Who is the shadow that walks beside you? I say.

Miller is still nodding, like he can't stop.

What? he says.

I shake my head. Never mind.

There is no dialogue, no foreplay. Molly has one camera, I have another. She weaves around the room, drifting close to the bed and then away. I am positioned against the wall on the far side of the room, shooting the wide angle. Molly moves in and out of my shot, but I'm not really paying attention to her. Jude takes off her boots and throws them across the room, sailing high then crashing to the wood floor. Now she lets the white dress fall from her shoulders. Miller sits on the edge of the bed, his lips wet. The dress slips slowly to the floor and she is naked before him. The long brown body that was once mine, and never mine. Molly moves across the room and for a moment my view is obscured. Miller reaches for the prize, dragging Jude roughly down onto the bed. He mashes her mouth with his. Jude groans and pulls at him and in a moment he is on top of her, grunting and trying to get inside and when he finds purchase there is a silence in the room like no other. There is no dialogue, no foreplay.

Jude makes a sobbing sound and Molly glances back at me, her eyes bright with shame.

I shake my head. Not yet, not yet.

Jude raises her head to look at me over Miller's shoulder, staring at me for a long, dreadful moment. Then closes her eyes as if in prayer.

Miller thrusts at her like a great hairless pig.

I place my camera on the floor and motion for Molly to do the same. She comes across the room as if it's five miles wide. She goes through the door behind me and her footsteps are brutal whispers falling down the stairs. I stare across the room at the two bodies grinding and rutting on the bare mattress until they become one, until they become a green shadow that is not man or woman.

Outside. The sky is white. I cross the yard and enter the garage, where I collect a small yellow funnel and one of the plastic red jugs of gasoline. In the kitchen, I gather four empty liquor bottles and line them up along the sink. My head is ringing like a church bell and my peripheral vision is gone. I have a tiny window of daylight in front of me and that's all I need. I am so fucking calm. My hands don't shake at all as I fill the bottles with gas. I take off my shirt and rip it into four pieces, which I twist into coiled rags and stuff into the mouths of the bottles. Molly comes through the kitchen, carrying the boy against her chest. Her face is pale and bloodless and when I look at her I see a corpse wrapped in a white sheet, sleeping beneath a window. I wonder how weak she must be. The boy wakes up and turns to look at me, his eyes bright with fever.

It's okay, I say. It's okay, Sam.

Molly takes him outside and I empty the rest of the gasoline in the kitchen, the hallway. I run through the living room and dining room splashing gasoline behind me and I remember Molly's monologue about families and the way they smell of furniture polish and dead flowers, of shampoo and dirty boots. They smell of ashtrays and garlic and spilled gin and gasoline.

Blackbirds slash the air around me. Molly walks up the long driveway with Sam in her arms. He weighs not quite fifty pounds but make no mistake, the boy is heavy, so heavy. One small child is enough to crush you. I stand maybe ninety feet from the house, the Molotov cocktails at my feet. I watch Molly and Sam until I'm satisfied they're safely away, then pick up the first bottle. I light the rag and let it burn a moment, then heave it through the living room window with a shocking crash of fire and light. I pick up another bottle, grinning like a fool. I light the rag and hurl the second bottle at the kitchen window. There is a gorgeous little explosion this time, showering me with glass.

I am sorry about the reptiles. They didn't ask for this. But they have been prepared for the apocalypse since the beginning of time. I throw the third bottle at what I think is the library, the last at an upstairs bathroom window, and already I hear the sirens. Impossible, I think. No one has a response time like that, but maybe we tripped a silent alarm. I turn and see that Molly has nearly made it to the road. The sirens are close and coming closer and I believe old Huck must have gotten his shit together and gone to the cops, or maybe it was the pretty motorcycle girl who turned to smile at me as she passed by with cigarettes that weren't hers.

Jude waited for Miller to come, I imagine. She tolerated his breath, his crushing weight, to allow us time to get outside. The stink of his skin. Then she cut his throat with my knife when he came and his body was trembling, defenseless. I imagine she cut out his eyes, then took his hair. And I think it's possible that she gathered her clothes and went out the window, swinging to the ground like a monkey with wings, but maybe not. Maybe she closed her eyes and curled up beside him as the bed filled with his blood, her blood. I see it in a wide, overhead shot.

The sirens are terribly loud and I think of dying angels and now three black and white police cars come down the driveway with blue lights flashing. Molly stops and stands at the mouth of the driveway with the boy in her arms. The first car slides to a stop in a mushroom cloud of dust. Two police officers come out of the white cloud, one male and one female. They are gentle with Molly, as if she might be Sam's sister, and I am glad for that. I don't think I could stand it, if they abused Molly. I might just pull the gun and then all would be lost. A third man gets out of the car and for a split second the sun and clouds are perfectly aligned so as to cast him in green shadow and I think this is Death coming for me, but then he steps out of the shadow and I see he's just a man, a tall blond man with a prosthetic hand.

The cops are coming toward me now with guns held high. They are screaming at me and I don't understand the words that fly jagged from their lips but they seem to want me to get on the ground. They don't look like they want to be so gentle with me. I need to stop them from reaching the house too quickly. I need to give Jude a minute to get away, just a minute could save her. I crouch down and gather fine white dust into my hand as the house of Miller burns furiously behind me. I raise my hands above my head to show that I am not armed and still the cops are screaming.

Down, get the fuck down.

I am not armed. I am not armed but I can show you fear in a handful of dust.

epilogue.

THREE MONTHS LATER I'M WATCHING A PINK MOON come up slow as a flower dying over the mountains. I've just stepped outside for a smoke, my hands stinking of bleach. The waffle shack has been about as popular today as a dead whore's bedroom and so I've had no dishes to wash. The boss has kept me busy all afternoon with disinfecting the floors, the fat wheezing fuck. I have inhaled so much bleach these past ninety days that on a lazy summer evening such as this I might come to think my soul had been covertly purified. I sit on a rock under a torn awning and stare out at northbound highway 77 shivering with bright cars and trucks on their way up to Waco and beyond. I can almost but not quite see the southbound traffic from this rock, which may be God's funny way of telling me something. I live in a rented trailer five miles south, in the desert.

The hailstones first come down in bursts, as if the sky is choking. They hit the asphalt and bounce high into the air, stones small as sweet baby peas. I look up and the pink moon is gone. The sky is the color of gunmetal. The traffic noise dies away and I feel relatively safe on my rock. In a minute the sky really opens up. The stones are now the size of goodly marbles and soon the parking lot is white, a lunar expanse. My skin is stinging. I toss my cigarette aside as a new silver Mercedes wobbles slowly into the lot with one flat tire, left rear. The crush of hailstones under the wheel are like gunshots and I find myself flinching, as if I should take cover. The car comes to rest but no one gets out. The hailstorm quits as suddenly as it began. The car just sits there, exhaust puffing from the tailpipe. The windows are tinted and I can't see the driver. I'm not interested, anyway. I need to get inside before the boss comes out and commences to share profanities in my direction but for some reason I don't move. I don't take my eyes off the silver car and now the driver's door opens and I glimmer a woman's profile.

For a heartbeat, I think it's Molly come back to me. And part of me wishes it were. Molly stuck by me in San Francisco like an angel. She stepped between me and the cops, before they started shooting. She held her ground until Sam broke away from his father and ran to her screaming don't shoot them, don't shoot. At which point the senator told the cops to stand down. Then in a cool calm very presidential voice, Senator Cody ordered the cops to get everyone to high ground and away from the fire, and said that they would figure this mess out later.

By then, the fire trucks had arrived.

I was in agreement with the senator, amputee geek or no. I wanted Sam and Molly away from that house. I allowed myself to be handcuffed and was deposited into the back of a black and white.

And at the police station, the interrogation came on pretty hardcore, but Molly swore on a stack of bibles that I'd had nothing to do with Miller or the kidnapping, that I was just an ex-cop who came out of nowhere and rescued her and the kid. She never breathed a word about Jude's involvement, and there was no breaking her of her story. And apparently Sam told his father pretty much the same thing, because the senator called in a pack of family favors and made all charges against me go away like he was blowing dust from his prosthetic fingers.

Make a wish, boy.

The woman who gets out of the Mercedes is sure as hell not Molly. She's a stranger but she looks so much like Jude that I think God must be fucking with me. Dark sunglasses and a scarf the color of spilled red wine around her neck. Tangled brown and gold hair. She wears a black T-shirt, a white jacket, and brown corduroys. Dark honey skin like Jude's with the same butterfly glow that just gets deeper in the sun. I see her in flashes, splinters. Jude's mouth. Jude's perfect ass, curved like a peach. But she is not Jude. She's an improbable echo, a body double. The woman walks around the car, cursing. She never glances my way. I watch as she removes jack and tire iron from the trunk. She handles them reluctantly, as if she's never changed a tire before, and soon she drops the tools. They crash to the ground and again I flinch. The hailstones are melting and the parking lot has taken on a lovely apocalyptic glow that makes me want to puke. The woman drags the spare tire from the trunk, then crouches beside the car and fumbles incompetently with the jack. I want to help her but something tells me to hold my ground. This scene is just a little too perfect for my taste and the woman in distress is therefore bad voodoo. If she were another amputee then I would have a hell of a story for the Internet. I don't have Internet access, however. And the woman appears to have all of her natural limbs. Thirty seconds wriggle past and now this woman who is not Jude turns to look at me.

Hey, she says.

I don't like people in sunglasses. I turn my head and spit. The woman frowns and promptly removes the sunglasses. Devastating. She turns back to the car and I watch for as long as I can stand it, then start walking toward her. It could be that two guys are going to hop out of the car and whack me on the head but what's the difference. I have nothing to steal. I walk across the parking lot to crouch beside her. I expect her to smell like expensive rainwater and fairy dust but all I can smell is bleach. I can smell nothing but my own disinfected skin and now the woman peers at me, grinning.

I'm hopeless with tools, she says.

I can see that.

She wears a silver and turquoise bracelet on her wrist and her left hand is covered in fine white scars, as if she got it tangled in a spider's web. The scars are beautiful as hell and I try not to stare at them. I have seen scars like that once before, when I was living on the psych ward at Fort Logan. There was a schizophrenic old guy called Sweet William who was a little claustrophobic and didn't like to be inside and the story behind those scars was that he once put both fists through a car windshield and maybe this strange woman is claustrophobic, maybe not. I reach for the tools and busy myself with the jack and pretty soon she moves away to give me some breathing room. I twist loose the lug nuts and spin the tire iron like a windmill, then slowly crank the silver car from the ground. The silence is heavy in my head. I glance over at the woman, who stands with her back to me, staring out at the desert with her hands on her hips. I wonder if she sees the same perfect wasteland that I see and now the jack slips and I rip two inches of perfectly good skin from the back of my hand.

Fuck, I say.

She glances at me and maybe it's my imagination but her eyes seem to flash at the sight of blood. She doesn't say a word. She slowly pulls the scarf from around her neck and gives it to me, then turns back to the desert. I suck on my hand a moment, staring. Her hair falls light as pale wildflowers just above her shoulders in back. I turn away and wrap my hand in her bandana and five minutes later, I'm finished with the tire. I toss the flat tire and tools into the trunk and light another cigarette. It's a miracle my boss has not shown himself and I think he must be camped out in the toilet with some very depressing porn. He tends to favor those magazines that promise sweet pubescent virgins but ultimately feature a lot of sad, fucked-up looking runaways with bad skin. The woman stands with her back to me and I don't know if she's contemplating the human condition or wondering how long it will take to get where she's going or praying or what, and intellectually speaking, I know it's unlikely but somewhere in the marrow I know this woman is Jude's sister, the one reputed to be in Toronto.

It's beautiful out here, she says.

I take a breath. It's like living on God's asshole.

She turns. Are you a religious man?

Lately, yes.

Flash of a smile and she nods.

Where are you going? I say.

Here, she says.

I cast a crooked eye at the diner.

Why? I say.

I'm looking for you.

I scratch my head. The woman must be joking because no one knows I'm out here, no one. I barely exist, legally.

Your name is Phineas Poe, she says. Is that right?

I don't mean to be nasty, I say. But what do you want?

Are you Phineas Poe? she says.

Yes.

The ex-cop?

The dishwasher, I say.

Whatever, she says. I have a package for you.

A package?

She smiles. It's just a small thing.

How small?

Well, she says. It's bigger than a loaf of bread.

I stare as she leans into the car and retrieves a black knapsack, then begins to dig through it, muttering softly to herself as if she's lost her keys. A wild strand of hair drifts between her lips as the breeze picks up and she blows it away impatiently. I get nervous when she drops the knapsack and the contents tumble onto the wet asphalt. Two packs of cigarettes and lipstick and pink chewing gum and handcuffs and a roll of electrician's tape and a screwdriver and a tin of Tiger Balm and a knife in a black nylon sheath and a pack of condoms and one pair of pink and white polka dot panties. There is a moment of pure, almost visible silence before she takes an exasperated breath and releases a short, violent, imaginative string of profanity and her voice has a Southern edge to it that I hadn't noticed before.

Oh my, she says. This is so fucking elegant.

She is so obviously Jude's sister that I feel like I might explode, but I don't want to spook her. I am tempted to tell her that nothing embarrasses me but I don't completely trust myself not to spit out something foolish or creepy so I go the safe route and say nothing. I crouch down beside her and together we gather her things. I pull the knife from its sheath and it's a tanto, a Japanese fighting knife. It isn't my knife, but it looks like mine. I test the edge and the narrow blade is sharp enough to skin a horse.

She smiles. Easy with that.

Beautiful knife, I say.

Take it, she says.

What do you mean?

She shrugs. I don't know. I'm trying to say thank you, for the tire.

I feel very strange and it's been a while but I think what I'm feeling is shy, or something along those lines. As if I'm seventeen and the new girl in town just smiled at me and my skull turned to rubber because I don't know what to say. I stare at her and her eyes are impossibly blue, with yellow and orange around the edges. Her eyes are the color of the sky gone to rust.

I mumble. Thank you.

You're welcome, she says. But give me a dollar.

What?

It's bad luck for a knife to change hands, otherwise.

I give her a crumpled dollar, which she slips into her left boot. Her eyes meet mine and dart away like bright fish behind glass and I wonder if she might be tempted to come home with me. But I have nothing to tempt her with. She rises and moves around to the trunk of the silver car, opens it and retrieves a plain brown box, unmarked, and a fat white envelope. The box looks heavy. She hands me the envelope first, holding it between thumb and finger. The name Phineas Poe is written on the front and I suck in my breath. I recognize the handwriting but I barely look at it. My eyes are on that box.

Merry Christmas, she says.

I stand there, blinking.

Are you going to open it?

Maybe tomorrow.

She shrugs. Whatever sets your world on fire.

Who gave this to you?

She turns to look at the desert, jingling her keys.

I think you know the answer to that.

Yeah. I'm just not sure I believe it.

Do you love her? she says.

I try not to breathe. Excuse me?

Do you love her?

Yeah, I say. I love her.

The woman nods. That's something, then.

Jude's sister gives me the box. It weighs maybe six pounds. I want to know how she found me. I want to know where she came from. I want to know if that punctured tire was sweet coincidence or some kind of test or psychological foreplay. I want to know what's in the box and at the same time, I don't want to know. I want to know how this package came into her possession but I doubt she would tell me and anyway I recognize the handwriting on the envelope. I just don't believe it. I watch as she climbs into the silver car and shakes out her hair, a dizzy flash of wildflowers.

The car rolls out of the lot.

I stare at the highway until the car is gone, then walk quickly over to the Dumpster at the edge of the gravel lot and shove the heavy cardboard box into the weeds next to the recycling bins. I slip the knife and envelope under my apron and into the waistband of my jeans and now I hear the crunch of gravel under heavy feet. My employer is behind me, wheezing. I let my face go slack and lifeless. I wet my lips and allow my mouth to fall open before I turn around.

Jack, he says. Ya sad fuckin retard.

Jack, I say. Sad fuckin.

Oh ya beggin to get fired. If ya weren't handicapped believe I'd kick your ass to the other side of the moon and you could fuck off all day with the moose and the fiddle.

My employer is a mean troll with a weird tendency to invoke mangled Mother Goose when framing an insult. If he sees the envelope, or the box, he will promptly confiscate them both. Which would be a shame because I would probably go ahead and give him the surprise of his life by cutting his throat. He is under the impression that I am retarded and suffer from a vague form of Tourette's that causes me to repeat everything he says, which irritates the hell out of him but by design prevents him from spewing too much garbage at me. He also believes that my name is Jack, that I live in a group home and that I cannot read or write. I find that it makes life easier, when people think you are simple. They ignore you.

The moose and the fiddle, I say. Fuck off all day.

Two hours later and it's dark out. The pink moon is gone. I sit in the doorway of my trailer, the fat white envelope unopened in my lap. The box sits beside me, to my right, unopened. On my left, a GI Joe action figure in jungle fatigues stands at attention, plastic M-16 slung low. I have a jelly jar full of whiskey in one hand. Early September and I have the radio tuned to the Diamondbacks game. They're tearing up the Cubs. I am again staring out at southbound traffic.

If I lift my head just so, I can see the lights of stars. I look at the box, give it a nudge. Bend over it and sniff around the edges. Nothing. The smell of cardboard. I take it in my hands once more, feel the weight of it. Five, maybe six pounds. This is the weight of the average human head. I can open the box, or not. I turn my attention to the envelope. The handwriting is strange and beautiful, at once jagged as broken glass and somehow curved and girlish. My skin feels cold. Like touching metal, or walking into church. The skin remembers. I first laid eyes on this handwriting in a hotel bathtub in Denver almost seven years ago.

This is Jude's hand, and I know whose head is in the box.

I open the envelope. It contains eleven hundred seven dollars and a one-way plane ticket to Amsterdam, first class. Eleven hundred and seven dollars. Jude has this thing about even numbers being unlucky. Taped inside the envelope is a silver hotel room key, number 9. There is also a photograph of a small boy with blond hair staring bullets at the camera.

Everson Poe, my son.

I stare back at him just as hard, trying with all my might to cross time and dimension to communicate with this tiny severed shadow of myself, this as yet perfect piece of me I've never met. In the envelope there is a jagged scrap of paper, thick white linen hotel stationery bearing the crest of the Dead Sea Hotel and an Amsterdam address.

On the back is a note, unsigned.

Come to us.

My name is Phineas Poe and this is how it begins.

acknowledgments.

DEEP THANKS TO Sterling Anderson, Will Yun Lee, Craig Clevenger, Ralph Hemecker, Shane Amaya, Jacopo De Michelis, Jeffrey Donovan, and above all Dan Mandel, for breathing life into Phineas and keeping him on his feet during the lean years. Thanks to David Poindexter, Scott Allen, and Pat Walsh for bringing me in from the cold. Thanks to Jason Wood for watching my back. Thanks to Stephen Graham Jones for closing the circle. Thanks to Jefferson Costa and Bonsai Ninja for their dead sexy interpretations of Phineas and Jude. Thanks to Dorothy Smith and Josh Brayer for making this beast of a collection look pretty. Thanks to Dennis Widmyer, Mirka Hodurova, and Kareem Badr for their unrivaled guidance and protection in the ether. Thanks to Roland G, Sparq, J.P. Moriarty, Julie Burton, and Dennis Hearne for tactical support. Thanks to Nick Campbell, Logan Frost, Drew M, and Naked Dan for the excellent glove work. Thanks to Craig Shindler for looking over my shoulder when I cross the street, when I step into oncoming traffic. Thanks to my family near and far for their unflinching faith. Thanks to Elias McCulloch, my son and shadow self, for inspiring me to see this thing through. Thanks to Emerson Jane, my daughter and favorite new creation, for coming into the work just when her mother and I needed her. And my undying thanks to Penelope Lee, for giving me a reason to keep my heart beating, for always being the best part of me. Thank you, patient weaver.